THE LIFE AND ADVENTURES OF
NICHOLAS NICKLEBY

CHARLES DICKENS

THE LIFE AND ADVENTURES OF
NICHOLAS NICKLEBY

Reproduced in facsimile from the
original monthly parts of 1838–9
with an essay by
MICHAEL SLATER

VOLUME ONE

CHAPTERS I TO XXXIII

UNIVERSITY OF PENNSYLVANIA PRESS
Philadelphia
1982

First published in monthly parts by Chapman and Hall
2 April 1838 to 1 October 1839
This edition first published in the United States by
the University of Pennsylvania Press, 1982
This edition first published in Great Britain by
Scolar Press, 1982
"The Composition and Monthly Publication of *Nicholas Nickleby*"
copyright © Michael Slater, 1972, 1982

Library of Congress Cataloging in Publication Data

Dickens, Charles, 1812-1870.
The life and adventures of Nicholas Nickleby.

Reprint. Originally published: London: Chapman and
Hall, 1838-1839.
I. Slater, Michael.   II. Title.
PR4565.A1   1982b   823'.8   82-21971
ISBN 0-8122-7873-9
ISBN 0-8122-1135-9 (pbk.)

Printed in the United States of America

CONTENTS

PUBLISHER'S NOTE

In the original parts of *Nicholas Nickleby* the illustrations relating to each issue were printed on a stiffer paper than the text and situated between the front advertisements and the chapters of the novel. On the completion of monthly publication the reader could have the whole text bound as a book with the illustrations inserted as closely as possible to the appropriate place in the narrative, as indicated in the List of Plates supplied with the other preliminary matter at the end of Part XX.

In the present facsimile the printing of the plates on the same paper as the narrative makes possible a closer relationship between illustrations and text. As a consequence the position of each illustration does not necessarily accord with that indicated in the 1839 List of Plates.

THE COMPOSITION AND MONTHLY PUBLICATION OF

NICHOLAS NICKLEBY

by Michael Slater

The evening of Saturday 18 November 1837 was a triumphant one for the 25-year-old Charles Dickens. He took the chair at a dinner, held at the Prince of Wales Tavern in Leicester Square, to celebrate the conclusion of the serial publication of *Pickwick Papers*, the monthly sales of which had risen to the astonishing figure of 40,000 copies. It had " fascinated everybody," wrote Dickens's friend and biographer, John Forster: "Judges on the bench and boys in the street, gravity and folly, the young and the old, those who were entering life and those who were quitting it, alike found it to be irresistible."[1] Its prodigious success had meant that Dickens had been able to give up his work as a Parliamentary reporter for the *Morning Chronicle* and devote himself to a full-time writing career. He had married Catherine, eldest daughter of George Hogarth, an eminent music critic and the editor of the *Evening Chronicle*, leased a pleasant modern house in Doughty Street, and taken his place among the leading lights of literary London. This last fact was demonstrated by the distinction of the guests assembled at the Prince of Wales's—such people as Harrison Ainsworth,. Macready the "eminent tragedian", William Jerdan, editor of the powerful *Literary Gazette* and Thomas Noon Talfourd (to whom Dickens had dedicated *Pickwick* in appreciation of his efforts as an M.P. to secure the passing of the Copyright Act). Also present, of course, were Dickens's publishers, Chapman and Hall, whose fortune had been made by Mr. Pickwick and his friends and who were understandably eager to publish more work by the " inimitable Boz ".

The dinner, Ainsworth wrote later, was " capital ". Just before Talfourd rose to toast Dickens's health, " the head waiter . . . entered, and placed a glittering temple of confectionery on the table, beneath the canopy of which stood a little figure of the

---

[1] John Forster, *The Life of Charles Dickens*, ed. J. W. T. Ley (1928). Hereafter referred to as Forster.

illustrious Mr. Pickwick. This was the work of the landlord.
As you may suppose, it was received with great applause ".[1]

But Dickens, neither then nor later, was a man to rest upon his
heaped up laurels. Mr. Pickwick might have ended his adventures and be serenely contemplating the pictures in Dulwich
Gallery but his creator had for nine months already been busy
chronicling the adventures of a very different hero, the workhouse boy who " asked for more ", in the pages of a new monthly
magazine, Bentley's Miscellany, of which he had become editor in
January 1837. For the same publisher, Richard Bentley, he was
about to begin editing for publication the memoirs of the great
clown Joey Grimaldi, who had died that year, and had also
promised to produce " Barnaby Rudge a Novel in 3 Vols Octavo "
by October 1838.

Despite his being thus committed to writing two other novels
already, Dickens signed an agreement with Chapman and Hall
a few days after the Pickwick celebration whereby he bound
himself to write for them " a new work the title whereof shall be
fixed upon and determined by him of a similar character and of
the same extent and contents in point of quantity as the said
work entitled ' The Posthumous Papers of the Pickwick Club '
and that the said new work shall consist of 20 parts or numbers
and shall be terminated and completed in the 20th part or number thereof ". Copy for the first number was to be delivered to
Chapman and Hall on 15 March 1838 ready for publication at
the end of the month and copy for the succeeding issues " on the
15th day of each of the nineteen months next following ". For
this Dickens was to receive £150 a month.[2] His initial remuneration for the monthly numbers of Pickwick—which he had
described to his fiancée as an " emolument . . . too tempting to
resist "—had been nine and a half guineas.

During the next two months Dickens was furiously busy not
only with editing Bentley's, writing instalments of Oliver Twist
and reducing the Grimaldi papers to some sort of order, but also
with writing a little book entitled Sketches of Young Gentlemen
to be published anonymously by Chapman and Hall. There was
also a notable domestic event, the christening of his son (born
January 1837) whom he facetiously referred to in letters as " the
infant phenomenon ". On 16 January 1838 he wrote to Forster,
who was struggling to meet a deadline of his own,

[1]   Forster, p. 109.
[2]   Dickens's Agreement with Chapman and Hall for Nickleby is given in full
       in Appendix C of Volume One (1820–1839) of the Pilgrim Edition of the
       Letters of Charles Dickens (1965), edited by Madeline House and Graham
       Storey. Unless otherwise stated, all subsequent quotations from Dickens's
       letters in this essay are taken from this edition, which will be referred
       to as Letters.

I am as badly off as you are.   I have not done the young
gentlemen, nor written the preface to Grimaldi, nor thought of
Oliver Twist, or even suggested a subject for the plate [each
instalment of *Oliver* in *Bentley's* was accompanied by a Cruik-
shank illustration].   Add to this, that I had no sleep last night
in consequence of some vagaries of my son and heir, and I
leave you to form some idea of my woeful plight.[1]

Nine days later, however, he could write to Ainsworth:

I should have written to you before, but my month's work has
been dreadful—Grimaldi, the anonymous book for Chapman
and Hall, Oliver and the Miscellany.   They are all done, thank
God, and I start on my pilgrimage to the cheap schools of
Yorkshire (a mighty secret, of course) next Monday Morning.[2]

One is not surprised that the Board of the Sun Life Assurance
Society, who interviewed Dickens on 9 January, " seemed
disposed to think [he worked] too much " and declined a proposal
to insure his life for £1000.[3]   It was a relentless pace that he
set himself and one that did not slacken as the years passed.

The mention of " the cheap schools of Yorkshire " in the letter
to Ainsworth is the first hint that we find, among Dickens's surviving correspondence, that he had settled upon a subject for his
new novel.   Forster tells us in his *Life of Dickens* that the novelist

went down into Yorkshire with Mr Hablot Browne to look up
the Cheap Schools in that county to which public attention had
been painfully drawn by a law case in the previous year; which
had before been notorious for cruelties committed in them,
whereof he had heard as early as his childish days; and which
he was bent upon destroying if he could.[4]

What were these scandalous Yorkshire schools that Dickens,
fresh from his championship of the child victims of the New Poor
Law, was now " bent upon destroying "?   And how had they
gained their notoriety?

In his preface to the Cheap Edition of *Nicholas Nickleby*, written
in 1848, Dickens begins by observing that when the novel was first
published there were " a good many cheap Yorkshire schools in
existence ".   He then adds, with an almost audible satisfaction,
" There are very few now ".   The next two paragraphs of the preface characterise the establishments and those who ran them:

[1] *Letters*, i, 355.
[2] *Letters*, i, 359.
[3] *Letters*, i, 630f. (extract from Dickens's diary).
[4] Forster, p. 123.

Of the monstrous neglect of education in England, and the disregard of it by the State as a means of forming good or bad citizens, and miserable or happy men, this class of schools long afforded a notable example. Although any man who had proved his unfitness for any other occupation in life, was free, without examination or qualification, to open a school anywhere; although preparation for the functions he undertook, was required in the surgeon who assisted to bring a boy into the world, or might one day assist, perhaps, to send him out of it,— in the chemist, the attorney, the butcher, the baker, the candlestick maker,—the whole round of crafts and trades, the schoolmaster excepted; and although schoolmasters, as a race, were the blockheads and impostors that might naturally be expected to arise from such a state of things, and to flourish in it; these Yorkshire schoolmasters were the lowest and most rotten round in the whole ladder. Traders in the avarice, indifference, or imbecility of parents, and the helplessness of children; ignorant, sordid, brutal men, to whom few considerate persons would have entrusted the board and lodging of a horse or a dog; they formed the worthy corner-stone of a structure, which, for absurdity and a magnificent high-handed *laissez-aller* neglect, has rarely been exceeded in the world.

We hear sometimes of an action for damages against the unqualified medical practitioner, who has deformed a broken limb in pretending to heal it. But, what about the hundreds of thousands of minds that have been deformed for ever by the incapable pettifoggers who have pretended to form them!

"The avarice, indifference or imbecility of parents." The Yorkshire schools had sprung up in the latter part of the 18th century,[1] mainly in the area round Barnard Castle, as places where children who were a nuisance or embarrassment to their parents or guardians could be sent and kept out of the way the whole year (the phrase " no vacations " was always prominent in the schoolmasters' advertisements) for very little cost. It was a convenient way of disposing of illegitimate children, for example; " We have a good many of them," Squeers tells Snawley in Chapter 4, and Dickens glances at this subject again in Chapter 8 when he notes that " Graymarsh's maternal aunt was strongly supposed, by her more intimate friends, to be no other than his maternal parent ". Mr. Snawley's anxiety to get his new-found step-children out of the way in case their mother should start squandering on them the little fortune for which he has married her is well understood by Mr. Squeers:

[1] In an article, " Yorkshire Schools ", in *The Dickensian*, vii (1911), 9, E. Hardy notes that the earliest known advertisement for a cheap Yorkshire school appears in the *London Advertiser*, September 1749.

1828.
—▶▷◀◀—

EDUCATION.
—▶▷◀◀—

At Brough Academy,

(LATE GILMONBY HALL,)

Near GRETABRIDGE, YORKSHIRE,

YOUNG GENTLEMEN are *liberally boarded, lodged,* and *clothed,* provided with Books, and all other Requisites, parentally treated, and expeditiously instructed in the English, Latin, and Greek Languages, Writing, Arithmetic, Book-keeping, Mensuration, Trigonometry, Plane and Spherical Navigation, Land Surveying, Guaging, Geography, with the Use of the Globes, &c. &c. at

Twenty Guineas per Annum,

BY MR. J. HORN,

And able Assistants.

A LIMITED NUMBER OF PARLOUR BOARDERS ADMITTED.

Under 12 *Years of Age...* 27 *Guineas per Annum.*
Above 12 *ditto ......* 30 *ditto ditto.*

The French Language by a Native of Paris, if required, 2 *Guineas per Annum*; also Drawing, Music, and other polite Accomplishments taught on reasonable Terms.

Brough is most beautifully situated, stands on the great north road, is better adapted for an Academy than any other establishment in the north of England, as the air is most salubrious and the premises very extensive, and has been in the same family and line of business upwards of a century.

There are no Vacations, and there will be no other expense whatever, except that of Medicines and Medical Attendance, in case of Sickness (rarely necessary in this salubrious part of the country); the utmost attention being paid to Health and Cleanliness.

At this Academy every attention is evinced to forward the general improvement of the Scholars, particular attention is paid to Reading, Writing, and Arithmetic, as these form the ground work of every other acquisition, and every inducement afforded to excite that emulation which so much tends to beneficial instruction, and strict attention is paid to the Sabbath.

Each Pupil is expected to be furnished with 2 Suits of Clothes, a great Coat, 2 Hats, 3 Pair of Shoes, 6 Shirts, 6 Pair of Stockings, 6 Pocket Handkerchiefs, and 4 Nightcaps; also a Bible and Prayer Book, or pay for any deficiencies.

Three Months' Notice required on any Pupil leaving School, or the Quarter charged.

~~~~~~~~~~~~~~~

Further information may be obtained of any of the very respectable Parties, whose Names form the List of Reference on the other side of this Card, all of whom are Parents of, or Guardians to Pupils now or late under Mr. HORN's parental care but more particularly of Mr. JOHNSTONE, Mr. Horn's Agent, 52, Burr Street, East Smithfield, London, to whom Quarterly Payments are expected to be made.

N.B At this Academy no Day-scholars are admitted.

[Turn over.

Mr. Horn's References.

Belle Sauvage Inn, Ludgate Hill.
Bowdon, Mr. J. 60, High Street, Borough.
Chapman, Mrs. 7, Park Place, East Lane, Walworth.
Dent, Mr. T. 43, Eldon Place, Vauxhall Road, Liverpool.
Eugley, E. Esq. 34, Westmoreland Place, City Road.
Evans, G. Esq London Hospital, Whitechapel Road.
Green, Harry, Esq. 4, Hadlow Street, Burton Crescent.
Lawless, Mr. 15, Tavistock Place, Tavistock Square.
Nelme, J. Esq. 90, Lower Thames Street.
Osborne, Mr. T. 2, King's Road, Grosvenor Place.
Quilter, S. S. Esq. Walton, Ipswich.
Ruth, Mr. 176, Brick Lane, Spitalfields.
Shelton, J. Esq. Merton, Surrey.
Sims, W. Esq. 16, Southampton Place, Camberwell.
Sturdy, J. Esq. Stock Exchange.
Tear, Mr. W. 44, Hatton Garden.
Turnbull, Mrs. 85, Well Street, Oxford Street.
Vanderkiste, Mr. Printer, Heden, Hull.
Williams, J. Esq. 10, Rodney Street, Pentonville.
Winterflood, Mr. Waterloo Bridge Wharf, Strand.

＊＊＊＊＊＊＊＊＊＊＊＊＊＊＊＊＊＊＊＊

Pupils, having worn out their Clothes, will be supplied with others at Mr. Horn's expense, and returned to their Parents, or Guardians, with 1 New Suit, 2 Shirts, 2 Pair of Stockings, 2 Handkerchiefs, and a New Hat each.

Parents, Guardians, or others, Friends of Children, being desirous of sending them to this Academy, have only to communicate their wishes to Mr. JOHNSTONE, the Agent, 52, Burr Street, by post, or otherwise, who will immediately wait on the Party, take charge of the Children, and get them safely conveyed, by land or water, to the Academy.

J. Horn's Prospectus Card (reverse side)

" Not too much writing home allowed, I suppose?" said the father-in-law,[1] hesitating.

"None, except a circular at Christmas, to say they never were so happy, and hope they may never be sent for," rejoined Squeers.

But many boys were also sent to these schools, in all good faith, by credulous parents of moderate means who were taken in by the high-flown language of the schoolmasters' advertisements with their great emphasis on wide-ranging academic tuition, " liberality " of treatment and attention to the boys' moral welfare. In his article " Benevolent Teachers of Youth " in the *Cornhill Magazine* (Vol. 169, 1957, pp. 361–82), the late V. C. Clinton-Baddeley quotes from the numerous advertisements for Yorkshire schools appearing in *The Times* during the 1820's and shows how the hilariously grotesque prospectus for Dotheboys Hall is, in fact, a brilliant distillation of these insertions in *The Times* of which the following (which appeared on 17 July 1826) is a representative example:

EDUCATION.—At the old established School, Woden Croft Lodge, near Barnard Castle, conducted by MR. LIONEL SIMPSON and able ASSISTANTS, YOUNG GENTLEMEN are liberally BOARDED, parentally treated, and carefully instructed in the English, Latin and Greek languages, writing, book-keeping, arithmetic, and all the branches of the mathematics, completely qualifying them for professional pursuits or trade, on the following terms:—Entrance one guinea. From 5 to 9 years old, 20 guineas a year. From 9 to 12 ditto, 25 guineas. The French language, drawing, &c. at a moderate extra charge. At this establishment unwearied attention is paid to forward the general improvement of the scholars, and every inducement practiced to excite the emulation that so much tends to beneficial instruction. There are no vacations or extra charge on that account. Mr. Simpson or his agent may be consulted, between the hours of 12 and 2 daily, at the Saracen's Head Inn, Snow-hill; and particulars had at 19, Stockbridge-terrace, Pimlico; and at Mr. Clarke's, bookseller, Finch-lane, Cornhill.

A comparison of the wording of this advertisement with that of the 1828 prospectus-card (reproduced opposite) of J. Horn, proprietor of Brough Academy near Greta-bridge, demonstrates the way in which the schoolmasters copied each other's phrases and strove to out-go each other's claims. Horn's prospectus is indeed even closer to Squeers's with its emphasis on the salubrious setting of Brough (" the delightful village of Dotheboys ") and one can see how his inclusion of " Plane and Spherical Navigation " among the subjects professed to be taught at Brough might have inspired

[1] See note 1, page xxiii

the gloriously absurd presence of " fortification and every other branch of classical literature " in Squeers's curriculum. " The French Language by a Native of Paris, if required " answers to Squeers's " single-stick (if required) ". As so often, one finds that what seem to be Dicken's wilder flights of fancy have a definite basis in reality.[1]

To return to Simpson of Woden Croft Lodge, he had among his pupils a boy named Bold Cooke who later came to believe that Simpson must have been the original of Squeers and one of his school-fellows the original of Smike. As Simpson died in 1828 and we have, as we shall see, Dickens's own authority for identifying Smike with the " ghost " of another boy, Mr. Cooke was wrong in his belief. But his reminiscences of his schooldays as recorded in *The Dickensian* Vol. 7 (1911) are nonetheless striking evidence that Dotheboys Hall was no unrecognisable exaggeration of the hideous conditions prevailing in at least some of the Yorkshire schools:

> It is true that Smike, whose home was at Higher Broughton, did run away from school because of the inhumanity and tyranny of the master, and he was captured and most unmercifully flogged in the sight of all the trembling boys.
>
> Mr. Cooke was wont to describe what actually took place with mingled indignation and pity. The poor runaway was well flogged in the first dormitory where there were twenty-three beds. He was there stripped naked and tied to the door, and then whipped till he was covered with livid marks and open wounds, all the rest of the boys sitting up in bed till the cruel work was half completed. Immediately after this he was dragged away to be finished off in the next dormitory, in which were twenty-four beds, and as many pallid and trembling eye-witnesses.
>
> It is true that the scholars were ill-fed and plied with disgusting doses of brimstone and treacle; and equally true that they were kept without fire in the coldest days of winter, and without sufficient food every day. In the former respect Cooke was wont to say that the only days in winter when he experienced a sense of heat was when he had been well thrashed at the beginning of the day. ' Thrashed,' as he used to say, ' to keep me warm.'

[1] After the first few numbers of *Nickleby* had appeared Lord Robert Grosvenor sent Dickens some Yorkshire school advertisements. Acknowledging receipt of them, Dickens wrote, " Mr. Charles Dickens presents his compliments to Lord Robert Grosvenor and begs to inform him that Mr. Squeers and Do-the-Boys Hall were originally suggested to him by such advertisements as Lord Robert Grosvenor has had the kindness to enclose." (*Letters*, i, 411).

It is true that the scholars were expected to wash their faces clean with the aid of clay instead of soap, and it is true that towels were a seldom seen luxury.

Some idea may be formed of the hatred which all the scholars of 'Dotheboys Hall' entertained towards Squeers and his wife by the following story, which is from the lips of Mr. Cooke himself, and that is a sufficient guarantee of its truth. 'When a certain usher, or tout, named Simpson, was sent into Broughton to canvass for scholars, Smike, who was then at home, resolved to murder him, and communicated his resolve to his mother in confidence. The usher, being secretly made aware of Smike's design, and knowing too well the implacable temper of his enemy, fled precipitately, and took not a single pupil with him. . .'.

The pages of *The Dickensian* for 1917 contain some equally vivid recollections of life at a Yorkshire school, reprinted from *The Life and Work of James Abernethy C.B.E.* (1897) written by Abernethy's son. Abernethy's account of his sufferings at an " academy " at Cotherstone, six miles from Barnard Castle, was apparently written down in 1835, before the publication of *Nickleby* and so " could not by any possibility have been copied from the picture of Dotheboys Hall ".[1] Abernethy first describes how he and his brother came to be sent to the school:

My father had long been speaking of putting me and my brother to a boarding school, and being taken with Mr. Smith's advertisement in a newspaper in which he described himself as a benevolent teacher of youth, called upon him at the Belle Sauvage Inn, Ludgate Hill, whither he used to repair periodically, for the purpose of securing new pupils, and was then staying on one of these ventures. Not finding him at home he left his card, and on the following day this worthy gentleman entered our house, demonstrated or at least attempted to demonstrate with great warmth the excellency of his system, called his scholars ' his dear children,' and, in fact, so won the respect of my unsuspecting parents that my father thought him a happy man and my mother regarded him as a saint. I was to learn ' good breeding ' and he engaged to teach me the classics, mathematics, etc., with board and lodging also, all for the moderate sum of £20 per annum.

Smith took the boys north by sea and enjoyed a tipsy re-union with his wife at Stockton-on-Tees where she had driven to meet him. Although it was a dark windy night and he was " so drunk that he could scarcely keep his seat " he then insisted on driving the 36 miles to the school where the Abernethy brothers' worst apprehensions were soon realised:

[1] See Editor's note, *The Dickensian*, xiii (1917), 260.

There were about fifty boys. The building had formerly been a nunnery, and was built in the form of a square, with a courtyard in the centre, into which all the windows looked, the exterior presenting dead walls. There were two gates at opposite sides of the square, which were locked every night at eight o'clock, thus debarring all exit. On one side of the square was a playground, out of which we were not allowed to go more than once or twice a month, and into which we were turned on the morning after our arrival. Never shall I forget the heart-sinking I felt at the sight of the crowd of unhealthy young ragamuffins, with their hardened faces, who surrounded us and treated us to jeers and laughter. Other realities of our situation were soon apparent: our clothes were taken from us, only to be returned on occasional Sundays when we attended church at the neighbouring village of Romaldkirk, and others of a workhouse quality substituted, while our shoes were replaced by wooden clogs. Our bed-rooms, three in number, were little better than granaries. In each room were fourteen or fifteen wooden beds with straw mattresses, and each with a couple of blankets. Our dining-room was a large gloomy apartment with an earthen floor, the only articles of furniture being long wooden benches, at which we stood and ate our miserable rations—yes, stood, for we had not even chairs. The schoolroom was a lofty chamber which I suppose had been the chapel. It had only one small stove and our suffering from cold in the winter was horrible. There were several large holes in the roof which let in water in rainy weather. We had two ruffians, who were styled teachers, beside our master, who seldom, or never entered the schoolroom but to assist at punishing the boys, which seemed to give him a hellish delight, like that with which the ministers of the Holy Inquisition witnessed the tortures of their victims. We rose at five, and at eight were assembled in the dining chamber to breakfast. This consisted of black bread, milk, and water, and when finished, we repaired to the play-ground, and school commenced at nine. At one, we again assembled to dine. This meal was varied every day; milk and bread, then soup, a small tureen of it among twelve boys, with about an ounce of meat to each, often in a putrid state. None of the teachers dined with us, they merely superintended the distribution of our often disgusting rations like huntmen feeding a kennel of hounds, which is no bad resemblance to our dinner parties. At five we supped off black bread and milk, played till seven, and were then sent off to bed.

Another regulation of this establishment was that no holidays were allowed, and fond parents as a consolation used to send from time to time hampers containing among other goods, biscuits and sweetmeats, which upon delivery were forthwith appropriated by the stronger young ruffians in the school.

It was not until an uncle of the Abernethy boys, chancing to be in the neighbourhood, paid a call at the school and discovered the brutal conditions in which his nephews were living under the " fatherly care " of Mr. Smith that the children were taken away.

In the 1848 preface to *Nickleby* from which I have already quoted Dickens writes:

> I cannot call to mind, now, how I came to hear about Yorkshire schools when I was a not very robust child, sitting in bye-places, near Rochester Castle, with a head full of Partridge, Strap, Tom Pipes and Sancho Panza; but I know that my first impressions of them were picked up at that time, and that they were, some-how or other, connected with a suppurated abscess that some boy had come home with, in consequence of his Yorkshire guide, philosopher, and friend, having ripped it open with an inky pen-knife. The impression made upon me, however, made, never left me. I was always curious about them—fell, long after-wards, and at sundry times, into the way of hearing more about them—at last, having an audience, resolved to write about them.

He did not fail to include in the novel a version of the incident which had so impressed him as a child: in Chapter 34 Mr. Squeers is praising his wife's resourcefulness to Ralph Nickleby and offers the following example: " One of our boys . . . got a abscess on him last week. To see how she operated upon him with a pen-knife! Oh Lor! what a member of society that woman is!" Several years after Dickens's death it was claimed in the *Newcastle Weekly Chronicle* (24 December 1886) that a certain John Brooks, who was born at Chatham in the same years as Dickens and who had been sent to a Yorkshire school called Bowes Hall, was the person who had told Dickens the abscess story. According to Brooks, however, he himself had caused the damage by cutting a pimple off his own nose with a pen-knife and his master, Clarkson, was in no way to blame.[1]

Whatever the truth was in this case, however, Dickens was not relying on this incident alone for documentary detail when scourg-ing the Yorkshire schools. His journey to Yorkshire mentioned by Forster was a swift fact-finding mission for the purpose of which, he wrote afterwards to Mrs. S. C. Hall (29 December 1838) he armed himself with " a plausible letter to an old Yorkshire attorney from another attorney in town, telling him how a friend had been left a widow, and wanted to place her boys at a Yorkshire

---

[1] See *Letters*, i, 482, note 2.

xviii THE COMPOSITION OF

school in hopes of thawing the frozen compassion of her relations."[1]

He made this "pious fraud" public in the 1848 Preface and described there also how, after he had passed a convivial evening with the old lawyer and had noticed how uneasy he seemed to become whenever the subject of schools came up, this "jovial, ruddy, broadfaced man"

> suddenly took up his hat, and leaning over the table and looking me full in the face, said, in a low voice: 'Weel, Misther, we've been vary pleasant toogather, and ar'll spak' my moind tiv'ee. Dinnot let the weedur send her lattle boy to yan o' our school-measthers, while there's a harse to hoold in a'Lunnun, or a gootther to lie asleep in. Ar wouldn't mak' ill words amang my neeburs, and ar speak tiv'ee quiet loike. But I'm dom'd if ar can gang to bed and not tell'ee, for weedur's sak', to keep the lattle boy from a'sike scoondrels while there's a harse to hoold in a'Lunnun, or a gootther to lie asleep in!' Repeating these words with great heartiness, and with a solemnity on his jolly face that made it look twice as large as before, he shook hands and went away. I never saw him afterwards, but I sometimes imagine that I descry a faint reflection of him in John Browdie.

We do not know precisely how many of the schools in the Barnard Castle area Dickens visited but we do know that he met the proprietor of one of the biggest of them. In his diary for 1838 the following entry appears under 2 February:

> [Mem. Shaw the schoolmaster we saw today, is the man in whose school several boys went blind sometime since, from gross neglect. The case was tried and the Verdict went against him. It must have been between 1823 and 1826. Look this out in the Newspapers.][2]

William Shaw had been running Bowes Academy, near Greta Bridge, since 1814 and, as Philip Collins observes,[3] it must have been a very profitable enterprise since he had been involved in costs of at least £1000 as a result of the case Dickens referred to. He had been the subject of two prosecutions in 1823 by parents of boys who had gone blind whilst in his care. The proceedings were fully reported in *The Times* for 31 October and 1 November 1823 and it is probable that Dickens did indeed look up these reports because at least one or two details from the evidence given by one of the boys, William Jones, are incorporated into his account of the "internal economy of Dotheboys Hall" as may be seen from the following quotation from the *Times* report:

[1] *Letters*, i, 482–83.
[2] *Letters*, i, 632.
[3] *Dickens and Education* (1963), p. 101. Chapter 5 of this book opens with a very full and interesting discussion of the Yorkshire schools and Dickens's treatment of them.

William Jones, sworn.—I shall be 12 years old the 3d of January next. I recollect going to Mr. Shaw's school, we went down on the stage. I could see as well as anybody then. I had the smallpox about a year before. It did not injure my sight. First week, they treated me well—gave me tea and toast for breakfast. Next week they turned me among the other boys, and gave me hasty-pudding for breakfast. There were from 260 to 300 boys. Gave us meat and potatoes four days in the week—bread and milk on Thursday—dumplings made of flour and water on Friday—and black potatoes, with a bit of butter, on Saturday. When any gentleman used to come to see the school, Mr. Shaw used to come in and tell the usher to make all the boys without jackets and trousers get under the table. When any of them got a hole in the jacket or trousers, they went without till they were mended. The boys washed in a long trough, like what horses drink out of: the biggest boys used to take advantage of the little boys, and get the dry part of the towel. There were two towels a day for the whole school. We had no supper; nothing after tea—we had dry bread, brown, and a drop of water and a drop of milk warmed. The flock of the bed was straw; one sheet and one quilt; four or five boys slept in a bed not very large. My brother and three more slept in my bed; about thirty beds in the room, and a great tub in the middle, full of . . . . There were not five boys in every bed. The tub used to be flowing all over the room. Every other morning we used to flea the beds. The usher used to cut the quills, and give us them to catch the fleas; and if you did not fill the quill, you caught a good beating. The pot-skimmings were called broth, and we used to have it for tea on Sunday; one of the ushers offered a penny a piece for every maggot, and there was a pot-full gathered: he never gave it them. No soap, except on Saturday, and then the wenches used to wash us. I was there nine months, and there was nothing the matter with me. One morning I could not write my copy. Next morning he sent me into the wash-house. There were other boys there; some quite blind. Mr. Shaw would not have us in his room. I was there a month. There were 18 boys at one time affected; some who were totally blind were sent into a room; I think two besides myself. In about a month I was removed to a private room, where there were nine totally blind. A doctor was sent for. Mr. Benning is his name. I was in the room two months: the doctor discharged me, saying I had lost one eye, and should preserve the other. I had lost one eye, but I could not see with the other. I was taken back to the washhouse and never had the doctor again; I was taken home in the month of March.

In Shaw's defence it was shown that he had called in an eminent London eye specialist, Sir W. Adams, at an expense of three hun-

dred guineas but, since the Jones boys had left the school before
Adams's arrival (his coming was clearly the result of last-minute
panic on Shaw's part), this evidence was not admitted and, despite
some loyal attempts on the part of members of Shaw's staff to
counter the boys' evidence, the verdict went against him and he
was ordered to pay damages of £300 to the boys' father.   The next
day, faced with another, similar, prosecution, Shaw threw in the
sponge: his counsel said that as the case would certainly go against
him, he " should be immediately disposed of and that the verdict
should be pronounced with the same damages which were given
in the action of yesterday . . . ".   One might have expected that
the judge, after hearing such evidence, would have animadverted
rather severely on Shaw's conduct of his school.   On the contrary,
Mr. Justice Park said that he

> was still of the opinion that there was nothing to impeach the
> general conduct of Mr. Shaw in the management of the School.
> But taking it for granted that the attention given to the morals,
> health, comfort and instruction of the boys was as much as
> could be expected, in all probability his unaccountable con-
> cealment of the calamity from the parents, when the boys were
> suffering the worst stages of the disease, had founded the
> verdict.[1]

The general public seems to have been quite as complacent as Mr.
Justice Park since, by the time Dickens visited Greta Bridge
fifteen years later, Bowes Academy was flourishing with between
two and three hundred pupils and seven assistant masters.   During
the publication of *Nickleby*, however, Mrs. Samuel Carter Hall
seems to have sent Dickens some anecdote relating to the 1823
trials and she was not the only one to make a connection between
Squeers and Shaw.   He became widely recognised as the original
of Dickens's character, despite the novelist's assertion in his
preface that " Mr. Squeers is the representative of a class, and
not of an individual."   Shaw was, in fact, the Editors of the
Pilgrim Letters observe, " the only local schoolmaster with one
eye—or, as a former pupil recalled, ' a slight scale covering the
pupil of one of his eyes ' ".[2]   According to Hablot Browne's son,
Dickens and his illustrator " seem to have fastened on one particular man as the model for Squeers.   I once asked my father what
the original man was really like.   He went so far as to say that the
etching was not unlike him."[3]   Presumably this is a discreet
reference to Shaw as Browne had beheld him on that February
morning in 1838.

[1] *The Times*, 1 November 1823, p. 3.
[2] *Letters*, i, 481, note 5.
[3] Edgar Browne, *Phiz and Dickens* (1913), p. 11*f*.

This " scoundrel ", as Dickens calls him in his reply to Mrs. Hall, certainly suffered, along with other Yorkshire schoolmasters, from the publication of *Nickleby*. The picture of Dotheboys Hall aroused public scorn and indignation against the " academies " as no law-report in *The Times* could. Philip Collins quotes an American traveller in Yorkshire in 1843 who noted in his diary:

We passed the veritable Dotheboys Hall of Dickens, exactly answering to his description in appearance, in situation, in all things. It is deserted utterly—*Nicholas Nickleby* ruined not this establishment alone, but many other schools with which the vicinity abounds, though some of the latter were in no way objectionable.[1]

And later Thackeray commented:

I remember, when that famous ' Nicholas Nickleby ' came out, seeing a letter from a pedagogue in the north of England, which, dismal as it was, was immensely comical. " Mr. Dickens's ill-advised publication," wrote the poor school-master, " has passed like a whirlwind over the schools of the North." He was a proprietor of a cheap school; Dotheboys Hall was a cheap school. There were many such establishments in the northern counties. Parents were ashamed that never were ashamed before until the kind satirist laughed at them; relatives were frightened; scores of little scholars were taken away; poor schoolmasters had to shut their shops up; every pedagogue was voted a Squeers, and many suffered, no doubt unjustly; but afterwards schoolboys' backs were not so much caned; schoolboys' meat was less tough and more plentiful; and schoolboys' milk was not so sky-blue.[2]

That Dickens was, in Henry James's phrase, " one of those people on whom nothing was lost " is clear if we compare his vivid account, in a letter home to his wife, of his journey to Yorkshire with the description of Nicholas and Squeers travelling the same route in the second number of *Nicholas Nickleby*. In the letter, written from the George and New Inn at Greta Bridge (where Nicholas and Squeers are put down by their coach) on Thursday 1 February, he writes:

We reached Grantham between 9 and 10 on Tuesday night, and found everything prepared for our reception in the very best Inn I have ever put up at. It is odd enough that an old

[1] *Dickens and Education*, p. 104.
[2] This passage forms part of the peroration of Thackeray's lecture entitled " Charity and Humour " first given in America in 1852.

lady who had been outside all day and came in towards dinner time turned out to be the Mistress of a Yorkshire School returning from the holiday-stay in London. She was a very queer old body, and shewed us a long letter she was carrying to one of the boys from his father, containing a severe lecture (enforced and aided by many texts from Scripture) *on his refusing to eat boiled meat*. She was very communicative, drank a great deal of brandy and water, and towards evening became insensible, in which state we left her.

Yesterday we were up again shortly after 7 and came on upon our journey by the Glasgow Mail which charged us the remarkably low sum of *six pounds, four* for two places inside. We had a very droll male companion until seven o'Clock in the evening, and a most delicious lady's maid for twenty miles who implored us to keep a sharp look-out at the coach windows as she expected her carriage was coming to meet her and she was afraid of missing it. We had many delightful vauntings of the same kind; and in the end it is scarcely necessary to say that the Coach did not come, and a very dirty girl did.

As we came further North, the snow grew deeper. About eight o'Clock it began to fall heavily, and as we crossed the wild heaths hereabout, there was no vestige of a track. The Mail kept on well, however, and at eleven we reached a bare place with a house standing alone in the midst of a dreary moor, which the Guard informed us was Greta Bridge. I was in a perfect agony of apprehension, for it was fearfully cold and there were no outward signs of anybody being up in the house. But to our great joy we discovered a comfortable room with drawn curtains and a most blazing fire. In half an hour they gave us a smoking supper and a bottle of mulled port (in which we drank your health) and then we retired to a couple of capital bedrooms in each of which was a rousing fire half way up the chimney.

We have had for breakfast, toasts, cakes, a yorkshire pie[,a] piece of beef about the size and much the shape of my portmanteau, tea, coffee, ham and eggs—and are now going to look about us. Having finished our discoveries, we start in a postchaise for Barnard Castle which is only four miles off, and there I deliver the letter given me by Mitton's friend. All the schools are round about that place, and a dozen old abbies besides, which we shall visit by some means or other tomorrow. We shall reach York on Saturday I hope, and (God willing) I trust I shall be at home on Wednesday morning. If anything should occur to prevent me, I will write to you from York, but I think that is not likely.[1]

[1] *Letters*, i, 365–66.

The extraordinary document shown to Dickens by the old schoolmistress clearly inspired the hilarious letter from Mobbs's step-mother[1] who " took to her bed on hearing he wouldn't eat fat, and has been very ill ever since," read out by Squeers in Chapter 8, and the schoolmistress's constant tippling must have suggested the detail about Squeer's frequent getting down from the coach " to stretch his legs " and returning from such excursions red-nosed and sleepy. The " delicious lady's maid " appears in the novel as Nicholas's fastidious travelling-companion " who loudly lamented . . . the non-arrival of her own carriage . . . and made the guard solemnly promise to stop every green chariot he saw coming ". And the disappearance of the road beneath heavy snow that Dickens mentions no doubt suggested to him, when he came to write up the journey as fiction, the overturning of the coach which occurs at the end of Chapter 5. It is pleasant, also, to find him publicly recording in these chapters his appreciation of particular inns. He refers to the George at Grantham as " one of the best inns in England " and has Newman Noggs recommend to Nicholas the " good ale " at the King's Head, Barnard Castle (chapter 7).[2] It was at this inn that Dickens's memorable interview with the " old Yorkshire attorney " must have taken place.

From Barnard Castle Dickens and Browne went on to the village of Bowes, three or four miles away, where they saw Shaw and received a powerfully gloomy impression of the district. In the letter to Mrs. Hall from which I have quoted earlier Dickens wrote:

The country for miles around was covered, when I was there, with deep snow. There is an old Church near the school, and the first grave-stone I stumbled on that dreary winter afternoon was placed above the grave of a boy, eighteen long years old, who had died—suddenly, the inscription said; I suppose his heart broke—the Camel falls down ' suddenly ' when they heap the last load on his back—died at that wretched place [Shaw's school]. I think his ghost put Smike into my head, upon the spot.[3]

---

[1] Originally Mobbs's mother-in-law (see p. 72 of Part Three). In 19th Century usage " mother-in-law " could mean " step-mother ". Dickens changed the words in a later edition.

[2] He also alludes playfully to the name of the landlord of the George and New Inn at Greta Bridge in 1838. This man's name was Martin and in Chapter 13 of *Nickleby*, after Smike has escaped, Mrs. Squeers tells her husband she will borrow " Swallow's " chaise to go in pursuit of the runaway.

[3] *Letters*, i, 482.

The inscription on 'Smike's" grave reads as follows:

Here lie
the remains of
GEORGE ASHTON TAYLOR
son of John Taylor
of Trowbridge, Wiltshire,
who died suddenly at Mr. William Shaw's Academy
of this place, April 13th, 1822
aged 19 years.
Young reader, thou must die, but after this the judgement.

If Dickens had inspected the Burial Registers as well as the gravestones " that dreary winter afternoon " he might have been given even more food for thought. T. P. Cooper, author of *With Dickens in Yorkshire* (1923), published in the 1939 volume of *The Dickensian* (pages 107–108) a list of boys from local schools buried in unrecorded graves in Bowes Churchyard between 1810 and 1834. Of the 29 boys listed there, aged between 7 and 15 with one aged 18, eleven had been pupils of Shaw's. Philip Collins rightly says that we should relate this list to " the mortality rates for boys of that period, locally and at other boarding schools, as well as nationally " before using it as evidence against Shaw and his fellow-schoolmasters.[1] But there is one desolate little detail, which, I think, Dickens might have noted: against the name of one 8-year-old boy, John Bell, a scholar at Mr. Horn's school, appear the words " supposed a native of Newcastle ". This seems to indicate an example of the kind of total abandonment of some children to the schools by their parents that Dickens dramatises in the figure of Smike who laments to Nicholas that no visions of former loved ones could ever come to cheer him on his deathbed: " They cannot come from home; they would frighten me, if they did, for I don't know what it is, and shouldn't know them."

Another name that appears in Mr. Cooper's list is that of John Dobson, " son of Mary Dobson, widow, London, a scholar of Mr. Shaw's school; aged 9 years ". Some letters written by this boy to his mother from Bowes Academy were presented to the Dickens House in 1936. That they were dictated by the schoolmaster seems clear from such an example as this:

Bowes, August 15th, 1818

Dear Mother
    I am sensible of the many obligations I am under to my dear Uncle and beg you to convey my acknowledgments to him in the best manner you can. His favors I will endeavour to

---

[1] *Dickens and Education*, p. 103. See also K.J. Fielding's "*Nicholas Nickleby Illustrated*" in *The Genealogist's Magazine*, xiv (1962), 101–07.

deserve. To you I also return my thanks for the present you
sent me by my kind Master; and in the hopes that you and my
kind Uncle are well and happy, I am

affectionately

Dear Mother

Your dutiful son

John C. Dobson.

Printing these letters in *The Dickensian* (Vol. 35, pages 32–36)
S. J. Rust remarks that " a great improvement in style is shown
as the year progresses, and we are forced to the conclusion that
Shaw could, and did, teach handwriting. I think we must also
admit that he taught spelling and English as well as did most
schools of that day." Mr. Rust seems to have been hoping to find
evidence that Shaw was as demonstrably illiterate as Squeers
whereas, of course, it is hardly likely that he would have been so
professionally flourishing if he had not been able to supply parents
with some assurance, in the form of well-written letters from their
children, that the boys really were being taught something.[1] He
could, of course, censor easily enough any allusions to bad food
and harsh living conditions that his pupils might venture on.
The real quality of the education he pretended to provide is shown,
however, by some exercise-books, belonging to two other pupils,
which were also presented to the Dickens House in 1936. The
perfect neatness of these books, Mr. Rust observes, " tells of
strong discipline " but it is also clear that the boys were merely
copying from text-books without any understanding—" the very
order of the study shows that the master, himself, knew nothing
of these subjects [trigonometry and algebra] ".

Dickens, however, did not need to research into burial registers
and school exercise-books as well as into *The Times* to give him
ammunition for his assault on the Yorkshire schools. He had
seen and heard enough on his northern excursion to feel confident
that, as he was to put it in the preface he wrote the following year,

---

[1] We learn from Mrs. Nickleby, in Chapter 26, that more respectable
schools than the Yorkshire ones were not above a little genteel decep-
tion in this respect. Recalling the " delightful " letters she and her
husband used to receive every half-year from Kate away at school,
" telling us she was the first pupil in the whole establishment, and had
made more progress than anybody else," Mrs. Nickleby adds: " The girls
wrote all the letters themselves . . . and the writing-master touched
them up afterwards with a magnifying glass and a silver pen; at least I
think they wrote them, though Kate was not quite certain about that,
because she didn't know the handwriting of hers again; but any way, I
know it was a circular which they all copied, and of course it was a very
gratifying thing—very gratifying."

" Mr. Squeers and his school are faint and feeble pictures of an existing reality, purposely subdued and kept down lest they should be deemed impossible." It was nearly three weeks, however, after his return before he was able to get down to the writing of the first chapter, so busy was he with writing *Oliver*, editing the *Miscellany*, persuading Bentley to let him postpone the writing of *Barnaby Rudge* (" The conduct of three different stories at the same time, and the production of a large portion of each, every month, would have been beyond Scott himself "[1]) and gathering contributors for a book he had undertaken to edit for the benefit of his first publisher's distressed widow. However, on 22 February he was at last able to inform Chapman and Hall that although he had been " decoyed to the play and seduced from Nicholas by a thousand blandishments . . . the first chapter is ready, and I mean (God willing) to begin in earnest tomorrow night, so you can begin to print as soon as you like. The sooner you begin, the faster I shall get on."[2] He did not " get on " all that fast, however. Domestic distractions such as the birth of his daughter, Mary, on 6 March and Catherine's subsequent illness, and the necessity of keeping up the instalments of *Oliver Twist* (on 13 March he wrote to Forster, " I am sitting patiently at home waiting for Oliver Twist who has not yet arrived ") made progress on the first number of *Nickleby* very difficult but, somehow, he managed to finish it in time for publication on 31 March. That night Dickens and Forster rode out to the Star and Garter Inn at Richmond, where Dickens had taken Catherine to recuperate, and Forster records in his biography, " The smallest hour was sounding into the night from St. Paul's before we started, and the night was none of the pleasantest; but we carried news that lightened every part of the road, for the sale of *Nickleby* had reached that day the astounding number of nearly fifty thousand!"[3]

Before publication Dickens and his publishers had made a forlorn attempt to protect the new work from the sort of piracy that *Pickwick Papers* and *Oliver Twist* were being subjected to. The unsatisfactory state of the copyright laws gave authors no redress if hack-writers chose to plagiarise them. All the literary pirate had to do was to alter the characters' names slightly and throw in a few distinguishing (and generally deplorable) touches of his own; he was then at liberty to copy the plot and incidents of the original novel as closely as he liked—the law would support him so long as there was no possibility of any purchaser's being unable to differentiate between his publication and the original. So Edward Lloyd had been able with impunity to begin issuing *The Posthumor-*

[1] *Letters*, i, 370.
[2] *Letters*, i, 379.
[3] Forster, p. 109.

ous Notes of the Pickwick Club, edited by " Bos " (identified by
Louis James as the hack-writer T. P. Prest[1]), in April or May 1837.
The weekly instalments were priced at one penny and the publica-
tion, a very crude and clumsily expanded version of *Pickwick
Papers*, continued to run until July 1839, a total of 112 instalments.
In December 1837 or January 1838 Lloyd began issuing *Oliver
Twiss*, also edited by " Bos ", and a rival piracy with the same
title but edited by " Poz " appeared in the field as well. " The
vagabonds have stuck placards on the walls—each to say *theirs*
is the only true Edition," Dickens reported indignantly to Richard
Bentley.[2]

Trying to protect *Nickleby* Dickens issued the so-called " Nickleby Proclamation " both as a separate leaflet and as an advertisement in the newspapers. Louis James comments that this
notice (reproduced overleaf) was " even by the contemporary
standards of journalism . . . a little puerile, although Dickens
probably felt these literary hacks should be spoken to in their own
language." All that happened, in fact, was that " Bos " parodied
the " Nickleby Proclamation " itself and Lloyd boldly published
on 31 March the first instalment of *Nickelas Nickelbery* in the usual
format of 8 pages plus one crude woodcut illustration, price one
penny. Louis James amusingly shows how the author of this
compilation (the inevitable " Bos "), having naturally no idea
of what would be contained in Dicken's first number, was forced
to pad out his pages as best he could until he was able to get hold
of a published copy. As soon as he had done so he was able to
" begin to bring his story round to his original with the appearance
of ' The New London Limited Hot-Baked Flourry Potatoe Conveyance and Delivery Company ! ! ! ' "[3]

Nickelas Nickelbery (or, to give it its full title, *Nickelas Nickelbery. Containing the Adventures, Mis-adventures, Chances, Mischances, Fortunes, Mis-fortunes, Mys-teries, Mis-eries and Miscellaneous Manoeuvres of the Family of Nickelbery*[4]) thereafter
carefully followed in Dickens's footsteps for the first ten monthly
parts of *Nicholas Nickleby*, stopping at the point where Nicholas
leaves Crummles's company to return to London to protect his
sister (the January 1839 instalment of *Nickleby*). " Bos " hastily

---

[1] See James, *Fiction for the Working Man 1830–1850* (1963), p. 50. For
much of what follows I am indebted to Dr. James's excellent discussion
of plagiarisms of Dickens in Chapter 4 of his book.

[2] *Letters*, i, 350.

[3] *Fiction for the Working Man*, p. 64.

[4] I have not been able to see a complete version of this plagiarism and have
inspected only some loose numbers of it (Part 4, nos. 13–16 and Part 11,
no. 42) in the Dexter Collection in the British Museum [press-mark:
DEX 303 (5)].

finishes off the story by having his Newman Noggs character discover that Roger Nickelbery (i.e. Ralph) had been concealing a
will which made Snike (i.e. Smike) heir to a fortune.   Evidently, as
Louis James comments, " Bos " found the imitation of *Nickleby*
a less congenial task than that of *Pickwick* or *Oliver*.

Some idea of the clumsy and coarsening elaboration that is
" Bos's " hallmark is given by the way in which he varies Dickens's
names (Sir Mulberry Hawk becomes Sir Grogsberry Raven, for
example, and Madame Mantalini becomes Madame Corsette de
Mantello) and by the following incident which occurs at the end
of his Chapter 12 (equivalent to Dickens's Chapter 9).   The
Squeers-character, here called Mr. Whackem Speres, and his wife
disagree about the desirability of having Nickelas Nickelbery at
the school, just as in Dickens but, instead of the dispute subsiding
into comic/horrific connubial complicity and mutual congratulation as in the original, " Bos " terminates it with some knockabout
farce:

> [Mr. Speres] was suddenly interrupted by Mrs. Speres raising the
> fire tongs, and before her husband had any power to defend
> himself, she applied the same with such force to his nose,
> dragging him at the same time all round the room, that he
> bawled a thousand murders, and writhed, danced and twisted
> in the most corkscrew fashion with the infliction he was under-
> going.   At length, however, he managed to release himself from
> the tongs, and immediately made an attack upon his wife, who
> resisted him heroically, pulling his hair out by handsfulls, and
> committing sad havoc on his cheeks with her finger-nails.   In
> this the amiable lady was assisted by master Speres, who made
> a violent attack on his father's legs, by kicking his hardest,
> and screaming himself black in the face.   At length, having
> completely exhausted themselves by beating and scratching
> one another, they made it up with a kiss and retired to bed.

There was little danger of anyone's mistaking such stuff as this
for " the true Dickens " but we can well understand how odious
he must have found this sort of cheapening of his works.   Nor
was it only the penny-number plagiarists he had to contend with;
as we shall see, he suffered even more vexation from the hack-
dramatists of the day.

The prodigious first-day sale of the first number was such,
however, that it would surely have taken more than " Bos's "
impudence to put Dickens out of temper in April 1838.   The
reception accorded to the number by the press seems, on the whole,
to have been very favourable.   " If the future numbers keep up
the promise given by this first," commented *The Age*,

THE NEW WORK BY THE AUTHOR OF "THE PICKWICK PAPERS."

Oᴺ the Thirty-first of March will be published, to be continued Monthly, price One Shilling, and completed in Twenty Parts, the First Number of " THE LIFE AND ADVENTURES OF NICHOLAS NICKLEBY ;" containing a faithful account of the Fortunes, Misfortunes, Uprisings, Downfallings, and Complete Career of the Nickleby Family— Edited by " BOZ."—And each Monthly Part embellished with Two Illustrations by " Pʜɪᴢ."

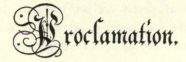

Proclamation.

Whereas we are the only true and lawful " Boz."

And Whereas it hath been reported to us, who are commencing a New Work, to be called—Tʜᴇ

LIFE & ADVENTURES

OF

NICHOLAS NICKLEBY

THAT some dishonest dullards, resident in the by-streets and cellars of this town, impose upon the unwary and

(*above and following pages*)
The "Nickleby Proclamation"

credulous, by producing cheap and wretched imitations of our delectable Works. 𝕬𝖓𝖉 𝖂𝖍𝖊𝖗𝖊𝖆𝖘 we derive but small comfort under this injury, from the knowledge that the dishonest dullards aforesaid, cannot, by reason of their mental smallness, follow near our heels, but are constrained to creep along by dirty and little-frequented ways, at a most respectful and humble distance behind.

𝕬𝖓𝖉 𝖂𝖍𝖊𝖗𝖊𝖆𝖘, in like manner, as some other vermin are not worth the killing for the sake of their carcases, so these kennel pirates are not worth the powder and shot of the law, inasmuch as whatever damages they may commit, they are in no condition to pay any.

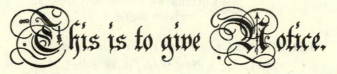

This is to give Notice.

FIRSTLY,

TO PIRATES.

THAT we have at length devised a mode of execution for them, so summary and terrible, that if any gang or gangs thereof presume to hoist but one shred of the colours of the good ship NICKLEBY, we will hang them on gibbets so lofty and enduring, that their remains shall be a monument of our just vengeance to all succeeding ages; and it shall not lie in the power of any Lord High Admiral, on earth, to cause them to be taken down again.

SECONDLY,

TO THE PUBLIC.

THAT in our new work, as in our preceding one, it will be our aim to amuse, by producing a rapid succession of characters and incidents, and describing them as cheerfully and pleasantly as in us lies; that we have wandered into fresh fields and pastures new, to seek materials for the purpose; and that, in behalf of NICHOLAS NICKLEBY, we confidently hope to enlist both their heartiest merriment, and their kindliest sympathies.

THIRDLY,

TO THE POTENTATES OF PATERNOSTER-ROW.

THAT from the THIRTIETH DAY OF MARCH next, until further notice, we shall hold our Levees, as heretofore, on the last evening but one of every month, between the hours of seven and nine, at our Board of Trade, Number ONE HUNDRED AND EIGHTY-SIX in the STRAND, LONDON; where we again request the attendance (in vast crowds) of their accredited agents and ambassadors. Gentlemen to wear knots upon their shoulders; and patent cabs to draw up with their doors towards the grand entrance, for the convenience of loading.

Given at the office of our Board of Trade aforesaid, in the presence of our Secretaries, EDWARD CHAPMAN & WILLIAM HALL, on this Twenty-eighth day of February, One Thousand Eight Hundred and Thirty-eight.

(Signed)

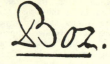

NICKELAS

NICKELBERY

EDITED BY "BOS."

The big Yorkshireman's curious behaviour at Miss Spere's tea party.

"I know it!" said Mrs. Speres pursuing her occupation of shirt mending.

"We might have spared her, I think, for a few weeks longer;" observed the schoolmaster, in a reflective manner, "no doubt she is very comfortable with the Gileses, as she always is, and it is a pity to disturb her happiness!"

"I think," replied Mrs. Speres putting down the shirt, and looking very

No. 13.

angry at her liege lord and master, "I think we had much better send her away altogether, if you mean to keep that Knockelbery here."

"What do you mean, my love?" asked Mr. Speres, with much amazement.

"What do I mean!" reiterated Mrs. Speres with a bitter sneer, "why any one would suppose that you had lost your senses, Mr. Speres;—what do I

First Page of Part 13 of *Nickelas Nickelbery*
(*J. F. Dexter Collection, British Museum*)

all we can say is, that poor Pickwick stands a chance of being soon forgotten. The scene between the Yorkshire schoolmaster at the Saracen's Head and his visitors is as rich and caustic as any ' Boz ' has ever penned, and the illustration of it by 'Phiz' is Capital. Newman Noggs, we strongly suspect, will eclipse ' Samivel Veller '.—Vivat Boz!

The *Weekly Chronicle* rejoiced that " the vainly-imitated and un-rivalled Boz has again made his devoirs at the shrine of humour " and regaled its readers with copious extracts. *The Sun* detected " more weight and earnestness of manner than [in] Pickwick " and noted that the author " bounds upon his characters at once "; it praised the characterisation of Ralph and Squeers especially, calling the latter a Fielding-like sketch which would " task all its author's tact and attention; but if well worked out—as we feel assured it will be—it will give him a foremost place among the novelists of the day." The founding of the Joint Stock Company in Chapter 2 the same reviewer found to be first-class stinging satire and " irresistably laughable ".

A less ecstatic note was struck by *Bell's New Weekly Messenger* which looked nostalgically back towards the glories of " Benevolent Pickwick " and " Immortal Sam " and feared that Dickens would ruin himself if he attempted to emulate Fielding and Smollett, writers who were out of his class, whatever his misguided admirers might pretend; *Nickleby* would need to recapture the " spirit, life and broad humour " of *Pickwick* if it was not to be regarded with " apathy and indifference ".[1]

But this review seems to have been very much a minority report and it seems that Dickens in this first number gripped his readers with Ancient-Mariner power. Nor is this surprising when we consider that these first four chapters introduce the reader to a hero and heroine who are all that heroes and heroines should be, to a " heavy " villain in the traditional guise of a Wicked Uncle, to some droll but sympathetic secondary characters such as Miss La Creevy (possibly based on Dickens's own miniature-painting aunt, Janet Barrow[2]) and Newman Noggs, and to a splendid grotesque villain in the shape of Mr. Squeers. Pleasurable anticipation is also provided in that readers, already fascinated by Squeers, learn that Nicholas is to start for Yorkshire and for Dotheboys

---

[1] *The Age*, 8 April 1838, p. 106; *The Weekly Chronicle*, 1 April 1838, p. 5; *The Sun*, 2 April 1838, p. 3; *Bell's New Weekly Messenger*, 8 April 1838, p. 6. I am much indebted to Professor J. Don Vann, of North Texas State University, for giving me references to these reviews (and to the notices of *Nickleby* in *The Penny Satirist* and *The Court Journal*, quoted below), and also to Miss Mary Ford of Birkbeck College (University of London) for her assistance in locating and copying them.

[2] See William J. Carlton's article, " Janet Barrow's Portrait Miniatures: an Australian Epilogue," in *The Dickensian*, lxviii (1972), 101–103.

Hall in the next number; they would be eagerly looking forward to finding out what the schoolmaster was like at home. The satirical presentation of the United Metropolitan Improved Hot Muffin and Crumpet Baking and Punctual Delivery Company may perhaps seem laboured to us today (especially as Dickens was to treat the same kind of subject so much more successfully in *Martin Chuzzlewit* and *Little Dorrit*) but Humphry House reminds us that still fresh in the public's memory would have been " the speculative rage which preceded the great crash of 1825–6, when steam-ovens, steam-laundries, and milk-and-egg companies competed with canals and railroads for the public's money ".[1]   Hence no doubt *The Sun*'s relish for this particular episode.

The second number appeared at the end of April and in this, as has been shown, Dickens begins to draw directly on his own trip to Yorkshire.   He also inserts two tales (a technique familiar to his readers from *Pickwick*) one of which, the Pilgrim Editors suggest, may have been the result of his having under-written the number; in a letter to Forster that the Editors tentatively date 15 April (the day on which he would be due to deliver copy for the May number to Chapman and Hall) he says, " I couldn't write a line 'till three o'Clock and have yet 5 slips to finish and don't know what to put in them for I have reached the point I meant to leave off with."[2]   The story of the Five Sisters of York would have been ready to his hand since he had visited York Cathedral on his way back from Barnard Castle in February and had had his attention firmly directed to the Five Sisters Window by the verger. His beloved young sister-in-law, Mary Hogarth, whose sudden death in his house at the age of 17 had so prostrated him with grief the previous year, had also been much in his thoughts on the northern journey: " I have dreamt of her ever since I left home, and no doubt shall 'till I return," he wrote to Catherine.   There can be little doubt that it was of Mary he was thinking when he described the youngest sister, Alice, on whose early death turns the story of the Five Sisters:

> The heart of this fair girl bounded with joy and gladness. Devoted attachment to her sisters, and a fervent love of all beautiful things in nature, were its pure affections. Her gleesome voice and merry laugh were the sweetest music of their home. She was its very light and life. . . .

Compare with this his comments on Mary in a letter to a friend written just after her death:

[1] H. House, *The Dickens World* (Oxford Paperback edition, 1950), p. 58. House notes that " the Muffin Company's meeting was to promote a Private Bill in Parliament: in 1825 438 petitions for such Bills were presented, and 286 Private Acts passed."
[2] *Letters*, i, 395–6.

From the day of our marriage the dear girl had been the grace and life of our home, our constant companion, and the sharer of our little pleasures. The love and affection which subsisted between her and her sister, no one can imagine the extent of. We might have known that we were too happy together to be long without a change.[1]

The dominant interest of the second number, however, is, of course, Dotheboys Hall and the introduction, towards the end of the number, of Smike, who is to be the chief focus for pathos in the novel (and whose prominence in the stage versions of the novel is some indication of the extent of his popularity; lacking the symbolic overtones of Oliver Twist or Little Nell, or the greater realism of poor Jo in *Bleak House*, he has had less success with modern readers). This interest is also continued strongly in the first two chapters of the third number (only one chapter of which Dickens had actually got written by 20 May) before the narrative reverts to London and " how Mr. Ralph Nickleby provided for his Niece and Sister-in-Law ". Here Dickens begins to develop the glorious personality of Mrs. Nickleby, destined to be the greatest comic triumph of this superlatively comic novel, and introduces also Mr. Mantalini and Madame, his " essential juice of pine-apple ". As with Smike, the prominence of Mr. Mantalini in all the stage versions of the novel shows that this character was a decided hit with the public. Mrs. Nickleby's wonderfully inconsequential monologues (which Dickens's mother failed, apparently, to recognise as based on her own conversational style) were no doubt less easily transferable to the stage than Mantalini's airy badinage but still it is surprising that this past-mistress of the hilarious non-sequitur did not commend herself more to the dramatisers of the novel.

The grimmer undertones of this last chapter would not have been lost upon Dickens's readers in 1838, however. Dickens himself had written in *Sketches by Boz* (" The Streets—Morning ") that milliners' apprentices were " the hardest worked, the worst paid, and too often, the worst used class of the community ". It is clear enough to modern readers that Ralph is placing Kate in a position where she will be overworked and miserably paid but the way in which he is exposing the fourteen-year-old girl to moral danger is perhaps less obvious, despite Mr. Mantalini's ogling. Richard Altick has written illuminatingly on this point:

the reasonably knowledgeable Victorian reader would have converted these vague hints [Mantalini's leers and the lecherous old lord in Chapter 18] into an explicit assurance, namely, that by the very fact of working in a dressmaking establishment, Kate

[1] *Letters*, i, 263.

was risking her virtue.   For it was well known that girls like her were exposed to the wiles of men both inside the shop and on the pavements outside as well.   By the mere deed of enrolling Kate in the dressmaking trade, therefore, Dickens was able to arouse in his readers a concern which he did not need to make explicit.   He was, in effect, laying the groundwork for the later development in which the danger of seduction was made explicit, Kate's becoming the prey of Lord Frederick Verisopht and Sir Mulberry Hawk.[1]

The fourth (July) number brings the Yorkshire part of the story to a climax with Nicholas's assault on Squeers and departure from Dotheboys Hall, followed by Smike and, just as in Number Three Dickens had introduced the Mantalinis at the end, so in this number the Kenwigs, Mr. Lillyvick and Miss Petowker (of the Theatre Royal, Drury Lane), a group done in his best *Sketches by Boz* vein, make their appearance in the last chapter as still another source of future comic interest.   It is worth noting Dickens's comment on the meekness of Mr. Lillyvick: " If he had been an author, who knew his place, he couldn't have been more humble." He had been particularly exasperated during June by the treatment accorded to him by Bentley, the publisher of the *Miscellany* that he was editing, and this tart comparison no doubt reflects his ire.

In June also Dickens rented a holiday villa at Twickenham where he continued his editorial work and the writing of *Oliver* and *Nickleby*, amidst a welter of visitors and pleasure-jaunts. On 10 July he was able to tell Bentley that he had not only completed the instalment of *Oliver* for publication in August but had also " planned the tale to the close " (it was intended to publish the complete novel in volume form in the autumn, before the serialisation in the *Miscellany* was finished).   But he foresaw that, " having the constant drawback of my monthly work " on *Nickleby* and as editor of the magazine he would be " sadly harassed " to get the whole of *Oliver* written in time.   On 18 July he informed some American publishers enquiring about the possibility of receiving early proof-sheets of the numbers of *Nickleby* that this could hardly be arranged since " I have been behind rather than in advance and have only completed each Number a day or two before its publication."

Number Five, the August number, of *Nickleby*, which he had begun on 10 July duly appeared at the end of July, however, complete with Fanny Squeers's immortal letter to Ralph which Leigh Hunt (for whom Dickens had just arranged that each number of the novel should be sent to him as soon as it was published) declared " surpassed the best things of the kind in Smollett that

---

[1] Richard D. Altick, " Victorian Readers and the Sense of the Present ", *Midway* (published by the University of Chicago), x, 95–119.

Mary Hogarth
(the only known portrait of her)
By "Phiz"

A page of Dickens's manuscript of *Nicholas Nickleby*
(instalment of August 1838; chapter 15)
(*British Museum*)   (*Reduced*)

A page of Dickens's manuscript of *Nicholas Nickleby*
(instalment of August 1838; chapter 15)
(*British Museum*)   (*Reduced*)

A page of Dickens's manuscript of *Nicholas Nickleby*
(instalment of August 1838; chapter 15)
(*British Museum*)   (*Reduced*)

he was able to call to mind ".[1]   In this number, too, Dickens gave
the world his second ludicrously fatuous M.P., Mr. Gregsbury,
successor to Cornelius Brook Dingwall in *Sketches by Boz*.   His
contempt for Parliament was a direct result of his experiences in
the reporters' gallery in the House of Commons between 1832 and
1836 and he was later to sum up his opinion very forcibly in the
words of his autobiographical hero, David Copperfield:

> Night after night, I record predictions that never come to pass,
> professions that are never fulfilled, explanations that are only
> meant to mystify.   I wallow in words.   Britannia, that un-
> fortunate female, is always before me, like a trussed fowl:
> skewered through and through with office-pens, and bound hand
> and foot with red tape.   I am sufficiently behind the scenes to
> know the worth of political life.   I am quite an Infidel about
> it, and shall never be converted.[2]

We notice that Dickens makes Mr. Gregsbury, M.P., particularly
scornful of " any preposterous bills [that might be] brought forward, for giving poor grubbing devils of authors a right to their
own property ".   This would have been a very topical allusion
in 1838 since Dickens's friend Talfourd had introduced a Copyright Bill into Parliament the previous year and it was being
bitterly opposed—it did not, in fact, become law until 1842 and
then only in an attenuated form.

Nickleby Number Six (September) introduces a new villain, Sir
Mulberry Hawk, and his dupe, Lord Frederick, and, in Hawk's
attempted seduction of Kate at her uncle's dinner-party, gives
the reader a scene of thrilling interest such as had been absent
from the previous number. Nicholas's thrashing of Squeers
in Number Four had been the last big theatrical moment. In
the September number there also appears briefly one of my
favourite minor characters in all Dickens, Miss Knag's brother,
the devotee of fashionable novels who " took to scorning everything, and became a genius ".   Dickens seldom missed an opportunity to mock Byronic affectation and had already done so once
earlier in the year in his *Sketches of Young Gentlemen* where " the
Poetical Young Gentlemen " is described being much addicted to
" gloomy and desponding " literature and " much given to opining, especially if he has taken anything strong to drink, that there
is nothing in [the world] worth living for."

The September number ends with Nicholas and Smike about to
set out once more upon their wanderings so that the same kind of
expectation of interesting new scenes is aroused as at the end
of the first number.   But, whereas then the reader knew that

[1] Forster, p. 122.
[2] *David Copperfield*, Chapter 43.

Nicholas was bound for Yorkshire, here his destination is mysterious to all concerned. It is quite likely that Dickens himself had no idea where Nicholas would make for when he wrote the end of Chapter 20 later in August but he had perhaps already the idea that he would make his hero fall in with an itinerant theatrical company. Dickens had been fascinated by the theatre since his childhood and had even, at one point, thought seriously of becoming a professional actor. The glorious Crummles company, who make their début in the October number (well answering the *Edinburgh Review*'s plea, published that month, that the " painful sombreness " of much of *Nickleby* should be relieved with " a sufficient portion of sunshine "[1]), are generally acknowledged to be one of the high points of Dickens's comic presentation of the world of the theatre, and it has also long been believed that the germ of inspiration for these characters was provided by an actual actor-manager, T. D. Davenport, his wife and his daughter, Jean, " the most celebrated Juvenile Actress of the day " (to quote the description of her given on the Davenports' playbills). It can, I think, be argued that the notion of sending Nicholas to Portsmouth and the idea of the Crummleses both came to Dickens simultaneously in September 1838.

He wrote to Bentley on 29 August, " I have some idea of sheltering myself for a week (for Oliver purposes) in the Isle of Wight next Monday " and did indeed go down to Alum Bay with Catherine on 3 September. They would probably have passed through Portsmouth (we know from Forster that Dickens did visit his native city at some point during the writing of *Nickleby*[2]) or Dickens may have visited it from the island. It seems likely that he would have had a look at the old theatre in the High Street which had just enjoyed a full and successful season for the first time for many years. In 1837 it had been opened only for a few nights in March and April when Davenport had leased it to display the precocious talents of his eight-year-old daughter. These talents, as we can see from the playbill, ranged from sustaining the role of Shylock to dancing highland flings and sailor's hornpipes and singing comic or pathetic songs in a variety of national costumes. As James Ollé pointed out in *The Dickensian* (1951 volume, p. 145), " The sight of a weather-worn playbill, clinging to the theatre's walls, advertising the Davenport season of the previous year, may be the simple explanation of the relationship between T. D. Davenport and his daughter, Jean, and Vincent Crummles and his daughter, ' The Infant Phenomenon ' ".

[1] Quoted in *Dickens: the Critical Heritage* (1971), ed. Philip Collins, p. 76.
[2] Forster, p. 2: " I perfectly recollect that, on our being at Portsmouth together while he was writing *Nickleby*, he recognized the exact shape of a military parade seen by him as a very infant, on the same spot, a quarter of a century before."

It is certainly significant, as Mr. Clinton-Baddeley has observed,[1] that Dickens describes the Crummles company as proceeding to Portsmouth " not for the regular season but in the course of a wandering speculation " since this had clearly been the case with the Davenports' Portsmouth venture.

During October Dickens finished writing *Oliver* (which was published in three volumes on 9 November) but somehow also found time to write the November number of *Nickleby* containing the account of " The Great Bespeak for Miss Snevellicci." He set off for a tour of the Midlands and North Wales with Browne on 29 October, and was delighted to find in Shrewsbury when he attended the theatre that it was, in fact, a bespeak night and " as like the Miss Snevellicci business as it could well be ". He also visited Stratford and Shakespeare's house which subsequently served him as a subject for a marvellously absurd conversation between the Wititterlys, Lord Frederick and Mrs. Nickleby in the December number. He was back in London in plenty of time to see the first stage version of the novel, dramatised by Edward Stirling and produced by Frederick Yates at the Adelphi Theatre on 19 November.

Stirling's version follows the first six numbers of *Nickleby* very closely, alternating Dotheboys Hall scenes with comic episodes dominated by Mr. Mantalini (played by Yates himself); and it is Mr. Mantalini, not Hawk, who tries to seduce Kate at Ralph's dinner, we notice. The dénouement is very simple: Newman Noggs finds a will made by Smike's father in Ralph Nickleby's accidentally-dropped pocket-book; the will leaves an immense property to Ralph in the event of Smike's death; the villainy is exposed at the dinner-party and Smike bestows all his new-found fortune on Nicholas, " my kind, my only friend ". After seeing the play Dickens praised many aspects of the production to Forster (who in his biography refers to this dramatisation as " an indecent assault " on the book), especially Mrs. Keeley's acting of Smike, " bating sundry choice sentiments and rubbish regarding the little robins in the fields which have been put into the boy's mouth by Mr. Stirling."[2] The passage to which Dickens objects occurs at the end of the third scene of the play:

SMIKE: He spoke kindly to me. I—I—can't bear it. (*Sighs.*) When—when shall I hear from home—from some one that loves me? To remain longer in this dreadful place will drive me mad. If I was a little bird, then I could fly far, far away, to live happy all the summer days among the green fields and wild flowers. Yes, yes—I'll go at once. (*Runs to window.*)

[1] In his fascinating lecture on Miss Snevellicci, printed in *The Dickensian*, lvii (1951), 43–52.
[2] *Letters*, i, 460.

But there are no flowers now. The cold, glistening snow is on the ground, and the green fields are buried under a large white shroud. If I left the house now I might be starved and drop helpless and frozen, like the poor birds! (*Pauses*) I've heard that good people that live away from this place feed the pretty harmless robins when the cold days and dark nights are on— perhaps they would feed me, too, for I am very harmless— very. I'll run to them at once and ask them. (*Quits the stage through the window, the reflection of the moon thrown upon him.*)

Mrs. Keeley was later reported to have said, " I shall never forget Dickens's face when he heard me repeating these lines. Turning to the prompter he said, ' Damn the robins; cut them out.' "[1]

To Yates himself Dickens wrote to say that the adaptation and production were so good that his general objection to the dramatisation of his unfinished works as tending " to vulgarise the characters . . . and . . . lessen the after-interest in their progress " did not apply in this case and that he had no objection to the play's publication.[2] It duly appeared in the 1838 volume of Chapman and Hall's *Acting National Drama* with a dedication to Dickens by Stirling and a note by the volume's editor, Benjamin Webster, recording Dickens's approval. Dickens had also privately complimented Yates highly on his " glorious Mantalini ".

The Adelphi dramatisation was apparently a great success, partly, of course, because of the great popularity of the novel itself—" its sale has left even that of Pickwick far behind," Dickens informed Yates. Another sign of *Nickleby*'s popularity in that same month was the devotion of the whole of the front page of *The Penny Satirist* for 3 November to portraits of characters from the book. A few days later, however, the same journal tempered this compliment by remarking that *Nickleby* was more of " a collection of capital sketches of character " than a story: " As a mere story teller [Dickens] is but so so. We think Reynolds far superior in this respect " (this would certainly have stung Dickens had he seen it since Reynolds, the author of *Pickwick Abroad*, was one of his most persistant plagiarisers). The *Satirist* had some criticism of Hablot Browne too:

the engraver has given Nickleby a most unphrenologically small head; it is like a man's fist stuck on the top of a man's shoulders. Surely Mr. Phiz has read of Gall and Vinegar, the great inventors of the human faculties?[3]

---

[1] Quoted from the *Westminster Gazette*, 13 March 1899, by the Editors of the Pilgrim *Letters* in note 1 on p. 460 of Vol. 1.

[2] *Letters*, i, 463.

[3] *The Penny Satirist*, 10 November 1838. Dr. Franz Joseph Gall (1758–1828) was one of the founders of the pseudo-science of phrenology, very popular in the 19th Century, which taught that a person's character could be learned from the shape of his skull.

FRIDAY EVENING, MARCH 31st, 1837.
PORTSMOUTH & PORTSEA THEATRE.
SECOND NIGHT
BY DESIRE, AND UNDER THE PATRONAGE OF

Colonel O'MALEY,
AND THE
Officers of the 88th Regt.

Great and Astonishing Success, of the most Celebrated

JUVENILE ACTRESS!
OF THE DAY

MISS DAVENPORT!
Who was received with Cheers of Applause!

On FRIDAY EVENING, MARCH 31st, 1837,
Will be presented the principal Scenes from Shakspeare's Tragedy of The

Merchant of Venice

The part of Shylock,   by   -   -   Miss DAVENPORT
(As Performed by her in London, and in the Theatre Royal Richmond with unbounded applause.)
Opposite Characters to the Child, by Mr. and Mrs. DAVENPORT.
AND OF TRAGEDY

A Favorite Song 'Rose of Lucerne,' Miss Davenport
after which, the admired favourite afters The

SPOIL'D CHILD

The Part of Little Pickle - Miss DAVENPORT

"The Ladies of Richmond after the Performance of Little Pickle, by MISS DAVENPORT ordered an elegant Gold Chain, which was presented to
her that astonishing Clever Child on Saturday last, as a mark of their delight at her performance and approval of her extraordinary talent." *Bell's Life
London Aera. 1836*

Old Pickle   -   -   Mr DAVENPORT | Miss Pickle -   -   -   Mrs DAVENPORT
John Maria &c
In the Course of this Piece Miss DAVENPORT will Sing
SONG 'SINCE NOW I'M DOOM'D.' SONG 'I'M A BRISK AND SPRIGHTLY LAD JUST COME HOME FROM SEA.'
Song—' Poll Dang .   .   hear my do,' and Dance a Sailor's Hornpipe.

The whole to conclude with a New Piece written expressly for Miss Davenport, by E. Lancaster, Esq. which was received with express-
cheers of applause on Tuesday Evening, with two appropriate Dresses, Properties, &c.

The Music composed expressly for Miss Davenport by the celebrated M. CORRI, Esq.—called the

Manager's Daughter!!

(Ir D. Manager of the Theatre Royal Richmond)   Mr. DAVENPORT (carpenter, &c
Mrs D.   .   .   .   .   Mrs. DAVENPORT
Miss Jean Margaret D.   .   .   .   the Manager's Daughter 8 years of age   .   .   .   .   Miss DAVENPORT!
CHARACTERS ASSUMED
Hector Lacryhier a man-about sketch of a genuine Yankee   .   .   .   .   Miss DAVENPORT

Miss Ella Heatherbloom is blooming from the Highlands in which she will Dance a Highland Fling   Miss DAVENPORT
Peggy O'Rafferty   .   .   comes from the Emerald Isle with her Irish Character all in all   Miss DAVENPORT
With New Song, My Father Lived near Cister Fair,
Paul a Mustard   .   .   .   .   .   .   Miss DAVENPORT, with new Song

Squintie Thorpe   .   .   .   .   .   Miss DAVENPORT
With Song "When I was a Young One, no Girl was like me.

The Theatre is perfectly Aired, LARGE FIRES have been kept in the Boxes, Pit, Lobbies, and on the Stage, for Several Days.

Boxes 4s. 6d., Saloon 3s. 6d., Pit 2s., Gallery 1s., Half Price at Half past eight &c.   Tickets and Places to be had at the Box Office, Library
office. Tickets to be had and Places to be had from Mr DAVENPORT, at Printer's. Portsmouth,
Gardiner, Printer, Portsea.

Yates as Mantalini, Miss Shaw as Madame Mantalini and Miss Potteril as Kate at the Adelphi Theatre, 1838. Drawn from life and etched on stone by J. W. Gear of 5 Charlotte Street, Fitzroy Square, and published by him.

T. W. Tyrrell Collection, Dickens House

Playbill advertising Stirling's dramatisation of *Nickleby*
Photo: D. Parry

Frontispiece to *Nicholas Nickleby, A Farce in Two Acts* by Edward
Stirling, published by Chapman and Hall in vol. 5 of Webster's *Acting
National Drama*, showing Browdie, Nicholas and Smike.
"An engraving by Pierce Egan the Younger from a drawing taken
during the representation".
(*British Museum*)

Another stage version entitled *Nicholas Nickleby, or, The Schoolmaster at Home and Abroad*, by George Dibden Pitt (the author of *Sweeney Todd*) was produced at the City of London Theatre on 17 December, according to Malcolm Morley,[1] but I have not been able to see a text of this. By this time the ninth monthly number of the novel had appeared and one very young reader, the five-year-old William Hughes (younger brother of the author of *Tom Brown's Schooldays*), was perturbed that no proper rewards and punishments had yet been distributed to the various characters. He dictated to his father a letter of remonstrance which was duly forwarded to Dickens, eliciting the following splendid reply which, as Philip Collins observes, " shows how charmingly [Dickens] could enter into the world of childish joys and fancies ''[2]:

Respected Sir.

I have given Squeers one cut on the neck and two on the head, at which he appeared much surprised and began to cry, which being a cowardly thing is just what I should have expected from him—wouldn't you?

I have carefully done what you told me in your letter, about the lamb and the two sheeps for the little boys. They have also had some good ale and porter, and some wine. I am sorry you didn't say *what* wine you would like them to have. I gave them some sherry which they liked very much, except one boy who was a little sick and choaked a good deal. He was rather greedy, and that's the truth, and I believe it went the wrong way, which I say served him right, and I hope you will say so, too.

Nicholas had his roast lamb as you said he was to, but he could not eat it all, and says if you do not mind his doing so, he should like to have the rest hashed tomorrow, with some greens which he is very fond of and so am I. I said I was sure you would give him leave. He said he did not like to have his porter hot, for he thought it spoilt the flavour, so I let him have it cold. You should have seen him drink it. I thought he never would have left off. I also gave him three pounds of money—all in six pences to make it seem more—and he said directly that he should give more than half of it to his mama and sister and divide the rest with poor Smike. And I say he is a good fellow for saying so, and if anybody says he isn't, I am ready to fight him whenever they like.—There.

Fanny Squeers shall be attended to, depend upon it. Your drawing of her is very like, except that I don't think the hair is

[1] See Morley's article, " Nicholas Nickleby on the Boards ", in *The Dickensian*, xliii (1947), 137–41.
[2] In *Dickens and Education* (p. 111).

quite curly enough. The nose is particularly like hers, and so are the legs. She is a nasty disagreeable thing and I know it will make her very cross when she sees it, and what I say is that I hope it may. You will say the same, I know—at least I think you will. . . .[1]

Young Master Hughes must have been delighted when the eleventh number of *Nickleby* made its appearance at the beginning of February for it introduced some characters who were clearly determined to see that Nicholas should get plenty of roast lamb and sixpences: " ' Brother Ned,' said [Charles Cheeryble], ' here is a young friend of mine whom we must assist . . . we must assist him, brother Ned.' " These Cheeryble brothers were drawn from life, Dickens stated in his preface, and their originals were widely recognised as the prominent Manchester merchants, William and Daniel Grant, whose energetic and extensive charitable activities Dickens had heard about from his Manchester-born friend, Harrison Ainsworth, and whom he may have met personally during a visit to Manchester in October 1838.[2]

The Grants had been brought to Lancashire from Scotland by their impoverished parents in 1783. The boys (there were seven children altogether) found employment as apprentices in a calico printing factory at Bury and their father began life again as a pedlar. He prospered sufficiently to open a shop and his sons later joined him in the business, adopting such agreeable means of attracting custom as " the playing of a small, but melodious organ at their shop on market days ".[3] Whether because of this spirited novelty or not, the shop flourished and the firm of William Grant and Brothers was soon well established. Sufficient capital was acquired to buy Peel's father's factory at Ramsbottom and, subsequently, other factories and a warehouse in Cannon Street, Manchester (this building was later re-named " Cheeryble House"). By the 1830's the firm was exceedingly prosperous and the brothers were widely celebrated for their apparently inexhaustible benevolence and acts of practical charity. When Number Eleven of *Nickleby* appeared Dickens's portrait of them was, it seems, unmistakeable. Their great-nephew, James Grant Taylor, recalled, in a letter written in 1898.

I was on my way along Market Street from Mosely Street when I saw old Aaron Lees from Gorton Mills and he said, ' James,

[1] *Letters*, i, 466–67.
[2] For a full discussion of the Grants and their relationship to the Cheerybles see Robert R. Carmyllie's *Charles Dickens and the ' Cheeryble ' Grants*, published by the Ramsbottom and District Local History Society (1972).
F. R. Dean, " The Cheeryble Brothers", *The Dickensian*, xxvi (1930), 146.

Sketches published on the front page of *The Penny Satirist*, 3 November 1838.

THE BOYS "DONE" FOR.

The purgative system, which begins by purifying the body, and endeth with the purification of the morals: but the end doth not yet appear.

MISS FANNY SQUEERS

In her three and twentieth year. If there be any one grace or loveliness inseparable from that particular period of life, Miss Squeers may be presumed to have been possessed of it. She was not tall like her mother, but short like her father. From the former she inherited a voice of harsh quality, and from the latter a remarkable expression of the right eye—something akin to having none at all.

Sketches published on the front page of *The Penny Satirist*, 3 November 1838.

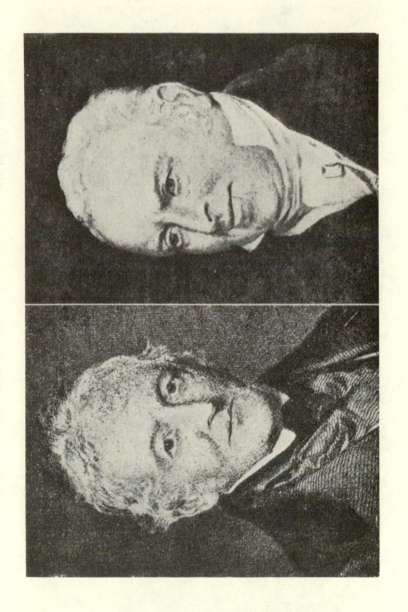

William and Daniel Grant

Staffordshire pottery figures representing characters from *Nicholas Nickleby*. Published 15 June 1839 by Ridgway and Robey of Hanley, Staffs.

have you seen this month's number of " Nicholas Nickleby "? '
I replied, ' No, is it out?' ' Yes and they have got your old
uncles in it,' he replied. I went to the first bookseller's shop,
and I read it at No. 11 Mosely Street—better known as ' The
Grant's Arms ' . . . everybody about Bury and for ten miles
around knew that we were the grandchildren of the eldest
brother of the Cheeryble Brothers. . . .[1]

So powerful was the effect of Dickens's portrayal, in fact, that, as
Mr. Carmyllie has shown, the historical Grants and the fictitious
Cheerybles became inextricably confused in reminiscences about
the former written later in the century. But we have no reason
to suppose that the engineer, James Nasmyth, was romancing in
the following anecdote of the Grants in 1834, related in his auto-
biography, closely parallel to Dickens though it is:

On this memorable day I had another introduction which proved
of great service to me. It was to the Messrs. Grant, the famous
Brothers Cheeryble of Dickens. I was taken to their counting-
house in Cannon Street, where I was introduced to Daniel Grant.
Although business was at its full height, he gave me a cordial
reception. But, to save time, he invited me to come after the
exchange was over, and taken ' tiffen ' with him at his hospitable
mansion in Mosely Street . . . . I went thither accordingly, and
the first thing Daniel did was to present me in the most cordial
manner to his ' noble brother William,' as he always affectionately called him. William was the head of the firm, and he, too,
gave me a warm and hearty welcome. He asked me to sit
beside him at the head of the table. . . . He took occasion to
inquire into the object of my visit to Manchester. I told him
as briefly as I could that I intended to begin the business of a
mechanical engineer on a very moderate scale, and that I had
been looking out for premises wherein to commence operations.
He seemed interested and asked more questions. I related to
him my little history, and told him of my desires, hopes and
aspirations. ' What was my age?' ' Twenty-six.' ' That is a
very young age to begin business on your own account. . . .'
' But what is your capital?' I told him that my capital in cash
was £63. ' What!' he said, ' that will do very little for you
when Saturday nights come round!' . . . He whispered to me
' to keep my heart up.' And if, he added, on any Saturday
night I wanted money to pay wages or other expenses, I would
find a credit for £500 at 3 per cent. at his office in Cannon Street,
and no security. These were his very words. What could
have been more generous?[2]

[1] Quoted by Mr. Carmyllie in his pamphlet on the Grants.
[2] Quoted by Arthur Humphreys in his article, " The Cheeryble Brothers,"
The Dickensian, i (1905), 94–96.

It is to be feared that no amount of parallels between the Cheerybles and their real-life originals will reconcile modern readers to these extravagant embodiments of zealous benevolence. Nor were they accepted without protest by some of the more intellectual of the novel's first readers. They are " irredeemable idiots," declared a reviewer in *Fraser's Magazine*:

> Mr. Dickens assures us in his preface that he has drawn these insufferable bores from actual life. It may be so; if it be, we recommend him to abstain from life academies which furnish no better subjects: for his hand was not intended for drawing such faultless monsters which the world ne'er saw, as these pot-bellied Sir Charles Grandisons of the ledger and day-book. The veritable Cheerybles may, no doubt, deserve all the compliments with which they are besplattered: but, in the novel, their appearance, or that of their nephew, or of Tim Linkinwater, is quite sufficient to warn the reader to skip the page with the utmost possible activity.[1]

Dickens may have been annoyed by such scornful dismissals of the Cheerybles as this but his greatest trouble with regard to them came from a different kind of reader, a kind less concerned with art than with making some easy money. Begging-letter writers plagued the novelist throughout his career and his statement in the preface that " the Brothers Cheeryble live " was, of course, certain to make these gentry reach for their pens. In the 1848 Preface he wrote, in comical desperation:

> If I were to attempt to sum up the hundreds upon hundreds of letters, from all sorts of people in all sorts of latitudes and climates, to which this unlucky paragraph has since given rise, I should get into an arithmetical difficulty from which I could not easily extricate myself. Suffice it to say, that I believe the applications for loans, gifts, and offices of profit that I have been requested to forward to the originals of the Brothers Cheeryble (with whom I never interchanged any communication in my life), would have exhausted the combined patronage of all the Lord Chancellors since the accession of the House of Brunswick, and would have broken the rest of the Bank of England.

To return to the story of the monthly publication of *Nickleby*, Dickens must have found the writing of each instalment not quite such a harrassing business from January 1839 onwards since he had *Oliver* behind him and now withdrew from the editorship of *Bentley's Miscellany*. In March, however, he was busy settling

---

[1] Quoted from *Fraser's Magazine* for April 1840 by Philip Collins in his *Dickens: the Critical Heritage*, p. 89.

his parents in a cottage at Alphington in Devon where he hoped they might manage to live in pleasant retirement, relieving him of the incessant financial worry that they had been causing him in London. By the middle of the month he was back at work in Doughty Street endeavouring, as he told Forster, " to get the Steam up " for the writing of the April number (Number Thirteen) which was to contain the account of Mrs. Nickleby's vegetable wooing by " the gentleman in small-clothes ", an episode which, in the event, fully justified his writing to Forster, " I think Mrs. Nickleby's love scene will come out rather unique ".[1] He was now thickening his plot in preparation for a series of dramatic revelations and dénouements in the last few numbers. The mysterious figure of Brooker appears in Number Fourteen making ominous hints that Ralph chooses to ignore. In Chapter 45 the united villains, Ralph, Snawley and Squeers, are foiled in a deter-mined attempt to recapture Smike but we are left in no doubt that they will return to the charge. Smike's hopeless love for Kate is delicately sketched in and the reader is kept in suspense about the progress of Nicholas's own love for " the young lady unknown ", the protégée of the Cheerybles, whom he had briefly encountered for the second time in Number Thirteen.

It must have been particularly irritating for Dickens at such a time to have yet another hack-dramatist sieze upon the novel, as far as it had gone, and put it on the stage with a botched-up ending. W. T. Moncrieff's *Nicholas Nickleby and Poor Smike or, The Victim of the Yorkshire School* was produced at the Strand Theatre on 20 May.[2] As the Strand was not a licensed theatre a number of songs had to feature in the piece so that it could be classified as a " burletta " rather than a straight play and these, of course, intensified the absurdity of the adaptation. The songs were mostly given to John Browdie but Kate also had a few sentimental ditties such as the following (which she sings on arrival at Madam Mantalini's):

> Ah what avails a glittering vest
> Unless the form it wraps is free
> For gay attire—what mortal breast
> Would yield dear precious liberty?

Most offensive to Dickens, however, must have been Moncrieff's grotesque dénouement. Smike turns out to be Ralph's son by a relative of Sir Mulberry Hawk. His mother having been repudi-ated by her rich uncle, General Hawk, Ralph had sent Smike to

[1] *Letters*, i, 527.
[2] The manuscript of Moncrieff's play is among the collection of the Lord Chamberlain's Plays in the British Museum (Add. MSS. 42951). Quotation from it here is made by courtesy of the Trustees of the British Museum.

Squeers's school. General Hawk then relented, after his niece's death, and settled all his fortune on Smike. The will and the letter about this have been maliciously kept secret by Brooker, however, and are only revealed by him, at the instigation of Newman Noggs, in the last scene, which takes the form of a grand assembly of all the characters at Sir Mulberry's house in Portman Square. The will appoints the Cheerybles as Smike's guardians and shows him to be the rightful owner of all Sir Mulberry's property. Lord Frederick Verisopht offers to marry Kate but she announces (with commendable prudence) that she proposes to devote her future life to Smike. Ralph is " foiled at all points " but departs snarling that he still has " the world to prey on " and Nicholas is hastily paired off with a niece of the Cheerybles.

One can well understand that Dickens, having planned to reveal Smike ultimately as Ralph's son but after the boy's death and with very different consequences for all concerned, must have been infuriated that Moncrieff (whose earlier dramatisation of *Pickwick* had, according to Forster " distinguished itself beyond the rest by a preface abusive of the writer plundered "[1]) had forestalled him in this, the main revelation, whilst at the same time presenting it so preposterously. He made his indignation public in the June number of *Nickleby* in which, at the Crummleses' farewell banquet, Nicholas, splendidly oblivious of his earlier plundering of French dramatists for the benefit of Mr. Crummles, harangues a " literary gentleman . . . who had dramatized in his time two hundred and forty-seven novels, as fast as they had come out— some of them faster than they had come out—and who *was* a literary gentleman in consequence ":

> you take the uncompleted books of living authors, fresh from their hands, wet from the press, cut, hack, and carve them to the powers and capacities of your actors, and the capability of your theatres, finish unfinished works, hastily and crudely vamp up ideas not yet fully worked out by their original projector, but which have doubtless cost him many thoughtful days and sleepless nights; by a comparison of incidents and dialogue, down to the very last word he may have written a fortnight before, do your utmost to anticipate his plot—all this without his permission, and against his will. . . .

To this " intemperate and vulgar caricature ", as he termed it, Moncrieff immediately replied in a long address to the public, dated from the New Strand Theatre 5 June 1839. It is reprinted by S. J. Adair Fitz-Gerald in his *Dickens and the Drama* (1910), pages 121–26, and needs to be read in full to appreciate the extent of its malice and insolence towards Dickens. Moncrieff, having

[1] Forster, p. 40.

noted that two other playwrights had dramatised the novel before him, " a cirumstance that did not seem displeasing either to Mr. Dickens or to his proprietors, Messrs. Chapman and Hall, as the latter themselves actually published one of the adaptations alluded to [i.e. Stirling's] ", goes on to say:

> . . . that I should unfortunately have hit upon the same ending of the history as that projected by Mr. Dickens . . . I really regret; but there is a very easy way of making me ' hide my diminished head.' Let Mr. Dickens—and he has five months before him—set his wits to work again and finish *his* ' Nicholas Nickleby ' better than I have done. . . .

Moncrieff then affects to deplore the unsatisfactory state of the copyright laws but says he is not to be blamed for this; he deplores also the fact that Dickens " has suffered his irritability to make him forget the good breeding of a gentleman " and follows this up with an unfair and spiteful reference to Dickens's own dramatic writings (which may have been based on the knowledge that Macready had found himself unable to accept for production a farce called *The Lamplighter* that Dickens had written for him the previous winter[1]):

> Having himself *unsuccessfully* tried the drama, there is some excuse for Mr. Dickens's petulance towards its professors; but it is somewhat illiberal and ungrateful that, being indebted to the stage for so many of his best characters—*Sam Weller*, from Beazley's ' Boarding House ', for example—he should deny it a few in return.[2]

[1] It is interesting to note that Dickens carefully salvages a good comic touch from *The Lamplighter* for Mr. Mantalini's benefit in the February number of *Nickleby*. The lamplighter, describing his father's suicide, says, " as he was a remarkably good husband, and never had any secrets from his wife, he put a note in the twopenny post, as he went along, to tell the widder where the body was." So Mr. Mantalini, announcing his intention to drown himself in the Thames, pathetically protests, " but I will not be angry with her [his wife], even then, for I will put a note in the twopenny post as I go along, to tell her where the body is."

[2] The two farces and the operetta by Dickens that were staged in London during the 1836-37 season were by no means unsuccessful so that Moncrieff's sneer is wholly unjustified. As to the suggestion that Dickens got Sam Weller from Beazley's farce, Fitz-Gerald comments: " This is not the case, though there is a slight resemblance to Sam in Simon Spatterdash, who has a trick of this kind of speech: ' I will, as the fly said when he hopped out of the mustard-pot,' which was quite a common practice with a certain class of ' smart ' youth, servants, and apprentices of the day. But I don't suppose Dickens ever saw the ' Boarding House '. It was produced at the Lyceum Theatre in 1811, revived there in 1815 and again at Drury Lane a few years later, and then it was heard no more. Where could he have seen the play?" (*Dickens and the Drama*, p. 127).

The address ends with an allusion to the writer's " long and
severe illness of nearly five years, with its consequent deprivation
of sight ", no doubt intended to convict Dickens of unfeeling
brutality as well as of bad temper.

Fortunately, Dickens did not allow himself to be drawn any
further into this particular dispute. He and his family were now
living at Elm Cottage, Petersham, which he had taken for four
months from 30 April and from which he visited the Hampton
Races, vividly described in the July number of *Nickleby* which
featured the fatal quarrel between Sir Mulberry and Lord Frederick
in a gambling-booth at the race-course. With Lord Frederick
dead and Sir Mulberry forced into exile abroad, Dickens was
beginning to clear his crowded stage for the final dénouement (the
Crummleses had made their bow in the June number): " It is
very difficult indeed to wind up so many people *in parts*, and
make each part tell by itself," Dickens wrote to Laman Blan-
chard in July, " but I hope to go out with flying colours notwithstanding."[1]

From Petersham Dickens sent Browne instruction for the first
plate in the August number, " Great excitement of Miss Kenwigs
at the hairdresser's Shop ":

—A hairdresser's shop at night—not a dashing one, but a
barber's. Morleena Kenwig[s] on a tall chair having her hair
dressed by an underbred attendant with his hair parted down the
middle, and frizzed up into curls at the sides. Another customer, who is being shaved, has just turned his head in the
direction of Miss Kenwigs, and she and Newman Noggs (who
has brought her there, and has been whiling away the time with
an old newspaper), recognise, with manifestations of surprise,
and Morleena with emotion, Mr. Lillyvick, the collector. Mr.
Lillyvick's bristly beard expresses great neglect of his person,
and he looks very grim and in the utmost despondency.[2]

At the end of August Dickens left Petersham and on 3 September
moved his family to Broadstairs "to close the fine season at the
seaside ". Here he had " pretty stiff work ", as he wrote to
Forster, for he had to write twice the usual amount for the final
October number which was to contain parts 19 and 20. His
diary from 5 September to 20 September contains little else
except the word " Work ". On the 18th he informed Forster,
" The discovery [of Smike's parentage] is made, Ralph is dead,
the loves have come all right, Tim Linkinwater has proposed, and
I have now only to break up Dotheboys and the book together ".[3]
And on the 20th his diary entry reads:

1 *Letters*, i, 561.
2 *Letters*, i, 560.
3 *Letters*, i, 581.

Sketch by Phiz for the second plate in the twelfth monthly number, "A sudden recognition, unexpected on both sides" (chapter 38). On the sketch Dickens has pencilled, "I don't think Smike is frightened enough or Squeers earnest enough—for my purposes."
(*Suzannet Collection, Dickens House*)
Photo: D. Parry

Sketch by Phiz for the first plate in the thirteenth monthly number,
"Nicholas recognizes the Young Lady unknown" (chapter 40).
(*Suzannet Collection, Dickens House*)
Photo: D. Parry

Work.

Finished Nickleby this day at 2 o'clock and went over to
Ramsgate with Fred and Kate, to send the last little chapter to
Bradbury and Evans in a parcel.

Thank God that I have lived to get through it happily.[1]

There only remained to dedicate the book to Macready, a " high
compliment " which deeply touched the great actor (" Surely here
is something to gratify me," he noted in his diary) and to arrange a
celebration dinner which came off at the Albion, Aldersgate Street,
on 5 October.   Reviewing the last number of *Nickleby* on that
same day the *Court Journal* wrote:

> So, here is the final close of ' Nicholas Nickleby, Esq. ' in a
> double number, illustrated by a portrait of Charles Dickens
> (worth all the cost), and three other plates. . . .   Moreover, here
> is an elucidatory preface which will not be read without interest.
> After the most exhaustless fund of enjoyment that we have, for
> the last eighteen months, derived from the labours of ' Boz' we
> should deem it the height of ingratitude, were we to say one
> word with reference to the dénouement; suffice it therefore to
> remark, that poetic justice is satisfied, and that everything is
> comme il faut.   We shall now look forward with interest to
> the announcement of Mr. Dickens's next work.

This next work should have been *Barnaby Rudge*, the manuscript
of which Dickens had promised Richard Bentley for January 1840,
but a final rupture between Dickens and Bentley took place in
December and Dickens's next appearance before the public was
to take a rather different form though still under the auspices of
Chapman and Hall.   It was that of a weekly miscellany entitled
Master Humphrey's Clock, the idea for which had been outlined
by Dickens in a letter to Forster from Petersham back in the
summer.   It was, in fact, to be another three years before Dickens
again published a novel in the same monthly-number format as
Pickwick and *Nickleby*.

But, although Dickens himself might now have finished with
Nickleby (apart from answering correspondents wishing to know
whether the lady in the cellar with Mr. Mantalini in Chapter 64
was actually Madame Mantalini or not—eventually he altered the
text to make it clear that it was *not* Madame), the playwrights and
plagiarists had by no means done so.   Another dramatisation
by Edward Stirling called *The Fortunes of Smike* was produced
at the Adelphi on 2 March 1840.   This managed to compress a
great deal of the second half of the novel into seven scenes and

[1] *Letters*, i, 642.

followed the plot fairly faithfully from the point at which Nicholas returns to London from Portsmouth to protect his sister. The only major departure from Dickens was the preservation of Ralph's life after the revelation that Smike was his son; in this play he simply collapses and is led from the room, Newman Noggs remarking, " His heart is broke—he'll never speak again ". According to Malcolm Morley, Dibden Pitt also produced a sequel to his *Nickleby* dramatisation for the City of London theatre about this time.[1] The most spirited stage adaptation of *Nickleby*, however, appeared not in London but in Paris where it was seen by a delighted Thackeray who wrote it up for *Fraser's Magazine* (March 1842) under the title of ' Dickens in France '.　His act-by-act description is marvellously funny but here I must content myself with quoting his report only of the

THIRD ACT

That scoundrel Squarrs before he kept the school was, as we have seen, a tumbler and *saltimbanque*, and, as such, a member of the great fraternity of cadgers, beggars, *gueux*, thieves, that have their club in London.　It is held in immense Gothic vaults under ground: here the beggars consort their plans, divide their spoil, and hold their orgies.

In returning to London Monsieur Squarrs instantly resumes his acquaintance with his old comrades, who appoint him, by the all-powerful interest of a *peculiar person*, head of the community of cadgers.

That person is no other than the banker Ralph, who, in secret, directs this godless crew, visits their haunts, and receives from them a boundless obedience.　A villain himself he has need of the aid of villany.　He pants for vengeance against his nephew, he has determined that his niece shall fall a prey to Milor Clarendon,—nay more, he has a dark suspicion that Smike— the orphan boy—the homeless fugitive from Yorkshire—is no other than the child who ten years ago—but, hush!

Where is his rebellious nephew and those whom he protects? The quick vigilance of Ralph soon discovered them; Nicholas, having taken the name of Edward Browne, was acting at a theatre in the neighbourhood of the Thames.　Haste, Squarrs, take a couple of trusty beggars with you, and hie thee to Wapping; seize young Smike and carry him to Cadger's Cavern, —haste, then!　The mind shudders to consider what is to happen.

In Nicholas's room at the theatre we find his little family assembled, and with them honest John Browdie, who has for-

---

[1] *The Dickensian*, xliii (1947), 139.　Morley also describes the earliest productions of stage versions of *Nickleby* in New York (the first appeared on 25 January 1839) in his " Early Dickens Drama in America," *The Dickensian*, xliv (1948), 153–57.

gotten his part on learning that Nicholas was attached, not to the *fermière*, but to the mistress; to them comes—gracious heavens!—Meess Annabel.[1] ' Fly,' says she, ' fly! I have overheard a plot concocted between my father and your uncle: the sheriff is to seize you for the abduction of Smeek and the assault upon Squarrs,' &c. &c. &c.

In short, it is quite impossible to describe this act, so much is there done in it. Lord Clarendon learns that he has pledged his life interest in his estates to Ralph.

His lordship *dies*, and Ralph seizes a paper, which proves beyond a doubt that young Smike is no other than Clarendon's long-lost son.

L'infâme Squarrs with his satellites carry off the boy; Browdie pitches Squarrs into the river; the sheriff carries Nickleby to prison; and VICE TRIUMPHS in the person of the odious Ralph. But vice does not always triumph; wait awhile and you will see. . . .

Moreover, just as Mr. Pickwick had been conducted by other hands to further adventures in France and in America after his creator had finished with him so there appeared in 1840 a sequel to *Nickleby*, published in sixpenny numbers. It was entitled *Scenes from the Life of Nickleby Married*, edited by " Guess " and illustrated by " Quiz " (who, whoever he was, was certainly no unworthy imitator of Phiz). Louis James admirably summarises this production in his *Fiction for the Working Man* (p. 67):

The Nickleby family are living happily together; Mrs. Squeers keeps a coffee house on the South Bank. After a cold reception back from prison, Wackford Squeers turns to writing begging letters. Mr. Mantalini insinuates himself back into his wife's favours, but is again rejected and humiliated by the end of the book. The main plot concerns the theft of over £3,000 from the firm of Nickleby and Cheeryble, when in the possession of Tim Linkinwater, and the recovery of £2,000 through a fortune teller operating in a London backstreet. Sir Mulberry Hawk attempts to rid himself of an innocent French wife, Matilda, and to marry the wealthy heiress, Mrs. Gambroon. He becomes implicated with the criminals involved in the robbery from Nickleby. Tom Brookes, who works for Nickleby, is instrumental in frustrating his design, and Hawk is killed. Brookes has discovered that Matilda is no other than his sister. He has been heading for ruin amid disreputable company: his eyes are opened just in time, and he reforms and marries Kate

[1] The audience has learned in Act One that Annabella is the daughter of Lord Clarendon, whose castle is next door to Squeers's school in Yorkshire; the first scene shows Nicholas giving her a French lesson at the school.

Nickleby—Nicholas's eldest daughter. Matilda becomes one of the family. While far short of Dickens, the writing is lively, and the quite incredible plot is partly compensated for by the vivid pictures of London low life: its music halls, fortune tellers, thieves, and labyrinths of dirty back streets. It is on a different plane to *Nickelas Nickelbery*.

A word should be said, finally, about Dickens's return to *Nickleby* in the 1860s, when he turned back to the book and devised from the chapters dealing with Dotheboys Hall a very successful public reading which he first introduced into his repertoire in the autumn of 1861. He wrote to Georgina Hogarth from Bury St. Edmunds that

> ... we had a splendid hall last night, and ... I think Nickleby tops all the readings. Somehow it seems to have got in it, by accident, exactly the qualities best suited to the purpose, and it went last night not only with roars, but with a general hilarity and pleasure that I have never seen surpassed.[1]

To Wilkie Collins he wrote of the audience's "fantastic and hearty enjoyment" of the reading at Norwich:

> The people were really quite ridiculous to see when Squeers read the boys' letters. And I am inclined to suspect that the impression of protection and hope derived from Nickleby's going away protecting Smike is exactly the impression—this is discovered by chance—that an Audience most likes to be left with.[2]

Dickens's prompt-copy for this reading, which was divided into four chapters and lasted about 75 minutes, is now in the Berg Collection in the New York Public Library and Philip Collins notes that it " contains not only numerous manuscript alterations and deletions but also at several points Dickens has expanded the text by pasting in passages from a copy of the novel ".[3] In 1866 he arranged a shorter version of this reading, omitting the section dealing with Fanny Squeers's tea-party, and the prompt-copy for this " short-time " version, entitled *Nicholas Nickleby at the Yorkshire School*, is now in the Suzannet Collection at the Dickens House. As may be seen from the page reproduced herewith, it also contains manuscript emendations and " stage-directions " to himself written in the margin by Dickens such as

---

[1] *Letters of Charles Dickens* (the Nonesuch Edition: Bloomsbury, 1938), iii, 246.

[2] Ibid., p. 248.

[3] Philip Collins, " The Texts of Dickens' Readings," *Bulletin of the New York Public Library*, lxxiv (1970), 372.

Mr Gambwoon makes preparations for her Wedding

Illustration from *Nickleby Married* by "Guess"
(*From the library of Mr. Leslie C. Staples*)
Photo: D. Parry

Mr Mantalini in Hot Water.

Illustration from *Nickleby Married* by "Guess"
(*From the library of Mr. Leslie C. Staples*)
Photo: D. Parry

24 NICHOLAS NICKLEBY

left unpaid, and so forth. This solemn proceeding always took place in the afternoon of the day succeeding his return. So, in the afternoon, the boys were recalled from house-window, garden, stable, and cow-yard, and the school were as-. sembled in full conclave, when Mr. Squeers, with a small bundle of papers in his hand, and Mrs. S. following with a pair of canes, entered the room and proclaimed silence.

Slapping the desk

" Let an boy speak a word without leave," said Mr. Squeers, " and I'll take the skin off that boy's back."

This special proclamation had the desired effect, and a deathlike silence immediately prevailed.

" Boys, I've been to London, and have returned to my family and you, as strong and as well as ever."

According to half-yearly custom, the boys gave three feeble cheers at this refreshing intelligence. Such cheers

" I have seen the parents of some boys," continued Squeers, turning over his papers, " and

A page from Dickens's prompt-copy of the "short time" reading version of *Nicholas Nickleby at the Yorkshire School*, showing deletions and stage-direction written in by Dickens
(*Suzannet Collection, Dickens House*)
Photo: D. Parry

Dickens giving a reading

" driving ", " breakfasting ", and so on. Professor Collins notes, however, that this shorter version was used only during one tour as " it was liked much less than the fuller version: audiences had particularly enjoyed Fanny, 'Tilda and John Browdie."[1]

It was with no thoughts, however, that he himself would later become, through his public readings, celebrated for his histrionic talents that Dickens listened to Macready proposing his health at the " Nicklebeian fête " in Aldersgate Street on 5 October 1839. About twenty people sat down to what the great actor described in his diary as a " *too* splendid dinner ". Among the guests were several, besides Macready, who had been present at the Pickwick dinner two years earlier—Jerdan and Talfourd and, of course, Forster and Chapman and Hall. Dickens's grateful publishers marked the occasion by presenting to him the portrait they had commissioned from his close friend, the artist Daniel Maclise (also present at the dinner) from which the frontispiece of *Nickleby* was engraved. Of this painting Thackeray said, " as a likeness it is perfectly amazing; a looking-glass could not render a better fac-simile. Here we have the real identical man Dickens; the artist must have understood the inward Boz as well as the outward, before he made this admirable representation of him."[2] According to Macready, neither he nor Dickens made very good speeches on this occasion but worth noting is Dickens's statement that " *Nickleby* had been to him a diary of the last two years: the various papers preserving to him the recollection of the events and feelings connected with their production."[3]

There were two other distinguished artists, as well as Maclise, among the dinner-guests, George Cattermole and Sir David Wilkie. The latter sent an interesting account of the event to his friend, Mrs. Ricketts. When proposing Dickens's health, Wilkie reported, Macready praised him for giving his readers not only " the bold adventure and the startling incident " but also " all the little details and minute feelings, of the every-day intercourse of life, so finely . . . characterised in the lines of Wordsworth as

Those nameless and unremembered acts,
That make the best part of a good man's life."

This, says Wilkie, led Dickens to talk about his great admiration for Wordsworth, whom he had lately seen, and about his particular love of the poem " We are Seven ": " What he seemed to like

---

[1] Philip Collins, " The Dickens Reading-Copies in Dickens House," *The Dickensian*, lxviii (1972), 178.
[2] Forster, p. 129.
[3] Macready's *Diaries*, quoted in *Letters*, i, 590, note 2.

in this was divesting death of its horror, by treating it as a separation and not an extinction.''[1] These remarks look forward, I think, to certain aspects of Dickens's next novel, *The Old Curiosity Shop*, which he was to begin serialising in *Master Humphrey's Clock* the following April.[2] This story with its saintly little heroine was destined to send Dickens's popularity soaring to an even greater height than that already triumphantly attained by *Pickwick, Oliver* and *Nickleby*.

[1] My quotations are taken from the extract from Wilkie's letter printed on p. 19 of Sotheby's Catalogue of items from the Suzannet Collection sold in London on 22 and 23 November 1971.
[2] He was later to write to Forster (*Letters*, ii, 188); " When I first began (on your valued suggestion) to keep my thoughts upon the ending of the tale [i.e. the death of Little Nell], I resolved to try and do something which might be read by people about whom Death had been,—with a softened feeling and with consolation."

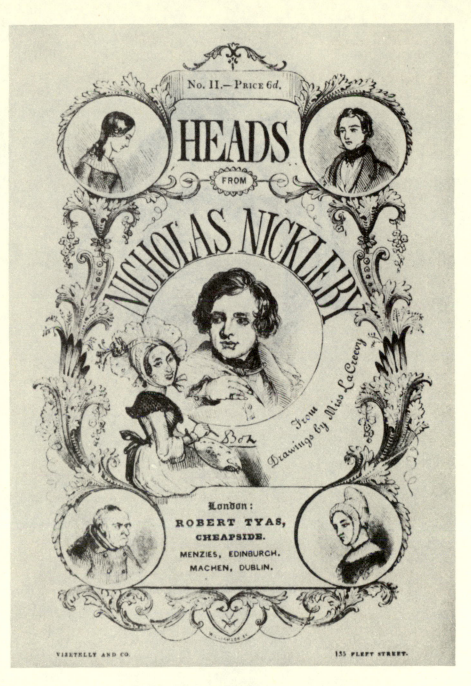

Cover of one of the instalments of *Heads from Nicholas Nickleby*
Photo: D. Parry

MR. MANTALINI

From *Heads of Nicholas Nickleby*, No. 2
Photo: D. Parry

APPENDIX

The Extra Illustrations to *Nicholas Nickleby*

The author and publisher of *Nickelas Nickelbery* and hack-dramatists like Stirling and Moncrieff were not the only people who sought to make money out of Dickens's novel whilst it was in course of publication. Readers of this reprint will have noticed in Number Seven an advertisement for some sheet music entitled " The Original Nicholas Nickleby Quadrilles, by Boz, Jun., author of the Pickwicks, danced at the Queen's balls". And they will also have seen in Number Four an announcement of the publication of the first part, price one shilling, of a set of extra illustrations to the novel by " Peter Palette ". This was the name adopted by the artist Thomas Onwhyn who had earlier produced a similar series of extra illustrations to *Pickwick Papers* " by Mr. Samuel Weller ". Subscribers to the monthly numbers of *Pickwick* or *Nickleby* would frequently buy these extra illustrations and have them bound up, as an additional embellishment, with their completed set of the parts of the novel. Onwhyn's publisher, Grattan, issued nine fascicules of his engravings and re-advertised them, with laudatory quotations from the press (" every admirer of Nickleby should possess these illustrations ") in later numbers of *Nickleby*. The advertisement in Number Fifteen announces that " portraits of the most interesting characters in the work " will also be included in the series. According to F. G. Kitton (*Dickens and his Illustrators*, 1899, p. 235), forty etchings in all, ten portraits and thirty scenes, were eventually published but I have only seen the thirty-two plates re-issued later (about 1847) by Grattan and Gilbert. These comprised two portraits, those of Nicholas and of Madeline Bray, and thirty scenes from the novels, some specimens of which are reproduced herewith.

A rival series of extra illustrations entitled *Heads from Nicholas Nickleby* was published by Robert Tyas. These were first advertised in *Nickleby* Number Eleven (February 1839) and were issued in six sixpenny fascicules, each containing four portraits (for a complete list of the subjects see Tyas's advertisement at the end of the last part of *Nickleby*). The artist was Kenny Meadows, masquerading as Miss La Creevy, and Tyas's advertisement in *Nickleby* Number Twelve promises that these portraits of the " most interesting " characters in the novel will be " selected at the period when their very actions define their true characters, and exhibit the inward mind by its outward manifestations." How far Meadows was able to fulfil this promise the reader may judge from the examples of his work shown here.

MR. CRUMMLES.

From Heads of Nicholas Nickleby, *No. 4*
Photo: D. Parry

LORD VERISOPHT

From *Heads of Nicholas Nickleby*, No. 3
Photo: *D. Parry*

BROOKER.

From *Heads of Nicholas Nickleby*, No. 6
Photo: D. Parry

The company being all ready Miss Petowker hummed a tune and Madame danced a ...

(*Above and following pages*) Specimen extra illustrations to *Nicholas Nickleby* by Onwhyn
Photos: D. Parry

"The procession up the aisle was beautiful"

The wedding of Miss Petowker and Mr. Lillyvick
(page 245)

Nicholas seized the heavy handle, and with it laid open one side of his antagonist's face from the eye to the lip.

Nicholas attacks Sir Mulberry Hawk
(page 315)

M'Crummles was moignmatiy glad to see him

Nicholas's reunion with Mr. Crummles
(page 473)

Arthur Gride and Peg Sliderskew
(page 505)

A BIBLIOGRAPHICAL NOTE

This reprint of the original parts of *Nicholas Nickleby* has been made from copies of Numbers One to Twelve of the novel in the possession of Dr. Robin Alston and from copies of Numbers Thirteen to Twenty in the Dr. Henry Collection at the Dickens House, London. This latter Collection includes variant issues of each part of *Nickleby*, as of other Dickens novels issued in the monthly-part format, showing different states of the plates and variations in the advertising supplements and traders' insets that were bound up with each part.

In their *Bibliography of the Periodical Works of Charles Dickens* (1933) Thomas Hatton and Arthur Cleaver, discussing the forty plates designed and etched for *Nickleby* by Hablot Browne (Phiz), state:

> Following on the experience gained in the publication of "Pickwick" and in anticipation of a monthly circulation reaching 40,000 to 50,000 copies, the Author and Publishers decided to continue the system of duplicate etchings for each subject. When, however, the circulation began to show definite signs of still further expansion, and owing to the fact that Dickens was never beforehand with his manuscript, it became necessary, beginning with Part 2, to have the plates etched in triplicate, and, in several cases after Part 6, in quadruplicate.
>
> There can be no question whatsoever as to priority of these duplicates, for they were, by reason of dire necessity, executed in rapid succession, and all of them were published simultaneously in the initial issue of the parts. Neither are there any outstanding variations of a major character in the "state" of impressions from the individual "steels". The variations, if any, are limited to those falling in the minor class.

In view of this authoritative pronouncement and bearing in mind that this reprint will, in the nature of things, hardly concern bibliophile collectors, I have not attempted to ensure that the parts used are in every case putative first issues. The only textual variants recorded by Hatton and Cleaver that indicate early issues will be found to be present, however, viz. the misprint of "visiter" for "sister" in Number Four (p. 123, l.17) and of "latter" for "letter" in Number Five (p. 160, six lines up from the bottom of the page). The first of these misprints was spotted by Dickens (see Pilgrim Edition of Dickens's letters, vol. 1,

p. 408).† Also present is the publishers' announcement in Number Fourteen explaining that no plates appear in that Number owing to the artist's indisposition and promising a compensatory double ration in the next Number.

Typical examples of the kind of variants found in the advertising supplements may be seen in the final double number (Parts 19/20). In three of the four copies of this Number in the Henry Collection the specimen illustration from *Valentine Vox* included in Tyas's 12-page inset at the back is a coaching scene entitled " A Mad Dog turning out a March Hare ". In the fourth copy (used for this reprint) the scene is a domestic interior entitled " Uncle John in extacies ". Similarly, both the illustrations included in the advertisement for a " New and Splendid Edition of Gulliver's Travels " vary in all four of the Dr. Henry copies. On at least one occasion, too, advertisements were transposed in different issues; in Number Eleven one issue in the Henry Collection has the advertisement for Ewer's Catalogue of Operas on p. 2 of the wrapper and the British College of Health advertisement on p. 3 whilst the three other copies of this Number show Ewer on p. 3 and the College of Health on p. 2.

Traders' insets feature in nearly all of the original monthly parts of *Nickleby* and it has not proved possible to reproduce every one of them in this reprint. Missing, for example, is the large folding sheet, printed both sides and with 15 woodcuts, advertising Amesbury's Patent Supports which should follow the National Loan Fund advertisement at the back of original copies of Number Three, and the small yellow slip advertising Charles Tilt's publications which should be pasted inside the front wrapper of Number Eleven. Nor has it always been possible to reproduce exactly certain other advertisements, e.g. Ackermann's 8-page inset at the back of Number Eleven. In original copies this is printed in blue and on smaller-sized paper than that used for the rest of the Number (the type area of the original is as shown in this reprint, however). Perhaps the most spectacular of all the *Nickleby* advertisements was the one for Hill's Seal Wafers at the end of the final double number. In all four copies of this Number in the Henry Collection the five specimen coloured wafers vary in all respects (colour, size, shape, imprint) but to have reproduced any one of these combinations in all its glory would have been prohibitively expensive.

M.S.

† Hatton and Cleaver's collation of the monthly number of *Nickleby* should be supplemented by E. H. Strange's "Notes on the Bibliography of *Nicholas Nickleby*" in *The Dickensian*, xxxiii (1937), 30–33.

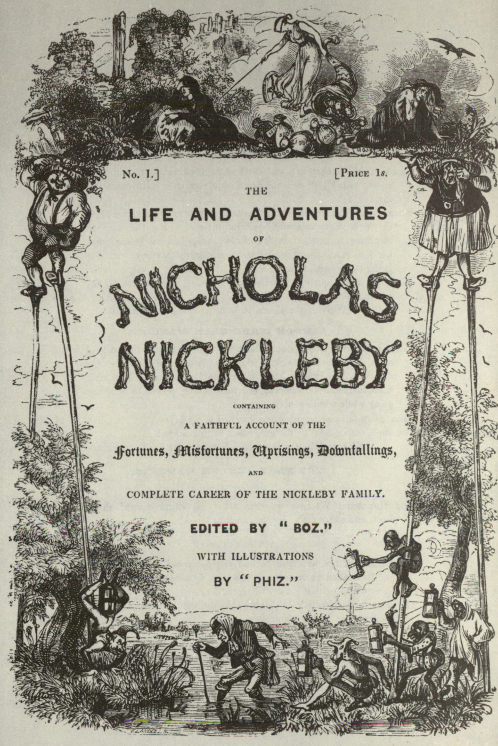

No. I.]   [PRICE 1s.

THE
LIFE AND ADVENTURES

OF

NICHOLAS
NICKLEBY

CONTAINING

A FAITHFUL ACCOUNT OF THE

Fortunes, Misfortunes, Uprisings, Downfallings,

AND

COMPLETE CAREER OF THE NICKLEBY FAMILY.

EDITED BY "BOZ."

WITH ILLUSTRATIONS

BY "PHIZ."

LONDON. CHAPMAN AND HALL, 186, STRAND.

GENTLEMEN'S WATCHES.

EVERY WATCH IS WARRANTED.

A. B. SAVORY & SONS,

WATCH MAKERS & JEWELLERS,

No. 9, CORNHILL, LONDON.

LONDON MADE SILVER WATCHES.

Fine Vertical Watches, in double-backed, engine-turned, or plain silver cases, with highly-finished jewelled movements, hard enamelled dials £4 4 0

Patent Lever Watches, in double-backed, plain, or engine-turned cases, the movements with the latest improvements, i. e. the detached escapement, jewelled in four holes, capped, hard enamel dial, hand to mark the seconds, and maintaining power to continue going while winding up 6 6 0

Ditto, the finest quality, jewelled in six holes, such as are usually mounted in gold 8 8 0

Either of the above, in hunting cases, 10s. 6d. extra.

LONDON MADE GOLD WATCHES.

Patent Lever Watches, in double-backed, plain, or engine-turned gold cases, the movements with the latest improvements, i. e. the detached escapement, jewelled in four holes, hard enamel dial, hand to mark the seconds, and maintaining power to continue going while winding up 14 14 0

Ditto, extra full size, capped, and jewelled in six holes 17 17 0

The same, with gold dial, the gold cases engine-turned 21 0 0

Either of the above, in gold hunting cases, £3 3s. extra.

THE FLAT GENEVA WATCHES.

(Silver Cases.)

Fine Horizontal Watches, in double-backed, engine-turned silver cases, and silver dials, jewelled in four holes 5 5 0

(Gold Cases.)

Horizontal Watches, in double-backed, engine-turned gold cases, with highly-finished movements, jewelled in four holes, with gold or silver dials, including a gold Brequet key 10 10 0

The same, with Brequet's celebrated skeleton movements, of various diameters, including a gold key 13 13 0

A Pamphlet containing detailed lists of the prices of various patterns of Silver Spoons and Forks, Silver Tea and Coffee Services, and of the different articles of Plated Ware, may be had on application, or will be sent into the country in answer to a paid letter; the Show Rooms of this Establishment contain a large selection of every article requisite to complete a service.

ILLUSTRATED EDITION OF FROISSART.

ON THE SECOND OF APRIL WAS PUBLISHED—PART II.—PRICE TWO SHILLINGS—OF

SIR JOHN FROISSART'S CHRONICLES OF ENGLAND, FRANCE, SPAIN, &c.

THIS Edition will be printed from the Translation of the late THOMAS JOHNES, Esq., and collated throughout with that of LORD BERNERS. Numerous additional Notes will also be given, and the whole will be embellished with upwards of ONE HUNDRED ENGRAVINGS ON WOOD, illustrating the Costume and Manners of the period, chiefly taken from the illuminated MS. Copies of the Author, in the British Museum, and elsewhere.

The Work will form about Thirteen Parts, of Ninety-six pages each, in super-royal octavo. A Part will be published every month, price 2s.

In demy 4to, half-bound morocco, gilt edges, price 36s.,

VOLUME THE FIRST,

THE FLORAL CABINET AND MAGAZINE OF EXOTIC BOTANY.

CONTAINING FORTY-FIVE FIGURES OF NEW AND BEAUTIFUL PLANTS,

Coloured after Nature, in the *most careful and accurate manner*, with Descriptions of the Plates, and other Original Matter.

THIS WORK,

⌊ Which has received the commendations of the best Authorities on the subject, for the *beauty* and *truth* of its Coloured Figures,

IS ALSO PUBLISHED MONTHLY, IN NUMBERS, CONTAINING FOUR PLATES EACH.
Price 2s. 6d.

LONDON : WILLIAM SMITH, 113, FLEET STREET.

PREPARING FOR PUBLICATION,

A HISTORY AND DESCRIPTION OF

THE LONDON AND BIRMINGHAM RAILWAY,

ILLUSTRATED BY NUMEROUS FINELY-ENGRAVED STEEL PLATES OF THE MOST INTERESTING BUILDINGS, VIADUCTS, BRIDGES, EMBANKMENTS, AND

POINTS OF SCENERY.

That portion of the Literary Department, comprising the highly-interesting *Historical* Details of this magnificent undertaking, will be written

BY LIEUTENANT LECOUNT, R.N., F.R.A.S., CIVIL ENGINEER,

Who has been connected with the Railway from its commencement ; and the *Descriptive* and *Popular* Account (of peculiar interest to the Resident or Tourist)

BY THOMAS ROSCOE, Esq., Author of " Wanderings and Excursions in Wales," &c.

LECOUNT AND ROSCOE'S LONDON AND BIRMINGHAM RAILWAY

Will be Published in Monthly Parts, demy 8vo, at Half-a-Crown each. A large paper edition, royal 8vo, will be printed, with *India proof impressions of Plates*, price Five Shillings.

Each Part will contain Twenty-four pages of Letter-press and Four fine Steel Plates, besides numerous Engravings on Wood. The First Part will be published in MAY, and the Work will be completed, as far as can be ascertained, in Five or Six Months.

WRIGHTSON AND WEBB, PUBLISHERS, NEW STREET, BIRMINGHAM ;
AND CHARLES TILT, FLEET STREET, LONDON.

TO ADVERTISERS.

The Publishers of this Work purpose inserting a few Advertising Pages in each Part. Upwards of Four Thousand copies will be issued, and the circulation will be very extensive in *London, Birmingham, Liverpool, Manchester,* and other large towns. It will be the Companion of the Tourist in his travels along the Line, or to and from it, and it will take its place as a permanent and elegant work on the library shelf or drawing-room table. Advertisers will therefore perceive that their announcements will not have merely the brief existence of a newspaper record, but will enjoy the advantage of continued and permanent reference. *Immediate application will be necessary for insertion in the First Part.*

LITERATURE & MUSIC COMBINED.

Published Weekly, price 3d., and Monthly in a neat
Wrapper,

THE SUNBEAM ; a Journal devoted
to Polite Literature and Music, embracing Original Papers and Poetry, by the first Writers of the day,
and New Music, by Bishop, Barnett, Bochsa, Kalkbrenner,
Loder, Neukomm, and Sola, with Adaptations and Arrangements from all the Old Masters.

No. VI. contains Authentic Particulars and a splendid
Portrait (gratis) of P. MURPHY, Esq., Author of the
" Weather Almanac."

" A pretty musical and literary medley. It promises
much, and its first number is a fair specimen, finishing
with a sweet ballad, composed by Barnett."—Lit. Gaz.

" A very clever publication."—Morning Post.

" The ' Sunbeam ' will shine in most houses where literature and music are duly estimated. No. 1 contains an
original song, by Barnett, composer of ' The Mountain
Sylph,' with upwards of six pages of agreeable literature,
for three-pence. The song is worth four times the
money."—Mark Lane Express.

" We strongly recommend this publication. No. 1
contains a new song, a beautiful and simple melody, by
J. Barnett. No. 2, a highly pleasing duet, by E. J.
Loder."—Weekly Chronicle.

" We have never met with a work more calculated to
please than this. It introduces a novel feature—original
songs, &c., with pianoforte accompaniments, by such
masters as Barnett, Loder, Bochsa, &c."—London and
Paris Ladies' Magazine.

" We have carefully looked through the pages of the
first part, and can safely recommend it to the support of
every respectable and intelligent family in the kingdom."
—Manchester Times.

" We have just seen the two first numbers of this new
weekly journal ; they contain interesting papers, with an
original song by Barnett and a duet by Loder, each of
which is worth four times the price of the periodical."—
Weekly True Sun.

London: Published for the Proprietors, by G. Berger.
Edinburgh: Messrs. Grant and Son. Glasgow : M'Phun.
Dublin: J. Cumming. And may be had of all Book-
sellers and Newsvenders.

Just published,

MOZART—A New and Correct Edition of the PIANOFORTE WORKS, with
and without Accompaniments, of this celebrated Composer. Edited by CIPRIANI POTTER.

Rondo, Posthumous, in A, No. 14, price 4s.

Introduction and Fuga for Two Performers, in D,
No. 15, 4s.

Concerto for Pianoforte, in A, No. 16, 8s.

Quartet for Pianoforte, Violin, Viola, and Violoncello,
No. 17, 8s.

JOHN SEBASTIAN BACH—Grand Studies for the
Organ, consisting of Preludes, Fugues, Toccatas, and
Fantasias, with a separate part for the Double Bass or
Violoncello ; arranged from the pedal by Signor Drago-
netti. Book I. to V., 7s. each.

W. S. BENNETT'S Overture, ' the Naiades,' performed at the Philharmonic Concerts, arranged as a Duet
for the Pianoforte, by the Composer, 5s.

W. S. BENNETT'S Third Concerto, performed at
the Concerts of the Philharmonic Society, and Society of
British Musicians, 8s.

W. S. BENNETT'S Three Musical Sketches for the
Pianoforte, entitled ' The Lake,' ' The Mill Stream,' and
' The Fountain,' 3s.

W. S. BENNETT'S Song, ' Gentle Zyphyr,' sung by
Herr Kroff, at the Quartet Concerts, 2s.

CIPRIANI POTTER—Overture to Shakspeare's Anthony and Cleopatra, arranged as a Duet for Pianoforte, 6s.

Coventry and Hollier, 71, Dean Street, Soho.

13, GREAT MARLBOROUGH STREET, MARCH 31.

MR. COLBURN'S NEW PUBLICATIONS.

I.

QUEEN ELIZABETH AND HER
TIMES, a Series of Original Letters. Selected
from the inedited private Correspondence of the Lord
Treasurer Burghley, the great Earl of Leicester, the
Secretaries Walsingham and Smith, Sir Christopher
Hatton, and most of the distinguished persons of the
period. Dedicated by permission to Her Majesty. 2
vols. 8vo, with Portraits.

II.

OUTWARD BOUND ; or, A MERCHANT'S
ADVENTURES. By the Author of " Rattlin the
Reefer," " The Old Commodore," &c. 3 vols.

III.

LIFE AND CORRESPONDENCE OF AD-
MIRAL EARL ST. VINCENT. By CAPTAIN BRENTON,
R.N., Author of " The Naval History of Great Britain,"
&c. Now first published from Official and Authentic
Documents, 2 vols. 8vo, with Portrait.

IV.

THE COURTIER'S DAUGHTER. By LADY
STEPNEY. 3 vols.

" A charming specimen of Lady Stepney's powers in
the world of fiction. Her ' Courtier's Daughter' mingles
enough of romance with the realities of modern life to
astonish as well as interest the reader."—John Bull.

V.

THE RIVER AND THE DESART. By
MISS PARDOE. Author of " The City of the Sultan," &c.
2 vols. 8vo, with Illustrations.

" This work is highly creditable to the author—discovering even more mind than any of Miss Pardoe's former
productions."—Atlas.

VI.

MEN OF CHARACTER. By DOUGLAS JER-
ROLD, Esq. 3 vols. post 8vo, with numerous characteristic
Etchings, after Thackeray.

" London folks and London scenes are here presented
to us, with a marvellous degree of freshness and truth ;
and many of the follies and evils of the times are lashed
in a style in which we know not whether most to approve
of the grotesqueness of their exhibition, the moral of
their exposure, or the caustic ridicule of their punishment."—Literary Gazette.

VII.

MEMOIRS OF THE BEAUTIES OF THE
COURT OF CHARLES II. With an Introductory
View of the State of Female Society, and its Influence
during that remarkable Reign. By Mrs. JAMESON. Comprising a Series of Twenty-one splendid Portraits, New
and cheaper Edition, with additions, to be completed in
Six Monthly Parts, at 7s. 6d. each. Part III. is now
ready.

VIII.

ROYSTON GOWER ; or, THE DAYS OF
KING JOHN. By THOMAS MILLER. Author of " A
Day in the Woods," " Beauties of the Country," &c.
3 vols.

" One of the best works in the Scott school that we
have read."—Athenæum.

HENRY COLBURN, Publisher, 13, Great Marlborough Street.

CORPORATION OF THE LONDON ASSURANCE,

ESTABLISHED BY ROYAL CHARTER, A.D. 1720,

FOR FIRE, LIFE, AND MARINE ASSURANCES.

OFFICES, 19, BIRCHIN LANE, CORNHILL, AND 10, REGENT STREET.

JOHN CLARK POWELL, Esq. Governor. ABEL CHAPMAN, Esq. Sub-Governor.
JOHN HILLERSDON, Esq. Deputy-Governor.

DIRECTORS.

Robert Allen, Esq.	John Deffell, Esq.	Alfred Latham, Esq.
George Barnes, Esq.	Richard Drew, Esq.	John Ord, Esq.
Henry Blanshard, Esq.	Joan Furse, Esq.	John Plummer, Esq.
J. Watson Borradaile, Esq.	George Henry Gibbs, Esq.	Daniel Stephenson, Esq.
Edward Burmester, Esq.	Edwin Gower, Esq.	Thomas Weeding, Esq.
Henry Cayley, Esq.	Edward Harnage, Esq.	James Williams, Esq.
Aaron Chapman, Esq., M.P.	Robert King, Esq.	Lestock P. Wilson, Esq.
Robert Cotesworth, Esq.	William King, Esq.	Henry Woodfall, Esq.

OFFICE, No. 10, BIRCHIN LANE.

Timothy Greated, Esq. *Manager of the Marine Department.*
Alexander Boetefeur, Esq. *Superintendent of the Fire Office.*
John Laurence, Esq. *Superintendent of the Life Office.*
John Rutherford, Esq. *Underwriter.* John Laurence, Esq. *Secretary.*

OFFICE, No. 10, REGENT STREET.

Abel Peyton Phelps, Esq. *Superintendent.*

Persons effecting Life Assurances with this Corporation have the choice of two Plans—
The one entitling them to an Annual Abatement of Premium after Five Years' payment.
The other at a lower fixed rate, without Abatement.
The leading features which distinguish the first of these plans from those of all other Life Assurance Offices are—That the business is carried on by the Corporation without any charge for management being deducted from the profits, and that the Assured are exempt from all liability of partnership.

ANNUAL PREMIUMS

REQUIRED FOR THE ASSURANCE, OF £100, FOR THE WHOLE PERIOD OF ANY SINGLE LIFE UNDER THE PLAN ENTITLING THE ASSURED TO AN ABATEMENT OF PREMIUM.

Age.	Premium.	Age.	Premium.	Age.	Premium.	Age.	Premium.
	£ s. d.		£ s. d.		£ s. d.		£ s. d.
16	2 0 3	31	2 13 1	46	4 1 9	61	7 10 0
17	2 1 5	32	2 14 3	47	4 5 0	62	7 17 1
18	2 2 5	33	2 15 6	48	4 8 6	63	8 4 10
19	2 3 5	34	2 16 11	49	4 12 2	64	8 13 1
20	2 4 3	35	2 18 4	50	4 16 1	65	9 1 11
21	2 5 0	36	2 19 11	51	5 0 3	66	9 11 3
22	2 5 8	37	3 1 7	52	5 4 6	67	10 0 9
23	2 6 3	38	3 3 3	53	5 8 9	68	10 10 9
24	2 6 10	39	3 5 1	54	5 13 3	69	11 1 4
25	2 7 6	40	3 7 0	55	5 17 9	70	11 12 6
26	2 8 2	41	3 9 0	56	6 2 6		
27	2 9 0	42	3 11 2	57	6 7 4		
28	2 9 11	43	3 13 7	58	6 12 5		
29	2 10 11	44	3 16 1	59	6 17 10		
30	2 11 11	45	3 18 9	60	7 3 8		

The Abatement of Premium for the year 1838, on Policies of Five Years' Standing, under the first of the above Plans, was £51. 12s. 3d. per cent.
The future Annual Abatement must vary according to the success of this Branch of the Corporation's Business.

IN THE FIRE DEPARTMENT,

ASSURANCES ARE EFFECTED AT THE LOWEST RATES.

Attendance daily, from Ten till Four, at both Offices, where Prospectuses and every information may be obtained.　　　　　　　　　　　　　　　　　　　JOHN LAURENCE, *Secretary.*

The Nickleby Advertiser.

FAMILY ENDOWMENT SOCIETY.

Empowered by Special Act of Parliament.

No. 12, CHATHAM PLACE, BLACKFRIARS.

CAPITAL, £500,000.

TRUSTEES.

PASCOE ST. LEGER GRENFELL, ESQ.

HENRY PORCHER, ESQ.   MARTIN TUCKER SMITH, ESQ.

DIRECTORS.

HENRY GEORGE WARD, ESQ., M.P., *Chairman.*

GEORGE ALFRED MUSKETT, ESQ., M.P., *Deputy-Chairman.*

WM. BUTTERWORTH BAYLEY, ESQ.   EDWARD LEE, ESQ.
HENRY BOWDEN, ESQ.   MAJOR JOHN LUARD.
SIR ROBERT COLQUHOUN, BART.   THOMAS WILLIS MUSKETT, ESQ.
JOHN FULLER, ESQ.   MAJOR GEORGE WILLOCK.

ENDOWMENT BRANCH.

NOVEL MODE OF ENDOWMENT PECULIAR TO THIS SOCIETY.

The peculiar object of this Society is to secure a given sum to each Child of a Marriage at a given age (or to the Parent or Guardian on its behalf).

The advantage it offers over all other systems of Endowment is, that it provides for the *future* as well as the *existing* Children, and that the premium is the same, whatever may eventually be the number of the after-born Children.

An explanatory Pamphlet and Prospectus may be had, *gratis*, at the Office, and of all the Society's Agents throughout the United Kingdom.

LIFE ASSURANCE BRANCH.

Includes Assurances for the whole term of Life, for short terms, for joint lives, for survivorships, and also on an ascending or descending scale.

Two sets of Tables have been constructed, admitting the parties to participate in the profits (*four-fifths*) or not, at their option.

ANNUAL PREMIUM FOR ASSURING £100
FOR THE WHOLE TERM OF LIFE.

Age.	WITH PROFITS.			WITHOUT PROFITS.		
	£.	s.	d.	£.	s.	d.
21	1	18	3	1	15	1
25	2	3	1	1	19	1
30	2	9	7	2	4	7
35	2	16	2	2	11	1
40	3	5	9	3	0	3
50	4	10	6	4	4	9
60	6	7	11	6	2	5

ANNUITY BRANCH.

Includes the granting of Immediate Annuities on Single or Joint Lives; the securing of Annuities to Wives after the decease of their Husbands, and all other Deferred, Reversionary, or Contingent Annuities.

IMMEDIATE ANNUITIES
GRANTED FOR EVERY £100 PAID THE SOCIETY.

Age.	Yearly.			Half-Yearly.		
	£.	s.	d.	£.	s.	d.
25	5	13	4	5	11	10
30	5	18	8	5	16	10
35	6	4	8	6	2	8
40	6	12	7	6	10	6
45	7	1	9	6	19	4
50	7	15	4	7	12	6
55	8	17	0	8	13	2
60	10	7	0	10	1	10
65	12	0	9	11	13	8
70	14	18	0	14	7	4
75	19	1	8	18	4	4
80	23	18	0	22	11	2

This Society also purchases Reversionary Property, advances Money on Mortgage or other Securities, and transacts generally all business appertaining to a Life Assurance Company.

JOHN CAZENOVE, *Secretary.*

[BRADBURY AND EVANS, PRINTERS, WHITEFRIARS.]

LIFE AND ADVENTURES

OF

NICHOLAS NICKLEBY.

CHAPTER I.

INTRODUCES ALL THE REST.

THERE once lived in a sequestered part of the county of Devonshire, one Mr. Godfrey Nickleby, a worthy gentleman, who taking it into his head rather late in life that he must get married, and not being young enough or rich enough to aspire to the hand of a lady of fortune, had wedded an old flame out of mere attachment, who in her turn had taken him for the same reason : thus two people who cannot afford to play cards for money, sometimes sit down to a quiet game for love.

Some ill-conditioned persons, who sneer at the life-matrimonial, may perhaps suggest in this place that the good couple would be better likened to two principals in a sparring match, who, when fortune is low and backers scarce, will chivalrously set to, for the mere pleasure of the buffetting; and in one respect indeed this comparison would hold good, for as the adventurous pair of the Fives' Court will after-wards send round a hat, and trust to the bounty of the lookers-on for the means of regaling themselves, so Mr. Godfrey Nickleby and *his* partner, the honey-moon being over, looked wistfully out into the world, relying in no inconsiderable degree upon chance for the improve-ment of their means. Mr. Nickleby's income, at the period of his marriage, fluctuated between sixty and eighty pounds *per annum*.

There are people enough in the world, heaven knows ! and even in London (where Mr. Nickleby dwelt in those days) but few complaints prevail of the population being scanty. It is extraordinary how long a man may look among the crowd without discovering the face of a friend, but it is no less true. Mr. Nickleby looked and looked till his eyes became sore as his heart, but no friend appeared ; and when, growing tired of the search, he turned his eyes homeward, he saw very little there to relieve his weary vision. A painter, who has gazed too long upon some glaring colour, refreshes his dazzled sight by looking upon a darker and more sombre tint; but everything that met Mr. Nickleby's gaze wore so black and gloomy a hue, that he would have been beyond description refreshed by the very reverse of the contrast.

At length, after five years, when Mrs. Nickleby had presented her husband with a couple of sons, and that embarrassed gentleman, impressed with the necessity of making some provision for his family, was seriously revolving in his mind a little commercial speculation of insuring his life next quarter-day, and then falling from the top of the Monument by accident, there came one morning, by the general post, a black-bordered letter to inform him how his uncle, Mr. Ralph Nickleby, was dead, and had left him the bulk of his little property, amounting in all to five thousand pounds sterling.

As the deceased had taken no further notice of his nephew in his life-time, than sending to his eldest boy (who had been christened after him, on desperate speculation) a silver spoon in a morocco case, which as he had not too much to eat with it, seemed a kind of satire upon his having been born without that useful article of plate in his mouth, Mr. Godfrey Nickleby could at first scarcely believe the tidings thus conveyed to him. On further examination, however, they turned out to be strictly correct. The amiable old gentleman, it seemed, had intended to leave the whole to the Royal Humane Society, and had indeed executed a will to that effect; but the Institution having been unfortunate enough, a few months before, to save the life of a poor relation to whom he paid a weekly allowance of three shillings and sixpence, he had in a fit of very natural exasperation, revoked the bequest in a codicil, and left it all to Mr. Godfrey Nickleby; with a special mention of his indignation, not only against the society for saving the poor relation's life, but against the poor relation also, for allowing himself to be saved.

With a portion of this property Mr. Godfrey Nickleby purchased a small farm near Dawlish, in Devonshire, whither he retired with his wife and two children, to live upon the best interest he could get for the rest of his money, and the little produce he could raise from his land. The two prospered so well together that, when he died, some fifteen years after this period, and some five after his wife, he was enabled to leave to his eldest son, Ralph, three thousand pounds in cash, and to his youngest son, Nicholas, one thousand and the farm; if indeed that can be called a farm, which, exclusive of house and paddock, is about the size of Russell Square, measuring from the street-doors of the houses.

These two brothers had been brought up together in a school at Exeter, and being accustomed to go home once a week, had often heard, from their mother's lips, long accounts of their father's sufferings in his days of poverty, and of their deceased uncle's importance in his days of affluence, which recitals produced a very different impression on the two: for while the younger, who was of a timid and retiring disposition, gleaned from thence nothing but forewarnings to shun the great world and attach himself to the quiet routine of a country life; Ralph, the elder, deduced from the often-repeated tale the two great morals that riches are the only true source of happiness and power, and that it is lawful and just to compass their acquisition by all means short of felony. "And," reasoned Ralph with himself, "if no good came of my uncle's money when he was alive, a great deal of good came of it after he was dead, inasmuch as my father has got it now, and is saving it up for me, which is a highly virtuous purpose; and, going back to the old gentleman, good *did* come of it to him too, for he had the pleasure of thinking of it all his life long, and of being envied and courted by all his family besides." And Ralph always wound up these mental soliloquies by arriving at the conclusion, that there was nothing like money.

Not confining himself to theory, or permitting his faculties to rust even at that early age in mere abstract speculations, this promising lad commenced usurer on a limited scale at school, putting out at good interest a small capital of slate-pencil and marbles, and gradually extending his operations until they aspired to the copper coinage of this realm, in which he speculated to considerable advantage. Nor did he trouble his borrowers with abstract calculations of figures, or references to ready-reckoners; his simple rule of interest being all comprised in the one golden sentence, "two-pence for every half-penny," which greatly simplified the accounts, and which, as a familiar precept, more easily acquired and retained in the memory than any known rule of arithmetic, cannot be too strongly recommended to the notice of capitalists, both large and small, and more especially of money-brokers and bill-discounters. Indeed, to do these gentlemen justice, many of them are to this day in the frequent habit of adopting it with eminent success.

In like manner, did young Ralph Nickleby avoid all those minute and intricate calculations of odd days, which nobody who has ever worked sums in simple-interest can fail to have found most embarrassing, by establishing the one general rule that all sums of principal and interest should be paid on pocket-money day, that is to say, on Saturday; and that whether a loan were contracted on the Monday or on the Friday, the amount of interest should be in both cases the same. Indeed he argued, and with great show of reason, that it ought to be rather more for one day than for five, inasmuch as the borrower might in the former case be very fairly presumed to be in great extremity, otherwise he would not borrow at all with such odds against him. This fact is interesting, as illustrating the secret connection and sympathy which always exists between great minds. Though master Ralph Nickleby was not at that time aware of it, the class of gentlemen before alluded to, proceed on just the same principle in all their transactions.

From what we have said of this young gentleman, and the natural admiration the reader will immediately conceive of his character, it may perhaps be inferred that he is to be the hero of the work which we shall presently begin. To set this point at rest for once and for ever, we hasten to undeceive them, and stride to its commencement.

On the death of his father, Ralph Nickleby, who had been some time before placed in a mercantile house in London, applied himself passionately to his old pursuit of money-getting, in which he speedily became so buried and absorbed, that he quite forgot his brother for many years; and if at times a recollection of his old play-fellow broke upon him through the haze in which he lived—for gold conjures up a mist about a man more destructive of all his old senses and lulling to his feelings than the fumes of charcoal—it brought along with it a companion thought, that if they were intimate he would want to borrow money of him: and Mr. Ralph Nickleby shrugged his shoulders, and said things were better as they were.

As for Nicholas, he lived a single man on the patrimonial estate until he grew tired of living alone, and then he took to wife the daughter of a neighbouring gentleman with a dower of one thousand pounds. This good lady bore him two children, a son and a daughter, and when the son was about nineteen, and the daughter fourteen, as near as we can guess—impartial records of young ladies' ages being, before the passing of the new act, nowhere preserved in the registries of this country—Mr. Nickleby looked about him for the means of repairing his capital, now sadly reduced by this increase in his family and the expenses of their education.

"Speculate with it," said Mrs. Nickleby.

"Spec—u—late, my dear?" said Mr. Nickleby, as though in doubt.

"Why not?" asked Mrs. Nickleby.

"Because, my dear, if we *should* lose it," rejoined Mr. Nickleby, who was a slow and time-taking speaker, "if we *should* lose it, we shall no longer be able to live, my dear."

"Fiddle," said Mrs. Nickleby.

"I am not altogether sure of that, my dear," said Mr. Nickleby.

"There's Nicholas," pursued the lady, "quite a young man—it's time he was in the way of doing something for himself; and Kate too, poor girl, without a penny in the world. Think of your brother; would he be what he is, if he hadn't speculated?"

"That's true," replied Mr. Nickleby. "Very good, my dear. Yes. I *will* speculate, my dear."

Speculation is a round game; the players see little or nothing of their cards at first starting; gains *may* be great—and so may losses. The run of luck went against Mr. Nickleby; a mania prevailed, a bubble burst, four stock-brokers took villa residences at Florence, four hundred nobodies were ruined, and among them Mr. Nickleby.

"The very house I live in," sighed the poor gentleman, "may be taken from me to-morrow. Not an article of my old furniture, but will be sold to strangers!"

The last reflection hurt him so much, that he took at once to his bed, apparently resolved to keep that, at all events.

"Cheer up, Sir!" said the apothecary.

"You mustn't let yourself be cast down, Sir," said the nurse.

"Such things happen every day," remarked the lawyer.

"And it is very sinful to rebel against them," whispered the clergy man.

" And what no man with a family ought to do," added the neighbours.

Mr. Nickleby shook his head, and motioning them all out of the room, embraced his wife and children, and having pressed them by turns to his languidly beating heart, sunk exhausted on his pillow. They were concerned to find that his reason went astray after this, for he babbled for a long time about the generosity and goodness of his brother, and the merry old times when they were at school together. This fit of wandering past, he solemnly commended them to One who never deserted the widow or her fatherless children, and smiling gently on them, turned upon his face, and observed, that he thought he could fall asleep.

CHAPTER II.

OF MR. RALPH NICKLEBY, AND HIS ESTABLISHMENT, AND HIS UNDER-
TAKINGS. AND OF A GREAT JOINT STOCK COMPANY OF VAST
NATIONAL IMPORTANCE.

MR. RALPH NICKLEBY was not, strictly speaking, what you would call a merchant : neither was he a banker, nor an attorney, nor a special pleader, nor a notary. He was certainly not a tradesman, and still less could he lay any claim to the title of a professional gentleman ; for it would have been impossible to mention any recognised profession to which he belonged. Nevertheless, as he lived in a spacious house in Golden Square, which, in addition to a brass plate upon the street-door, had another brass plate two sizes and a half smaller upon the left hand door-post, surmounting a brass model of an infant's fist grasping a fragment of a skewer, and displaying the word " Office," it was clear that Mr. Ralph Nickleby did, or pretended to do, business of some kind ; and the fact, if it required any further circumstantial evidence, was abundantly demonstrated by the diurnal attendance, between the hours of half-past nine and five, of a sallow-faced man in rusty brown, who sat upon an uncommonly hard stool in a species of butler's pantry at the end of the passage, and always had a pen behind his ear when he answered the bell.

Although a few members of the graver professions live about Golden Square, it is not exactly in anybody's way to or from anywhere. It is one of the squares that have been ; a quarter of the town that has gone down in the world, and taken to letting lodgings. Many of its first and second floors are let furnished to single gentlemen, and it takes boarders besides. It is a great resort of foreigners. The dark-complexioned men who wear large rings, and heavy watch-guards and bushy whiskers, and who congregate under the Opera colonnade, and about the box-office in the season, between four and five in the after-noon, when Mr. Seguin gives away the orders,—all live in Golden Square, or within a street of it. Two or three violins and a wind instrument from the Opera band reside within its precincts. Its boarding-houses are musical, and the notes of pianos and harps float in the evening time round the head of the mournful statue, the guardian genius of a little wilderness of shrubs, in the centre of the square. On a summer's night, windows are thrown open, and groups of swarthy mustachio'd men are seen by the passer-by lounging at the casements, and smoking fearfully. Sounds of gruff voices practising vocal music invade the evening's silence, and the fumes of choice tobacco scent the air. There, snuff and cigars, and German pipes and flutes, and violins, and violoncellos, divide the supremacy between them. It is the region of song and smoke. Street bands are on their mettle in Golden Square, and itinerant glee-singers quaver involuntarily as they raise their voices within its boundaries.

This would not seem a spot very well adapted to the transaction of business; but Mr. Ralph Nickleby had lived there notwithstanding for many years, and uttered no complaint on that score. He knew nobody round about and nobody knew him, although he enjoyed the reputation of being immensely rich. The tradesmen held that he was a sort of lawyer, and the other neighbours opined that he was a kind of general agent; both of which guesses were as correct and definite as guesses about other people's affairs usually are, or need to be.

Mr. Ralph Nickleby sat in his private office one morning, ready dressed to walk abroad. He wore a bottle-green spencer over a blue coat; a white waistcoat, grey mixture pantaloons, and Wellington boots drawn over them: the corner of a small-plaited shirt frill struggled out, as if insisting to show itself, from between his chin and the top button of his spencer, and the garment was not made low enough to conceal a long gold watch-chain, composed of a series of plain rings, which had its beginning at the handle of a gold repeater in Mr. Nickleby's pocket, and its termination in two little keys, one belonging to the watch itself, and the other to some patent padlock. He wore a sprinkling of powder upon his head, as if to make himself look benevolent; but if that were his purpose, he would perhaps have done better to powder his countenance also, for there was something in its very wrinkles, and in his cold restless eye, which seemed to tell of cunning that would announce itself in spite of him. However this might be, there he was; and as he was all alone, neither the powder nor the wrinkles, nor the eyes, had the smallest effect, good or bad, upon anybody just then, and are consequently no business of ours just now.

Mr. Nickleby closed an account-book which lay on his desk, and throwing himself back in his chair, gazed with an air of abstraction through the dirty window. Some London houses have a melancholy little plot of ground behind them, usually fenced in by four high white-washed walls and frowned upon by stacks of chimneys, in which there withers on from year to year a crippled tree, that makes a show of putting forth a few leaves late in autumn, when other trees shed theirs, and drooping in the effort, lingers on all crackled and smoke-dried till the following season, when it repeats the same process, and perhaps if the weather be particularly genial, even tempts some rheumatic sparrow to chirrup in its branches. People sometimes call these dark yards " gardens ;" it is not supposed that they were ever planted, but rather that they are pieces of unreclaimed land, with the withered vegetation of the original brick-field. No man thinks of walking in this desolate place, or of turning it to any account. A few hampers, half-a-dozen broken bottles, and such-like rubbish, may be thrown there when the tenant first moves in, but nothing more ; and there they remain till he goes away again, the damp straw taking just as long to moulder as it thinks proper, and mingling with the scanty box, and stunted everbrowns, and broken flower-pots, that are scattered mournfully about—a prey to " blacks" and dirt.

It was into a place of this kind that Mr. Ralph Nickleby gazed as he sat with his hands in his pockets looking out at window. He had fixed his eyes upon a distorted fir-tree, planted by some former tenant in a tub that had once been green, and left there years before, to rot away piecemeal. There was nothing very inviting in the object, but Mr. Nickleby was wrapt in a brown study, and sat contemplating it with far greater attention than, in a more conscious mood, he would have deigned to bestow upon the rarest exotic. At length his eyes wandered to a little dirty window on the left, through which the face of the clerk was dimly visible, and that worthy chancing to look up, he beckoned him to attend.

In obedience to this summons the clerk got off the high stool (to which he had communicated a high polish, by countless gettings off and on), and presented himself in Mr. Nickleby's room. He was a tall man of middle-age with two goggle eyes whereof one was a fixture, a rubicund nose, a cadaverous face, and a suit of clothes (if the term be allowable when they suited him not at all) much the worse for wear, very much too small, and placed upon such a short allowance of buttons that it was quite marvellous how he contrived to keep them on.

" Was that half-past twelve, Noggs ?" said Mr. Nickleby, in a sharp and grating voice.

" Not more than five-and-twenty minutes by the—" Noggs was going to add public-house clock, but recollecting himself, he substituted " regular time."

" My watch has stopped," said Mr. Nickleby ; " I don't know from what cause."

" Not wound up" said Noggs.

" Yes, it is," said Mr. Nickleby.

" Over-wound then" rejoined Noggs.

" That can't very well be," observed Mr. Nickleby.

" Must be," said Noggs.

" Well !" said Mr. Nickleby, putting the repeater back in his pocket ; " perhaps it is."

Noggs gave a peculiar grunt as was his custom at the end of all disputes with his master, to imply that he (Noggs) triumphed, and (as he rarely spoke to anybody unless somebody spoke to him) fell into a grim silence, and rubbed his hands slowly over each other, cracking the joints of his fingers, and squeezing them into all possible distortions.

The incessant performance of this routine on every occasion, and the communication of a fixed and rigid look to his unaffected eye, so as to make it uniform with the other, and to render it impossible for anybody to determine where or at what he was looking, were two among the numerous peculiarities of Mr. Noggs, which struck an inexperienced observer at first sight.

"I am going to the London Tavern this morning," said Mr. Nickleby.

"Public meeting?" inquired Noggs.

Mr. Nickleby nodded. "I expect a letter from the solicitor respecting that mortgage of Ruddle's. If it comes at all, it will be here by the two o'clock delivery. I shall leave the city about that time and walk to Charing-Cross on the left-hand side of the way; if there are any letters, come and meet me, and bring them with you."

Noggs nodded; and as he nodded, there came a ring at the office bell: the master looked up from his papers, and the clerk calmly remained in a stationary position.

"The bell," said Noggs, as though in explanation; "at home?"

"Yes."

"To anybody?"

"Yes."

"To the tax-gatherer?"

"No! Let him call again."

Noggs gave vent to his usual grunt, as much as to say "I thought so!" and, the ring being repeated, went to the door, whence he presently returned ushering in, by the name of Mr. Bonney, a pale gentleman in a violent hurry, who, with his hair standing up in great disorder all over his head, and a very narrow white cravat tied loosely round his throat, looked as if he had been knocked up in the night and had not dressed himself since.

"My dear Nickleby," said the gentleman, taking off a white hat which was so full of papers that it would scarcely stick upon his head, "there's not a moment to lose; I have a cab at the door. Sir Matthew Pupker takes the chair, and three members of Parliament are positively coming. I have seen two of them safely out of bed; and the third, who was at Crockford's all night, has just gone home to put a clean shirt on, and take a bottle or two of soda-water, and will certainly be with us in time to address the meeting. He is a little excited by last night, but never mind that; he always speaks the stronger for it."

"It seems to promise pretty well," said Mr. Ralph Nickleby, whose deliberate manner was strongly opposed to the vivacity of the other man of business.

"Pretty well!" echoed Mr. Bonney; "It's the finest idea that was ever started. 'United Metropolitan Improved Hot Muffin and Crumpet Baking and Punctual Delivery Company. Capital, five millions, in five hundred thousand shares of ten pounds each.' Why the very name will get the shares up to a premium in ten days."

"And when they *are* at a premium," said Mr. Ralph Nickleby, smiling.

" When they are, you know what to do with them as well as any man alive, and how to back quietly out at the right time," said Mr. Bonney, slapping the capitalist familiarly on the shoulder. " By the bye, what a *very* remarkable man that clerk of yours is."

" Yes, poor devil !" replied Ralph, drawing on his gloves. " Though Newman Noggs kept his horses and hounds once."

" Aye, aye ?" said the other carelessly.

" Yes," continued Ralph, " and not many years ago either; but he squandered his money, invested it anyhow, borrowed at interest, and in short made first a thorough fool of himself, and then a beggar. He took to drinking, and had a touch of paralysis, and then came here to borrow a pound, as in his better days I had—had—"

" Had done business with him," said Mr. Bonney with a meaning look.

" Just so," replied Ralph ; " I couldn't lend it, you know."

" Oh, of course not."

" But as I wanted a clerk just then, to open the door and so forth, I took him out of charity, and he has remained with me ever since. He is a little mad, I think," said Mr. Nickleby, calling up a charitable look, " but he is useful enough, poor creature—useful enough."

The kind-hearted gentleman omitted to add that Newman Noggs, being utterly destitute, served him for rather less than the usual wages of a boy of thirteen; and likewise failed to mention in his hasty chronicle, that his eccentric taciturnity rendered him an especially valuable person in a place where much business was done, of which it was desirable no mention should be made out of doors. The other gentleman was plainly impatient to be gone, however, and as they hurried into the hackney cabriolet immediately afterwards, perhaps Mr. Nickleby forgot to mention circumstances so unimportant.

There was a great bustle in Bishopsgate Street Within, as they drew up, and (it being a windy day) half a dozen men were tacking across the road under a press of paper, bearing gigantic announcements that a Public Meeting would be holden at one o'clock precisely, to take into consideration the propriety of petitioning Parliament in favour of the United Metropolitan Improved Hot Muffin and Crumpet Baking and Punctual Delivery Company, capital five millions, in five hundred thousand shares of ten pounds each; which sums were duly set forth in fat black figures of considerable size. Mr. Bonney elbowed his way briskly up stairs, receiving in his progress many low bows from the waiters who stood on the landings to show the way, and, followed by Mr. Nickleby, dived into a suite of apartments behind the great public room, in the second of which was a business-looking table, and several business-looking people.

" Hear !" cried a gentleman with a double chin, as Mr. Bonney presented himself. " Chair, gentlemen, chair."

The new comers were received with universal approbation, and Mr. Bonney bustled up to the top of the table, took off his hat, ran his fingers through his hair, and knocked a hackney-coachmen's knock on the table with a little hammer: whereat several gentlemen cried

"Hear!" and nodded slightly to each other, as much as to say what spirited conduct that was.   Just at this moment a waiter, feverish with agitation, tore into the room, and throwing the door open with a crash, shouted "Sir Matthew Pupker."

The committee stood up and clapped their hands for joy; and while they were clapping them, in came Sir Matthew Pupker, attended by two live members of Parliament, one Irish and one Scotch, all smiling and bowing, and looking so pleasant that it seemed a perfect marvel how any man could have the heart to vote against them. Sir Matthew Pupker especially, who had a little round head with a flaxen wig on the top of it, fell into such a paroxysm of bows, that the wig threatened to be jerked off every instant.   When these symptoms had in some degree subsided, the gentlemen who were on speaking terms with Sir Matthew Pupker, or the two other members, crowded round them in three little groups, near one or other of which the gentlemen who were *not* on speaking terms with Sir Matthew Pupker or the two other members, stood lingering, and smiling, and rubbing their hands, in the desperate hope of something turning up which might bring them into notice.   All this time Sir Matthew Pupker and the two other members were relating to their separate circles what the intentions of government were about taking up the bill, with a full account of what the government had said in a whisper the last time they dined with it, and how the government had been observed to wink when it said so; from which premises they were at no loss to draw the conclusion, that if the government had one object more at heart than another, that one object was the welfare and advantage of the United Metropolitan Improved Hot Muffin and Crumpet Baking and Punctual Delivery Company.

Meanwhile, and pending the arrangement of the proceedings, and a fair division of the speechifying, the public in the large room were eyeing, by turns, the empty platform, and the ladies in the Music Gallery.   In these amusements the greater portion of them had been occupied for a couple of hours before, and as the most agreeable diversions pall upon the taste on a too protracted enjoyment of them, the sterner spirits now began to hammer the floor with their boot-heels, and to express their dissatisfaction by various hoots and cries.   These vocal exertions, emanating from the people who had been there longest, naturally proceeded from those who were nearest to the platform and furthest from the policemen in attendance, who having no great mind to fight their way through the crowd, but entertaining nevertheless a praiseworthy desire to do something to quell the disturbance, immediately began to drag forth by the coat tails and collars all the quiet people near the door; at the same time dealing out various smart and tingling blows with their truncheons, after the manner of that ingenious actor, Mr. Punch, whose brilliant example, both in the fashion of his weapons and their use, this branch of the executive occasionally follows.

Several very exciting skirmishes were in progress, when a loud shout attracted the attention even of the belligerents, and then there poured on to the platform, from a door at the side, a long line of gentlemen with their hats off, all looking behind them, and uttering vociferous cheers; the cause whereof was sufficiently explained when Sir Matthew Pupker and the two other real members of Parliament came to the front, amidst deafening shouts, and testified to each other in dumb motions that they had never seen such a glorious sight as that in the whole course of their public career.

At length, and at last, the assembly left off shouting, but Sir Matthew Pupker being voted into the chair, they underwent a relapse which lasted five minutes. This over, Sir Matthew Pupker went on to say what must be his feelings on that great occasion, and what must be that occasion in the eyes of the world, and what must be the intelligence of his fellow-countrymen before him, and what must be the wealth and respectability of his honourable friends behind him; and lastly, what must be the importance to the wealth, the happiness, the comfort, the liberty, the very existence of a free and great people, of such an Institution as the United Metropolitan Improved Hot Muffin and Crumpet Baking and Punctual Delivery Company.

Mr. Bonney then presented himself to move the first resolution, and having run his right hand through his hair, and planted his left in an easy manner in his ribs, he consigned his hat to the care of the gentleman with the double chin (who acted as a species of bottle-holder to the orators generally), and said he would read to them the first resolution—"That this meeting views with alarm and apprehension, the existing state of the Muffin Trade in this Metropolis and its neighbourhood; that it considers the Muffin Boys, as at present constituted, wholly undeserving the confidence of the public, and that it deems the whole Muffin system alike prejudicial to the health and morals of the people, and subversive of the best interests of a great commercial and mercantile community." The honourable gentleman made a speech which drew tears from the eyes of the ladies, and awakened the liveliest emotions in every individual present. He had visited the houses of the poor in the various districts of London, and had found them destitute of the slightest vestige of a muffin, which there appeared too much reason to believe some of these indigent persons did not taste from year's end to year's end. He had found that among muffin sellers there existed drunkenness, debauchery, and profligacy, which he attributed to the debasing nature of their employment as at present exercised; he had found the same vices among the poorer class of people who ought to be muffin consumers, and this he attributed to the despair engendered by their being placed beyond the reach of that nutritious article, which drove them to seek a false stimulant in intoxicating liquors. He would undertake to prove before a committee of the House of Commons, that there existed a combination to keep up the price of muffins, and to give the bellman a monopoly; he would prove it by bellmen at the bar of that House; and he would also prove, that these men corresponded with each other by secret words and signs, as, "Snooks," "Walker," "Ferguson," "Is Murphy right?" and many others. It was this melancholy state of things that the Company proposed to correct; firstly, by prohibiting under heavy penalties all private muffin trading of every description; and secondly, by themselves supplying the public generally, and the poor at their own homes, with muffins of first quality at reduced prices. It was with this object that a bill had been introduced into Parliament by their patriotic chairman Sir Mathew Pupker; it was this bill that they had met to support; it was the supporters of this bill who would confer undying brightness and splendour upon England, under the name of the United Metropolitan Improved Hot Muffin and Crumpet Baking and Punctual Delivery Company; he would add, with a capital of Five Millions, in five hundred thousand shares of ten pounds each.

Mr. Ralph Nickleby seconded the resolution, and another gentleman having moved that it be amended by the insertion of the words " and crumpet" after the word "muffin," whenever it occurred, it was carried triumphantly; only one man in the crowd cried " No !" and he was promptly taken into custody, and straightway borne off.

The second resolution, which recognised the expediency of immediately abolishing " all muffin (or crumpet) sellers, all traders in muffins (or crumpets) of whatsoever description, whether male or female, boys or men, ringing hand-bells or otherwise," was moved by a grievous gentleman of semi-clerical appearance, who went at once into such deep pathetics, that he knocked the first speaker clean out of the course in no time. You might have heard a pin fall—a pin ! a feather—as he described the cruelties inflicted on muffin boys by their masters, which he very wisely urged were in themselves a sufficient reason for the establishment of that inestimable company. It seemed that the unhappy youths were nightly turned out into the wet streets at the most inclement periods of the year, to wander about in darkness and rain—or it might be hail or snow—for hours together, without shelter, food, or warmth; and let the public never forget upon the latter point, that while the muffins were provided with warm clothing and blankets, the boys were wholly unprovided for, and left to their own miserable resources. (Shame !) The honourable gentleman related one case of a muffin boy, who having been exposed to this inhuman and barbarous system for no less than five years, at length fell a victim to a cold in the head, beneath which he gradually sunk until he fell into a perspiration and recovered; this he could vouch for, on his own authority, but he had heard (and he had no reason to doubt the fact) of a still more heart-rending and appalling circumstance. He had heard of the case of an orphan muffin boy, who, having been run over by a hackney carriage, had been removed to the hospital, had undergone the amputation of his leg below the knee, and was now actually pursuing his occupation on crutches. Fountain of justice, were these things to last !

This was the department of the subject that took the meeting, and this was the style of speaking to enlist their sympathies. The men shouted, the ladies wept into their pocket-handkerchiefs till they were moist, and waved them till they were dry; the excitement was tremendous, and Mr. Nickleby whispered his friend that the shares were thenceforth at a premium of five-and twenty per cent.

The resolution was of course carried with loud acclamations, every man holding up both hands in favour of it, as he would in his enthusiasm have held up both legs also, if he could have conveniently accomplished it. This done, the draft of the proposed petition was read at length ; and the petition said, as all petitions *do* say, that the petitioners were very humble, and the petitioned very honorable, and the object very virtuous, therefore (said the petition) the bill ought to be passed into a law at once, to the everlasting honor and glory of that most honorable and glorious Commons of England in Parliament assembled.

Then the gentleman who had been at Crockford's all night, and who looked something the worse about the eyes in consequence, came forward to tell his fellow-countrymen what a speech he meant to make in favour of that petition whenever it should be presented, and how desperately he meant to taunt the parliament if they rejected the bill ; and to inform them also that he regretted his honorable friends had not inserted a clause rendering the purchase of muffins and crumpets compulsory upon all classes of the community, which he—opposing all half measures, and preferring to go the extreme animal—pledged himself to propose and divide upon in committee. After announcing this determination, the honorable gentleman grew jocular ; and as patent boots, lemon-coloured kid gloves, and a fur coat collar, assist jokes materially, there was immense laughter and much cheering, and moreover such a brilliant display of ladies' pocket-handkerchiefs, as threw the grievous gentleman quite into the shade.

And when the petition had been read and was about to be adopted, there came forward the Irish member (who was a young gentleman of ardent temperament), with such a speech as only an Irish member can make, breathing the true soul and spirit of poetry, and poured forth with such fervour, that it made one warm to look at him ; in the course whereof he told them how he would demand the extension of that great boon to his native country ; how he would claim for her equal rights in the muffin laws as in all other laws ; and how he yet hoped to see the day when crumpets should be toasted in her lowly cabins, and muffin bells should ring in her rich green valleys. And after him came the Scotch member, with various pleasant allusions to the probable amount of profits, which increased the good humour that the poetry had awakened ; and all the speeches put together did exactly what they were intended to do, and established in the hearers' minds that there was no speculation so promising, or at the same time so praiseworthy, as the United Metropolitan Improved Hot Muffin and Crumpet Baking and Punctual Delivery Company.

So, the petition in favour of the bill was agreed upon, and the meeting adjourned with acclamations, and Mr. Nickleby and the other directors went to the office to lunch, as they did every day at half-past one o'clock ; and to remunerate themselves for which trouble, (as the company was yet in its infancy,) they only charged three guineas each man for every such attendance.

CHAPTER III.

MR. RALPH NICKLEBY RECEIVES SAD TIDINGS OF HIS BROTHER, BUT BEARS UP NOBLY AGAINST THE INTELLIGENCE COMMUNICATED TO HIM. THE READER IS INFORMED HOW HE LIKED NICHOLAS, WHO IS HEREIN INTRODUCED, AND HOW KINDLY HE PROPOSED TO MAKE HIS FORTUNE AT ONCE.

HAVING rendered his zealous assistance towards despatching the lunch, with all that promptitude and energy which are among the most important qualities that men of business can possess, Mr. Ralph Nickleby took a cordial farewell of his fellow speculators, and bent his steps westward in unwonted good humour. As he passed Saint Paul's he stepped aside into a doorway to set his watch, and with his hand on the key and his eye on the cathedral dial, was intent upon so doing, when a man suddenly stopped before him. It was Newman Noggs.

"Ah! Newman," said Mr. Nickleby, looking up as he pursued his occupation. "The letter about the mortgage has come, has it? I thought it would."

"Wrong," replied Newman.

"What! and nobody called respecting it?" inquired Mr. Nickleby, pausing. Noggs shook his head.

"What has come, then?" inquired Mr. Nickleby.

"I have," said Newman.

"What else?" demanded the master, sternly.

"This," said Newman, drawing a sealed letter slowly from his pocket. "Post-mark, Strand, black wax, black border, woman's hand, C. N. in the corner."

"Black wax," said Mr. Nickleby, glancing at the letter. "I know something of that hand, too. Newman, I shouldn't be surprised if my brother were dead."

"I don't think you would," said Newman, quietly.

"Why not, sir?" demanded Mr. Nickleby.

"You never are surprised," replied Newman, "that's all."

Mr. Nickleby snatched the letter from his assistant, and fixing a cold look upon him, opened, read it, put it in his pocket, and having now hit the time to a second, began winding up his watch.

"It is as I expected, Newman," said Mr. Nickleby, while he was thus engaged. "He is dead. Dear me. Well, that's a sudden thing. I shouldn't have thought it, really." With these touching expressions of sorrow, Mr. Nickleby replaced his watch in his fob, and fitting on his gloves to a nicety, turned upon his way, and walked slowly westward with his hands behind him.

"Children alive?" inquired Noggs, stepping up to him.

"Why, that's the very thing," replied Mr. Nickleby, as though his thoughts were about them at that moment. "They are both alive."

"Both!" repeated Newman Noggs, in a low voice.

"And the widow, too," added Mr. Nickleby, "and all three in London, confound them; all three here, Newman."

Newman fell a little behind his master, and his face was curiously twisted as by a spasm, but whether of paralysis, or grief, or inward laughter, nobody but himself could possibly explain. The expression of a man's face is commonly a help to his thoughts, or glossary on his speech; but the countenance of Newman Noggs, in his ordinary moods, was a problem which no stretch of ingenuity could solve.

"Go home!" said Mr. Nickleby after they had walked a few paces, looking round at the clerk as if he were his dog. The words were scarcely uttered when Newman darted across the road, slunk among the crowd, and disappeared in an instant.

"Reasonable, certainly!" muttered Mr. Nickleby to himself, as he walked on, "very reasonable! My brother never did anything for me, and I never expected it; the breath is no sooner out of his body than I am to be looked to, as the support of a great hearty woman and a grown boy and girl. What are they to me? _I_ never saw them."

Full of these and many other reflections of a similar kind, Mr. Nickleby made the best of his way to the Strand, and referring to his letter as if to ascertain the number of the house he wanted, stopped at a private door about half-way down that crowded thoroughfare.

A miniature painter lived there, for there was a large gilt frame screwed upon the street-door, in which were displayed, upon a black velvet ground, two portraits of naval dress coats with faces looking out of them and telescopes attached; one of a young gentleman in a very vermilion uniform, flourishing a sabre; and one of a literary character with a high forehead, a pen and ink, six books, and a curtain. There was moreover a touching representation of a young lady reading a manuscript in an unfathomable forest, and a charming whole length of a large-headed little boy, sitting on a stool with his legs fore-shortened to the size of salt-spoons. Besides these works of art, there were a great many heads of old ladies and gentlemen smirking at each other out of blue and brown skies, and an elegantly-written card of terms with an embossed border.

Mr. Nickleby glanced at these frivolities with great contempt, and gave a double knock, which having been thrice repeated was answered by a servant girl with an uncommonly dirty face.

"Is Mrs. Nickleby at home, girl?" demanded Ralph, sharply.

"Her name ain't Nickleby," said the girl, "La Creevy, you mean."

Mr. Nickleby looked very indignant at the handmaid on being thus corrected, and demanded with much asperity what she meant; which she was about to state, when a female voice, proceeding from a perpendicular staircase at the end of the passage, inquired who was wanted.

"Mrs. Nickleby" said Ralph.

"It's the second floor, Hannah," said the same voice; "what a stupid thing you are! Is the second floor at home?"

" Somebody went out just now, but I think it was the attic which had been a cleaning of himself," replied the girl.

" You had better see," said the invisible female. " Show the gentleman where the bell is, and tell him he mustn't knock double knocks for the second floor; I can't allow a knock except when the bell's broke, and then it must be two single ones."

" Here," said Ralph, walking in without more parley, " I beg your pardon; is that Mrs. La what's-her-name ? "

" Creevy—La Creevy," replied the voice, as a yellow head-dress bobbed over the bannisters.

" I'll speak to you a moment, ma'am, with your leave," said Ralph.

The voice replied that the gentleman was to walk up; but he had walked up before it spoke, and stepping into the first floor, was received by the wearer of the yellow head-dress, who had a gown to correspond, and was of much the same colour herself. Miss La Creevy was a mincing young lady of fifty, and Miss La Creevy's apartment was the gilt frame down stairs on a larger scale and something dirtier.

" Hem ! " said Miss La Creevy, coughing delicately behind her black silk mitten. " A miniature, I presume. A very strongly-marked countenance for the purpose, Sir. Have you ever sat before ? "

" You mistake my purpose, I see, Ma'am," replied Mr. Nickleby, in his usual blunt fashion. " I have no money to throw away on miniatures, ma'am, and nobody to give one to (thank God) if I had. Seeing you on the stairs, I wanted to ask a question of you, about some lodgers here."

Miss La Creevy coughed once more—this cough was to conceal her disappointment—and said, " Oh, indeed ! "

" I infer from what you said to your servant, that the floor above belongs to you, ma'am ? " said Mr. Nickleby.

Yes it did, Miss La Creevy replied. The upper part of the house belonged to her, and as she had no necessity for the second-floor rooms just then, she was in the habit of letting them. Indeed, there was a lady from the country and her two children in them, at that present speaking.

" A widow, ma'am ? " said Ralph.

" Yes, she is a widow," replied the lady.

" A *poor* widow, ma'am ? " said Ralph, with a powerful emphasis on that little adjective which conveys so much.

" Well, I am afraid she *is* poor," rejoined Miss La Creevy.

" I happen to know that she is, ma'am," said Ralph. " Now what business has a poor widow in such a house as this, ma'am ? "

" Very true," replied Miss La Creevy, not at all displeased with this implied compliment to the apartments. " Exceedingly true."

" I know her circumstances intimately, ma'am," said Ralph; " in fact, I am a relation of the family; and I should recommend you not to keep them here, ma'am."

" I should hope, if there was any incompatibility to meet the pecuniary obligations," said Miss La Creevy with another cough, " that the lady's family would—— "

" No they wouldn't, ma'am," interrupted Ralph, hastily. " Don't think it."

" If I am to understand that ;" said Miss La Creevy, " the case wears a very different appearance."

" You may understand it then, ma'am," said Ralph, " and make your arrangements accordingly. I am the family, ma'am—at least, I believe I am the only relation they have, and I think it right that you should know I can't support them in their extravagances. How long have they taken these lodgings for ?"

" Only from week to week," replied Miss La Creevy. " Mrs. Nickleby paid the first week in advance."

" Then you had better get them out at the end of it," said Ralph. " They can't do better than go back to the country, ma'am; they are in everybody's way here."

" Certainly," said Miss La Creevy, rubbing her hands; " if Mrs. Nickleby took the apartments without the means of paying for them, it was very unbecoming a lady."

" Of course it was, ma'am," said Ralph.

" And naturally," continued Miss La Creevy, " I who am *at present* —hem—an unprotected female, cannot afford to lose by the apartments."

" Of course you can't, ma'am," replied Ralph.

" Though at the same time," added Miss La Creevy who was plainly wavering between her good-nature and her interest, " I have nothing whatever to say against the lady, who is extremely pleasant and affable, though, poor thing, she seems terribly low in her spirits; nor against the young people either, for nicer, or better-behaved young people cannot be."

" Very well, ma'am," said Ralph, turning to the door, for these encomiums on poverty irritated him; " I have done my duty, and perhaps more than I ought : of course nobody will thank me for saying what I have."

" I am sure I am very much obliged to you at least, Sir," said Miss La Creevy in a gracious manner. " Would you do me the favour to look at a few specimens of my portrait painting ?"

" You're very good, ma'am," said Mr. Nickleby, making off with great speed; " but as I have a visit to pay up stairs, and my time is precious, I really can't."

" At any other time when you are passing, I shall be most happy," said Miss La Creevy. " Perhaps you will have the kindness to take a card of terms with you ? Thank you—good morning."

" Good morning, ma'am," said Ralph, shutting the door abruptly after him to prevent any further conversation. " Now for my sister-in-law. Bah !"

Climbing up another perpendicular flight, composed with great mechanical ingenuity of nothing but corner stairs, Mr. Ralph Nickleby stopped to take breath on the landing, when he was overtaken by the handmaid, whom the politeness of Miss La Creevy had despatched to announce him, and who had apparently been making a variety of unsuccessful attempts since their last interview, to wipe her dirty face clean upon an apron much dirtier.

" What name ?" said the girl.

" Nickleby," replied Ralph.

" Oh ! Mrs. Nickleby," said the girl, throwing open the door, " here's Mr. Nickleby."

A lady in deep mourning rose as Mr. Ralph Nickleby entered, but appeared incapable of advancing to meet him, and leant upon the arm of a slight but very beautiful girl of about seventeen, who had been sitting by her. A youth, who appeared a year or two older, stepped forward and saluted Ralph as his uncle.

" Oh," growled Ralph, with an ill-favoured frown, " you are Nicholas, I suppose ?"

" That is my name, Sir," replied the youth.

" Put my hat down," said Ralph, imperiously. " Well, ma'am, how do you do ? You must bear up against sorrow, ma'am ; I always do."

" Mine was no common loss !" said Mrs. Nickleby, applying her handkerchief to her eyes.

" It was no *uncommon* loss, ma'am," returned Ralph, as he coolly unbuttoned his spencer. " Husbands die every day, ma'am, and wives too."

" And brothers also, Sir," said Nicholas, with a glance of indignation.

" Yes, Sir, and puppies, and pug-dogs likewise," replied his uncle, taking a chair. " You didn't mention in your letter what my brother's complaint was, ma'am."

" The doctors could attribute it to no particular disease," said Mrs. Nickleby, shedding tears. " We have too much reason to fear that he died of a broken heart."

" Pooh !" said Ralph, " there's no such thing. I can understand a man's dying of a broken neck, or suffering from a broken arm, or a broken head, or a broken leg, or a broken nose ; but a broken heart—nonsense, it's the cant of the day. If a man can't pay his debts, he dies of a broken heart, and his widow's a martyr."

" Some people, I believe, have no hearts to break," observed Nicholas, quietly.

" How old is this boy, for God's sake ?" inquired Ralph, wheeling back his chair, and surveying his nephew from head to foot with intense scorn.

" Nicholas is very nearly nineteen," replied the widow.

" Nineteen, eh !" said Ralph, " and what do you mean to do for your bread, Sir ?"

" Not to live upon my mother," replied Nicholas, his heart swelling as he spoke.

" You'd have little enough to live upon, if you did," retorted the uncle, eyeing him contemptuously.

" Whatever it be," said Nicholas, flushed with anger, " I shall not look to you to make it more."

" Nicholas, my dear, recollect yourself," remonstrated Mrs. Nickleby.

Mr. Ralph Nickleby's first visit to his poor relations.

London, Chapman & Hall, 186, Strand.

" Dear Nicholas, pray," urged the young lady.

" Hold your tongue, Sir," said Ralph. " Upon my word! Fine beginnings, Mrs. Nickleby—fine beginnings."

Mrs. Nickleby made no other reply than entreating Nicholas by a gesture to keep silent, and the uncle and nephew looked at each other for some seconds without speaking. The face of the old man was stern, hard-featured and forbidding; that of the young one, open, handsome, and ingenuous. The old man's eye was keen with the twinklings of avarice and cunning; the young man's, bright with the light of intelligence and spirit. His figure was somewhat slight, but manly and well-formed; and apart from all the grace of youth and comeliness, there was an emanation from the warm young heart in his look and bearing which kept the old man down.

However striking such a contrast as this, may be to lookers-on, none ever feel it with half the keenness or acuteness of perfection with which it strikes to the very soul of him whose inferiority it marks. It galled Ralph to the heart's core, and he hated Nicholas from that hour.

The mutual inspection was at length brought to a close by Ralph withdrawing his eyes with a great show of disdain, and calling Nicholas " a boy." This word is much used as a term of reproach by elderly gentlemen towards their juniors, probably with the view of deluding society into the belief that if they could be young again, they wouldn't on any account.

" Well, ma'am," said Ralph, impatiently, " the creditors have administered, you tell me, and there's nothing left for you?"

" Nothing," replied Mrs. Nickleby.

" And you spent what little money you had, in coming all the way to London, to see what I could do for you?" pursued Ralph.

" I hoped," faltered Mrs. Nickleby, " that you might have an opportunity of doing something for your brother's children. It was his dying wish that I should appeal to you in their behalf."

" I don't know how it is," muttered Ralph, walking up and down the room, " but whenever a man dies without any property of his own, he always seems to think he has a right to dispose of other people's. What is your daughter fit for, ma'am?"

" Kate has been well educated," sobbed Mrs. Nickleby. " Tell your uncle, my dear, how far you went in French and extras."

The poor girl was about to murmur forth something, when her uncle stopped her very unceremoniously.

" We must try and get you apprenticed at some boarding-school," said Ralph. " You have not been brought up too delicately for that, I hope?"

" No, indeed, uncle," replied the weeping girl. " I will try to do anything that will gain me a home and bread."

" Well, well," said Ralph, a little softened, either by his niece's beauty or her distress (stretch a point, and say the latter). " You must try it, and if the life is too hard, perhaps dress-making or tambour-work will come lighter. Have *you* ever done anything, Sir?" (turning to his nephew.)

" No," replied Nicholas, bluntly.

" No, I thought not!" said Ralph. " This is the way my brother brought up his children, ma'am."

" Nicholas has not long completed such education as his poor father could give him," rejoined Mrs. Nickleby, " and he was thinking of—"

" Of making something of him some day," said Ralph. " The old story; always thinking, and never doing. If my brother had been a man of activity and prudence, he might have left you a rich woman, ma'am : and if he had turned his son into the world, as my father turned me, when I wasn't as old as that boy by a year and a half, he would have been in a situation to help you, instead of being a burden upon you, and increasing your distress. My brother was a thoughtless, inconsiderate man, Mrs. Nickleby, and nobody, I am sure, can have better reason to feel that, than you."

This appeal set the widow upon thinking that perhaps she might have made a more successful venture with her one thousand pounds, and then she began to reflect what a comfortable sum it would have been just then ; which dismal thoughts made her tears flow faster, and in the excess of these griefs she (being a well-meaning woman enough, but rather weak withal) fell first to deploring her hard fate, and then to remarking, with many sobs, that to be sure she had been a slave to poor Nicholas, and had often told him she might have married better (as indeed she had, very often), and that she never knew in his life-time how the money went, but that if he had confided in her they might all have been better off that day ; with other bitter recollections common to most married ladies either during their coverture, or after-wards, or at both periods. Mrs. Nickleby concluded by lamenting that the dear departed had never deigned to profit by her advice, save on one occasion : which was a strictly veracious statement, inasmuch as he had only acted upon it once, and had ruined himself in consequence.

Mr. Ralph Nickleby heard all this with a half smile ; and when the widow had finished, quietly took up the subject where it had been left before the above outbreak.

" Are you willing to work, Sir ?" he inquired, frowning on his nephew.

" Of course I am," replied Nicholas haughtily.

" Then see here, Sir," said his uncle. " This caught my eye this morning, and you may thank your stars for it."

With this exordium, Mr. Ralph Nickleby took a newspaper from his pocket, and after unfolding it, and looking for a short time among the advertisements, read as follows.

" EDUCATION.—At Mr. Wackford Squeers's Academy, Dotheboys Hall, at the delightful village of Dotheboys, near Greta Bridge in Yorkshire.   Youth are boarded, clothed, booked, furnished with pocket-money, provided with all necessaries, instructed in all languages, living and dead, mathematics, orthography, geometry, astronomy, tri-gonometry, the use of the globes, algebra, single stick (if required), writing, arithmetic, fortification, and every other branch of classical literature.   Terms, twenty guineas per annum.   No extras, no vacations, and diet unparalleled. Mr. Squeers is in town, and attends daily, from one 'till four, at the Saracen's Head, Snow Hill. N.B. An able assistant wanted. Annual salary £5. A Master of Arts would be preferred."

"There," said Ralph, folding the paper again. "Let him get that situation, and his fortune is made."

"But he is not a Master of Arts," said Mrs. Nickleby.

"That," replied Ralph, "that, I think, can be got over."

"But the salary is so small, and it is such a long way off, uncle!" faltered Kate.

"Hush, Kate my dear," interposed Mrs. Nickleby; "your uncle must know best."

"I say," repeated Ralph, tartly, "let him get that situation, and his fortune is made. If he don't like that, let him get one for himself. Without friends, money, recommendation, or knowledge of business of any kind, let him find honest employment in London which will keep him in shoe leather, and I'll give him a thousand pounds. At least," said Mr. Ralph Nickleby, checking himself, "I would if I had it."

"Poor fellow!" said the young lady. "Oh! uncle, must we be separated so soon!"

"Don't teaze your uncle with questions when he is thinking only for our good, my love," said Mrs. Nickleby. "Nicholas, my dear, I wish you would say something."

"Yes, mother, yes," said Nicholas, who had hitherto remained silent and absorbed in thought. "If I am fortunate enough to be appointed to this post, Sir, for which I am so imperfectly qualified, what will become of those I leave behind?"

"Your mother and sister, Sir," replied Ralph, "will be provided for in that case (not otherwise), by me, and placed in some sphere of life in which they will be able to be independent. That will be my immediate care; they will not remain as they are, one week after your departure, I will undertake."

"Then," said Nicholas, starting gaily up, and wringing his uncle's hand, "I am ready to do anything you wish me. Let us try our fortune with Mr. Squeers at once; he can but refuse."

"He won't do that," said Ralph. "He will be glad to have you on my recommendation. Make yourself of use to him, and you'll rise to be a partner in the establishment in no time. Bless me, only think! if he were to die, why your fortune's made at once."

"To be sure, I see it all," said poor Nicholas, delighted with a thousand visionary ideas, that his good spirits and his inexperience were conjuring up before him. "Or suppose some young nobleman who is being educated at the Hall, were to take a fancy to me, and get his father to appoint me his travelling tutor when he left, and when we come back from the continent, procured me some handsome appointment. Eh! uncle?"

"Ah, to be sure!" sneered Ralph.

"And who knows, but when he came to see me when I was settled (as he would of course), he might fall in love with Kate, who would be keeping my house, and—and—marry her, eh! uncle? Who knows?"

" Who, indeed !" snarled Ralph.

" How happy we should be !" cried Nicholas with enthusiasm. " The pain of parting is nothing to the joy of meeting again. Kate will be a beautiful woman, and I so proud to hear them say so, and mother so happy to be with us once again, and all these sad times forgotten, and—" The picture was too bright a one to bear, and Nicholas, fairly overpowered by it, smiled faintly, and burst into tears.

This simple family, born and bred in retirement, and wholly unacquainted with what is called the world—a conventional phrase which, being interpreted, signifieth all the rascals in it—mingled their tears together at the thought of their first separation ; and, this first gush of feeling over, were proceeding to dilate with all the buoyancy of untried hope on the bright prospects before them, when Mr. Ralph Nickleby suggested, that if they lost time, some more fortunate candidate might deprive Nicholas of the stepping-stone to fortune which the advertisement pointed out, and so undermine all their air-built castles. This timely reminder effectually stopped the conversation, and Nicholas having carefully copied the address of Mr. Squeers, the uncle and nephew issued forth together in quest of that accomplished gentleman ; Nicholas firmly persuading himself that he had done his relative great injustice in disliking him at first sight, and Mrs. Nickleby being at some pains to inform her daughter that she was sure he was a much more kindly disposed person than he seemed, which Miss Nickleby dutifully remarked he might very easily be.

To tell the truth, the good lady's opinion had been not a little influenced by her brother-in-law's appeal to her better understanding and his implied compliment to her high deserts ; and although she had dearly loved her husband and still doted on her children, he had struck so successfully on one of those little jarring chords in the human heart (Ralph was well acquainted with its worst weaknesses, though he knew nothing of its best), that she had already begun seriously to consider herself the amiable and suffering victim of her late husband's imprudence.

CHAPTER IV.

NICHOLAS AND HIS UNCLE (TO SECURE THE FORTUNE WITHOUT LOSS OF TIME) WAIT UPON MR. WACKFORD SQUEERS, THE YORKSHIRE SCHOOLMASTER.

SNOW HILL ! What kind of place can the quiet town's-people who see the words emblazoned in all the legibility of gilt letters and dark shading on the north-country coaches, take Snow Hill to be ? All people have some undefined and shadowy notion of a place whose name is frequently before their eyes or often in their ears, and what a vast

number of random ideas there must be perpetually floating about, regarding this same Snow Hill. The name is such a good one. Snow
Hill—Snow Hill too, coupled with a Saracen's Head : picturing to us
by a double association of ideas, something stern and rugged. A bleak
desolate tract of country, open to piercing blasts and fierce wintry
storms—a dark, cold, and gloomy heath, lonely by day, and scarcely to
be thought of by honest folks at night—a place which solitary wayfarers shun, and where desperate robbers congregate ;—this, or something
like this, we imagine must be the prevalent notion of Snow Hill
in those remote and rustic parts, through which the Saracen's Head,
like some grim apparition, rushes each day and night with mysterious
and ghost-like punctuality, holding its swift and headlong course in all
weathers, and seeming to bid defiance to the very elements themselves.

The reality is rather different, but by no means to be despised notwithstanding. There, at the very core of London, in the heart of its
business and animation, in the midst of a whirl of noise and motion :
stemming as it were the giant currents of life that flow ceaselessly on
from different quarters, and meet beneath its walls, stands Newgate ;
and in that crowded street on which it frowns so darkly—within a few
feet of the squalid tottering houses—upon the very spot on which the
venders of soup and fish and damaged fruit are now plying their trades
—scores of human beings, amidst a roar of sounds to which even the
tumult of a great city is as nothing, four, six, or eight strong men at a
time, have been hurried violently and swiftly from the world, when the
scene has been rendered frightful with excess of human life ; when curious
eyes have glared from casement, and house-top, and wall and pillar, and
when, in the mass of white and upturned faces, the dying wretch, in his
all-comprehensive look of agony, has met not one—not one—that bore
the impress of pity or compassion.

Near to the jail, and by consequence near to Smithfield also, and the
Compter and the bustle and noise of the city ; and just on that particular part of Snow Hill where omnibus horses going eastwards seriously
think of falling down on purpose, and where horses in hackney cabrio-
lets going westwards not unfrequently fall by accident, is the coach-
yard of the Saracen's-Head Inn, its portal guarded by two Saracens'
heads and shoulders, which it was once the pride and glory of the
choice spirits of this metropolis to pull down at night, but which have
for some time remained in undisturbed tranquillity ; possibly because
this species of humour is now confined to Saint James's parish, where
door knockers are preferred, as being more portable, and bell-wires
esteemed as convenient tooth-picks. Whether this be the reason or
not, there they are, frowning upon you from each side of the gateway,
and the inn itself, garnished with another Saracen's Head, frowns upon
you from the top of the yard ; while from the door of the hind boot of
all the red coaches that are standing therein, there glares a small Saracen's
Head with a twin expression to the large Saracen's Heads below, so
that the general appearance of the pile is of the Saracenic order.

When you walk up this yard, you will see the booking-office on your

left, and the tower of Saint Sepulchre's church darting abruptly up
into the sky on your right, and a gallery of bed-rooms on both sides.
Just before you, you will observe a long window with the words
" coffee-room " legibly painted above it ; and looking out of that window, you would have seen in addition, if you had gone at the right
time, Mr. Wackford Squeers with his hands in his pockets.

Mr. Squeers's appearance was not prepossessing. He had but one
eye, and the popular prejudice runs in favour of two. The eye he had
was unquestionably useful, but decidedly not ornamental, being of a
greenish grey, and in shape resembling the fanlight of a street door.
The blank side of his face was much wrinkled and puckered up, which
gave him a very sinister appearance, especially when he smiled, at
which times his expression bordered closely on the villanous. His
hair was very flat and shiny, save at the ends, where it was brushed
stiffly up from a low protruding forehead, which assorted well with
his harsh voice and coarse manner. He was about two or three and
fifty, and a trifle below the middle size ; he wore a white neckerchief
with long ends, and a suit of scholastic black, but his coat sleeves being
a great deal too long, and his trousers a great deal too short, he appeared ill at ease in his clothes, and as if he were in a perpetual state
of astonishment at finding himself so respectable.

Mr. Squeers was standing in a box by one of the coffee-room fire-
places, fitted with one such table as is usually seen in coffee-rooms,
and two of extraordinary shapes and dimensions made to suit the
angles of the partition. In a corner of the seat was a very small deal
trunk, tied round with a scanty piece of cord ; and on the trunk was
perched—his lace-up half-boots and corduroy trowsers dangling in the
air—a diminutive boy, with his shoulders drawn up to his ears, and his
hands planted on his knees, who glanced timidly at the schoolmaster
from time to time with evident dread and apprehension.

" Half-past three," muttered Mr. Squeers, turning from the window,
and looking sulkily at the coffee-room clock. " There will be nobody
here to-day."

Much vexed by this reflection, Mr. Squeers looked at the little boy
to see whether he was doing anything he could beat him for : as he
happened not to be doing anything at all, he merely boxed his ears, and
told him not to do it again.

" At Midsummer," muttered Mr. Squeers, resuming his complaint, " I
took down ten boys ; ten twentys—two hundred pound. I go back
at eight o'clock to-morrow morning, and have got only three—three
oughts an ought—three twos six—sixty pound. What's come of all
the boys ? what's parents got in their heads ? what does it all mean ?"

Here the little boy on the top of the trunk gave a violent sneeze.

" Halloa, Sir ! " growled the schoolmaster, turning round. " What's
that, Sir ? "

" Nothing, please Sir," replied the little boy.

" Nothing, Sir ! " exclaimed Mr. Squeers.

" Please Sir, I sneezed," rejoined the boy, trembling till the little
trunk shook under him.

The Yorkshire Schoolmaster at "The Saracen's Head."

London, Chapman & Hall, 186 Strand.

" Oh! sneezed, did you ? " retorted Mr. Squeers. " Then what did you say ' nothing ' for, Sir ? "

In default of a better answer to this question, the little boy screwed a couple of knuckles into each of his eyes and began to cry, wherefore Mr. Squeers knocked him off the trunk with a blow on one side of his face, and knocked him on again with a blow on the other.

" Wait till I get you down into Yorkshire, my young gentleman," said Mr. Squeers, " and then I'll give you the rest. Will you hold that noise, Sir ? "

" Ye—ye—yes," sobbed the little boy, rubbing his face very hard with the Beggar's Petition in printed calico.

" Then do so at once, Sir," said Squeers. " Do you hear ? "

As this admonition was accompanied with a threatening gesture, and uttered with a savage aspect, the little boy rubbed his face harder, as if to keep the tears back; and, beyond alternately sniffing and choking, gave no further vent to his emotions.

" Mr. Squeers," said the waiter, looking in at this juncture; " here's a gentleman asking for you at the bar."

" Show the gentleman in, Richard," replied Mr. Squeers, in a soft voice. " Put your handkerchief in your pocket, you little scoundrel, or I'll murder you when the gentleman goes."

The schoolmaster had scarcely uttered these words in a fierce whisper, when the stranger entered. Affecting not to see him, Mr. Squeers feigned to be intent upon mending a pen, and offering benevolent advice to his youthful pupil.

" My dear child," said Mr. Squeers, " all people have their trials. This early trial of yours that is fit to make your little heart burst, and your very eyes come out of your head with crying, what is it ? Nothing; less than nothing. You are leaving your friends, but you will have a father in me, my dear, and a mother in Mrs. Squeers. At the delightful village of Dotheboys, near Greta Bridge, in Yorkshire, where youth are boarded, clothed, booked, washed, furnished with pocket-money, provided with all necessaries—"

" It *is* the gentleman," observed the stranger, stopping the schoolmaster in the rehearsal of his advertisement. " Mr. Squeers, I believe, Sir ? "

" The same, Sir," said Mr. Squeers, with an assumption of extreme surprise.

" The gentleman," said the stranger, " that advertised in the Times newspaper ? "

—" Morning Post, Chronicle, Herald, and Advertiser, regarding the Academy called Dotheboys Hall at the delightful village of Dotheboys, near Greta Bridge, in Yorkshire," added Mr. Squeers. " You come on business, Sir. I see by my young friends. How do you do, my little gentleman ? and how do *you* do, Sir ? " With this salutation Mr. Squeers patted the heads of two hollow-eyed, small-boned little boys, whom the applicant had brought with him, and waited for further communications.

" I am in the oil and colour way. My name is Snawley, Sir," said the stranger.

Squeers inclined his head as much as to say, "And a remarkably pretty name, too."

The stranger continued. "I have been thinking, Mr. Squeers, of placing my two boys at your school."

"It is not for me to say so, Sir," replied Mr. Squeers, "but I don't think you could possibly do a better thing."

"Hem!" said the other. "Twenty pounds per annewum, I believe, Mr. Squeers?"

"Guineas," rejoined the schoolmaster, with a persuasive smile.

"Pounds for two, I think, Mr. Squeers," said Mr. Snawley solemnly.

"I don't think it could be done, Sir," replied Squeers, as if he had never considered the proposition before. "Let me see; four fives is twenty, double that, and deduct the—well, a pound either way shall not stand betwixt us. You must recommend me to your connection, Sir, and make it up that way."

"They are not great eaters," said Mr. Snawley.

"Oh! that doesn't matter at all," replied Squeers. "We don't consider the boys' appetites at our establishment." This was strictly true; they did not.

"Every wholesome luxury, Sir, that Yorkshire can afford," continued Squeers; "every beautiful moral that Mrs. Squeers can instil; every—in short, every comfort of a home that a boy could wish for, will be theirs, Mr. Snawley."

"I should wish their morals to be particularly attended to," said Mr. Snawley.

"I am glad of that, Sir," replied the schoolmaster, drawing himself up. "They have come to the right shop for morals, Sir."

"You are a moral man yourself," said Mr. Snawley.

"I rather believe I am, Sir," replied Squeers.

"I have the satisfaction to know you are, Sir," said Mr. Snawley. "I asked one of your references, and he said you were pious."

"Well, Sir, I hope I am a little in that way," replied Squeers.

"I hope I am also," rejoined the other. "Could I say a few words with you in the next box?"

"By all means," rejoined Squeers, with a grin. "My dears, will you speak to your new playfellow a minute or two? That is one of my boys, Sir. Belling his name is,—a Taunton boy that, Sir."

"Is he, indeed?" rejoined Mr. Snawley, looking at the poor little urchin as if he were some extraordinary natural curiosity.

"He goes down with me to-morrow, Sir," said Squeers. "That's his luggage that he is sitting upon now. Each boy is required to bring, Sir, two suits of clothes, six shirts, six pair of stockings, two nightcaps, two pocket-handkerchiefs, two pair of shoes, two hats, and a razor."

"A razor!" exclaimed Mr. Snawley, as they walked into the next box. "What for?"

"To shave with," replied Squeers, in a slow and measured tone.

There was not much in these three words, but there must have been something in the manner in which they were said, to attract attention, for the schoolmaster and his companion looked steadily at each other for a few seconds, and then exchanged a very meaning smile. Snawley was a sleek flat-nosed man, clad in sombre garments, and long black gaiters, and bearing in his countenance an expression of much mortification and sanctity, so that his smiling without any obvious reason was the more remarkable.

" Up to what age do you keep boys at your school then ?" he asked at length.

" Just as long as their friends make the quarterly payments to my agent in town, or until such time as they run away," replied Squeers. " Let us understand each other; I see we may safely do so. What are these boys ;—natural children ?"

" No," rejoined Snawley, meeting the gaze of the schoolmaster's one eye. " They an't."

" I thought they might be," said Squeers, coolly. " We have a good many of them; that boy's one."

" Him in the next box ?" said Snawley.

Squeers nodded in the affirmative, and his companion took another peep at the little boy on the trunk, and turning round again, looked as if he were quite disappointed to see him so much like other boys, and said he should hardly have thought it.

" He is," cried Squeers. " But about these boys of yours; you wanted to speak to me ?"

" Yes," replied Snawley. " The fact is, I am not their father, Mr. Squeers. I'm only their father-in-law."

" Oh! Is that it ?" said the schoolmaster. " That explains it at once. I was wondering what the devil you were going to send them to Yorkshire for. Ha! ha! Oh, I understand now."

" You see I have married the mother," pursued Snawley; " it's expensive keeping boys at home, and as she has a little money in her own right, I am afraid (women are so very foolish, Mr. Squeers) that she might be led to squander it on them, which would be their ruin, you know."

" *I* see," returned Squeers, throwing himself back in his chair, and waving his hand.

" And this," resumed Snawley, " has made me anxious to put them to some school a good distance off, where there are no holidays—none of those ill-judged comings home twice a year that unsettle children's minds so—and where they may rough it a little—you comprehend ?"

" The payments regular, and no questions asked," said Squeers, nodding his head.

" That's it, exactly," rejoined the other. " Morals strictly attended to, though."

" Strictly," said Squeers.

" Not too much writing home allowed, I suppose ?" said the father-in-law, hesitating.

" None, except a circular at Christmas, to say that they never were so happy, and hope they may never be sent for," rejoined Squeers.

" Nothing could be better," said the father-in-law, rubbing his hands.

" Then, as we understand each other," said Squeers, " will you allow me to ask you whether you consider me a highly virtuous, exemplary, and well-conducted man in private life ; and whether, as a person whose business it is to take charge of youth, you place the strongest confidence in my unimpeachable integrity, liberality, religious principles and ability ?"

" Certainly I do," replied the father-in-law, reciprocating the school-master's grin.

" Perhaps you won't object to say that, if I make you a reference ?"

" Not the least in the world."

" That's your sort," said Squeers, taking up a pen; " this is doing business, and that's what I like."

Having entered Mr. Snawley's address, the schoolmaster had next to perform the still more agreeable office of entering the receipt of the first quarter's payment in advance, which he had scarcely completed, when another voice was heard inquiring for Mr. Squeers.

" Here he is," replied the schoolmaster ; " what is it ?"

" Only a matter of business, Sir," said Ralph Nickleby, presenting himself, closely followed by Nicholas. " There was an advertisement of yours in the papers this morning ?"

" There was, Sir. This way, if you please," said Squeers, who had by this time got back to the box by the fire-place. " Won't you be seated?"

" Why, I think I will," replied Ralph, suiting the action to the word, and placing his hat on the table before him. " This is my nephew, Sir, Mr. Nicholas Nickleby."

" How do you do, Sir ?" said Squeers.

Nicholas bowed: said he was very well, and seemed very much asto-nished at the outward appearance of the proprietor of Dotheboys Hall, as indeed he was.

" Perhaps you recollect me ? " said Ralph, looking narrowly at the schoolmaster.

" You paid me a small account at each of my half-yearly visits to town, for some years, I think, Sir," replied Squeers.

" I did," rejoined Ralph.

" For the parents of a boy named Dorker, who unfortunately—"

" —unfortunately died at Dotheboys Hall," said Ralph, finishing the sentence.

" I remember very well, Sir," rejoined Squeers. " Ah ! Mrs. Squeers, Sir, was as partial to that lad as if he had been her own ; the attention, Sir, that was bestowed upon that boy in his illness—dry toast and warm tea offered him every night and morning when he couldn't swallow anything—a candle in his bed-room on the very night he died—the best dictionary sent up for him to lay his head upon.— I don't regret it though. It is a pleasant thing to reflect that one did one's duty by him."

Ralph smiled as if he meant anything but smiling, and looked round at the strangers present.

" These are only some pupils of mine," said Wackford Squeers, pointing to the little boy on the trunk and the two little boys on the floor, who had been staring at each other without uttering a word, and writhing their bodies into most remarkable contortions, according to the custom of little boys when they first become acquainted. " This gentleman, Sir, is a parent who is kind enough to compliment me upon the course of education adopted at Dotheboys Hall, which is situated, Sir, at the delightful village of Dotheboys, near Greta Bridge, in Yorkshire, where youth are boarded, clothed, booked, washed, furnished with pocket-money——"

" Yes, we know all about that, Sir," interrupted Ralph, testily. " It's in the advertisement."

" You are very right, Sir; it *is* in the advertisement," replied Squeers.

" And in the matter of fact besides," interrupted Mr. Snawley. " I feel bound to assure you, Sir, and I am proud to have this opportunity *of* assuring you, that I consider Mr. Squeers a gentleman highly virtuous, exemplary, well-conducted, and——"

" I make no doubt of it, Sir," interrupted Ralph, checking the torrent of recommendation ; " no doubt of it at all. Suppose we come to business ?"

" With all my heart, Sir," rejoined Squeers. " ' Never postpone business,' is the very first lesson we instil into our commercial pupils. Master Belling, my dear, always remember that ; do you hear ?"

" Yes, Sir," repeated Master Belling.

" He recollects what it is, does he ?" said Ralph.

" Tell the gentleman," said Squeers.

" ' Never,' " repeated Master Belling.

" Very good," said Squeers ; " go on."

" Never, " repeated Master Belling again.

" Very good indeed," said Squeers. " Yes."

" P," suggested Nicholas, good-naturedly.

" Perform—business !" said Master Belling. " Never—perform—business !"

" Very well, Sir," said Squeers, darting a withering look at the culprit. " You and I will perform a little business on our private account bye and bye."

" And just now," said Ralph, " we had better transact our own, perhaps."

" If you please," said Squeers.

" Well," resumed Ralph, " it's brief enough ; soon broached, and I hope easily concluded. You have advertised for an able assistant, Sir ? "

" Precisely so," said Squeers.

" And you really want one ? "

" Certainly," answered Squeers.

" Here he is," said Ralph. " My nephew Nicholas, hot from school, with everything he learnt there, fermenting in his head, and nothing fermenting in his pocket, is just the man you want."

" I am afraid," said Squeers, perplexed with such an application from a youth of Nicholas's figure, " I am afraid the young man won't suit me."

" Yes, he will," said Ralph ; " I know better. Don't be cast down, Sir; you will be teaching all the young noblemen in Dotheboys Hall in less than a week's time, unless this gentleman is more obstinate than I take him to be."

" I fear, Sir," said Nicholas, addressing Mr. Squeers, " that you object to my youth, and my not being a Master of Arts ?"

" The absence of a college degree *is* an objection," replied Squeers, looking as grave as he could, and considerably puzzled, no less by the contrast between the simplicity of the nephew and the worldly manner of the uncle, than by the incomprehensible allusion to the young noblemen under his tuition.

" Look here, Sir," said Ralph ; " I'll put this matter in its true light in two seconds."

" If you'll have the goodness," rejoined Squeers.

" This is a boy, or a youth, or a lad, or a young man, or a hobbledehoy, or whatever you like to call him, of eighteen or nineteen, or thereabouts," said Ralph.

" That I see," observed the schoolmaster.

" So do I," said Mr. Snawley, thinking it as well to back his new friend occasionally.

" His father is dead, he is wholly ignorant of the world, has no resources whatever, and wants something to do," said Ralph. " I recommend him to this splendid establishment of yours, as an opening which will lead him to fortune, if he turns it to proper account. Do you see that ? "

" Every body must see that," replied Squeers, half imitating the sneer with which the old gentleman was regarding his unconscious relative.

" I do, of course," said Nicholas eagerly.

" He does, of course, you observe," said Ralph, in the same dry, hard manner. " If any caprice of temper should induce him to cast aside this golden opportunity before he has brought it to perfection, I consider myself absolved from extending any assistance to his mother and sister. Look at him, and think of the use he may be to you in half a dozen ways. Now the question is, whether, for some time to come at all events, he won't serve your purpose better than twenty of the kind of people you would get under ordinary circumstances. Isn't that a question for consideration ? "

" Yes, it is," said Squeers, answering a nod of Ralph's head with a nod of his own.

" Good," rejoined Ralph. " Let me have two words with you."

The two words were had apart, and in a couple of minutes Mr. Wackford Squeers announced that Mr. Nicholas Nickleby was from that moment thoroughly nominated to, and installed in, the office of first assistant-master at Dotheboys Hall.

" Your uncle's recommendation has done it, Mr. Nickleby," said Wackford Squeers.

Nicholas, overjoyed at his success, shook his uncle's hand warmly, and could have worshipped Squeers upon the spot.

" He is an odd-looking man," thought Nicholas. " What of that? Porson was an odd-looking man, and so was Doctor Johnson; all these bookworms are."

" At eight o'clock to-morrow morning, Mr. Nickleby," said Squeers, " the coach starts. You must be here at a quarter before, as we take these boys with us."

" Certainly, Sir," said Nicholas.

" And your fare down, I have paid," growled Ralph. " So you'll have nothing to do but keep yourself warm."

Here was another instance of his uncle's generosity. Nicholas felt his unexpected kindness so much, that he could scarcely find words to thank him; indeed, he had not found half enough, when they took leave of the schoolmaster and emerged from the Saracen's Head gateway.

" I shall be here in the morning to see you fairly off," said Ralph. " No skulking!"

" Thank you, Sir," replied Nicholas; " I never shall forget this kindness."

" Take care you don't," replied his uncle. " You had better go home now, and pack up what you have got to pack. Do you think you could find your way to Golden Square first?"

" Certainly," said Nicholas, " I can easily inquire."

" Leave these papers with my clerk, then," said Ralph, producing a small parcel, " and tell him to wait till I come home."

Nicholas cheerfully undertook the errand, and bidding his worthy uncle an affectionate farewell, which that warm-hearted old gentleman acknowledged by a growl, hastened away to execute his commission.

He found Golden Square in due course; and Mr. Noggs, who had stepped out for a minute or so to the public-house, was opening the door with a latch-key as he reached the steps.

" What's that?" inquired Noggs, pointing to the parcel.

" Papers from my uncle," replied Nicholas; " and you're to have the goodness to wait till he comes home, if you please."

" Uncle!" cried Noggs.

" Mr. Nickleby," said Nicholas in explanation.

" Come in," said Newman.

Without another word he led Nicholas into the passage, and thence into the official pantry at the end of it, where he thrust him into a chair, and mounting upon his high stool, sat with his arms hanging straight down by his sides, gazing fixedly upon him as from a tower of observation.

" There is no answer," said Nicholas, laying the parcel on a table beside him.

Newman said nothing, but folding his arms, and thrusting his head forward so as to obtain a nearer view of Nicholas's face, scanned his features closely.

" No answer," said Nicholas, speaking very loud, under the impression that Newman Noggs was deaf.

Newman placed his hands upon his knees, and without uttering a syllable, continued the same close scrutiny of his companion's face.

This was such a very singular proceeding on the part of an utter stranger, and his appearance was so extremely peculiar, that Nicholas, who had a sufficiently keen sense of the ridiculous, could not refrain from breaking into a smile as he inquired whether Mr. Noggs had any commands for him.

Noggs shook his head and sighed; upon which Nicholas rose, and remarking that he required no rest, bade him good morning.

It was a great exertion for Newman Noggs, and nobody knows to this day how he ever came to make it, the other party being wholly unknown to him, but he drew a long breath and actually said out loud, without once stopping, that if the young gentleman did not object to tell, he should like to know what his uncle was going to do for him.

Nicholas had not the least objection in the world, but on the contrary was rather pleased to have an opportunity of talking on the subject which occupied his thoughts; so he sat down again, and (his sanguine imagination warming as he spoke) entered into a fervent and glowing description of all the honours and advantages to be derived from his appointment at that seat of learning, Dotheboys Hall.

" But, what's the matter—are you ill?" said Nicholas, suddenly breaking off, as his companion, after throwing himself into a variety of uncouth attitudes, thrust his hands under the stool and cracked his finger-joints as if he were snapping all the bones in his hands.

Newman Noggs made no reply, but went on shrugging his shoulders and cracking his finger-joints, smiling horribly all the time, and looking stedfastly at nothing, out of the tops of his eyes, in a most ghastly manner.

At first Nicholas thought the mysterious man was in a fit, but on further consideration decided that he was in liquor, under which circumstances he deemed it prudent to make off at once. He looked back when he had got the street-door open. Newman Noggs was still indulging in the same extraordinary gestures, and the cracking of his fingers sounded louder than ever.

From an Original Sketch taken on the spot by G. Chambers, Esq.

A VIEW IN FLEET STREET, Nov. 9, 1837,

When Her Most Gracious Majesty, QUEEN VICTORIA, visited the City of London.

The Right Honourable John Cowan, Lord Mayor.

WEST, OPTICIAN—A curious but superb illumination. In double rows appeared, in amber lamps, "A GRAND," and below, a device in blue lamps, a representation of a Pair of Spectacles—the meaning of this worthy citizen being, "A Grand Spectacle." In addition to these were numerous Banners, inscribed with the Queen's name; and over the roof, mast high, the Royal Standard. Festoons of lamps along the parapet, railing, &c. &c.—*Vide Morning Herald, Nov.* 10.

Sixth Edition, now ready,
WEST'S TREATISE ON THE EYE—(Price Sixpence.)

Containing practical rules, that will enable all to judge what Spectacles are best calculated to preserve their eyes to extreme old age. Illustrated by *Three correct Diagrams of the Human Eye.*

IMPORTANT

TO ALL WHO REQUIRE

SPECTACLES

FOR

OUT-DOOR EXERCISE.

———◦✕◦———

FRANCIS WEST,

(SUCCESSOR TO MR. ADAMS)

OPTICIAN TO HIS LATE MAJESTY,

83, FLEET STREET, LONDON,

Respectfully begs to call the attention of the Nobility and Public to his CORRECTUS SPECULATUS, or NEWLY-CONSTRUCTED SPECTACLES, which will be found particularly advantageous to Sportsmen, Pedestrians, or any other person taking violent exercise, as it is not possible to displace them. The lenses are ground with F. W.'s usual care, of the finest Bohemian Glass or Pebble; and as they are always concentric with the pupil of the Eye, they may be pronounced the most perfect Spectacles that have hitherto been constructed for walking, riding, public exhibitions, &c. &c.

———

" A FAMILIAR TREATISE ON THE HUMAN EYE: *by F. West, Fleet Street.*—This work is chiefly intended for the direction of persons who are under the necessity of making use of spectacles, and to all such we recommend it, as containing plain and easy rules by which they may ascertain what sort of glasses are best calculated to assist their sight, without injuring the eyes. The subject is philosophically treated, and the great experience of the author will warrant a confident reliance in the principles he has so clearly developed."—*Weekly Dispatch, Sept.* 20, 1829.

" THE SIGHT.—Of all our organs that of sight is at once the most important and the most delicate; it behoves us, therefore, to be extremely cautious, where defects natural or accidental may arise, how we attempt to remedy them. It is but too frequently the practice to try experiments and have recourse to aids which produce the most pernicious consequences, and often render the evil still greater. These remarks are induced by the perusal of a treatise on the Structure of the Eye, published by Mr. West, the optician, in Fleet Street, which, in a plain and familiar manner, illustrates the construction of this organ, by the assistance of three diagrams, and lays downs practical rules for the adoption of such artificial helps as may remedy existing inconveniences, or prevent those injuries which injudicious treatment or ignorance of the science of optics may naturally give rise to. The experience of Mr. West in his profession must render his work highly valuable, while the trifling price at which it is published, brings it within the attainment of all classes."—*Bell's Life in London, Nov.* 29, 1829.

" A FAMILIAR TREATISE ON THE HUMAN EYE: *by F. West, Fleet Street, London.*—A Third Edition of a pamphlet on this subject has just appeared. The author does not indulge in the technicalities of science, but treats his subject in a clear, intelligible manner; it is well worth the attention of persons who value the preservation of their sight."—*Kent and Essex Mercury, Oct.* 6, 1829.

" A FAMILIAR TREATISE ON THE HUMAN EYE: *by F. West.*—This is a very useful little treatise, which conveys much valuable information for the preservation of the sight, illustrated with three correct diagrams of the structure of the eye. The contents of the pamphlet are calculated to remove the numerous popular errors, and to induce those who require optical aid to apply to respectable and intelligent opticians, who manufacture their spectacles with professional skill and critical precision, for the aid and preservation of the sight, and not to purchase glasses from ignorant impostors, which are faulty in every respect, and consequently extremely injurious to the visual organ of those who use them. The author points out, with clearness and perspicuity, the time and the indications when persons should have immediate recourse to the use of spectacles, for the preservation of their sight, and for their ease and comfort; and those who do not avail themselves of this information and advice, founded on experience and correct principles, will have reason, we will venture to add, to lament and deplore their neglect."—*Morning Advertiser, Sept.* 25, 1829.

———

JUST PUBLISHED, BY F. WEST,

" An Anatomical Diagram of the Human Eye; in which all the Internal Structures of the Eye are accurately developed;" price 2*s.* coloured.—" Companion to the Microscope."—" Chemical Recreations."—" A Key to the Study of Astronomy."—" How to Chose and how to Use the Camera Lucida."—" Description and Use of Mathematical Instruments."—" Brief Account of the Barometer and Comparative Scales of the Thermometer."—" Description of the Air-Pump, and Use of the various Apparatus."—" Electrician's Guide."—" An Account of Intellectual Toys."—" Brief View of the Solar System."—" Method of placing Horizontal Sun-Dials, Ring Dials, and Joint Dials."

N.B. *Optical, Mathematical, and Philosophical Instruments of every description, wholesale and for exportation, of the best workmanship, and on the most reasonable terms.*

ACKERMANN & CO.,

PRINTSELLERS AND PUBLISHERS TO HER MAJESTY,

AND

TO HER ROYAL HIGHNESS THE DUCHESS OF KENT,

HAVE THE HONOUR TO ANNOUNCE THAT THEY HAVE JUST PUBLISHED

A SUPERB PORTRAIT

OF HER MOST GRACIOUS MAJESTY

THE QUEEN:

ENGRAVED IN THE FIRST STYLE OF MEZZOTINT, BY W. O. GELLER,

𝔉𝔯𝔬𝔪 𝔱𝔥𝔢 𝔒𝔯𝔦𝔤𝔦𝔫𝔞𝔩 𝔞𝔫𝔡 ℭ𝔢𝔩𝔢𝔟𝔯𝔞𝔱𝔢𝔡 𝔓𝔦𝔠𝔱𝔲𝔯𝔢

BY C. SWANDALE, ESQ.

PRICE TO SUBSCRIBERS.

Prints, £1. 1s.　　Proofs, £2. 2s.　　Fine Proofs before letters, £3. 3s.

Size of the Engraving—Twenty-six Inches and a Half by Twenty, including Margin.

" This portrait may be considered a surprising resemblance of the illustrious original."—*Literary Gaz.*

" Mr. Swandale's portrait of her Majesty is a dignified work, excellently conceived and executed."—*Athenæum.*

" This is a splendid production. The likeness is the best we have seen."—*Literary Journal.*

" This is the first portrait—at least the first worthy of being called a portrait, of her Majesty."—*Morning Advertiser.*

" This very graceful picture presents us with the best likeness we have seen of her Majesty."—*Morning Chronicle.*

" This is a faithful likeness."—*Sunday Times.*

" The composition of the whole picture is excellently conceived, and in the best taste ; as a portrait it is admirable."—*Naval and Military Gazette.*

" The posture is easy and natural, and reflects the highest credit on Mr. Swandale."—*Conservative Journal.*

" This is an admirable resemblance of the illustrious original."—*Bell's Life.*

" As a national work of art, it rivals any we have ever had the good fortune to notice."—*Weekly Chronicle.*

" We recommend this admirable portrait by Mr. Swandale as a most interesting likeness of the Queen. The attitude is graceful, and the one into which her Majesty habitually falls."—*Age.*

" This is a work of infinite merit, and reflects great credit both on the painter and engraver. The charming expression of our gracious young Queen is successfully portrayed."—*Bell's Weekly Messenger.*

" This is certainly the best-finished likeness we have seen."—*Liverpool Mail.*

" A lovely picture of a lovely Queen ; and among the many portraits of our youthful sovereign, this will most decidedly take the lead."—*Derbyshire Courier.*

" An engraving honourable to British art, from a striking and characteristic likeness of our beloved Queen."—*Manchester Times.*

** Subscribers are respectfully informed, that, in order to secure early impressions, it will be necessary to give immediate orders, either direct, or through their respective Printsellers, to the Publishers—the Proofs, with very few exceptions, being all engaged.

LONDON : ACKERMANN AND CO., 96, STRAND.

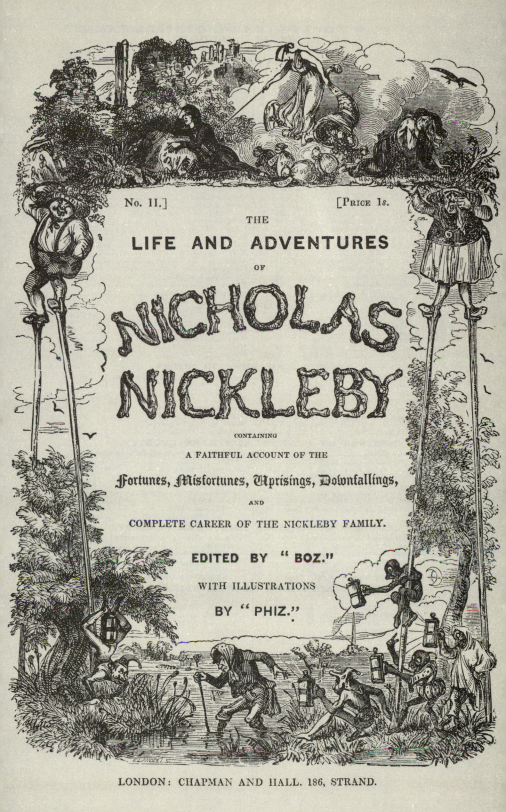

No. II.] [Price 1s.

THE
LIFE AND ADVENTURES
OF
NICHOLAS NICKLEBY

CONTAINING

A FAITHFUL ACCOUNT OF THE

Fortunes, Misfortunes, Uprisings, Downfallings,

AND

COMPLETE CAREER OF THE NICKLEBY FAMILY.

EDITED BY "BOZ."

WITH ILLUSTRATIONS

BY "PHIZ."

LONDON: CHAPMAN AND HALL, 186, STRAND.

PRICES OF THE GRAY'S INN WINE ESTABLISHMENT, 23, HIGH HOLBORN.

WINES IN WOOD.

Duty paid; delivered to any part of London, free of Expense.

	Per Pipe.	Hhd.	Qr. Cask.
Port, very good	£60	£30 10	£15 10
Do. superior	65	33 0	17 0
Do. for immediate bottling	75	38 0	19 10
Do. do.	84	42 10	21 10
A few pipes of extraordinary old Wines, of high character, and full of flavour	93 & 100		
Masdeu	66	33 10	16 16
Sherries (golden)	55	28 10	14 10
Do. pale or brown	60	30 10	15 10
Do. superior	68	34 10	17 10
Do. very superior	75	38 0	19 5

	Per Pipe.	Hhd.	Qr. Cask.
Sherries, any colour	£84	£42 10	£21 10
Do. very old do.	93	47 0	21 10
Do. very high character, scarce	100	50 0	—
Do. very choice old East India	120	60 0	—
Vidonia	45	23 0	12 0
Do. London Particular	55	28 0	—
Marsala, the best	45	23 0	12 0
Cape, good and clean	25	13 0	6 15
Do. superior	30	15 10	8 0
Do. Madeira or Sherry character	36	19 10	9 10
Pontac, superior	36	18 10	9 10

WINES IN BOTTLE.

	24s.	30
Port, from the wood	24s.	30
Do. superior, best Marks	34	36
Do. old crusted	32	36
Do. superior, 5 to 8 years in bottle	42	48
Do. very choice, 10 years in bottle	—	54
Masdeu	—	28
Do. old crusted, 2 years in bottle	—	32
Sherries, good quality	24	30
Do. superior pale, gold, or brown	36	42
Do. very choice, of rare quality	48	54
Do. the Amontillado, very old	48	54
Do. very superior old East India	54	60

Madeira (direct)	30s. 36s.	42
Do. West India		48 54
Do. East India		60 72
Bucellas, very old		30 26
Lisbon, rich and dry		28 34
Calcavella		— 33
Vidonia		— 28
Marsala		24 —
Arinto		— 28
Cape, good quality		12 15
Do. old and superior		18 21
Pontac		18 21

• All the above wines in Pints at proportionate prices.

DRAUGHT WINES.

	Per Gallon.
Port, good stout wine	10s. 6d. & 12s.
Do. very superior	15
Sherries, straw colour	10 6 12
Do. superior, any colour	15 0 18
Cape, good and clean	5s. 9d. 6 6 7 6d.

	Per Gallon.
Cape, very best	9s. 0
Pontac	9 6
West India Madeira	14 6
Marsala, Lisbon, or Vidonia	12 0
Masdeu	13 0

FRENCH AND RHENISH WINES.

Champagne, sparkling	54s.	60
Do. first quality	72	84
Do. in Pints	36	42
Claret, second growths	36	42
Do. St. Julien, vintage 1827		48
Do. Larose and Leoville		60
Do. Lafitte, Latour, and Chateau Margeaux	72	84
Moselle	48	54

Sparkling St. Peray, in high condition, and very fine		72
Sauterne and Barsac	30s.	36 48
Hock		36 48 60
Do. Rudesheim Berg, 1819		84 —
Do. do. 1811		90 —
Hermitage (the choicest quality)		90 105
Burgundy do.		

WINES OF CURIOUS AND RARE QUALITY.

Muscatel, very choice	42s.
Mountain	38
Rota Tent, very superior	42
Old East India Madeira, South-side Wine, and two years in India	70
Malmsey, old East India	60
Very old East India Brown Sherry, two voyages	70
Very curious Old Sherry, many years in bottle	63

A bin of high-flavoured old Port, ten years in bottle	60s.
Paxaretta, of exquisite quality (in Pints)	36
Constantia, red and white (do.)	26
Frontiguac	30
The Liqueur Sherry, shipped expressly to this establishment (do.)	45
Very old Canary Sack (do.)	36
Ausbruch Tokay, very scarce (do.)	36

SPIRITS OF CURIOUS AND RARE QUALITY.

A beautiful article of Pure Pale Brandy	72s. per doz.
A few cases of extraordinary Old Brandy, well worthy the attention of the Connoisseur	84 100
Milk Punch, very superior	32
Very old Pine-apple Rum, over proof	18 per gal.

Jamieson's Dublin Whiskey, seven years old	21s. per gal.
Very Superior English Gin	12 „
Rum Shrub, very superior	16 „
East India Nectar (in Pints)	60s. per doz.
Scotch Whiskey (various)	21

FOREIGN AND BRITISH SPIRITS.

	Per Gallon.
Genuine Cognac Brandy	24s. 0d. 26s. 6d.
Finest Old Champagne do.	28 0 32 0
Jamaica Rum	10 8 12 0
Wedderburn do. best marks	14 0
Whiskey (Scotch & Irish) various strengths	12s. 16s. 18 0

	Per Gallon.
Hollands (Schiedam)	26s. 6d. 28s. 0d
Rum Shrub	10 8 13 4
English Gin, various strengths	6s. 8 0 9 4
Best do.	10 8

N. B. Also, imported in one-dozen cases, containing two gallons, very superior Schiedam Hollands, at 60s. per dozen, which will be delivered from the Docks in the original package. Bottles and Cases included.

The attention of Innkeepers is requested to the article of Milk Punch, by which, with the addition of a small quantity of hot water, a tumbler of the finest Punch is produced, and at a less price than by the usual tedious process.

Country residents visiting London, and others, are respectfully invited to inspect the different departments of this Establishment, which now ranks among the greatest curiosities of the Metropolis.

• Bottles charged 2s. per doz.; Hampers or Cases, 1s.; Stone Bottles, 6d. per Gallon, which will be allowed if returned.

GEO. HENEKEY AND COMPY.

PUBLISHED BY CHAPMAN AND HALL.

THE CORONATION.

In one volume, small 8vo, price 5s. 6d., cloth boards,

REGAL RECORDS;

OR, A CHRONICLE OF

The Coronations of the Queens Regnant of England,

COMPILED FROM CONTEMPORARY ACCOUNTS AND OFFICIAL DOCUMENTS,

BY J. R. PLANCHE, F.S.A.

WITH NUMEROUS ILLUSTRATIONS.

DEDICATED BY PERMISSION TO HER GRACE THE DUCHESS OF SUTHERLAND, MISTRESS OF THE ROBES TO HER MAJESTY.

" A seasonable little book by Mr. J. R. Planche, whose antiquarian learning is relieved by a lively and ingenious turn of thinking."—*Times*.

" An interesting work, showing much research, and abounding in historical detail."—*Post*.

" An exceedingly well-timed and popular publication. Mr. Planche has gone into the subject with his usual taste and attention, giving us all that was necessary and no more, and bestowing the care they deserve upon the points chiefly applicable to the present day."—*Literary Gazette*.

THE PICKWICK PAPERS COMPLETE.

In one volume 8vo, bound in cloth, price 1l. 1s.

THE

POSTHUMOUS PAPERS OF THE PICKWICK CLUB.

BY " BOZ."

WITH FORTY-THREE ILLUSTRATIONS BY " PHIZ."

SEVENTH EDITION.

In one volume, small 8vo, price 3s. boards,

SKETCHES OF YOUNG LADIES;

WITH SIX ILLUSTRATIONS BY " PHIZ."

The Busy Young Lady.
The Romantic Young Lady.
The Matter-of-Fact Young Lady.
The Young Lady who Sings.
The Plain Young Lady.
The Evangelical Young Lady.
The Manly Young Lady.
The Literary Young Lady.

The Young Lady who is engaged.
The Petting Young Lady.
The Natural Historian Young Lady.
The Indirect Young Lady.
The Stupid Young Lady.
The Hyperbolical Young Lady.
The Interesting Young Lady.
The Abstemious Young Lady.

The Whimsical Young Lady.
The Sincere Young Lady.
The Affirmative Young Lady.
The Natural Young Lady.
The Clever Young Lady.
The Mysterious Young Lady.
The Lazy Young Lady.
The Young Lady from School.

FOURTH EDITION.

In one volume, small 8vo, price 3s. boards,

SKETCHES OF YOUNG GENTLEMEN;

CONTENTS.

Dedication to the Young Ladies.
The Out-and-out Young Gentleman.
The Domestic Young Gentleman.
The Bashful Young Gentleman.
The very Friendly Young Gentleman.

The ' Throwing-off' Young Gentleman.
The Poetical Young Gentleman.
The Funny Young Gentleman.
The Theatrical Young Gentleman.

The Military Young Gentleman.
The Political Young Gentleman.
The Censorious Young Gentleman.
The Young Ladies' Young Gentleman.

WITH SIX ILLUSTRATIONS BY " PHIZ."

SPLENDID NEW EDITION OF PLAYS!

WEBSTER'S
ACTING NATIONAL DRAMA.

UNDER THE AUSPICES OF

THE DRAMATIC AUTHORS' SOCIETY.

This Edition comprises every successful New Play, Farce, Melo-Drama, &c., produced at the London Theatres, correctly printed from the Prompter's Copy.

A NUMBER WILL BE PUBLISHED EVERY FORTNIGHT, PRICE SIXPENCE.

(THE MORE EXPENSIVE COPYRIGHTS ONE SHILLING.)

Each Play will be illustrated by an Etching of the most interesting Scene, taken during the representation, By PIERCE EGAN THE YOUNGER.

VOLUME I.

With a Portrait of J. R. PLANCHE, F.S.A. price 7s. in cloth, contains :—

1. THE TWO FIGAROS.
2. THE COUNTRY SQUIRE.
3. THE QUEER SUBJECT.
4. THE SENTINEL.
5. THE MODERN ORPHEUS
6. A PECULIAR POSITION.
7. WALTER TYRRELL.
8. THE TIGER AT LARGE.
9. THE BRIDAL, 1s.
10. MY YOUNG WIFE AND MY OLD UMBRELLA.
11. THE MIDDLE TEMPLE.
12. RIQUET WITH THE TUFT.

VOLUME II.

With a Portrait of TYRONE POWER, Esq., price 7s. cloth, contains :—

13. A QUARTER TO NINE.
14. BLANCHE OF JERSEY.
15. THE BOTTLE IMP.
16. COURT FAVOUR.
17. THE SPITFIRE.
18. RORY O'MORE.
19. ADVICE GRATIS.
20. THE ORIGINAL.
21. BARBERS OF BASSORA.
22. WHY DID YOU DIE?
23. VALSHA.
24. BENGAL TIGER.
25. ST. PATRICK'S EVE.

VOLUME III.

With a Portrait of Mr. C. MATTHEWS, price 7s. cloth, contains :—

26. PUSS IN BOOTS.
27. THE RINGDOVES.
28. BLACK DOMINO.
29. OUR MARY ANNE.
30. SHOCKING EVENTS.
31. THE CULPRIT.
32. CONFOUNDED FOREIGNERS.
33. THE DANCING BARBER.
34. ALL FOR LOVE, OR THE LOST PLEIAD.
35. THE SPITALFIELDS WEAVER.
36. THE RIFLE BRIGADE.
37. ANGELINE.
38.

39. YOU CAN'T MARRY YOUR GRANDMOTHER.   40. SPRING LOCK.   41. THE VALET-DE-SHAM.

JUST READY.

THE GROVES OF BLARNEY.   A HASTY CONCLUSION.

CHESS.

One volume, royal 16mo, neatly bound, price 5s. 6d.,

CHESS FOR BEGINNERS;

In a Series of Progressive Lessons,

SHOWING THE MOST APPROVED METHODS OF BEGINNING AND ENDING THE GAME, TOGETHER WITH VARIOUS SITUATIONS AND CHECK MATES.

BY WILLIAM LEWIS,

Author of several Works on the Game.

WITH TWENTY-FOUR DIAGRAMS PRINTED IN COLOURS. SECOND EDITION, CORRECTED.

ORNAMENTAL PAINTING, &c.

One volume, foolscap, handsomely bound in embossed cloth, gilt edges, price 12s.; or in morocco, 16s.,

THE ARTIST;

Or, Young Ladies' Instructor in Ornamental Painting, Drawing, &c.

CONSISTING OF LESSONS IN

| GRECIAN PAINTING | ORIENTAL TINTING | TRANSFERRING |
| JAPAN PAINTING | MEZZOTINTING | INLAYING |

AND MANUFACTURING ARTICLES FOR FANCY FAIRS, ETC.

BY B. F. GANDEE, Teacher.

EMBELLISHED WITH A BEAUTIFUL FRONTISPIECE AND TITLE-PAGE, PRINTED IN OIL COLOURS BY BAXTER, AND SEVENTEEN OTHER ILLUSTRATIVE ENGRAVINGS.

FRENCH POETRY.

In one volume 12mo, neatly bound in cloth, gilt edges, price 4s.,

FLEURS DE POESIE MODERNE;

CONTAINING

THE BEAUTIES OF A. DE LAMARTINE, VICTOR HUGO, DE BERANGER, C. DE LAVIGNE.

" A selection made in the spirit of the day. Instead of a collection from other and old collections, the compiler has chosen the best of modern French writers, and presented us with the very best of their thoughts."—*Spectator.*

MRS. BARWELL.

In two volumes, small 8vo, with Frontispieces, price 9s.,

EDWARD, THE CRUSADER'S SON.

A Tale.

ILLUSTRATING THE HISTORY, MANNERS, AND CUSTOMS OF ENGLAND IN THE ELEVENTH CENTURY.

BY MRS. BARWELL

" The intelligent and accomplished lady who has written these volumes was urged to the undertaking by an idea that a tale founded on, and illustrating the manners, customs, architecture, and costume of the eleventh century, would be valuable, not only to the young, but to that class of instructors who disapprove of the too stimulating pages f historical romance, and yet desire something more than dull details for their pupils. The task was difficult, but has been fully conquered."—*New Monthly Magazine.*

One Volume, small 8vo, elegantly bound, gilt leaves, price 6s., or in silk, 7s,

A GARLAND OF LOVE,

WREATHED OF CHOICE FLOWERS GATHERED IN THE FIELD OF ENGLISH POETRY

With a beautiful Frontispiece,

FROM A DESIGN BY HARVEY, PRINTED IN SEPIA, BY BAXTER.

" A charming little volume, selected with much taste, and elegantly put together. We have to bestow unqualified praise on the judgment which has avoided the slightest approach to what might bring a blush upon the modest cheek." —*Literary Gazette.*

In One Volume, small 8vo, bound, gilt leaves, price 7s.

THE POETIC WREATH;

CONSISTING OF

SELECT PASSAGES FROM THE WORKS OF ENGLISH POETS,

FROM CHAUCER TO WORDSWORTH.

Alphabetically Arranged,

WITH

TWENTY-SIX VIGNETTE LETTERS, BEAUTIFULLY ENGRAVED ON WOOD,

FROM DESIGNS BY S. W. ARNALD.

" This volume chancing to fall into our hands, has charmed us by the taste with which it has been prepared, both with respect to the literary materials, and the paper, print, embellishment, and binding. The pieces are arranged alphabetically under their titles, and at the beginning of each of the twenty-four letters is a beautiful device, in wood engraving, representing each letter by a combination of cherubs. Being satisfied, upon inspection, that the volume does not contain one trashy piece, we earnestly recommend it to general notice."—*Chambers' Journal.*

Complete in Two Volumes 8vo, price 16s., bound in cloth,

WITH TWENTY-EIGHT ILLUSTRATIONS,

THE LIBRARY OF FICTION;

OR, FAMILY STORY-TELLER.

These cheap and entertaining Volumes, admirably adapted for fireside reading, contain Sketches and Tales written expressly for the Work, by

" BOZ."	MISS MITFORD.
THE COUNTESS OF BLESSINGTON.	DOUGLAS JERROLD.
SHERIDAN KNOWLES.	C. WHITEHEAD, AUTHOR OF " THE CAVALIER."
E. MAYHEW, AUTHOR OF " MAKE YOUR WILLS."	T. K. HERVEY.
CHARLES OLLIER, AUTHOR OF " INESILLA."	THE GENTLEMAN IN BLACK.
G. P. R. JAMES.	AUTHOR OF " RATTLIN THE REEFER."

" We should be doing an injustice to the Publishers did we not remark, that in all the novelties that have appeared in ' The Library of Fiction,' there is not one that has contained aught that might shock the purity of the most rigid moralist, or wound the feelings of the most serious Christian. It may safely be admitted into families."—*Metropolitan.*

CHAPMAN AND HALL.

SKETCHES BY "BOZ."

COMPLETE IN ONE VOLUME,

UNIFORM WITH THE "PICKWICK PAPERS."

PUBLISHING MONTHLY, TO BE COMPLETED IN TWENTY NUMBERS, OCTAVO,

Price One Shilling each,

SKETCHES BY "BOZ."

ILLUSTRATIVE OF EVERY-DAY LIFE AND EVERY-DAY PEOPLE.

A New Edition.

COMPRISING BOTH THE SERIES,

AND EMBELLISHED WITH FORTY ILLUSTRATIONS,

BY GEORGE CRUIKSHANK.

THIS EDITION WILL BE REVISED BY THE AUTHOR, AND ARRANGED AS FOLLOWS:—

SEVEN SKETCHES FROM OUR PARISH.

THE BEADLE—THE PARISH ENGINE—THE SCHOOLMASTER—THE CURATE—THE OLD LADY—THE RETIRED CAPTAIN—THE FOUR SISTERS—THE ELECTION FOR BEADLE—THE BROKER'S MAN—THE LADIES' SOCIETIES— OUR NEXT-DOOR NEIGHBOURS.

SCENES.

THE STREET, MORNING, NOON, AND NIGHT—SHOPS AND THEIR TENANTS—SCOTLAND YARD—SEVEN DIALS— MONMOUTH STREET—HACKNEY COACH STANDS—DOCTORS'-COMMONS—LONDON RECREATIONS—THE RIVER— ASTLEY'S—GREENWICH FAIR—PRIVATE THEATRES—VAUXHALL GARDENS BY DAY—EARLY COACHES—OMNIBUSES —THE LAST CAB-DRIVER AND THE FIRST OMNIBUS CAD—THE HOUSE OF COMMONS—PUBLIC DINNERS— THE FIRST OF MAY—BROKERS AND MARINE STORE SHOPS—GIN SHOPS—THE PAWNBROKERS—THE CRIMINAL COURT—NEWGATE.

CHARACTERS.

SOME THOUGHTS ABOUT SOME PEOPLE—A CHRISTMAS FAMILY DINNER—A NEW YEAR'S PARTY—MISS JEMIMA EVANS—THE PARLOUR ORATOR—THE HOSPITAL PATIENT—MR. DOUNCE, THE WIDOWER—THE MISTAKEN MIL- LINER—THE DANCING ACADEMY—SHABBY GENTEEL PEOPLE—MAKING A NIGHT OF IT—THE PRISONERS' VAN·

TALES.

THE BOARDING HOUSE—MR. MINNS AND HIS COUSIN—SENTIMENT—THE TUGGS AT RAMSGATE—HORATIO SPARKINS—THE BLACK VEIL—THE STEAM EXCURSION—THE GREAT WINGLEBURY DUEL—MRS. JOSEPH PORTER —MR. WATKINS TOTTLE—THE BLOOMSBURY CHRISTENING—THE DRUNKARD'S DEATH.

PRICE ONE SHILLING,

A FEW WORDS ON A FEW WINES.

CHAPTER I.—CHOICE OF WINE.

PORT IN THE WOOD—GOOD WINE—WHAT IT SHOULD NOT BE—WHAT IT SHOULD BE—HOW TO OBTAIN WHAT YOU WANT—MATURITY—BOTTLED WINE—CONDITION—BEES-WING—CLARETY PORT—THE WAY TO PURCHASE —THE BEST SORT—KNOW YOUR OWN MIND—WHITE WINE—ACIDITY—SHERRY—MADEIRA.

CHAPTER II.—MANAGEMENT OF WINE

DIRECTIONS FOR—FINING PORT—CONDITION—WHEN FIT TO BOTTLE—WHITE WINE FINING—DIRECTION FOR BOTTLING—BOTTLES—CORKS—IMPLEMENTS—PIERCING—DRAWING—CORKING—PACKING—THE CELLAR.

CHAPTER III.—TREATMENT OF BOTTLED WINE.

CORKSCREW—DRAWING THE CORK—DECANTING THE WINE—WINE STRAINERS—DRINKING WINE—TOO MUCH— ENOUGH—USE OF WINE—ABUSE OF WINE—DINING AT HOME—DINING OUT—LIGHT WINE—ICING WINE—WINE COOLERS—WINE GLASSES.

TRAVELLING AND HUNTING MAPS.

MOUNTED IN CASES ADAPTED TO THE WAISTCOAT POCKET, 1s. 6d. EACH,

MAPS OF THE ENGLISH COUNTIES,

ENGRAVED BY SYDNEY HALL.

WITH THE MAIL AND COACH ROADS CORRECTLY COLOURED.

BEDFORDSHIRE	HEREFORDSHIRE	NORTHUMBERLAND
BERKSHIRE	HERTFORDSHIRE	NOTTINGHAMSHIRE
BUCKINGHAMSHIRE	HUNTINGDONSHIRE	OXFORDSHIRE
CAMBRIDGESHIRE	ISLE OF WIGHT	RUTLANDSHIRE
CHESHIRE	ISLES OF MAN,	SHROPSHIRE
CORNWALL	JERSEY, AND GUERNSEY }	SOMERSETSHIRE
CUMBERLAND	KENT	STAFFORDSHIRE
DERBYSHIRE	LANCASHIRE	SUFFOLK
DEVONSHIRE	LEICESTERSHIRE	SURREY
DORSETSHIRE	LINCOLNSHIRE	SUSSEX
DURHAM	MIDDLESEX	WARWICKSHIRE
ENGLAND	MONMOUTHSHIRE	WESTMORELAND
ESSEX	NORFOLK	WILTSHIRE
GLOUCESTERSHIRE	NORTHAMPTONSHIRE	WORCESTERSHIRE.
HAMPSHIRE		

Price 2s., double the size of the above,

YORKSHIRE, IRELAND, SCOTLAND, AND WALES.

COMPLETE SETS OF THE ABOVE, UNIFORMLY MOUNTED AND LETTERED,

IN A NEAT CASE,

MAY BE HAD, PRICE FOUR GUINEAS.

DISTORTION of the SPINE.—MRS.
HART, the late Widow and Successor of Mr.
CALLAM, respectfully begs to announce that she continues
the application of her much-approved Support for the
Assistance and Cure of DISTORTED SPINES, which
has received the patronage of her Majesty the Queen
Dowager, and is recommended by Sir Astley Cooper,
Mr. Keate, Dr. Davies, Dr. Ashwell, and several gentle-
men of the Faculty.

MRS. HART manufactures a new and peculiar descrip-
tion of Ladies' Stays, to improve the Figure and con-
ceal Deformity in Adults ; Leg Irons of every description ;
Trusses for Hernia ; Back Boards and Collars ; Laced
Stockings ; Knee Caps ; every description of Bandage ;
Reclining Boards ; Crutches ; Dumb Bells ; Belts for
Corpulency and Pregnancy ; Lunatic Belts, &c.

Address, MRS. HART, 57, Great Queen Street, Lincoln's
Inn, four doors from the Freemasons' Tavern.

LABERN'S BOTANIC CREAM.—
By appointment, patronised by her Most Gracious
Majesty, celebrated for strengthening and promoting the
growth of Hair, and completely freeing it from Scurf.—
Sold by the Proprietor, H. Labern, Perfumer to her
Majesty, 49, Judd Street, Brunswick Square, in pots,
1s. 6d., 2s. 6d., 3s. 6d., and 5s. each, and by all Perfumers
and Medicine Venders. Beware of counterfeits. Ask
for " Labern's Botanic Cream."

PATRONISED BY THE ROYAL FAMILY AND
THE NOBILITY.

SHARP'S ROYAL BRITISH CERATES & LINIMENT.

THESE valuable medical applications,
long privately known, and highly appreciated by
some of the most eminent medical men in the metropolis,
constitute, in their various modifications, rapid and effectual remedies for Gout—in some states, Rheumatic Affections, Lumbago, Glandular Swellings, many instances
of Scrofulous Sores and Swellings, Tumours, Relaxed
Sore Throats, Swelled Face or Gums, some cases of
Deafness, external Inflammation—in all its shapes, Boils,
Ulcerated and other wounds, Sprains, Bruises, Burns,
Scalds, Erysipelas, Venomous Stings, Itch, Ringworm,
Scaldhead, Grocer's Itch, Chilblains, Bunions, Corns,
Tender Feet, Paralysis of a local character, and Tic-douloureux. As no class of society is exempt from the
liability to some or other of these attacks, so to every rank
must access to such a powerful series of simple, but effec-
tual, remedies be highly desirable.

The series consist of a Liniment, with the Plain, and
four combinations of Cerates—Namely, No. 1, Plain ;
No. 2, Camphorated ; No. 3, Emollient ; No. 4, Balsamic ; and No. 5, Sulphurated ; severally applicable to
the cure of the above diseases and injuries, in the manner clearly laid down in the full printed directions which
accompany each packet.

The Proprietors give their solemn assurance, that
there is not a fact stated with respect to the powers of
these substances, which is not fully established in every
class of cases, in the private practice of medical men of
great respectability in the metropolis and elsewhere ; and
that each of the preparations, although most effectual in
its remedial character, is in the highest degree innocent
in its entire composition ; and may, consequently, be
used with perfect safety.

The Royal British Cerates are made up, in all their
modifications, in Boxes of four Sizes, at 13½d., 2s. 9d.,
4s. 6d., and 11s. each ; and the Liniment in Bottles of
three Sizes, with ground-glass Stoppers, at 2s. 9d., 4s. 6d.,
and 11s. each ; Stamps in all Cases included.

Sold by SHARP & Co., 153, Fleet Street, London, sole
Proprietors, whose name and address are upon the
Stamp ; and by the established Licensed Medicine Vend-
ers throughout the three kingdoms.

TO EPICURES.

CROSSE and BLACKWELL'S celebrated SOHO SAUCE for Fish, Game, Steaks, Made
Dishes, &c.

CROSSE and BLACKWELL'S FLORENCE CREAM for
Salads, Lobsters, &c.

DINMORE'S ESSENCE OF SHRIMPS for every description of boiled and fried Fish.

DINMORE'S SHRIMP PASTE, a superior delicacy for
Breakfast, Sandwiches, &c.—The above to be had of
most Sauce Venders throughout the Kingdom, and
wholesale at their manufactory, 11, King-Street, Soho.

BEDS, FEATHERS, BEDTICKS, MAT-
TRESSES.

SEASONED FEATHER-BEDS, 18s.
to 5l.; Prime Dressed Feathers, 9d. to 2s. 6d.
per lb. ; Ticks, 3s. to 24s.; Field Tent Bedsteads, 20s.;
Alva Marina Mattresses to fit, 10s.; Soft Wool Flocks,
2d., 3d., and 4d. per lb. Every description of Bedsteads,
Mattresses, Palliasses, and Bedding, full 30 per cent.
cheaper. Merchants, Captains, Upholsterers, Brokers,
and Proprietors of Schools, supplied at D. TIMOTHY'S
old-established Manufactory, No. 31, Barbican, corner of
Redcross-street, City.

PATENT PORTABLE WATER CLOSETS

ON WISS and HAWKINS'S PRIN-
CIPLE.—Fifteen years' labour and experience
have not only established their superiority, but the decided conviction that they cannot be improved. ROBERT
WISS, the actual inventor and holder of the patent,
feels justified in calling attention to the above, as the
most simple and perfect article of the kind. Also
WATER-CLOSETS for fixing, on the same principle,
particularly recommended for the country and exportation, the machinery and cistern requiring no more room
than is occupied by the seat. To be seen in great
variety at the manufactory. Plumber's work of every
description executed in town and country.—Address to
No. 38, Charing-cross, near the Admiralty, London.

HOSIERY.

POPE and Co. have removed from 28, Friday Street, to
4, *Waterloo Place, Pall Mall.*

THEY continue to manufacture every
description of HOSIERY, in the old-fashioned
substantial manner, the greatest attention being paid to
Elasticity and Durability.—Orders and Patterns to be
forwarded to 4, Waterloo Place, or to their manufactory,
Mount Street, Nottingham.

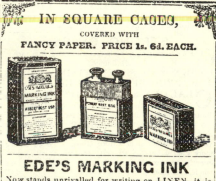

IN SQUARE CASES,

COVERED WITH

FANCY PAPER. PRICE 1s. 6d. EACH.

EDE'S MARKING INK

Now stands unrivalled for writing on LINEN, it is
scrupulously manufactured from a delicate composition of Silver, and warranted never to wash out, or
become pale.

WHOLESALE LONDON DEPOT,
for the Trade and Public,
79, BISHOPSGATE STREET WITHIN.

HEAL AND SON'S FRENCH MATTRESSES.

The very frequent inquiries for MATTRESSES made after the manner of the French, have induced F. HEAL and SON to turn their attention to the making of mattresses on the same principles. The essential difference between FRENCH MATTRESSES and ENGLISH consists in the Materials of which they are made, and consequently a difference in the making. The French use long Fleece Wool, and therefore but little work is requisite, leaving to the Wool the whole of its elasticity. English Mattresses are made of short Wool, the refuse of other Manufacturings, and a great deal of work is necessarily required to keep the material together, which makes them comparatively *Non-Elastic.* The advantages F. HEAL and SON possess by being exclusively Manufacturers of Bedding, enable them to offer Mattresses of *fine long Wool,* equal to the best that are made in France, at the same prices that are usually charged for those generally made in this Country.—F. HEAL & SON, Bedding Manufacturers, 203, Tottenham Court Road.

C. & A. OLDRIDGE'S BALM OF COLUMBIA,

PREVENTS

THE HAIR FROM

FALLING OFF;

MAKES IT

CURL

BEAUTIFULLY,

AND COMPLETELY

FREES IT

FROM SCURF ON

THE

FIRST OR SECOND

APPLICATION.

Abundance of Gertificates, of the first respectability, from those who have been Bald and had their Hair restored, are shown by the Proprietors, No. 1, WELLINGTON STREET, STRAND, LONDON;

Where the BALM is sold, and by most of the respectable Perfumers and Chemists, price 3s. 6d., 6s., and 11s. per Bottle; no other prices are genuine.——N.B. Oldridge's Balm produces Whiskers and Eyebrows.

ASK FOR OLDRIDGE'S BALM.

LAMING'S EFFERVESCING CHELTENHAM SALTS,

Are recommended and personally employed by many of the faculty, as the safest aperient known. They contain the constituents of the Cheltenham Waters, which are so advantageously used for correcting errors of Digestion and Biliary attacks during hot weather, and afford a highly agreeable beverage exactly resembling Soda Water.—" They are the invention of a surgeon of the highest respectability."—*Journ. of Lit. and Science.* "We know of no preparation of which we can speak more highly."—*Oriental Herald.* "The traveller should not fail to take them with him."—*Brockedon's Italy.* "They are particularly agreeable, and highly efficacious."—*Lancet.* "We cannot recommend a better thing than Laming's Salts."—*Literary Gazette.* "For free livers, bilious persons, and those troubled with indigestion, they are admirable."—*Times.*

Mothers of families will find this a most valuable Family Medicine, as it is quite destitute of all taste, and is equally efficient when taken in the doses marked on the labels, as any of the common aperients, and much safer. Sold in Bottles, at 2s. 6d., 4s., and 10s., by R. E. DEAR, 89, Bishopsgate Within, and all respectable Chemists.

IMPROVED ACHROMATIC TELESCOPES,

Made by THOMAS HARRIS and SON, of the very best quality, at prices considerably lower than any other house,

viz.:—

A Pocket Telescope, to discern objects 8 miles £0 18 0
| | | | |
Ditto | ditto | 12 ditto .... | 1 10 0 |
Ditto | ditto | 16 ditto .... | 2 2 0 |
Ditto | ditto | 20 ditto .... | 4 0 0 |

N.B. A distant object to test them with.

THOMAS HARRIS and SON, Opticians to the Royal Family, 52, Great Russell Street, opposite the British Museum. Established sixty years. No other connexion.

NICHOLAS NICKLEBY:
BY "BOZ."

ADVERTISEMENTS WILL BE INSERTED IN THE MONTH'S NUMBER OF THIS POPULAR PERIODICAL ON THE FOLLOWING

TERMS.

NOT EXCEEDING EIGHT LINES	£0 10	6
EACH LINE BEYOND EIGHT	0 1	0
HALF A COLUMN	2 2	0
A COLUMN	3 10	0
A WHOLE PAGE	6 6	0
PROSPECTUSES, &c., OF WHICH 32,000 ARE REQUIRED, NOT EXCEEDING		
HALF A SHEET	5 5	0
,, ,, A WHOLE SHEET . . .	6 6	0

PLATE.—A. B. SAVORY and SONS, Manufacturing Silversmiths, 14, Cornhill. London, opposite the Bank of England. The best wrought Silver Spoons and Forks, Fiddle Pattern, 7s. 2d. per ounce ; the King's Pattern, 7s. 4d. pa. ounce. The following are the weights recommended, but the articles may be ha. lighter or heavier, at the same price per ounce :—

FIDDLE PATTERN.	oz.	s.	d.	£	s.	d.	KING'S PATTERN.	oz.	s.	d.	£	s.	d.
12 Table Spoons	30 at 7	2	...	10	15	0	12 Table Spoons	40 at 7	4	...	14	13	4
12 Dessert ditto	20	7	2	7	3	4	12 Dessert ditto	26	7	4	9	10	8
12 Table Forks	30	7	2	10	15	0	12 Table Forks	40	7	4	14	13	4
12 Dessert ditto	20	7	2	7	3	4	12 Dessert ditto	26	7	4	9	10	8
9 Gravy Spoons	10	7	2	3	11	8	2 Gravy Spoons	12	7	4	4	8	0
1 Soup Ladle	10	7	2	3	11	8	1 Soup Ladle	12	7	4	4	8	0
4 Sauce ditto	10	7	8	3	16	8	4 Sauce ditto	12	7	10	4	14	0
4 Salt Spoons (gilt strong)				1	0	0	4 Salt ditto (strong gilt)				2	2	0
1 Fish Slice				2	10	0	1 Fish Slice				3	5	0
12 Tea Spoons	10	7	8	3	16	8	12 Tea Spoons	14	7	10	5	9	8
1 Pair Sugar Tongs				0	15	0	1 Pair Sugar Tongs				1	5	0

A Pamphlet containing detailed lists of the prices of various patterns of Silver Spoons and Forks, Silver Tea and Coffee Services, and of the different articles of Plated Ware, may be had on application, free of cost, or will be sent into the country in answer to a paid letter. The Plate Rooms of the Establishment, which are extensive, contain a arge and choice selection of Silver Plate. Plated Goods and every article requisite to complete a service.

ENGLISH GOLD WATCHES.—A. B. SAVORY & SONS, Watchmakers, No. 9, Cornhill, London, opposite the Bank of England, submit for selection a very large STOCK of GOLD WATCHES, the whole of which are made and finished under the careful inspection of experienced workmen on their own premises, and each warranted for correct performance.

SIZE FOR LADIES.

Fine Vertical Watches, jewelled, in engine-turned gold cases, and gold dials, warranted ....£ 10 10 0

Fine Vertical Watches, jewelled, with double-backed engine-turned gold cases, and gold dials, warranted ....£ 12 12 0

Patent Detached Lever Watches, jewelled in four holes, with double-backed gold cases, and gold dials, warranted ....£ 14 14 0

SIZE FOR GENTLEMEN.

Patent Detached Lever Watches, jewelled in four holes, seconds, and double-backed gold cases, warranted...................£ 14 14 0

Patent Detached Lever Watches, capped, jewelled in six holes, seconds, double-backed gold cases and enamel dials, warranted.£ 17 17 0

Patent Detached Lever Watches, capped, jewelled in six holes, seconds, double-backed gold cases and gold dials, warranted ..£ 21 0 0

Either of the Gentlemen's Watches may be had in gold hunting cases for £ 3 3s. each extra.

N. B. Second-hand Watches purchased in exchange.

[BRADBURY AND EVANS, PRINTERS, WHITEFRIARS.]

CHAPTER V.

NICHOLAS STARTS FOR YORKSHIRE.—OF HIS LEAVE-TAKING AND HIS
FELLOW-TRAVELLERS, AND WHAT BEFEL THEM ON THE ROAD.

IF tears dropped into a trunk were charms to preserve its owner from
sorrow and misfortune, Nicholas Nickleby would have commenced his
expedition under most happy auspices. There was so much to be done,
and so little time to do it in, so many kind words to be spoken, and
such bitter pain in the hearts in which they rose to impede their utterance, that the little preparations for his journey were made mournfully
indeed. A hundred things which the anxious care of his mother and
sister deemed indispensable for his comfort, Nicholas insisted on leaving
behind, as they might prove of some after use, or might be convertible
into money if occasion required. A hundred affectionate contests on
such points as these, took place on the sad night which preceded his
departure; and, as the termination of every angerless dispute brought
them nearer and nearer to the close of their slight preparations, Kate
grew busier and busier, and wept more silently.

The box was packed at last, and then there came supper, with some
little delicacy provided for the occasion, and as a set-off against the
expense of which, Kate and her mother had feigned to dine when
Nicholas was out. The poor lad nearly choked himself by attempting
to partake of it, and almost suffocated himself in affecting a jest or two,
and forcing a melancholy laugh. Thus they lingered on till the hour
of separating for the night was long past : and then they found that they
might as well have given vent to their real feelings before, for they could
not suppress them, do what they would. So they let them have their
way, and even that was a relief.

Nicholas slept well till six next morning; dreamed of home, or of
what was home once—no matter which, for things that are changed or
gone will come back as they used to be, thank God, in sleep—and rose
quite brisk and gay. He wrote a few lines in pencil to say the good
bye which he was afraid to pronounce himself, and laying them with
half his scanty stock of money at his sister's door, shouldered his box and
crept softly down stairs.

" Is that you, Hannah ?" cried a voice from Miss La Creevy's sitting-
room, whence shone the light of a feeble candle.

" It is I, Miss La Creevy," said Nicholas, putting down the box and
looking in.

" Bless us !" exclaimed Miss La Creevy, starting and putting her
hand to her curl-papers ; " You're up very early, Mr. Nickleby."

" So are you," replied Nicholas.

" It's the fine arts that bring me out of bed, Mr. Nickleby," returned
the lady. " I'm waiting for the light to carry out an idea."

Miss La Creevy had got up early to put a fancy nose into a miniature of an ugly little boy, destined for his grandmother in the country, who was expected to bequeath him property if he was like the family.

"To carry out an idea," repeated Miss La Creevy; "and that's the great convenience of living in a thoroughfare like the Strand. When I want a nose or an eye for any particular sitter, I have only to look out of window and wait till I get one."

"Does it take long to get a nose, now?" inquired Nicholas, smiling.

"Why, that depends in a great measure on the pattern," replied Miss La Creevy. "Snubs and romans are plentiful enough, and there are flats of all sorts and sizes when there's a meeting at Exeter Hall; but perfect aquilines, I am sorry to say, are scarce, and we generally use them for uniforms or public characters."

"Indeed!" said Nicholas. "If I should meet with any in my travels, I'll endeavour to sketch them for you."

"You don't mean to say that you are really going all the way down into Yorkshire this cold winter's weather, Mr. Nickleby?" said Miss La Creevy. "I heard something of it last night."

"I do, indeed," replied Nicholas. "Needs must, you know, when somebody drives. Necessity is my driver, and that is only another name for the same gentleman."

"Well, I am very sorry for it, that's all I can say," said Miss La Creevy; "as much on your mother's and sister's account as on yours. Your sister is a very pretty young lady, Mr. Nickleby, and that is an additional reason why she should have somebody to protect her. I persuaded her to give me a sitting or two, for the street-door case. Ah! she'll make a sweet miniature." As Miss La Creevy spoke, she held up an ivory countenance intersected with very perceptible sky-blue veins, and regarded it with so much complacency, that Nicholas quite envied her.

"If you ever have an opportunity of showing Kate some little kindness," said Nicholas, presenting his hand, "I think you will."

"Depend upon that," said the good-natured miniature painter; "and God bless you, Mr. Nickleby; and I wish you well."

It was very little that Nicholas knew of the world, but he guessed enough about its ways to think, that if he gave Miss La Creevy one little kiss, perhaps she might not be the less kindly disposed towards those he was leaving behind. So he gave her three or four with a kind of jocose gallantry, and Miss La Creevy evinced no greater symptoms of displeasure than declaring, as she adjusted her yellow turban, that she had never heard of such a thing, and couldn't have believed it possible.

Having terminated the unexpected interview in this satisfactory manner, Nicholas hastily withdrew himself from the house. By the time he had found a man to carry his box it was only seven o'clock, so he walked slowly on, a little in advance of the porter, and very probably with not half as light a heart in his breast as the man had, although he had no waistcoat to cover it with, and had evidently, from the appearance of his other garments, been spending the night in a stable, and taking his breakfast at a pump.

Regarding with no small curiosity and interest all the busy preparations for the coming day which every street and almost every house displayed; and thinking now and then that it seemed rather hard that so many people of all ranks and stations could earn a livelihood in London, and that he should be compelled to journey so far in search of one, Nicholas speedily arrived at the Saracen's Head, Snow Hill. Having dismissed his attendant, and seen the box safely deposited in the coach-office, he looked into the coffee-room in search of Mr. Squeers.

He found that learned gentleman sitting at breakfast, with the three little boys before noticed, and two others who had turned up by some lucky chance since the interview of the previous day, ranged in a row on the opposite seat. Mr. Squeers had before him a small measure of coffee, a plate of hot toast, and a cold round of beef; but he was at that moment intent on preparing breakfast for the little boys.

" This is twopenn'orth of milk is it, waiter ? " said Mr. Squeers, looking down into a large blue mug, and slanting it gently so as to get an accurate view of the quantity of liquid contained in it.

" That's twopenn'orth, Sir," replied the waiter.

" What a rare article milk is, to be sure, in London ! " said Mr. Squeers with a sigh. " Just fill that mug up with lukewarm water, William, will you ? "

" To the wery top, Sir ? " inquired the waiter. " Why, the milk will be drownded."

" Never you mind that," replied Mr. Squeers. " Serve it right for being so dear. You ordered that thick bread and butter for three, did you ? "

" Coming directly, Sir."

" You needn't hurry yourself," said Squeers; " there's plenty of time. Conquer your passions, boys, and don't be eager after vittles." As he uttered this moral precept, Mr. Squeers took a large bite out of the cold beef, and recognised Nicholas.

" Sit down, Mr. Nickleby," said Squeers. " Here we are, a breakfasting you see."

Nicholas did *not* see that anybody was breakfasting except Mr. Squeers; but he bowed with all becoming reverence, and looked as cheerful as he could.

" Oh ! that's the milk and water, is it, William ? " said Squeers. " Very good; don't forget the bread and butter presently."

At this fresh mention of the bread and butter, the five little boys looked very eager, and followed the waiter out with their eyes; meanwhile Mr. Squeers tasted the milk and water.

" Ah ! " said that gentleman, smacking his lips, " here's richness ! Think of the many beggars and orphans in the streets that would be glad of this, little boys. A shocking thing hunger is, isn't it, Mr. Nickleby ? "

" Very shocking, Sir," said Nicholas.

" When I say number one," pursued Mr. Squeers, putting the mug before the children, " the boy on the left hand nearest the window may take a drink ; and when I say number two the boy next him will go in, and so till we come to number five, which is the last boy. Are you ready?"

"Yes, Sir," cried all the little boys with great eagerness.

"That's right," said Squeers, calmly getting on with his breakfast; "keep ready till I tell you to begin. Subdue your appetites, my dears, and you've conquered human natur. This is the way we inculcate strength of mind, Mr. Nickleby," said the schoolmaster, turning to Nicholas, and speaking with his mouth very full of beef and toast.

Nicholas murmured something—he knew not what—in reply, and the little boys dividing their gaze between the mug, the bread and butter (which had by this time arrived), and every morsel which Mr. Squeers took into his mouth, remained with strained eyes in torments of expectation.

"Thank God for a good breakfast," said Squeers when he had finished. "Number one may take a drink."

Number one seized the mug ravenously, and had just drunk enough to make him wish for more, when Mr. Squeers gave the signal for number two, who gave up at the same interesting moment to number three, and the process was repeated till the milk and water terminated with number five.

"And now," said the schoolmaster, dividing the bread and butter for three into as many portions as there were children, "you had better look sharp with your breakfast, for the horn will blow in a minute or two, and then every boy leaves off."

Permission being thus given to fall to, the boys began to eat voraciously, and in desperate haste, while the schoolmaster (who was in high good humour after his meal) picked his teeth with a fork and looked smilingly on. In a very short time the horn was heard.

"I thought it wouldn't be long," said Squeers, jumping up and producing a little basket from under the seat; "put what you haven't had time to eat, in here, boys! You'll want it on the road!"

Nicholas was considerably startled by these very economical arrangements, but he had no time to reflect upon them, for the little boys had to be got up to the top of the coach, and their boxes had to be brought out and put in, and Mr. Squeers's luggage was to be seen carefully deposited in the boot, and all these offices were in his department. He was in the full heat and bustle of concluding these operations, when his uncle, Mr. Ralph Nickleby, accosted him.

"Oh! here you are, Sir?" said Ralph. "Here are your mother and sister, Sir."

"Where!" cried Nicholas, looking hastily round.

"Here!" replied his uncle. "Having too much money and nothing at all to do with it, they were paying a hackney coach as I came up, Sir."

"We were afraid of being too late to see him before he went away from us," said Mrs. Nickleby, embracing her son, heedless of the unconcerned lookers-on in the coach-yard.

"Very good, ma'am," returned Ralph, "you're the best judge of course. I merely said that you were paying a hackney coach. I never pay a hackney coach, ma'am, I never hire one. I hav'n't been in a hackney coach of my own hiring for thirty years, and I hope I shan't be for thirty more, if I live as long."

" I should never have forgiven myself if I had not seen him," said Mrs. Nickleby. " Poor dear boy—going away without his breakfast too, because he feared to distress us."

" Mighty fine certainly," said Ralph, with great testiness. " When I first went to business, ma'am, I took a penny loaf and a ha'porth of milk for my breakfast as I walked to the city every morning ; what do you say to that, ma'am ? Breakfast ! Pshaw !"

" Now, Nickleby," said Squeers, coming up at the moment button- ing his great-coat ; " I think you'd better get up behind. I'm afraid of one of them boys falling off, and then there's twenty pound a year gone."

" Dear Nicholas," whispered Kate, touching her brother's arm, " who is that vulgar man ?"

" Eh !" growled Ralph, whose quick ears had caught the inquiry. " Do you wish to be introduced to Mr. Squeers, my dear ?"

" That the schoolmaster ! No, uncle. Oh, no !" replied Kate, shrinking back.

" I'm sure I heard you say as much, my dear," retorted Ralph in his cold sarcastic manner. " Mr. Squeers, here's my niece, Nicholas's sister ?"

" Very glad to make your acquaintance, Miss," said Squeers, raising his hat an inch or two. " I wish Mrs. Squeers took gals, and we had you for a teacher. I don't know though whether she mightn't grow jealous if we had. Ha ! Ha ! Ha !"

If the proprietor of Dotheboys Hall could have known what was passing in his assistant's breast at that moment, he would have disco- vered with some surprise, that he was as near being soundly pummelled as he had ever been in his life. Kate Nickleby having a quicker per- ception of her brother's emotions led him gently aside, and thus pre- vented Mr. Squeers from being impressed with the fact in a peculiarly disagreeable manner.

" My dear Nicholas," said the young lady, " who is this man ? What kind of place can it be that you are going to ?"

" I hardly know, Kate," replied Nicholas, pressing his sister's hand. " I suppose the Yorkshire folks are rather rough and uncultivated, that's all."

" But this person," urged Kate.

" Is my employer, or master, or whatever the proper name may be," replied Nicholas quickly, " and I was an ass to take his coarseness ill. They are looking this way, and it is time I was in my place. Bless you love, and good bye. Mother ; look forward to our meeting again some day. Uncle, farewell ! Thank you heartily for all you have done and all you mean to do. Quite ready, Sir."

With these hasty adieux, Nicholas mounted nimbly to his seat, and waved his hand as gallantly as if his heart went with it.

At this moment, when the coachman and guard were comparing

notes for the last time before starting, on the subject of the way-bill; when porters were screwing out the last reluctant sixpences, itinerant newsmen making the last offer of a morning paper, and the horses giving the last impatient rattle to their harness, Nicholas felt somebody pulling softly at his leg. He looked down, and there stood Newman Noggs, who pushed up into his hand a dirty letter.

" What's this ?" inquired Nicholas.

" Hush !" rejoined Noggs, pointing to Mr. Ralph Nickleby, who was saying a few earnest words to Squeers a short distance off. " Take it. Read it. Nobody knows. That's all."

" Stop !" cried Nicholas.

" No," replied Noggs.

Nicholas cried stop, again, but Newman Noggs was gone.

A minute's bustle, a banging of the coach doors, a swaying of the vehicle to one side, as the heavy coachman, and still heavier guard, climbed into their seats ; a cry of all right, a few notes from the horn, a hasty glance of two sorrowful faces below and the hard features of Mr. Ralph Nickleby—and the coach was gone too, and rattling over the stones of Smithfield.

The little boys' legs being too short to admit of their feet resting upon anything as they sat, and the little boys' bodies being consequently in imminent hazard of being jerked off the coach, Nicholas had enough to do to hold them on : and between the manual exertion and the mental anxiety attendant upon this task, he was not a little relieved when the coach stopped at the Peacock at Islington. He was still more relieved when a hearty-looking gentleman, with a very good-humoured face, and a very fresh colour, got up behind and proposed to take the other corner of the seat.

" If we put some of these youngsters in the middle," said the new comer, " they'll be safer in case of their going to sleep ; eh ? "

" If you'll have the goodness, Sir," replied Squeers, " that'll be the very thing. Mr. Nickleby, take three of them boys between you and the gentleman. Belling and the youngest Snawley can sit between me and the guard. Three children," said Squeers, explaining to the stranger, " books as two."

" I have not the least objection I am sure," said the fresh-coloured gentleman ; " I have a brother who wouldn't object to book his six children as two at any butcher's or baker's in the kingdom, I dare say. Far from it."

" Six children, Sir !" exclaimed Squeers.

" Yes, and all boys," replied the stranger.

" Mr. Nickleby," said Squeers, in great haste, " catch hold of that basket. Let me give you a card, Sir, of an establishment where those six boys can be brought up in an enlightened, liberal, and moral manner, with no mistake at all about it, for twenty guineas a year each—twenty guineas, Sir ; or I'd take all the boys together upon a average right through, and say a hundred pound a year for the lot."

" Oh !" said the gentleman, glancing at the card, " You are the Mr. Squeers mentioned here, I presume ? "

Nicholas starts for Yorkshire.

"Yes I am, Sir," replied the worthy pedagogue; " Mr. Wackford Squeers is my name, and I'm very far from being ashamed of it. These are some of my boys, Sir; that's one of my assistants, Sir—Mr. Nickleby, a gentleman's son, and a good scholar, mathematical, classical, and commercial. We don't do things by halves at our shop. All manner of learning my boys take down, Sir; the expense is never thought of, and they get paternal treatment and washing in."

" Upon my word," said the gentleman, glancing at Nicholas with a half smile, and a more than half expression of surprise, " these are advantages indeed."

" You may say that, Sir," rejoined Squeers, thrusting his hands into his great-coat pockets. " The most unexceptionable references are given and required. I wouldn't take a reference with any boy that was not responsible for the payment of five pound five a quarter, no, not if you went down on your knees, and asked me with the tears running down your face to do it."

" Highly considerate," said the passenger.

" It's my great aim and end to be considerate, Sir," rejoined Squeers. " Snawley, junior, if you don't leave off chattering your teeth, and shaking with the cold, I'll warm you with a severe thrashing in about half a minute's time."

" Sit fast here, genelmen," said the guard as he clambered up.

" All right behind there, Dick?" cried the coachman.

" All right," was the reply. " Off she goes." And off she did go, —if coaches be feminine—amidst a loud flourish from the guard's horn, and the calm approval of all the judges of coaches and coach-horses congregated at the Peacock, but more especially of the helpers, who stood with the cloths over their arms, watching the coach till it disappeared, and then lounged admiringly stablewards, bestowing various gruff encomiums on the beauty of the turn-out.

When the guard (who was a stout old Yorkshireman) had blown himself quite out of breath, he put the horn into a little tunnel of a basket fastened to the coach-side for the purpose, and giving himself a plentiful shower of blows on the chest and shoulders, observed it was uncommon cold, after which he demanded of every person separately whether he was going right through, and if not where he *was* going. Satisfactory replies being made to these queries, he surmised that the roads were pretty heavy arter that fall last night, and took the liberty of asking whether any of them gentlemen carried a snuff-box. It happening that nobody did, he remarked with a mysterious air that he had heard a medical gentleman as went down to Grantham last week say how that snuff-taking was bad for the eyes; but for his part he had never found it so, and what he said was, that every body should speak as they found. Nobody attempting to controvert this position, he took a small brown paper parcel out of his hat, and putting on a pair of horn spectacles (the writing being crabbed) read the direction half a dozen times over, having done which he consigned the parcel to its old place, put up his spectacles again, and stared at every body in turn. After this, he took another blow at the horn by way

of refreshment, and having now exhausted his usual topics of conversation folded his arms as well as he could in so many coats, and
falling into a solemn silence, looked carelessly at the familiar objects
which met his eye on every side as the coach rolled on; the only
things he seemed to care for, being horses and droves of cattle, which
he scrutinised with a critical air as they were passed upon the
road.

The weather was intensely and bitterly cold; a great deal of snow
fell from time to time, and the wind was intolerably keen. Mr. Squeers
got down at almost every stage—to stretch his legs as he said, and as
he always came back from such excursions with a very red nose, and
composed himself to sleep directly, there is reason to suppose that he
derived great benefit from the process. The little pupils having been
stimulated with the remains of their breakfast, and further invigorated
by sundry small sups of a curious cordial carried by Mr. Squeers,
which tasted very like toast and water put into a brandy bottle by
mistake, went to sleep, woke, shivered, and cried, as their feelings
prompted. Nicholas and the good-tempered man found so many things
to talk about, that between conversing together, and cheering up the
boys, the time passed with them as rapidly as it could, under such
adverse circumstances.

So the day wore on. At Eton Slocomb there was a good coach
dinner, of which the box, the four front outsides, the one inside, Nicholas,
the good-tempered man, and Mr. Squeers, partook; while the five
little boys were put to thaw by the fire, and regaled with sandwiches. A stage or two further on, the lamps were lighted, and a great
to-do occasioned by the taking up at a road-side inn of a very fastidious
lady with an infinite variety of cloaks and small parcels, who loudly lamented for the behoof of the outsides the non-arrival of her own carriage
which was to have taken her on, and made the guard solemnly promise
to stop every green chariot he saw coming; which, as it was a dark
night and he was sitting with his face the other way, that officer undertook, with many fervent asseverations, to do. Lastly, the fastidious
lady, finding there was a solitary gentleman inside, had a small lamp
lighted which she carried in her reticule; and being after much
trouble shut in, the horses were put into a brisk canter and the coach
was once more in rapid motion.

The night and the snow came on together, and dismal enough they
were. There was no sound to be heard but the howling of the wind;
for the noise of the wheels and the tread of the horses' feet were rendered inaudible by the thick coating of snow which covered the earth,
and was fast increasing every moment. The streets of Stamford were
deserted as they passed through the town, and its old churches rose
frowning and dark from the whitened ground. Twenty miles further
on, two of the front outside passengers wisely availing themselves of
their arrival at one of the best inns in England, turned in for the night
at the George at Grantham. The remainder wrapped themselves more
closely in their coats and cloaks, and leaving the light and warmth of
the town behind them, pillowed themselves against the luggage and pre-

pared, with many half-suppressed moans, again to encounter the piercing blast which swept across the open country.

They were little more than a stage out of Grantham, or about half way between it and Newark, when Nicholas, who had been asleep for a short time, was suddenly roused by a violent jerk which nearly threw him from his seat. Grasping the rail, he found that the coach had sunk greatly on one side, though it was still dragged forward by the horses; and while—confused by their plunging and the loud screams of the lady inside—he hesitated for an instant whether to jump off or not, the vehicle turned easily over, and relieved him from all further uncertainty by flinging him into the road.

CHAPTER VI.

IN WHICH THE OCCURRENCE OF THE ACCIDENT MENTIONED IN THE LAST CHAPTER, AFFORDS AN OPPORTUNITY TO A COUPLE OF GENTLEMEN TO TELL STORIES AGAINST EACH OTHER.

" Wo ho !" cried the guard, on his legs in a minute, and running to the leaders' heads. " Is there ony genelmen there, as can len' a hand here? Keep quiet, dang ye. Wo ho !"

" What's the matter?" demanded Nicholas, looking sleepily up.

" Matther mun, matther eneaf for one neight," replied the guard; " dang the wall-eyed bay, he's gane mad wi' glory I think, carse t'coorch is over. Here, can't ye len' a hond? Dom it, I'd ha' dean it if all my boans were brokken."

" Here!" cried Nicholas, staggering to his feet, " I'm ready. I'm only a little abroad, that's all."

" Hoold 'em toight," cried the guard, " while ar coot treaces. Hang on tiv 'em sumhoo. Weel deame, my lad. That's it. Let 'em goa noo. Dang 'em, they'll gang whoam fast eneaf."

In truth, the animals were no sooner released than they trotted back with much deliberation to the stable they had just left, which was distant not a mile behind.

" Can you blo' a harn?" asked the guard, disengaging one of the coach-lamps.

" I dare say I can," replied Nicholas.

" Then just blo' away into that 'un as lies on the grund, fit to wakken the deead, will'ee," said the man, " while I stop sum o' this here squealing inside. Cumin', cumin'; dean't make that noise, wooman."

As the man spoke he proceeded to wrench open the uppermost door of the coach, while Nicholas seizing the horn, awoke the echoes far and wide with one of the most extraordinary performances on that instrument ever heard by mortal ears. It had its effect however, not only in rousing such of the passengers as were recovering from the stunning effects of their fall, but in summoning assistance to their relief, for lights gleamed in the distance, and the people were already astir.

In fact, a man on horseback galloped down before the passengers were well collected together, and a careful investigation being instituted it appeared that the lady inside had broken her lamp, and the gentleman his head; that the two front outsides had escaped with black eyes, the box with a bloody nose, the coachman with a contusion on the temple, Mr. Squeers with a portmanteau bruise on his back, and the remaining passengers without any injury at all—thanks to the softness of the snow-drift in which they had been overturned. These facts were no sooner thoroughly ascertained than the lady gave several indications of fainting, but being forewarned that if she did, she must be carried on some gentleman's shoulders to the nearest public-house, she prudently thought better of it, and walked back with the rest.

They found on reaching it, that it was a lonely place with no very great accommodation in the way of apartments—that portion of its resources being all comprised in one public room with a sanded floor, and a chair or two. However, a large faggot and a plentiful supply of coals being heaped upon the fire, the appearance of things was not long in mending, and by the time they had washed off all effaceable marks of the late accident, the room was warm and light, which was a most agreeable exchange for the cold and darkness out of doors.

"Well, Mr. Nickleby," said Squeers, insinuating himself into the warmest corner, "you did very right to catch hold of them horses. I should have done it myself if I had come to in time, but I am very glad you did it. You did it very well; very well."

"So well," said the merry-faced gentleman, who did not seem to approve very much of the patronising tone adopted by Squeers, "that if they had not been firmly checked when they were, you would most probably have had no brains left to teach with."

This remark called up a discourse relative to the promptitude Nicholas had displayed, and he was overwhelmed with compliments and commendations.

"I am very glad to have escaped, of course," observed Squeers; "every man is glad when he escapes from danger, but if any one of my charges had been hurt—if I had been prevented from restoring any one of these little boys to his parents whole and sound as I received him—what would have been my feelings? Why the wheel a-top of my head would have been far preferable to it."

"Are they all brothers, Sir?" inquired the lady who had carried the "Davy" or safety-lamp.

"In one sense they are, ma'am," replied Squeers, diving into his great-coat pocket for cards. "They are all under the same parental and affectionate treatment. Mrs. Squeers and myself are a mother and father to every one of 'em. Mr. Nickleby, hand the lady them cards, and offer these to the gentlemen. Perhaps they might know of some parents that would be glad to avail themselves of the establishment."

Expressing himself to this effect, Mr. Squeers, who lost no opportunity of advertising gratuitously, placed his hands upon his knees and looked at the pupils with as much benignity as he could possibly affect, while Nicholas, blushing with shame, handed round the cards as directed.

" I hope you suffer no inconvenience from the overturn, ma'am ?" said the merry-faced gentleman addressing the fastidious lady, as though he were charitably desirous to change the subject.

" No bodily inconvenience," replied the lady.

" No mental inconvenience, I hope ?"

" The subject is a very painful one to my feelings, Sir," replied the lady with strong emotion; " and I beg you, as a gentleman, not to refer to it."

" Dear me," said the merry-faced gentleman, looking merrier still, " I merely intended to inquire——"

" I hope no inquiries will be made," said the lady, " or I shall be compelled to throw myself on the protection of the other gentlemen. Landlord, pray direct a boy to keep watch outside the door—and if a green chariot passes in the direction of Grantham, to stop it instantly."

The people of the house were evidently overcome by this request, and when the lady charged the boy to remember, as a means of identifying the expected green chariot, that it would have a coachman with a gold-laced hat on the box, and a footman most probably in silk stockings behind, the attentions of the good woman of the inn were redoubled. Even the box-passenger caught the infection, and growing wonderfully deferential, immediately inquired whether there was not very good society in that neighbourhood, to which the lady replied yes, there was, in a manner which sufficiently implied that she moved at the very tip-top and summit of it all.

" As the guard has gone on horseback to Grantham to get another coach," said the good-tempered gentleman when they had been all sitting round the fire for some time in silence, " and as he must be gone a couple of hours at the very least, I propose a bowl of hot punch. What say you, Sir ? "

This question was addressed to the broken-headed inside, who was a man of very genteel appearance, dressed in mourning. He was not past the middle age, but his hair was grey; it seemed to have been prematurely turned by care or sorrow. He readily acceded to the proposal, and appeared to be prepossessed by the frank good-nature of the individual from whom it emanated.

This latter personage took upon himself the office of tapster when the punch was ready, and after dispensing it all round, led the conversation to the antiquities of York, with which both he and the grey-haired gentleman appeared well acquainted. When this topic flagged, he turned with a smile to the grey-headed gentleman and asked if he could sing.

" I cannot indeed," replied the gentleman, smiling in his turn.

" That's a pity," said the owner of the good-humoured countenance. " Is there nobody here who can sing a song to lighten the time ?"

The passengers one and all protested that they could not; that they wished they could, that they couldn't remember the words of anything without the book, and so forth.

" Perhaps the lady would not object," said the president with great respect, and a merry twinkle in his eye. " Some little Italian thing out of the last opera brought out in town, would be most acceptable I am sure."

As the lady condescended to make no reply, but tossed her head contemptuously, and murmured some further expression of surprise regarding the absence of the green chariot, one or two voices urged upon the president himself the propriety of making an attempt for the general benefit.

" I would if I could," said he of the good-tempered face; " for I hold that in this, as in all other cases where people who are strangers to each other are thrown unexpectedly together, they should endeavour to render themselves as pleasant for the joint sake of the little community as possible."

" I wish the maxim were more generally acted on in all cases," said the grey-headed gentleman.

" I'm glad to hear it," returned the other. " Perhaps, as you can't sing, you'll tell us a story ? "

" Nay. I should ask you."

" After you, I will, with pleasure."

" Indeed !" said the grey-haired gentleman, smiling. " Well, let it be so. I fear the turn of my thoughts is not calculated to lighten the time you must pass here; but you have brought this upon yourselves, and shall judge. We were speaking of York Minster just now. My story shall have some reference to it. Let us call it

THE FIVE SISTERS OF YORK.

After a murmur of approbation from the other passengers, during which the fastidious lady drank a glass of punch unobserved, the grey-headed gentleman thus went on :—

" A great many years ago—for the fifteenth century was scarce two years old at the time, and King Henry the Fourth sat upon the throne of England—there dwelt in the ancient city of York, five maiden sisters, the subjects of my tale.

" These five sisters were all of surpassing beauty. The eldest was in her twenty-third year, the second a year younger, the third a year younger than the second, and the fourth a year younger than the third. They were tall stately figures, with dark flashing eyes and hair of jet; dignity and grace were in their every movement, and the fame of their great beauty had spread through all the country round.

" But if the four elder sisters were lovely, how beautiful was the youngest, a fair creature of sixteen ! The blushing tints in the soft bloom on the fruit, or the delicate painting on the flower, are not more exquisite than was the blending of the rose and lily in her gentle face, or the deep blue of her eye. The vine in all its elegant luxuriance is not more graceful, than were the clusters of rich brown hair that sported around her brow.

The Five Sisters of York.

" If we all had hearts like those which beat so lightly in the bosoms of the young and beautiful, what a heaven this earth would be! If, while our bodies grew old and withered, our hearts could but retain their early youth and freshness, of what avail would be our sorrows and sufferings! But the faint image of Eden which is stamped upon them in childhood, chafes and rubs in our rough struggles with the world, and soon wears away: too often to leave nothing bu' ¬ mournful blank remaining

" The heart of this fair girl bounded with joy and gladness. Devoted attachment to her sisters, and a fervent love of all beautiful things in nature, were its pure affections. Her gleesome voice and merry laugh were the sweetest music of their home. She was its very light and life. The brightest flowers in the garden were reared by her; the caged birds sang when they heard her voice, and pined when they missed its sweetness. Alice, dear Alice; what living thing within the sphere of her gentle witchery, could fail to love her!

" You may seek in vain, now, for the spot on which these sisters lived, for their very names have passed away, and dusty antiquaries tell of them as of a fable. But they dwelt in an old wooden house— old even in those days—with overhanging gables and balconies of rudely-carved oak, which stood within a pleasant orchard, and was surrounded by a rough stone wall, whence a stout archer might have winged an arrow to Saint Mary's abbey. The old abbey flourished then, and the five sisters living on its fair domains, paid yearly dues to the black monks of Saint Benedict, to which fraternity it belonged.

" It was a bright and sunny morning in the pleasant time of summer when one of these black monks emerged from the abbey portal, and bent his steps towards the house of the fair sisters. Heaven above was blue, and earth beneath was green; the river glistened like a path of diamonds in the sun, the birds poured forth their songs from the shady trees, the lark soared high above the waving corn, and the deep buzz of insects filled the air. Everything looked gay and smiling; but the holy man walked gloomily on, with his eyes bent upon the ground. The beauty of the earth is but a breath, and man is but a shadow. What sympathy should a holy preacher have with either?

" With eyes bent upon the ground, then, or only raised enough to prevent his stumbling over such obstacles as lay in his way, the religious man moved slowly forward until he reached a small postern in the wall of the sisters' orchard, through which he passed, closing it behind him. The noise of soft voices in conversation and of merry laughter fell upon his ear ere he had advanced many paces; and raising his eyes higher than was his humble wont, he descried, at no great distance, the five sisters seated on the grass, with Alice in the centre, all busily plying their customary task of embroidering.

" ' Save you, fair daughters,' said the friar; and fair in truth they were. Even a monk might have loved them as choice master-pieces of his Maker's hand.

" The sisters saluted the holy man with becoming reverence, and the eldest motioned him to a mossy seat beside them. But the good friar shook his head, and bumped himself down on a very hard stone,—at which, no doubt, approving angels were gratified.

" ' Ye were merry daughters,' said the monk.

" ' You know how light of heart sweet Alice is,' replied the eldest sister, passing her fingers through the tresses of the smiling girl.

" ' And what joy and cheerfulness it wakes up within us, to see all nature beaming in brightness and sunshine, father,' added Alice, blushing beneath the stern look of the recluse.

" The monk answered not, save by a grave inclination of the head, and the sisters pursued their task in silence.

" ' Still wasting the precious hours,' said the monk at length, turning to the eldest sister as he spoke, ' still wasting the precious hours on this vain trifling. Alas, alas! that the few bubbles on the surface of eternity—all that Heaven wills we should see of that dark deep stream —should be so lightly scattered!'

" ' Father,' urged the maiden, pausing, as did each of the others, in her busy task, ' we have prayed at matins, our daily alms have been distributed at the gate, the sick peasants have been tended,—all our morning tasks have been performed. I hope our occupation is a blameless one?'

" ' See here,' said the friar, taking the frame from her hand, ' an intricate winding of gaudy colours without purpose or object, unless it be that one day it is destined for some vain ornament, to minister to the pride of your frail and giddy sex. Day after day has been employed upon this senseless task, and yet it is not half accomplished. The shade of each departed day falls upon our graves, and the worm exults as he beholds it, to know that we are hastening thither. Daughters, is there no better way to pass the fleeting hours?'

" The four elder sisters cast down their eyes as if abashed by the holy man's reproof, but Alice raised hers, and bent them mildly on the friar.

" ' Our dear mother,' said the maiden; ' Heaven rest her soul.'

" ' Amen!' cried the Friar in a deep voice.

" ' Our dear mother!' faltered the fair Alice, ' was living when these long tasks began, and bade us, when she should be no more, ply them in all discretion and cheerfulness in our leisure hours: she said that if in harmless mirth and maidenly pursuits we passed those hours together, they would prove the happiest and most peaceful of our lives, and that if in later times we went forth into the world, and mingled with its cares and trials—if, allured by its temptations and dazzled by its glitter, we ever forgot that love and duty which should bind in holy ties the children of one loved parent—a glance at the old work of our common girlhood would awaken good thoughts of by-gone days, and soften our hearts to affection and love.'

" ' Alice speaks truly, father,' said the elder sister, somewhat proudly. And so saying she resumed her work, as did the others.

" It was a kind of sampler of large size, that each sister had before her; the device was of a complex and intricate description, and the pattern and colours of all five were the same. The sisters bent gracefully over their work, and the monk resting his chin upon his hands, looked from one to the other in silence.

" ' How much better,' he said at length, ' to shun all such thoughts and chances, and in the peaceful shelter of the church devote your lives to Heaven! Infancy, childhood, the prime of life, and old age, wither as rapidly as they crowd upon each other. Think how human dust rolls onward to the tomb, and turning your faces steadily towards that goal, avoid the cloud which takes its rise among the pleasures of the world and cheats the senses of their votaries. The veil, daughters, the veil !'

" ' Never, sisters,' cried Alice. ' Barter not the light and air of heaven, and the freshness of earth and all the beautiful things which breathe upon it, for the cold cloister and the cell. Nature's own blessings are the proper goods of life, and we may share them sinlessly together. To die is our heavy portion, but, oh, let us die with life about us ; when our cold hearts cease to beat, let warm hearts be beating near ; let our last look be upon the bounds which God has set to his own bright skies, and not on stone walls and bars of iron. Dear sisters, let us live and die, if you list, in this green garden's compass ; only shun the gloom and sadness of a cloister, and we shall be happy.'

" The tears fell fast from the maiden's eyes as she closed her impassioned appeal, and hid her face in the bosom of her sister.

" ' Take comfort, Alice,' said the eldest, kissing her fair forehead. ' The veil shall never cast its shadow on thy young brow. How say you, sisters ? For yourselves you speak, and not for Alice, or for me.'

" The sisters, as with one accord, cried that their lot was cast together, and that there were dwellings for peace and virtue beyond the convent's walls.

" ' Father,' said the eldest lady, rising with dignity, ' you hear our final resolve. The same pious care which enriched the abbey of Saint Mary, and left us, orphans, to its holy guardianship, directed that no constraint should be imposed upon our inclinations, but that we should be free to live according to our choice. Let us hear no more of this, we pray you. Sisters, it is nearly noon. Let us take shelter until evening !' With a reverence to the Friar, the lady rose and walked towards the house hand in hand with Alice ; and the other sisters followed.

" The holy man, who had often urged the same point before, but had never met with so direct a repulse, walked some little distance behind, with his eyes bent upon the earth, and his lips moving *as if* in prayer. As the sisters reached the porch, he quickened his pace and called upon them to stop.

" ' Stay,' said the monk, raising his right hand in the air, and directing an angry glance by turns at Alice and the eldest sister, ' Stay, and hear from me what these recollections are, which you would cherish above eternity, and awaken—if in mercy they slumbered—by means of idle toys. The memory of earthly things is charged in after life with bitter disappointment, affliction, and death ; with dreary change and wasting sorrow. The time will one day come when a glance at those unmeaning baubles shall tear open deep wounds in the hearts of some among you, and strike to your inmost souls. When that hour arrives—and, mark me, come it will—turn from the world to which you clung, to the refuge which you spurned. Find me the cell which shall be colder than the fire of mortals grows when dimmed by calamity and trial, and there weep for the dreams of youth. These things are Heaven's will, not mine,' said the friar, subduing his voice as he looked round upon the shrinking girls. 'The Virgin's blessing be upon you, daughters!'

"With these words he disappeared through the postern, and the sisters hastening into the house were seen no more that day.

"But nature will smile though priests may frown, and next day the sun shone brightly, and on the next, and the next again. And in the morning's glare and the evening's soft repose, the five sisters still walked, or worked, or beguiled the time by cheerful conversation in their quiet orchard.

"Time passed away as a tale that is told; faster indeed than many tales that are told, of which number I fear this may be one. The house of the five sisters stood where it did, and the same trees cast their pleasant shade upon the orchard grass. The sisters too were there, and lovely as at first, but a change had come over their dwelling. Sometimes there was the clash of armour, and the gleaming of the moon on caps of steel, and at others jaded coursers were spurred up to the gate, and a female form glided hurriedly forth as if eager to demand tidings of the weary messenger. A goodly train of knights and ladies lodged one night within the abbey walls, and next day rode away with two of the fair sisters among them. Then horsemen began to come less frequently, and seemed to bring bad tidings when they did, and at length they ceased to come at all, and foot-sore peasants slunk to the gate after sunset and did their errand there by stealth. Once a vassal was despatched in haste to the abbey at dead of night, and when morning came there were sounds of woe and wailing in the sisters' house; and after this a mournful silence fell upon it, and knight or lady, horse or armour, was seen about it no more.

"There was a sullen darkness in the sky, and the sun had gone angrily down, tinting the dull clouds with the last traces of his wrath, when the same black monk walked slowly on with folded arms, within a stone's-throw of the abbey. A blight had fallen on the trees and shrubs; and the wind at length beginning to break the unnatural stillness that had prevailed all day, sighed heavily from time to time, as though foretelling in grief the ravages of the coming storm. The bat skimmed in fantastic flights through the heavy air, and the ground was alive with crawling things, whose instinct brought them forth to swell and fatten in the rain.

"No longer were the friar's eyes directed to the earth; they were cast abroad, and roamed from point to point, as if the gloom and desolation of the scene found a quick response in his own bosom. Again he paused near the sisters' house, and again he entered by the postern.

"But not again did his ear encounter the sound of laughter, or his eyes rest upon the beautiful figures of the five sisters. All was silent and deserted. The boughs of the trees were bent and broken, and the grass had grown long and rank. No light feet had pressed it for many, many, a day.

" With the indifference or abstraction of one well accustomed to the change, the monk glided into the house, and entered a low, dark room. Four sisters sat there. Their black garments made their pale faces whiter still, and time and sorrow had worked deep ravages. They were stately yet ; but the flush and pride of beauty were gone.

" And Alice—where was she ? In heaven.

" The monk—even the monk—could bear with some grief here ; for it was long since these sisters had met, and there were furrows in their blanched faces which years could never plough. He took his seat in silence, and motioned them to continue their speech.

" ' They are here, sisters,' said the elder lady in a trembling voice. ' I have never borne to look upon them since, and now I blame myself for my weakness. What is there in her memory that we should dread ? To call up our old days shall be a solemn pleasure yet.'

" She glanced at the monk as she spoke, and, opening a cabinet, brought forth the five frames of work, completed long before. Her step was firm, but her hand trembled as she produced the last one ; and when the feelings of the other sisters gushed forth at sight of it, her pent-up tears made way, and she sobbed ' God bless her !'

" The monk rose and advanced towards them. ' It was almost the last thing she touched in health,' he said in a low voice.

" ' It was,' cried the elder lady, weeping bitterly.

" The monk turned to the second sister.

" ' The gallant youth who looked into thine eyes, and hung upon thy very breath when first he saw thee intent upon this pastime, lies buried on a plain whereof the turf is red with blood. Rusty fragments of armour once brightly burnished, lie rotting on the ground, and are as little distinguishable for his, as are the bones that crumble in the mould !'

" The lady groaned and wrung her hands.

" ' The policy of courts,' he continued, turning to the two other sisters, ' drew ye from your peaceful home to scenes of revelry and splendour. The same policy, and the restless ambition of proud and fiery men, have sent ye back, widowed maidens, and humbled out-casts. Do I speak truly ?'

" The sobs of the two sisters were their only reply.

" ' There is little need,' said the monk, with a meaning look, ' to fritter away the time in gewgaws which shall raise up the pale ghosts of hopes of early years. Bury them, heap penance and mortification on their heads, keep them down, and let the convent be their grave !'

" The sisters asked for three days to deliberate, and felt that night as though the veil were indeed the fitting shroud for their dead joys. But morning came again, and though the boughs of the orchard trees drooped and ran wild upon the ground, it was the same orchard still. The grass was coarse and high, but there was yet the spot on which

they had so often sat together when change and sorrow were but names.
There was every walk and nook which Alice had made glad, and in the
minster nave was one flat stone beneath which she slept in peace.

" And could they, remembering how her young heart had sickened
at the thought of cloistered walls, look upon her grave in garbs which
would chill the very ashes within it ? Could they bow down in prayer,
and when all Heaven turned to hear them bring the dark shade of
sadness on one angel's face ? No.

" They sent abroad to artists of great celebrity in those times, and
having obtained the church's sanction to their work of piety, caused to
be executed in five large compartments of richly stained glass a faithful
copy of their old embroidery work. These were fitted into a large window until that time bare of ornament, and when the sun shone brightly,
as she had so well loved to see it, the familiar patterns were reflected in
their original colours, and throwing a stream of brilliant light upon the
pavement, fell warmly on the name of 𝔄𝔩𝔦𝔠𝔢.

" For many hours in every day the sisters paced slowly up and
down the nave, or knelt by the side of the flat broad stone. Only
three were seen in the customary place after many years, then but
two, and for a long time afterwards, but one solitary female bent with
age. At length she came no more, and the stone bore five plain
Christian names.

" That stone has worn away and been replaced by others, and many
generations have come and gone since then. Time has softened down
the colours, but the same stream of light still falls upon the forgotten
tomb, of which no trace remains ; and to this day the stranger is shown
in York cathedral an old window called The Five Sisters."

" That's a melancholy tale," said the merry-faced gentleman, emptying his glass.

" It is a tale of life, and life is made up of such sorrows," returned
the other, courteously, but in a grave and sad tone of voice.

" There are shades in all good pictures, but there are lights too, if we
choose to contemplate them," said the gentleman with the merry face.
" The youngest sister in your tale was always light-hearted."

" And died early," said the other, gently.

" She would have died earlier, perhaps, had she been less happy,"
said the first speaker, with much feeling. " Do you think the sisters
who loved her so well, would have grieved the less if her life had been
one of gloom and sadness ? If anything could soothe the first sharp
pain of a heavy loss, it would be—with me—the reflection, that those
I mourned, by being innocently happy here, and loving all about them,
had prepared themselves for a purer and happier world. The sun does
not shine upon this fair earth to meet frowning eyes, depend upon it."

" I believe you are right," said the gentleman who had told the story.

" Believe !" retorted the other, " can anybody doubt it ? Take any
subject of sorrowful regret, and see with how much of pleasure it is
associated. The recollection of past pleasure may become pain——"

" It does," interposed the other.

" Well; it does. To remember happiness which cannot be restored is pain, but of a softened kind. Our recollections are unfortunately mingled with much that we deplore, and with many actions which we bitterly repent; still in the most chequered life I firmly think there are so many little rays of sunshine to look back upon, that I do not believe any mortal (unless he had put himself without the pale of hope) would deliberately drain a goblet of the waters of Lethe, if he had it in his power."

" Possibly you are correct in that belief," said the grey-haired gentleman after a short reflection. " I am inclined to think you are."

" Why, then," replied the other, " the good in this state of existence preponderates over the bad, let miscalled philosophers tell us what they will. If our affections be tried, our affections are our consolation and comfort ; and memory, however sad, is the best and purest link between this world and a better.

" But come ; I'll tell you a story of another kind."

After a very brief silence the merry-faced gentleman sent round the punch, and glancing slily at the fastidious lady, who seemed desperately apprehensive that he was going to relate something improper, began

THE BARON OF GROGZWIG.

" The Baron Von Koëldwethout, of Grogzwig in Germany, was as likely a young baron as you would wish to see. I needn't say that he lived in a castle, because that's of course ; neither need I say that he lived in an old castle, for what German baron ever lived in a new one ? There were many strange circumstances connected with this venerable building, among which not the least startling and mysterious were, that when the wind blew, it rumbled in the chimneys, or even howled among the trees in the neighbouring forest ; and that when the moon shone, she found her way through certain small loopholes in the wall, and actually made some parts of the wide halls and galleries quite light, while she left others in gloomy shadow. I believe that one of the baron's ancestors, being short of money, had inserted a dagger in a gentleman who called one night to ask his way, and it *was* supposed that these miraculous occurrences took place in consequence. And yet I hardly know how that could have been, either, because the baron's ancestor, who was an amiable man, felt very sorry afterwards for having been so rash, and laying violent hands upon a quantity of stone and timber which belonged to a weaker baron, built a chapel as an apology, and so took a receipt from Heaven in full of all demands.

" Talking of the baron's ancestor puts me in mind of the baron's great claims to respect on the score of his pedigree. I am afraid to say, I am sure, how many ancestors the baron had; but I know that he had a great many more than any other man of his time, and I only wish that he had lived in these latter days that he might have had more. It is a very hard thing upon the great men of past centuries, that they should have come into the world so soon, because a man who was born three or four hundred years ago, cannot reasonably be expected to have had as many relations before him as a man who is born now. The last man, whoever he is—and he may be a cobbler or some low vulgar dog for aught we know—will have a longer pedigree than the greatest nobleman now alive : and I contend that this is not fair.

" Well, but the Baron Von Koëldwethout of Grogzwig—he was a fine swarthy fellow, with dark hair and large mustachios, who rode a-hunting in clothes of Lincoln green, with russet boots on his feet, and a bugle slung over his shoulder like the guard of a long stage. When he blew this bugle, four-and-twenty other gentlemen of inferior rank, in Lincoln green a little coarser, and russet boots with a little thicker soles, turned out directly, and away galloped the whole train, with spears in their hands like lackered area railings, to hunt down the boars, or perhaps encounter a bear, in which latter case the baron killed him first and greased his whiskers with him afterwards.

" This was a merry life for the Baron of Grogzwig, and a merrier still for the baron's retainers, who drank Rhine wine every night till they fell under the table, and then had the bottles on the floor, and called for pipes.   Never were such jolly, roystering, rollicking, merry-making blades, as the jovial crew of Grogzwig.

" But the pleasures of the table, or the pleasures of under the table, require a little variety ; especially when the same five-and-twenty people sit daily down to the same board, to discuss the same subjects, and tell the same stories.   The baron grew weary, and wanted excite-ment.   He took to quarrelling with his gentlemen, and tried kicking two or three of them every day after dinner.   This was a pleasant change at first ; but it became monotonous after a week or so, and the baron fell quite out of sorts, and cast about in despair for some new amusement.

" One night, after a day's sport in which he had outdone Nimrod or Gillingwater, and slaughtered ' another fine bear ' and brought him home in triumph, the Baron Von Koëldwethout sat moodily at the head of his table, eyeing the smoky roof of the hall with a discontented aspect. He swallowed huge bumpers of wine, but the more he swallowed, the more he frowned : the gentlemen who had been honoured with the dangerous distinction of sitting on his right and left, imitated him to a miracle in the drinking, and frowned at each other.

" ' I will !' cried the baron suddenly, smiting the table with his right hand, and twirling his moustache with his left. ' Fill to the Lady of Grogzwig.'

" The four-and-twenty Lincoln greens turned pale, with the excep-tion of their four-and-twenty noses, which were unchangeable.

" ' I said to the Lady of Grogzwig,' repeated the baron, looking round the board.

" ' To the Lady of Grogzwig !' shouted the Lincoln greens ; and down their four-and-twenty throats went four-and-twenty imperial pints of such rare old hock, that they smacked their eight-and-forty lips, and winked again.

" ' The fair daughter of the Baron Von Swillenhausen,' said Koëld-wethout, condescending to explain. ' We will demand her in marriage of her father, ere the sun goes down to-morrow. If he refuse our suit, we will cut off his nose.'

" A hoarse murmur arose from the company, and every man touched, first the hilt of his sword, and then the tip of his nose, with appalling significance.

" What a pleasant thing filial piety is to contemplate! If the daughter of the Baron Von Swillenhausen had pleaded a pre-occupied heart, or fallen at her father's feet and corned them in tears, or only fainted away, and complimented the old gentleman in frantic ejaculations, the odds are a hundred to one, but Swillenhausen castle would have been turned out at window, or rather the baron turned out at window, and the castle demolished. The damsel held her peace however when an early messenger bore the request of Von Koëldwethout next morning, and modestly retired to her chamber, from the casement of which she watched the coming of the suitor and his retinue. She was no sooner assured that the horseman with the large moustachios was her proffered husband, than she hastened to her father's presence, and expressed her readiness to sacrifice herself to secure his peace. The venerable baron caught his child to his arms, and shed a wink of joy.

" There was great feasting at the castle that day. The four-and-twenty Lincoln greens of Von Koëldwethout exchanged vows of eternal friendship with twelve Lincoln greens of Von Swillenhausen, and promised the old baron that they would drink his wine ' Till all was blue' —meaning probably until their whole countenances had acquired the same tint as their noses. Everybody slapped everybody else's back when the time for parting came ; and the Baron Von Koëldwethout and his followers rode gaily home.

" For six mortal weeks the bears and boars had a holiday. The houses of Koëldwethout and Swillenhausen were united; the spears rusted, and the baron's bugle grew hoarse for lack of blowing.

" These were great times for the four-and-twenty ; but, alas! their high and palmy days had taken boots to themselves, and were already walking off.

" ' My dear,' said the baroness.

" ' My love,' said the baron.

" ' Those coarse, noisy men—'

" ' Which, ma'am ?' said the baron starting.

" The baroness pointed from the window at which they stood, to the court-yard beneath, where the unconscious Lincoln greens were taking a copious stirrup-cup preparatory to issuing forth after a boar or two.

" ' My hunting train, ma'am,' said the baron.

" ' Disband them, love,' murmured the baroness.

" ' Disband them !' cried the baron, in amazement.

" ' To please me love,' replied the baroness.

" ' To please the devil ma'am,' answered the baron.

" Whereupon the baroness uttered a great cry, and swooned away at the baron's feet.

" What could the baron do? He called for the lady's maid, and roared for the doctor; and then rushing into the yard, kicked the two Lincoln greens who were the most used to it, and cursing the others all round, bade them go to——but never mind where. I don't know the German for it, or I would put it delicately that way.

" It is not for me to say by what means or by what degrees, some wives manage to keep down some husbands as they do, although I may have my private opinion on the subject, and may think that no Member of Parliament ought to be married, inasmuch as three married members out of every four, must vote according to their wives' consciences (if there be such things), and not according to their own. All I need say just now is, that the Baroness Von Koëldwethout somehow or other acquired great control over the Baron Von Koëldwethout, and that little by little, and bit by bit, and day by day, and year by year, the baron got the worst of some disputed question, or was slily unhorsed from some old hobby; and that by the time he was a fat hearty fellow of forty-eight or thereabouts, he had no feasting, no revelry, no hunting train, and no hunting—nothing in short that he liked, or used to have; and that although he was as fierce as a lion and as bold as brass, he was decidedly snubbed and put down by his own lady, in his own castle of Grogzwig.

" Nor was this the whole extent of the baron's misfortunes. About a year after his nuptials there came into the world a lusty young baron, in whose honour a great many fireworks were let off, and a great many dozens of wine drunk ; but next year there came a young baroness, and next year another young baron, and so on every year either a baron or baroness (and one year both together), until the baron found himself the father of a small family of twelve. Upon every one of these anniversaries the venerable Baroness Von Swillenhausen was nervously sensitive for the well-being of her child the Baroness Von Koëldwethout, and although it was not found that the good lady ever did anything material towards contributing to her child's recovery, still she made it a point of duty to be as nervous as possible at the castle of Grogzwig, and to divide her time between moral observations on the baron's housekeeping, and bewailing the hard lot of her unhappy daughter. And if the Baron of Grogzwig, a little hurt and irritated at this, took heart and ventured to suggest that his wife was at least no worse off than the wives of other barons, the Baroness Von Swillenhausen begged all persons to take notice, that nobody but she sympathised with her dear daughter's sufferings ; upon which her relations and friends remarked, that to be sure she did cry a great deal more than her son-in-law, and that if there was a hard-hearted brute alive, it was that Baron of Grogzwig.

" The poor baron bore it all as long as he could, and when he could bear it no longer lost his appetite and his spirits, and sat himself gloomily and dejectedly down. But there were worse troubles yet in store for him, and as they came on, his melancholy and sadness increased. Times changed. He got into debt. The Grogzwig coffers ran low, though the Swillenhausen family had looked upon them as inexhaustible, and just when the baroness was on the point of making a thirteenth addition to the family pedigree, Von Koëldwethout discovered that he had no means of replenishing them.

" ' I don't see what is to be done,' said the Baron. ' I think I'll kill myself.'

" This was a bright idea. The baron took an old hunting-knife from a cupboard hard by, and having sharpened it on his boot, made what boys call ' an offer ' at his throat.

" ' Hem !' said the Baron, stopping short. ' Perhaps it's not sharp enough.'

" The baron sharpened it again, and made another offer, when his hand was arrested by a loud screaming among the young barons and baronesses, who had a nursery in an up-stairs tower with iron bars outside the window, to prevent their tumbling out into the moat.

" ' If I had been a bachelor,' said the baron sighing ; ' I might have done it fifty times over, without being interrupted. Hallo. Put a flask of wine and the largest pipe in the little vaulted room behind the hall.'

" One of the domestics in a very kind manner executed the baron's order in the course of half an hour or so, and Von Koëldwethout being apprised thereof, strode to the vaulted room, the walls of which being of dark shining wood gleamed in the light of the blazing logs which were piled upon the hearth. The bottle and pipe were ready, and upon the whole the place looked very comfortable.

" ' Leave the lamp,' said the baron.

" ' Anything else, my lord ?' inquired the domestic.

" ' The room,' replied the baron. The domestic obeyed, and the baron locked the door.

" ' I'll smoke a last pipe,' said the baron, ' and then I'll be off.' So, putting the knife upon the table till he wanted it, and tossing off a goodly measure of wine, the Lord of Grogzwig threw himself back in his chair, stretched his legs out before the fire, and puffed away.

" He thought about a great many things—about his present troubles and past days of bachelorship, and about the Lincoln greens long since dispersed up and down the country no one knew whither, with the exception of two who had been unfortunately beheaded, and four who had killed themselves with drinking. His mind was running upon bears and boars, when in the process of draining his glass to the bottom he raised his eyes, and saw for the first time and with unbounded asto- nishment, that he was not alone.

" No, he was not ; for on the opposite side of the fire there sat with folded arms a wrinkled hideous figure, with deeply sunk and bloodshot eyes, and an immensely long cadaverous face, shadowed by jagged and matted locks of coarse black hair. He wore a kind of tunic of a dull blueish colour, which the baron observed on regarding it attentively, was clasped or ornamented down the front with coffin handles. His legs too, were encased in coffin plates as though in armour, and over his left shoulder he wore a short dusky cloak, which seemed made of a remnant of some pall. He took no notice of the baron, but was in- tently eyeing the fire.

" ' Halloa !' said the baron, stamping his foot to attract attention.

" ' Halloa !' replied the stranger, moving his eyes towards the baron, but not his face or himself. ' What now ?'

" ' What now !' replied the baron, nothing daunted by his hollow voice and lustreless eyes, ' *I* should ask that question. How did you get here ?'

" ' Through the door,' replied the figure.

" ' What are you ?' says the baron.

" ' A man,' replied the figure.

" ' I don't believe it,' says the baron.

" ' Disbelieve it then,' says the figure.

" ' I will,' rejoined the baron.

" The figure looked at the bold Baron of Grogzwig for some time, and then said familiarly,

" ' There's no coming over you, I see. I'm not a man !'

" ' What are you then ?' asked the baron.

" ' A genius,' replied the figure.

" ' You don't look much like one,' returned the Baron scornfully.

" ' I am the Genius of Despair and Suicide,' said the apparition. ' Now you know me.'

" With these words the apparition turned towards the baron as if composing himself for a talk—and what was very remarkable was, that he threw his cloak aside, and displaying a stake which was run through the centre of his body, pulled it out with a jerk, and laid it on the table as composedly as if it had been his walking-stick.

" ' Now,' said the figure, glancing at the hunting knife, ' are you ready for me ?'

" ' Not quite,' rejoined the baron ; ' I must finish this pipe first.'

" ' Look sharp then,' said the figure.

" ' You seem in a hurry,' said the baron.

" ' Why, yes, I am,' answered the figure ; ' they're doing a pretty brisk business in my way over in England and France just now, and my time is a good deal taken up.'

" ' Do you drink ?' said the baron, touching the bottle with the bowl of his pipe.

" ' Nine times out of ten, and then very hard,' rejoined the figure, drily.

" ' Never in moderation ?' asked the baron.

" ' Never,' replied the figure, with a shudder, ' that breeds cheerfulness.'

" The baron took another look at his new friend, whom he thought an uncommonly queer customer, and at length enquired whether he took any active part in such little proceedings as that which he had in contemplation.

" ' No,' replied the figure, evasively ; ' but I am always present.'

" ' Just to see fair, I suppose,' said the baron.

" ' Just that,' replied the figure, playing with his stake, and examining the ferrule. ' Be as quick as you can, will you, for there's a young gentleman who is afflicted with too much money and leisure wanting me now, I find.'

" ' Going to kill himself because he has too much money !' exclaimed the baron, quite tickled ; 'Ha! ha! that's a good one.' (This was the first time the baron had laughed for many a long day.)

" 'I say,' expostulated the figure, looking very much scared ; 'don't do that again.'

" 'Why not ?' demanded the baron.

" 'Because it gives me a pain all over,' replied the figure. 'Sigh as much as you please ; that does me good.'

" The baron sighed mechanically at the mention of the word, and the figure brightening up again, handed him the hunting-knife with most winning politeness.

" 'It's not a bad idea though,' said the baron, feeling the edge of the weapon ; 'a man killing himself because he has too much money.'

" 'Pooh!' said the apparition, petulantly, 'no better than a man's killing himself because he has got none or little.'

" Whether the genius unintentionally committed himself in saying this, or whether he thought the baron's mind was so thoroughly made up that it didn't matter what he said, I have no means of knowing. I only know that the baron stopped his hand all of a sudden, opened his eyes wide, and looked as if quite a new light had come upon him for the first time.

" 'Why, certainly,' said Von Koëldwethout, 'nothing is too bad to be retrieved.'

" 'Except empty coffers,' cried the genius.

" 'Well ; but they may be one day filled again,' said the baron.

" 'Scolding wives,' snarled the genius.

" 'Oh! They may be made quiet,' said the baron.

" 'Thirteen children,' shouted the genius.

" 'Can't all go wrong, surely,' said the baron.

" The genius was evidently growing very savage with the baron for holding these opinions all at once, but he tried to laugh it off, and said if he would let him know when he had left off joking he should feel obliged to him.

" 'But I am not joking ; I was never farther from it,' remonstrated the baron.

" 'Well, I am glad to hear that,' said the genius, looking very grim, 'because a joke, without any figure of speech, is the death of me. Come. Quit this dreary world at once.'

" 'I don't know,' said the baron, playing with the knife ; 'it's a dreary one certainly, but I don't think yours is much better, for you have not the appearance of being particularly comfortable. That puts me in mind—what security have I that I shall be any the better for going out of the world after all!' he cried, starting up ; 'I never thought of that.'

" 'Dispatch,' cried the figure, gnashing its teeth.

" 'Keep off,' said the baron. 'I'll brood over miseries no longer, but put a good face on the matter, and try the fresh air and the bears again ; and if that don't do, I'll talk to the baroness soundly, and cut the Von Swillenhausens dead.' With this, the baron fell into his chair and laughed so loud and boisterously, that the room rang with it.

" The figure fell back a pace or two, regarding the baron meanwhile with a look of intense terror, and when he had ceased, caught up the stake, plunged it violently into its body, uttered a frightful howl, and disappeared.

" Von Koëldwethout never saw it again. Having once made up his mind to action, he soon brought the baroness and the Von Swillenhausens to reason, and died many years afterwards, not a rich man that I am aware of, but certainly a happy one : leaving behind him a numerous family, who had been carefully educated in bear and boar-hunting under his own personal eye. And my advice to all men is, that if ever they become hipped and melancholy from similar causes (as very many men do), they look at both sides of the question, applying a magnifying glass to the best one ; and if they still feel tempted to retire without leave, that they smoke a large pipe and drink a full bottle first, and profit by the laudable example of the Baron of Grogzwig."

———

" The fresh coach is ready, ladies and gentlemen, if you please," said a new driver, looking in.

This intelligence caused the punch to be finished in a great hurry, and prevented any discussion relative to the last story. Mr. Squeers was observed to draw the grey-headed gentleman on one side and to ask a question with great apparent interest ; it bore reference to the Five Sisters of York, and was in fact an enquiry whether he could inform him how much per annum the Yorkshire convents got in those days with their boarders.

The journey was then resumed. Nicholas fell asleep towards morning, and when he awoke found, with great regret, that during his nap both the Baron of Grogzwig and the grey-haired gentleman had got down and were gone. The day dragged on uncomfortably enough, and about six o'clock that night he and Mr. Squeers, and the little boys, and their united luggage, were all put down together at the George and New Inn, Greta Bridge.

———

CHAPTER VII.

MR. AND MRS. SQUEERS AT HOME

MR. SQUEERS being safely landed, left Nicholas and the boys standing with the luggage in the road, to amuse themselves by looking at the coach as it changed horses, while he ran into the tavern and went through the leg-stretching process at the bar. After some minutes he returned with his legs thoroughly stretched, if the hue of his nose and a short hiccup afforded any criterion, and at the same time there came out of the yard a rusty pony-chaise and a cart, driven by two labouring men.

" Put the boys and the boxes into the cart," said Squeers, rubbing his hands ; " and this young man and me will go on in the chaise. Get in, Nickleby."

Nicholas obeyed, and Mr. Squeers with some difficulty inducing the pony to obey also, they started off, leaving the cart-load of infant misery to follow at leisure.

" Are you cold, Nickleby ?" inquired Squeers, after they had travelled some distance in silence.

" Rather, Sir, I must say."

" Well, I don't find fault with that," said Squeers ; " it's a long journey this weather."

" Is it much further to Dotheboys Hall, Sir ?" asked Nicholas.

" About three mile from here," replied Squeers. " But you needn't call it a Hall down here."

Nicholas coughed, as if he would like to know why.

" The fact is, it ain't a Hall," observed Squeers drily.

" Oh, indeed !" said Nicholas, whom this piece of intelligence much astonished.

" No," replied Squeers. " We call it a Hall up in London, because it sounds better, but they don't know it by that name in these parts. A man may call his house an island if he likes ; there's no act of Parliament against that, I believe."

" I believe not, Sir," rejoined Nicholas.

Squeers eyed his companion slily at the conclusion of this little dialogue, and finding that he had grown thoughtful and appeared in nowise disposed to volunteer any observations, contented himself with lashing the pony until they reached their journey's end.

" Jump out," said Squeers. " Hallo there ! come and put this horse up. Be quick, will you."

While the schoolmaster was uttering these and other impatient cries, Nicholas had time to observe that the school was a long cold-looking house, one story high, with a few straggling outbuildings behind, and a barn and stable adjoining. After the lapse of a minute or two, the noise of somebody unlocking the yard gate was heard, and presently a tall lean boy, with a lantern in his hand, issued forth.

" Is that you, Smike ?" cried Squeers.

" Yes, Sir," replied the boy.

" Then why the devil didn't you come before ? "

" Please, Sir, I fell asleep over the fire," answered Smike, with humility.

" Fire ! what fire ? Where's there a fire ?" demanded the schoolmaster, sharply.

" Only in the kitchen, Sir," replied the boy. " Missus said as I was sitting up, I might go in there, for a warm."

" Your missus is a fool," retorted Squeers. " You'd have been a deuced deal more wakeful in the cold, I'll engage."

By this time Mr. Squeers had dismounted ; and after ordering the boy to see to the pony, and to take care that he hadn't any more corn that night, he told Nicholas to wait at the front door a minute while he went round and let him in.

A host of unpleasant misgivings, which had been crowding upon Nicholas during the whole journey, thronged into his mind with redoubled force when he was left alone. His great distance from home and the impossibility of reaching it, except on foot, should he feel ever so anxious to return, presented itself to him in most alarming colours ; and as he looked up at the dreary house and dark windows, and upon the wild country round covered with snow, he felt a depression of heart and spirit which he had never experienced before.

" Now then," cried Squeers, poking his head out at the front door. " Where are you, Nickleby ? "

" Here, Sir ?" replied Nicholas.

" Come in then," said Squeers, " the wind blows in at this door fit to knock a man off his legs."

Nicholas sighed and hurried in. Mr. Squeers having bolted the door to keep it shut, ushered him into a small parlour scantily furnished with a few chairs, a yellow map hung against the wall, and a couple of tables, one of which bore some preparations for supper ; while on the other, a tutor's assistant, a Murray's grammar, half a dozen cards of terms, and a worn letter directed to Wackford Squeers, Esquire, were arranged in picturesque confusion.

They had not been in this apartment a couple of minutes when a female bounced into the room, and seizing Mr. Squeers by the throat gave him two loud kisses, one close after the other, like a postman's knock. The lady, who was of a large raw-boned figure, was about half a head taller than Mr. Squeers, and was dressed in a dimity night jacket with her hair in papers ; she had also a dirty night-cap on, relieved by a yellow cotton handkerchief which tied it under the chin.

" How is my Squeery ?" said this lady in a playful manner, and a very hoarse voice.

" Quite well, my love," replied Squeers. " How are the cows ?"

" All right, every one of 'em," answered the lady.

" And the pigs ?" said Squeers.

" As well as they were when you went away."

" Come ; that's a blessing," said Squeers, pulling off his great-coat. " The boys are all as they were, I suppose ? "

" Oh, yes, they're well enough," replied Mrs. Squeers, snappishly. " That young Pitcher's had a fever."

" No ! " exclaimed Squeers. " Damn that boy, he's always at something of that sort."

" Never was such a boy, I do believe," said Mrs. Squeers ; " whatever he has, is always catching too. I say it's obstinacy, and nothing shall ever convince me that it isn't. I'd beat it out of him, and I told you that six months ago."

" So you did, my love," rejoined Squeers. " We'll try what can be done."

Pending these little endearments, Nicholas had stood awkwardly enough in the middle of the room, not very well knowing whether he was expected to retire into the passage, or to remain where he was. He was now relieved from his perplexity by Mr. Squeers.

" This is the new young man, my dear," said that gentleman.

" Oh," replied Mrs. Squeers, nodding her head at Nicholas, and eyeing him coldly from top to toe.

" He'll take a meal with us to-night," said Squeers, "and go among the boys to-morrow morning. You can give him a shake-down here to-night, can't you? "

" We must manage it somehow," replied the lady. " You don't much mind how you sleep, I suppose, Sir ?"

" No, indeed," replied Nicholas, " I am not particular."

" That's lucky," said Mrs. Squeers. And as the lady's humour was considered to lie chiefly in retort, Mr. Squeers laughed heartily, and seemed to expect that Nicholas should do the same.

After some further conversation between the master and mistress relative to the success of Mr. Squeers's trip, and the people who had paid, and the people who had made default in payment, a young servant girl brought in a Yorkshire pie and some cold beef, which being set upon the table, the boy Smike appeared with a jug of ale.

Mr. Squeers was emptying his great-coat pockets of letters to different boys, and other small documents, which he had brought down in them. The boy glanced with an anxious and timid expression at the papers, as if with a sickly hope that one among them might relate to him. The look was a very painful one, and went to Nicholas's heart at once, for it told a long and very sad history.

It induced him to consider the boy more attentively, and he was surprised to observe the extraordinary mixture of garments which formed his dress. Although he could not have been less than eighteen or nineteen years old, and was tall for that age, he wore a skeleton suit, such as is usually put upon very little boys, and which, though most absurdly short in the arms and legs, was quite wide enough for his attenuated frame. In order that the lower part of his legs might be in perfect keeping with this singular dress, he had a very large pair of boots originally made for tops, which might have been once worn by some stout farmer, but were now too patched and tattered for a beggar. God knows how long he had been there, but he still wore the same linen which he had first taken down; for round his neck was a tattered child's frill, only half concealed by a coarse man's neckerchief. He was lame; and as he feigned to be busy in arranging the table, glanced at the letters with a look so keen, and yet so dispirited and hopeless, that Nicholas could hardly bear to watch him.

" What are you bothering about there, Smike ?" cried Mrs. Squeers; " let the things alone, can't you."

" Eh !" said Squeers, looking up. " Oh! it's you, is it ?"

" Yes, Sir," replied the youth, pressing his hands together, as though to control by force the nervous wandering of his fingers ; " Is there—"

" Well !" said Squeers.

" Have you—did anybody—has nothing been heard—about me ?"

" Devil a bit," replied Squeers testily.

The lad withdrew his eyes, and putting his hand to his face moved towards the door.

" Not a word," resumed Squeers, " and never will be. Now, this is a pretty sort of thing, isn't it, that you should have been left here all these years and no money paid after the first six—nor no notice taken, nor no clue to be got who you belong to? It's a pretty sort of thing that I should have to feed a great fellow like you, and never hope to get one penny for it, isn't it?"

The boy put his hand to his head as if he were making an effort to recollect something, and then looking vacantly at his questioner, gradually broke into a smile and limped away.

" I'll tell you what, Squeers," remarked his wife as the door closed, " I think that young chap's turning silly."

" I hope not," said the schoolmaster; " for he's a handy fellow out of doors, and worth his meat and drink any way. I should think he'd have wit enough for us though, if he was. But come; let's have supper, for I am hungry and tired, and want to get to bed."

This reminder brought in an exclusive steak for Mr. Squeers, who speedily proceeded to do it ample justice. Nicholas drew up his chair, but his appetite was effectually taken away.

" How's the steak, Squeers?" said Mrs. S.

" Tender as a lamb," replied Squeers. " Have a bit."

" I couldn't eat a morsel," replied his wife. " What'll the young man take, my dear?"

" Whatever he likes that's present," rejoined Squeers, in a most unusual burst of generosity.

" What do you say, Mr. Knuckleboy?" inquired Mrs. Squeers.

" I'll take a little of the pie, if you please," replied Nicholas. " A very little, for I'm not hungry."

" Well, it's a pity to cut the pie if you're not hungry, isn't it?" said Mrs. Squeers. " Will you try a piece of the beef?"

" Whatever you please," replied Nicholas abstractedly; " it's all the same to me."

Mrs. Squeers looked vastly gracious on receiving this reply; and nodding to Squeers, as much as to say that she was glad to find the young man knew his station, assisted Nicholas to a slice of meat with her own fair hands.

" Ale, Squeery?" inquired the lady, winking and frowning to give him to understand that the question propounded was, whether Nicholas should have ale, and not whether he (Squeers) would take any.

" Certainly," said Squeers, re-telegraphing in the same manner. " A glassful."

So Nicholas had a glassful, and being occupied with his own reflections, drank it in happy innocence of all the foregone proceedings.

" Uncommon juicy steak that," said Squeers as he laid down his knife and fork, after plying it in silence for some time.

" It's prime meat," rejoined his lady. " I bought a good large piece of it myself on purpose for——"

" For what!" exclaimed Squeers hastily. " Not for the——"

" No, no; not for them," rejoined Mrs. Squeers; " on purpose for you against you came home. Lor! you didn't think I could have made such a mistake as that."

' Upon my word, my dear, I didn't know what you were going to say," said Squeers, who had turned very pale.

" You needn't make yourself uncomfortable," remarked his wife, laughing heartily. " To think that I should be such a noddy ! Well !"

This part of the conversation was rather unintelligible ; but popular rumour in the neighbourhood asserted that Mr. Squeers, being amiably opposed to cruelty to animals, not unfrequently purchased for boy consumption the bodies of horned cattle who had died a natural death, and possibly he was apprehensive of having unintentionally devoured some choice morsel intended for the young gentlemen.

Supper being over, and removed by a small servant girl with a hungry eye, Mrs. Squeers retired to lock it up, and also to take into safe custody the clothes of the five boys who had just arrived, and who were half way up the troublesome flight of steps which leads to death's door, in consequence of exposure to the cold. They were then regaled with a light supper of porridge, and stowed away side by side in a small bedstead, to warm each other and dream of a substantial meal with something hot after it if their fancies set that way, which it is not at all improbable they did.

Mr. Squeers treated himself to a stiff tumbler of brandy and water, made on the liberal half and half principle, allowing for the dissolution of the sugar ; and his amiable helpmate mixed Nicholas the ghost of a small glassfull of the same compound. This done, Mr. and Mrs. Squeers drew close up to the fire, and sitting with their feet on the fender talked confidentially in whispers ; while Nicholas, taking up the tutor's assistant, read the interesting legends in the miscellaneous questions, and all the figures into the bargain, with as much thought or consciousness of what he was doing, as if he had been in a magnetic slumber.

At length Mr. Squeers yawned fearfully, and opined that it was high time to go to bed ; upon which signal Mrs. Squeers and the girl dragged in a small straw mattress and a couple of blankets, and arranged them into a couch for Nicholas.

" We'll put you into your regular bed-room to-morrow, Nickleby," said Squeers. " Let me see, who sleeps in Brooks's bed, my dear ?"

" In Brooks's," said Mrs. Squeers, pondering. " There's Jennings, little Bolder, Graymarsh, and what's his name."

" So there are," rejoined Squeers. " Yes ! Brooks is full."

" Full !" thought Nicholas, " I should think he was."

" There's a place somewhere I know," said Squeers ; " but I can't at this moment call to mind where it is. However, we'll have that all settled to-morrow. Good night, Nickleby. Seven o'clock in the morning, mind."

" I shall be ready, Sir," replied Nicholas. " Good night."

" I'll come in myself and show you where the well is," said Squeers. " You'll always find a little bit of soap in the kitchen window ; that belongs to you."

Nicholas opened his eyes, but not his mouth ; and Squeers was again going away, when he once more turned back.

" I don't know, I am sure," he said, " whose towel to put you on ; but if you'll make shift with something to-morrow morning, Mrs.

Squeers will arrange that, in the course of the day. My dear, don't forget."

"I'll take care," replied Mrs. Squeers; "and mind *you* take care, young man, and get first wash. The teacher ought always to have it; but they get the better of him if they can."

Mr. Squeers then nudged Mrs. Squeers to bring away the brandy bottle, lest Nicholas should help himself in the night; and the lady having seized it with great precipitation, they retired together.

Nicholas being left alone, took half a dozen turns up and down the room in a condition of much agitation and excitement, but growing gradually calmer, sat himself down in a chair and mentally resolved that, come what come might, he would endeavour for a time to bear whatever wretchedness might be in store for him, and that remembering the helplessness of his mother and sister, he would give his uncle no plea for deserting them in their need. Good resolutions seldom fail of producing some good effects in the mind from which they spring. He grew less desponding, and—so sanguine and buoyant is youth—even hoped that affairs at Dotheboys Hall might yet prove better than they promised.

He was preparing for bed with something like renewed cheerfulness, when a sealed letter fell from his coat pocket. In the hurry of leaving London it had escaped his attention and had not occurred to him since, but it at once brought back to him the recollection of the mysterious behaviour of Newman Noggs.

"Dear me!" said Nicholas; "what an extraordinary hand!"

It was directed to himself, was written upon very dirty paper, and in such cramped and crippled writing as to be almost illegible. After great difficulty and much puzzling, he contrived to read as follows:—

'My dear young Man.

"I know the world. Your father did not, or he would not have done me a kindness when there was no hope of return. You do not, or you would not be bound on such a journey.

"If ever you want a shelter in London, (don't be angry at this, *I* once thought I never should), they know where I live at the sign of the Crown, in Silver Street, Golden Square. It is at the corner of Silver Street and James Street, with a bar door both ways. You can come at night. Once nobody was ashamed—never mind that. It's all over.

"Excuse errors. I should forget how to wear a whole coat now. I have forgotten all my old ways. My spelling may have gone with them.   "NEWMAN NOGGS.

"P.S. If you should go near Barnard Castle, there is good ale at the King's Head. Say you know me, and I am sure they will not charge you for it. You may say *Mr.* Noggs there, for I was a gentleman then. I was indeed."

It may be a very undignified circumstance to record, but after he had folded this letter and placed it in his pocket-book, Nicholas Nickleby's eyes were dimmed with a moisture that might have been taken for tears.

About the middle of May will be published, price 2s., with neat Engravings, an entirely new Work, entitled

THE PREMATURE MARRIAGE;

OR, THE HISTORY OF FREDERICK AND SOPHIA.

A TALE OF TRUTH. BY AN OBSERVER.

Also, price 2s. 6d., beautifully printed,

THE BREAKFAST-TABLE COMPANION.

DARTON AND CLARKE, HOLBORN HILL; AND ALL BOOKSELLERS.

REFORM YOUR TAILORS' BILLS!

LADIES' ELEGANT
RIDING HABITS.

Summer Cloth	- - -	£3	3	0
Ladies' Cloth	- - - -	4	4	0
Saxony Cloth	- - -	5	5	0

GENTLEMAN'S

Superfine Dress Coat	- -	2	7	6
Extra Saxony, the best that is made	- -	2	15	0
Superfine Frock Coat, silk facings	- - -	2	10	0
Buckskin Trousers	- - -	1	1	0
Cloth or double-milled Cassimere ditto	- 17s. 6d. to	1	5	0
New Patterns, Summer Trousers, 10s. 6d. per pr. or 3 pr.		1	10	0
Summer Waistcoats, 7s.; or 3,		1	0	0
Splendid Silk Valencia Dress Waistcoats, 10s.6d. each, or 3,		1	10	0

FIRST-RATE
BOYS' CLOTHING.

Skeleton Dresses	- -	£0	15	0
Tunic and Hussar Suits,	-	1	10	0
Camlet Cloaks	- - -	0	8	6
Cloth Cloaks	- - -	0	15	6

GENTLEMAN'S

Morning Coats and Dressing Gowns	- - -	0	18	0
Petersham Great Coats and Pilot P Jackets, bound, and Velvet Collar	- -	1	10	0
Camlet Cloak, lined all through	1	1	0
Cloth Opera Cloak	- -	1	10	0
Army Cloth Blue Spanish Cloak, 9½ yards round	-	2	10	0
Super Cloth ditto	- -	3	3	0
Cloth or Tweed Fishing or Travelling Trousers	. -	0	13	6

THE CELEBRITY THE

CITY CLOTHING ESTABLISHMENT

Has so many years maintained, being the

BEST AS WELL AS THE CHEAPEST HOUSE,

Renders any Assurance as to STYLE and QUALITY unnecessary. The NOBILITY and GENTRY are invited to the

SHOW-ROOMS, TO VIEW THE IMMENSE & SPLENDID STOCK.

The numerous Applications for

REGIMENTALS & NAVAL UNIFORMS,

Have induced E. P. D. & SON to make ample Arrangements for an extensive Business in this particular Branch: a perusal of their List of Prices (which can be had gratis) will show the EXORBITANT CHARGES to which OFFICERS OF THE ARMY AND NAVY HAVE SO LONG BEEN SUBJECTED.

CONTRACTS BY THE YEAR,

Originated by E. P. D. & SON, are universally adopted by CLERGYMEN and PROFESSIONAL GENTLEMEN, as being MORE REGULAR and ECONOMICAL. THE PRICES ARE THE LOWEST EVER OFFERED:—

Two Suits per Year, Superfine,	7 7—Extra Saxony, the best that is made,	8 5
Three Suits per Year, ditto	10 17—Extra Saxony, ditto	- 12 6
Four Suits per Year, ditto	14 6—Extra Saxony, ditto	- 15 18

(THE OLD SUITS TO BE RETURNED.)

Capital Shooting Jackets, 21s. The new Waterproof Cloak, 21s.

COUNTRY GENTLEMEN,

Preferring their Clothes Fashionably made, at a FIRST-RATE LONDON HOUSE, are respectfully informed, that by a Post-paid Application, they will receive a Prospectus explanatory of the System of Business, Directions for Measurement, and a Statement of Prices. Or if Three or Four Gentlemen unite, one of the Travellers will be dispatched immediately to wait on them.

STATE LIVERIES SPLENDIDLY MADE.

Footman's Suit of Liveries, £3 3. Scarlet Hunting Coat, £3 3

E. P. DOUDNEY AND SON,
49, LOMBARD-STREET. 1784.

Established

LONDON : BRADBURY AND EVANS, PRINTERS, WHITEFRIARS.

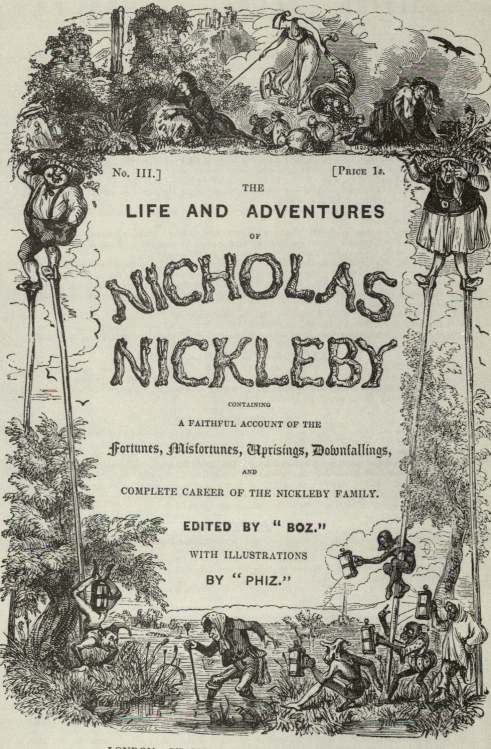

No. III.]   [Price 1s.

THE

LIFE AND ADVENTURES

OF

NICHOLAS NICKLEBY

CONTAINING

A FAITHFUL ACCOUNT OF THE

Fortunes, Misfortunes, Uprisings, Downfallings,

AND

COMPLETE CAREER OF THE NICKLEBY FAMILY.

EDITED BY "BOZ."

WITH ILLUSTRATIONS

BY "PHIZ."

LONDON: CHAPMAN AND HALL, 186, STRAND.

BRITISH COLLEGE OF HEALTH,
HAMILTON PLACE, NEW ROAD.

CASE OF THE HYGEISTS AGAINST THE MEDICAL PROFESSION.

That a strong case, borne out by the most indubitable testimony, has been made, and stands recorded in favour of the Hygeian theory of medicine, and against medical practice, it is presumed cannot be called in question. That, notwithstanding the persecution those connected with the honest promulgation of that system have endured from medical men for the last five years, the Hygeian system remains unshaken, and, at this moment, is triumphantly spreading itself throughout the world.

That, were medical men honest in their opposition to that system, and were they impressed with a *bona fide* belief that Hygeism was not founded in truth, they ought (if they can) first to show, in contradiction of that which Hygeists assert to be the truth, and upon which they act,

First—That the vital principle is not contained in the blood—and why?

Second—That every thing in the body is not derived from the blood—and why?

Third—That all constitutions are not radically the same—and why?

Fourth—That all diseases do not arise from impurity of the blood—and why?

Fifth—That this impurity, which degenerates the blood, has not three sources, namely, the maternine, the contagious, and the personal—and why?

Sixth—That pain and disease have not the same origin, and should not, therefore, be considered synonymous terms—and why?

Seventh—That purgation by vegetables is not the effectual mode of eradicating disease—and why?

Eighth—That there is not an intimate connexion subsisting between the mind and the body, and that the health of the one does not conduce to the serenity of the other—and why?

When any member of the medical profession shall have satisfactorily proved the reverse of the above (which are the principles of the Hygeian theory) to be fallacious, more especially the seventh proposition, then, and then only, ought faith to be placed by the public in what medical men (as interested individuals) are pleased to assert in reference to the doctrine of Hygeism, which every-day experience clearly shows to be founded in truth.

The important Letter of Dr. Lynch, on the Nature, Cause, and Treatment of Inflammation, is just published, and may be had at the Medical Dissenter Office, 368, Strand, and of all the regularly appointed agents and sub-agents throughout the country.—British College of Health, Hamilton Place, New Road.

PETITION TO PARLIAMENT.

HYGEISM.—A petition (which was signed by upwards of 10,000 persons) was presented, in the House of Commons, by Mr. Hall, the Member for Marylebone, on Tuesday evening, praying that a Committee be appointed to inquire into the merits of Hygeism. The petition was ordered to lie on the table.—*Bell's Weekly Messenger*, 11th *March*, 1838.

TO MISSIONARIES.

It has been said by some of our most celebrated Travellers, that a knowledge of Medicine, or, more properly speaking, the art of curing disease, is absolutely necessary to the office or calling of Missionaries. The Hygeian System is founded upon unerring principles, and within the comprehension of all persons. It can be proved that the most successful results have followed from the administration of MORISON'S PILLS by non-medical persons in all parts of India, and in fact in every other part of the World. What Medicine, therefore, can be better suited for the purpose before mentioned? Missionaries desirous of taking out a quantity of the Medicine with them, will have a liberal allowance made.

British College of Health, 2, Hamilton Place, King's Cross, London.

CAUTION.

Whereas spurious imitations of my Medicines are now in circulation, I, James Morison, the Hygeist, hereby give notice, That I am in nowise connected with the following Medicines purporting to be mine, and sold under the various names of " Dr. Morrison's Pills," " The Hygeian Pills," " The Improved Vegetable Universal Pills," " The Original Morison's Pills, as compounded by the late Mr. Moat," " The Original Hygeian Vegetable Pills," " The Original Morison's Pills," &c. &c.

That my Medicines are prepared only at the British College of Health, Hamilton Place, King's Cross, and sold by the General Agents to the British College of Health and their Sub-Agents, and that no Chemist or Druggist is authorised by me to dispose of the same. None can be genuine without the words " Morison's Universal Medicines " are engraved on the Government Stamp, in white letters upon a red ground.—In witness whereof, I have hereunto set my hand,

British College of Health, New Road, April 20, 1838.   JAMES MORISON, the Hygeist.

The following is a List of the principal Depots where the Medicines may be had in London:—Medical Dissenter Office, 368, Strand; Mr. Field, Bookseller, 65, Quadrant, Regent Street; Mr. Lofts, City Agent, Park Place, Mile. End; Mr. Chappell, Bookseller, 19, Cornhill, late of 97, Royal Exchange; Mr. Haslett, 118, Ratcliff Highway; Mrs. Twell, 10, Hand Court, Holborn; Western Branch, 72, Edgeware Road; Messrs. Hannay and Co., Perfumers, 63, Oxford Street, corner of Wells Street; Mr. Cowell, 22, Terrace, Pimlico; British College of Health, Hamilton Place, King's Cross; and of their Sub-Agents.

N.B.—Dr. LYNCH can be consulted at the British College of Health, New Road, from 12 till 2, and at the Medical Dissenter Office, from 3 till 5 daily.

FOREIGN GENERAL AGENTS.—Mr. Anderson, St. John's, New Brunswick; Mr. James Cochrane, Guernsey; Mr. Charles Edwards, Sydney; Mr. V. Formosa, Malta; Mr. Thomas Gardner, Calcutta; Mr. Edward Linington, Barbadoes; Messrs. John Legge and Co., Quebec; Mr. Lobe, Cuba; Lieut. J. M'Kinnon, Cape Breton, North America and Newfoundland; Mr. T. H. Roberts, Church-street, Gibraltar; Messrs. Stiffel and Co., Odessa; Dr. Tollhausen, Jassey, Bucharest, Constantinople, and the whole of Turkey; Dr. George Taylor, 6½, Wall Street, New York general agent for the United States of America; Mr. H. W. Wells, British Guiana, George Town, Demerara

On the 30th of June will be published, Part I., price 1s., to be completed in Eight Parts, of

ILLUSTRATIONS TO NICHOLAS NICKLEBY.
BY PETER PALETTE.

Also, on Saturday, June 30, will be published, No. I., Price One Penny, to be continued Weekly, of a New Work, entitled

THE WONDERS OF THE WORLD IN NATURE, ART, AND MIND.
EDITED BY HENRY INCE, M.A.
ASSISTED BY CONTRIBUTIONS FROM EMINENT LITERARY CHARACTERS.

On a subject embracing so vast a range as the rich and innumerable wonders of "Nature's Store-house," the Proprietors are desirous of producing a Work in every way commensurate with its soul-expanding importance.

The contemplation of the numerous objects contained in the fossil, vegetable, mineral, and animal kingdoms—lavished so bountifully before us, displays facts of an interesting and extraordinary character, and *alone* presents abundant materials for intellectual energy and research.

The wonders of the Antediluvian World—the massive mountain rising above the neighbouring hills—the volcano and earthquake, each spreading devastation in its course—the ever-sounding and boundless deep—the blue clear vault of heaven, studded through space illimitable with countless orbs—are phenomena that must enlarge and elevate the mind, induce ennobling views of the Universal Governor, and teach us our dependence upon His power, His wisdom, and goodness.

In the varied Works of Art on which man has exercised his genius and industry, in which science and philosophy have aided his efforts, we shall record all that is rare, curious, and admirable, mark-ing the gradual progress and advancing stages of improvement.

The Wonders of the Mind—the Creator's highest work, his mirror and representative, will not inaptly engage our thoughts. The Mind is, in itself, a microcosm—man's chief and noblest distinction—a transcript of that intellectual energy that first gave birth to Nature.

To select these jewels, and to seize the beauties everywhere presented to notice, will be the features of the WONDERS OF THE WORLD. On all subjects reference will be made to every available source of information. The veil of error and credulity, which too often obscures the narrative of the traveller, will be carefully withdrawn—the most recent and best accredited authorities (whether English or foreign) compared, and *data* given for farther research, so that truth without alloy will usher in the varied departments of Nature's "ample bound."

The Work will be embellished with spirited Engravings, derived from authentic sources, which, if regarded as highly finished specimens of art, or vivid pictorial illustrations of the subject, will, we trust, be found superior to most contemporary productions.

THE WONDERS OF THE WORLD
WILL APPEAR IN WEEKLY NUMBERS, PRICE ONE PENNY,
AND IN MONTHLY PARTS AT SIXPENCE.

. To enable Subscribers resident in the country to receive the Work simultaneously with the inhabitants of the Metropolis, it will be issued to the order of All Country Booksellers, a week in advance.

LONDON: PUBLISHED FOR THE PROPRIETORS, BY
E. GRATTAN, 51, PATERNOSTER ROW.
SOLD BY ALL BOOKSELLERS, ETC.

Of whom may be had,

COMPLETE IN EIGHT PARTS, PRICE 1s. EACH, OR IN FANCY BINDING, PRICE 9s.,

ILLUSTRATIONS TO THE PICKWICK PAPERS.
BY SAMUEL WELLER.

" Among the decided clever things of the day, Weller's Illustrations to Pickwick stand prominent."—*Chronicle.*

" We advise all the readers of this inimitable work to possess themselves of these Illustrations; they will form a valuable acquisition to the work or the scrap-book."—*Observer.*

" Very clever prints, and delightfully etched."—*Atlas.*

" There is a refinement about the humour of his pencil which we do not find in that of many of his brother artists."—*Bell's Messenger.*

New Works
PUBLISHED BY CHAPMAN AND HALL.

THE CORONATION.

In one volume, small 8vo, price 5s. 6d., cloth boards,

REGAL RECORDS;
OR, A CHRONICLE OF
The Coronations of the Queens Regnant of England,
COMPILED FROM CONTEMPORARY ACCOUNTS AND OFFICIAL DOCUMENTS,

BY J. R. PLANCHE, F.S.A.
WITH NUMEROUS ILLUSTRATIONS.
DEDICATED BY PERMISSION TO HER GRACE THE DUCHESS OF SUTHERLAND, MISTRESS OF THE ROBES TO HER MAJESTY.

" A seasonable little book by Mr. J. R. Planche, whose antiquarian learning is relieved by a lively and ingenious turn of thinking."—*Times.*

" An interesting work, showing much research, and abounding in historical detail."—*Post.*

" An exceedingly well-timed and popular publication. Mr. Planche has gone into the subject with his usu al taste and attention, giving us all that was necessary and no more, and bestowing the care they deserve upon the points chiefly applicable to the present day."—*Literary Gazette.*

THE PICKWICK PAPERS COMPLETE.

In one volume 8vo, bound in cloth, price 1l. 1s.

THE
POSTHUMOUS PAPERS OF THE PICKWICK CLUB.
BY " BOZ."
WITH FORTY-THREE ILLUSTRATIONS BY " PHIZ."

SEVENTH EDITION.

In one volume, small 8vo, price 3s. boards,

SKETCHES OF YOUNG LADIES;
WITH SIX ILLUSTRATIONS BY " PHIZ."

The Busy Young Lady.	The Young Lady who is engaged.	The Whimsical Young Lady.
The Romantic Young Lady.	The Petting Young Lady.	The Sincere Young Lady.
The Matter-of-Fact Young Lady.	The Natural Historian Young Lady.	The Affirmative Young Lady.
The Young Lady who Sings.	The Indirect Young Lady.	The Natural Young Lady.
The Plain Young Lady.	The Stupid Young Lady.	The Clever Young Lady.
The Evangelical Young Lady.	The Hyperbolical Young Lady.	The Mysterious Young Lady.
The Manly Young Lady.	The Interesting Young Lady.	The Lazy Young Lady.
The Literary Young Lady.	The Abstemious Young Lady.	The Young Lady from School.

FOURTH EDITION.

In one volume, small 8vo, price 3s. boards,

SKETCHES OF YOUNG GENTLEMEN;
CONTENTS.

Dedication to the Young Ladies.	The ' Throwing-off' Young Gentleman	The Military Young Gentleman.
The Out-and-out Young Gentleman.	The Poetical Young Gentleman.	The Political Young Gentleman.
The Domestic Young Gentleman.	The Funny Young Gentleman.	The Censorious Young Gentleman.
The Bashful Young Gentleman.	The Theatrical Young Gentleman.	The Young Ladies' Young Gentleman.
The very Friendly Young Gentleman.		

WITH SIX ILLUSTRATIONS BY " PHIZ."

POPULAR JUVENILE BOOKS,
ELEGANTLY EMBELLISHED.

Neatly bound, price 2*s.* 6*d.*, THE

NOVEL ADVENTURES OF TOM THUMB THE GREAT,
SHOWING HOW HE VISITED THE INSECT WORLD, AND LEARNED MUCH WISDOM.

BY MRS. BARWELL.
WITH ILLUSTRATIONS.

Neatly bound, price 2*s.* 6*d.*,

REMEMBER; OR, MAMMA'S BIRTHDAY.
BY MRS. BARWELL.
WITH ILLUSTRATIONS.

Neatly bound, price 2*s.* 6*d.*,

POETRY FOR CHILDREN.
SELECTED BY THE LATE WM. BURDON.
A NEW EDITION. WITH ILLUSTRATIONS PRINTED IN COLOURS.

Neatly bound, price 2*s.* 6*d.*,

THE TWO COUSINS; AND OTHER TALES.
BY THE AUTHORESS OF " POETIC SKETCHES."
WITH ILLUSTRATIONS.

Neatly bound, price 1*s.* 6*d.*,

ROSE AND ANNE.
A FIRST BOOK, IN MONOSYLLABLES, WITH SIX ILLUSTRATIONS.

Neatly bound, price 2*s.* 6*d.*,

NEW SCENES FOR YOUTH.
DESIGNED FOR THE INSTRUCTION AND AMUSEMENT OF YOUNG LADIES AND GENTLEMEN.

BY MRS. RODWELL.
WITH ILLUSTRATIONS.

Neatly bound in cloth, price 2*s.* 6*d.*,

CAROLINE; OR THE PLEASURES OF A BIRTHDAY.
BY M. M. RODWELL.
Author of " Geography of the British Isles." With SIX ILLUSTRATIONS.

Neatly bound, price 2*s.* 6*d.*,

THE SPOILED CHILD RECLAIMED.
BY M. M. RODWELL.
WITH ILLUSTRATIONS.

" Two works brought out with great taste and neatness, for the amusement of children. The stories are well told, the moral lessons they inculcate precisely those which it is of most importance to impress on the youthful mind."—*Athenæum.*

SECOND EDITION. Neatly bound, price 3*s.* 6*d.*

THE JUVENILE PIANIST;
Or, A Mirror of Music for Infant Minds.
BY ANN RODWELL.
Teacher of the Pianoforte.
ILLUSTRATED BY UPWARDS OF ONE HUNDRED MUSICAL DIAGRAMS.

" This instructive little work, which is illustrated with numerous engravings and diagrams explanatory of its interesting art, is truly what it professes to be, a Mirror of Music for Infant Minds, constructed with such simplicity and clearness, that it would be impossible, even for a very young child, to read without deriving the wished for instruction. It is admirably calculated to render the early practice of the piano easy and attractive."—*Morning Post.*

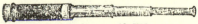

CEREMONIALS.

SPLENDOUR, GAIETY, and EFFECT, pleasing concomitants upon memorable occasions of public ceremony, are anticipated in that which is approaching, in a degree not previously witnessed, one sentiment of loyal and affectionate participation pervading a whole people. Of the August Ceremonial alluded to, and indeed of every other, whether celebrated in palaces or private circles, Female Beauty is the chief grace and ornament. The preservation and enhancement of this charm of society may be confided to

GOWLAND'S LOTION,

With a reliance founded upon the successful experience of more than Eighty Years, SAFETY, and an early removal of all cutaneous irritability, attending its use. In the department of the TOILET, more particularly the advantages derived from the Lotion, are continued purity of the Skin, with a bright and lively tint of the Complexion, unaffected by incidental HEAT or change of Season, and a style of preparation and refreshing qualities peculiarly adapted to meet approbation where elegance and utility are appreciated.

GOWLAND'S LOTION is prepared only by the Proprietor, **ROBERT SHAW, 33. QUEEN STREET, CHEAPSIDE, LONDON,** whose Name and Address are Engraved on the Government Stamp, a notice of which is respectfully solicited from Purchasers, as an effectual barrier to the danger of Substitutions and Imposture.

SHAW'S MINDORA OIL.

Purity and delicacy of flavour, united with highly restorative properties, distinguish this favourite article for the Hair from all the COLOURED and factitious compounds heretofore resorted to: CLEANLINESS, preservation of the TRUE COLOUR, with luxuriant growth, and fine texture of the Hair, are ensured by its use, and the firmness of curl, and generally perfect condition acquired, will be found both pleasing and important auxiliaries to personal appearance in both Sexes.

Prepared only for the Toilet by the Proprietor, ROBERT SHAW, 33, QUEEN STREET, CHEAP-SIDE, LONDON, in Bottles bearing his Signature on the label and wrapper at 3s., 5s. 6d.. and in Stoppered Bottles at 10s. 6d. A Practical Treatise on the Hair accompanies each genuine Package. Sold as above, and by the most respectable Perfumers and Medicine Venders.

BEDS, FEATHERS, BEDTICKS, AND MATTRESSES.

Seasoned Feather Beds, 18s. to 5d.; Prime Dressed Feathers, 9d. to 2s. 6d. per lb.; Ticks, 3s. to 24s.; Field Tent Bedsteads, 20s.; Alva Marina Mattresses to fit, 10s.; Soft Wool Flocks, 2d., 3d., and 4d. per lb. Every description of Bedsteads, Mattresses, Palliasses, and Bedding, full 30 per cent. cheaper. Merchants, Captains, Upholsterers, Brokers, and Proprietors of Schools, supplied at D. TIMOTHY'S old-established Manufactory, No. 31, Barbican, corner of Redcross-street, City.

HEAL AND SON'S FRENCH MATTRESSES.

The very frequent inquiries for MATTRESSES made after the manner of the French, have induced F. HEAL and SON to turn their attention to the making of mattresses on the same principles. The essential difference between FRENCH MATTRESSES and ENGLISH consists in the Materials of which they are made, and consequently a difference in the making. The French use long Fleece Wool, and therefore but little work is requisite, leaving to the Wool the whole of its elasticity. English Mattresses are made of short Wool, the refuse of other Manufacturings, and a great deal of work is necessarily required to keep the material together, which makes them comparatively *Non-Elastic*. The advantages F. HEAL and SON possess by being exclusively Manufacturers of Bedding, enable them to offer Mattresses of *fine long Wool*, equal to the best that are made in France, at the same prices that are usually charged for those generally made in this Country.—F. HEAL & SON, Bedding Manufacturers. 203, Tottenham Court Road.

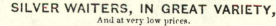

T. COX SAVORY, WATCHMAKER, 47, CORNHILL, LONDON.

SILVER WAITERS, IN GREAT VARIETY,
And at very low prices.

SILVER TEA AND COFFEE SERVICES, AND SILVER PLATE
Of every description. Plated Goods, &c. arranged in
THREE EXTENSIVE SHOW ROOMS.

THE NEW FLAT GOLD WATCHES
Are offered
in engine-turned cases, with vertical movements, jewelled, for Seven Guineas each, or with highly-finished horizontal movements, warranted, at Nine Guineas each, at

T. COX SAVORY'S,
Working Goldsmith, Silversmith, and Watchmaker, 47, Cornhill, London.

THE HORIZONTAL CONSTRUCTION IS STRONGLY RECOMMENDED FOR ITS SUPERIOR ACCURACY.

A Pamphlet, illustrated with Engravings of the most useful and ornamental Articles in Silver Plate, Plated Goods. Watches, Clocks, Jewellery, &c. with the weight and prices affixed, may be obtained Gratis, or will be transmitted in answer to a post paid application.

BEAUFOY AND Co., SOUTH LAMBETH, LONDON.

BEAUFOY'S INSTANT CURE

FOR THE

TOOTHACHE.

THE GENUINE PACKAGES CONTAIN
A FAC-SIMILE
OF ONE OR THE OTHER OF THESE
VIGNETTES.

SOLD BY MOST RESPECTABLE DRUGGISTS, WITH AMPLE DIRECTIONS FOR USE,
In Bottles, Price 1s. 1½d. each, Stamp included.

BEAUFOY AND CO., SOUTH LAMBETH, LONDON.

[BRADBURY AND EVANS, PRINTERS, WHITEFRIARS.]

TO READING CLUBS AND FAMILIES,

IN TOWN AND COUNTRY.

TERMS OF SUBSCRIPTION

TO

CHURTON'S

BRITISH AND FOREIGN LIBRARY,

26, HOLLES STREET,

THREE DOORS FROM OXFORD STREET.

FOR A SINGLE FAMILY.

Class .. I. £5 5 0 per annum, 12 Vols. in Town, 24 in the Country.
" .. II. 4 4 0 " 8 " 16 "
Extra Class * 10 10 0 " 15 " 30 "

The only system by which Subscribers can be supplied with all the New Publications, BRITISH AND FOREIGN, MAGAZINES, &c., is that pursued at the above Establishment, namely, to place at the disposal of Subscribers an UNLIMITED SUPPLY of every Work on the day it issues from the Press; besides this advantage, the Standard Collection consists of 25,000 Volumes in the

ENGLISH, FRENCH, ITALIAN, GERMAN, SPANISH, AND PORTUGUESE LANGUAGES.

The more valuable and interesting New Works being added to the Library in far greater quantities than is required, after their popularity has in some degree subsided, E. CHURTON informs his Subscribers that they are offered for sale, at one-third the price at which they were published; thus for an additional Guinea per annum the Subscriber may have

THREE GUINEAS' WORTH OF BOOKS.

* This Class is designed for the accommodation of those who wish for the NEW WORKS CHIEFLY; an extra supply being provided expressly for their use, they are allowed 15 Volumes in Town and 30 in the Country, and are entitled to have purchased for them any Work not previously added to the Library.

TERMS FOR BOOK CLUBS.

CLASS I.

CLUBS paying 6l. 6s. the Year, are entitled to 20 Vols. at one time, including 10 Vols. of the Newest Works.

CLASS II.

CLUBS paying 8l. 8s. the Year, are entitled to 30 Vols. at one time, including 15 Vols. of the Newest Works.

CLASS III.

CLUBS paying 10l. 10s. the Year, are entitled to 30 Vols. at one time, two-thirds of which may be of the Newest Works.

CLASS IV.

CLUBS paying 13l. 13s. the Year, are entitled to 36 Vols. at one time, including 25 Vols. of the Newest Works.

CLASS V.

CLUBS paying 16l. 16s. the Year, are entitled to 42 Vols., including 30 Vols. of the Newest Works at one time.

And so on, adding 2l. 2s. for every additional 6 Volumes required.

The advantage to Members of Reading Clubs, of a subscription over the old method of purchasing Books, will be obvious, after reading the following statement.

Take, for illustration, a Club consisting of Twelve Members—
The usual subscription of one guinea per annum £12 12 0
Sale of 14 guineas' worth of books to the members at half-price,
the 12 guineas being increased to that sum by the discount al- } 7 7 0
lowed to Clubs ....
Gross amount per annum .... ——— £19 19 0

For this sum the Club would have had in their possession 47 Volumes, calculating the average price per volume, after deducting the discount, at 8s. 6d.; whereas, by a subscription paying 10l. 10s., and leaving 2l. 2s. for expenses of carriage, &c., the Club would have *Two Hundred and Forty Volumes*, or, *One Hundred and Ninety-three* more than by purchasing.

BRADBURY AND EVANS, PRINTERS, WHITEFRIARS.

CHAPTER VIII.

OF THE INTERNAL ECONOMY OF DOTHEBOYS HALL.

A RIDE of two hundred and odd miles in severe weather, is one of the best softeners of a hard bed that ingenuity can devise. Perhaps it is even a sweetener of dreams, for those which hovered over the rough couch of Nicholas, and whispered their airy nothings in his ear, were of an agreeable and happy kind. He was making his fortune very fast indeed, when the faint glimmer of an expiring candle shone before his eyes, and a voice he had no difficulty in recognising as part and parcel of Mr. Squeers, admonished him that it was time to rise.

" Past seven, Nickleby," said Mr. Squeers.

" Has morning come already ?" asked Nicholas, sitting up in bed.

" Ah ! that has it," replied Squeers, " and ready iced too. Now, Nickleby, come ; tumble up, will you ?"

Nicholas needed no further admonition, but " tumbled up " at once, and proceeded to dress himself by the light of the taper which Mr. Squeers carried in his hand.

" Here's a pretty go," said that gentleman ; " the pump's froze."

" Indeed !" said Nicholas, not much interested in the intelligence.

" Yes," replied Squeers. " You can't wash yourself this morning."

" Not wash myself !" exclaimed Nicholas.

" No, not a bit of it," rejoined Squeers tartly. " So you must be content with giving yourself a dry polish till we break the ice in the well, and can get a bucketful out for the boys. Don't stand staring at me, but do look sharp, will you ?"

Offering no further observation, Nicholas huddled on his clothes, and Squeers meanwhile opened the shutters and blew the candle out, when the voice of his amiable consort was heard in the passage, demanding admittance.

" Come in, my love," said Squeers.

Mrs. Squeers came in, still habited in the primitive night-jacket which had displayed the symmetry of her figure on the previous night, and further ornamented with a beaver bonnet of some antiquity, which she wore with much ease and lightness upon the top of the nightcap before mentioned.

" Drat the things," said the lady, opening the cupboard ; " I can't find the school spoon anywhere."

" Never mind it, my dear," observed Squeers in a soothing manner ; " it's of no consequence."

" No consequence, why how you talk !" retorted Mrs. Squeers sharply ; " isn't it brimstone morning ?"

" I forgot, my dear," rejoined Squeers ; " yes, it certainly is. We purify the boys' bloods now and then, Nickleby."

" Purify fiddlesticks' ends," said his lady. " Don't think, young man, that we go to the expense of flower of brimstone and molasses just to purify them; because if you think we carry on the business in that way, you'll find yourself mistaken, and so I tell you plainly."

" My dear," said Squeers frowning.   " Hem!"

" Oh! nonsense," rejoined Mrs. Squeers.   " If the young man comes to be a teacher here, let him understand at once that we don't want any foolery about the boys.   They have the brimstone and treacle, partly because if they hadn't something or other in the way of medicine they'd be always ailing and giving a world of trouble, and partly because it spoils their appetites and comes cheaper than breakfast and dinner.   So it does them good and us good at the same time, and that's fair enough I'm sure."

Having given this explanation, Mrs. Squeers put her head into the closet and instituted a stricter search after the spoon, in which Mr. Squeers assisted.   A few words passed between them while they were thus engaged, but as their voices were partially stifled by the cupboard all that Nicholas could distinguish was, that Mr. Squeers said what Mrs. Squeers had said was injudicious, and that Mrs. Squeers said what Mr. Squeers said was " stuff."

A vast deal of searching and rummaging succeeded, and it proving fruitless, Smike was called in, and pushed by Mrs. Squeers and boxed by Mr. Squeers, which course of treatment brightening his intellects, enabled him to suggest that possibly Mrs. Squeers might have the spoon in her pocket, as indeed turned out to be the case.   As Mrs. Squeers had previously protested, however, that she was quite certain she had not got it, Smike received another box on the ear for presuming to contradict his mistress, together with a promise of a sound threshing if he were not more respectful in future; so that he took nothing very advantageous by his motion.

" A most invaluable woman, that, Nickleby," said Squeers when his consort had hurried away, pushing the drudge before her.

" Indeed, Sir!" observed Nicholas.

" I don't know her equal," said Squeers; " I do not know her equal. That woman, Nickleby, is always the same—always the same bustling, lively, active, saving creetur that you see her now."

Nicholas sighed involuntarily at the thought of the agreeable domestic prospect thus opened to him; but Squeers was, fortunately, too much occupied with his own reflections to perceive it.

" It's my way to say, when I am up in London," continued Squeers, " that to them boys she is a mother.   But she is more than a mother to them, ten times more.   She does things for them boys, Nickleby, that I don't believe half the mothers going would do for their own sons."

" I should think they would not, Sir," answered Nicholas.

Now, the fact was, that both Mr. and Mrs. Squeers viewed the boys in the light of their proper and natural enemies; or, in other words, they held and considered that their business and profession was to get as much from every boy as could by possibility be screwed out of him. On this point they were both agreed, and behaved in unison accordingly.   The only difference between them was, that Mrs. Squeers waged war against the enemy openly and fearlessly, and that Squeers covered his rascality, even at home, with a spice of his habitual deceit,

The internal economy of Dotheboys Hall.

as if he really had a notion of some day or other being able to take himself in, and persuade his own mind that he was a very good fellow.

" But come," said Squeers, interrupting the progress of some thoughts to this effect in the mind of his usher, " let's go to the school-room; and lend me a hand with my school-coat, will you?"

Nicholas assisted his master to put on an old fustian shooting-jacket, which he took down from a peg in the passage; and Squeers arming himself with his cane, led the way across a yard to a door in the rear of the house.

" There," said the schoolmaster as they stepped in together; " this is our shop, Nickleby."

It was such a crowded scene, and there were so many objects to attract attention, that at first Nicholas stared about him, really without seeing anything at all. By degrees, however, the place resolved itself into a bare and dirty room with a couple of windows, whereof a tenth part might be of glass, the remainder being stopped up with old copybooks and paper. There were a couple of long old rickety desks, cut and notched, and inked and damaged, in every possible way; two or three forms, a detached desk for Squeers, and another for his assistant. The ceiling was supported like that of a barn, by cross beams and rafters, and the walls were so stained and discoloured, that it was impossible to tell whether they had ever been touched with paint or whitewash.

But the pupils—the young noblemen! How the last faint traces of hope, the remotest glimmering of any good to be derived from his efforts in this den, faded from the mind of Nicholas as he looked in dismay around! Pale and haggard faces, lank and bony figures, children with the countenances of old men, deformities with irons upon their limbs, boys of stunted growth, and others whose long meagre legs would hardly bear their stooping bodies, all crowded on the view together; there were the bleared eye, the hare-lip, the crooked foot, and every ugliness or distortion that told of unnatural aversion conceived by parents for their offspring, or of young lives which, from the earliest dawn of infancy, had been one horrible endurance of cruelty and neglect. There were little faces which should have been handsome, darkened with the scowl of sullen dogged suffering; there was childhood with the light of its eye quenched, its beauty gone, and its helplessness alone remaining; there were vicious-faced boys brooding, with leaden eyes, like malefactors in a jail; and there were young creatures on whom the sins of their frail parents had descended, weeping even for the mercenary nurses they had known, and lonesome even in their loneliness. With every kindly sympathy and affection blasted in its birth, with every young and healthy feeling flogged and starved down, with every revengeful passion that can fester in swollen hearts, eating its evil way to their core in silence, what an incipient Hell was breeding there!

And yet this scene, painful as it was, had its grotesque features, which, in a less interested observer than Nicholas, might have provoked a smile. Mrs. Squeers stood at one of the desks, presiding over an immense basin of brimstone and treacle, of which delicious compound she administered a large instalment to each boy in succession, using for the purpose a common wooden spoon, which might have been originally manufactured for some gigantic top, and which widened every young gentleman's mouth considerably, they being all obliged, under heavy corporal penalties, to take in the whole of the bowl at a gasp. In another corner, huddled together for companionship, were the little boys who had arrived on the preceding night, three of them in very large leather breeches, and two in old trousers, a something tighter fit than drawers are usually worn ; at no great distance from them was seated the juvenile son and heir of Mr. Squeers—a striking likeness of his father—kicking with great vigour under the hands of Smike, who was fitting upon him a pair of new boots that bore a most suspicious resemblance to those which the least of the little boys had worn on the journey down, as the little boy himself seemed to think, for he was regarding the appropriation with a look of most rueful amazement. Besides these, there was a long row of boys waiting, with countenances of no pleasant anticipation, to be treacled, and another file who had just escaped from the infliction, making a variety of wry mouths indicative of any thing but satisfaction. The whole were attired in such motley, ill-assorted, extraordinary garments, as would have been irresistibly ridiculous, but for the foul appearance of dirt, disorder, and disease, with which they were associated.

" Now," said Squeers, giving the desk a great rap with his cane, which made half the little boys nearly jump out of their boots, " is that physicking over ? "

" Just over," said Mrs. Squeers, choking the last boy in her hurry, and tapping the crown of his head with the wooden spoon to restore him. " Here, you Smike; take away now. Look sharp."

Smike shuffled out with the basin, and Mrs. Squeers having called up a little boy with a curly head, and wiped her hands upon it, hurried out after him into a species of wash-house, where there was a small fire and a large kettle, together with a number of little wooden bowls which were arranged upon a board.

Into these bowls Mrs. Squeers, assisted by the hungry servant, poured a brown composition which looked like diluted pincushions without the covers, and was called porridge. A minute wedge of brown bread was inserted in each bowl, and when they had eat their porridge by means of the bread, the boys eat the bread itself, and had finished their breakfast ; whereupon Mr. Squeers said, in a solemn voice, " For what we have received may the Lord make us truly thankful ! "—and went away to his own.

Nicholas distended his stomach with a bowl of porridge, for much the same reason which induces some savages to swallow earth—lest they should be inconveniently hungry when there is nothing to eat. Having further disposed of a slice of bread and butter, allotted to him in virtue of his office, he sat himself down to wait for school-time.

He could not but observe how silent and sad the boys all seemed to be. There was none of the noise and clamour of a school-room, none of its boisterous play or hearty mirth. The children sat crouching and shivering together, and seemed to lack the spirit to move about. The only pupil who evinced the slightest tendency towards locomotion or playfulness was Master Squeers, and as his chief amusement was to tread upon the other boys' toes in his new boots, his flow of spirits was rather disagreeable than otherwise.

After some half-hour's delay Mr. Squeers reappeared, and the boys took their places and their books, of which latter commodity the average might be about one to eight learners. A few minutes having elapsed, during which Mr. Squeers looked very profound, as if he had a perfect apprehension of what was inside all the books, and could say every word of their contents by heart if he only chose to take the trouble, that gentleman called up the first class.

Obedient to this summons there ranged themselves in front of the schoolmaster's desk, half-a-dozen scarecrows, out at knees and elbows, one of whom placed a torn and filthy book beneath his learned eye.

" This is the first class in English spelling and philosophy, Nickleby," said Squeers, beckoning Nicholas to stand beside him. " We'll get up a Latin one, and hand that over to you. Now, then, where's the first boy ? "

" Please, Sir, he's cleaning the back parlour window," said the temporary head of the philosophical class.

" So he is, to be sure," rejoined Squeers. " We go upon the practical mode of teaching, Nickleby ; the regular education system. C-l-e-a-n, clean, verb active, to make bright, to scour. W-i-n, win, d-e-r, der, winder, a casement. When the boy knows this out of book, he goes and does it. It's just the same principle as the use of the globes. Where's the second boy ? "

" Please, Sir, he's weeding the garden," replied a small voice.

" To be sure," said Squeers, by no means disconcerted. " So he is. B-o-t, bot, t-i-n, tin, bottin, n-e-y, ney, bottinney, noun substantive, a knowledge of plants. When he has learned that bottinney means a knowledge of plants, he goes and knows 'em. That's our system, Nickleby : what do you think of it ? "

" It's a very useful one, at any rate," answered Nicholas significantly.

" I believe you," rejoined Squeers, not remarking the emphasis of his usher. " Third boy, what's a horse ? "

" A beast, Sir," replied the boy.

" So it is," said Squeers. " Ain't it, Nickleby ? "

" I believe there is no doubt of that, Sir," answered Nicholas.

" Of course there isn't," said Squeers. " A horse is a quadruped, and quadruped's Latin for beast, as every body that's gone through the grammar knows, or else where's the use of having grammars at all ? "

" Where, indeed ! " said Nicholas abstractedly.

" As you're perfect in that," resumed Squeers, turning to the boy, " go and look after *my* horse, and rub him down well, or I'll rub you down. The rest of the class go and draw water up till somebody tells you to leave off, for it's washing day to-morrow, and they want the coppers filled."

So saying he dismissed the first class to their experiments in practical philosophy, and eyed Nicholas with a look half cunning and half doubtful, as if he were not altogether certain what he might think of him by this time.

" That's the way we do it, Nickleby," he said, after a long pause.

Nicholas shrugged his shoulders in a manner that was scarcely perceptible, and said he saw it was.

" And a very good way it is, too," said Squeers. " Now, just take those fourteen little boys and hear them some reading, because you know you must begin to be useful, and idling about here won't do."

Mr. Squeers said this as if it had suddenly occurred to him, either that he must not say too much to his assistant, or that his assistant did not say enough to him in praise of the establishment. The children were arranged in a semicircle round the new master, and he was soon listening to their dull, drawling, hesitating recital of those stories of engrossing interest which are to be found in the more antiquated spelling books.

In this exciting occupation the morning lagged heavily on. At one o'clock, the boys having previously had their appetites thoroughly taken away by stir-about and potatoes, sat down in the kitchen to some hard salt beef, of which Nicholas was graciously permitted to take his portion to his own solitary desk, and to eat there in peace. After this there was another hour of crouching in the school-room and shivering with cold, and then school began again.

It was Mr. Squeers's custom to call the boys together, and make a sort of report after every half-yearly visit to the metropolis regarding the relations and friends he had seen, the news he had heard, the letters he had brought down, the bills which had been paid, the accounts which had been left unpaid, and so forth. This solemn proceeding always took place in the afternoon of the day succeeding his return ; perhaps because the boys acquired strength of mind from the suspense of the morning, or possibly because Mr. Squeers himself acquired greater sternness and inflexibility from certain warm potations in which he was wont to indulge after his early dinner. Be this as it may, the boys were recalled from house-window, garden, stable, and cow-yard, and the school were assembled in full conclave, when Mr. Squeers, with a small bundle of papers in his hand, and Mrs. S. following with a pair of canes, entered the room and proclaimed silence.

" Let any boy speak a word without leave," said Mr. Squeers, mildly, " and I'll take the skin off his back."

This special proclamation had the desired effect, and a deathlike silence immediately prevailed, in the midst of which Mr. Squeers went on to say—

" Boys, I've been to London, and have returned to my family and you, as strong and well as ever."

According to half-yearly custom, the boys gave three feeble cheers at this refreshing intelligence. Such cheers ! Sighs of extra strength with the chill on.

" I have seen the parents of some boys," continued Squeers, turning over his papers, " and they're so glad to hear how their sons are getting on that there's no prospect at all of their going away, which of course is a very pleasant thing to reflect upon for all parties."

Two or three hands went to two or three eyes when Squeers said this, but the greater part of the young gentlemen having no particular parents to speak of, were wholly uninterested in the thing one way or other.

" I have had disappointments to contend against," said Squeers, looking very grim, " Bolder's father was two pound ten short. Where is Bolder ? "

" Here he is, please Sir," rejoined twenty officious voices. Boys are very like men to be sure.

" Come here, Bolder," said Squeers.

An unhealthy-looking boy, with warts all over his hands, stepped from his place to the master's desk, and raised his eyes imploringly to Squeers's face ; his own quite white from the rapid beating of his heart.

" Bolder," said Squeers, speaking very slowly, for he was considering, as the saying goes, where to have him. " Bolder, if your father thinks that because—why what's this, Sir ? "

As Squeers spoke, he caught up the boy's hand by the cuff of his jacket, and surveyed it with an edifying aspect of horror and disgust.

" What do you call this, Sir ? " demanded the schoolmaster, administering a cut with the cane to expedite the reply.

" I can't help it, indeed, Sir," rejoined the boy, crying. " They will come ; it's the dirty work I think, Sir—at least I don't know what it is, Sir, but it's not my fault."

" Bolder," said Squeers, tucking up his wristbands and moistening the palm of his right hand to get a good grip of the cane, " you're an incorrigible young scoundrel, and as the last thrashing did you no good, we must see what another will do towards beating it out of you.",

With this, and wholly disregarding a piteous cry for mercy, Mr. Squeers fell upon the boy and caned him soundly : not leaving off indeed, until his arm was tired out.

" There," said Squeers, when he had quite done ; " rub away as hard as you like, you won't rub that off in a hurry. Oh ! you won't hold that noise, won't you ? Put him out, Smike."

The drudge knew better from long experience, than to hesitate about obeying, so he bundled the victim out by a side door, and Mr. Squeers perched himself again on his own stool, supported by Mrs. Squeers, who occupied another at his side.

" Now let us see," said Squeers. " A letter for Cobbey. Stand up, Cobbey."

Another boy stood up, and eyed the letter very hard while Squeers made a mental abstract of the same.

" Oh ! " said Squeers : " Cobbey's grandmother is dead, and his uncle John has took to drinking, which is all the news his sister sends, except eighteenpence, which will just pay for that broken square of glass. Mrs. Squeers, my dear, will you take the money ? "

The worthy lady pocketed the eighteenpence with a most business-like air, and Squeers passed on to the next boy as coolly as possible.

" Graymarsh," said Squeers, " he's the next. Stand up, Graymarsh."

Another boy stood up, and the schoolmaster looked over the letter as before.

" Graymarsh's maternal aunt," said Squeers when he had possessed himself of the contents, " is very glad to hear he's so well and happy, and sends her respectful compliments to Mrs. Squeers, and thinks she must be an angel. She likewise thinks Mr. Squeers is too good for this world; but hopes he may long be spared to carry on the business. Would have sent the two pair of stockings as desired, but is short of money, so forwards a tract instead, and hopes Graymarsh will put his trust in Providence. Hopes above all, that he will study in everything to please Mr. and Mrs. Squeers, and look upon them as his only friends; and that he will love Master Squeers, and not object to sleeping five in a bed, which no Christian should. Ah!" said Squeers, folding it up, " a delightful letter. Very affecting, indeed."

It was affecting in one sense, for Graymarsh's maternal aunt was strongly supposed, by her more intimate friends, to be no other than his maternal parent; Squeers however, without alluding to this part of the story (which would have sounded immoral before boys), proceeded with the business by calling out " Mobbs," whereupon another boy rose, and Graymarsh resumed his seat.

" Mobbs's mother-in-law," said Squeers, " took to her bed on hearing that he would not eat fat, and has been very ill ever since. She wishes to know by an early post where he expects to go to, if he quarrels with his vittles; and with what feelings he could turn up his nose at the cow's liver broth, after his good master had asked a blessing on it. This was told her in the London newspapers—not by Mr. Squeers, for he is too kind and too good to set anybody against anybody—and it has vexed her so much, Mobbs can't think. She is sorry to find he is discontented, which is sinful and horrid, and hopes Mr. Squeers will flog him into a happier state of mind; with which view she has also stopped his halfpenny a week pocket-money, and given a double-bladed knife with a corkscrew in it to the Missionaries, which she had bought on purpose for him."

" A sulky state of feeling," said Squeers, after a terrible pause, during which he had moistened the palm of his right hand again, " won't do; cheerfulness and contentment must be kept up. Mobbs, come to me."

Mobbs moved slowly towards the desk, rubbing his eyes in anticipation of good cause for doing so; and he soon afterwards retired by the side door, with as good cause as a boy need have.

Mr. Squeers then proceeded to open a miscellaneous collection of letters, some enclosing money, which Mrs. Squeers " took care of;" and others referring to small articles of apparel, as caps and so forth, all of which the same lady stated to be too large or too small, and calculated for nobody but young Squeers, who would appear indeed to have had most accommodating limbs, since everything that came into the school fitted him to a nicety. His head, in particular, must have been singularly elastic, for hats and caps of all dimensions were alike to him.

This business despatched, a few slovenly lessons were performed, and Squeers retired to his fireside, leaving Nicholas to take care of the boys in the school-room, which was very cold, and where a meal of bread and cheese was served out shortly after dark.

There was a small stove at that corner of the room which was nearest to the master's desk, and by it Nicholas sat down, so depressed and self-degraded by the consciousness of his position, that if death could have come upon him at that time he would have been almost happy to meet it. The cruelty of which he had been an unwilling witness, the coarse and ruffianly behaviour of Squeers even in his best moods, the filthy place, the sights and sounds about him, all contributed to this state of feeling; but when he recollected that being there as an assistant, he actually seemed—no matter what unhappy train of circumstances had led him to that pass—to be the aider and abettor of a system which filled him with honest disgust and indignation, he loathed himself, and felt for the moment as though the mere consciousness of his present situation must, through all time to come, prevent his raising his head in society again.

But for the present his resolve was taken, and the resolution he had formed on the preceding night remained undisturbed. He had written to his mother and sister, announcing the safe conclusion of his journey, and saying as little about Dotheboys Hall, and saying that little as cheerfully, as he possibly could. He hoped that by remaining where he was, he might do some good, even there, and at all events others depended too much on his uncle's favour to admit of his awakening his wrath just then.

One reflection disturbed him far more than any selfish considerations arising out of his own position. This was the probable destination of his sister Kate. His uncle had deceived him, and might he not consign her to some miserable place where her youth and beauty would prove a far greater curse than ugliness and decrepitude ? To a caged man, bound hand and foot, this was a terrible idea ;—but no, he thought, his mother was by ; there was the portrait-painter, too—simple enough, but still living in the world, and of it. He was willing to believe that Ralph Nickleby had conceived a personal dislike to himself. Having pretty good reason by this time to reciprocate it, he had no great difficulty in arriving at that conclusion, and tried to persuade himself that the feeling extended no farther than between them.

As he was absorbed in these meditations he all at once encountered the upturned face of Smike, who was on his knees before the stove, picking a few stray cinders from the hearth and planting them on the fire. He had paused to steal a look at Nicholas, and when he saw that he was observed, shrunk back as if expecting a blow.

" You need not fear me," said Nicholas kindly. " Are you cold ?"

" N-n-o."

" You are shivering."

" I am not cold," replied Smike quickly. " I am used to it."

There was such an obvious fear of giving offence in his manner, and he was such a timid, broken-spirited creature, that Nicholas could not help exclaiming, " Poor fellow ! "

If he had struck the drudge, he would have slunk away without a word. But now he burst into tears.

" Oh dear, oh dear ! " he cried, covering his face with his cracked and horny hands. " My heart will break. It will, it will."

" Hush ! " said Nicholas, laying his hand upon his shoulder. " Be a man ; you are nearly one by years, God help you."

" By years ! " cried Smike. " Oh dear, dear, how many of them !

How many of them since I was a little child, younger than any that are here now! Where are they all!"

" Whom do you speak of?" inquired Nicholas, wishing to rouse the poor half-witted creature to reason. " Tell me."

" My friends," he replied, " myself—my—oh! what sufferings mine have been!"

" There is always hope," said Nicholas; he knew not what to say.

" No," rejoined the other, " no; none for me. Do you remember the boy that died here?"

" I was not here you know," said Nicholas gently; " but what of him?"

" Why," replied the youth, drawing closer to his questioner's side, " I was with him at night, and when it was all silent he cried no more for friends he wished to come and sit with him, but began to see faces round his bed that came from home; he said they smiled, and talked to him, and died at last lifting his head to kiss them. Do you hear?"

" Yes, yes," rejoined Nicholas.

" What faces will smile on me when I die!" said his companion, shivering. " Who will talk to me in those long nights? They cannot come from home; they would frighten me if they did, for I don't know what it is, and shouldn't know them. Pain and fear, pain and fear for me, alive or dead. No hope, no hope."

The bell rang to bed, and the boy subsiding at the sound into his usual listless state, crept away as if anxious to avoid notice. It was with a heavy heart that Nicholas soon afterwards—no, not retired; there was no retirement there—followed—to his dirty and crowded dormitory.

CHAPTER IX.

OF MISS SQUEERS, MRS. SQUEERS, MASTER SQUEERS, AND MR. SQUEERS; AND VARIOUS MATTERS AND PERSONS CONNECTED NO LESS WITH THE SQUEERSES THAN WITH NICHOLAS NICKLEBY.

When Mr. Squeers left the school-room for the night, he betook himself, as has been before remarked, to his own fire-side, which was situated—not in the room in which Nicholas had supped on the night of his arrival, but in a smaller apartment in the rear of the premises, where his lady wife, his amiable son, and accomplished daughter, were in the full enjoyment of each other's society: Mrs. Squeers being engaged in the matronly pursuit of stocking-darning, and the young lady and gentleman occupied in the adjustment of some youthful differences by means of a pugilistic contest across the table, which, on the approach of their honoured parent, subsided into a noiseless exchange of kicks beneath it.

And in this place it may be as well to apprise the reader, that Miss Fanny Squeers was in her three-and-twentieth year. If there be any one grace or loveliness inseparable from that particular period of life, Miss Squeers may be presumed to have been possessed of it, as there is no reason to suppose that she was a solitary exception to a universal rule. She was not tall like her mother, but short like her father; from the former she inherited a voice of harsh quality, and from the latter a remarkable expression of the right eye, something akin to having none at all.

Miss Squeers had been spending a few days with a neighbouring friend, and had only just returned to the parental roof. To this circumstance may be referred her having heard nothing of Nicholas, until Mr. Squeers himself now made him the subject of conversation.

" Well, my dear," said Squeers, drawing up his chair, " what do you think of him by this time?"

" Think of who?" inquired Mrs. Squeers; who (as she often remarked) was no grammarian, thank God.

" Of the young man—the new teacher—who else could I mean?"

"Oh! that Knuckleboy," said Mrs. Squeers impatiently; "I hate him."

" What do you hate him for, my dear?" asked Squeers.

" What's that to you?" retorted Mrs. Squeers. " If I hate him that's enough, ain't it?"

" Quite enough for him, my dear, and a great deal too much I dare say, if he knew it," replied Squeers in a pacific tone. " I only asked from curiosity, my dear."

" Well, then, if you want to know," rejoined Mrs. Squeers, " I'll tell you. Because he's a proud, haughty, consequential, turned-up-nosed peacock."

Mrs. Squeers when excited was accustomed to use strong language, and moreover to make use of a plurality of epithets, some of which were of a figurative kind, as the word peacock, and furthermore the allusion to Nicholas's nose, which was not intended to be taken in its literal sense, but rather to bear a latitude of construction according to the fancy of the hearers. Neither were they meant to bear reference to each other, so much as to the object on whom they were bestowed, as will be seen in the present case: a peacock with a turned-up-nose being a novelty in ornithology, and a thing not commonly seen.

" Hem!" said Squeers, as if in mild deprecation of this outbreak. " He is cheap, my dear; the young man is very cheap."

" Not a bit of it," retorted Mrs. Squeers.

" Five pound a year," said Squeers.

" What of that; it's dear if you don't want him, isn't it?" replied his wife.

" But we do want him," urged Squeers.

" I don't see that you want him any more than the dead," said Mrs. Squeers. " Don't tell me. You can put on the cards and in the advertisements, ' Education by Mr. Wackford Squeers and able assistants,' without having any assistants, can't you? Isn't it done every day by all the masters about? I've no patience with you."

" Haven't you!" said Squeers, sternly. " Now I'll tell you what, Mrs. Squeers. In this matter of having a teacher, I'll take my own way, if you please. A slave driver in the West Indies is allowed a man under him, to see that his blacks don't run away, or get up a rebellion ; and I'll have a man under me to do the same with *our* blacks, till such time as little Wackford is able to take charge of the school."

"Am I to take care of the school when I grow up a man, father?" said Wackford junior, suspending, in the excess of his delight, a vicious kick which he was administering to his sister.

"You are, my son," replied Mr. Squeers, in a sentimental voice.

"Oh my eye, won't I give it to the boys !" exclaimed the interesting child, grasping his father's cane.   "Oh father, won't I make 'em squeak again ! "

It was a proud moment in Mr. Squeers's life to witness that burst of enthusiasm in his young child's mind, and to see in it a foreshadowing of his future eminence.   He pressed a penny into his hand, and gave vent to his feelings (as did his exemplary wife also), in a shout of approving laughter.   The infantine appeal to their common sympathies at once restored cheerfulness to the conversation, and harmony to the company.

"He's a nasty stuck-up monkey, that's what I consider him," said Mrs. Squeers, reverting to Nicholas.

"Supposing he is," said Squeers, "he is as well stuck up in our school-room as anywhere else, isn't he?—especially as he don't like it."

"Well," observed Mrs. Squeers, "there's something in that.   I hope it'll bring his pride down, and it shall be no fault of mine if it don't."

Now, a proud usher in a Yorkshire school was such a very extraordinary and unaccountable thing to hear of,—any usher at all being a novelty, but a proud one a being of whose existence the wildest imagination could never have dreamt—that Miss Squeers, who seldom troubled herself with scholastic matters, inquired with much curiosity who this Knuckleboy was that gave himself such airs.

"Nickleby," said Squeers, spelling the name according to some eccentric system which prevailed in his own mind, "your mother always calls things and people by their wrong names."

"No matter for that," said Mrs. Squeers, "I see them with right eyes, and that's quite enough for me.   I watched him when you were laying on to little Bolder this afternoon.   He looked as black as thunder all the while, and one time started up as if he had more than got it in his mind to make a rush at you ; I saw him, though he thought I didn't."

"Never mind that, father," said Miss Squeers, as the head of the family was about to reply.   "Who is the man?"

"Why, your father has get some nonsense in his head that he's the son of a poor gentleman that died the other day," said Mrs. Squeers.

"The son of a gentleman ! "

"Yes; but I don't believe a word of it.   If he's a gentleman's son at all he's a fondling, that's my opinion."

Mrs. Squeers intended to say "foundling," but, as she frequently remarked when she made any such mistake, it would be all the same a hundred years hence ; with which axiom of philosophy indeed she was in the constant habit of consoling the boys when they laboured under more than ordinary ill usage.

" He's nothing of the kind," said Squeers in answer to the above remark, " for his father was married to his mother, years before he was born, and she is alive now. If he was it would be no business of ours, for we make a very good friend by having him here, and if he likes to learn the boys anything besides minding them, I have no objection I am sure."

" I say again I hate him worse than poison," said Mrs. Squeers vehemently.

" If you dislike him, my dear," returned Squeers, " I don't know anybody who can show dislike better than you, and of course there's no occasion, with him, to take the trouble to hide it."

" I don't intend to, I assure you," interposed Mrs. S.

" That's right," said Squeers ; " and if he has a touch of pride about him, as I think he has, I don't believe there's a woman in all England that can bring anybody's spirit down as quick as you can, my love."

Mrs. Squeers chuckled vastly on the receipt of these flattering compliments, and said, she hoped she had tamed a high spirit or two in her day. It is but due to her character to say, that in conjunction with her estimable husband, she had broken many and many a one.

Miss Fanny Squeers carefully treasured up this and much more conversation on the same subject until she retired for the night, when she questioned the hungry servant minutely regarding the outward appearance and demeanour of Nicholas ; to which queries the girl returned such enthusiastic replies, coupled with so many laudatory remarks touching his beautiful dark eyes, and his sweet smile, and his straight legs—upon which last-named articles she laid particular stress, the general run of legs at Dotheboys Hall being crooked—that Miss Squeers was not long in arriving at the conclusion that the new usher must be a very remarkable person, or as she herself significantly phrased it, " something quite out of the common." And so Miss Squeers made up her mind that she would take a personal observation of Nicholas the very next day.

In pursuance of this design, the young lady watched the opportunity of her mother being engaged and her father absent, and went accidentally into the school-room to get a pen mended, where, seeing nobody but Nicholas presiding over the boys, she blushed very deeply, and exhibited great confusion.

" I beg your pardon," faltered Miss Squeers ; " I thought my father was—or might be—dear me, how very awkward !"

" Mr. Squeers is out," said Nicholas, by no means overcome by the apparition, unexpected though it was.

" Do you know will he be long, Sir ? " asked Miss Squeers, with bashful hesitation.

" He said about an hour," replied Nicholas—politely of course, but without any indication of being stricken to the heart by Miss Squeers's charms.

" I never knew any thing happen so cross," exclaimed the young lady. " Thank you ; I am very sorry I intruded I am sure. If I hadn't thought my father was here, I wouldn't upon any account have —it is very provoking—must look so very strange," murmured Miss

Squeers, blushing once more, and glancing from the pen in her hand, to Nicholas at his desk, and back again.

"If that is all you want," said Nicholas, pointing to the pen, and smiling, in spite of himself, at the affected embarrassment of the school-master's daughter, "perhaps I can supply his place."

Miss Squeers glanced at the door as if dubious of the propriety of advancing any nearer to an utter stranger, then round the school-room as though in some measure reassured by the presence of forty boys, and finally sidled up to Nicholas, and delivered the pen into his hand with a most winning mixture of reserve and condescension.

"Shall it be a hard or a soft nib?" inquired Nicholas, smiling to prevent himself from laughing outright.

"He *has* a beautiful smile," thought Miss Squeers.

"Which did you say?" asked Nicholas.

"Dear me, I was thinking of something else for the moment, I declare," replied Miss Squeers—"Oh! as soft as possible, if you please." With which words Miss Squeers sighed; it might be to give Nicholas to understand that her heart was soft, and that the pen was wanted to match.

Upon these instructions Nicholas made the pen; when he gave it to Miss Squeers, Miss Squeers dropped it, and when he stooped to pick it up, Miss Squeers stooped also, and they knocked their heads together, whereat five-and-twenty little boys laughed aloud, being positively for the first and only time that half year.

"Very awkward of me," said Nicholas, opening the door for the young lady's retreat.

"Not at all, Sir," replied Miss Squeers; "it was my fault. It was all my foolish—a—a—good morning."

"Good bye," said Nicholas. "The next I make for you, I hope will be made less clumsily. Take care, you are biting the nib off now."

"Really," said Miss Squeers; "so embarrassing that I scarcely know what I—very sorry to give you so much trouble."

"Not the least trouble in the world," replied Nicholas, closing the school-room door.

"I never saw such legs in the whole course of my life!" said Miss Squeers, as she walked away.

In fact, Miss Squeers was in love with Nicholas Nickleby.

To account for the rapidity with which this young lady had conceived a passion for Nicholas, it may be necessary to state that the friend from whom she had so recently returned was a miller's daughter of only eighteen, who had contracted herself unto the son of a small corn-factor resident in the nearest market town. Miss Squeers and the miller's daughter being fast friends, had covenanted together some two years before, according to a custom prevalent among young ladies, that whoever was first engaged to be married should straightway confide the mighty secret to the bosom of the other, before communicating it to any living soul, and bespeak her as bridesmaid without loss of time; in fulfilment of which pledge the miller's daughter, when her engagement was formed, came out express at eleven o'clock at night as the corn-factor's son made an offer of his hand and heart at twenty-five minutes past ten by the Dutch clock in the kitchen, and rushed into Miss Squeers's bed-room with the gratifying intelligence. Now, Miss Squeers being five years older, and out of her teens (which is also a great matter), had since been more than commonly anxious to return the compliment, and possess her friend with a similar secret ; but either in consequence of finding it hard to please herself, or harder still to please any body else, had never had an opportunity so to do, inasmuch as she had no such secret to disclose. The little interview with Nicholas had no sooner passed as above described, however, than Miss Squeers, putting on her bonnet, made her way with great precipitation to her friend's house, and upon a solemn renewal of divers old vows of secrecy, revealed how that she was—not exactly engaged, but going to be—to a gentleman's son—(none of your corn-factors, but a gentleman's son of high descent)—who had come down as teacher to Dotheboys Hall under most mysterious and remarkable circumstances—indeed, as Miss Squeers more than once hinted she had good reason to believe—induced by the fame of her many charms to seek her out, and woo and win her.

" Isn't it an extraordinary thing ? " said Miss Squeers, emphasising the adjective strongly.

" Most extraordinary," replied the friend. " But what has he said to you ? "

" Don't ask me what he said, my dear," rejoined Miss Squeers. " If you had only seen his looks and smiles ! I never was so overcome in all my life."

" Did he look in this way ? " inquired the miller's daughter, counterfeiting as nearly as she could a favourite leer of the corn-factor.

" Very like that—only more genteel," replied Miss Squeers.

" Ah ! " said the friend, " then he means something depend on it."

Miss Squeers, having slight misgivings on the subject, was by no means ill pleased to be confirmed by a competent authority; and discovering, on further conversation and comparison of notes, a great many points of resemblance between the behaviour of Nicholas and that of the corn-factor, grew so exceedingly confidential, that she intrusted her friend with a vast number of things Nicholas had *not* said, which were all so very complimentary as to be quite conclusive. Then she dilated on the fearful hardship of having a father and mother strenuously opposed to her intended husband, on which unhappy circumstance she dwelt at great length ; for the friend's father and mother were quite agreeable to her being married, and the whole courtship was in consequence as flat and common-place an affair as it was possible to imagine.

" How I should like to see him ! " exclaimed the friend.

" So you shall, 'Tilda," replied Miss Squeers. " I should consider myself one of the most ungrateful creatures alive, if I denied you. I think mother's going away for two days to fetch some boys, and when she does, I'll ask you and John up to tea, and have him to meet you."

This was a charming idea, and having fully discussed it, the friends parted.

It so fell out that Mrs. Squeers's journey to some distance, to fetch three new boys, and dun the relations of two old ones for the balance of a small account, was fixed that very afternoon for the next day but one; and on the next day but one Mrs. Squeers got up outside the coach as it stopped to change at Greta Bridge, taking with her a small bundle containing something in a bottle and some sandwiches, and carrying besides a large white top coat to wear in the night-time; with which baggage she went her way.

Whenever such opportunities as these occurred, it was Squeers's custom to drive over to the market town every evening on pretence of urgent business, and stop till ten or eleven o'clock at a tavern he much affected. As the party was not in his way therefore, but rather afforded a means of compromise with Miss Squeers, he readily yielded his full assent thereunto, and willingly communicated to Nicholas that he was expected to take his tea in the parlour that evening at five o'clock.

To be sure Miss Squeers was in a desperate flutter as the time approached, and to be sure she was dressed out to the best advantage: with her hair—it had more than a tinge of red, and she wore it in a crop—curled in five distinct rows up to the very top of her head, and arranged dexterously over the doubtful eye; to say nothing of the blue sash which floated down her back, or the worked apron, or the long gloves, or the green gauze scarf worn over one shoulder and under the other, or any of the numerous devices which were to be as so many arrows to the heart of Nicholas. She had scarcely completed these arrangements to her entire satisfaction when the friend arrived with a whitey-brown parcel—flat and three-cornered—containing sundry small adornments which were to be put on up stairs, and which the friend put on, talking incessantly. When Miss Squeers had " done" the friend's hair, the friend " did" Miss Squeers's hair, throwing in some striking improvements in the way of ringlets down the neck; and then, when they were both touched up to their entire satisfaction, they went down stairs in full state with the long gloves on, all ready for company.

" Where's John, 'Tilda?" said Miss Squeers.

" Only gone home to clean himself," replied the friend. " He will be here by the time the tea's drawn."

" I do so palpitate," observed Miss Squeers.

" Ah! I know what it is," replied the friend.

" I have not been used to it, you know, 'Tilda," said Miss Squeers, applying her hand to the left side of her sash.

" You'll soon get the better of it, dear," rejoined the friend. While they were talking thus the hungry servant brought in the tea things, and soon afterwards somebody tapped at the room door.

" There he is!" cried Miss Squeers. " Oh 'Tilda!"

" Hush!" said 'Tilda. " Hem! Say, come in."

" Come in," cried Miss Squeers faintly. And in walked Nicholas.

" Good evening," said that young gentleman, all unconscious of his conquest. " I understood from Mr. Squeers that"——

" Oh yes; it's all right," interposed Miss Squeers. " Father don't tea with us, but you won't mind that I dare say." (This was said archly.)

Nicholas opened his eyes at this, but he turned the matter off very coolly—not caring particularly about any thing just then—and went through the ceremony of introduction to the miller's daughter with so much grace, that that young lady was lost in admiration.

" We are only waiting for one more gentleman," said Miss Squeers, taking off the tea-pot lid, and looking in, to see how the tea was getting on.

It was matter of equal moment to Nicholas whether they were waiting for one gentleman or twenty, so he received the intelligence with perfect unconcern ; and being out of spirits, and not seeing any especial reason why he should make himself agreeable, looked out of the window and sighed involuntarily.

As luck would have it, Miss Squeers's friend was of a playful turn, and hearing Nicholas sigh, she took it into her head to rally the lovers on their lowness of spirits.

" But if it's caused by my being here," said the young lady, " don't mind me a bit, for I'm quite as bad. You may go on just as you would if you were alone."

" 'Tilda," said Miss Squeers, colouring up to the top row of curls, " I am ashamed of you ;" and here the two friends burst into a variety of giggles, and glanced from time to time over the tops of their pocket-handkerchiefs at Nicholas, who, from a state of unmixed astonishment, gradually fell into one of irrepressible laughter—occasioned partly by the bare notion of his being in love with Miss Squeers, and partly by the preposterous appearance and behaviour of the two girls ; the two causes of merriment taken together, struck him as being so keenly ridiculous, that despite his miserable condition, he laughed till he was thoroughly exhausted.

" Well," thought Nicholas, " as I am here, and seem expected for some reason or other to be amiable, it's of no use looking like a goose. I may as well accommodate myself to the company."

We blush to tell it, but his youthful spirits and vivacity getting for a time the better of his sad thoughts, he no sooner formed this resolution than he saluted Miss Squeers and the friend with great gallantry, and drawing a chair to the tea-table, began to make himself more at home than in all probability an usher has ever done in his employer's house since ushers were first invented.

The ladies were in the full delight of this altered behaviour on the part of Mr. Nickleby, when the expected swain arrived with his hair very damp from recent washing; and a clean shirt, whereof the collar might have belonged to some giant ancestor, forming, together with a white waistcoat of similar dimensions, the chief ornament of his person.

" Well, John," said Miss Matilda Price (which, by-the-bye, was the name of the miller's daughter).

" Weel," said John, with a grin that even the collar could not conceal.

" I beg your pardon," interposed Miss Squeers, hastening to do the honours, " Mr. Nickleby—Mr. John Browdie."

" Servant, Sir," said John, who was something over six feet high, with a face and body rather above the due proportion than below it.

" Yours to command, Sir," replied Nicholas, making fearful ravages on the bread and butter.

Mr. Browdie was not a gentleman of great conversational powers, so he grinned twice more, and having now bestowed his customary mark of recognition on every person in company, grinned at nothing particular and helped himself to food.

" Old wooman awa,' beant she?" said Mr. Browdie, with his mouth full. Miss Squeers nodded assent.

Mr. Browdie gave a grin of special width, as if he thought that really was something to laugh at, and went to work at the bread and butter with increased vigour. It was quite a sight to behold how he and Nicholas emptied the plate between them.

" Ye weant get bread and butther ev'ry neight I expect, mun," said Mr. Browdie, after he had sat staring at Nicholas a long time over the empty plate.

Nicholas bit his lip and coloured, but affected not to hear the remark.

" Ecod," said Mr. Browdie, laughing boisterously, " they dean't put too much intiv 'em. Ye'll be nowt but skeen and boans if you stop here long eneaf. Ho! ho! ho!"

" You are facetious, Sir," said Nicholas, scornfully.

" Na; I deant know," replied Mr. Browdie, " but t'oother teacher, 'cod he wur a learn 'un, he wur." The recollection of the last teacher's leanness seemed to afford Mr. Browdie the most exquisite delight, for he laughed until he found it necessary to apply his coat-cuffs to his eyes.

" I don't know whether your perceptions are quite keen enough, Mr. Browdie, to enable you to understand that your remarks are very offensive," said Nicholas in a towering passion, " but if they are, have the goodness to——"

" If you say another word, John," shrieked Miss Price, stopping her admirer's mouth as he was about to interrupt, " only half a word, I'll never forgive you, or speak to you again."

" Weel, my lass, I deant care aboot 'un," said the corn-factor, bestowing a hearty kiss on Miss Matilda; " let 'un gang on, let 'un gang on."

It now became Miss Squeers's turn to intercede with Nicholas, which she did with many symptoms of alarm and horror; the effect of the double intercession was that he and John Browdie shook hands across the table with much gravity, and such was the imposing nature of the ceremonial, that Miss Squeers was overcome and shed tears.

" What's the matter, Fanny?" said Miss Price.

" Nothing, 'Tilda," replied Miss Squeers, sobbing.

" There never was any danger," said Miss Price, " was there, Mr. Nickleby?"

" None at all," replied Nicholas. " Absurd."

" That's right," whispered Miss Price, " say something kind to her, and she'll soon come round. Here, shall John and I go into the little kitchen, and come back presently?"

" Not on any account," rejoined Nicholas, quite alarmed at the proposition. " What on earth should you do that for?"

" Well," said Miss Price, beckoning him aside, and speaking with some degree of contempt—" you *are* a one to keep company."

" What do you mean ?" said Nicholas; " I am not one to keep company at all—here at all events. I can't make this out."

" No, nor I neither," rejoined Miss Price ; " but men are always fickle, and always were, and always will be; that I can make out, very easily."

" Fickle !" cried Nicholas ; " what do you suppose ? You don't mean to say that you think——"

" Oh no, I think nothing at all," retorted Miss Price pettishly. " Look at her, dressed so beautiful and looking so well—really *almost* handsome. I am ashamed at you."

" My dear girl, what have I got to do with her dressing beautifully or looking well ?" inquired Nicholas.

" Come, don't call me a dear girl," said Miss Price—smiling a little though, for she was pretty, and a coquette too in her small way, and Nicholas was good-looking, and she supposed him the property of somebody else, which were all reasons why she should be gratified to think she had made an impression on him, " or Fanny will be saying it's my fault. Come ; we're going to have a game at cards." Pronouncing these last words aloud, she tripped away and rejoined the big Yorkshireman.

This was wholly unintelligible to Nicholas, who had no other distinct impression on his mind at the moment, than that Miss Squeers was an ordinary-looking girl, and her friend Miss Price a pretty one ; but he had not time to enlighten himself by reflection, for the hearth being by this time swept up, and the candle snuffed, they sat down to play speculation.

" There are only four of us, 'Tilda," said Miss Squeers, looking slyly at Nicholas ; " so we had better go partners, two against two."

" What do you say, Mr. Nickleby ?" inquired Miss Price.

" With all the pleasure in life," replied Nicholas. And so saying, quite unconscious of his heinous offence, he amalgamated into one common heap those portions of a Dotheboys Hall card of terms, which represented his own counters, and those allotted to Miss Price, respectively.

" Mr. Browdie," said Miss Squeers hysterically, " shall we make a bank against them ?"

The Yorkshireman assented—apparently quite overwhelmed by the new usher's impudence—and Miss Squeers darted a spiteful look at her friend, and giggled convulsively.

The deal fell to Nicholas, and the hand prospered.

" We intend to win every thing," said he.

" 'Tilda *has* won something she didn't expect I think, haven't you, dear ? " said Miss Squeers, maliciously.

" Only a dozen and eight, love," replied Miss Price, affecting to take the question in a literal sense.

" How dull you are to-night !" sneered Miss Squeers.

" No, indeed," replied Miss Price, " I am in excellent spirits. I was thinking *you* seemed out of sorts."

" Me !" cried Miss Squeers, biting her lips, and trembling with very jealousy ; " Oh no !"

" That's well," remarked Miss Price. " Your hair's coming out of curl, dear."

" Never mind me," tittered Miss Squeers; " you had better attend to your partner."

" Thank you for reminding her," said Nicholas.   " So she had."

The Yorkshireman flattened his nose once or twice with his clenched fist, as if to keep his hand in, till he had an opportunity of exercising it upon the features of some other gentleman; and Miss Squeers tossed her head with such indignation, that the gust of wind raised by the multitudinous curls in motion, nearly blew the candle out.

" I never had such luck, really," exclaimed coquettish Miss Price, after another hand or two.   " It's all along of you, Mr. Nickleby, I think.   I should like to have you for a partner always."

" I wish you had."

" You'll have a bad wife, though, if you always win at cards," said Miss Price.

" Not if your wish is gratified," replied Nicholas.   " I am sure I shall have a good one in that case."

To see how Miss Squeers tossed her head, and the corn-factor flattened his nose, while this conversation was carrying on!   It would have been worth a small annuity to have beheld that; let alone Miss Price's evident joy at making them jealous, and Nicholas Nickleby's happy unconsciousness of making anybody uncomfortable.

" We have all the talking to ourselves, it seems," said Nicholas, looking good-humouredly round the table as he took up the cards for a fresh deal.

" You do it so well," tittered Miss Squeers, " that it would be a pity to interrupt, wouldn't it, Mr. Browdie?   He! he! he!"

" Nay," said Nicholas, " we do it in default of having anybody else to talk to."

" We'll talk to you, you know, if you'll say anything," said Miss Price.

" Thank you, 'Tilda, dear," retorted Miss Squeers, majestically.

" Or you can talk to each other, if you don't choose to talk to us," said Miss Price, rallying her dear friend.   " John, why don't you say something?"

" Say summat?" repeated the Yorkshireman.

" Ay, and not sit there so silent and glum."

" Wool, then!" said the Yorkshireman, striking the table heavily with his fist, " what I say's this—Dang my boans and boddy, if I stan' this ony longer.   Do ye gang whoam wi' me; and do yon loight an' toight young whipster, look sharp out for a brokken head next time he cums under my hond."

" Mercy on us, what's all this?" cried Miss Price, in affected astonishment.

" Cum whoam, tell'e, cum whoam," replied the Yorkshireman, sternly.   And as he delivered the reply Miss Squeers burst into a shower of tears; arising in part from desperate vexation, and in part from an impotent desire to lacerate somebody's countenance with her fair finger-nails.

This state of things had been brought about by divers means and workings.   Miss Squeers had brought it about by aspiring to the high state and condition of being matrimonially engaged without good grounds for so doing; Miss Price had brought it about by indulging in three motives of action; first, a desire to punish her friend for laying claim to a rivalship in dignity, having no good title; secondly, the gratification of her own vanity in receiving the compliments of a smart young man; and thirdly, a wish to convince the corn-factor of the great danger he ran, in deferring the celebration of their expected nuptials: while Nicholas had brought it about by half an hour's gaiety and thoughtlessness, and a very sincere desire to avoid the imputation of inclining at all to Miss Squeers. So, that the means employed, and the end produced, were alike the most natural in the world: for young ladies will look forward to being married, and will jostle each other in the race to the altar, and will avail themselves of all opportunities of displaying their own attractions to the best advantage, down to the very end of time as they have done from its beginning.

" Why, and here's Fanny in tears now!" exclaimed Miss Price, as if in fresh amazement. " What can be the matter?"

" Oh! you don't know, Miss, of course you don't know. Pray don't trouble yourself to inquire," said Miss Squeers, producing that change of countenance which children call making a face.

" Well, I'm sure," exclaimed Miss Price.

" And who cares whether you are sure or not, ma'am?" retorted Miss Squeers, making another face.

" You are monstrous polite, ma'am," said Miss Price.

" I shall not come to you to take lessons in the art, ma'am," retorted Miss Squeers.

" You needn't take the trouble to make yourself plainer than you are, ma'am, however," rejoined Miss Price, " because that's quite unnecessary."

Miss Squeers in reply turned very red, and thanked God that she hadn't got the bold faces of some people, and Miss Price in rejoinder congratulated herself upon not being possessed of the envious feeling of other people; whereupon Miss Squeers made some general remark touching the danger of associating with low persons, in which Miss Price entirely coincided, observing that it was very true indeed, and she had thought so a long time.

" 'Tilda," exclaimed Miss Squeers with dignity, " I hate you."

" Ah! There's no love lost between us I assure you," said Miss Price, tying her bonnet strings with a jerk. " You'll cry your eyes out when I'm gone, you know you will."

" I scorn your words. Minx," said Miss Squeers.

" You pay me a great compliment when you say so," answered the miller's daughter, curtseying very low. " Wish you a very good night, ma'am, and pleasant dreams attend your sleep."

With this parting benediction Miss Price swept from the room, followed by the huge Yorkshireman, who exchanged with Nicholas at parting, that peculiarly expressive scowl with which the cut-and-thrust counts in melo-dramatic performances inform each other they will meet again,

They were no sooner gone than Miss Squeers fulfilled the prediction of her quondam friend by giving vent to a most copious burst of tears.

and uttering various dismal lamentations and incoherent words. Nicholas stood looking on for a few seconds, rather doubtful what to do, but feeling uncertain whether the fit would end in his being embraced or scratched, and considering that either infliction would be equally agreeable, he walked off very quietly while Miss Squeers was moaning in her pocket-handkerchief.

"This is one consequence," thought Nicholas, when he had groped his way to the dark sleeping-room, " of my cursed readiness to adapt myself to any society into which chance carries me. If I had sat mute and motionless, as I might have done, this would not have happened."

He listened for a few minutes, but all was quiet.

" I was glad," he murmured, " to grasp at any relief from the sight of this dreadful place, or the presence of its vile master. I have set these people by the ears and made two new enemies, where, Heaven knows, I needed none. Well, it is a just punishment for having forgotten, even for an hour, what is around me now."

So saying, he felt his way among the throng of weary-hearted sleepers, and crept into his poor bed.

CHAPTER X.

HOW MR. RALPH NICKLEBY PROVIDED FOR HIS NIECE AND SISTER-IN-LAW.

ON the second morning after the departure of Nicholas for Yorkshire, Kate Nickleby sat in a very faded chair raised upon a very dusty throne in Miss La Creevy's room, giving that lady a sitting for the portrait upon which she was engaged; and towards the full perfection of which, Miss La Creevy had had the street-door case brought up stairs, in order that she might be the better able to infuse into the counterfeit countenance of Miss Nickleby a bright salmon flesh-tint which she had originally hit upon while executing the miniature of a young officer therein contained, and which bright salmon flesh-tint was considered by Miss La Creevy's chief friends and patrons, to be quite a novelty in art : as indeed it was.

" I think I have caught it now," said Miss La Creevy. " The very shade. This will be the sweetest portrait I have ever done, certainly."

" It will be your genius that makes it so, then, I am sure," replied Kate, smiling.

" No, no, I won't allow that, my dear," rejoined Miss La Creevy. " It's a very nice subject—a very nice subject, indeed—though of course, something depends upon the mode of treatment."

" And not a little," observed Kate.

" Why, my dear, you are right there," said Miss La Creevy, " in the main you are right there; though I don't allow that it is of such very great importance in the present case. Ah! The difficulties of art my dear, are great."

Kate Nickleby sitting to Miss La Creevy.

" They must be, I have no doubt," said Kate, humouring her good-natured little friend.

" They are beyond anything you can form the faintest conception of," replied Miss La Creevy. "What with bringing out eyes with all one's power, and keeping down noses with all one's force, and adding to heads, and taking away teeth altogether, you have no idea of the trouble one little miniature is."

" The remuneration can scarcely repay you," said Kate.

" Why, it does not, and that's the truth," answered Miss La Creevy; " and then people are so dissatisfied and unreasonable, that nine times out of ten there's no pleasure in painting them. Sometimes they say, ' Oh, how very serious you have made me look, Miss La Creevy !' and at others, ' La, Miss La Creevy, how very smirking !' when the very essence of a good portrait is, that it must be either serious or smirking, or it's no portrait at all."

" Indeed !" said Kate, laughing.

" Certainly, my dear ; because the sitters are always either the one or the other," replied Miss La Creevy. " Look at the Royal Academy. All those beautiful shiny portraits of gentlemen in black velvet waist-coats, with their fists doubled up on round tables or marble slabs, are serious, you know ; and all the ladies who are playing with little parasols, or little dogs, or little children—it's the same rule in art, only varying the objects—are smirking. In fact," said Miss La Creevy, sinking her voice to a confidential whisper, " there are only two styles of por-trait painting, the serious and the smirk ; and we always use the serious for professional people (except actors sometimes), and the smirk for pri-vate ladies and gentlemen who don't care so much about looking clever."

Kate seemed highly amused by this information, and Miss La Creevy went on painting and talking with immovable complacency.

" What a number of officers you seem to paint !" said Kate, availing herself of a pause in the discourse, and glancing round the room.

" Number of what, child?" inquired Miss La Creevy, looking up from her work. " Character portraits, oh yes—they're not real military men, you know."

" No !"

" Bless your heart, of course not ; only clerks and that, who hire a uniform coat to be painted in and send it here in a carpet bag. Some artists," said Miss La Creevy, " keep a red coat, and charge seven-and-sixpence extra for hire and carmine ; but I don't do that myself, for I don't consider it legitimate."

Drawing herself up as though she plumed herself greatly upon not resorting to these lures to catch sitters, Miss La Creevy applied herself more intently to her task, only raising her head occasionally to look with unspeakable satisfaction at some touch she had just put in, and now and then giving Miss Nickleby to understand what particular feature she was at work upon at the moment ; " not," she expressly observed, " that you should make it up for painting, my dear, but because it's our custom sometimes, to tell sitters what part we are upon, in order that if there's any particular expression they want introduced, they may throw it in at the time, you know."

" And when," said Miss La Creevy, after a long silence, to wit, an interval of full a minute and a half, " when do you expect to see your uncle again ? "

" I scarcely know ; I had expected to have seen him before now," replied Kate. " Soon I hope, for this state of uncertainty is worse than anything."

" I suppose he has money, hasn't he ? " inquired Miss La Creevy.

" He is very rich I have heard," rejoined Kate. " I don't know that he is, but I believe so."

" Ah, you may depend upon it he is, or he wouldn't be so surly," remarked Miss La Creevy, who was an odd little mixture of shrewdness and simplicity. " When a man's a bear he is generally pretty independent."

" His manner is rough," said Kate.

" Rough ! " cried Miss La Creevy, " a porcupine's a feather-bed to him. I never met with such a cross-grained old savage."

" It is only his manner, I believe," observed Kate, timidly, " he was disappointed in early life I think I have heard, or has had his temper soured by some calamity. I should be sorry to think ill of him until I knew he deserved it."

" Well ; that's very right and proper," observed the miniature painter, " and Heaven forbid that I should be the cause of your doing so. But now mightn't he, without feeling it himself, make you and your mama some nice little allowance that would keep 'you both comfortable until you were well married, and be a little fortune to her afterwards ? What would a hundred a year, for instance, be to him ? "

" I don't know what it would be to him," said Kate, with great energy, " but it would be that to me I would rather die than take."

" Heyday ! " cried Miss La Creevy.

" A dependence upon him," said Kate, " would embitter my whole life. I should feel begging a far less degradation."

" Well ! " exclaimed Miss La Creevy. " This of a relation whom you will not hear an indifferent person speak ill of, my dear, sounds oddly enough, I confess."

" I dare say it does," replied Kate, speaking more gently, " indeed I am sure it must. I—I—only mean that with the feelings and recollection of better times upon me, I could not bear to live on anybody's bounty—not his particularly, but anybody's."

Miss La Creevy looked slyly at her companion, as if she doubted whether Ralph himself were not the subject of dislike, but seeing that her young friend was distressed, made no remark.

" I only ask of him," continued Kate, whose tears fell while she spoke, " that he will move so little out of his way in my behalf, as to enable me by his recommendation—only by his recommendation—to earn, literally, my bread and remain with my mother. Whether we shall ever taste happiness again, depends upon the fortunes of my dear brother ; but if he will do this, and Nicholas only tells us that he is well and cheerful, I shall be contented."

As she ceased to speak there was a rustling behind the screen which stood between her and the door, and some person knocked at the wainscot.

" Come in whoever it is," cried Miss La Creevy.

The person complied, and coming forward at once, gave to view the form and features of no less an individual than Mr. Ralph Nickleby himself.

" Your servant, ladies," said Ralph, looking sharply at them by turns. " You were talking so loud that I was unable to make you hear."

When the man of business had a more than commonly vicious snarl lurking at his heart, he had a trick of almost concealing his eyes under their thick and protruding brows for an instant, and then displaying them in their full keenness. As he did so now, and tried to keep down the smile which parted his thin compressed lips, and puckered up the bad lines about his mouth, they both felt certain that some part, if not the whole, of their recent conversation had been overheard.

" I called in on my way up stairs, more than half expecting to find you here," said Ralph, addressing his niece, and looking contemptuously at the portrait. " Is that my niece's portrait, ma'am ? "

" Yes it is, Mr. Nickleby," said Miss La Creevy, with a very sprightly air, " and between you and me and the post, Sir, it will be a very nice portrait too, though I say it who am the painter."

" Don't trouble yourself to show it to me, ma'am," cried Ralph, moving away, " I have no eye for likenesses. Is it nearly finished ? "

" Why, yes," replied Miss La Creevy, considering with the pencil-end of her brush in her mouth. " Two sittings more will "——

" Have them at once, ma'am," said Ralph. " She'll have no time to idle over fooleries after to-morrow. Work, ma'am, work ; we must all work. Have you let your lodgings, ma'am ? "

" I have not put a bill up yet, Sir."

" Put it up at once, ma'am ; they won't want the rooms after this week, or if they do, can't pay for them. Now, my dear, if you're ready, we'll lose no more time."

With an assumption of kindness which sat worse upon him, even than his usual manner, Mr. Ralph Nickleby motioned to the young lady to precede him, and bowing gravely to Miss La Creevy, closed the door and followed up stairs, where Mrs. Nickleby received him with many expressions of regard. Stopping them somewhat abruptly, Ralph waved his hand with an impatient gesture, and proceeded to the object of his visit.

" I have found a situation for your daughter, ma'am," said Ralph.

" Well," replied Mrs. Nickleby. " Now, I will say that that is only just what I have expected of you. ' Depend upon it,' I said to Kate only yesterday morning at breakfast, ' that after your uncle has provided in that most ready manner for Nicholas, he will not leave us until he has done at least the same for you.' These were my very words as near as I remember. Kate, my dear, why don't you thank your "——

" Let me proceed, ma'am, pray," said Ralph, interrupting his sister-in-law in the full torrent of her discourse.

" Kate, my love, let your uncle proceed," said Mrs. Nickleby.

" I am most anxious that he should, mama," rejoined Kate.

" Well, my dear, if you are anxious that he should, you had better allow your uncle to say what he has to say, without interruption," observed Mrs. Nickleby, with many small nods and frowns. " Your uncle's time is very valuable, my dear ; and however desirous you may be—and naturally desirous, as I am sure any affectionate relations who have seen so little of your uncle as we have, must naturally be—to protract the pleasure of having him among us, still we are bound not to be selfish, but to take into consideration the important nature of his occupations in the city."

" I am very much obliged to you, ma'am," said Ralph with a scarcely perceptible sneer. " An absence of business habits in this family leads apparently to a great waste of words before business—when it does come under .consideration—is arrived at, at all."

" I fear it is so indeed," replied Mrs. Nickleby with a sigh. " Your poor brother— "

" My poor brother, ma'am," interposed Ralph tartly, " had no idea what business was—was unacquainted, I verily believe, with the very meaning of the word."

" I fear he was," said Mrs. Nickleby, with her handkerchief to her eyes. " If it hadn't been for me, I don't know what would have become of him."

What strange creatures we are! The slight bait so skilfully thrown out by Ralph on their first interview was dangling on the hook yet. At every small deprivation or discomfort which presented itself in the course of the four-and-twenty hours to remind her of her straitened and altered circumstances, peevish visions of her dower of one thousand pounds had arisen before Mrs. Nickleby's mind, until at last she had come to persuade herself that of all her late husband's creditors she was the worst used and the most to be pitied. And yet she had loved him dearly for many years, and had no greater share of selfishness than is the usual lot of mortals. Such is the irritability of sudden poverty. A decent annuity would have restored her thoughts to their old train at once.

" Repining is of no use, ma'am," said Ralph. " Of all fruitless errands, sending a tear to look after a day that is gone is the most fruit-less."

" So it is," sobbed Mrs. Nickleby. " So it is."

" As you feel so keenly in your own purse and person the conse-quences of inattention to business, ma'am," said Ralph, " I am sure you will impress upon your children the necessity of attaching them-selves to it early in life."

" Of course I must see that," rejoined Mrs. Nickleby. " Sad expe-rience, you know, brother-in-law—. Kate, my dear, put that down in the next letter to Nicholas, or remind me to do it if I write."

Ralph paused for a few moments, and seeing that he had now made pretty sure of the mother in case the daughter objected to his proposi-tion, went on to say—

" The situation that I have made interest to procure, ma'am, is with —with a milliner and dress-maker, in short."

" A milliner ! " cried Mrs. Nickleby.

" A milliner and dress-maker, ma'am," replied Ralph. " Dress-makers in London, as I need not remind you, ma'am, who are so well acquainted with all matters in the ordinary routine of life, make large fortunes, keep equipages, and become persons of great wealth and fortune."

Now, the first ideas called up in Mrs. Nickleby's mind by the words milliner and dress-maker were connected with certain wicker baskets lined with black oilskin, which she remembered to have seen carried to and fro in the streets, but as Ralph proceeded these disappeared, and were replaced by visions of large houses at the West End, neat private carriages, and a banker's book, all of which images succeeded each other with such rapidity, that he had no sooner finished speaking than she nodded her head and said, " Very true," with great appearance of satisfaction.

" What your uncle says is very true, Kate, my dear," said Mrs. Nickleby. " I recollect when your poor papa and I came to town after we were married, that a young lady brought me home a chip cottage bonnet, with white and green trimming, and green persian lining, in her own carriage, which drove up to the door full gallop ;— at least, I am not quite certain whether it was her own carriage or a hackney chariot, but I remember very well that the horse dropped down dead as he was turning round, and that your poor papa said he hadn't had any corn for a fortnight."

This anecdote, so strikingly illustrative of the opulence of milliners, was not received with any great demonstration of feeling, inasmuch as Kate hung down her head while it was relating, and Ralph manifested very intelligible symptoms of extreme impatience.

" The lady's name," said Ralph, hastily striking in, " is Mantalini— Madame Mantalini. I know her. She lives near Cavendish Square. If your daughter is disposed to try after the situation, I'll take her there directly."

" Have you nothing to say to your uncle, my love ? " inquired Mrs. Nickleby.

" A great deal," replied Kate ; " but not now. I would rather speak to him when we are alone ;—it will save his time if I thank him and say what I wish to say to him as we walk along."

With these words Kate hurried away, to hide the traces of emotion that were stealing down her face, and to prepare herself for the walk, while Mrs. Nickleby amused her brother-in-law by giving him, with many tears, a detailed account of the dimensions of a rosewood cabinet piano they had possessed in their days of affluence, together with a minute description of eight drawing-room chairs with turned legs and green chintz squabs to match the curtains, which had cost two pounds fifteen shillings a-piece, and went at the sale for a mere nothing.

These reminiscences were at length cut short by Kate's return in her walking dress, when Ralph, who had been fretting and fuming during the whole time of her absence, lost no time, and used very little ceremony, in descending into the street.

" Now," he said, taking her arm, " walk as fast as you can, and you'll get into the step that you'll have to walk to business with every morning." So saying, he led Kate off at a good round pace towards Cavendish Square.

" I am very much obliged to you, uncle," said the young lady, after they had hurried on in silence for some time ; " very."

" I'm glad to hear it," said Ralph.   " I hope you'll do your duty."

" I will try to please, uncle," replied Kate; " indeed I—"

" Don't begin to cry," growled Ralph; " I hate crying."

" It's very foolish, I know, uncle," began poor Kate.

" It is," replied Ralph, stopping her short, "and very affected besides.   Let me see no more of it."

Perhaps this was not the best way to dry the tears of a young and sensitive female about to make her first entry on an entirely new scene of life, among cold and uninterested strangers ; but it had its effect notwithstanding.   Kate coloured deeply, breathed quickly for a few moments, and then walked on with a firmer and more determined step.

It was a curious contrast to see how the timid country girl shrunk through the crowd that hurried up and down the streets, giving way to the press of people, and clinging closely to Ralph as though she feared to lose him in the throng ; and how the stern and hard-featured man of business went doggedly on, elbowing the passengers aside, and now and then exchanging a gruff salutation with some passing acquaintance, who turned to look back upon his pretty charge with looks expressive of surprise, and seemed to wonder at the ill-assorted companionship.   But it would have been a stranger contrast still, to have read the hearts that were beating side by side ; to have had laid bare the gentle innocence of the one, and the rugged villany of the other ; to have hung upon the guileless thoughts of the affectionate girl, and been amazed that among all the wily plots and calculations of the old man, there should not be one word or figure denoting thought of death or of the grave.   But so it was ; and stranger still —though this is a thing of every day—the warm young heart palpitated with a thousand anxieties and apprehensions, while that of the old worldly man lay rusting in its cell, beating only as a piece of cunning mechanism, and yielding no one throb of hope, or fear, or love, or care, for any living thing.

" Uncle," said Kate, when she judged they must be near their destination, " I must ask one question of you. I am to live at home?"

" At home ! " replied Ralph ; " where's that ? "

" I mean with my mother—the widow," said Kate, emphatically.

" You will live, to all intents and purposes, here," rejoined Ralph ; " for here you will take your meals, and here you will be from morning till night ; occasionally perhaps till morning again."

" But at night, I mean," said Kate ; " I cannot leave her, uncle. I must have some place that I can call a home ; it will be wherever she is, you know, and may be a very humble one."

" May be ! " said Ralph, walking faster in the impatience provoked by the remark, "must be, you mean.   May be a humble one !   Is the girl mad ? "

" The word slipped from my lips, I did not mean it indeed," urged Kate.

" I hope not," said Ralph.

" But my question, uncle ; you have not answered it."

" Why, I anticipated something of the kind," said Ralph ; " and —though I object very strongly, mind—have provided against it. I spoke of you as an out-of-door worker; so you will go to this home that may be humble, every night."

There was comfort in this. Kate poured forth many thanks for her uncle's consideration, which Ralph received as if he had deserved them all, and they arrived without any further conversation at the dress-maker's door, which displayed a very large plate, with Madame Mantalini's name and occupation, and was approached by a handsome flight of steps. There was a shop to the house, but it was let off to an importer of otto of roses. Madame Mantalini's show-rooms were on the first floor, a fact which was notified to the nobility and gentry by the casual exhibition near the handsomely curtained windows of two or three elegant bonnets of the newest fashion, and some costly garments in the most approved taste.

A liveried footman opened the door, and in reply to Ralph's inquiry whether Madame Mantalini was at home, ushered them through a handsome hall, and up a spacious staircase, into the show saloon, which comprised two spacious drawing-rooms, and exhibited an immense variety of superb dresses and materials for dresses, some arranged on stands, others laid carelessly on sofas, and others again scattered over the carpet, hanging upon the cheval glasses, or mingling in some other way with the rich furniture of various descriptions, which was profusely displayed.

They waited here a much longer time than was agreeable to Mr. Ralph Nickleby, who eyed the gaudy frippery about him with very little concern, and was at length about to pull the bell, when a gentleman suddenly popped his head into the room, and seeing somebody there as suddenly popped it out again.

" Here. Hollo !" cried Ralph. " Who's that ? "

At the sound of Ralph's voice the head reappeared, and the mouth displaying a very long row of very white teeth, uttered in a mincing tone the words, " Demmit. What, Nickleby ! oh, demmit !" Having uttered which ejaculations, the gentleman advanced, and shook hands with Ralph with great warmth. He was dressed in a gorgeous morning gown, with a waistcoat and Turkish trousers of the same pattern, a pink silk neckerchief, and bright green slippers, and had a very copious watch-chain wound round his body. Moreover, he had whiskers and a moustache, both dyed black and gracefully curled.

" Demmit, you don't mean to say you want me, do you, demmit ?" said this gentleman, smiting Ralph on the shoulder.

" Not yet," said Ralph, sarcastically.

" Ha ! ha ! demmit," cried the gentleman ; when wheeling round to laugh with greater elegance, he encountered Kate Nickleby, who was standing near.

" My niece," said Ralph.

" I remember," said the gentleman, striking his nose with the knuckle of his forefinger as a chastening for his forgetfulness. "Demmit, I remember what you come for. Step this way, Nickleby; my dear, will you follow me? Ha! ha! They all follow me, Nickleby; always did, demmit, always."

Giving loose to the playfulness of his imagination after this fashion, the gentleman led the way to a private sitting-room on the second floor scarcely less elegantly furnished than the apartment below, where the presence of a silver coffee-pot, an egg-shell, and sloppy china for one, seemed to show that he had just breakfasted.

"Sit down, my dear," said the gentleman: first staring Miss Nickleby out of countenance, and then grinning in delight at the achievement. "This cursed high room takes one's breath away. These infernal sky parlours—I'm afraid I must move, Nickleby."

"I would, by all means," replied Ralph, looking bitterly round.

"What a demd rum fellow you are, Nickleby," said the gentleman, "the demdest, longest-headed, queerest-tempered old coiner of gold and silver ever was—demmit."

Having complimented Ralph to this effect, the gentleman rang the bell, and stared at Miss Nickleby till it was answered, when he left off to bid the man desire his mistress to come directly; after which he began again, and left off no more till Madame Mantalini appeared.

The dress-maker was a buxom person, handsomely dressed and rather good-looking, but much older than the gentleman in the Turkish trousers, whom she had wedded some six months before. His name was originally Muntle; but it had been converted, by an easy transition, into Mantalini: the lady rightly considering that an English appellation would be of serious injury to the business. He had married on his whiskers, upon which property he had previously subsisted in a genteel manner for some years, and which he had recently improved after patient cultivation by the addition of a moustache, which promised to secure him an easy independence: his share in the labours of the business being at present confined to spending the money, and occasionally when that ran short, driving to Mr. Ralph Nickleby to procure discount—at a per centage—for the customers' bills.

"My life," said Mr. Mantalini, "what a demd devil of a time you have been!"

"I didn't even know Mr. Nickleby was here, my love," said Madame Mantalini.

"Then what a doubly demd infernal rascal that footman must be, my soul," remonstrated Mr. Mantalini.

"My dear," said Madame, "that is entirely your fault."

'My fault, my heart's joy?"

"Certainly," returned the lady; "what can you expect, dearest, if you will not correct the man?"

"Correct the man, my soul's delight!"

"Yes; I am sure he wants speaking to, badly enough," said Madame, pouting.

"Then do not vex itself," said Mr. Mantalini; "he shall be horse-whipped till he cries out demnebly." With this promise Mr. Mantalini kissed Madame Mantalini, and after that performance Madame

Mantalini pulled Mr. Mantalini playfully by the ear, which done they
descended to business.

" Now, ma'am," said Ralph, who had looked on at all this, with
such scorn as few men can express in looks, " this is my niece."

" Just so, Mr. Nickleby," replied Madame Mantalini, surveying Kate
from head to foot and back again. " Can you speak French, child ?"

" Yes, ma'am," replied Kate, not daring to look up ; for she felt that
the eyes of the odious man in the dressing-gown were directed towards
her.

" Like a demd native ?" asked the husband.

Miss Nickleby offered no reply to this inquiry, but turned her back
upon the questioner, as if addressing herself to make answer to what his
wife might demand.

" We keep twenty young women constantly employed in the establishment," said Madame.

" Indeed, ma'am !" replied Kate, timidly.

" Yes ; and some of 'em demd handsome, too," said the master.

" Mantalini !" exclaimed his wife, in an awful voice.

" My senses' idol !" said Mantalini.

" Do you wish to break my heart ? "

" Not for twenty thousand hemispheres populated with—with—
with little ballet-dancers," replied Mantalini in a poetical strain.

" Then you will, if you persevere in that mode of speaking," said his
wife. " What can Mr. Nickleby think when he hears you ? "

" Oh ! Nothing, ma'am, nothing," replied Ralph. " I know his
amiable nature, and yours,—mere little remarks that give a zest to
your daily intercourse; lovers' quarrels that add sweetness to those
domestic joys which promise to last so long—that's all ; that's all."

If an iron door could be supposed to quarrel with its hinges, and to
make a firm resolution to open with slow obstinacy, and grind them to
powder in the process, it would emit a pleasanter sound in so doing,
than did these words in the rough and bitter voice in which they were
uttered by Ralph. Even Mr. Mantalini felt their influence, and turning
affrighted round, exclaimed—" What a demd horrid croaking ! "

" You will pay no attention, if you please, to what Mr. Mantalini
says," observed his wife, addressing Miss Nickleby.

" I do not, ma'am," said Kate, with quiet contempt.

" Mr. Mantalini knows nothing whatever about any of the young
women," continued Madame, looking at her husband, and speaking
to Kate. " If he has seen any of them, he must have seen them in
the street going to, or returning from, their work, and not here. He
was never even in the room. I do not allow it. What hours of work
have you been accustomed to ? "

" I have never yet been accustomed to work at all, ma'am," replied
Kate, in a low voice.

" For which reason she'll work all the better now," said Ralph,
putting in a word, lest this confession should injure the negotiation.

" I hope so," returned Madame Mantalini ; " our hours are from
nine to nine, with extra work when we're very full of business, for
which I allow payment as over-time."

Kate bowed her head to intimate that she heard, and was satisfied.

"Your meals," continued Madame Mantalini, "that is, dinner and tea, you will take here.   I should think your wages would average from five to seven shillings a-week ; but I can't give you any certain information on that point until I see what you can do."

Kate bowed her head again.

"If you're ready to come," said Madame Mantalini, "you had better begin on Monday morning at nine exactly, and Miss Knag the forewoman shall then have directions to try you with some easy work at first.   Is there anything more, Mr. Nickleby ? "

"Nothing more, ma'am," replied Ralph, rising.

"Then I believe that's all," said the lady.   Having arrived at this natural conclusion, she looked at the door, as if she wished to be gone, but hesitated notwithstanding, as though unwilling to leave to Mr. Mantalini the sole honour of showing them down stairs.   Ralph relieved her from her perplexity by taking his departure without delay: Madame Mantalini making many gracious inquiries why he never came to see them, and Mr. Mantalini anathematizing the stairs with great volubility as he followed them down, in the hope of inducing Kate to look round,—a hope, however, which was destined to remain ungratified.

"There !" said Ralph when they got into the street ; " now you're provided for."

Kate was about to thank him again, but he stopped her.

"I had some idea," he said, " of providing for your mother in a pleasant part of the country—(he had a presentation to some alms-houses on the borders of Cornwall, which had occurred to him more than once) —but as you want to be together, I must do something else for her. She has a little money ? "

"A very little," replied Kate.

"A little will go a long way if it's used sparingly," said Ralph. "She must see how long she can make it last, living rent free.   You leave your lodgings on Saturday ?"

"You told us to do so, uncle."

"Yes ; there is a house empty that belongs to me, which I can put you into till it is let, and then, if nothing else turns up, perhaps I shall have another.   You must live there."

"Is it far from here, Sir ?" inquired Kate.

"Pretty well," said Ralph ; " in another quarter of the town—at the East end ; but I'll send my clerk down to you at five o'clock on Saturday to take you there.   Good bye.   You know your way ?   Straight on."

Coldly shaking his niece's hand, Ralph left her at the top of Regent Street, and turned down a bye thoroughfare, intent on schemes of money-getting.   Kate walked sadly back to their lodgings in the Strand.

Shower Baths, Japanned Bamboo, with Brass Force-pump attached, to throw the water into the shower cistern, & curtains complete   £4 10

Ditto, the very best made, with copper conducting tubes, brass force-pump, and curtains   .   5 10

Hot Water Baths, self-heating, slipper shaped, full size, japanned wainscot, with copper fire-place, so attached that the Bath may, with the greatest safety be heated in any room in 20 minutes   .   .   .   .   - 7 0

Hip Baths, Japanned Bamboo   .   . 1 2

Spunging Baths, Round, 30 inches diameter, 7 inches deep 1 1

Open Baths, 3 ft. 6 in. long, 30s.; 4 ft. long, 35s.; 4 ft. 6in. long, 50s.; 5 ft. long, 60s.; 5 ft. 6 in. long, 70s.

Feet Baths, Japanned Bamboo, small size, 6s. 6d.; large, 7s 6d.; tub shape, with hoops, 11s.

Bottle Jacks, Japanned, 7s. 6d.; Brass, 9s. 6d. each.

Brass Stair Rods, per doz. 21 inches long, 3s. 6d.; 24 in. 4s. 3d.; 27 in. 5s.; 30 in. 5s. 6d.

Brass Curtain Poles, warranted solid, 1½ inch diameter, 1s. 6d. per foot; 2 in. 2s. 2d. per foot.

Brass Poles, complete with end ornaments, rings, hooks & brackets, 3ft. long, 15s.; 3ft. 6 in. 17s.; 4ft. 20s.

Brass Curtain Bands, 1¼ in. wide, 2s. 6d. per pair, 1½ in. 3s.; 2 in. 4s. Richer patterns, 1½ in. 4s.; 2 in. 5s.

Finger Plates for Doors, newest and richest patterns, long, 1s. 2d.; short, 10d. each.

Copper Coal Scoops, small, 10s. 6d.; middle, 13s. large, 14s. 6d.. Helmet Shape, 14s. 6d., 18s., 20s.; Square Shape, with Hand Scoop, 28s.

Copper Tea Kettles, Oval Shape, very strong, with barrel handle, 2 quarts, 5s. 6d.; 3 quarts, 6s.; 4 quarts, 7s. The strongest quality made, 2 quarts 8s.; 3 quarts, 10s.; 4 quarts, 11s.

Copper Stewpans; Soup or Stock Pots, and Fish Kettles, with Brazing Pan; Saucepans & Preserving Pans; Cutlet Pans, Frying Pans, and Omelette Pans, at prices proportionate with the above.

Copper Warming Pans, with handles, for fire, 6s. 6d. to 9s. 6d.; Ditto, for water, 25s.

Fire Irons.

Large strong Wrought Iron, for Kitchens, 5s. 6d. to 12s. 0
Wrought Iron, suitable for Servants' Bed Rooms 2 0
Small Polished Steel, for better Bed Rooms   . 5 0
Large ditto, for Libraries   .   :   . 7 0
Ditto ditto, for Dining Rooms   .   . 8 6
Ditto ditto, with Cut Heads, for ditto   . 11 6
Ditto very highly polished Steel, plain good pattern 20 0
Ditto ditto, richly cut   .   . 25s. to 50 0

Corkscrews, Patent, 3s. 6d. each ; Common ditto, 6d.; 9d., 1s.; 1s. 6d., and 2s.

Smoke Jack, with Chains and Spit, £6. Superior Self-acting do. with Dangle and Horizontal Spit, £10.

N. B. Experienced Workmen employed to clean, repair, and oil Smoke Jacks, which are so constantly put out of order by the treatment they meet with from chimney sweepers.

Captains' Cabin Lamps, with 1 quart kettles, 6s.

Britannia Metal Goods.

	To hold . -	1½ Pts.	1 Qt.	2½ Pts.
Teapots, with Black Handles and Black Knobs	.	1s. 6d.	2s. 0d.	2s. 9d.
Ditto, very strong	.	3 0	3 6	4 0
Ditto, with Pearl Knobs	.	4 6	5 6	6 6
Ditto with Pearl Knobs and Metal Handles	.	6 6	8 0	9 6

Coffee Biggins, 1s. 6d. each size extra.

Table Candlesticks, 8 in. 3s. per pair; 9 in. 4s. 6d.; 10 in. 6s.
Chamber Candlesticks with Extinguishers, 2s. each.
Ditto with Gadroon Edges, complete with Snuffers and Extinguisher, 4s. each.
Mustards, with Blue Earthen Lining, 1s. each.
Salt Cellars with ditto, 1s. 4d. per pair.
Pepper Boxes, 1s. each.

Britannia Metal Hot Water Dishes, with wells for gravy, and gadroon edges, 16 inches long, 30s.; 18in., 35s.; 20 in., 42s.; 22 in., 50s.; 24 in., 55s.
Hot Water Plates, 6s. 6d. each.

Cruet Frames, Black Japanned, with 3 Glasses, 3s. 8d.; 4 Glasses, 4s. 9d.; 5 Glasses, 6s.; 6 Glasses, 7s.

Reading Candlesticks, with Shade and Light to slide, one light, 5s. 6d.; two lights, 7s. 6d.

Coffee Filterers, for making Coffee without boiling.

To hold .	1½ Pts.	1 Qt.	3 Pts.	2 Qts.
Best Block Tin .	4s. 6d.	5s. 6d.	7s. 0d.	9s. 0d.
Bronzed . . .	6 6	7 6	9 6	11 0

Etnas, for boiling a Pint of Water in three minutes, 3s. each.

Coffee and **Pepper Mills,** small, 3s.; middle, 4s.; large, 4s. 6d.
Ditto, to fix, small, 4s. 6d.; middle, 5s. 6d.; large, 6s. 6d.

Iron Digesters, for making Soup, to hold 2 galls. 9s.; 3 galls. 10s. 6d.; 4 galls. 16s.

Tea Urns, Globe shape. to hold four quarts, 27s. each. Modern Shapes, to hold 6 quarts, 45s. to 60s. each.

Improved Wove Wire Gauze Window Blinds, in mahogany frames, made to any size, and painted to any shade of colour, 2s. 3d. per square foot.
Ornamenting with shaded lines, 1s. 6d. each blind.
Ditto, with lines and corner ornaments, 2s. 6d. each blind.
Blinds, ornamented with landscape, in mahogany frames, 4s. per square foot.
Old Blind Frames filled with new wire, and painted any colour, at 1s. 4d. per square foot.

Servants' Wire Lanterns, Open Tops, with Doors, 1s. 6d. each. Closed Tops, with Doors, 2s.

Rush Safes, Open Tops, 2s. 3d. each. Closed Tops, with Doors, 2s. 9d. each.

Fire Guards, painted Green, with Dome Tops, 14 inch, 1s. 6d.; 16 in. 1s. 9d.; 18 in. 2s. 3d. Brass Wire, 6d., 9d., 1s., and Per 6d.

Egg Whisks, Tinned Wire, 9d. each.

Wire Work.—All kinds of useful and ornamental Wire Work made to order.

Family Weighing Machines, or Balances, complete, with weights from ¼ oz. to 14lbs., 26s.

Ditto Patent Spring Weighing Machines, which do not require weights, 6s. 6d. to 20s.

DISH COVERS.

Inches long .	9	10	11	12	14	16	18	Set of 6.	Set of 7.
The commonest are in sets of the six first sizes, which cannot be separated .	...	...	...	...	...	...	£0 6s. 0d		
Block Tin	1s. 6d.	1s. 9d	2s. 0d	2s. 6d.	3s. 3d	3s. 6d	5s. 6d	0 11 6	£0 17s. 0d
Ditto, Anti-Patent shape . .	1 9	2 0	2 6	3 0	4 0	4 6	8 0	0 16 0	1 4 0
Ditto, O. G. shape . .	2 0	2 6	3 0	3 6	4 6	6 0	8 6	1 1 0	1 9 6
Ditto, Patent Imperial Silver shape. The Tops raised in one piece . .	2 3	2 9	3 6	4 6	5 6	7 6	9 0	1 6 0	1 15 0
Ditto, the very best made, except Plated or Silver	3 6	4 0	4 9	6 0	7 6	9 6	11 6	1 15 0	2 5 0
Wove Wire Fly-proof, tin rims, japanned	...	2 6	...	3 3	6	5 0	5 6		

FENDERS.

The immense variety which the Show Rooms contain, and the constant change of patterns of Fenders, render it impossible to give the prices of but a small portion of them. The following Scale, however, may be taken as a guide, and the prices generally will be found about 25 per cent. below any other house whatever.

	3 Feet.	3 Feet 3.	3 Feet 6.	3 Feet 9.	4 Feet.
Green, with Brass Top, suitable for Bed Rooms . .	3s. 0d.	3s. 6d.	4s. 0d.		
All Brass	9 6	10 6	12 0	13s. 6d.	15s. 0d.
Black Iron for Dining Rooms or Libraries . . .	12 0	13 0	14 0	15 0	16 0
Bronzed for ditto	15 0	16 0	17 0	18 0	19 0
Ditto, with bright Steel Tops	18 0	20 0	21 0	23 0	25 0
Ditto, very handsome, with Steel Tops and Steel Bottom Moulding	21 0	23 0	25 0	27 0	29 0
Very rich Pattern, with Scroll Centre, Steel Rod and Steel Ends, for Drawing Rooms [all sizes]	...	...	...	...	50 0
Green painted Wire Nursery Guard Fenders, Brass Tops, 18 in. high	15 0	16 3	17 6	18 9	20 0
Ditto, 24 inches high	18 0	19 6	21 0	22 6	24 0
Iron Kitchen Fenders, with Sliding Bars . . .	6 0	6 6	7 0	7 6	

STOVES.

Inches wide . .	18	20	22	24	26	28	30	32	34	36
Elliptic or Rumford Stoves, for Bed Rooms .	6s. 0d.	6s. 8d.	7s. 4d.	8s. 0d.	8s. 8d.	9s. 4d.	10s. 0d	10s. 8d	11s. 4d	12s. 0d
Common half register Stoves . .	9 0	10 0	11 0	12 0	13 0	14 0	15 0	16 0	17 0	18 0
Best do. bold Fronts and Bannister Bars .	-	-	-	-	-	-	-	28 0	30 0	32 0
Register Stoves of superior patterns .	-	-	18 0	19 6	21 0	22 6	24 0	25 6	27 0	

Register Stoves, fine Cast, 3 feet wide, 2*l.* 5*s.*, 2*l.* 10*s.*, and 3*l.*—Ground Bright Front Register Stoves with Bronzed and Steel Ornaments, and with bright and black bars, 3 feet wide, 4*l.* 10*s.*, 5*l.* and 5*l.* 10*s.*

Ironing Stoves for Laundries, complete, with Frame and Ash Pan, 1*l.* 6*s.*

KITCHEN RANGES.

To fit an opening of .	3 Ft. 2.	3 Ft. 4.	3 Ft. 6.	4 Ft.	4 Ft. 4.	5 Ft.
With Oven and Boiler	50s.	54s.	58s.			
Self-acting ditto, with Oven and Boiler, Sl'ding Cheek, and Wrought Iron Bars (recommended)	90	95	100	110s.	126s.	140s.

Iron Saucepans and Tea Kettles.

	1 pint.	1½ pint.	1 Quart.	3 pint.	2 Quart.	3 Quart.	4 Quart.	6 Quart.	8 Quart.
Iron Saucepan and Cover . .	1s. 0d.	1s. 2d.	1s. 4d.	1s. 8d.	1s. 10d	2s. 3d	2s. 9d.	3s. 6d.	4s. 0d.
Iron Stewpan and Cover . .	...	...	1 4	1 10	2 3	3 3	4 0	5 6	6 6
Round Iron Tea Kettles . .	...	...	...	...	3 0	4 3	5 0	7 0	9 0
Oval ditto . . . . :	...	...	...	...	3 6	4 9	5 6	7 6	9 6

Iron Boiling Pots.

	2½ Gall.	3 Gall.	3½ Gall.	4 Gall.	5 Gall.	6 Gall.
Oval Iron Boiling Pot and Cover	5s. 6d.	6s. 6d.	7s. 6d.	9s. 6d.	11s. 6d.	12s. 6d.
Tea Kitchens, or Water Fountains, with Brass Pipe & Cock		13 0	14 0	14 6	16 0	18 6

Iron Coal Scoops and Boxes.

	14 in. long.	16 in. long.	18 in. long.
Coal Boxes, Japanned with Covers, ornamented with Gold Lines . .	12s. 0d.	14s. 0d.	16s. 0d.
Coal Scoops. Iron, for Kitchen Use . .	1 9	2 6	3 6
Ditto, lined with Zinc, the most serviceable article of the kind ever made .	5 0	6 6	7 6
Upright Hods	1 9	2 6	3 6

Japanned Goods.

Inches long . .	18	20	22	24	26	28	30
TEA TRAYS, good common quality . .	1s. 3d.	1s. 6d.	1s. 9d.	2s. 3d.	2s. 9d.	3s. 3d.	3s. 9d.
Ditto, best common quality . . .	2 6	3 0	3 6	4 6	5 6	6 0	7 0
Ditto, paper shape, black . . .	5 6	7 0	8 0	9 6	11 0	12 6	14 0
Ditto, Gothic paper shape, black . .	9 6	11 0	12 6	14 0	15 6	17 0	19 0
Ditto, ditto, Marone, ornamented all over .	11 0	12 6	14 0	16 0	17 6	19 0	21 0

Bread and Knife Trays, each 9d., 1s., 1s. 6d., 2s. & 2s. 6d.
Middle quality ditto, at 2s. and 2s. 6d.
Best ditto, Gothic shape, 3s. 6d., 4s. 6d. and 5s. 6d. each.
Tea Trays, paper, Gothic shape, in sets of one each of 18, 24, and 30 inches, £3. 10s.
Ditto, ornamented, the set, £4. 5s.
Ditto, richest patterns, ditto, £5. 5s. and £6.
Toast Racks, plain black, 1s. 6d. Ornamented, 2s.
Ditto, marone or green, ornamented all over, 2s. 9d.
Cheese Trays, 2s., 2s. 6d., 3s., and 3s. 6d.
Snuffer Trays, Cd., 9d., 1s., 1s. 3d., and 1s. 6d.
Paper ditto, 2s., 2s. 6d., 3s., 3s. 6d., and 4s.
Paper Decanter Stands, plain black, 3s. 6d. per pair.
Ditto, ditto, red, 4s. per pair.
Ditto, ornamented black or marone, 4s. 6d per pair.

Plate Warmers, upright shape, with gilt lines, 18s.
Ditto, long shape, £1. 5s.
Toilet Cans and Toilet Pails, 7s. 6d. each.
Chamber Slop Pails, japanned green outside and red inside, small, 3s.; middle, 4s.; large, 5s. 6d.
Chamber Candlesticks, complete, with Snuffers and Extinguisher, 6d. Ditto, better, 9d. to 3s.
Cash Boxes, with Tumbler Locks, small size, 5s. 6d.
Ditto, ditto, middle size, 6s. 6d.; large size, 7s. 6d.
Ditto, ditto, with Patent Locks, 10s. 6d.
Deed Boxes, Japanned Brown, with Locks, 12 inches long, 11s.; 14 in. 15s.; 16 in. 18s.; 18 in. 21s.
Candle Boxes, 1s. 4d. each.
Candle or Rush Safes, 2s. 6d. each.
Cinder Pails or Sifters, Japanned Brown, 11s. each.

TIN GOODS.

To hold	1 Pt.	1 Qt.	3 Pt.	2 Qt.	3 Qt.	4 Qt.	6 Qt.	8 Qt.	9 Qt.	10 Qt.
SAUCEPANS, strong common. with Covers	0s. 4d	0s. 5d	0s. 6d	0s. 8d	0s. 10	1s. 2d	1s. 3d	1s. 4d	1s. 8d	2s. 0d
Strongest Tin, with Iron Handles	0 9	1 0	1 4	1 10	2 2	2 9	3 6	4 0	4 6	5 0
Block Tin	1 4	2 0	2 6	3 0	3 9	4 6	6 0			
Saucepans and Steamers	—	—	—	—	2 9	3 6	4 0	4 6		

Coffee and Chocolate Pots, Block Tin, to hold 1 quart, 1s. 4d. ; 3 pints, 1s. 10d.; 2 quarts, 2s. 3d	Turbot Pans, or Kettles, Turbot shape, 21s.
Colanders, small, 1s.; large, 1s. 6d.	Meat Screens for Bottle Jacks, 15s. each.
Ditto, Block Tin, small, 3s. 6d.; large, 4s. 6d.	Ditto, Wood, Elliptic Shape, lined with Tin, upon Rollers, with Shelf and Door, 3 feet wide, £1. 10s.
Dripping Pans, with wells, small, 3s.; mid., 5s.; large. 7s.	Larger sizes in proportion.
Fish Kettles, small, 4s. 6d.; middle, 5s. 6d. ; large, 6s. 6d.	Stomach Warmers, each 2s. 6d.

To hold	3 Pts.	2 Qts.	3 Qts.	4 Qts.
TEA KETTLES, Oval shape, strong Common Tin	1s. 0d.	1s. 2d.	1s. 4d.	1s. 6d.
Ditto, strongest Tin	2 0	2 6	3 0	3 6
Block Tin, with Iron Handles and Iron Spouts	4 0	4 3	5 9	6 0
Oblong shape, with round Barrel Handles and Iron Spout	4 9	5 6	6 0	6 6

RIPPON & BURTON'S Prices of STRONG SETS of IRON and TIN

KITCHEN FURNITURE.

Small Set.

1 Bread Grater	0s. 6
1 Pair Brass Candlesticks	2 6
1 Bottle Jack	7 6
1 Tin Candlestick	1 3
1 Candle Box	0 10
1 Meat Chopper	1 6
1 Cinder Sifter	1 0
1 Coffee Pot	1 0
1 Colander	1 0
1 Dripping Pan & Stand	5 0
1 Dust Pan	0 6
1 Slice	0 6
1 Fish Kettle	4 0
1 Flour Box	0 8
2 Flat Irons	1 8
1 Fryingpan	1 2
1 Gridiron	1 0
1 Mustard Pot	1 0
1 Salt Cellar	0 8
1 Pepper Box	0 6
1 Block Tin Butter Saucepan	1 6
2 Iron Saucepans	6 0
2 Iron Stewpans	3 6
1 Boiling Pot, Iron	7 0
1 Set of Skewers	0 6
6 Knives and Forks	4 6
3 Spoons	0 9
1 Tea Pot and 1 Tea Tray	6 0
1 Toasting Fork	0 6
1 Tea Kettle	4 6
	£3 10 0

Middle Set.

1 Bread Grater	1s. 0
1 Pair Brass Candlesticks	3 0
1 Bottle Jack	7 6
1 Pair of Bellows	1 4
2 Tin Candlesticks	2 6
1 Candle Box	1 4
1 Cheese Toaster	1 4
1 Chopper	1 9
1 Cinder Sifter	1 3
1 Coffee Pot	1 3
1 Colander	1 3
1 Dripping Pan & Stand	5 6
1 Dust Pan	0 8
1 Fish Slice	1 0
1 Fish Kettle	5 6
Pepper and Flour Boxes	1 2
3 Flat Irons	2 0
1 Fryingpan	1 9
1 Gridiron	1 3
2 Jelly Moulds	4 0
1 Mustard Pot	1 0
1 Salt Cellar	0 8
1 Plate Basket	5 6
2 Block Tin Saucepans	3 6
3 Iron Saucepans	7 6
1 Saucepan and Steamer	3 6
1 Large Boiling Pot	9 6
3 Stewpans	7 0
1 Set of Skewers	0 6
6 Knives and Forks	5 6
6 Iron Spoons	1 6
1 Tea Pot & 1 Tea Tray	6 0
1 Toasting Fork	0 6
1 Tea Kettle	6 6
	£5 5 0

Large Set.

1 Bread Grater	1s. 0
1 Pair Brass Candlesticks	3 6
1 Bottle Jack	9 6
1 Pair of Bellows	2 0
2 Deep Tin Candlesticks	2 6
1 Candle Box	1 4
1 Cheese Toaster	1 10
1 Chopper, for Meat	2 0
1 Cinder Sifter	1 6
1 Coffee Pot	2 3
1 Coal Shovel	2 6
1 Colander	1 6
1 Dripping Pan and Stand	7 0
1 Dust Pan	0 8
1 Egg Slice	0 6
1 Fish Slice	1 3
2 Fish Kettles	10 6
1 Flour Box	1 0
3 Flat Irons	3 0
2 Fryingpans	4 6
1 Gridiron, with fluted Bars	3 6
1 Wood Meat Screen	30 0
3 Jelly Moulds	6 0
1 Mustard Pot	1 0
1 Salt Cellar	0 8
1 Pepper Box	0 6
1 Wicker Plate Basket, lined with Tin	7 6
3 Block Tin Saucepans	5 6
4 Iron Saucepans	12 3
1 Saucepan and Steamer	4 6
1 Large Boiling Pot, Iron	10 6
4 Stewpans, Iron	9 0
2 Sets of Skewers	1 0
6 Knives and Forks	5 6
6 Iron Spoons	1 6
1 Tea Pot	3 0
1 Tea Tray	4 0
1 Toasting Fork	1 0
1 Egg Whisk	0 9
1 Tea Kettle	7 6
	£7 15 0

In submitting to the Public the foregoing Catalogue, RIPPON & BURTON beg to state, that they will continue to offer Articles of the VERY BEST MANUFACTURE only, as they have hitherto done, at prices which, when compared with others of the same quality, will be found much lower than any that have ever yet been quoted. The knowledge which RIPPON & BURTON have obtained by their long connexion with the largest Manufacturers, and the principle upon which they conduct their business, afford great advantages to the purchaser; all Articles being bought in very large quantities for Cash, and marked for sale at Cash prices, which are not subject to discount or abatement of any kind; thus giving the ready money purchaser all the advantages that can be obtained over the plan usually adopted by others, of marking their goods at prices which will enable them to give credit, and pay for that credit which they take; allowing those, who pay cash, 5 per cent. discount from prices 25 per cent. higher than they should fairly be charged. The many years RIPPON & BURTON'S business has been established, and the very extensive patronage they have met with, will be some proof that the public have not been deceived by them; but, as a further security against the impositions practised by many, RIPPON & BURTON will continue to exchange, or return the money for every article that is not approved of, if returned in good condition and free of expense within one month of the time it was purchased.

J. Bradley, Printer, 78, Great Titchfield-street, London.

⁎ *This Pamphlet is stitched by itself, and may be separated from the Publication it accompanies ; and it is requested that the widest circulation may be given to it amongst the Members of each Family, and the Industrious Classes generally.*

NATIONAL LOAN FUND
LIFE ASSURANCE SOCIETY.

CAPITAL, £500,000.

DEFERRED ANNUITIES.

Patron.
HIS GRACE THE DUKE OF SOMERSET, F.R.S.

Directors.

T. LAMIE MURRAY, Esq., Chairman.

Col. Sir BURGES CAMAC, K.C.S.	ROBERT HOLLOND, Esq., M.P.
J. ELLIOTSON, M.D., F.R.S.	GEORGE LUNGLEY, Esq.
C. FAREBROTHER, Esq., Ald.	KENNETH MACKENZIE, Esq.
H. GORDON, Esq.	JOHN RAWSON, Esq.

JOSEPH THOMPSON, Esq.

Auditor.
PROFESSOR WHEATSTONE, F.R.S.

Physician.	Surgeon.
J. ELLIOTSON, M.D., F.R.S.	E. S. SYMES, Esq.
37, Conduit Street.	38, Hill Street, Berkeley Square.

Actuary.	Bankers.
W. S. B. WOOLHOUSE, Esq.	Messrs. WRIGHT & CO.,
F.R.A.S.	5, Henrietta Street, Covent Garden.

Standing Counsel.	Solicitors.
W. MILBOURNE JAMES, Esq.	Messrs. WEBBER and BLAND,
Stone Buildings, Lincoln's Inn.	43, Bedford Row.

Secretary.
F. FERGUSON CAMROUX, Esq.

NATIONAL LOAN FUND

LIFE ASSURANCE SOCIETY.

DEFERRED ANNUITIES.

I. Amongst the several remedies proposed to mitigate or diminish the burthen of poor-laws, none has hitherto been brought forward or adopted that would either induce or afford facilities to the able-bodied members of society, to be responsible for their own support.

II. In a state of employment and health every one may be assumed capable of self-support; competition has, no doubt, reduced the rewards of labour to the standard of existence, rendering it the more necessary that the smallest surplus, over exigencies, should be carefully husbanded, in order that, by the best facilities given to economy and the application of means to ends, it may be rendered capable of supplying the deficiencies, caused by want of employment, sickness, the several casualties of life, and by old age. Over the frequent fluctuations in the quantity of employment, the employed have no control; and, as the cause is not dependent on fixed laws, but most frequently on the contingencies which affect the quantity of money, their duration or occurrence cannot be submitted to calculation,—at any rate the remedy is beyond their reach. The laws of sickness have been sufficiently ascertained, for fixing a provision apportioned to the value of a given contribution; but although such a provision is not to be overlooked, it is of trifling importance, compared to the hardships resulting from want of employment, and unprovided old age. Want of employment, sickness, and old age, may fairly be classed under one head, viz. :—a state of *non-productiveness*. To those, therefore, who solely depend on their labour, which is seldom too highly remunerated, it must be a matter of importance, out of their earnings when employed, to provide for every period of non-productiveness, from whichever of the foregoing causes it may arise.

III. The two institutions open to the productive classes, are Savings Banks and Benefit Societies, whose nature and scope, when examined, will be found to offer but a very imperfect remedy against the evil, being institutions wherein the limited means of this class are not best made applicable to their several ends.

Savings Banks are of unquestionable utility, but they afford no contingent future advantage, and, besides, the sum that can be hoarded is incommensurate with the wants of the middle productive classes.

Benefit Societies propose to offer provision in sickness and old age, but their construction will be found imperfect, and their plan the least profitable application of the means of economy.

1. Because sickness itself is not a calamity of equally probable duration to the fluctuations in the quantity of employment and other casualties, and misfortune, against which they offer no protection.

2. Because, out of a given means, the sum laid aside for sickness must diminish the provision for old age.

3. Because many must contribute to the sick fund who never become chargeable upon it, and the value of such contributions is lost to themselves and families.

4. Because sickness, being a state of non-productiveness, must necessarily be included in any protection against such an occurrence.

IV. Various observations have been made on the duration of sickness, amongst the industrious classes, from an early

period of life until its close. Those most in use are,—the sickness amongst the Benefit Societies in Scotland, given by the
Highland Society;—the sickness amongst the labourers in the
East India Company's Service;—the sickness amongst persons
employed in Cotton, Silk, Wool, Flax, and in the Potteries,
by the Factory Commissioners;—and the sickness amongst
the English Benefit Societies, from returns made to the Society
for the Diffusion of Useful Knowledge.

These results, though varied, show how inconsiderable is
the amount of sickness during that period of life, between the
ages of 20 and 65, when each individual is more immediately
thrown on his own resources;—they are as follows:—

Class of Persons.	Period.	Average amount of Sickness.		Average yearly Sickness in the period.
		Months.	Days.	Days.
Highland Societies' return . .	20 to 65	16	4	11
East India Company's labourers .	20 to 65	9	0	6$\frac{7}{15}$
Factory Commissioners—				
Cotton	21 to 61	7	27	
Wool, Yorkshire . .	21 to 61	10	29	
Ditto, West of England .	21 to 61	8	13	7$\frac{1}{4}$
Flax, Yorkshire . .	21 to 61	9	1	
Silk	21 to 61	11	4	
Society for Diffusion of Useful Knowledge	20 to 65	18	21	12$\frac{1}{4}$

Thus, it appears that the highest expectation of sickness,
amongst males, is twelve and a half days, and the lowest six
days, in each year from the age of twenty to sixty-five; its
mean duration, inclusive of accidents of all kinds, would be nine
and a quarter days, during which, from these causes, an individual may expect to be abstracted from productive employment throughout a period of forty-five years: while, it may
be observed, his religious observation of the seventh day, in
which he "shall do no work," has diminished his productiveness, by its recurrence in the same period, six years and 156
days.

V. From the foregoing facts it must be obvious that provision in sickness, or a Health Assurance by means of a separate contribution, is unnecessary, more particularly as such separate contribution must tend to waste the resources out of which the industrious classes have to provide for the future. It also in effect throws the burthen of the permanently sick on one class exclusively, instead of society at large; who are thus called on for an act of benevolence, while they are scarce able to do justice to the claims of their own families. Besides this, no compensation is given out of the contribution for a provision in sickness and old age to the families of those who never reach the age of 65, though death should happen immediately preceding it; and, if an assumed hypothesis is correct, that sickness before death is not more than five weeks, and taking bed-lying-pay at 10s. per week, it will not unfrequently happen the only return a man may obtain as a long and steady contributor to a Benefit Society, will not exceed 50s., a sum scarcely equal to one year's payment at a shilling per week, while by his death he leaves his family entirely unprovided for.

VI. It is to remedy these defects, inherent in the constitution of Benefit Societies, that the National Loan Fund Life Assurance Society proposes to submit a plan of Deferred Annuities on a new principle, which will not only afford a more ample provision for old age, and protection against sickness and misfortune—but in addition, the means, at all times, of putting his energies in motion, and in the event of premature death, a better protection to his family.

The plan proposed will embody several essential objects :—

1. To secure an increased provision for old age out of a given saving, by applying it exclusively to the purchase of a Deferred Annuity.

2. To render the purchase of a protection in sickness unnecessary, by enabling the purchaser of a Deferred Annuity to withdraw or borrow two-thirds of his previous payments.

3. By the use of two-thirds of all his payments when required, to limit misfortune and want of employment, and extend the power of productiveness by an increasing command, in each year, of capital, so that, while providing for old age, each successive contribution renders him more secure against present misfortune.

4. To afford, at the age at which the Deferred Annuity would commence, without reference to his then state of health, the option of receiving, instead of his annuity, its value in money, according to the value fixed on the contract, or a larger sum payable at his death.

5. In the event of death before the age at which he would be entitled to his Deferred Annuity, to return two-thirds of his payments to his family, or such fixed Life Assurance as may be settled on the contract.

6. In all such cases where the power of productiveness fails, either from disease or accident, to enable the assured on equal terms to convert his Deferred Annuity into a present Annuity.

VII. Notwithstanding the obvious and manifold advantages of this plan over every other hitherto proposed, for securing present and future competence to the industrious population, still more striking advantages will be exhibited by contrasting its prospective provision for old age with that offered by Benefit Societies. This arises from the non-abstraction of a given sum for a separate benefit in sickness; which protection, by the operation of the Loan Fund on the Deferred Annuity, is not only more ample, but other misfortunes are provided against, which if calculated, and a separate contribution made for each, whose duration equals that of sickness; the purchase of them would entirely absorb the means of providing for old age, while such a system must tend to discourage productiveness, and afford no protection to a family in the event of premature death. The object this plan embraces is to open facilities to the efforts of self support, to stimulate the independence of one class above the forced benevolence of another, while it recommends itself to the latter by diminishing the burthen of poor laws, which has been at all times irksome, disturbing the harmony and fomenting the mutual distrusts of society.

The following is a comparison of the benefits to be derived from the contribution of 1s. per week paid into a Benefit Society, or to purchase a Deferred Annuity from the National Loan Fund Society:

Age 20.	Annuity.	Cash.	Policy.	Sickness.	Loan.	Death.
National Loan Fund Deferred Annuities Option of Benefits, at 65	£. s. 47 16	£. s. 394 11	£. s. 466 0	⅔ of the payments	⅔ of the payments	⅔ of the payments received
Benefit Societies ditto	26 0	Nil.	Nil.	allowances in sickness	Nil.	Nil.
National Loan Fund Option of Benefits, at 60	27 11	269 11	346 15	⅔ of the payments	⅔ of the payments	⅔ of the payments received

It is not alone to the industrious classes this plan of Deferred Annuities will be found efficient, in securing an ample competency for old age; but also to that important class of the community who derive their income from a combination of capital and personal labour. To this class, the Savings Banks do not afford a sufficiently profitable investment; and, indeed, the framework of such institutions as have been designed for the more humble classes, has not been made to suit their wants or consult their interests, and there exists no institution, at present, to which they can resort, that would at the same time foster their industry,—secure to them a competency in old age,—and protect them against the varied casualties of life.

The Tables of Deferred Annuities have been constructed with a view to exhibit the benefits that may be secured by the smallest effort of frugality, and to suit the circumstances and convenience of all classes.

The object of Tables No. I. is to show the option of benefits the payment of 1s. per week, or £2. 12s. per annum, will secure at the period of attaining the age of 65, 60, 55, or 50.

The Tables No. II. show the Annual Premiums required to secure the option of given benefits at these ages,—the sum required at each age to be paid down at once to purchase them,—and also the sum at any age to be paid as disparity, so as to enable the purchaser, instead of paying the premium at his own age, to pay that set down for the age of 20, and by this means enabling the owner of a little saving to turn it to the best account. The society will, moreover, receive all this sum by instalments, and two-thirds of the amount paid may, at any time, be withdrawn on deposit of the policy; and in the event of death before the stipulated age, two-thirds of the payments will be returned to the family.

I. BENEFITS

Secured, on attaining the AGE OF **65**, by an Annual Premium
of £2. 12s.

AGE.	Annuity.			Cash.			Policy.		
	£.	s.	d.	£.	s.	d.	£.	s.	d.
20	47	16	6	394	11	0	466	0	0
21	45	4	8	373	3	0	440	14	0
22	42	15	3	352	16	0	416	13	0
23	40	8	2	333	7	0	393	15	0
24	38	3	4	314	17	0	371	18	0
25	36	0	8	297	5	0	351	2	0
26	33	19	11	280	9	0	331	5	0
27	32	1	2	264	10	0	312	7	0
28	30	4	4	249	5	0	294	8	0
29	28	9	2	234	16	0	277	6	0
30	26	15	10	221	0	0	261	0	0
31	25	4	0	207	18	0	245	11	0
32	23	13	9	195	8	0	230	16	0
33	22	5	0	183	11	0	216	15	0
34	20	17	7	172	5	0	203	9	0
35	19	11	7	161	10	0	190	16	0
36	18	6	11	151	7	0	178	15	0
37	17	3	5	141	13	0	167	6	0
38	16	1	1	132	9	0	156	8	0
39	14	19	11	123	14	0	146	2	0
40	13	19	9	115	8	0	136	6	0
41	13	0	7	107	10	0	126	19	0
42	12	2	6	100	0	0	118	2	0
43	11	5	3	92	18	0	109	14	0
44	10	8	10	86	2	0	101	14	0
45	9	13	3	79	14	0	94	3	0
46	8	18	6	73	12	0	86	19	0
47	8	4	6	67	10	0	80	2	0
48	7	11	1	62	7	0	73	12	0
49	6	18	6	57	2	0	67	9	0
50	6	6	6	52	3	0	61	12	0

The basis on which this table is calculated is the payment of 1s. per week, or 2l. 12s. per annum; but any payment may be made, and the benefits secured in proportion thereto.

EXAMPLE.—A person, aged 23, by the payment of 1s. per week, or 2l. 12s. per annum, will secure, on attaining the age of 65, the option of an annuity of 40l. 8s. 2d., cash down 333l. 7s., or a policy on his life for 393l. 15s.

By one-half the payment, that is, 6d. per week, or 1l. 6s. per annum, he will secure the option of half the benefits. By five times the payment, he will be entitled to the option of five times the benefits; and the same may be extended to any other proportion.

All premiums to terminate with the period.

Two thirds of the payments may at any time be withdrawn, on deposit of the policy; and should the party not survive, two-thirds of his payments will be returned to his representatives.

II. PREMIUMS.

To secure, on attaining the
AGE OF **65,** the option of
$$\begin{cases} \text{Annuity,} & \pounds10 \quad 0 \quad 0 \\ \text{Cash,} & 82 \quad 10 \quad 0 \\ \text{Policy,} & 97 \quad 8 \quad 6 \end{cases}$$

AGE.	Payable Annually.			Payable in One Sum.			Payable for Disparity.		
	£.	s.	d.	£.	s.	d.	£.	s.	d.
20	0	10	11	10	0	10	0	0	0
21	0	11	7	10	10	8	0	11	5
22	0	12	2	11	1	1	1	3	5
23	0	12	11	11	12	0	1	16	0
24	0	13	8	12	3	7	2	9	3
25	0	14	6	12	15	8	3	3	1
26	0	15	4	13	8	6	3	17	8
27	0	16	3	14	2	0	4	13	0
28	0	17	3	14	16	2	5	9	1
29	0	18	4	15	11	3	6	6	1
30	0	19	6	16	7	1	7	3	11
31	1	0	8	17	3	11	8	2	9
32	1	2	0	18	1	7	9	2	7
33	1	3	5	19	0	3	10	3	4
34	1	5	0	20	0	0	11	5	4
35	1	6	7	21	0	11	12	8	8
36	1	8	5	22	2	11	13	13	0
37	1	10	4	23	6	2	14	18	10
38	1	12	5	24	10	9	16	6	0
39	1	14	9	25	16	7	17	14	8
40	1	17	3	27	3	11	19	4	10
41	2	0	0	28	12	8	20	16	8
42	2	3	0	30	2	11	22	10	1
43	2	6	3	31	14	10	24	5	4
44	2	9	10	33	8	5	26	2	6
45	2	13	10	35	3	11	28	1	8
46	2	18	4	37	1	3	30	2	11
47	3	3	3	39	0	8	32	6	6
48	3	8	11	41	2	2	34	12	3
49	3	15	2	43	6	0	37	0	7
50	4	2	3	45	12	2	39	11	7

The basis on which these tables, No. II., are calculated, is the purchase of a deferred annuity of 10*l.*; but any amount of annuity may be similarly purchased by making the payments in proportion.

EXAMPLE.—A person, age 30, may secure, on attaining the age of 65, the option of an annuity of 10*l.*, cash down 82*l.* 10*s.*, or a policy on his life for 97*l.* 8*s.* by the annual payment of 19*s.* 6*d.*, or a single payment of 16*l.* 7*s.* 1*d.*; or by payment of 7*l.* 3*s.* 11*d.* for disparity of age, he will be entitled to the same benefits by the same annual payment as for the age of 20, *viz.* 10*s.* 11*d.* per annum.

An annuity of 50*l.*, or five times the other benefits, may be secured by five times the payment; and, in like manner, any other annuity and corresponding benefits may be purchased by making the payment accordingly.

All premiums to terminate with the period.

Two-thirds of the amount paid may at any time be withdrawn on deposit of the policy; and should the party not survive, two-thirds of his payments will be returned to his representatives.

I. BENEFITS

Secured, on attaining the AGE OF **60,** by an Annual Premium
of £2. 12s.

AGE.	Annuity.			Cash.			Policy.		
	£.	s.	d.	£.	s.	d.	£.	s.	d.
20	27	11	4	269	11	0	346	15	0
21	26	1	1	254	15	0	327	14	0
22	24	12	2	240	12	0	309	11	0
23	23	4	8	227	3	0	292	5	0
24	21	18	5	214	6	0	275	14	0
25	20	13	4	202	1	0	259	19	0
26	19	9	6	190	8	0	244	19	0
27	18	6	9	179	6	0	230	13	0
28	17	5	1	168	14	0	217	1	0
29	16	4	5	158	12	0	204	1	0
30	15	4	9	148	19	0	191	13	0
31	14	6	0	139	16	0	179	17	0
32	13	8	2	131	2	0	168	13	0
33	12	11	2	122	16	0	157	19	0
34	11	15	0	114	17	0	147	16	0
35	10	19	7	107	7	0	138	2	0
36	10	4	11	100	4	0	128	18	0
37	9	11	0	93	7	0	120	2	0
38	8	17	9	86	18	0	111	16	0
39	8	5	1	80	14	0	103	17	0
40	7	13	1	74	17	0	96	6	0
41	7	1	8	69	5	0	89	2	0
42	6	10	10	63	19	0	82	5	0
43	6	0	6	58	18	0	75	15	0
44	5	10	7	54	1	0	69	11	0
45	5	1	3	49	10	0	63	14	0

EXAMPLE.—A person, aged 25, by the payment of £2. 12s. per annum, will
secure, on attaining the age of 60, the option of an annuity of £20. 13s. 4d.,
cash down £202. 1s.; or a policy on his life for £259, 19s.

II. PREMIUMS.

To secure, on attaining the ⎰Annuity, £ 10 0 0
AGE OF **60,** the option of ⎱Cash, 97 15 0
⎱Policy, 125 15 6

AGE.	Payable Annually.			Payable in One Sum.			Payable for Disparity.		
	£.	s.	d.	£.	s.	d.	£.	s.	d.
20	0	18	11	17	3	7	0	0	0
21	1	0	0	18	0	2	0	19	9
22	1	1	2	18	17	8	2	0	7
23	1	2	5	19	16	1	3	2	3
24	1	3	9	20	15	6	4	5	2
25	1	5	2	21	15	10	5	9	1
26	1	6	9	22	17	3	6	14	3
27	1	8	5	23	19	10	8	0	9
28	1	10	2	25	3	7	9	8	5
29	1	12	1	26	8	7	10	17	7
30	1	14	2	27	15	0	12	8	3
31	1	16	5	29	2	10	14	0	6
32	1	18	10	30	12	2	15	14	5
33	2	1	6	32	3	0	17	10	1
34	2	4	4	33	15	7	19	7	8
35	2	7	5	35	9	11	21	7	2
36	2	10	10	37	6	0	23	8	9
37	2	14	6	39	4	0	25	12	5
38	2	18	7	41	4	0	27	18	4
39	3	3	0	43	6	1	30	6	9
40	3	7	11	45	10	3	32	17	5
41	3	13	5	47	16	8	35	10	10
42	3	19	7	50	5	3	38	6	9
43	4	6	1	52	16	4	41	5	6
44	4	14	1	55	9	11	44	7	3
45	5	2	9	58	6	2	47	12	0

EXAMPLE.—A person aged 26 may secure, on attaining the age of 60, an Annuity of £10, with the other options, by the annual payment of £1. 6s. 9d., or a single payment of £22. 17s. 3d.; or on payment of £6. 14s. 3d. for disparity, he will be entitled to the same benefits by an annual payment of 18s. 11d., the same as for age 20

I. BENEFITS

Secured, on attaining the AGE OF **55**, by an Annual Premium
of £2. 12s.

AGE.	Annuity.			Cash.			Policy.		
	£.	s.	d.	£.	s.	d.	£.	s.	d.
20	16	16	6	190	11	0	269	15	0
21	15	17	5	179	16	0	254	10	0
22	14	19	3	169	10	0	239	18	0
23	14	1	11	159	13	0	226	0	0
24	13	5	4	150	6	0	212	15	0
25	12	9	7	141	6	0	200	1	0
26	11	14	6	132	16	0	188	0	0
27	11	0	1	124	13	0	176	9	0
28	10	6	5	116	18	0	165	10	0
29	9	13	4	109	10	0	155	0	0
30	9	0	11	102	8	0	145	0	0
31	8	9	0	95	14	0	135	10	0
32	7	17	8	89	6	0	126	8	0
33	7	6	11	83	3	0	117	15	0
34	6	16	7	77	7	0	109	10	0
35	6	6	9	71	16	0	101	13	0
36	5	17	5	66	10	0	94	3	0
37	5	8	6	61	9	0	87	0	0
38	5	0	0	56	13	0	80	4	0
39	4	12	0	52	2	0	73	15	0
40	4	4	3	47	14	0	67	11	0

EXAMPLE.—A person, aged 25, by the payment of £2. 12s. per annum, will secure, on attaining the age of 55, the option of an Annuity of £12. 9s. 7d. ; Cash down £141. 6s. ; or a Policy on his Life for £200. 1s.

II. PREMIUMS.

To secure, on attaining the $\left\{\begin{array}{l}\text{Annuity,}\\\text{Cash,}\\\text{Policy,}\end{array}\right.$ £ 10 0 0
AGE OF **55,** the option of   113 5 0
                           160 6 6

AGE.	Payable Annually.			Payable in One Sum.			Payable for Disparity.		
	£.	s.	d.	£.	s.	d.	£.	s.	d.
20	1	11	0	27	5	11	0	0	0
21	1	12	10	28	12	0	1	12	6
22	1	14	10	29	19	5	3	6	5
23	1	16	11	31	8	3	5	2	0
24	1	19	3	32	18	6	6	19	4
25	2	1	9	34	10	3	8	18	4
26	2	4	5	36	3	7	10	19	5
27	2	7	3	37	18	9	13	2	6
28	2	10	5	39	15	7	15	7	7
29	2	13	10	41	14	5	17	15	1
30	2	17	7	43	15	3	20	4	10
31	3	1	7	45	18	2	22	17	1
32	3	6	0	48	3	4	25	12	0
33	3	10	10	50	10	10	28	9	8
34	3	16	2	53	0	9	31	10	3
35	4	2	1	55	13	3	34	13	10
36	4	8	7	58	8	4	38	0	7
37	4	15	11	61	6	3	41	10	9
38	5	4	0	64	7	0	45	4	4
39	5	13	1	67	10	8	49	1	6
40	6	3	5	70	17	5	53	2	6

EXAMPLE.—A person aged 25 may secure, on attaining the age of 55, an annuity of £10, with the other options, by the annual payment of £2. 1s. 9d., or a single payment of £34. 10s. 3d. ; or on payment of £8. 18s. 4d. for disparity, he will be entitled to the same benefits by an annual payment of £1. 11s., the same as for age 20.

I. BENEFITS

Secured, on attaining the AGE OF **50,** by an Annual Premium
of £2. 12s.

AGE next Birth-Day.	Annuity.			Cash.			Policy.		
	£.	s.	d.	£.	s.	d.	£.	s.	d.
20	10	12	6	136	12	0	214	15	0
21	9	19	11	128	9	0	201	19	0
22	9	7	10	120	14	0	189	15	0
23	8	16	3	113	6	0	178	1	0
24	8	5	2	106	4	0	166	19	0
25	7	14	8	99	8	0	156	6	0
26	7	4	8	92	19	0	146	3	0
27	6	15	0	86	16	0	136	9	0
28	6	5	11	80	18	0	127	4	0
29	5	17	2	75	6	0	118	7	0
30	5	8	10	69	19	0	109	19	0
31	5	0	10	64	16	0	101	18	0
32	4	13	3	59	19	0	94	5	0
33	4	6	0	55	6	0	86	18	0
34	3	19	1	50	17	0	79	19	0
35	0	12	0	46	12	0	73	6	0

EXAMPLE.—A person, aged 23, by the payment of £2. 12s. per annum,
will secure, on attaining the age of 50, the option of an Annuity of £8. 16s. 3d.,
cash down, £113. 6s.; or a Policy on his Life for £178. 1s.

II. PREMIUMS.

To secure, on attaining the ⎧ Annuity, £ 10 0 0
AGE OF **50,** the option of ⎨ Cash, 128 11 0
⎩ Policy, 202 1 6

Age next Birth-Day.	Payable Annually.			Payable in One Sum.			Payable for Disparity.		
	£.	s.	d.	£.	s.	d.	£.	s.	d.
20	2	9	0	41	1	0	0	0	0
21	2	12	1	42	19	10	2	11	4
22	2	15	5	45	0	6	5	4	11
23	2	19	1	47	3	3	8	1	2
24	3	3	0	49	8	0	11	0	1
25	3	7	3	51	15	0	14	1	9
26	3	11	11	54	4	3	17	6	5
27	3	17	1	56	16	1	20	14	3
28	4	2	8	59	10	4	24	5	4
29	4	8	10	62	7	5	27	19	10
30	4	15	7	65	7	4	31	18	0
31	5	3	2	68	10	3	36	0	0
32	5	11	6	71	16	4	40	6	0
33	6	0	11	75	5	8	44	16	3
34	6	11	6	78	18	5	49	10	10
35	7	3	5	82	14	8	54	10	0

EXAMPLE.—A person, aged 24, may secure, on attaining the age of 50, an Annuity of £10, with the other options, by the annual payment of £3. 3s., or a single payment of £49. 8s.; or on payment of £11. 0s. 1d. for disparity, he will be entitled to the same benefits, by an annual payment of £2. 9s., the same as for age 20.

NATIONAL LOAN FUND,

Life Assurance,

AND

REVERSIONARY INTEREST SOCIETY;

FOR GRANTING

ASSURANCES AND ANNUITIES ON LIVES
AND SURVIVORSHIPS;

Endowments;

AND FOR THE PURCHASE AND SALE OF REVERSIONARY
PROPERTY AND LIFE INTERESTS.

~~~~~~~~~

CHIEF OFFICES :—

26, CORNHILL, LONDON.
67, NEW BUILDINGS, NORTH BRIDGE, EDINBURGH.
36, WESTMORLAND STREET, DUBLIN.
45, SOUTH CASTLE STREET, LIVERPOOL.
AND 9, CLARE STREET, BRISTOL.

~~~~~~~~~

LONDON:
PRINTED BY A. H. BAILY & CO., 83, CORNHILL.

———

MDCCCXXXVIII.

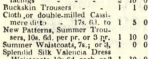

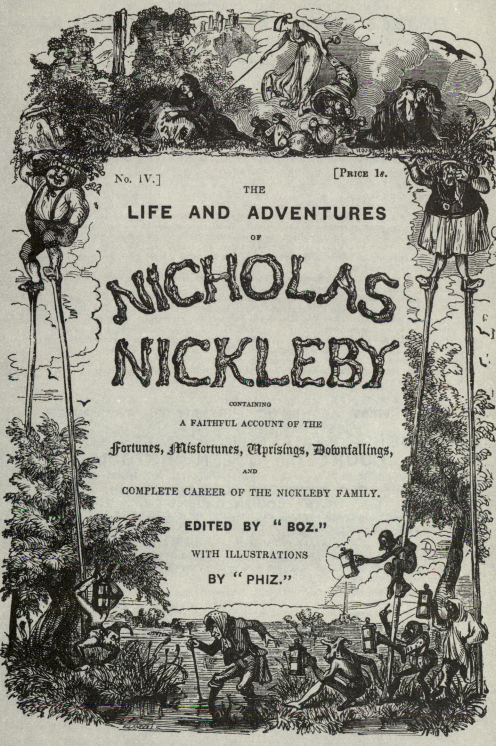

No. IV.]   [Price 1s.

THE

LIFE AND ADVENTURES

OF

NICHOLAS NICKLEBY

CONTAINING

A FAITHFUL ACCOUNT OF THE

Fortunes, Misfortunes, Uprisings, Downfallings,

AND

COMPLETE CAREER OF THE NICKLEBY FAMILY.

EDITED BY " BOZ."

WITH ILLUSTRATIONS

BY " PHIZ."

LONDON: CHAPMAN AND HALL, 186, STRAND.

(A NEW MONTHLY MAGAZINE.)

Price only 1s. 6d.

CONTAINING SIX SHEETS OF LETTER-PRESS,

SHERWOOD'S MONTHLY MISCELLANY.

A Magazine of General Literature,

SCIENCE, THE FINE ARTS, MANNERS, CONTINENTAL INFORMATION, &c. &c.

EMBELLISHED WITH TWO STEEL ENGRAVINGS

BY ALFRED CROWQUILL.

In announcing a new and cheap Periodical, the Publishers beg to observe, that the contributions of the first-rate literary talent have been engaged in the interest of the work; and it is determined that, as a Miscellany of Amusement and Instruction, this Magazine shall be rivalled by no competitor.

THE FIRST NUMBER WILL BE PUBLISHED ON THE

31ST OF JULY NEXT.

LONDON:

SHERWOOD, GILBERT, AND PIPER, PATERNOSTER ROW.

SCALE OF ADVERTISEMENTS.

One entire page . . . £3 0 0	Four pages £9 0 0
Two pages 5 0 0	Bills to sew in, &c. . . . 1 10 0

There will be a page in the body of the Magazine devoted entirely to Select Literary Intelligence, the rates of Advertisement in which are as follow:

The entire page £4 0 0
Half the page 2 5 0
A quarter 1 5 0

ARRANGEMENT OF THE ARTICLES

Tales, Poetry, and light Literature in general	3 Sheets
Biography, Translations from Foreign Works, &c.	1 Sheet
Scientific and learned Disquisitions	1 Sheet
Reviews of New Works, Obituary of Eminent Men, Literary Intelligence, the Fine Arts, Exhibitions, Theatrical Notices, the Gazette, &c. . . .	1 Sheet

* *This Magazine will contain no Political Articles.*

This day is published,

CHALON'S PORTRAIT OF THE QUEEN.

Prints on India paper, 1*l.* 1*s.* Proofs on India paper, 2*l.* 2*s.* A few copies coloured as perfect fac-similes of the original drawings, 3*l.* 3*s.* ; beautifully drawn on stone, by R. J. LANE, Esq., A.R.A.

" A beautiful full length, and a happy instance of Chalon's power of doing justice to female beauty."—*Sunday Times.*
" The likeness is wonderfully faithful."—*Blackwood's Lady's Mag.*
" The likeness of the Queen is the best we have hitherto seen."—*Naval and Military Gazette.*
" As a drawing, it is pleasing : and the colouring exquisite. The attitude, too, is easy, and the accessories of the picture pretty."—*Morning Post.*

* Please, with the order, to name the price, to prevent mistake.

LONDON : THOMAS BOYS, PRINTSELLER TO HER ROYAL HIGHNESS
THE DUCHESS OF KENT, 11, GOLDEN SQUARE.

TO TRAVELLERS IN EUROPE.

M. A LEIGH and SON, 421, Strand (removed from 18), beg to announce to the Travelling Public that their Summer Stock of Guides, Maps, &c is completed, and that the Tourist will find at their Establishment every species of Topographical information calculated to render a Tour to the Continent, or a Home Journey, an object of instruction and entertainment.

Leigh's Traveller's Guides may be obtained of their Agents in the principal towns of England, Wales, Scotland, and Ireland ; also of all Booksellers in London.

Catalogues to be had gratis, at 421, Strand.

Road and Posting Books, Guides, Maps, Plans, Tours, and Journals ; Grammars and Dictionaries ; Manuels du Voyageur and Interpreters ; Note Books ; Passport Cases ; Panoramas ; Views, &c.

Maps mounted and coloured. Binding in all its branches.

Just published, price 2*s.*,

THE SUMMER TOURIST'S POCKET COMPANION : or, Continental Note Book. No. I. The Rhine ; exhibiting the course of that River from the Sea to Schaffhausen, describing the Towns, Villages, &c., on each Bank ; with an Account of the Modes of Conveyance, Passports, Coins, Inns, &c.

* London : Leigh and Son, 421, Strand.

On the 26th day of June, royal 8vo, price 2*s* ; India proofs, ditto, 3*s.*—Demy 4to, 4*s.* ; India proofs, ditto, 5*s.* With a beautiful Likeness of her Majesty, the Queen, Part I.

WINDSOR CASTLE, and its EN-VIRONS : with three highly-finished Line-Engravings, from Original Drawings, by J. CARTER, Esq., and twenty-four pages of Letter-press, containing Anecdotes of the Royal Founders of the Towns and Seats, &c. By the author of the " Landscape Annual," " Wanderings in North and in South Wales," &c. &c.

Published for the proprietors by J. Carter, 21, Aldenham Terrace, St. Pancras Road ; Ackermann and Co., Strand ; J. Rickerby, Sherbourn Lane, King William Street ; and W. Lloyd, 36, Chandos Street, Strand. Subscribers' names received by all Booksellers in town and country. Advertisements for Part II. to be sent to J. Rickerby, Publisher, Sherbourn Lane, King William Street.

TO FLUTE PLAYERS.

W. & N. BOAG solicit the attention of Flute Players to an extensive collection of their FLUTES, which combine every desirable quality of the instrument, being finished in the first style of workmanship, well-seasoned, possessing great power and sweetness of tone, correctly in tune, and at more than 30 per cent. under the prices usually charged for first-rate Flutes. An extensive variety of excellent Second-hand Flutes by Rudall, Monzani, Prowse, and other makers. An assortment of Eight-Keyed (German Silver) Cocoa Flutes, Three Guineas each. Flutes exchanged or purchased. Repairs in a superior style. No 11, Great Turnstile, Holborn.

THE CORONATION.

In one volume, small 8vo, price 5*s.* 6*d.*, cloth boards.

REGAL RECORDS;

OR, A CHRONICLE OF

The Coronations of the Queens Regnant of England,

COMPILED FROM CONTEMPORARY ACCOUNTS AND OFFICIAL DOCUMENTS,

BY J. R. PLANCHE, F.S.A.

WITH NUMEROUS ILLUSTRATIONS.

DEDICATED BY PERMISSION TO HER GRACE THE DUCHESS OF SUTHERLAND, MISTRESS OF THE ROBES TO HER MAJESTY.

" A seasonable little book by Mr. J. R. Planche, whose antiquarian learning is relieved by a lively and ingenious turn of thinking."—*Times.*
" An interesting work, showing much research, and abounding in historical detail."—*Post.*
" An exceedingly well-timed and popular publication. Mr. Planche has gone into the subject with his usual taste and attention, giving us all that was necessary and no more, and bestowing the care they deserve upon the points chiefly applicable to the present day."—*Literary Gazette.*

CHAPMAN AND HALL, 186, STRAND.

PLATE.—A. B. SAVORY and SONS, Manufacturing Silversmiths, 14, Cornhill, London, opposite the Bank of England. The best wrought Silver Spoons and Forks, Fiddle Pattern, 7s. 2d. per ounce ; the King's Pattern, 7s. 4d per ounce. The following are the weights recommended, but the articles may be had lighter or heavier, at the same price per ounce :—

FIDDLE PATTERN.	oz.	s.	d.	£	s.	d.	KING'S PATTERN.	oz.	s.	d.	£	s.	d.
12 Table Spoons	30 at 7	2		10	15	0	12 Table Spoons	40 at 7	4		14	13	4
12 Dessert ditto	20	7	2	7	3	4	12 Dessert ditto	26	7	4	9	10	8
12 Table Forks	30	7	2	10	15	0	12 Table Forks	40	7	4	14	13	4
12 Dessert ditto	20	7	2	7	3	4	12 Dessert ditto	26	7	4	9	10	8
2 Gravy Spoons	10	7	2	3	11	8	2 Gravy Spoons	12	7	4	4	8	0
1 Soup Ladle	10	7	2	3	11	8	1 Soup Ladle	12	7	4	4	8	0
4 Sauce ditto	10	7	8	3	16	8	4 Sauce ditto	12	7	10	4	14	0
4 Salt Spoons (gilt strong)				1	0	0	4 Salt ditto (strong gilt)				2	2	0
1 Fish Slice				2	10	0	1 Fish Slice				3	5	0
12 Tea Spoons	10	7	8	3	16	8	12 Tea Spoons	14	7	10	5	9	8
1 Pair Sugar Tongs				0	15	0	1 Pair Sugar Tongs				1	5	0

A Pamphlet containing detailed lists of the prices of various patterns of Silver Spoons and Forks, Silver Tea and Coffee Services, and of the different articles of Plated Ware, may be had on application, free of cost, or will be sent into the country in answer to a paid letter.

The Plate Rooms of the Establishment, which are extensive, contain a large and choice selection of Silver Plate, Plated Goods, and every article requisite to complete a service.

ENGLISH GOLD WATCHES.—A. B. SAVORY & SONS, Watchmakers, No. 9, Cornhill, London, opposite the Bank of England, submit for selection a very large STOCK of GOLD WATCHES, the whole of which are made and finished under the careful inspection of experienced workmen on their own premises, and each warranted for correct performance.

SIZE FOR LADIES

Fine Vertical Watches, jewelled, in engine-turned gold cases, and gold dials, warranted £10 10 0

Fine Vertical Watches, jewelled, with double-backed engine-turned gold cases, and gold dials, warranted £12 12 0

Patent Detached Lever Watches, jewelled in four holes, with double-backed gold cases, and gold dials, warranted £14 14 0

SIZE FOR GENTLEMEN.

Patent Detached Lever Watches, jewelled in four holes, seconds, and double-backed gold cases, warranted....................£14 14 0

Patent Detached Lever Watches, capped, jewelled in six holes, seconds, double-backed gold cases and enamel dials, warranted.£17 17 0

Patent Detached Lever Watches, capped, jewelled in six holes, seconds, double-backed gold cases and gold dials, warranted ..£21 0 0

Either of the Gentlemen's Watches may be had n gold hunting cases for £3 3s. each extra.

N.B. Second-hand Watches purchased in exchange.

LONDON: BRADBURY AND EVANS, PRINTERS, WHITEFRIARS,

CHAPTER XI.

MR. NEWMAN NOGGS INDUCTS MRS. AND MISS NICKLEBY INTO THEIR
NEW DWELLING IN THE CITY.

Miss Nickleby's reflections as she wended her way homewards, were
of that desponding nature which the occurrences of the morning had
been sufficiently calculated to awaken. Her uncle's was not a manner
likely to dispel any doubts or apprehensions she might have formed in
the outset, neither was the glimpse she had had of Madame Mantalini's
establishment by any means encouraging. It was with many gloomy
forebodings and misgivings, therefore, that she looked forward with a
heavy heart to the opening of her new career.

If her mother's consolations could have restored her to a pleasanter
and more enviable state of mind, there were abundance of them to produce the effect. By the time Kate reached home, the good lady had
called to mind two authentic cases of milliners who had been possessed
of considerable property, though whether they had acquired it all in
business, or had had a capital to start with, or had been lucky and
married to advantage, she could not exactly remember. However, as
she very logically remarked, there must have been *some* young person in
that way of business who had made a fortune without having anything
to begin with, and that being taken for granted, why should not Kate
do the same? Miss La Creevy, who was a member of the little council,
ventured to insinuate some doubts relative to the probability of Miss
Nickleby's arriving at this happy consummation in the compass of an
ordinary lifetime; but the good lady set that question entirely at rest,
by informing them that she had a presentiment on the subject—a species
of second-sight with which she had been in the habit of clenching every
argument with the deceased Mr. Nickleby, and in nine cases and three-
quarters out of every ten, determining it the wrong way.

" I am afraid it is an unhealthy occupation," said Miss La Creevy.
" I recollect getting three young milliners to sit to me when I first began
to paint, and I remember that they were all very pale and sickly."

" Oh! that's not a general rule, by any means," observed Mrs.
Nickleby; " for I remember as well as if it was only yesterday, em-
ploying one that I was particularly recommended to, to make me a
scarlet cloak at the time when scarlet cloaks were fashionable, and she
had a very red face—a very red face, indeed."

" Perhaps she drank," suggested Miss La Creevy.

" I don't know how that may have been," returned Mrs. Nickleby;
" but I know she had a very red face, so your argument goes for nothing."

In this manner, and with like powerful reasoning, did the worthy
matron meet every little objection that presented itself to the new
scheme of the morning. Happy Mrs. Nickleby! A project had but to
be new, and it came home to her mind brightly varnished and gilded as
a glittering toy.

H

This question disposed of, Kate communicated her uncle's desire about the empty house, to which Mrs. Nickleby assented with equal readiness, characteristically remarking, that on the fine evenings it would be a pleasant amusement for her to walk to the west-end to fetch her daughter home; and no less characteristically forgetting, that there were such things as wet nights and bad weather to be encountered in almost every week of the year.

" I shall be sorry—truly sorry to leave you, my kind friend," said Kate, on whom the good feeling of the poor miniature-painter had made a deep impression.

" You shall not shake me off, for all that," replied Miss La Creevy, with as much sprightliness as she could assume. " I shall see you very often, and come and hear how you get on ; and if in all London, or all the wide world besides, there is no other heart that takes an interest in your welfare, there will be one little lonely woman that prays for it night and day."

With this the poor soul, who had a heart big enough for Gog, the guardian genius of London, and enough to spare for Magog to boot, after making a great many extraordinary faces which would have secured her an ample fortune, could she have transferred them to ivory or canvass, sat down in a corner, and had what she termed " a real good cry."

But no crying, or talking, or hoping, or fearing, could keep off the dreaded Saturday afternoon, or Newman Noggs either ; who, punctual to his time, limped up to the door and breathed a whiff of cordial gin through the keyhole, exactly as such of the church clocks in the neighbourhood as agreed among themselves about the time, struck five. Newman waited for the last stroke, and then knocked.

" From Mr. Ralph Nickleby," said Newman, announcing his errand when he got up stairs with all possible brevity.

" We shall be ready directly," said Kate. " We have not much to carry, but I fear we must have a coach."

" I'll get one," replied Newman.

" Indeed you shall not trouble yourself," said Mrs. Nickleby.

" I will," said Newman.

" I can't suffer you to think of such a thing," said Mrs. Nickleby.

" You can't help it," said Newman.

" Not help it ! "

" No. I thought of it as I came along ; but didn't get one, thinking you mightn't be ready. I think of a great many things. Nobody can prevent that."

" Oh yes, I understand you, Mr. Noggs," said Mrs. Nickleby. " Our thoughts are free, of course. Everybody's thoughts are their own, clearly."

" They wouldn't be if some people had their way," muttered Newman.

" Well, no more they would, Mr. Noggs, and that's very true," rejoined Mrs. Nickleby. " Some people, to be sure, are such—how's your master ?"

Newman darted a meaning glance at Kate, and replied with a strong emphasis on the last word of his answer, that Mr. Ralph Nickleby was well, and sent his—*love*.

" I am sure we are very much obliged to him," observed Mrs. Nickleby.

" Very," said Newman. " I'll tell him so."

It was no very easy matter to mistake Newman Noggs after having once seen him, and as Kate, attracted by the singularity of his manner (in which on this occasion, however, there was something respectful and even delicate, notwithstanding the abruptness of his speech), looked at him more closely. She recollected having caught a passing glimpse of that strange figure before.

" Excuse my curiosity," she said, " but did I not see you in the coach-yard on the morning my brother went away to Yorkshire ?"

Newman cast a wistful glance on Mrs. Nickleby, and said " No," most unblushingly.

" No !" exclaimed Kate, " I should have said so anywhere."

" You'd have said wrong," rejoined Newman. " It's the first time I've been out for three weeks. I've had the gout."

Newman was very, very far from having the appearance of a gouty subject, and so Kate could not help thinking; but the conference was cut short by Mrs. Nickleby's insisting on having the door shut lest Mr. Noggs should take cold, and further persisting in sending the servant girl for a coach, for fear he should bring on another attack of his disorder. To both conditions Newman was compelled to yield. Presently the coach came ; and, after many sorrowful farewells, and a great deal of running backwards and forwards across the pavement on the part of Miss La Creevy, in the course of which the yellow turban came into violent contact with sundry foot passengers, it (that is to say the coach, not the turban) went away again with the two ladies and their luggage inside ; and Newman—despite all Mrs. Nickleby's assurances that it would be his death—on the box beside the driver.

They went into the City, turning down by the river side ; and after a long and very slow drive, the streets being crowded at that hour with vehicles of every kind, stopped in front of a large old dingy house in Thames Street, the door and windows of which were so bespattered with mud, that it would have appeared to have been uninhabited for years.

The door of this deserted mansion Newman opened with a key which he took out of his hat—in which, by-the-bye, in consequence of the dilapidated state of his pockets he deposited everything, and would most likely have carried his money if he had had any—and the coach being discharged, he led the way into the interior of the mansion.

Old and gloomy and black in truth it was, and sullen and dark were the rooms once so bustling with life and enterprise. There was a wharf behind, opening on the Thames. An empty dog-kennel, some bones of animals, fragments of iron hoops and staves of old casks, lay strewn about, but no life was stirring there. It was a picture of cold, silent decay.

" This house depresses and chills one," said Kate, " and seems as if some blight had fallen on it. If I were superstitious, I should be almost inclined to believe that some dreadful crime had been perpetrated within these old walls, and that the place had never prospered since. How frowning and dark it looks ! "

" Lord, my dear," replied Mrs. Nickleby, " don't talk in that way, or you'll frighten me to death."

" It is only my foolish fancy, mama," said Kate, forcing a smile.

" Well, then, my love, I wish you would keep your foolish fancy to yourself, and not wake up *my* foolish fancy to keep it company," retorted Mrs. Nickleby. " Why didn't you think of all this before—you are so careless—we might have asked Miss La Creevy to keep us company, or borrowed a dog, or a thousand things—but it always was the way, and was just the same with your poor dear father. Unless I thought or everything——" This was Mrs. Nickleby's usual commencement of a general lamentation, running through a dozen or so of complicated sentences addressed to nobody in particular, and into which she now launched until her breath was exhausted.

Newman appeared not to hear these remarks, but preceded them to a couple of rooms on the first floor, which some kind of attempt had been made to render habitable. In one were a few chairs, a table, an old hearth-rug, and some faded baize ; and a fire was ready laid in the grate. In the other stood an old tent bedstead, and a few scanty articles of chamber furniture.

" Well, my dear," said Mrs. Nickleby, trying to be pleased, " now isn't this thoughtful and considerate of your uncle ? Why, we should not have had anything but the bed we bought yesterday to lie down upon, if it hadn't been for his thoughtfulness."

" Very kind, indeed," replied Kate, looking round.

Newman Noggs did not say that he had hunted up the old furniture they saw, from attic or cellar; or that he had taken in the halfpenny-worth of milk for tea that stood upon a shelf, or filled the rusty kettle on the hob, or collected the wood-chips from the wharf, or begged the coals. But the notion of Ralph Nickleby having directed it to be done tickled his fancy so much, that he could not refrain from cracking all his ten fingers in succession, at which performance Mrs. Nickleby was rather startled at first, but supposing it to be in some remote manner connected with the gout, did not remark upon.

" We need detain you no longer, I think," said Kate.

" Is there nothing I can do ?" asked Newman.

" Nothing, thank you," rejoined Miss Nickleby.

" Perhaps my dear, Mr. Noggs would like to drink our healths," said Mrs. Nickleby, fumbling in her reticule for some small coin.

" I think, mama," said Kate hesitating, and remarking Newman's averted face, " you would hurt his feelings if you offered it."

Newman Noggs, bowing to the young lady more like a gentleman than the miserable wretch he seemed, placed his hand upon his breast, and, pausing for a moment, with the air of a man who struggles to speak but is uncertain what to say, quitted the room.

As the jarring echoes of the heavy house-door closing on its latch reverberated dismally through the building, Kate felt half tempted to call him back, and beg him to remain a little while ; but she was ashamed to own her fears, and Newman Noggs was on his road homewards.

Newman Noggs leaves the ladies in the empty house.

CHAPTER XII.

WHEREBY THE READER WILL BE ENABLED TO TRACE THE FURTHER
COURSE OF MISS FANNY SQUEERS'S LOVE, AND TO ASCERTAIN
WHETHER IT RAN SMOOTHLY OR OTHERWISE.

IT was a fortunate circumstance for Miss Fanny Squeers, that when
her worthy papa returned home on the night of the small tea-party, he
was what the initiated term "too far gone" to observe the numerous
tokens of extreme vexation of spirit which were plainly visible in her
countenance. Being, however, of a rather violent and quarrelsome
mood in his cups, it is not impossible that he might have fallen out
with her, either on this or some imaginary topic, if the young lady had
not, with a foresight and prudence highly commendable, kept a boy up
on purpose to bear the first brunt of the good gentleman's anger; which
having vented itself in a variety of kicks and cuffs, subsided sufficiently
to admit of his being persuaded to go to bed; which he did with his
boots on, and an umbrella under his arm.

The hungry servant attended Miss Squeers in her own room according
to custom, to curl her hair, perform the other little offices of her toilet,
and administer as much flattery as she could get up for the purpose; for
Miss Squeers was quite lazy enough (and sufficiently vain and frivolous
withal) to have been a fine lady, and it was only the arbitrary distinctions of rank and station which prevented her from being one.

"How lovely your hair do curl to-night, Miss!" said the hand-
maiden. "I declare if it isn't a pity and a shame to brush it out!"

"Hold your tongue," replied Miss Squeers wrathfully.

Some considerable experience prevented the girl from being at all
surprised at any outbreak of ill-temper on the part of Miss Squeers.
Having a half perception of what had occurred in the course of the
evening, she changed her mode of making herself agreeable, and proceeded on the indirect tack.

"Well, I couldn't help saying, miss, if you was to kill me for it,"
said the attendant, "that I never see anybody look so vulgar as Miss
Price this night."

Miss Squeers sighed, and composed herself to listen.

"I know it's very wrong in me to say so, miss," continued the girl,
delighted to see the impression she was making, "Miss Price being a
friend of yours and all; but she do dress herself out so, and go in such
a manner to get noticed, that—oh—well, if people only saw themselves."

"What do you mean, Phib?" asked Miss Squeers, looking in her
own little glass, where, like most of us, she saw—not herself, but the
reflection of some pleasant image in her own brain. "How you talk!"

"Talk, miss! It's enough to make a Tom cat talk French grammar,
only to see how she tosses her head," replied the handmaid.

"She *does* toss her head," observed Miss Squeers, with an air of
abstraction.

" So vain, and so very—very plain," said the girl.

" Poor 'Tilda !" sighed Miss Squeers, compassionately.

" And always laying herself out so to get to be admired," pursued the servant.   " Oh dear !   It's positive indelicate."

" I can't allow you to talk in that way, Phib," said Miss Squeers. " 'Tilda's friends are low people, and if she don't know any better, it's their fault, and not hers."

" Well, but you know, miss," said Phœbe, for which name " Phib " was used as a patronising abbreviation, " if she was only to take copy by a friend—oh ! if she only knew how wrong she was, and would but set herself right by you, what a nice young woman she might be in time!"

" Phib," rejoined Miss Squeers, with a stately air, " it's not proper for me to hear these comparisons drawn ; they make 'Tilda look a coarse improper sort of person, and it seems unfriendly in me to listen to them. I would rather you dropped the subject, Phib ; at the same time I must say, that if 'Tilda Price would take pattern by somebody—not me particularly——"

" Oh yes ; you miss," interposed Phib.

" Well, me Phib, if you will have it so," said Miss Squeers.   " I must say that if she would, she would be all the better for it."

" So somebody else thinks, or I am much mistaken," said the girl mysteriously.

" What do you mean ?" demanded Miss Squeers.

" Never mind, miss," replied the girl ; " I know what I know, that's all."

" Phib," said Miss Squeers dramatically, " I insist upon your explaining yourself.   What is this dark mystery ?   Speak."

" Why, if you will have it, miss, it's this," said the servant girl. " Mr. John Browdie thinks as you think ; and if he wasn't too far gone to do it creditable, he'd be very glad to be off with Miss Price, and on with Miss Squeers."

" Gracious Heavens !" exclaimed Miss Squeers, clasping her hands with great dignity.   " What is this ?"

" Truth, ma'am, and nothing but truth," replied the artful Phib.

" What a situation !" cried Miss Squeers ; " on the brink of unconsciously destroying the peace and happiness of my own 'Tilda.   What is the reason that men fall in love with me, whether I like it or not, and desert their chosen intendeds for my sake !"

" Because they can't help it, miss," replied the girl ; " the reason's plain."   (If Miss Squeers were the reason, it was very plain.)

" Never let me hear of it again," retorted Miss Squeers.   " Never ; do you hear ?   'Tilda Price has faults—many faults—but I wish her well, and above all I wish her married ; for I think it highly desirable —most desirable from the very nature of her failings—that she should be married as soon as possible.   No, Phib.   Let her have Mr. Browdie. I may pity him, poor fellow ; but I have a great regard for 'Tilda, and only hope she may make a better wife than I think she will."

With this effusion of feeling Miss Squeers went to bed.

Spite is a little word ; but it represents as strange a jumble of feelings and compound of discords, as any polysyllable in the language.   Miss

Squeers knew as well in her heart of hearts, that what the miserable serving girl had said was sheer coarse lying flattery, as did the girl herself; yet the mere opportunity of venting a little ill-nature against the offending Miss Price, and affecting to compassionate her weaknesses and foibles, though only in the presence of a solitary dependant, was almost as great a relief to her spleen as if the whole had been gospel truth. Nay more. We have such extraordinary powers of persuasion when they are excited over ourselves, that Miss Squeers felt quite high-minded and great after her noble renunciation of John Browdie's hand, and looked down upon her rival with a kind of holy calmness and tranquillity, that had a mighty effect in soothing her ruffled feelings.

This happy state of mind had some influence in bringing about a reconciliation; for when a knock came at the front door next day, and the miller's daughter was announced, Miss Squeers betook herself to the parlour in a Christian frame of spirit perfectly beautiful to behold.

"Well, Fanny," said the miller's daughter, "you see I have come to see you, although we *had* some words last night."

"I pity your bad passions, 'Tilda," replied Miss Squeers; "but I bear no malice. I am above it."

"Don't be cross, Fanny," said Miss Price. "I have come to tell you something that I know will please you."

"What may that be, 'Tilda?" demanded Miss Squeers; screwing up her lips, and looking as if nothing in earth, air, fire, or water, could afford her the slightest gleam of satisfaction.

"This," rejoined Miss Price. "After we left here last night, John and I had a dreadful quarrel."

"That doesn't please me," said Miss Squeers—relaxing into a smile though.

"Lor! I wouldn't think so bad of you as to suppose it did," rejoined her companion. "That's not it."

"Oh!" said Miss Squeers, relapsing into melancholy. "Go on."

"After a great deal of wrangling and saying we would never see each other any more," continued Miss Price, "we made it up, and this morning John went and wrote our names down to be put up for the first time next Sunday, so we shall be married in three weeks, and I give you notice to get your frock made."

There was mingled gall and honey in this intelligence. The prospect of the friend's being married so soon was the gall, and the certainty of her not entertaining serious designs upon Nicholas was the honey. Upon the whole, the sweet greatly preponderated over the bitter, so Miss Squeers said she would get the frock made, and that she hoped 'Tilda might be happy, though at the same time she didn't know, and would not have her build too much upon it, for men were strange creatures, and a great many married women were very miserable, and wished themselves single again with all their hearts; to which condolences Miss Squeers added others equally calculated to raise her friend's spirits and promote her cheerfulness of mind.

"But come now, Fanny," said Miss Price, "I want to have a word or two with you about young Mr. Nickleby."

" He is nothing to me," interrupted Miss Squeers, with hysterical symptoms. " I despise him too much !"

" Oh, you don't mean that, I am sure ?" replied her friend. " Confess, Fanny ; don't you like him now ?"

Without returning any direct reply Miss Squeers all at once fell into a paroxysm of spiteful tears, and exclaimed that she was a wretched, neglected, miserable, castaway.

" I hate everybody," said Miss Squeers, " and I wish that everybody was dead—that I do."

" Dear, dear !" said Miss Price, quite moved by this avowal of misanthropical sentiments. " You are not serious, I am sure."

" Yes, I am," rejoined Miss Squeers, tying tight knots in her pocket-handkerchief and clenching her teeth. " And I wish I was dead too. There."

" Oh ! you'll think very differently in another five minutes," said Matilda. " How much better to take him into favour again, than to hurt yourself by going on in that way ; wouldn't it be much nicer now to have him all to yourself on good terms, in a company-keeping, love-making, pleasant sort of manner ?"

" I don't know but what it would," sobbed Miss Squeers. " Oh ! 'Tilda, how could you have acted so mean and dishonourable ! I wouldn't have believed it of you if anybody had told me."

Heyday !" exclaimed Miss Price, giggling. " One would suppose I had been murdering somebody at least."

" Very nigh as bad," said Miss Squeers passionately.

" And all this because I happen to have enough of good looks to make people civil to me," cried Miss Price. " Persons don't make their own faces, and it's no more my fault if mine is a good one than it is other people's fault if theirs is a bad one."

" Hold your tongue," shrieked Miss Squeers, in her shrillest tone ; " or you'll make me slap you, 'Tilda, and afterwards I should be sorry for it."

It is needless to say that by this time the temper of each young lady was in some slight degree affected by the tone of the conversation, and that a dash of personality was infused into the altercation in consequence. Indeed the quarrel, from slight beginnings, rose to a considerable height, and was assuming a very violent complexion, when both parties, falling into a great passion of tears, exclaimed simultaneously, that they had never thought of being spoken to in that way, which exclamation, leading to a remonstrance, gradually brought on an explanation, and the upshot was that they fell into each other's arms and vowed eternal friendship ; the occasion in question, making the fifty-second time of repeating the same impressive ceremony within a twelvemonth.

Perfect amicability being thus restored, a dialogue naturally ensued upon the number and nature of the garments which would be indispensable for Miss Price's entrance into the holy state of matrimony, when Miss Squeers clearly showed that a great many more than the miller could, or would, afford were absolutely necessary, and could not decently be dispensed with. The young lady then, by an easy digression, led the discourse to her own wardrobe, and after recounting its principal beauties at some length, took her friend up stairs to make inspection thereof. The treasures of two drawers and a closet having been displayed, and all the smaller articles tried on, it was time for Miss Price to return home, and as she had been in raptures with all the frocks, and had been stricken quite dumb with admiration of a new pink scarf, Miss Squeers said in high good humour, that she would walk part of the way with her for the pleasure of her company ; and off they went together, Miss Squeers dilating, as they walked along, upon her father's accomplishments, and multiplying his income by ten, to give her friend some faint notion of the vast importance and superiority of her family.

It happened that that particular time, comprising the short daily interval which was suffered to elapse between what was pleasantly called the dinner of Mr. Squeers's pupils and their return to the pursuit of useful knowledge, was precisely the hour when Nicholas was accustomed to issue forth for a melancholy walk, and to brood, as he sauntered listlessly through the village, upon his miserable lot. Miss Squeers knew this perfectly well, but had perhaps forgotten it, for when she caught sight of that young gentleman advancing towards them, she evinced many symptoms of surprise and consternation, and assured her friend that she " felt fit to drop into the earth."

" Shall we turn back, or run into a cottage ?" asked Miss Price. " He don't see us yet."

" No, 'Tilda," replied Miss Squeers, " it is my duty to go through with it, and I will."

As Miss Squeers said this in the tone of one who has made a high moral resolution, and was besides taken with one or two chokes and catchings of breath, indicative of feelings at a high pressure, her friend made no farther remark, and they bore straight down upon Nicholas, who, walking with his eyes bent upon the ground, was not aware of their approach until they were close upon him ; otherwise he might perhaps have taken shelter himself.

" Good morning," said Nicholas, bowing and passing by.

" He is going," murmured Miss Squeers. " I shall choke, 'Tilda."

" Come back, Mr. Nickleby, do," cried Miss Price, affecting alarm at her friend's threat, but really actuated by a malicious wish to hear what Nicholas would say ; " come back, Mr. Nickleby."

Mr. Nickleby came back, and looked as confused as might be, as he inquired whether the ladies had any commands for him.

" Don't stop to talk," urged Miss Price, hastily ; " but support her on the other side. How do you feel now, dear ? "

" Better," sighed Miss Squeers, laying a beaver bonnet of reddish brown with a green veil attached, on Mr. Nickleby's shoulder. " This foolish faintness !"

" Don't call it foolish, dear," said Miss Price, her bright eye dancing with merriment as she saw the perplexity of Nicholas ; " you have no reason to be ashamed of it. It's those who are too proud to come round again without all this to-do, that ought to be ashamed."

" You are resolved to fix it upon me, I see," said Nicholas, smiling, " although I told you last night it was not my fault."

" There; he says it was not his fault, my dear," remarked the wicked Miss Price. "Perhaps you were too jealous or too hasty with him? He says it was not his fault, you hear; I think that's apology enough."

" You will not understand me," said Nicholas. " Pray dispense with this jesting, for I have no time, and really no inclination, to be the subject or promoter of mirth just now."

" What do you mean ? " asked Miss Price, affecting amazement.

" Don't ask him, 'Tilda," cried Miss Squeers; " I forgive him."

" Dear me," said Nicholas, as the brown bonnet went down on his shoulder again, " this is more serious than I supposed; allow me. Will you have the goodness to hear me speak ? "

Here he raised up the brown bonnet, and regarding with most unfeigned astonishment a look of tender reproach from Miss Squeers, shrunk back a few paces to be out of the reach of the fair burden, and went on to say—

" I am very sorry—truly and sincerely sorry—for having been the cause of any difference among you last night. I reproach myself most bitterly for having been so unfortunate as to cause the dissension that occurred, although I did so, I assure you, most unwittingly and heedlessly."

" Well; that's not all you have got to say surely," exclaimed Miss Price as Nicholas paused.

" I fear there is something more," stammered Nicholas with a half smile, and looking towards Miss Squeers, " it is a most awkward thing to say—but—the very mention of such a supposition makes one look like a puppy—still—may I ask if that lady supposes that I entertain any—in short does she think that I am in love with her ? "

" Delightful embarrassment," thought Miss Squeers, " I have brought him to it at last. Answer for me, dear," she whispered to her friend.

" Does she think so ? " rejoined Miss Price; " of course she does."

" She does ! " exclaimed Nicholas with such energy of utterance as might have been for the moment mistaken for rapture.

" Certainly," replied Miss Price.

" If Mr. Nickleby has doubted that, 'Tilda," said the blushing Miss Squeers in soft accents, " he may set his mind at rest. His sentiments are recipro—"

" Stop," cried Nicholas hurriedly; " pray hear me. This is the grossest and wildest delusion, the completest and most signal mistake, that ever human being laboured under or committed. I have scarcely seen the young lady half a dozen times, but if I had seen her sixty times, or am destined to see her sixty thousand, it would be and will be precisely the same. I have not one thought, wish, or hope, connected with her unless it be—and I say this, not to hurt her feelings, but to impress her with the real state of my own—unless it be the one object dear to my heart as life itself, of being one day able to turn my back upon this accursed place, never to set foot in it again or to think of it—even think of it—but with loathing and disgust."

With this particularly plain and straight-forward declaration, which he made with all the vehemence that his indignant and excited feelings could bring to bear upon it, Nicholas slightly bowed, and waiting to hear no more, retreated.

But poor Miss Squeers! Her anger, rage, and vexation; the rapid succession of bitter and passionate feelings that whirled through her mind, are not to be described. Refused! refused by a teacher picked up by advertisement at an annual salary of five pounds payable at indefinite periods, and "found" in food and lodging like the very boys themselves; and this too in the presence of a little chit of a miller's daughter of eighteen, who was going to be married in three weeks' time to a man who had gone down on his very knees to ask her! She could have choked in right good earnest at the thought of being so humbled.

But there was one thing clear in the midst of her mortification, and that was that she hated and detested Nicholas with all the narrowness of mind and littleness of purpose worthy a descendant of the house of Squeers. And there was one comfort too; and that was, that every hour in every day she could wound his pride and goad him with the infliction of some slight, or insult, or deprivation, which could not but have some effect on the most insensible person, and must be acutely felt by one so sensitive as Nicholas. With these two reflections uppermost in her mind, Miss Squeers made the best of the matter to her friend by observing, that Mr. Nickleby was such an odd creature, and of such a violent temper, that she feared she should be obliged to give him up; and parted from her.

And here it may be remarked, that Miss Squeers having bestowed her affections (or whatever it might be that in the absence of anything better represented them) on Nicholas Nickleby, had never once seriously contemplated the possibility of his being of a different opinion from herself in the business. Miss Squeers reasoned that she was prepossessing and beautiful, and that her father was master and Nicholas man, and that her father had saved money and Nicholas had none, all of which seemed to her conclusive arguments why the young man should feel only too much honoured by her preference. She had not failed to recollect, either, how much more agreeable she could render his situation if she were his friend, and how much more disagreeable if she were his enemy; and doubtless, many less scrupulous young gentlemen than Nicholas would have encouraged her extravagance had it been only for this very obvious and intelligible reason. However, he had thought proper to do otherwise, and Miss Squeers was outrageous.

" Let him see," said the irritated young lady when she had regained her own room, and eased her mind by committing an assault on Phib, "if I don't set mother against him a little more when she comes back."

It was scarcely necessary to do this, but Miss Squeers was as good as her word; and poor Nicholas, in addition to bad food, dirty lodgement, and the being compelled to witness one dull unvarying round of squalid misery, was treated with every special indignity that malice could suggest, or the most grasping cupidity put upon him.

Nor was this all. There was another and deeper system of annoyance which made his heart sink, and nearly drove him wild by its injustice and cruelty.

The wretched creature, Smike, since the night Nicholas had spoken kindly to him in the school-room, had followed him to and fro with an ever restless desire to serve or help him, anticipating such little wants as his humble ability could supply, and content only to be near him. He would sit beside him for hours looking patiently into his face, and a word would brighten up his care-worn visage, and call into it a passing gleam even of happiness. He was an altered being; he had an object now, and that object was to show his attachment to the only person—that person a stranger—who had treated him, not to say with kindness, but like a human creature.

Upon this poor being all the spleen and ill-humour that could not be vented on Nicholas were unceasingly bestowed. Drudgery would have been nothing—he was well used to that. Buffetings inflicted without cause would have been equally a matter of course, for to them also he had served a long and weary apprenticeship; but it was no sooner observed that he had become attached to Nicholas, than stripes and blows, stripes and blows, morning, noon, and night, were his only portion. Squeers was jealous of the influence which his man had so soon acquired, and his family hated him, and Smike paid for both. Nicholas saw it, and ground his teeth at every repetition of the savage and cowardly attack.

He had arranged a few regular lessons for the boys, and one night as he paced up and down the dismal school-room, his swoln heart almost bursting to think that his protection and countenance should have increased the misery of the wretched being whose peculiar destitution had awakened his pity, he paused mechanically in a dark corner where sat the object of his thoughts.

The poor soul was poring hard over a tattered book with the traces of recent tears still upon his face, vainly endeavouring to master some task which a child of nine years old, possessed of ordinary powers, could have conquered with ease, but which to the addled brain of the crushed boy of nineteen was a sealed and hopeless mystery. Yet there he sat, patiently conning the page again and again, stimulated by no boyish ambition, for he was the common jest and scoff even of the uncouth objects that congregated about him, but inspired by the one eager desire to please his solitary friend.

Nicholas laid his hand upon his shoulder.

" I can't do it," said the dejected creature, looking up with bitter disappointment in every feature. " No, no."

" Do not try," replied Nicholas.

The boy shook his head, and closing the book with a sigh, looked vacantly round, and laid his head upon his arm. He was weeping.

" Do not for God's sake," said Nicholas, in an agitated voice; " I cannot bear to see you."

" They are more hard with me than ever," sobbed the boy.

" I know it," rejoined Nicholas. " They are."

" But for you," said the outcast, " I should die. They would kill me; they would, I know they would."

" You will do better, poor fellow," replied Nicholas, shaking his head mournfully, " when I am gone."

" Gone!" cried the other, looking intently in his face.

" Softly!" rejoined Nicholas. " Yes."

" Are you going ?" demanded the boy, in an earnest whisper.

" I cannot say," replied Nicholas, " I was speaking more to my own thoughts than to you."

" Tell me," said the boy imploringly. " Oh do tell me, *will* you go—*will* you ?"

" I shall be driven to that at last !" said Nicholas. " The world is before me, after all."

" Tell me," urged Smike, " is the world as bad and dismal as this place ?"

" Heaven forbid," replied Nicholas, pursuing the train of his own thoughts, " its hardest, coarsest toil, were happiness to this."

" Should I ever meet you there ?" demanded the boy, speaking with unusual wildness and volubility.

" Yes," replied Nicholas, willing to soothe him.

" No, no !" said the other, clasping him by the hand. " Should I—should I—tell me that again. Say I should be sure to find you."

" You would," replied Nicholas, with the same humane intention, " and I would help and aid you, and not bring fresh sorrow on you as I have done here."

The boy caught both the young man's hands passionately in his, and hugging them to his breast, uttered a few broken sounds which were unintelligible. Squeers entered at the moment, and he shrunk back into his old corner.

CHAPTER XIII.

NICHOLAS VARIES THE MONOTONY OF DOTHEBOYS HALL BY A MOST VIGOROUS AND REMARKABLE PROCEEDING, WHICH LEADS TO CONSEQUENCES OF SOME IMPORTANCE.

The cold feeble dawn of a January morning was stealing in at the windows of the common sleeping-room, when Nicholas, raising himself upon his arm, looked among the prostrate forms which on every side surrounded him, as though in search of some particular object.

It needed a quick eye to detect from among the huddled mass of sleepers, the form of any given individual. As they lay closely packed together, covered, for warmth's sake, with their patched and ragged clothes, little could be distinguished but the sharp outlines of pale faces, over which the sombre light shed the same dull heavy colour, with here and there a gaunt arm thrust forth : its thinness hidden by no covering, but fully exposed to view in all its shrunken ugliness. There were some who, lying on their backs with upturned faces and clenched hands, just visible in the leaden light, bore more the aspect of dead bodies than of living creatures, and there were others coiled up into strange and fantastic postures, such as might have been taken for the uneasy efforts of pain to gain some temporary relief, rather than the freaks of slumber. A few—and these were among the youngest of the children—slept peacefully on with smiles upon their faces, dreaming perhaps of home; but ever and again a deep and heavy sigh, breaking the stillness of the room, announced that some new sleeper had awakened to the misery of another day, and, as morning took the place of night, the smiles gradually faded away with the friendly darkness which had given them birth.

Dreams are the bright creatures of poem and legend, who sport on earth in the night season, and melt away in the first beam of the sun, which lights grim care and stern reality on their daily pilgrimage through the world.

Nicholas looked upon the sleepers, at first with the air of one who gazes upon a scene which, though familiar to him, has lost none of its sorrowful effect in consequence, and afterwards, with a more intense and searching scrutiny, as a man would who missed something his eye was accustomed to meet, and had expected to rest upon. He was still occupied in this search, and had half risen from his bed in the eagerness of his quest, when the voice of Squeers was heard calling from the bottom of the stairs.

" Now then," cried that gentleman, " are you going to sleep all day, up there—"

" You lazy hounds?" added Mrs. Squeers, finishing the sentence, and producing at the same time a sharp sound like that which is occasioned by the lacing of stays.

" We shall be down directly, Sir," replied Nicholas.

" Down directly!" said Squeers. " Ah! you had better be down directly, or I'll be down upon some of you in less. Where's that Smike?"

Nicholas looked hurriedly round again, but made no answer.

" Smike!" shouted Squeers.

" Do you want your head broke in a fresh place, Smike?" demanded his amiable lady in the same key.

Still there was no reply, and still Nicholas stared about him, as did the greater part of the boys who were by this time roused.

" Confound his impudence," muttered Squeers, rapping the stair-rail impatiently with his cane. " Nickleby."

" Well, Sir."

" Send that obstinate scoundrel down ; don't you hear me calling?"

" He is not here, Sir," replied Nicholas.

" Don't tell me a lie," retorted the schoolmaster. " He is."

" He is not," retorted Nicholas angrily, " don't tell me one."

" We shall soon see that," said Mr. Squeers, rushing up stairs. " I'll find him I warrant you."

With which assurance Mr. Squeers bounced into the dormitory, and swinging his cane in the air ready for a blow, darted into the corner where the lean body of the drudge was usually stretched at night. The cane descended harmlessly upon the ground. There was nobody there.

" What does this mean?" said Squeers, turning round with a very
pale face. " Where have you hid him?"

" I have seen nothing of him since last night," replied Nicholas.

" Come," said Squeers, evidently frightened, though he endeavoured
to look otherwise, " you won't save him this way. Where is he?"

" At the bottom of the nearest pond for aught I know," rejoined
Nicholas in a low voice, and fixing his eyes full on the master's face.

" D—n you, what do you mean by that?" retorted Squeers in great
perturbation. And without waiting for a reply, he inquired of the
boys whether any one among them knew anything of their missing
schoolmate.

There was a general hum of anxious denial, in the midst of which
one shrill voice was heard to say (as, indeed, everybody thought)—

" Please, Sir, I think Smike's run away, Sir."

" Ha!" cried Squeers, turning sharp round ; " Who said that?"

" Tomkins, please Sir," rejoined a chorus of voices. Mr. Squeers
made a plunge into the crowd, and at one dive caught a very little boy
habited still in his night gear, and the perplexed expression of whose
countenance as he was brought forward, seemed to intimate that he
was as yet uncertain whether he was about to be punished or rewarded
for the suggestion. He was not long in doubt.

" You think he has run away, do you, Sir?" demanded Squeers.

" Yes, please Sir," replied the little boy.

" And what, Sir," said Squeers, catching the little boy suddenly by
the arms and whisking up his drapery in a most dexterous manner,
" what reason have you to suppose that any boy would want to run
away from this establishment? Eh, Sir?"

The child raised a dismal cry by way of answer, and Mr. Squeers,
throwing himself into the most favourable attitude for exercising his
strength, beat him till the little urchin in his writhings actually rolled
out of his hands, when he mercifully allowed him to roll away as he
best could.

" There," said Squeers. " Now if any other boy thinks Smike has
run away, I shall be glad to have a talk with him."

There was of course a profound silence, during which, Nicholas
showed his disgust as plainly as looks could show it.

" Well, Nickleby," said Squeers, eyeing him maliciously. " *You*
think he has run away, I suppose?"

" I think it extremely likely," replied Nicholas, in a very quiet manner.

" Oh, you do, do you?" sneered Squeers. " Maybe you know he
has?"

" I know nothing of the kind."

" He did'nt tell you he was going, I suppose, did he?" sneered
Squeers.

" He did not," replied Nicholas ; " I am very glad he did not, for it
would then have been my duty to have warned you in time."

" Which no doubt you would have been devilish sorry to do," said
Squeers in a taunting fashion.

" I should, indeed," replied Nicholas. " You interpret my feelings
with great accuracy."

Mrs. Squeers had listened to this conversation from the bottom of the stairs, but now losing all patience, she hastily assumed her night-jacket and made her way to the scene of action.

" What's all this here to do ?" said the lady, as the boys fell off right and left to save her the trouble of clearing a passage with her brawny arms. " What on earth are you a talking to him for, Squeery !"

" Why, my dear," said Squeers, " the fact is, that Smike is not to be found."

" Well, I know that," said the lady, " and where's the wonder ? If you get a parcel of proud-stomached teachers that set the young dogs a rebelling, what else can you look for ? Now, young man, you just have the kindness to take yourself off to the school-room, and take the boys off with you, and don't you stir out of there 'till you have leave given you, or you and I may fall out in a way that'll spoil your beauty, handsome as you think yourself, and so I tell you."

" Indeed ! " said Nicholas, smiling.

" Yes ; and indeed and indeed again, Mister Jackanapes," said the excited lady ; " and I wouldn't keep such as you in the house another hour if I had my way."

" Nor would you, if I had mine," replied Nicholas. " Now, boys."

" Ah ! Now boys," said Mrs. Squeers, mimicking, as nearly as she could, the voice and manner of the usher. " Follow your leader, boys, and take pattern by Smike if you dare. See what he'll get for himself when he is brought back, and mind I tell you that you shall have as bad, and twice as bad, if you so much as open your mouths about him."

" If I catch him," said Squeers, " I'll only stop short of flaying him alive, I give you notice, boys."

" If you catch him," retorted Mrs. Squeers contemptuously, " you are sure to ; you can't help it, if you go the right way to work.   Come, away with you !"

With these words, Mrs. Squeers dismissed the boys, and after a little light skirmishing with those in the rear who were pressing forward to get out of the way, but were detained for a few moments by the throng in front, succeeded in clearing the room, when she confronted her spouse alone.

" He is off," said Mrs. Squeers. " The cow-house and stable are locked up, so he can't be there ; and he's not down stairs anywhere, for the girl has looked. He must have gone York way, and by a public road too."

" Why must he ? " inquired Squeers.

" Stupid !" said Mrs. Squeers angrily. " He hadn't any money, had he ? "

" Never had a penny of his own in his whole life, that I know of," replied Squeers.

" To be sure," rejoined Mrs. Squeers, " and he didn't take anything to eat with him, that I'll answer for.   Ha ! ha ! ha ! "

" Ha ! ha ! ha !" cried Squeers.

" Then of course," said Mrs. S., " he must beg his way, and he could do that nowhere but on the public road."

" That's true," exclaimed Squeers, clapping his hands.

" True! Yes; but you would never have thought of it for all that, if I hadn't said so," replied his wife. " Now, if you take the chaise and go one road, and I borrow Swallows's chaise, and go the other, what with keeping our eyes open and asking questions, one or other of us is pretty certain to lay hold of him."

The worthy lady's plan was adopted and put in execution without a moment's delay. After a very hasty breakfast, and the prosecution of some inquiries in the village, the result of which seemed to show that he was on the right track, Squeers started forth in the pony-chaise, intent upon discovery and vengeance. Shortly afterwards Mrs. Squeers, arrayed in the white top-coat, and tied up in various shawls and handkerchiefs, issued forth in another chaise and another direction, taking with her a good-sized bludgeon, several odd pieces of strong cord, and a stout labouring man : all provided and carried upon the expedition with the sole object of assisting in the capture, and (once caught) ensuring the safe custody of the unfortunate Smike.

Nicholas remained behind in a tumult of feeling, sensible that whatever might be the upshot of the boy's flight, nothing but painful and deplorable consequences were likely to ensue from it. Death from want and exposure to the weather was the best that could be expected from the protracted wandering of so poor and helpless a creature, alone and unfriended, through a country of which he was wholly ignorant. There was little, perhaps, to choose between this fate and a return to the tender mercies of the Yorkshire school, but the unhappy being had established a hold upon his sympathy and compassion, which made his heart ache at the prospect of the suffering he was destined to undergo. He lingered on in restless anxiety, picturing a thousand possibilities, until the evening of next day, when Squeers returned alone and unsuccessful.

" No news of the scamp," said the schoolmaster, who had evidently been stretching his legs, on the old principle, not a few times during the journey. " I'll have consolation for this out of somebody, Nickleby, if Mrs. Squeers don't hunt him down, so I give you warning."

" It is not in my power to console you, Sir," said Nicholas. " It is nothing to me."

" Isn't it?" said Squeers in a threatening manner. " We shall see !"

" We shall," rejoined Nicholas.

" Here's the pony run right off his legs, and me obliged to come home with a hack cob, that'll cost fifteen shillings besides other expenses," said Squeers ; " who's to pay for that, do you hear ?"

Nicholas shrugged his shoulders and remained silent.

" I'll have it out of somebody I tell you," said Squeers, his usual harsh crafty manner changed to open bullying. " None of your whining vapourings here, Mr. Puppy, but be off to your kennel, for it's past your bed-time. Come. Get out."

Nicholas bit his lip and knit his hands involuntarily, for his finger-ends tingled to avenge the insult, but remembering that the man was drunk, and that it could come to little but a noisy brawl, he contented

I

himself with darting a contemptuous look at the tyrant, and walked as majestically as he could up stairs, not a little nettled however to observe that Miss Squeers and Master Squeers, and the servant girl, were enjoying the scene from a snug corner; the two former indulging in many edifying remarks about the presumption of poor upstarts; which occasioned a vast deal of laughter, in which even the most miserable of all miserable servant girls joined, while Nicholas, stung to the quick, drew over his head such bedclothes as he had, and sternly resolved that the out-standing account between himself and Mr. Squeers should be settled rather more speedily than the latter anticipated.

Another day came, and Nicholas was scarcely awake when he heard the wheels of a chaise approaching the house. It stopped. The voice of Mrs. Squeers was heard, and in exultation, ordering a glass of spirits for somebody, which was in itself a sufficient sign that something extraordinary had happened. Nicholas hardly dared to look out of the window, but he did so, and the very first object that met his eyes was the wretched Smike; so bedabbled with mud and rain, so haggard and worn, and wild, that, but for his garments being such as no scarecrow was ever seen to wear, he might have been doubtful, even then, of his identity.

" Lift him out," said Squeers, after he had literally feasted his eyes in silence upon the culprit. " Bring him in; bring him in."

" Take care," cried Mrs. Squeers, as her husband proffered his assistance. " We tied his legs under the apron and made 'em fast to the chaise, to prevent his giving us the slip again."

With hands trembling with delight, Squeers unloosened the cord, and Smike, to all appearance more dead than alive, was brought into the house and securely locked up in a cellar, until such time as Mr. Squeers should deem it expedient to operate upon him in presence of the assembled school.

Upon a hasty consideration of the circumstances, it may be matter of surprise to some persons, that Mr. and Mrs. Squeers should have taken so much trouble to repossess themselves of an incumbrance of which it was their wont to complain so loudly; but their surprise will cease when they are informed that the manifold services of the drudge, if performed by anybody else, would have cost the establishment some ten or twelve shillings per week in the shape of wages; and furthermore, that all runaways were, as a matter of policy, made severe examples of at Dotheboys Hall, inasmuch as in consequence of the limited extent of its attractions there was but little inducement, beyond the powerful impulse of fear, for any pupil provided with the usual number of legs and the power of using them, to remain.

The news that Smike had been caught and brought back in triumph, ran like wild-fire through the hungry community, and expectation was on tiptoe all the morning. On tiptoe it was destined to remain, however, until afternoon; when Squeers, having refreshed himself with his dinner, and further strengthened himself by an extra libation or so, made his appearance (accompanied by his amiable partner) with a countenance of portentous import, and a fearful instrument of flagellation, strong, supple, wax-ended, and new—in short, purchased that morning expressly for the occasion.

" Is every boy here ?" asked Squeers, in a tremendous voice.

Every boy was there, but every boy was afraid to speak ; so Squeers glared along the lines to assure himself, and every eye drooped and every head cowered down as he did so.

" Each boy keep his place," said Squeers, administering his favourite blow to the desk, and regarding with gloomy satisfaction the universal start which it never failed to occasion. " Nickleby, to your desk, Sir."

It was remarked by more than one small observer, that there was a very curious and unusual expression in the usher's face, but he took his seat without opening his lips in reply ; and Squeers casting a triumphant glance at his assistant and a look of most comprehensive despotism on the boys, left the room, and shortly afterwards returned dragging Smike by the collar—or rather by that fragment of his jacket which was nearest the place where his collar would have been, had he boasted such a decoration.

In any other place the appearance of the wretched, jaded, spiritless object would have occasioned a murmur of compassion and remonstrance. It had some effect even there ; for the lookers-on moved uneasily in their seats, and a few of the boldest ventured to steal looks at each other, expressive of indignation and pity.

They were lost on Squeers, however, whose gaze was fastened on the luckless Smike as he inquired, according to custom in such cases, whether he had anything to say for himself.

" Nothing, I suppose ?" said Squeers, with a diabolical grin.

Smike glanced round, and his eye rested for an instant on Nicholas, as if he had expected him to intercede ; but his look was riveted on his desk.

" Have you anything to say ?" demanded Squeers again : giving his right arm two or three flourishes to try its power and suppleness. " Stand a little out of the way, Mrs. Squeers, my dear ; I've hardly got room enough."

" Spare me, Sir," cried Smike.

" Oh ! that's all, is it ?" said Squeers. " Yes, I'll flog you within an inch of your life, and spare you that."

" Ha, ha, ha," laughed Mrs. Squeers, " that's a good 'un."

" I was driven to do it," said Smike faintly ; and casting another imploring look about him.

" Driven to do it, were you ?" said Squeers. " Oh ! it wasn't your fault ; it was mine, I suppose—eh ?"

" A nasty, ungrateful, pig-headed, brutish, obstinate, sneaking dog," exclaimed Mrs. Squeers, taking Smike's head under her arm, and administering a cuff at every epithet ; " what does he mean by that ?"

" Stand aside, my dear," replied Squeers. " We'll try and find out."

Mrs. Squeers being out of breath with her exertions, complied. Squeers caught the boy firmly in his grip ; one desperate cut had fallen on his body—he was wincing from the lash and uttering a scream of pain—it was raised again, and again about to fall—when Nicholas

Nickleby suddenly starting up, cried " Stop !" in a voice that made the rafters ring.

" Who cried stop ? " said Squeers, turning savagely round.

" I," said Nicholas, stepping forward.   " This must not go on."

" Must not go on !" cried Squeers, almost in a shriek.

" No !" thundered Nicholas.

Aghast and stupified by the boldness of the interference, Squeers released his hold of Smike, and falling back a pace or two, gazed upon Nicholas with looks that were positively frightful.

" I say must not," repeated Nicholas, nothing daunted ; " shall not. I will prevent it."

Squeers continued to gaze upon him, with his eyes starting out of his head ; but astonishment had actually for the moment bereft him of speech.

" You have disregarded all my quiet interference in the miserable lad's behalf," said Nicholas ; " returned no answer to the letter in which I begged forgiveness for him, and offered to be responsible that he would remain quietly here.   Don't blame me for this public inter- ference.   You have brought it upon yourself ; not I."

" Sit down, beggar !" screamed Squeers, almost beside himself with rage, and seizing Smike as he spoke.

" Wretch," rejoined Nicholas, fiercely, " touch him at your peril ! I will not stand by and see it done ; my blood is up, and I have the strength of ten such men as you.   Look to yourself, for by Heaven I will not spare you, if you drive me on."

" Stand back," cried Squeers, brandishing his weapon.

" I have a long series of insults to avenge," said Nicholas, flushed with passion ; " and my indignation is aggravated by the dastardly cruelties practised on helpless infancy in this foul den.   Have a care ; for if you do raise the devil within me, the consequences shall fall heavily upon your own head."

He had scarcely spoken when Squeers, in a violent outbreak of wrath and with a cry like the howl of a wild beast, spat upon him, and struck him a blow across the face with his instrument of torture, which raised up a bar of livid flesh as it was inflicted.   Smarting with the agony of the blow, and concentrating into that one moment all his feelings of rage, scorn, and indignation, Nicholas sprang upon him, wrested the weapon from his hand, and, pinning him by the throat, beat the ruffian till he roared for mercy.

The boys—with the exception of Master Squeers, who, coming to his father's assistance, harassed the enemy in the rear—moved not hand or foot ; but Mrs. Squeers, with many shrieks for aid, hung on to the tail of her partner's coat and endeavoured to drag him from his infuriated adversary ; while Miss Squeers, who had been peeping through the key- hole in expectation of a very different scene, darted in at the very beginning of the attack, and after launching a shower of inkstands at the usher's head, beat Nicholas to her heart's content, animating herself at every blow with the recollection of his having refused her proffered love, and thus imparting additional strength to an arm which (as she took after her mother in this respect) was at no time one of the weakest.

Nicholas astonishes Mr. Squeers and family.

Nicholas, in the full torrent of his violence, felt the blows no more than if they had been dealt with feathers; but becoming tired of the noise and uproar, and feeling that his arm grew weak besides, he threw all his remaining strength into half-a-dozen finishing cuts, and flung Squeers from him with all the force he could muster. The violence of his fall precipitated Mrs. Squeers completely over an adjacent form, and Squeers, striking his head against it in his descent, lay at his full length on the ground, stunned and motionless.

Having brought affairs to this happy termination, and ascertained to his thorough satisfaction that Squeers was only stunned, and not dead (upon which point he had had some unpleasant doubts at first), Nicholas left his family to restore him, and retired to consider what course he had better adopt. He looked anxiously round for Smike as he left the room, but he was nowhere to be seen.

After a brief consideration he packed up a few clothes in a small leathern valise, and finding that nobody offered to oppose his progress, marched boldly out by the front-door, and shortly afterwards struck into the road which led to Greta Bridge.

When he had cooled sufficiently to be enabled to give his present circumstances some little reflection, they did not appear in a very encouraging light, for he had only four shillings and a few pence in his pocket, and was something more than two hundred and fifty miles from London, whither he resolved to direct his steps, that he might ascertain, among other things, what account of the morning's proceedings Mr. Squeers transmitted to his most affectionate uncle.

Lifting up his eyes, as he arrived at the conclusion that there was no remedy for this unfortunate state of things, he beheld a horseman coming towards him, whom, on his nearer approach, he discovered, to his infinite chagrin, to be no other than Mr. John Browdie, who, clad in cords and leather leggings, was urging his animal forward by means of a thick ash stick, which seemed to have been recently cut from some stout sapling.

"I am in no mood for more noise and riot," thought Nicholas, "and yet, do what I will, I shall have an altercation with this honest blockhead, and perhaps a blow or two from yonder staff."

In truth there appeared some reason to expect that such a result would follow from the encounter, for John Browdie no sooner saw Nicholas advancing, than he reined in his horse by the footpath, and waited until such time as he should come up; looking meanwhile very sternly between the horse's ears at Nicholas, as he came on at his leisure.

"Servant, young genelman," said John.

"Yours," said Nicholas.

"Weel; we ha' met at last," observed John, making the stirrup ring under a smart touch of the ash stick.

"Yes," replied Nicholas, hesitating. "Come," he said, frankly, after a moment's pause, "we parted on no very good terms the last time we met; it was my fault, I believe; but I had no intention of offending you, and no idea that I was doing so. I was very sorry for it afterwards. Will you shake hands?"

"Shake honds!" cried the good-humoured Yorkshireman; "ah!

that I weel;" at the same time he bent down from the saddle, and
gave Nicholas's fist a huge wrench; "but wa'at be the matther wi' thy
feace, mun? it be all brokken loike."

"It is a cut," said Nicholas, turning scarlet as he spoke,—"a blow;
but I returned it to the giver, and with good interest too."

"Noa, did 'ee though?" exclaimed John Browdie. "Weel deane,
I loike 'un for thot."

"The fact is," said Nicholas, not very well knowing how to make
the avowal, "the fact is, that I have been ill-treated."

"Noa!" interposed John Browdie, in a tone of compassion; for he
was a giant in strength and stature, and Nicholas very likely in his
eyes seemed a mere dwarf; "dean't say thot."

"Yes, I have," replied Nicholas, "by that man Squeers, and I have
beaten him soundly, and am leaving this place in consequence."

"What!" cried John Browdie, with such an ecstatic shout, that the
horse quite shyed at it. "Beatten the schoolmeasther! Ho! ho! ho!
Beatten the schoolmeasther! who ever heard o' the loike o' that noo!
Giv' us thee hond agean, yoongster. Beatten a schoolmeasther! Dang
it, I loove thee for't."

With these expressions of delight, John Browdie laughed and laughed
again—so loud that the echoes far and wide sent back nothing but
jovial peals of merriment—and shook Nicholas by the hand meanwhile
no less heartily. When his mirth had subsided, he inquired what
Nicholas meant to do; on his informing him, to go straight to London,
he shook his head doubtfully, and inquired if he knew how much the
coaches charged to carry passengers so far.

"No, I do not," said Nicholas; "but it is of no great consequence
to me, for I intend walking."

"Gang awa' to Lunnun afoot!" cried John, in amazement.

"Every step of the way," replied Nicholas. "I should be many
steps further on by this time, and so good bye."

"Nay noo," replied the honest countryman, reining in his impatient
horse, "stan' still, tellee. Hoo much cash hast thee gotten?"

"Not much," said Nicholas, colouring, "but I can make it enough.
Where there's a will there's a way, you know."

John Browdie made no verbal answer to this remark, but putting
his hand in his pocket, pulled out an old purse of soiled leather, and
insisted that Nicholas should borrow from him whatever he required
for his present necessities.

"Dean't be afeard, mun," he said; "tak' eneaf to carry thee whoam.
Thee'lt pay me yan day, a' warrant."

Nicholas could by no means be prevailed upon to borrow more than
a sovereign, with which loan Mr. Browdie, after many entreaties that
he would accept of more (observing, with a touch of Yorkshire caution,
that if he didn't spend it all he could put the surplus by, till he had an
opportunity of remitting it carriage free), was fain to content himself.

"Tak' that bit o' timber to help thee on wi', mun," he added, pressing his stick on Nicholas, and giving his hand another squeeze; "keep
a good hart, and bless thee. Beatten a schoolmeasther! 'Cod its the
best thing a've heerd this twenty year!"

So saying, and indulging, with more delicacy than could have been expected from him, in another series of loud laughs, for the purpose of avoiding the thanks which Nicholas poured forth, John Browdie set spurs to his horse, and went off at a smart canter, looking back from time to time as Nicholas stood gazing after him; and waving his hand cheerily, as if to encourage him on his way. Nicholas watched the horse and rider until they disappeared over the brow of a distant hill, and then set forward on his journey.

He did not travel far that afternoon, for by this time it was nearly dark, and there had been a heavy fall of snow, which not only rendered the way toilsome, but the track uncertain and difficult to find after daylight, save by experienced wayfarers. He lay that night at a cottage, where beds were let at a cheap rate to the more humble class of travellers, and rising betimes next morning, made his way before night to Boroughbridge. Passing through that town in search of some cheap resting-place, he stumbled upon an empty barn within a couple of hundred yards of the road side; in a warm corner of which he stretched his weary limbs, and soon fell asleep.

When he awoke next morning, and tried to recollect his dreams, which had been all connected with his recent sojourn at Dotheboys Hall, he sat up, rubbed his eyes, and stared—not with the most composed countenance possible—at some motionless object which seemed to be stationed within a few yards in front of him.

"Strange!" cried Nicholas; "can this be some lingering creation of the visions that have scarcely left me! It cannot be real—and yet I— I am awake. Smike?"

The form moved, rose, advanced, and dropped upon its knees at his feet. It was Smike indeed.

"Why do you kneel to me?" said Nicholas, hastily raising him.

"To go with you—anywhere—everywhere—to the world's end—to the churchyard grave," replied Smike, clinging to his hand. "Let me, oh do let me. You are my home—my kind friend—take me with you, pray."

"I am a friend who can do little for you," said Nicholas, kindly. "How came you here?"

He had followed him, it seemed; had never lost sight of him all the way; had watched while he slept, and when he halted for refreshment; and had feared to appear before, lest he should be sent back. He had not intended to appear now, but Nicholas had awakened more suddenly than he looked for, and he had no time to conceal himself.

"Poor fellow!" said Nicholas, "your hard fate denies you any friend but one, and he is nearly as poor and helpless as yourself."

"May I—may I go with you?" asked Smike, timidly. "I will be your faithful hard-working servant, I will, indeed. I want no clothes," added the poor creature, drawing his rags together; "these will do very well. I only want to be near you."

"And you shall," cried Nicholas. "And the world shall deal by you as it does by me, till one or both of us shall quit it for a better. Come."

With these words he strapped his burden on his shoulders, and taking his stick in one hand, extended the other to his delighted charge, and so they passed out of the old barn together.

CHAPTER XIV.

HAVING THE MISFORTUNE TO TREAT OF NONE BUT COMMON PEOPLE, IS
NECESSARILY OF A MEAN AND VULGAR CHARACTER.

In that quarter of London in which Golden Square is situated, there
is a by-gone, faded, tumble-down street, with two irregular rows
of tall meagre houses, which seem to have stared each other out of
countenance years ago. The very chimneys appear to have grown
dismal and melancholy, from having had nothing better to look at than
the chimneys over the way. Their tops are battered, and broken,
and blackened with smoke; and here and there some taller stack than
the rest, inclining heavily to one side, and toppling over the roof,
seems to meditate taking revenge for half a century's neglect, by
crushing the inhabitants of the garrets beneath.
  The fowls who peck about the kennels, jerking their bodies hither
and thither with a gait which none but town fowls are ever seen to
adopt, and which any country cock or hen would be puzzled to understand, are perfectly in keeping with the crazy habitations of their
owners. Dingy, ill-plumed, drowsy flutterers, sent, like many of the
neighbouring children, to get a livelihood in the streets, they hop
from stone to stone in forlorn search of some hidden eatable in the mud,
and can scarcely raise a crow among them. The only one with anything approaching to a voice is an aged bantam at the baker's, and
even he is hoarse in consequence of bad living in his last place.
  To judge from the size of the houses, they have been at one time
tenanted by persons of better condition than their present occupants,
but they are now let off by the week in floors or rooms, and every
door has almost as many plates or bell-handles as there are apartments within. The windows are for the same reason sufficiently
diversified in appearance, being ornamented with every variety of
common blind and curtain that can easily be imagined, while every
doorway is blocked up and rendered nearly impassable by a motley
collection of children and porter pots of all sizes, from the baby in
arms and the half-pint pot, to the full-grown girl and half-gallon can.
  In the parlour of one of these houses, which was perhaps a thought
dirtier than any of its neighbours; which exhibited more bell-handles,
children, and porter pots, and caught in all its freshness the first gust
of the thick black smoke that poured forth night and day from a large
brewery hard by, hung a bill announcing that there was yet one room
to let within its walls, although on what story the vacant room could
be—regard being had to the outward tokens of many lodgers which
the whole house front displayed, from the mangle in the kitchen-window to
the flower-pots on the parapet—it would have been beyond the power
of a calculating boy to discover.
  The common stairs of this mansion were bare and carpetless; but a
curious visitor who had to climb his way to the top, might have

observed that there were not wanting indications of the progressive poverty of the inmates, although their rooms were shut. Thus the first-floor lodgers, being flush of furniture, kept an old mahogany table —real mahogany—on the landing-place outside, which was only taken in when occasion required. On the second story the spare furniture dwindled down to a couple of old deal chairs, of which one, belonging to the back room, was shorn of a leg and bottomless. The story above boasted no greater excess than a worm-eaten wash-tub: and the garret landing-place displayed no costlier articles than two crippled pitchers, and some broken blacking-bottles.

It was on this garret landing-place that a hard-featured square-faced man, elderly and shabby, stopped to unlock the door of the front attic, into which, having surmounted the task of turning the rusty key in its still more rusty wards, he walked with the air of its legal owner.

This person wore a wig of short, coarse, red hair, which he took off with his hat, and hung upon a nail. Having adopted in its place a dirty cotton nightcap, and groped about in the dark till he found a remnant of candle, he knocked at the partition which divided the two garrets, and inquired in a loud voice whether Mr. Noggs had got a light.

The sounds that came back were stifled by the lath and plaster, and it seemed moreover as though the speaker had uttered them from the interior of a mug or other drinking vessel; but they were in the voice of Newman, and conveyed a reply in the affirmative.

" A nasty night, Mr. Noggs," said the man in the night-cap, stepping in to light his candle.

" Does it rain?" asked Newman.

" Does it?" replied the other pettishly. " I am wet through."

" It doesn't take much to wet you and me through, Mr. Crowl," said Newman, laying his hand upon the lappel of his threadbare coat.

" Well; and that makes it the more vexatious," observed Mr. Crowl, in the same pettish tone.

Uttering a low querulous growl, the speaker, whose harsh countenance was the very epitome of selfishness raked the scanty fire nearly out of the grate, and, emptying the glass which Noggs had pushed towards him, inquired where he kept his coals.

Newman Noggs pointed to the bottom of a cupboard, and Mr. Crowl, seizing the shovel, threw on half the stock, which Noggs very deliberately took off again without saying a word.

" You have not turned saving at this time of day, I hope?" said Crowl.

Newman pointed to the empty glass, as though it were a sufficient refutation of the charge, and briefly said that he was going down stairs to supper.

" To the Kenwigses?" asked Crowl.

Newman nodded assent.

" Think of that now!" said Crowl. " If I didn't—thinking that you were certain not to go, because you said you wouldn't—tell Kenwigs I couldn't come, and make up my mind to spend the evening with you."

" I was obliged to go," said Newman. " They would have me."

" Well; but what's to become of me?" urged the selfish man, who never thought of anybody else. " It's all your fault. I'll tell you what—I'll sit by your fire till you come back again."

Newman cast a despairing glance at his small store of fuel, but not having the courage to say no, a word which in all his life he never could say at the right time, either to himself or any one else, gave way to the proposed arrangement, and Mr. Crowl immediately went about making himself as comfortable with Newman Noggs's means, as circumstances would admit of his being.

The lodgers to whom Crowl had made allusion under the designation of " the Kenwigses," were the wife and olive branches of one Mr. Kenwigs, a turner in ivory, who was looked upon as a person of some consideration on the premises, inasmuch as he occupied the whole of the first floor, comprising a suite of two rooms. Mrs. Kenwigs, too, was quite a lady in her manners, and of a very genteel family, having an uncle who collected a water-rate; besides which distinction, the two eldest of her little girls went twice a week to a dancing school in the neighbourhood, and had flaxen hair tied with blue ribands hanging in luxuriant pigtails down their backs, and wore little white trousers with frills round the ancles—for all of which reasons and many more, equally valid but too numerous to mention, Mrs. Kenwigs was considered a very desirable person to know, and was the constant theme of all the gossips in the street, and even three or four doors round the corner at both ends.

It was the anniversary of that happy day on which the church of England as by law established, had bestowed Mrs. Kenwigs upon Mr. Kenwigs, and in grateful commemoration of the same, Mrs. Kenwigs had invited a few select friends to cards and supper in the first floor, and put on a new gown to receive them in, which gown, being of a flaming colour and made upon a juvenile principle, was so successful that Mr. Kenwigs said the eight years of matrimony and the five children seemed all a dream, and Mrs. Kenwigs younger and more blooming than the very first Sunday he kept company with her.

Beautiful as Mrs. Kenwigs looked when she was dressed though, and so stately that you would have supposed she had a cook and housemaid at least, and nothing to do but order them about, she had had a world of trouble with the preparations; more indeed than she, being of a delicate and genteel constitution, could have sustained, had not the pride of housewifery upheld her. At last, however, all the things that had to be got together were got together, and all the things that had to be got out of the way were got out of the way, and everything was ready, and the collector himself having promised to come, fortune smiled upon the occasion.

The party was admirably selected. There were first of all Mr. Kenwigs and Mrs. Kenwigs, and four olive Kenwigses who sat up to supper, firstly, because it was but right that they should have a treat on such a day; and secondly, because their going to bed in presence of the company, would have been inconvenient, not to say improper. Then there was the young lady who had made Mrs. Kenwigs's dress, and who—it was the most convenient thing in the world—living in the two-pair back, gave up her bed to the baby, and got a little girl to watch it. Then, to match this young lady, was a young man, who had known Mr. Kenwigs when he was a bachelor, and was much esteemed by the ladies, as bearing the reputation of a rake. To these were added a newly-married couple, who had visited Mr. and Mrs. Kenwigs in their courtship, and a sister of Mrs. Kenwigs's, who was quite a beauty; besides whom, there was another young man supposed to entertain honourable designs upon the lady last mentioned, and Mr. Noggs, who was a genteel person to ask, because he had been a gentleman once. There were also an elderly lady from the back parlour, and one more young lady, who, next to the collector, perhaps was the great lion of the party, being the daughter of a theatrical fireman, who " went on" in the pantomime, and had the greatest turn for the stage that was ever known, being able to sing and recite in a manner that brought the tears into Mrs. Kenwigs's eyes. There was only one drawback upon the pleasure of seeing such friends, and that was, that the lady in the back parlour, who was very fat, and turned of sixty, came in a low book-muslin dress and short kid gloves, which so exasperated Mrs. Kenwigs, that that lady assured her visiter in private, that if it hadn't happened that the supper was cooking at the back-parlour grate at that moment, she certainly would have requested its representative to withdraw.

" My dear," said Mr. Kenwigs, " wouldn't it be better to begin a round game ? "

" Kenwigs, my dear," returned his wife, " I am surprised at you. Would you begin without my uncle ? "

" I forgot the collector," said Kenwigs; " oh no, that would never do."

" He's so particular," said Mrs. Kenwigs, turning to the other married lady, " that if we began without him, I should be out of his will for ever."

" Dear ! " cried the married lady.

" You've no idea what he is," replied Mrs. Kenwigs; " and yet as good a creature as ever breathed."

" The kindest-hearted man that ever was," said Kenwigs.

" It goes to his heart, I believe, to be forced to cut the water off when the people don't pay," observed the bachelor friend, intending a joke.

" George," said Mr. Kenwigs, solemnly, " none of that, if you please."

" It was only my joke," said the friend, abashed.

" George," rejoined Mr. Kenwigs, " a joke is a wery good thing—a wery good thing—but when that joke is made at the expense of Mrs. Kenwigs's feelings, I set my face against it. A man in public life expects to be sneered at—it is the fault of his elewated sitiwation, not of himself. Mrs. Kenwigs's relation is a public man, and that he knows, George, and that he can bear; but putting Mrs. Kenwigs out of the question (if I *could* put Mrs. Kenwigs out of the question on such an occasion as this), I have the honour to be connected with the collector by marriage; and I cannot allow these remarks in my—" Mr. Kenwigs was going to say " house," but he rounded the sentence with " apartments."

At the conclusion of these observations, which drew forth evidences of acute feeling from Mrs. Kenwigs, and had the intended effect of impressing the company with a deep sense of the collector's dignity, a ring was heard at the bell.

" That's him," whispered Mr. Kenwigs, greatly excited. " Morleena, my dear, run down and let your uncle in, and kiss him directly you get the door open. Hem ! Let's be talking."

Adopting Mr. Kenwigs's suggestion, the company spoke very loudly, to look easy and unembarrassed ; and almost as soon as they had begun to do so, a short old gentleman, in drabs and gaiters, with a face that might have been carved out of *lignum vitæ*, for anything that appeared to the contrary, was led playfully in by Miss Morleena Kenwigs, regarding whose uncommon Christian name it may be here remarked that it was invented and composed by Mrs. Kenwigs previous to her first lying-in, for the special distinction of her eldest child, in case it should prove a daughter.

" Oh uncle, I am *so* glad to see you," said Mrs. Kenwigs, kissing the collector affectionately on both cheeks. " So glad."

" Many happy returns of the day, my dear," replied the collector, returning the compliment.

Now this was an interesting thing. Here was a collector of water-rates without his book, without his pen and ink, without his double knock, without his intimidation, kissing—actually kissing—an agreeable female, and leaving taxes, summonses, notices that he had called, or announcements that he would never call again for two quarters' due, wholly out of the question. It was pleasant to see how the company looked on, quite absorbed in the sight, and to behold the nods and winks with which they expressed their gratification at finding so much humanity in a tax-gatherer.

" Where will you sit, uncle ? " said Mrs. Kenwigs, in the full glow of family pride, which the appearance of her distinguished relation occasioned.

" Anywheres, my dear," said the collector, " I am not particular."

Not particular ! What a meek collector. If he had been an author, who knew his place, he couldn't have been more humble.

" Mr. Lillyvick," said Kenwigs, addressing the collector, " some friends here, sir, are very anxious for the honour of—thank you—Mr. and Mrs. Cutler, Mr. Lillyvick."

" Proud to know you, Sir," said Mr. Cutler, " I've heerd of you very often." These were not mere words of ceremony; for Mr. Cutler, having kept house in Mr. Lillyvick's parish, had heard of him very often indeed. His attention in calling had been quite extraordinary.

" George, you know, I think, Mr. Lillyvick," said Kenwigs ; " lady from down stairs—Mr. Lillyvick, Mr. Snewkes—Mr. Lillyvick. Miss Green—Mr. Lillyvick. Mr. Lillyvick. Miss Petowker of the Theatre Royal Drury Lane. Very glad to make two public characters acquainted. Mrs. Kenwigs, my dear, will you sort the counters ?"

Mrs. Kenwigs, with the assistance of Newman Noggs, (who, as he performed sundry little acts of kindness for the children at all times and seasons, was humoured in his request to be taken no notice of, and was merely spoken about in a whisper as the decayed gentleman), did as he was desired, and the greater part of the guests sat down to speculation, while Newman himself, Mrs. Kenwigs, and Miss Petowker of the Theatre Royal Drury Lane, looked after the supper-table.

While the ladies were thus busying themselves, Mr. Lillyvick was intent upon the game in progress, and as all should be fish that comes to a water-collector's net, the dear old gentleman was by no means scrupulous in appropriating to himself the property of his neigh-- bours, which, on the contrary, he abstracted whenever an opportunity presented itself, smiling good-humouredly all the while, and making so many condescending speeches to the owners, that they were delighted with his amiability, and thought in their hearts that he deserved to be Chancellor of the Exchequer at least.

After a great deal of trouble, and the administration of many slaps on the head to the infant Kenwigses, whereof two of the most rebellious were summarily banished, the cloth was laid with great elegance, and a pair of boiled fowls, a large piece of pork, apple-pie, potatoes and greens, were served; at sight of which the worthy Mr. Lillyvick vented a great many witticisms, and plucked up amazingly, to the immense delight and satisfaction of the whole body of admirers.

Very well and very fast the supper went off; no more serious diffi- culties occurring than those which arose from the incessant demand for clean knives and forks, which made poor Mrs. Kenwigs wish more than once that private society adopted the principle of schools, and required that every guest should bring his own knife, fork, and spoon, which doubtless would be a great accommodation in many cases, and to no one more so than to the lady and gentleman of the house, espe- cially if the school principle were carried out to the full extent, and the articles were expected, as a matter of delicacy, not to be taken away again.

Everybody having eaten everything, the table was cleared in a most alarming hurry, and with great noise; and the spirits, whereat the eyes of Newman Noggs glistened, being arranged in order with water both hot and cold, the party composed themselves for conviviality, Mr. Lilly- vick being stationed in a large arm-chair by the fire-side, and the four little Kenwigses disposed on a small form in front of the company with their flaxen tails towards them, and their faces to the fire; an arrange- ment which was no sooner perfected than Mrs. Kenwigs was over- powered by the feelings of a mother, and fell upon the left shoulder of Mr. Kenwigs dissolved in tears.

" They are so beautiful," said Mrs. Kenwigs, sobbing.

" Oh, dear," said all the ladies, " so they are, it's very natural you should feel proud of that ; but don't give way, don't."

" I can—not help it, and it don't signify," sobbed Mrs. Kenwigs ; " oh ! they're too beautiful to live, much too beautiful."

On hearing this alarming presentiment of their being doomed to an early death in the flower of their infancy, all four little girls raised a hideous cry, and, burying their heads in their mother's lap simulta- neously, screamed until the eight flaxen tails vibrated again : Mrs. Kenwigs meanwhile clasping them alternately to her bosom with attitudes expressive of distraction, which Miss Petowker herself might have copied.

At length the anxious mother permitted herself to be soothed into a more tranquil state, and the little Kenwigses being also composed, were distributed among the company, to prevent the possibility of Mrs. Kenwigs being again overcome by the blaze of their combined beauty. Which done, the ladies and gentlemen united in prophesying that they would live for many, many years, and that there was no occasion at all for Mrs. Kenwigs to distress herself : which in good truth there did not appear to be, the loveliness of the children by no means justifying her apprehensions.

"This day eight year," said Mr. Kenwigs, after a pause. "Dear me—ah !"

This reflection was echoed by all present, who said "Ah!" first, and "dear me" afterwards.

"I was younger then," tittered Mrs. Kenwigs.

"No," said the collector.

"Certainly not," added everybody.

"I remember my niece," said Mr. Lillyvick, surveying his audience with a grave air ; "I remember her, on that very afternoon when she first acknowledged to her mother a partiality for Kenwigs. 'Mother,' she says, 'I love him.'"

"'Adore him,' I said, uncle," interposed Mrs. Kenwigs.

"'Love him,' I think, my dear," said the collector, firmly.

"Perhaps you are right, uncle," replied Mrs. Kenwigs, submissively. "I thought it was 'adore.'"

"'Love,' my dear," retorted Mr. Lillyvick. "'Mother, 'she says, 'I love him.' 'What do I hear?' cries her mother; and instantly falls into strong convulsions."

A general exclamation of astonishment burst from the company.

"Into strong convulsions," repeated Mr. Lillyvick, regarding them with a rigid look. "Kenwigs will excuse my saying, in the presence of friends, that there was a very great objection to him, on the ground that he was beneath the family, and would disgrace it. You remember that, Kenwigs?"

"Certainly," replied that gentleman, in no way displeased at the reminiscence, inasmuch as it proved beyond all doubt what a high family Mrs. Kenwigs came of.

"I shared in that feeling," said Mr. Lillyvick : "perhaps it was natural ; perhaps it wasn't."

A gentle murmur seemed to say, that in one of Mr. Lillyvick's station the objection was not only natural, but highly praiseworthy.

"I came round to him in time," said Mr. Lillyvick. "After they were married, and there was no help for it, I was one of the first to say that Kenwigs must be taken notice of. The family *did* take notice of him in consequence, and on my representation ; and I am bound to say—and proud to say—that I have always found him a very honest, well-behaved, upright, respectable sort of man. Kenwigs, shake hands."

"I am proud to do it, Sir," said Mr. Kenwigs.

" So am I, Kenwigs," rejoined Mr. Lillyvick.

" A very happy life I have led with your niece, Sir," said Kenwigs.

" It would have been your own fault if you had not, Sir," remarked Mr. Lillyvick.

" Morleena Kenwigs," cried her mother, at this crisis, much affected, " kiss your dear uncle."

The young lady did as she was requested, and the three other little girls were successively hoisted up to the collector's countenance, and subjected to the same process, which was afterwards repeated by the majority of those present.

" Oh dear, Mrs. Kenwigs," said Miss Petowker, " while Mr. Noggs is making that punch to drink happy returns in, do let Morleena go through that figure dance before Mr. Lillyvick."

" No, no, my dear," replied Mrs. Kenwigs, " it will only worry my uncle."

" It can't worry him, I am sure," said Miss Petowker. " You will be very much pleased, won't you, Sir —

" That I am sure I shall," replied the collector, glancing at the punch mixer.

" Well then, I'll tell you what," said Mrs. Kenwigs, " Morleena shall do the steps, if uncle can persuade Miss Petowker to recite us the Blood-Drinker's Burial afterwards."

There was a great clapping of hands and stamping of feet at this proposition, the subject whereof gently inclined her head several times, in acknowledgment of the reception.

" You know," said Miss Petowker, reproachfully, " that I dislike doing anything professional in private parties."

" Oh, but not here?" said Mrs. Kenwigs. " We are all so very friendly and pleasant, that you might as well be going through it in your own room; besides, the occasion——"

" I can't resist that," interrupted Miss Petowker, " anything in my humble power I shall be delighted to do."

Mrs. Kenwigs and Miss Petowker had arranged a small *programme* of the entertainments between them, of which this was the prescribed order, but they had settled to have a little pressing on both sides, because it looked more natural. The company being all ready, Miss Petowker hummed a tune, and Morleena danced a dance, having previously had the soles of her shoes chalked with as much care as if she were going on the tight-rope. It was a very beautiful figure, comprising a great deal of work for the arms, and was received with unbounded applause.

" If I was blessed with a—a child—" said Miss Petowker, blushing, " of such genius as that, I would have her out at the Opera instantly."

Mrs. Kenwigs sighed and looked at Mr. Kenwigs, who shook his head, and observed that he was doubtful about it.

" Kenwigs is afraid," said Mrs. K.

" What of?" enquired Miss Petowker, " not of her failing?"

" Oh no," replied Mrs. Kenwigs, " but if she grew up what she is now,—only think of the young dukes and marquises."

" Very right," said the collector.

" Still," submitted Miss Petowker, " if she has a proper pride in herself, you know—"

" There's a good deal in that," observed Mrs. Kenwigs, looking at her husband.

" I only know—" faltered Miss Petowker,—" it may be no rule to be sure—but *I* have never found any inconvenience or unpleasantness of that sort."

Mr. Kenwigs, with becoming gallantry, said that settled the question at once, and that he would take the subject into his serious consideration : this being resolved upon, Miss Petowker was entreated to begin the Blood-Drinker's Burial, to which end, that young lady let down her back hair, and taking up her position at the other end of the room, with the bachelor friend posted in a corner, to rush out at the cue " in death expire," and catch her in his arms when she died raving mad, went through the performance with extraordinary spirit, and to the great terror of the little Kenwigses, who were all but frightened into fits.

The ecstacies consequent upon the effort had not yet subsided, and Newman (who had not been thoroughly sober at so late an hour for a long long time,) had not yet been able to put in a word of announcement that the punch was ready, when a hasty knock was heard at the room-door, which elicited a shriek from Mrs. Kenwigs, who immediately divined that the baby had fallen out of bed.

" Who is that ? " demanded Mr. Kenwigs, sharply.

" Don't be alarmed, it's only me," said Crowl, looking in, in his nightcap. " The baby is very comfortable, for I peeped into the room as I came down, and it's fast asleep, and so is the girl ; and I don't think the candle will set fire to the bed-curtain, unless a draught gets into the room—it's Mr. Noggs that's wanted."

" Me ! " cried Newman, much astonished.

" Why it *is* a queer hour, isn't it ? " replied Crowl, who was not best pleased at the prospect of losing his fire ; " and they are queer-looking people, too, all covered with rain and mud. Shall I tell them to go away ? "

" No," said Newman, rising. " People ? How many ? "

" Two," rejoined Crowl.

" Want me ! By name ! " asked Newman.

" By name," replied Crowl. " Mr. Newman Noggs, as pat as need be."

Newman reflected for a few seconds, and then hurried away, muttering that he would be back directly. He was as good as his word ; for in an exceedingly short time he burst into the room, and seizing, without a word of apology or explanation, a lighted candle and tumbler of hot punch from the table, darted away like a madman.

" What the deuce is the matter with him ! " exclaimed Crowl, throwing the door open. " Hark ! Is there any noise above ? "

The guests rose in great confusion, and, looking in each other's faces with much perplexity and some fear, stretched their necks forward, and listened attentively.

GRAVESEND
STAR STEAM PACKETS

LEAVE

LONDON BRIDGE.
MORNING . . **9, 10.**
AFTERNOON . . **1, 4, 6.**

ROYAL TERRACE PIER, GRAVESEND.
MORNING . . **7, 9.**
AFTERNOON . . **3, 6, 7.**

Monday Mornings an Extra Packet at . . **6.**

SUNDAYS.

LONDON BRIDGE.
MORNING . . **8, 9, 10.**
AFTERNOON . . **1.**

FROM GRAVESEND.
MORNING . . **9.**
AFTERNOON . . **5, 6, 7.**

With such Extra Packets as the Public convenience may from time to time require.

At the ROYAL TERRACE PIER, GRAVESEND, to which the Star Packets resort, there is in connection with it a beautiful Shrubbery of several acres, from which Carriages for Rochester, Chatham, Maidstone, &c., start on the arrival of the Packets.

Tickets, available in the Packets of the Star and Diamond Companies to the 1st of November next, to be had at the Star Offices, Gravesend and London Bridge Wharf, and of the Captains on Board the Packets.

ANNUAL TICKETS £6 6 0
SEASON TICKETS, to October 31st, ... 4 4 0
TICKETS for 3 MONTHS (from date) 2 12 6

FARES,—*SALOON, 2s.*——*FORE CABIN, 1s. 6d.*
On SUNDAYS, 2s. each Passenger.

JUNE 13th, 1838.

[Johnston & Barrett, Printers, 13, Mark Lane.

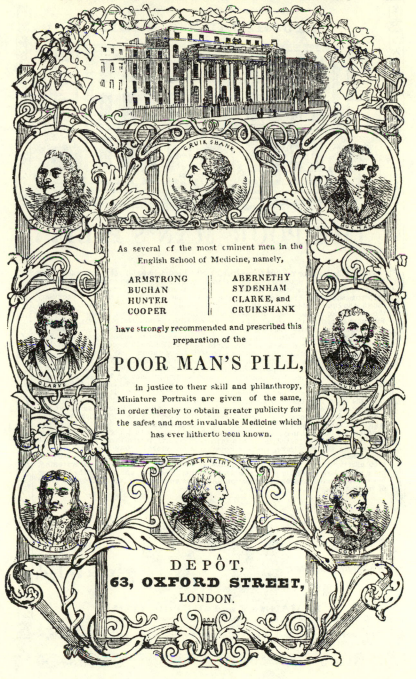

Prepared from Drugs purchased direct from

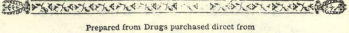

APOTHECARIES' HALL.

THE POOR MAN'S PILL.

THESE Pills, now for the first time offered to the Public, have for years been extensively prescribed in private practice by a physician of great eminence and experience. It were to be regretted, for the benefit of humanity, that a medicine possessing such valuable properties should have remained so long a secret, or could be procured at a pecuniary sacrifice so considerable as to render it available only to the wealthy classes. Through the exercise of extraordinary interest, the original recipe has been procured; and the Pills now advertised are warranted to be prepared with the minutest exactness, according to the directions given. They are not put forth as a universal nostrum, calculated to cure all the diseases incident to humanity, but rather as the means of preventing them; at the same time, in certain chronic disorders, they will be found a remedy of unrivalled efficacy. It may be stated, without the slightest exaggeration, that nine-tenths of the most serious maladies arise from an unhealthy action of the stomach, bowels, or liver, inducing, as a natural consequence, indigestion and its results, such as head-ache, acidity upon the stomach, heartburn, flatulency, nausea, despondency or lowness of spirits, jaundice, and a whole catalogue of other complaints, which may be entirely obviated by conforming to the directions appended to each box of these Pills. It might be inferred from the above title that they are adapted exclusively for one sex; this is not intended: the most delicate female, when an aperient is required, may at all times have recourse to them, and they will act as a preventive against those nervous and hysterical affections which so frequently arise from constipation. The last symptom is almost universally a concomitant of pregnancy, and here they may be taken with the greatest safety and benefit. The most cogent objection to aperients in general, is from their containing some drastic drug, that they leave, after their operation has ceased, a torpidity of the stomach and bowels, producing consequences which their administration was intended to correct; such effects will not ensue after the action of these Pills. To individuals travelling, more particularly seafaring persons, when from change of habit and climate the liver and bowels become inactive, and constipation follows as an invariable result, they will prove of invaluable service.

SOLD

Wholesale and Retail,

IN BOXES AT

$7\frac{1}{2}d.$ & $1s.1\frac{1}{2}d.$

By HANNAY and DIETRICHSEN,

63, Oxford-street, London, by whom the trade are supplied on the usual terms; Johnston, Cornhill; Butler, Cheapside; Barclay, Farringdon-street; Heywood, Manchester; Riches, Norwich; Riches, Lynn; Gardner, Portsea; Watts, Birmingham; Smith, Liverpool; and by most Patent Medicine Venders in every Town in the kingdom.

BRITISH COLLEGE OF HEALTH,
HAMILTON PLACE, NEW ROAD.

ON QUACKERY.—Quackery has been defined as "mean, bad acts in physic—deceit." Let us just ask whether we are to consider the system practised by the majority of the Faculty as answering the definition above quoted. To administer a medicine, of the properties of which they know little, perhaps nothing—to prescribe (although in infinitesimal doses) a poison, by way of experiment, upon a fellow-creature—to extend the sufferings of human nature by what may be termed nostrums or specifics, and thus retard the progress of nature—and for what? Is it the interests of science? is it to "allay the sufferings which man is heir to?" No? is it not, then, for personal aggrandisement? To give restoratives to-day which are nullified and neutralised by the treatment of the morrow—to play with the fears and prejudices of the effeminate and debilitated hypochondriac, calculated to distress and harass their already debilitated frames—to further attenuate by further abstraction of the stream of existence—to reprobate simplicity, and extend the arm of fellowship to the propounders of the most absurd and metaphorical doctrines—may tend, and forcibly tend, to convince the sentient portions of the community in what direction the practice of empiricism and ignorance, divested of every particle of sound medical philosophy, may be found. Alas! sanctioned by a diploma, too frequently obtained without the proper test of the possession of sound medical and scientific knowledge on the part of the individual, thus extending to such individual the power of injuring a credulous and unwary public. Let but men be valued according to the ability and merit evinced; let freedom of action, and, above all, freedom of practice, be generally allowed and divested of prejudice; and the public will at once have a means, and a certain means, of judging whether simplicity of medical practice, or that bordering on necromancy, is to be considered as most acceptable.

Previously to the Christian era, man was as subject to disease as he is at present: had our forefathers recourse to mineral poisons? Most assuredly not. Refer to the sacred volume, and you will find that the age of man was prolonged by means of the simples of the fields. Our forefathers knew not of the poisonous ingredients which are administered in the present day, yet they "slept with their fathers" in the vigour of their strength, and closed lives of aged simplicity with calmness and resignation.

Why, then, let it be asked, should the march of science in modern times exclude simplicity in alleviating the sufferings of that great machine—the human frame—which has known no alteration from man's first creation. Among the various arguments that have been advanced in support of the Hygeian theory of medicine, several have doubted the power of one medicine possessing the attribute of curing all disease. Let them but reflect and consider that there is but one disease—impurity of the blood. Those impurities being deposited in different organs in different individuals, thus apparently creating a multitude of diseases, taking on directly different forms, and affording different symptoms, but one and all still arising from the same source—impurity of what Plato terms "the pabulum, or, food of the flesh." This being allowed (and it is anticipated it cannot be denied or controverted by legitimate argument), where lies the absurdity of concocting a vegetable remedy, efficacious as a depurator of that fluid in a state of disease? and such medicament acting as an aperient, mild or transcendently powerful at will of the practitioner, as symptoms may indicate a necessity of administration, thus rendering the first passages the outlet of impurity existing in the system, and preparing the digestive organs for the elaboration of healthy chyle for further admixture with the blood.

In conclusion, let it be remembered, that such is the practice adopted under the Hygeian theory of medicine, from which practices, be it remembered, thousands have experienced that which ordinary practice failed to afford—the restoration to health after years of suffering.—*British College of Health, New Road, May 24, 1838.*

Another Letter from Lady Sophia Grey, confirmatory of the truth of the Hygeian Practice.
Ashton Hayes, Oct. 30th, 1837.

SIR,—I have received your letter dated the 20th of this month, and can assure you that it will ever give me real pleasure to do anything that may benefit your noble cause. I have not the least objection to your publishing what I said at the end of my letter:—that to your medicines, through the mercy of Heaven, I attribute the wonderful improvement, almost restoration of my health; and that from having taken it for three years in large quantities—even up to 50 pills—It is a convincing proof it is not dangerous, and it never weakens the digestion, but strengthens it; as before I took that medicine I had a very bad digestion, and after taking calomel was weeks before I could take solid meat. I now rarely ever want medicine, and when I do, one pill is sufficient. A gentleman lately come from Paris informs me that you live there, and are greatly patronised. In short, justice seems done you in every country but your own. I remain, Sir, your sincerely obliged,
S. GREY.
To JAMES MORISON, Esq., British College of Health, New Road, near King's Cross.

CAUTION.

Whereas spurious imitations of my Medicines are now in circulation, I, James Morison, the Hygeist, hereby give notice, That I am in nowise connected with the following Medicines purporting to be mine, and sold under the various names of "Dr. Morrison's Pills," "The Hygeian Pills," "The Improved Vegetable Universal Pills," "The Original Morison's Pills, as compounded by the late Mr. Moat," "The Original Hygeian Vegetable Pills," "The Original Morison's Pills," &c. &c.

That my Medicines are prepared only at the British College of Health, Hamilton Place, King's Cross, and sold by the General Agents to the British College of Health and their Sub-Agents, and that no Chemist or Druggist is authorized by me to dispose of the same. None can be genuine without the words "Morison's Universal Medicines" are engraved on the Government Stamp, in white letters upon a red ground.—In witness whereof I have hereunto set my hand,
British College of Health, New Road, April 20, 1838.   JAMES MORISON, the Hygeist.

The following is a List of the principal Depôts where the Medicines may be had in London:—Medical Dissenter Office, 368, Strand; Mr. Field, Bookseller, 65, Quadrant, Regent Street; Mr. Lofts, City Agent, Park Place, Mile End; Mr. Chappell, Bookseller, 19, Cornhill, late of 97, Royal Exchange; Mr. Haslett, 118, Ratcliff Highway; Mrs. Twell, 10, Hand Court, Holborn; Western Branch, 72, Edgeware Road; Messrs. Hannay and Co., Perfumers, 63, Oxford Street, corner of Wells Street; Mr. Cowell, 22, Terrace, Pimlico; British College of Health, Hamilton Place, King's Cross; and of their Sub-Agents.

N.B.—Dr. LYNCH can be consulted at the British College of Health, New Road, from 12 till 2, and at the Medical Dissenter Office, from 3 till 5, daily.

FOREIGN GENERAL AGENTS.—Mr. Anderson, St. John's, New Brunswick; Mr. James Cochrane, Guernsey; Mr. Charles Edwards, Sydney; Mr. V. Formosa, Malta; Mr. Thomas Gardner, Calcutta; Mr. Edwin Linington, Barbadoes; Messrs. John Legge and Co., Quebec; Mr. Lobe, Cuba; Lieut. J. M'Kinnon, Cape Breton, North America, and Newfoundland; Mr. T. H. Roberts, Church-street, Gibraltar; Messrs. Stiffel and Co., Odessa; Dr. Tolihausen, Jassey, Bucharest, Constantinople, and the whole of Turkey; Dr. George Taylor, 6½, Wall-street, New York, general agent for the United States of America; Mr. H. W. Wells, British Guiana, George Town, Demerara.

REFORM YOUR TAILORS' BILLS!

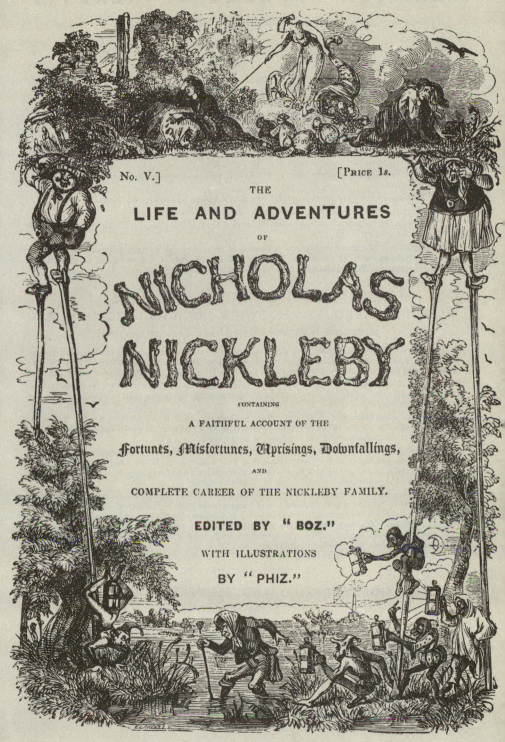

No. V.]   [Price 1s.

THE

LIFE AND ADVENTURES

OF

NICHOLAS NICKLEBY

CONTAINING

A FAITHFUL ACCOUNT OF THE

Fortunes, Misfortunes, Uprisings, Downfallings,

AND

COMPLETE CAREER OF THE NICKLEBY FAMILY.

EDITED BY "BOZ."

WITH ILLUSTRATIONS

BY "PHIZ."

LONDON: CHAPMAN AND HALL, 186, STRAND.

BRITISH COLLEGE OF HEALTH,

HAMILTON PLACE, NEW ROAD

THE PRINCIPLES OF THE HYGEIAN THEORY, AS LAID DOWN BY JAMES MORISON, ARE CONTAINED IN THE FOLLOWING PROPOSITIONS.

I. The vital principle is contained in the blood.

II. Everything in the body is derived from the blood.

III. All constitutions are radically the same.

IV. All diseases arise from impurity of the blood, or, in other words, from acrimonious humours lodged in the body.

V. This *impurity*, which degenerates the blood, has three sources—the *maternine*, the *contagious*, and the *personal*.

VI. Pain and disease have the same origin; and may therefore be considered synonimous terms.

VII. Purgation by vegetables is the only effectual mode of eradicating disease.

VIII. From the intimate connexion subsisting between the mind and body, the health of the one must conduce to the serenity of the other.

In elucidation of the above propositions, the reader is referred to the Lecture delivered by Dr. Lynch at Exeter Hall, published at the Medical Dissenter Office, 368, Strand, and to be had of all regularly appointed Agents and Sub-Agents for the sale of Morison's Pills, price 6*d.*

BLEEDING, MERCURY, ANODYNES, SUCH AS LAUDANUM, &c.,

CONTRASTED WITH THE HYGEIAN TREATMENT OF DISEASE.

These agents of medical practice have proved the cause of more lamentable and fatal consequences to the health and lives of the community, than can possibly be imagined by the public, who have hitherto supposed that medical science was founded on the best basis for alleviating the sufferings of the human race.

Bleeding, though productive of momentary ease, by creating a void in the circulation, is not only an unnatural palliative, but highly injurious to the body, by abstracting that which must be considered the very stream of existence.

Mercury (the next remedy to which the medical profession pin their faith) not only lays the foundation for diseases of a chronic nature, but is creative of disease much worse, much more destructive in its ravages, than any of the maladies for which it is asserted to be a specific.

Anodynes, as Laudanum, &c.—That the whole class of remedies in our pharmacopœias bearing these titles are to be considered as the positive enemies of health and vigour, is but using the mildest phrase. True, they are sedative in their nature, as professed, but they are also frequently so transcendently sedative as to lull the patient into " that sleep which knows no waking."

The Hygeian treatment does not seek to abstract the stream of existence; does not administer remedies so transcendently pernicious as to be productive of diseases worse in their character than those sought to be cured; does not call to its assistance remedies which produce premature disease, and an easy exit from this world's sufferings. On the contrary, it produces depuration of the blood, by administration of vegetable and powerful purgative medicaments, and by deflection of existing impurities of the blood to the first passages, induce a restoration to health and vigour.

THE HOMŒOPATHIC AND MESMERIC, OR ANIMAL MAGNETISM QUACKERY.

Can any argument more strongly prove the miserable and degraded condition at which the art of medicine (because not founded on a certain or proper basis) has arrived in this country, than the fact of medical men of repute lending themselves to the support of the most absurd and metaphorical doctrines that ever disgraced an age of reason? If poor and ignorant persons are to be brought before a Magistrate for obtaining money as fortune-tellers and practising the art of necromancy, where lies the reason that those pursuing a similar, but much worse system, should not be dealt with accordingly? So long, therefore, it now is made apparent, as the medical profession of this or any other country does not properly systematize the art of medicine, and at once adopt one uniform practice; it will always be subject to the quackery, however gross, of this and other nations. In further illustration of the above, reference is made to the *Medical Gazette* of Saturday, June 30, page 587.

THE
NICKLEBY ADVERTISER.

ECARTE.

Neatly bound, with gilt edges, price 2*s.* 6*d.*

A TREATISE ON THE GAME OF ECARTE;

COMPRISING

THE RULES OF THE GAME, AND TABLES SHOWING THE ODDS AT ANY
POINT OF IT.

ALSO,

EXAMPLES OF DIFFICULT HANDS,

WITH DIRECTIONS FOR PLAYING THEM; TO WHICH ARE ADDED, RULES FOR CALCULATING
BETS ON ANY EVENTS.

SEVENTH EDITION.

In one volume, small 8vo, price 3*s.* boards,

SKETCHES OF YOUNG LADIES;

WITH SIX ILLUSTRATIONS BY "PHIZ."

The Busy Young Lady.
The Romantic Young Lady.
The Matter-of-Fact Young Lady.
The Young Lady who Sings.
The Plain Young Lady.
The Evangelical Young Lady.
The Manly Young Lady.
The Literary Young Lady.

The Young Lady who is engaged.
The Petting Young Lady.
The Natural Historian Young Lady.
The Indirect Young Lady.
The Stupid Young Lady.
The Hyperbolical Young Lady.
The Interesting Young Lady.
The Abstemious Young Lady.

The Whimsical Young Lady.
The Sincere Young Lady.
The Affirmative Young Lady.
The Natural Young Lady.
The Clever Young Lady.
The Mysterious Young Lady.
The Lazy Young Lady.
The Young Lady from School.

FOURTH EDITION.

In one volume, small 8vo, price 3*s.* boards,

SKETCHES OF YOUNG GENTLEMEN;

CONTENTS.

Dedication to the Young Ladies.
The Out-and-out Young Gentleman.
The Domestic Young Gentleman.
The Bashful Young Gentleman.
The very Friendly Young Gentleman.

The 'Throwing-off' Young Gentleman
The Poetical Young Gentleman.
The Funny Young Gentleman.
The Theatrical Young Gentleman.

The Military Young Gentleman.
The Political Young Gentleman.
The Censorious Young Gentleman.
The Young Ladies' Young Gentleman.

WITH SIX ILLUSTRATIONS BY "PHIZ."

CHAPMAN AND HALL, 186, STRAND.

GOWLAND'S LOTION.

The constant effects of HEAT and relaxation upon the Texture and Colour of the Skin, visible in DIS-COLOURATIONS or Freckle, are prevented and removed by the use of this elegant preparation, which the experience of nearly a CENTURY recommends as

A PRESERVATIVE OF THE COMPLEXION;

Of uniformly SAFE and Congenial Character, and equally remarkable for its refreshing qualities, whether Tension or Languor affect the elasticity so essential to personal comfort: in Cutaneous affections of the Eruptive kind, all Irritability subsides upon application of the Lotion, and a pure surface and clear tint is re-established, with the pleasing facility which renders it the most acceptable article offered for selection as a permanent appendage of the TOILET.

GOWLAND'S LOTION has the Name and Address of the Proprietor, **ROBERT SHAW, 33, QUEEN STREET, CHEAPSIDE, LONDON,** Engraved on the Government Stamp, by whom only (as Successor to the late Mrs. Vincent) this celebrated article is faithfully prepared from the original MS. Recipe of the late Doctor Gowland. The popular work, "The Theory of Beauty," accompanies each genuine package. Prices 2s. 9d., 5s. 6d., quarts 8s. 6d.; and in Cases, from One to Five Guineas.

SHAW'S MINDORA OIL.

The valuable peculiarities of this Exotic (for general purposes) are, its native purity, fragrance, and entire freedom from CHEMICAL admixture, by which CLEANLINESS and preservation of the true COLOUR of the Hair are decidedly obtained. COMPARISON will satisfactorily prove, that in these requisites Mindora Oil is widely removed from the class of COLOURED Oils and Compounds, while its restorative properties become speedily evident in a renewed and even growth, with the vigour which ensures the disposition to curl, so much desired by both sexes.

Prepared for the Toilet only by the Proprietor, ROBERT SHAW, 33, QUEEN STREET, CHEAPSIDE, LONDON, in Bottles bearing his Signature on the label and wrapper at 3s., 5s. 6d., and in Stoppered Bottles at 10s. 6d. A Practical Treatise on the Hair accompanies each genuine Package. Sold as above, and generally by respectable Perfumers and Medicine Venders.

IMPORTANT TO GENTLEMEN GOING ABROAD.

R. KIPLING,

SHIRT MAKER AND GENERAL OUTFITTER, 7, LEICESTER SQUARE,

Respectfully invites the attention of the Nobility, Gentry, and Public, to his extensive Stock of Ready-made Linen. R. K. rests his claim for patronage upon superior quality and style, at the most moderate prices.

Where despatch is required, Gentlemen can be supplied with Ready-made Linen or India Cloth Shirts, of any size or quality, washed and ready for immediate use, at the following scale of prices :—

India Cloth			£1 16 0 per doz.	Stout Linen			8 6 each.
Do. with Linen Fronts, } Collars, and Wristbands }		3 0 0		Do. Fine Fronts			9 6
				Superfine do.			10 6
Fine do.			3 18 0	Fine do. Finest Fronts, Collars,			
Best do.			4 4 0	and Wrists			12 6
Aquatic do.			2 0 0	Superfine			14 6
Night Shirts			2 2 0	Do. with French Cambric Fronts		16 6	

The above articles made to order on the shortest possible notice.

An extensive assortment of every description of Woollen, Cotton, and Silk Hosiery, and Under-Clothing. Bed and Table Linen, Flannels, Blankets, Calicoes, Linens, &c. &c.

7, LEICESTER SQUARE.—Two Doors East of Miss Linwood's Exhibition.

TRY MECHI's MAGIC STROP

THE MECHIAN DRESSING-CASE,

The most portable ever invented, only six and three quarter inches long, three and a quarter wide, and three-fourths of an inch deep, the size of a pocket-book, contains one pair of Mechi's ivory-handle peculiar steel razors, his magic strop and comb, badger-hair shaving-brush, his patent castellated tooth-brush, and a neat nail-brush; price only 25s. The same with hair-brush and soap dish, 35s. To military men, and as a steam-boat or travelling companion, this invention must prove invaluable, the articles therein being all of the first quality. An immense variety of other Dressing-Cases, for both Gentlemen and Ladies, either in fancy woods or leather, at all prices, from 20s. to 30 guineas. At Mechi's Cutlery and Dressing-Case Manufactory, 4, Leadenhall-street, London, four doors from Cornhill. An extensive stock of Leather Writing Cases, Work Boxes, Bagatelle Tables, Razors, Razor Strops, Sheffield Plated Goods, Tea Trays, Tea Caddies, &c. cheaper than any house in London. Every article warranted, money returned if not approved.

SPLENDID REAL SHEFFIELD PLATE,

BEAUFOY'S
INSTANT CURE FOR THE TOOTH-ACHE.

This article has been extensively and successfully used for some time past in a populous Neighbourhood, and has proved to be an INSTANT CURE in most cases.

The Selling Price to the Public has been fixed purposely so low as
to render the

" INSTANT CURE FOR THE TOOTH-ACHE '

accessible to all Classes.

MADE BY BEAUFOY & CO. SOUTH LAMBETH, LONDON

And Sold by most Respectable Druggists and Patent Medicine Vendors
in Town and Country.

The Bottles, with ample Directions for Use, Price 1s. 1½d. each, Stamp included.

LONDON: BRADBURY AND EVANS, PRINTERS, WHITEFRIARS.

CHAPTER XV.

NEWMAN NOGGS scrambled in violent haste up stairs with the steaming beverage, which he had so unceremoniously snatched from the table
of Mr. Kenwigs, and indeed from the very grasp of the water-rate
collector, who was eyeing the contents of the tumbler at the moment of
its unexpected abstraction, with lively marks of pleasure visible in his
countenance, and bore his prize straight to his own back garret, where,
footsore and nearly shoeless, wet, dirty, jaded, and disfigured with every
mark of fatiguing travel, sat Nicholas, and Smike, at once the cause and
partner of his toil: both perfectly worn out by their unwonted and
protracted exertion.

Newman's first act was to compel Nicholas, with gentle force, to
swallow half of the punch at a breath, nearly boiling as it was, and his
next to pour the remainder down the throat of Smike, who, never
having tasted anything stronger than aperient medicine in his whole
life, exhibited various odd manifestations of surprise and delight, during
the passage of the liquor down his throat, and turned up his eyes most
emphatically when it was all gone.

" You are wet through," said Newman, passing his hand hastily
over the coat which Nicholas had thrown off; " and I—I—haven't
even a change," he added, with a wistful glance at the shabby clothes
he wore himself.

" I have dry clothes, or at least such as will serve my turn well, in
my bundle," replied Nicholas. " If you look so distressed to see me,
you will add to the pain I feel already, at being compelled for one night
to cast myself upon your slender means for aid and shelter."

Newman did not look the less distressed to hear Nicholas talking in
this strain; but upon his young friend grasping him heartily by
the hand, and assuring him that nothing but implicit confidence in the
sincerity of his professions, and kindness of feeling towards himself,
would have induced him, on any consideration, even to have made him
acquainted with his arrival in London, Mr. Noggs brightened up again,
and went about making such arrangements as were in his power for
the comfort of his visitors, with extreme alacrity.

These were simple enough, poor Newman's means halting at a very
considerable distance short of his inclinations; but, slight as they were,
they were not made without much bustling and running about. As
Nicholas had husbanded his scanty stock of money so well that it was
not yet quite expended, a supper of bread and cheese, with some
cold beef from the cook's shop, was soon placed upon the table; and
these viands being flanked by a bottle of spirits and a pot of porter,

K

there was no ground for apprehension on the score of hunger and thirst, at all events. Such preparations as Newman had it in his power to make, for the accommodation of his guests during the night, occupied no very great time in completing; and as he had insisted, as an express preliminary, that Nicholas should change his clothes, and that Smike should invest himself in his solitary coat (which no entreaties would dissuade him from stripping off for the purpose), the travellers partook of their frugal fare, with more satisfaction than one of them at least had derived from many a better meal.

They then drew near the fire, which Newman Noggs had made up as well as he could, after the inroads of Crowl upon the fuel; and Nicholas, who had hitherto been restrained by the extreme anxiety of his friend that he should refresh himself after his journey, now pressed him with earnest questions concerning his mother and sister.

" Well;" replied Newman, with his accustomed taciturnity; " both well."

" They are living in the city still ?" inquired Nicholas.

" They are," said Newman.

" And my sister"—added Nicholas. " Is she still engaged in the business which she wrote to tell me she thought she should like so much ? "

Newman opened his eyes rather wider than usual, but merely replied by a gasp, which, according to the action of the head that accompanied it, was interpreted by his friends as meaning yes or no. In the present instance, the pantomime consisted of a nod, and not a shake, so Nicholas took the answer as a favourable one.

" Now listen to me," said Nicholas, laying his hand on Newman's shoulder. " Before I would make an effort to see them, I deemed it expedient to come to you, lest, by gratifying my own selfish desire, I should inflict an injury upon them which I can never repair. What has my uncle heard from Yorkshire ? "

Newman opened and shut his mouth several times, as though he were trying his utmost to speak, but could make nothing of it, and finally fixed his eyes on Nicholas with a grim and ghastly stare.

" What has he heard?" urged Nicholas, colouring. " You see that I am prepared to hear the very worst that malice can have suggested. Why should you conceal it from me ? I must know it sooner or later; and what purpose can be gained by trifling with the matter for a few minutes, when half the time would put me in possession of all that has occurred ? Tell me at once, pray."

" To-morrow morning," said Newman; " hear it to-morrow."

" What purpose would that answer ? " urged Nicholas.

" You would sleep the better," replied Newman.

" I should sleep the worse," answered Nicholas, impatiently. "Sleep! Exhausted as I am, and standing in no common need of rest, I cannot hope to close my eyes all night, unless you tell me everything."

" And if I should tell you everything," said Newman, hesitating.

" Why, then you may rouse my indignation or wound my pride," rejoined Nicholas; " but you will not break my rest; for if the scene were acted over again, I could take no other part than I have taken;

and whatever consequences may accrue to myself from it, I shall never regret doing as I have—never, if I starve or beg in consequence. What is a little poverty or suffering, to the disgrace of the basest and most inhuman cowardice! I tell you, if I had stood by, tamely and passively, I should have hated myself, and merited the contempt of every man in existence. The black-hearted scoundrel!"

With this gentle allusion to the absent Mr. Squeers, Nicholas repressed his rising wrath, and relating to Newman exactly what had passed at Dotheboys Hall, entreated him to speak out without further pressing. Thus adjured, Mr. Noggs took from an old trunk a sheet of paper, which appeared to have been scrawled over in great haste; and after sundry extraordinary demonstrations of reluctance, delivered himself in the following terms.

"My dear young man, you mustn't give way to—this sort of thing will never do, you know—as to getting on in the world, if you take everybody's part that 's ill-treated—Damn it, I am proud to hear of it; and would have done it myself!"

Newman accompanied this very unusual outbreak with a violent blow upon the table, as if, in the heat of the moment, he had mistaken it for the chest or ribs of Mr. Wackford Squeers; and having, by this open declaration of his feelings, quite precluded himself from offering Nicholas any cautious worldly advice (which had been his first intention), Mr. Noggs went straight to the point.

"The day before yesterday," said Newman, "your uncle received this letter. I took a hasty copy of it while he was out. Shall I read it?"

"If you please," replied Nicholas. Newman Noggs accordingly read as follows:—

> "Dotheboys Hall,
> "Thursday Morning.

"SIR,

"My pa requests me to write to you. The doctors considering it doubtful whether he will ever recuvver the use of his legs which prevents his holding a pen.

"We are in a state of mind beyond everything, and my pa is one mask of brooses both blue and green likewise two forms are steepled in his Goar. We were kimpelled to have him carried down into the kitchen where he now lays. You will judge from this that he has been brought very low.

"When your nevew that you recommended for a teacher had done this to my pa and jumped upon his body with his feet and also langwedge which I will not pollewt my pen with describing, he assaulted my ma with dreadful violence, dashed her to the earth, and drove her back comb several inches into her head. A very little more and it must have entered her skull. We have a medical certifiket that if it had, the tortershell would have affected the brain.

"Me and my brother were then the victims of his feury since which we have suffered very much which leads us to the arrowing belief that we have received some injury in our insides, especially as no marks of violence are visible externally. I am screaming out loud all

K 2

the time I write and so is my brother which takes off my attention
rather, and I hope will excuse mistakes.

" The monster having satiated his thirst for blood ran away, taking
with him a boy of desperate caracter that he had excited to rebellyon,
and a garnet ring belonging to my ma, and not having been apprehended
by the constables is supposed to have been took up by some stage-
coach.   My pa begs that if he comes to you the ring may be returned,
and that you will let the thief and assassin go, as if we prosecuted him
he would only be transported, and if he is let go he is sure to be hung
before long, which will save us trouble, and be much more satisfactory.
Hoping to hear from you when convenient

" I remain
" Yours and cetrer
" FANNY SQUEERS.

" P.S. I pity his ignorance and despise him."

A profound silence succeeded to the reading of this choice epistle,
during which Newman Noggs, as he folded it up, gazed with a kind of
grotesque pity at the boy of desperate character therein referred to ;
who, having no more dist'nct perception of the matter in hand, than
that he had been the unfortunate cause of heaping trouble and falsehood
upon Nicholas, sat mute and dispirited, with a most woe-begone and
heart-stricken look.

" Mr. Noggs," said Nicholas, after a few moments' reflection, " I must
go out at once."

" Go out !" cried Newman.

" Yes," said Nicholas, " to Golden Square. Nobody who knows
me would believe this story of the ring ; but it may suit the purpose, or
gratify the hatred, of Mr. Ralph Nickleby to feign to attach credence
to it. It is due—not to him, but to myself—that I should state the
truth ; and moreover, I have a word or two to exchange with him,
which will not keep cool."

" They must," said Newman.

" They must not, indeed," rejoined Nicholas firmly, as he prepared
to leave the house.

" Hear me speak," said Newman, planting himself before his impetuous young friend.   " He is not there.   He is away from town.   He
will not be back for three days ; and I know that letter will not be
answered before he returns."

" Are you sure of this ?" asked Nicholas, chafing violently, and pacing
the narrow room with rapid strides.

" Quite," rejoined Newman.   " He had hardly read it when he was
called away. Its contents are known to nobody but himself and us."

" Are you certain ?" demanded Nicholas, precipitately ; " not even
to my mother or sister ?   If I thought that they—I will go there—I
must see them.   Which is the way ?   Where is it ?"

" Now be advised by me," said Newman, speaking for the moment,
in his earnestness, like any other man—" make no effort to see even
them, till he comes home. I know the man. Do not seem to have
been tampering with anybody.   When he returns, go straight to him,

and speak as boldly as you like. Guessing at the real truth, he knows it as well as you or I. Trust him for that."

" You mean well to me, and should know him better than I can," replied Nicholas, after some further thought. " Well; let it be so."

Newman, who had stood during the foregoing conversation with his back planted against the door ready to oppose any egress from the apartment by force, if necessary, resumed his seat with much satisfaction ; and as the water in the kettle was by this time boiling, made a glass-full of spirits and water for Nicholas, and a cracked mug-full for the joint accommodation of himself and Smike, of which the two partook in great harmony, while Nicholas, leaning his head upon his hand, remained buried in melancholy meditation.

Meanwhile the company below stairs, after listening attentively and not hearing any noise which would justify them in interfering for the gratification of their curiosity, returned to the chamber of the Kenwigses, and employed themselves in hazarding a great variety of conjectures relative to the cause of Mr. Noggs's sudden disappearance and detention.

" Lor, I'll tell you what ;" said Mrs. Kenwigs. " Suppose it should be an express sent up to say that his property has all come back again !"

" Dear me," said Mr. Kenwigs ; " it's not impossible. Perhaps, in that case, we'd better send up and ask if 'e won't take a little more punch."

" Kenwigs," said Mr. Lillyvick, in a loud voice, " I'm surprised at you."

" What's the matter, Sir ?" asked Mr. Kenwigs, with becoming submission to the collector of water rates.

" Making such a remark as that, Sir," replied Mr. Lillyvick, angrily. " He has had punch already, has he not, Sir ? I consider the way in which that punch was cut off, if I may use the expression, highly disrespectful to this company ; scandalous, perfectly scandalous. It may be the custom to allow such things in this house, but it's not the kind of behaviour that I've been used to see displayed, and so I don't mind telling you, Kenwigs. A gentleman has a glass of punch before him to which he is just about to set his lips, when another gentleman comes and collars that glass of punch, without a ' with your leave,' or ' by your leave,' and carries that glass of punch away. This may be good manners—I dare say it is—but I don't understand it, that's all ; and what's more, I don't care if I never do. It's my way to speak my mind, Kenwigs, and that is my mind ; and if you don't like it, it's past my regular time for going to bed, and I can find my way home without making it later."

Here was an untoward event. The collector had sat swelling and fuming in offended dignity for some minutes, and had now fairly burst out. The great man—the rich relation—the unmarried uncle—who had it in his power to make Morleena an heiress, and the very baby a legatee—was offended. Gracious Powers, where was this to end !

" I am very sorry, Sir," said Mr. Kenwigs, humbly.

" Don't tell me you're sorry," retorted Mr. Lillyvick, with much sharpness. " You should have prevented it, then."

The company were quite paralysed by this domestic crash. The back parlour sat with her mouth wide open, staring vacantly at the collector in a stupor of dismay, and the other guests were scarcely less overpowered by the great man's irritation. Mr. Kenwigs not being skilful in such matters, only fanned the flame in attempting to extinguish it.

" I didn't think of it, I am sure, Sir," said that gentleman. " I didn't suppose that such a little thing as a glass of punch would have put you out of temper."

" Out of temper ! What the devil do you mean by that piece of impertinence, Mr. Kenwigs ?" said the collector. " Morleena, child— give me my hat."

" Oh, you're not going, Mr. Lillyvick, Sir," interposed Miss Petowker, with her most bewitching smile.

But still Mr. Lillyvick, regardless of the siren, cried obdurately, " Morleena, my hat !" upon the fourth repetition of which demand Mrs. Kenwigs sunk back in her chair, with a cry that might have softened a water-butt, not to say a water collector ; while the four little girls (privately instructed to that effect) clasped their uncle's corduroy shorts in their arms, and prayed him in imperfect English to remain.

" Why should I stop here, my dears ?" said Mr. Lillyvick ; " I'm not wanted here."

" Oh, do not speak so cruelly, uncle," sobbed Mrs. Kenwigs, " unless you wish to kill me."

" I shouldn't wonder if some people were to say I did," replied Mr. Lillyvick, glancing angrily at Kenwigs. " Out of temper !"

" Oh ! I cannot bear to see him look so at my husband," cried Mrs. Kenwigs. " It's so dreadful in families. Oh !"

" Mr. Lillyvick," said Kenwigs, " I hope, for the sake of your niece, that you won't object to be reconciled."

The collector's features relaxed, as the company added their entreaties to those of his nephew-in-law. He gave up his hat and held out his hand.

" There, Kenwigs," said Mr. Lillyvick ; " and let me tell you at the same time, to show you how much out of temper I was, that if I had gone away without another word, it would have made no difference respecting that pound or two which I shall leave among your children when I die."

" Morleena Kenwigs," cried her mother, in a torrent of affection. " Go down upon your knees to your dear uncle, and beg him to love you all his life through, for he's more a angel than a man, and I've always said so."

Miss Morleena approaching to do homage in compliance with this injunction, was summarily caught up and kissed by Mr. Lillyvick, and thereupon Mrs. Kenwigs darted forward and kissed the collector, and an irrepressible murmur of applause broke from the company who had witnessed his magnanimity.

The worthy gentleman then became once more the life and soul of the society, being again reinstated in his old post of lion, from which high station the temporary distraction of their thoughts had for a moment dispossessed him. Quadruped lions are said to be savage only when they are hungry; biped lions are rarely sulky longer than when their appetite for distinction remains unappeased. Mr. Lillyvick stood higher than ever, for he had shown his power, hinted at his property and testamentary intentions; gained great credit for disinterestedness and virtue; and in addition to all, he was finally accommodated with a much larger tumbler of punch than that which Newman Noggs had so feloniously made off with.

" I say, I beg everybody's pardon for intruding again," said Crowl, looking in at this happy juncture ; " but what a queer business this is, isn't it ? Noggs has lived in this house now going on for five years, and nobody has ever been to see him before within the memory of the oldest inhabitant."

" It's a strange time of night to be called away, Sir, certainly," said the collector ; " and the behaviour of Mr. Noggs himself is, to say the least of it, mysterious."

" Well, so it is," rejoined Crowl; " and I'll tell you what's more— I think these two geniuses, whoever they are, have run away from somewhere."

" What makes you think that, Sir ?" demanded the collector, who seemed by a tacit understanding to have been chosen and elected mouthpiece to the company. " You have no reason to suppose that they have run away from anywhere without paying the rates and taxes due, I hope ?"

Mr. Crowl, with a look of some contempt, was about to enter a general protest against the payment of rates or taxes, under any circumstances, when he was checked by a timely whisper from Kenwigs, and several frowns and winks from Mrs. K., which providentially stopped him.

" Why the fact is," said Crowl, who had been listening at Newman's door, with all his might and main ; " the fact is, that they have been talking so loud, that they quite disturbed me in my room, and so I couldn't help catching a word here, and a word there ; and all I heard certainly seemed to refer to their having bolted from some place or other. I don't wish to alarm Mrs. Kenwigs ; but I hope they haven't come from any jail or hospital, and brought away a fever or some unpleasantness of that sort, which might be catching for the children."

Mrs. Kenwigs was so overpowered by this supposition, that it needed all the tender attentions of Miss Petowker, of the Theatre Royal, Drury Lane, to restore her to anything like a state of calmness; not to mention the assiduity of Mr. Kenwigs, who held a fat smelling-bottle to his lady's nose, until it became matter of some doubt whether the tears which coursed down her face, were the result of feelings or *sal volatile*.

The ladies, having expressed their sympathy, singly and separately, fell, according to custom, into a little chorus of soothing expressions, among which, such condolences as " Poor dear !"—" I should feel just the same, if I was her"—" To be sure, it's a very trying thing"— and " Nobody but a mother knows what a mother's feelings is," were among the most prominent and most frequently repeated. In short, the opinion of the company was so clearly manifested, that Mr. Kenwigs was on the point of repairing to Mr. Noggs's room, to demand an explanation; and had indeed swallowed a preparatory glass of punch, with great inflexibility and steadiness of purpose, when the attention of all present was diverted by a new and terrible surprise.

This was nothing less than the sudden pouring forth of a rapid succession of the shrillest and most piercing screams, from an upper story; and to all appearance from the very two-pair back in which the infant Kenwigs was at that moment enshrined. They were no sooner audible, than Mrs. Kenwigs, opining that a strange cat had come in, and sucked the baby's breath while the girl was asleep, made for the door, wringing her hands, and shrieking dismally; to the great consternation and confusion of the company.

"Mr. Kenwigs, see what it is; make haste!" cried the sister, laying violent hands upon Mrs. Kenwigs, and holding her back by force. "Oh don't twist about so, dear, or I can never hold you."

"My baby, my blessed, blessed, blessed, blessed baby," screamed Mrs. Kenwigs, making every blessed louder than the last. "My own darling, sweet, innocent Lillyvick—Oh let me go to him. Let me go-o-o-o."

Pending the utterance of these frantic cries, and the wails and lamentations of the four little girls, Mr. Kenwigs rushed up stairs to the room whence the sounds proceeded, at the door of which he encountered Nicholas, with the child in his arms, who darted out with such violence, that the anxious father was thrown down six stairs, and alighted on the nearest landing-place, before he had found time to open his mouth to ask what was the matter.

"Don't be alarmed," cried Nicholas, running down; "here it is; it's all out, it's all over; pray compose yourselves; there's no harm done;" and with these, and a thousand other assurances, he delivered the baby (whom, in his hurry, he had carried upside down), to Mrs. Kenwigs, and ran back to assist Mr. Kenwigs, who was rubbing his head very hard, and looking much bewildered by his tumble.

Reassured by this cheering intelligence, the company in some degree recovered from their fears, which had been productive of some most singular instances of a total want of presence of mind; thus the bachelor friend had for a long time supported in his arms Mrs. Kenwigs's sister, instead of Mrs. Kenwigs; and the worthy Mr. Lillyvick had been actually seen, in the perturbation of his spirits, to kiss Miss Petowker several times, behind the room door, as calmly as if nothing distressing were going forward.

"It is a mere nothing," said Nicholas, returning to Mrs. Kenwigs; "the little girl, who was watching the child, being tired I suppose, fell asleep, and set her hair on fire."

"Oh you malicious little wretch!" cried Mrs. Kenwigs, impressively shaking her fore-finger at the small unfortunate, who might be thirteen years old, and was looking on with a singed head and a frightened face.

"I heard her cries," continued Nicholas, "and ran down in time to prevent her setting fire to any thing else. You may depend upon it that the child is not hurt; for I took it off the bed myself, and brought it here to convince you."

This brief explanation over, the infant, who, as he was christened after the collector, rejoiced in the names of Lillyvick Kenwigs, was partially suffocated under the caresses of the audience, and squeezed to his mother's bosom, until he roared again. The attention of the company was then directed, by a natural transition, to the little girl who had had the audacity to burn her hair off, and who, after receiving sundry small slaps and pushes from the more energetic of the ladies, was mercifully sent home ; the ninepence, with which she was to have been rewarded, being escheated to the Kenwigs family.

" And whatever we are to say to you, Sir," exclaimed Mrs. Kenwigs, addressing young Lillyvick's deliverer, " I am sure I don't know."

" You need say nothing at all," replied Nicholas. " I have done nothing to found any very strong claim upon your eloquence, I am sure."

" He might have been burnt to death, if it hadn't been for you, Sir," simpered Miss Petowker.

" Not very likely, I think," replied Nicholas ; " for there was abundance of assistance here, which must have reached him before he had been in any danger."

" You will let us drink your health, anyvays, Sir ? " said Mr. Kenwigs, motioning towards the table.

" — In my absence, by all means," rejoined Nicholas, with a smile. " I have had a very fatiguing journey, and should be most indifferent company—a far greater check upon your merriment, than a promoter of it, even if I kept awake, which I think very doubtful. If you will allow me, I'll return to my friend, Mr. Noggs, who went up stairs again, when he found nothing serious had occurred. Good night."

Excusing himself in these terms from joining in the festivities, Nicholas took a most winning farewell of Mrs. Kenwigs and the other ladies, and retired, after making a very extraordinary impression upon the company.

" What a delightful young man ! " cried Mrs. Kenwigs.

" Uncommon gentlemanly, really," said Mr. Kenwigs. " Don't you think so, Mr. Lillyvick ? "

" Yes," said the collector, with a dubious shrug of his shoulders. " He *is* gentlemanly, very gentlemanly—in appearance."

" I hope you don't see anything against him, uncle ? " inquired Mrs. Kenwigs.

" No, my dear," replied the collector, " no. I trust he may not turn out—well—no matter—my love to you, my dear, and long life to the baby."

" Your namesake," said Mrs. Kenwigs, with a sweet smile.

" And I hope a worthy namesake," observed Mr. Kenwigs, willing to propitiate the collector. " I hope a baby as will never disgrace his godfather, and as may be considered in arter years of a piece with the Lillyvicks whose name he bears. I do say—and Mrs. Kenwigs is of the same sentiment, and feels it as strong as I do—that I consider his being called Lillyvick one of the greatest blessings and *h*onours of my existence."

" *The* greatest blessing, Kenwigs," murmured his lady.

"*The* greatest blessing," said Mr. Kenwigs, correcting himself. "A blessing that I hope one of these days I may be able to deserve."

This was a politic stroke of the Kenwigses, because it made Mr. Lillyvick the great head and fountain of the baby's importance. The good gentleman felt the delicacy and dexterity of the touch, and at once proposed the health of the gentleman, name unknown, who had signalised himself that night by his coolness and alacrity.

"Who, I don't mind saying," observed Mr. Lillyvick, as a great concession, "is a good-looking young man enough, with manners that I hope his character may be equal to."

"He has a very nice face and style, really," said Mrs. Kenwigs.

"He certainly has," added Miss Petowker. "There's something in his appearance quite—dear, dear, what's that word again?"

"What word?" inquired Mr. Lillyvick.

"Why—dear me, how stupid I am," replied Miss Petowker, hesitating. "What do you call it when Lords break off door-knockers and beat policemen, and play at coaches with other people's money, and all that sort of thing?"

"Aristocratic?" suggested the collector.

"Ah! aristocratic," replied Miss Petowker; "something very aristocratic about him, isn't there?"

The gentlemen held their peace and smiled at each other, as who should say, "Well! there's no accounting for tastes;" but the ladies resolved unanimously that Nicholas had an aristocratic air, and nobody caring to dispute the position, it was established triumphantly.

The punch being by this time drunk out and the little Kenwigses (who had for some time previously held their little eyes open with their little fore-fingers) becoming fractious, and requesting rather urgently to be put to bed, the collector made a move by pulling out his watch, and acquainting the company that it was nigh two o'clock; whereat some of the guests were surprised and others shocked, and hats and bonnets being groped for under the tables, and in course of time found, their owners went away, after a vast deal of shaking of hands, and many remarks how they had never spent such a delightful evening, and how they marvelled to find it so late, expecting to have heard that it was half-past ten at the very latest, and how they wished that Mr. and Mrs. Kenwigs had a wedding-day once a week, and how they wondered by what hidden agency Mrs. Kenwigs could possibly have managed so well; and a great deal more of the same kind. To all of which flattering expressions Mr. and Mrs. Kenwigs replied, by thanking every lady and gentleman, *seriatim*, for the favour of their company, and hoping they might have enjoyed themselves only half as well as they said they had.

As to Nicholas, quite unconscious of the impression he had produced, he had long since fallen asleep, leaving Mr. Newman Noggs and Smike to empty the spirit bottle between them; and this office they performed with such extreme good will, that Newman was equally at a loss to determine whether he himself was quite sober, and whether he had ever seen any gentleman so heavily, drowsily, and completely intoxicated as his new acquaintance.

CHAPTER XVI.

NICHOLAS SEEKS TO EMPLOY HIMSELF IN A NEW CAPACITY, AND
BEING UNSUCCESSFUL, ACCEPTS AN ENGAGEMENT AS TUTOR IN A
PRIVATE FAMILY.

THE first care of Nicholas next morning was, to look after some room
in which, until better times dawned upon him, he could contrive to
exist, without trenching upon the hospitality of Newman Noggs, who
would have slept upon the stairs with pleasure, so that his young friend
was accommodated.

The vacant apartment to which the bill in the parlour window bore
reference, appeared on inquiry to be a small back room on the second
floor, reclaimed from the leads, and overlooking a soot-bespeckled
prospect of tiles and chimney-pots. For the letting of this portion of
the house from week to week, on reasonable terms, the parlour lodger
was empowered to treat, he being deputed by the landlord to dispose of
the rooms as they became vacant, and to keep a sharp look-out that the
lodgers didn't run away. As a means of securing the punctual discharge
of which last service he was permitted to live rent-free, lest he should
at any time be tempted to run away himself.

Of this chamber Nicholas became the tenant; and having hired a few
common articles of furniture from a neighbouring broker, and paid the
first week's hire in advance, out of a small fund raised by the conversion
of some spare clothes into ready money, he sat himself down to ruminate
upon his prospects, which, like that outside his window, were sufficiently
confined and dingy. As they by no means improved on better acquaintance, and as familiarity breeds contempt, he resolved to banish them
from his thoughts by dint of hard walking. So, taking up his hat, and
leaving poor Smike to arrange and re-arrange the room with as much
delight as if it had been the costliest palace, he betook himself to the
streets, and mingled with the crowd which thronged them.

Although a man may lose a sense of his own importance when he is
a mere unit among a busy throng, all utterly regardless of him, it by no
means follows that he can dispossess himself, with equal facility, of a
very strong sense of the importance and magnitude of his cares. The
unhappy state of his own affairs was the one idea which occupied the
brain of Nicholas, walk as fast as he would; and when he tried to dis-
lodge it by speculating on the situation and prospects of the people who
surrounded him, he caught himself in a few seconds contrasting their
condition with his own, and gliding almost imperceptibly back into his
old train of thought again.

Occupied in these reflections, as he was making his way along one of
the great public thoroughfares of London, he chanced to raise his eyes
to a blue board, whereon was inscribed in characters of gold, " General
Agency Office; for places and situations of all kinds inquire within."
It was a shop-front, fitted up with a gauze blind and an inner door; and

in the window hung a long and tempting array of written placards, announcing vacant places of every grade, from a secretary's to a footboy's.

Nicholas halted instinctively before this temple of promise, and ran his eye over the capital-text openings in life which were so profusely displayed. When he had completed his survey he walked on a little way, and then back, and then on again; at length, after pausing irresolutely several times before the door of the General Agency Office, he made up his mind and stepped in.

He found himself in a little floor-clothed room, with a high desk railed off in one corner, behind which sat a lean youth with cunning eyes and a protruding chin, whose performances in capital-text darkened the window. He had a thick ledger lying open before him, and with the fingers of his right hand inserted between the leaves, and his eyes fixed on a very fat old lady in a mob-cap—evidently the proprietress of the establishment—who was airing herself at the fire, seemed to be only waiting her directions to refer to some entries contained within its rusty clasps.

As there was a board outside, which acquainted the public that servants-of-all-work were perpetually in waiting to be hired from ten till four, Nicholas knew at once that some half-dozen strong young women, each with pattens and an umbrella, who were sitting upon a form in one corner, were in attendance for that purpose, especially as the poor things looked anxious and weary. He was not quite so certain of the callings and stations of two smart young ladies who were in conversation with the fat lady before the fire, until—having sat himself down in a corner, and remarked that he would wait until the other customers had been served—the fat lady resumed the dialogue which his entrance had interrupted.

" Cook, Tom," said the fat lady, still airing herself as aforesaid.

" Cook," said Tom, turning over some leaves of the ledger. " Well."

" Read out an easy place or two," said the fat lady.

" Pick out very light ones, if you please, young man," interposed a genteel female in shepherd's-plaid boots, who appeared to be the client.

" ' Mrs. Marker,' " said Tom, reading, " ' Russell Place, Russell Square; offers eighteen guineas, tea and sugar found. Two in family, and see very little company. Five servants kept. No man. No followers.' "

" Oh Lor!" tittered the client. " *That* won't do. Read another, young man, will you?"

" ' Mrs. Wrymug,' " said Tom. " ' Pleasant Place, Finsbury. Wages, twelve guineas. No tea, no sugar. Serious family—' "

" Ah! you needn't mind reading that," interrupted the client.

" ' Three serious footmen,' " said Tom, impressively.

" Three, did you say?" asked the client, in an altered tone.

" Three serious footmen," replied Tom. " ' Cook, housemaid, and nursemaid; each female servant required to join the Little Bethel Congregation three times every Sunday—with a serious footman. If the cook is more serious than the footman, she will be expected to improve the footman; if the footman is more serious than the cook, he will be expected to improve the cook.' "

"I'll take the address of that place," said the client; "I don't know but what it mightn't suit me pretty well."

"Here's another," remarked Tom, turning over the leaves; "'Family of Mr. Gallanbile, M.P. Fifteen guineas, tea and sugar, and servants allowed to see male cousins, if godly. Note. Cold dinner in the kitchen on the Sabbath, Mr. Gallanbile being devoted to the Observance question. No victuals whatever cooked on the Lord's Day, with the exception of dinner for Mr. and Mrs. Gallanbile, which, being a work of piety and necessity, is exempted. Mr. Gallanbile dines late on the day of rest, in order to prevent the sinfulness of the cook's dressing herself.'"

"I don't think that'll answer as well as the other," said the client, after a little whispering with her friend. "I'll take the other direction, if you please, young man. I can but come back again, if it don't do."

Tom made out the address, as requested, and the genteel client, having satisfied the fat lady with a small fee meanwhile, went away, accompanied by her friend.

As Nicholas opened his mouth, to request the young man to turn to letter S, and let him know what secretaryships remained undisposed of, there came into the office an applicant, in whose favour he immediately retired, and whose appearance both surprised and interested him.

This was a young lady who could be scarcely eighteen, of very slight and delicate figure, but exquisitely shaped, who, walking timidly up to the desk, made an inquiry, in a very low tone of voice, relative to some situation as governess, or companion to a lady. She raised her veil for an instant, while she preferred the inquiry, and disclosed a countenance of most uncommon beauty, although shaded by a cloud of sadness, which in one so young was doubly remarkable. Having received a card of reference to some person on the books, she made the usual acknowledgment, and glided away.

She was neatly, but very quietly attired; so much so, indeed, that it seemed as though her dress, if it had been worn by one who imparted fewer graces of her own to it, might have looked poor and shabby. Her attendant—for she had one—was a red-faced, round-eyed, slovenly girl, who, from a certain roughness about the bare arms that peeped from under her draggled shawl, and the half-washed-out traces of smut and blacklead which tattooed her countenance, was clearly of a kin with the servants-of-all-work on the form, between whom and herself there had passed various grins and glances, indicative of the freemasonry of the craft.

This girl followed her mistress; and before Nicholas had recovered from the first effects of his surprise and admiration, the young lady was gone. It is not a matter of such complete and utter improbability as some sober people may think, that he would have followed them out, had he not been restrained by what passed between the fat lady and her book-keeper.

"When is she coming again, Tom?" asked the fat lady.

"To-morrow morning," replied Tom, mending his pen.

"Where have you sent her to?" asked the fat lady.

"Mrs. Clark's," replied Tom.

" She'll have a nice life of it, if she goes there," observed the fat lady, taking a pinch of snuff from a tin box.

Tom made no other reply than thrusting his tongue into his cheek, and pointing the feather of his pen towards Nicholas—reminders which elicited from the fat lady an inquiry of " Now, Sir, what can we do for you ? "

Nicholas briefly replied, that he wanted to know whether there was any such post as secretary or amanuensis to a gentleman to be had.

" Any such!" rejoined the mistress; " a dozen such. An't there, Tom ? "

" *I* should think so," answered that young gentleman ; and as he said it, he winked towards Nicholas, with a degree of familiarity which he no doubt intended for a rather flattering compliment, but with which Nicholas was most ungratefully disgusted.

Upon reference to the book, it appeared that the dozen secretaryships had dwindled down to one. Mr. Gregsbury, the great member of parliament, of Manchester Buildings, Westminster, wanted a young man, to keep his papers and correspondence in order ; and Nicholas was exactly the sort of young man that Mr. Gregsbury wanted.

" I don't know what the terms are, as he said he'd settle them himself with the party," observed the fat lady ; " but they must be pretty good ones, because he 's a member of parliament."

Inexperienced as he was, Nicholas did not feel quite assured of the force of this reasoning, or the justice of this conclusion ; but without troubling himself to question it, he took down the address, and resolved to wait upon Mr. Gregsbury without delay.

" I don't know what the number is," said Tom ; " but Manchester Buildings isn't a large place ; and if the worst comes to the worst, it won't take you very long to knock at all the doors on both sides of the way 'till you find him out. I say, what a good-looking gal that was, wasn't she ? "

" What girl, Sir," demanded Nicholas, sternly.

" Oh yes. I know—what gal, eh ? " whispered Tom, shutting one eye, and cocking his chin in the air. " You didn't see her, you didn't— I say, don't you wish you was me, when she comes to-morrow morning ? "

Nicholas looked at the ugly clerk, as if he had a mind to reward his admiration of the young lady by beating the ledger about his ears, but he refrained, and strode haughtily out of the office ; setting at defiance, in his indignation, those ancient laws of chivalry, which not only made it proper and lawful for all good knights to hear the praise of the ladies to whom they were devoted, but rendered it incumbent upon them to roam about the world, and knock at head all such matter-of-fact and unpoetical characters, as declined to exalt, above all the earth, damsels whom they had never chanced to look upon or hear of—as if that were any excuse.

Thinking no longer of his own misfortunes, but wondering what could be those of the beautiful girl he had seen, Nicholas, with many wrong turns, and many inquiries, and almost as many misdirections, bent his steps towards the place whither he had been directed.

Within the precincts of the ancient city of Westminster, and within half a quarter of a mile of its ancient sanctuary, is a narrow and dirty region, the sanctuary of the smaller members of Parliament in modern days. It is all comprised in one street of gloomy lodging-houses, from whose windows in vacation time there frown long melancholy rows of bills, which say as plainly as did the countenances of their occupiers, ranged on ministerial and opposition benches in the session which slumbers with its fathers, " To Let"—" To Let." In busier periods of the year these bills disappear, and the houses swarm with legislators. There are legislators in the parlours, in the first floor, in the second, in the third, in the garrets ; the small apartments reek with the breath of deputations and delegates. In damp weather the place is rendered close by the steams of moist acts of parliament and frowzy petitions ; general postmen grow faint as they enter its infected limits, and shabby figures in quest of franks, flit restlessly to and fro like the troubled ghosts of Complete Letter-writers departed. This is Manchester Buildings ; and here, at all hours of the night, may be heard the rattling of latch-keys in their respective keyholes, with now and then—when a gust of wind sweeping across the water which washes the Buildings' feet, impels the sound towards its entrance—the weak, shrill voice of some young member practising the morrow's speech. All the live-long day there is a grinding of organs and clashing and clanging of little boxes of music, for Manchester Buildings is an eel-pot, which has no outlet but its awkward mouth—a case-bottle which has no thoroughfare, and a short and narrow neck—and in this respect it may be typical of the fate of some few among its more adventurous residents, who, after wriggling themselves into Parliament by violent efforts and contortions, find that it too is no thoroughfare for them ; that, like Manchester Buildings, it leads to nothing beyond itself; and that they are fain at last to back out, no wiser, no richer, not one whit more famous, than they went in.

Into Manchester Buildings Nicholas turned, with the address of the great Mr. Gregsbury in his hand ; and as there was a stream of people pouring into a shabby house not far from the entrance, he waited until they had made their way in, and then making up to the servant, ventured to inquire if he knew where Mr. Gregsbury lived.

The servant was a very pale, shabby boy, who looked as if he had slept under ground from his infancy, as very likely he had. " Mr. Gregsbury ?" said he ; " Mr. Gregsbury lodges here. It's all right. Come in."

Nicholas thought he might as well get in while he could, so in he walked ; and he had no sooner done so, than the boy shut the door and made off.

This was odd enough, but what was more embarrassing was, that all along the narrow passage, and all along the narrow stairs, blocking up the window, and making the dark entry darker still, was a confused crowd of persons with great importance depicted in their looks ; who were, to all appearance, waiting in silent expectation of some coming event ; from time to time one man would whisper his neighbour, or a little group would whisper together, and then the whisperers would nod fiercely to each other, or give their heads a relentless shake, as if they were bent upon doing something very desperate, and were determined not to be put off, whatever happened.

As a few minutes elapsed without anything occurring to explain this phenomenon, and as he felt his own position a peculiarly uncomfortable one, Nicholas was on the point of seeking some information from the man next him, when a sudden move was visible on the stairs, and a voice was heard to cry, " Now, gentlemen, have the goodness to walk up."

So far from walking up, the gentlemen on the stairs began to walk down with great alacrity, and to entreat, with extraordinary politeness, that the gentlemen nearest the street would go first; the gentlemen nearest the street retorted, with equal courtesy, that they couldn't think of such a thing on any account; but they did it without thinking of it, inasmuch as the other gentlemen pressing some half-dozen (among whom was Nicholas) forward, and closing up behind, pushed them, not merely up the stairs, but into the very sitting-room of Mr. Gregsbury, which they were thus compelled to enter with most unseemly precipitation, and without the means of retreat; the press behind them more than filling the apartment.

" Gentlemen," said Mr. Gregsbury, " you are welcome. I am rejoiced to see you."

For a gentleman who was rejoiced to see a body of visitors, Mr. Gregsbury looked as uncomfortable as might be; but perhaps this was occasioned by senatorial gravity, and a statesmanlike habit of keeping his feelings under control. He was a tough, burly, thick-headed gentleman, with a loud voice, a pompous manner, a tolerable command of sentences with no meaning in them, and in short every requisite for a very good member indeed.

" Now, gentlemen," said Mr. Gregsbury, tossing a great bundle of papers into a wicker basket at his feet, and throwing himself back in his chair with his arms over the elbows, " you are dissatisfied with my conduct, I see by the newspapers."

" Yes, Mr. Gregsbury, we are," said a plump old gentleman in a violent heat, bursting out of the throng, and planting himself in the front.

" Do my eyes deceive me," said Mr. Gregsbury, looking towards the speaker, " or is that my old friend Pugstyles?"

" I am that man, and no other, Sir," replied the plump old gentleman.

" Give me your hand, my worthy friend," said Mr. Gregsbury. " Pugstyles, my dear friend, I am very sorry to see you here."

" I am very sorry to be here, Sir," said Mr. Pugstyles; " but your conduct, Mr. Gregsbury, has rendered this deputation from your constituents imperatively necessary."

" My conduct, Pugstyles," said Mr. Gregsbury, looking round upon the deputation with gracious magnanimity—" My conduct has been, and ever will be, regulated by a sincere regard for the true and real interests of this great and happy country. Whether I look at home or abroad, whether I behold the peaceful industrious communities of our island home, her rivers covered with steam-boats, her roads with loco-motives, her streets with cabs, her skies with balloons of a power and magnitude hitherto unknown in the history of aeronautics in this or any other nation—I say, whether I look merely at home, or stretching my eyes further, contemplate the boundless prospect of conquest and possession—achieved by British perseverance and British valour—which is outspread before me, I clasp my hands, and turning my eyes to the broad expanse above my head, exclaim, ' Thank Heaven, I am a Briton!'"

The time had been when this burst of enthusiasm would have been cheered to the very echo; but now the deputation received it with chilling coldness. The general impression seemed to be, that as an explanation of Mr. Gregsbury's political conduct, it did not enter quite enough into detail, and one gentleman in the rear did not scruple to remark aloud, that for his purpose it savoured rather too much of a " gammon" tendency.

" The meaning of that term—gammon," said Mr. Gregsbury, " is unknown to me. If it means that I grow a little too fervid, or perhaps even hyperbolical, in extolling my native land, I admit the full justice of the remark. I *am* proud of this free and happy country. My form dilates, my eye glistens, my breast heaves, my heart swells, my bosom burns, when I call to mind her greatness and her glory."

" We wish, Sir," remarked Mr. Pugstyles, calmly, " to ask you a few questions."

" If you please, gentlemen; my time is yours—and my country's— and my country's—" said Mr. Gregsbury.

This permission being conceded, Mr. Pugstyles put on his spectacles, and referred to a written paper which he drew from his pocket, where-upon nearly every other member of the deputation pulled a written paper from *his* pocket, to check Mr. Pugstyles off, as he read the questions. This done, Mr. Pugstyles proceeded to business.

" Question number one.—Whether, Sir, you did not give a voluntary pledge previous to your election, that in the event of your being returned you would immediately put down the practice of coughing and groaning in the House of Commons. And whether you did not submit to be coughed and groaned down in the very first debate of the session, and have since made no effort to effect a reform in this respect? Whether you did not also pledge yourself to astonish the government, and make them shrink in their shoes. And whether you have astonished them and made them shrink in their shoes, or not?"

" Go on to the next one, my dear Pugstyles," said Mr. Gregsbury.

" Have you any explanation to offer with reference to that question, Sir?" asked Mr. Pugstyles.

" Certainly not," said Mr. Gregsbury.

The members of the deputation looked fiercely at each other, and afterwards at the member, and " dear Pugstyles" having taken a very long stare at Mr. Gregsbury over the tops of his spectacles, resumed his list of inquiries.

" Question number two.—Whether, Sir, you did not likewise give a voluntary pledge that you would support your colleague on every occasion; and whether you did not, the night before last, desert him and vote upon the other side, because the wife of a leader on that other side had invited Mrs. Gregsbury to an evening party?"

L

" Go on," said Mr. Gregsbury.

" Nothing to say on that, either, Sir ?" asked the spokesman.

" Nothing whatever," replied Mr. Gregsbury.   The deputation, who
had only seen him at canvassing or election time, were struck dumb by
his coolness.   He didn't appear like the same man; then he was all
milk and honey—now he was all starch and vinegar.   But men *are* so
different at different times !

" Question number three—and last—" said Mr. Pugstyles, emphatically.   " Whether, Sir, you did not state upon the hustings, that it
was your firm and determined intention to oppose everything proposed ;
to divide the house upon every question, to move for returns on every
subject, to place a motion on the books every day, and, in short, in your
own memorable words, to play the devil with everything and everybody ?"   With this comprehensive inquiry Mr. Pugstyles folded up his
list of questions, as did all his backers.

Mr. Gregsbury reflected, blew his nose, threw himself further back
in his chair, came forward again, leaning his elbows on the table, made
a triangle with his two thumbs and his two forefingers, and tapping
his nose with the apex thereof, replied (smiling as he said it), " I deny
everything."

At this unexpected answer a hoarse murmur arose from the deputation ; and the same gentleman who had expressed an opinion relative to
the gammoning nature of the introductory speech, again made a mono-
syllabic demonstration, by growling out " Resign ;" which growl being
taken up by his fellows, swelled into a very earnest and general remonstrance.

" I am requested, Sir, to express a hope," said Mr. Pugstyles, with
a distant bow, " that on receiving a requisition to that effect from a great
majority of your constituents, you will not object at once to resign your
seat in favour of some candidate whom they think they can better trust."

To which Mr. Gregsbury read the following reply, which, anticipating the request, he had composed in the form of a letter, whereof
copies had been made to send round to the newspapers.

" MY DEAR PUGSTYLES,

" Next to the welfare of our beloved Island—this great and free and
happy country, whose powers and resources are, I sincerely believe,
illimitable—I value that noble independence which is an Englishman's
proudest boast, and which I fondly hope to bequeath to my children
untarnished and unsullied.   Actuated by no personal motives, but
moved only by high and great constitutional considerations which I will
not attempt to explain, for they are really beneath the comprehension
of those who have not made themselves masters, as I have, of the intricate and arduous study of politics, I would rather keep my seat, and
intend doing so.

" Will you do me the favour to present my compliments to the con-
stituent body, and acquaint them with this circumstance ?

" With great esteem,

" My dear Pugstyles,

" &c.   &c."

" Then you will not resign, under any circumstances?" asked the spokesman.

Mr. Gregsbury smiled, and shook his head.

" Then good morning, Sir," said Pugstyles, angrily.

" God bless you," said Mr. Gregsbury. And the deputation, with many growls and scowls, filed off as quickly as the narrowness of the staircase would allow of their getting down.

The last man being gone, Mr. Gregsbury rubbed his hands and chuckled, as merry fellows will, when they think they have said or done a more than commonly good thing ; he was so engrossed in this self-congratulation, that he did not observe that Nicholas had been left behind in the shadow of the window-curtains, until that young gentleman fearing he might otherwise overhear some soliloquy intended to have no listeners, coughed twice or thrice to attract the member's notice.

" What's that ?" said Mr. Gregsbury, in sharp accents.

Nicholas stepped forward and bowed.

" What do you do here, Sir ? " asked Mr. Gregsbury ; " a spy upon my privacy ! A concealed voter ! You have heard my answer, Sir. Pray follow the deputation."

" I should have done so if I had belonged to it, but I do not," said Nicholas.

" Then how came you here, Sir ?" was the natural inquiry of Mr. Gregsbury, M.P. " And where the devil have you come from, Sir ?" was the question which followed it.

" I brought this card from the General Agency Office, Sir," said Nicholas, " wishing to offer myself as your secretary, and understanding that you stood in need of one."

" That's all you have come for, is it ? " said Mr. Gregsbury, eyeing him in some doubt.

Nicholas replied in the affirmative.

" You have no connexion with any of these rascally papers, have you ? " said Mr. Gregsbury. " You didn't get into the room to hear what was going forward, and put it in print, eh ? "

" I have no connexion, I am sorry to say, with anything at present," rejoined Nicholas,—politely enough, but quite at his ease.

" Oh ! " said Mr. Gregsbury. " How did you find your way up here, then ? "

Nicholas related how he had been forced up by the deputation.

" That was the way, was it ? " said Mr. Gregsbury. " Sit down."

Nicholas took a chair, and Mr. Gregsbury stared at him for a long time, as if to make certain, before he asked any further questions, that there were no objections to his outward appearance.

" You want to be my secretary, do you ? " he said at length.

" I wish to be employed in that capacity," replied Nicholas.

" Well, " said Mr. Gregsbury ; " Now what can you do ?"

" I suppose," replied Nicholas, smiling, " that I can do what usually falls to the lot of other secretaries."

" What's that ? " inquired Mr. Gregsbury.

" What is it ? " replied Nicholas.

" Ah! What is it ? " retorted the member, looking shrewdly at him, with his head on one side.

" A secretary's duties are rather difficult to define, perhaps," said Nicholas, considering. " They include, I presume, correspondence."

" Good," interposed Mr. Gregsbury.

" The arrangement of papers and documents—"

" Very good."

" Occasionally, perhaps, the writing from your dictation ; and possibly,"—said Nicholas, with a half smile, " the copying of your speech, for some public journal, when you have made one of more than usual importance."

" Certainly," rejoined Mr. Gregsbury. " What else ? "

" Really," said Nicholas, after a moment's reflection, " I am not able, at this instant, to recapitulate any other duty of a secretary, beyond the general one of making himself as agreeable and useful to his employer as he can, consistently with his own respectability, and without overstepping that line of duties which he undertakes to perform, and which the designation of his office is usually understood to imply."

Mr. Gregsbury looked fixedly at Nicholas for a short time, and then glancing warily round the room, said in a suppressed voice—

" This is all very well, Mr. — what is your name ? "

" Nickleby."

" This is all very well, Mr. Nickleby, and very proper, so far as it goes—so far as it goes, but it doesn't go far enough. There are other duties, Mr. Nickleby, which a secretary to a parliamentary gentleman must never lose sight of. I should require to be crammed, Sir."

" I beg your pardon," interposed Nicholas, doubtful whether he had heard aright.

" — To be crammed, Sir," repeated Mr. Gregsbury.

" May I beg your pardon again, if I inquire what you mean ?" said Nicholas.

" My meaning, Sir, is perfectly plain," replied Mr. Gregsbury, with a solemn aspect. " My secretary would have to make himself master of the foreign policy of the world, as it is mirrored in the newspapers ; to run his eye over all accounts of public meetings, all leading articles, and accounts of the proceedings of public bodies; and to make notes of anything which it appeared to him might be made a point of, in any little speech upon the question of some petition lying on the table, or anything of that kind. Do you understand ? "

" I think I do, Sir," replied Nicholas.

" Then," said Mr. Gregsbury, " it would be necessary for him to make himself acquainted from day to day with newspaper paragraphs on passing events ; such as ' Mysterious disappearance, and supposed suicide of a pot-boy,' or anything of that sort, upon which I might found a question to the Secretary of State for the Home Department. Then he would have to copy the question, and as much as I remembered of the answer (including a little compliment about my independence and good sense) ; and to send the manuscript in a frank to the local paper, with perhaps half a dozen lines of leader, to the effect, that I was always to be found in my place in parliament, and never shrunk from the discharge of my responsible and arduous duties, and so forth. You see?"

Nicholas bowed.

" Besides which," continued Mr. Gregsbury, " I should expect him now and then to go through a few figures in the printed tables, and to pick out a few results, so that I might come out pretty well on timber duty questions, and finance questions, and so on; and I should like him to get up a few little arguments about the disastrous effects of a return to cash payments and a metallic currency, with a touch now and then about the exportation of bullion, and the Emperor of Russia, and bank notes, and all that kind of thing, which it's only necessary to talk fluently about, because nobody understands it. Do you take me?"

" I think I understand," said Nicholas.

" With regard to such questions as are not political," continued Mr. Gregsbury, warming ; " and which one can't be expected to care a damn about, beyond the natural care of not allowing inferior people to be as well off as ourselves, else where are our privileges? I should wish my secretary to get together a few little flourishing speeches, of a patriotic cast. For instance, if any preposterous bill were brought forward for giving poor grubbing devils of authors a right to their own property, I should like to say, that I for one would never consent to opposing an insurmountable bar to the diffusion of literature among *the people*,—you understand? that the creations of the pocket, being man's, might belong to one man, or one family ; but that the creations of the brain, being God's, ought as a matter of course to belong to the people at large—and if I was pleasantly disposed, I should like to make a joke about posterity, and say that those who wrote for posterity, should be content to be rewarded by the approbation *of* posterity ; it might take with the house, and could never do me any harm, because posterity can't be expected to know anything about me or my jokes either—don't you see?"

" I see that, Sir," replied Nicholas.

" You must always bear in mind, in such cases as this, where our interests are not affected," said Mr. Gregsbury, " to put it very strong about the people, because it comes out very well at election-time; and you could be as funny as you liked about the authors ; because I believe the greater part of them live in lodgings, and are not voters. This is a hasty outline of the chief things you'd have to do, except waiting in the lobby every night, in case I forgot anything, and should want fresh cramming; and now and then, during great debates, sitting in the front row of the gallery, and saying to the people about—' You see that gentleman, with his hand to his face, and his arm twisted round the pillar—that's Mr. Gregsbury—the celebrated Mr. Gregsbury—' with any other little eulogium that might strike you at the moment. And for salary," said Mr. Gregsbury, winding up with great rapidity; for he was out of breath—" And for salary, I don't mind saying at once in round numbers, to prevent any dissatisfaction—though it's more than I've been accustomed to give— fifteen shillings a week, and find yourself. There."

With this handsome offer Mr. Gregsbury once more threw himself back in his chair, and looked like a man who has been most profligately liberal, but is determined not to repent of it notwithstanding.

" Fifteen shillings a week is not much," said Nicholas, mildly.

" Not much ! Fifteen shillings a week not much, young man ?" cried Mr. Gregsbury. " Fifteen shillings a——"

" Pray do not suppose that I quarrel with the sum," replied Nicholas ; " for I am not ashamed to confess, that whatever it may be in itself, to me it is a great deal. But the duties and responsibilities make the recompense small, and they are so very heavy that I fear to undertake them."

" Do you decline to undertake them, Sir ?" inquired Mr. Gregsbury, with his hand on the bell-rope.

" I fear they are too great for my powers, however good my will may be," replied Nicholas.

" That is as much as to say that you had rather not accept the place, and that you consider fifteen shillings a week too little," said Mr. Gregsbury, ringing. " Do you decline it, Sir ?"

" I have no alternative but to do so," replied Nicholas.

" Door, Matthews," said Mr. Gregsbury, as the boy appeared.

" I am sorry I have troubled you unnecessarily, Sir," said Nicholas.

" I am sorry you have," rejoined Mr. Gregsbury, turning his back upon him. " Door, Matthews."

" Good morning," said Nicholas.

" Door, Matthews," cried Mr. Gregsbury.

The boy beckoned Nicholas, and tumbling lazily down stairs before him, opened the door and ushered him into the street. With a sad and pensive air he retraced his steps homewards.

Smike had scraped a meal together from the remnant of last night's supper, and was anxiously awaiting his return. The occurrences of the morning had not improved Nicholas's appetite, and by him the dinner remained untasted. He was sitting in a thoughtful attitude, with the plate which the poor fellow had assiduously filled with the choicest morsels untouched, by his side, when Newman Noggs looked into the room.

" Come back ?" asked Newman.

" Yes," replied Nicholas, " tired to death ; and what is worse, might have remained at home for all the good I have done."

" Couldn't expect to do much in one morning," said Newman.

" May be so, but I am sanguine, and did expect," said Nicholas, " and am proportionately disappointed." Saying which, he gave Newman an account of his proceedings.

" If I could do anything," said Nicholas, " anything however slight, until Ralph Nickleby returns, and I have eased my mind by confronting him, I should feel happier. I should think it no disgrace to work, Heaven knows. Lying indolently here like a half-tamed sullen beast distracts me."

" I don't know," said Newman; " small things offer—they would pay the rent, and more—but you wouldn't like them ; no, you could hardly be expected to undergo it—no, no."

" What could I hardly be expected to undergo ?" asked Nicholas, raising his eyes. " Show me, in this wide waste of London, any honest means by which I could even defray the weekly hire of this poor room, and see if I shrink from resorting to them. Undergo! I have undergone too much, my friend, to feel pride or squeamishness now. Except—" added Nicholas hastily, after a short silence, " except such squeamishness as is common honesty, and so much pride as constitutes self-respect. I see little to choose, between the assistant to a brutal pedagogue, and the toad-eater of a mean and ignorant upstart, be he member or no member."

" I hardly know whether I should tell you what I heard this morning or not," said Newman.

" Has it reference to what you said just now?" asked Nicholas.

" It has."

" Then in Heaven's name, my good friend, tell it me," said Nicholas. " For God's sake consider my deplorable condition; and while I promise to take no step without taking counsel with you, give me, at least, a vote in my own behalf."

Moved by this entreaty, Newman stammered forth a variety of most unaccountable and entangled sentences, the upshot of which was, that Mrs. Kenwigs had examined him at great length that morning touching the origin of his acquaintance with, and the whole life, adventures, and pedigree of Nicholas; that Newman had parried these questions as long as he could, but being at length hard pressed and driven into a corner, had gone so far as to admit, that Nicholas was a tutor of great accomplishments, involved in some misfortunes which he was not at liberty to explain, and bearing the name of Johnson. That Mrs. Kenwigs, impelled by gratitude, or ambition, or maternal pride, or maternal love, or all four powerful motives conjointly, had taken secret conference with Mr. Kenwigs, and finally returned to propose that Mr. Johnson should instruct the four Miss Kenwigses in the French language as spoken by natives, at the weekly stipend of five shillings current coin of the realm, being at the rate of one shilling per week per each Miss Kenwigs, and one shilling over, until such time as the baby might be able to take it out in grammar.

" Which, unless I am very much mistaken," observed Mrs. Kenwigs in making the proposition, " will not be very long; for such clever children, Mr. Noggs, never were born into this world I do believe."

" There," said Newman, " that's all. It's beneath you, I know; but I thought that perhaps you might——"

" Might!" said Nicholas, with great alacrity; " of course I shall. I accept the offer at once. Tell the worthy mother so without delay, my dear fellow; and that I am ready to begin whenever she pleases."

Newman hastened with joyful steps to inform Mrs. Kenwigs of his friend's acquiescence, and soon returning, brought back word that they would be happy to see him in the first floor as soon as convenient; that Mrs. Kenwigs had upon the instant sent out to secure a second-hand French grammar and dialogues, which had long been fluttering in the sixpenny box at the book-stall round the corner; and that the family, highly excited at the prospect of this addition to their gentility, wished the initiatory lesson to come off immediately.

And here it may be observed, that Nicholas was not, in the ordinary sense of the word, a young man of high spirit. He would resent an affront to himself, or interpose to redress a wrong offered to another, as

boldly and freely as any knight that ever set lance in rest; but he
lacked that peculiar excess of coolness and great-minded selfishness, which
invariably distinguish gentlemen of high spirit. In truth, for our own
part, we are rather disposed to look upon such gentlemen as being rather
incumbrances than otherwise in rising families, happening to be acquainted
with several whose spirit prevents their settling down to any grovelling
occupation, and only displays itself in a tendency to cultivate mustachios,
and look fierce; and although mustachios and ferocity are both very
pretty things in their way, and very much to be commended, we confess
to a desire to see them bred at the owner's proper cost, rather than at
the expense of low-spirited people.

Nicholas, therefore, not being a high-spirited young man according to
common parlance, and deeming it a greater degradation to borrow, for
the supply of his necessities, from Newman Noggs, than to teach French
to the little Kenwigses for five shillings a week, accepted the offer with
the alacrity already described, and betook himself to the first floor with
all convenient speed.

Here he was received by Mrs. Kenwigs with a genteel air, kindly
intended to assure him of her protection and support; and here too he
found Mr. Lillyvick and Miss Petowker: the four Miss Kenwigses on
their form of audience, and the baby in a dwarf porter's chair with a
deal tray before it, amusing himself with a toy horse without a head;
the said horse being composed of a small wooden cylinder supported on
four crooked pegs, not unlike an Italian iron, and painted in ingenious
resemblance of red wafers set in blacking.

"How do you do, Mr. Johnson?" said Mrs. Kenwigs. "Uncle—
Mr. Johnson."

"How do you do, Sir?" said Mr. Lillyvick—rather sharply; for he
had not known what Nicholas was, on the previous night, and it was
rather an aggravating circumstance if a tax collector had been too polite
to a teacher.

"Mr. Johnson is engaged as private master to the children, uncle,"
said Mrs. Kenwigs.

"So you said just now, my dear," replied Mr. Lillyvick.

"But I hope," said Mrs. Kenwigs, drawing herself up, "that that
will not make them proud; but that they will bless their own good
fortune, which has born them superior to common people's children. Do
you hear, Morleena?"

"Yes, ma," replied Miss Kenwigs.

"And when you go out in the streets, or elsewhere, I desire that you
don't boast of it to the other children," said Mrs. Kenwigs; "and that
if you must say anything about it, you don't say no more than 'We've
got a private master comes to teach us at home, but we ain't proud,
because ma says it's sinful.' Do you hear, Morleena?"

"Yes, ma," replied Miss Kenwigs again.

"Then mind you recollect, and do as I tell you," said Mrs. Kenwigs.
"Shall Mr. Johnson begin, uncle?"

"I am ready to hear, if Mr. Johnson is ready to commence, my
dear," said the collector, assuming the air of a profound critic. "What
sort of language do you consider French, Sir?"

Nicholas engaged as Tutor in a private family.

" How do you mean ? " asked Nicholas.

" Do you consider it a good language, Sir ? " said the collector ; " a pretty language, a sensible language ? "

" A pretty language, certainly," replied Nicholas ; " and as it has a name for everything, and admits of elegant conversation about everything, I presume it is a sensible one."

" I don't know," said Mr. Lillyvick, doubtfully.   " Do you call it a cheerful language, now ? "

" Yes," replied Nicholas, " I should say it was, certainly."

" It's very much changed since my time, then," said the collector, " very much."

" Was it a dismal one in your time ? " asked Nicholas, scarcely able to repress a smile.

" Very," replied Mr. Lillyvick, with some vehemence of manner. " It 's the war time that I speak of ; the last war. It may be a cheerful language.   I should be sorry to contradict anybody ; but I can only say that I've heard the French prisoners, who were natives, and ought to know how to speak it, talking in such a dismal manner, that it made one miserable to hear them.   Ay, that I have, fifty times, Sir —fifty times."

Mr. Lillyvick was waxing so cross, that Mrs. Kenwigs thought it expedient to motion to Nicholas not to say anything ; and it was not until Miss Petowker had practised several blandishments, to soften the excellent old gentleman, that he deigned to break silence, by asking,

" What's the water in French, Sir ? "

" L'Eau," replied Nicholas.

"Ah! " said Mr. Lillyvick, shaking his head mournfully, "I thought as much. Lo, eh ? I don't think anything of that language—nothing at all."

" I suppose the children may begin, uncle ? " said Mrs. Kenwigs.

" Oh yes ; they may begin, my dear," replied the collector, discontentedly.   " I have no wish to prevent them."

This permission being conceded, the four Miss Kenwigses sat in a row, with their tails all one way, and Morleena at the top, while Nicholas, taking the book, began his preliminary explanations.   Miss Petowker and Mrs. Kenwigs looked on, in silent admiration, broken only by the whispered assurances of the latter, that Morleena would have it all by heart in no time ; and Mr. Lillyvick regarded the group with frowning and attentive eyes, lying in wait for something upon which he could open a fresh discussion on the language.

CHAPTER XVII.

FOLLOWS THE FORTUNES OF MISS NICKLEBY.

IT was with a heavy heart, and many sad forebodings which no effort could banish, that Kate Nickleby, on the morning appointed for the commencement of her engagement with Madame Mantalini, left the city when its clocks yet wanted a quarter of an hour of eight, and threaded her way alone, amid the noise and bustle of the streets, towards the west end of London.

At this early hour many sickly girls, whose business, like that of the poor worm, is to produce with patient toil the finery that bedecks the thoughtless and luxurious, traverse our streets, making towards the scene of their daily labour, and catching, as if by stealth, in their hurried walk, the only gasp of wholesome air and glimpse of sunlight which cheers their monotonous existence during the long train of hours that make a working day. As she drew nigh to the more fashionable quarter of the town, Kate marked many of this class as they passed by, hurrying like herself to their painful occupation, and saw, in their unhealthy looks and feeble gait, but too clear an evidence that her misgivings were not wholly groundless.

She arrived at Madame Mantalini's some minutes before the appointed hour, and after walking a few times up and down, in the hope that some other female might arrive and spare her the embarrassment of stating her business to the servant, knocked timidly at the door, which after some delay was opened by the footman, who had been putting on his striped jacket as he came up stairs, and was now intent on fastening his apron.

" Is Madame Mantalini in ?" faltered Kate.

" Not often out at this time, Miss," replied the man in a tone which rendered ' Miss,' something more offensive than ' My dear.'

" Can I see her ?" asked Kate.

" Eh ?" replied the man, holding the door in his hand, and honouring the inquirer with a stare and a broad grin, " Lord, no."

" I came by her own appointment," said Kate; " I am—I am—to be employed here."

" Oh! you should have rung the workers' bell," said the footman, touching the handle of one in the door-post. " Let me see, though, I forgot—Miss Nickleby, is it ?"

" Yes," replied Kate.

" You're to walk up stairs then, please," said the man. " Madame Mantalini wants to see you—this way—take care of these things on the floor."

Cautioning her in these terms not to trip over a heterogeneous litter of pastry cook's trays, lamps, waiters full of glasses, and piles of rout seats which were strewn about the hall, plainly bespeaking a late party on the previous night, the man led the way to the second story, and ushered Kate into a back room, communicating by folding-doors with the apartment in which she had first seen the mistress of the establishment.

" If you'll wait here a minute," said the man, " I'll tell her presently." Having made this promise with much affability, he retired and left Kate alone.

There was not much to amuse in the room; of which the most attractive feature was, a half-length portrait in oil of Mr. Mantalini, whom the artist had depicted scratching his head in an easy manner, and thus displaying to advantage a diamond ring, the gift of Madame Mantalini before her marriage. There was, however, the sound of voices in conversation in the next room; and as the conversation was loud and the partition thin, Kate could not help discovering that they belonged to Mr. and Mrs. Mantalini.

" If you will be odiously, demnebly, outri*g*eously jealous, my soul," said Mr. Mantalini, " you will be very miserable—horrid miserable— demnition miserable." And then there came a sound as though Mr. Mantalini were sipping his coffee.

" I *am* miserable," returned Madame Mantalini, evidently pouting.

" Then you are an ungrateful, unworthy, demd unthankful little fairy," said Mr. Mantalini.

" I am not," returned Madame, with a sob.

" Do not put itself out of humour," said Mr. Mantalini, breaking an egg. " It is a pretty bewitching little demd countenance, and it should not be out of humour, for it spoils its loveliness, and makes it cross and gloomy like a frightful, naughty, demd hobgoblin."

" I am not to be brought round in that way, always," rejoined Madame, sulkily.

" It shall be brought round in any way it likes best, and not brought round at all if it likes that better," retorted Mr. Mantalini, with his egg-spoon in his mouth.

" It's very easy to talk," said Mrs. Mantalini.

" Not so easy when one is eating a demnition egg," replied Mr. Mantalini; " for the yolk runs down the waistcoat, and yolk of egg does not match any waistcoat but a yellow waistcoat, demmit."

" You were flirting with her during the whole night," said Madame Mantalini, apparently desirous to lead the conversation back to the point from which it had strayed.

" No, no, my life."

" You were," said Madame; " I had my eye upon you all the time."

" Bless the little winking twinkling eye; was it on me all the time!" cried Mantalini, in a sort of lazy rapture. " Oh, demmit!"

" And I say once more," resumed Madame, " that you ought not to waltz with anybody but your own wife; and I will not bear it, Mantalini, if I take poison first."

" She will not take poison and have horrid pains, will she?" said Mantalini; who, by the altered sound of his voice, seemed to have moved his chair and taken up his position nearer to his wife. " She will not take poison, because she had a demd fine husband who might have married two countesses and a dowager——"

" Two countesses," interposed Madame. " You told me one before!"

" Two!" cried Mantalini. " Two demd fine women, real countesses and splendid fortunes, demmit."

" And why didn't you?" asked Madame, playfully.

" Why didn't I!" replied her husband. " Had I not seen at a morning concert the demdest little fascinator in all the world, and while that little fascinator is my wife, may not all the countesses and dowagers in England be"——

Mr. Mantalini did not finish the sentence, but he gave Madame Mantalini a very loud kiss, which Madame Mantalini returned; after which there seemed to be some more kissing mixed up with the progress of the breakfast.

"And what about the cash, my existence's jewel?" said Mantalini, when these endearments ceased. "How much have we in hand?"

"Very little indeed," replied Madame.

"We must have some more," said Mantalini; "we must have some discount out of old Nickleby to carry on the war with, demmit."

"You can't want any more just now," said Madame coaxingly.

"My life and soul," returned her husband, "there is a horse for sale at Scrubbs's, which it would be a sin and crime to lose—going, my senses' joy, for nothing."

"For nothing," cried Madame, "I am glad of that."

"For actually nothing," replied Mantalini. "A hundred guineas down will buy him; mane, and crest, and legs, and tail, all of the demdest beauty. I will ride him in the park before the very chariots of the rejected countesses. The demd old dowager will faint with grief and rage; the other two will say 'He is married, he has made away with himself, it is a demd thing, it is all up.' They will hate each other demnebly, and wish you dead and buried. Ha! ha! Demmit."

Madame Mantalini's prudence, if she had any, was not proof against these triumphal pictures; after a little jingling of keys, she observed that she would see what her desk contained, and rising for that purpose, opened the folding-door, and walked into the room where Kate was seated.

"Dear me, child!" exclaimed Madame Mantalini, recoiling in surprise. "How came you here?"

"Child!" cried Mantalini, hurrying in. "How came it—eh!—oh—demmit, how d'ye do?"

"I have been waiting here some time, ma'am," said Kate, addressing Madame Mantalini. "The man must have forgotten to let you know that I was here, I think."

"You really must see to that man," said Madame, turning to her husband. "He forgets everything."

"I will twist his demd nose off his countenance for leaving such a very pretty creature all alone by herself," said her husband.

"Mantalini," cried Madame, "you forget yourself."

"I don't forget you, my soul, and never shall, and never can," said Mantalini, kissing his wife's hand, and grimacing, aside, to Miss Nickleby, who turned contemptuously away.

Appeased by this compliment, the lady of the business took some papers from her desk, which she handed over to Mr. Mantalini, who received them with great delight. She then requested Kate to follow her, and after several feints on the part of Mr. Mantalini to attract the young lady's attention, they went away, leaving that gentleman extended at full length on the sofa, with his heels in the air and a newspaper in his hand.

Madame Mantalini led the way down a flight of stairs, and through a passage, to a large room at the back of the premises, where were a number of young women employed in sewing, cutting out, making up, altering, and various other processes known only to those who are cun-

Madame Mantalini introduces Kate to Miss Knag.

ning in the arts of millinery and dress-making. It was a close room with a sky-light, and as dull and quiet as a room could be.

On Madame Mantalini calling aloud for Miss Knag, a short, bust-ling, over-dressed female, full of importance, presented herself, and all the young ladies suspending their operations for the moment, whispered to each other sundry criticisms upon the make and texture of Miss Nic-kleby's dress, her complexion, cast of features, and personal appearance, with as much good-breeding as could have been displayed by the very best society in a crowded ball-room.

" Oh, Miss Knag," said Madame Mantalini, " this is the young per-son I spoke to you about."

Miss Knag bestowed a reverential smile upon Madame Mantalini, which she dexterously transformed into a gracious one for Kate, and said that certainly, although it was a great deal of trouble, to have young people, who were wholly unused to the business, still she was sure the young person would try to do her best—impressed with which conviction she (Miss Knag) felt an interest in her already.

" I think that, for the present at all events, it will be better for Miss Nickleby to come into the show-room with you, and try things on for people," said Madame Mantalini. " She will not be able for the present to be of much use in any other way ; and her appearance will—"

" Suit very well with mine, Madame Mantalini," interrupted Miss Knag. " So it will ; and to be sure I might have known that you would not be long in finding that out ; for you have so much taste in all those matters, that really, as I often say to the young ladies, I do not know how, when, or where, you possibly could have acquired all you know—hem—Miss Nickleby and I are quite a pair, Madam Mantalini, only I am a little darker than Miss Nickleby, and—hem—I think my foot may be a little smaller. Miss Nickleby, I am sure, will not be offended at my saying that, when she hears that our family always have been celebrated for small feet ever since—hem—ever since our family had any feet at all, indeed, I think. I had an uncle once, Madame Mantalini, who lived in Cheltenham, and had a most excellent business as a tobacconist—hem—who had such small feet, that they were no bigger than those which are usually joined to wooden legs—the most symmetrical feet, Madame Mantalini, that even you can imagine."

" They must have had something the appearance of club feet, Miss Knag," said Madame.

" Well now, that is so like you," returned Miss Knag. " Ha ! ha ! ha ! Of club feet ! Oh very good ! As I often remark to the young ladies, ' Well I must say, and I do not care who knows it, of all the ready humour—hem—I ever heard anywhere'—and I have heard a good deal ; for when my dear brother was alive (I kept house for him, Miss Nickleby), we had to supper once a week two or three young men, highly celebrated in those days for their humour, Madame Mantalini— ' Of all the ready humour,' I say to the young ladies, ' *I* ever heard, Madame Mantalini's is the most remarkable—hem. It is so gentle, so sarcastic, and yet so good-natured (as I was observing to Miss Sim-monds only this morning), that how, or when, or by what means she acquired it, is to me a mystery indeed.' "

Here Miss Knag paused to take breath, and while she pauses, it may be observed—not that she was marvellously loquacious and marvel-lously deferential to Madame Mantalini, since these are facts which require no comment; but that every now and then she was accustomed, in the torrent of her discourse, to introduce a loud, shrill, clear " hem !" the import and meaning of which was variously interpreted by her acquaintance ; some holding that Miss Knag dealt in exaggeration, and introduced the monosyllable, when any fresh invention was in course of coinage in her brain ; and others, that when she wanted a word, she threw it in to gain time, and prevent anybody else from striking into the conversation. It may be further remarked, that Miss Knag still aimed at youth, though she had shot beyond it years ago ; and that she was weak and vain, and one of those people who are best described by the axiom, that you may trust them as far as you can see them, and no farther.

" You'll take care that Miss Nickleby understands her hours, and so forth," said Madame Mantalini ; " and so I'll leave her with you. You'll not forget my directions, Miss Knag ? "

Miss Knag of course replied, that to forget anything Madame Man-talini had directed, was a moral impossibility ; and that lady, dispensing a general good morning among her assistants, sailed away.

" Charming creature, isn't she, Miss Nickleby ? " said Miss Knag, rubbing her hands together.

" I have seen very little of her," said Kate. " I hardly know yet."

" Have you seen Mr. Mantalini ? " inquired Miss Knag.

" Yes ; I have seen him twice. "

" Isn't *he* a charming creature ? "

" Indeed he does not strike me as being so, by any means," replied Kate.

" No, my dear !" cried Miss Knag, elevating her hands. " Why, goodness gracious mercy, where's your taste ? Such a fine tall, full-whiskered dashing gentlemanly man, with such teeth and hair, and—hem—well now, you *do* astonish me."

" I dare say I am very foolish," replied Kate, laying aside her bonnet ; " but as my opinion is of very little importance to him or any one else, I do not regret having formed it, and shall be slow to change it, I think."

" He is a very fine man, don't you think so ! " asked one of the young ladies.

" Indeed he may be, for anything I could say to the contrary," replied Kate.

" And drives very beautiful horses, doesn't he ? " inquired another.

" I dare say he may, but I never saw them," answered Kate.

" Never saw them !" interposed Miss Knag. " Oh, well, there it is at once you know ; how can you possibly pronounce an opinion about a gentleman—hem—if you don't see him as he turns out altogether ? "

There was so much of the world—even of the little world of the country girl—in this idea of the old milliner, that Kate, who was anxious for every reason to change the subject, made no further remark, and left Miss Knag in possession of the field.

After a short silence, during which most of the young people made a closer inspection of Kate's appearance, and compared notes respecting it, one of them offered to help her off with her shawl, and the offer being accepted, inquired whether she did not find black very uncomfortable wear.

" I do indeed," replied Kate, with a bitter sigh.

" So dusty and hot," observed the same speaker, adjusting her dress for her.

Kate might have said, that mourning was the coldest wear which mortals can assume; that it not only chills the breasts of those it clothes, but extending its influence to summer friends, freezes up their sources of good-will and kindness, and withering all the buds of promise they once so liberally put forth, leaves nothing but bared and rotten hearts exposed. There are few who have lost a friend or relative constituting in life their sole dependence, who have not keenly felt this chilling influence of their sable garb. She had felt it acutely, and feeling it at the moment, could not restrain her tears.

" I am very sorry to have wounded you by my thoughtless speech," said her companion. " I did not think of it. You are in mourning for some near relation."

" For my father," answered Kate, weeping.

" For what relation, Miss Simmonds?" asked Miss Knag in an audible voice.

" Her father," replied the other softly.

" Her father, eh?" said Miss Knag, without the slightest depression of her voice. " Ah! A long illness, Miss Simmonds?"

" Hush—pray," replied the girl; " I don't know."

" Our misfortune was very sudden," said Kate, turning away, " or I might perhaps, at a time like this, be enabled to support it better."

There had existed not a little desire in the room, according to invariable custom when any new " young person" came, to know who Kate was, and what she was, and all about her; but although it might have been very naturally increased by her appearance and emotion, the knowledge that it pained her to be questioned, was sufficient to repress even this curiosity, and Miss Knag, finding it hopeless to attempt extracting any further particulars just then, reluctantly commanded silence, and bade the work proceed.

In silence, then, the tasks were plied until half-past one, when a baked leg of mutton, with potatoes to correspond, were served in the kitchen. The meal over, and the young ladies having enjoyed the additional relaxation of washing their hands, the work began again, and was again performed in silence, until the noise of carriages rattling through the streets, and of loud double knocks at doors, gave token that the day's work of the more fortunate members of society was proceeding in its turn.

One of these double knocks at Madame Mantalini's door announced the equipage of some great lady—or rather rich one, for there is occasionally a wide distinction between riches and greatness—who had come with her daughter to approve of some court-dresses which had been a long time preparing, and upon whom Kate was deputed to wait, accompanied by Miss Knag, and officered of course by Madame Mantalini.

Kate's part in the pageant was humble enough, her duties being limited to holding articles of costume until Miss Knag was ready to try them on, and now and then tying a string or fastening a hook-and-eye. She might, not unreasonably, have supposed herself beneath the reach of any arrogance, or bad humour; but it happened that the rich lady and the rich daughter were both out of temper that day, and the poor girl came in for her share of their revilings. She was awkward—her hands were cold—dirty—coarse—she could do nothing right; they wondered how Madame Mantalini could have such people about her: requested they might see some other young woman the next time they came, and so forth.

So common an occurrence would be hardly deserving of mention, but for its effect. Kate shed many bitter tears when these people were gone, and felt, for the first time, humbled by her occupation. She had, it is true, quailed at the prospect of drudgery and hard service; but she had felt no degradation in working for her bread, until she found herself exposed to insolence and the coarsest pride. Philosophy would have taught her that the degradation was on the side of those who had sunk so low as to display such passions habitually, and without cause; but she was too young for such consolation, and her honest feeling was hurt. May not the complaint, that common people are above their station, often take its rise in the fact of *uncommon* people being below theirs?

In such scenes and occupations the time wore on until nine o'clock, when Kate, jaded and dispirited with the occurrences of the day, hastened from the confinement of the work-room, to join her mother at the street corner, and walk home :—the more sadly, from having to disguise her real feelings, and feign to participate in all the sanguine visions of her companion.

" Bless my soul, Kate," said Mrs. Nickleby; " I 've been thinking all day, what a delightful thing it would be for Madame Mantalini to take you into partnership—such a likely thing too, you know. Why your poor dear papa's cousin's sister-in-law—a Miss Browndock—was taken into partnership by a lady that kept a school at Hammersmith, and made her fortune in no time at all ; I forget, by the bye, whether that Miss Browndock was the same lady that got the ten thousand pounds prize in the lottery, but I think she was ; indeed, now I come to think of it, I am sure she was. ' Mantalini and Nickleby,' how well it would sound !—and if Nicholas has any good fortune, you might have Doctor Nickleby, the head-master of Westminster School, living in the same street."

" Dear Nicholas ! " cried Kate, taking from her reticule her brother's latter from Dotheboys Hall. " In all our misfortunes, how happy it makes me, mamma, to hear he is doing well, and to find him writing in such good spirits. It consoles me for all we may undergo, to think that he is comfortable and happy."

Poor Kate ! she little thought how weak her consolation was, and how soon she would be undeceived.

STEAM NAVIGATION UP THE RHINE

BY THE

SPLENDID BOATS OF

THE COLOGNE ÇOMPANY,

FROM

COLOGNE AS FAR AS STRASBURG, IN CONNEXION WITH THE NETHERLAND STEAM BOAT COMPANY,

AND WITH THE BATAVIER STEAMER TO ROTTERDAM.

Travellers by the Boats of the COLOGNE COMPANY enjoy the privilege of disembarking at any place, and resuming their journey at their pleasure ; and untransferable Tickets are given for the voyage, out and home, at a reduction of one-fourth from the fares, to be made use of at any time and by any of the Company's Boats, within the current year.

Passengers embark and disembark *free of expense ;* and at the places where the Boats are changed, Luggage and Carriages are transhipped *free of expense ;* and if the Baggage is properly directed and a list of it given to the Conductor of the Boats, he will be *responsible* for it.

The Batavier leaves London for Rotterdam every Sunday, and Boats start every morning from Rotterdam to Nymegen and Cologne.

The COLOGNE COMPANY have three splendid Steam Boats daily from Cologne up the Rhine. The first leaves Cologne at Seven o'clock in the morning, arrives at Coblentz the same afternoon, goes on to Mayence at half-past Six the following morning, and arrives there at Five o'clock in the evening.   The second Boat starts at Nine o'clock in the morning, arrives at Coblentz the same evening, stops there one hour, continues the voyage during the night, and arrives at Mayence the next morning; stops there one hour, and arrives at Manheim in the afternoon, whence a Boat starts at Nine o'clock in the evening for Carlsruhe and Strasbur.   The third Boat leaves Cologne at Five o'clock in the afternoon, and arrives at Coblentz in time for the passengers to proceed to Mayence with the Boats that start from Coblen z at half-past Six in the morning.   In this Boat there is a separate Cabin for the Ladies during the night.

Down the Rhine the Boats leave Strasburg daily for Manheim, Mayence, and Coblentz, to Cologne. The journey from Strasburg to Cologne is done in two days, and from Manheim to Cologne in one day. Passengers leaving Cologne on Sunday, arrive at Rotterdam in time for the Batavier which leaves for London on Tuesday.

To prevent any mistake, passengers are requested to take notice that, at Cologne, the Offices for the Steamers of the

COLOGNE COMPANY ARE, 26, THURMARKT STREET, AND AT THE LANDING-PLACE WHERE THE COMPANY'S BOATS ARRIVE AND DEPART.

The fares, which have, since the beginning of the year, been again considerably reduced, are now—

IN THE FIRST CABIN, FOR THE JOURNEY,

	Out *or* home.			Out *and* home.		
From Cologne to Mayence	£0	14	6	£1	1	6
———— to Frankfort	0	18	6	1	10	0
———— to Manheim	0	18	4	1	7	6
———— to Carlsruhe	1	2	7	1	14	6
———— to Strasburg	1	5	3	1	17	10
AND						
From London to Cologne	3	0	0	4	10	0
———— to Mayence	3	11	0	5	6	6
———— to Frankfort	3	16	0	5	15	0
———— to Manheim	3	12	2	5	8	3
———— to Carlsruhe	3	14	6	5	11	9
———— to Strasburg	3	17	6	5	16	3

Further particulars and books containing the reduced fares and all necessary information may be obtained *gratis* from Mr. WM. MAY, 123, Fenchurch Street ; at 61, Charing Cross ; CHAPLIN's, Regent Circus ; and 56, Haymarket ; where Tickets for the whole distance from London to Strasburg, as well as for all intermediate places, may be obtained.

Inserted by order of the **COLOGNE STEAM BOAT COMPANY.**

26, THURMARKT STREET, COLOGNE.

30th June, 1838.

VALUABLE BOOKS

OFFERED, AT REDUCED PRICES, BY

JAMES BOHN, 12, KING WILLIAM STREET,

STRAND.

LODGE'S PORTRAITS.

	Published at £ s. d.	Reduced to £ s. d.
LODGE'S (ED.) PORTRAITS OF ILLUSTRIOUS PERSONS OF GREAT BRITAIN, with Biographical Memoirs, 4 vols. royal folio, LARGE PAPER, PROOF IMPRESSIONS ON INDIA PAPER of the 240 fine Engravings	182 14 0	45 0 0
—— Another Copy, WITH 20 ADDITIONAL ENGRAVERS' PROOFS INSERTED, royal folio, cloth bds.	203 14 0	55 0 0

These copies were reserved by Mr. Harding. Copies may be had in morocco, extra, gilt edges, by LEWIS, for £14. 14s. additional.

As a Collection of Portraits of the Illustrious Persons of our Country, the work of Lodge holds the foremost rank. The outlay of the spirited proprietors exceeded £40,000, and as the copper-plates were all destroyed, the copies cannot be multiplied. The *reimpression in the small size* was from steel plates, which, however they may please the multitude, cannot be said to merit a place in the library of the Amateur.

DUGDALE'S MONASTICON.

	Published at £ s. d.	Reduced to £ s. d.
DUGDALE'S (SIR W.) MONASTICON ANGLICANUM, a History of the Abbeys and other Monasteries, and CATHEDRAL AND COLLEGIATE CHURCHES, IN ENGLAND AND WALES, and of Scotch, Irish, and French Monasteries connected with the Religious Houses in England. A new edition, greatly enlarged, and continued from Leiger Books, and other National Documents, by MESSRS. CALEY, ELLIS, and BANDINEL, 8 vols. folio, plates, cloth bds.	141 15 0	36 15 0
—— Another Copy, LARGE PAPER, 8 vols. royal folio, WITH PROOF IMPRESSIONS of the Plates	238 10 0	55 0 0

JAMES BOHN, being in possession of the entire stock of the above important work, *reserved by Mr. Harding, the original publisher*, will be glad to treat for any copies, which, owing to the death of Subscribers, or other causes, still remain in an unfinished state: or should the possessors of such copies prefer completing them, he will have great pleasure in doing so at a moderate rate, according to the number of parts required.

Copies of the small paper may be had in morocco, gilt edges, by LEWIS, for £20. additional, or on LARGE PAPER, superbly bound by the same artist, for £30. 0s. additional.

DUGDALE'S ST. PAUL'S.

	Published at £ s. d.	Reduced to £ s. d.
DUGDALE'S HISTORY OF ST. PAUL'S CATHEDRAL IN LONDON, extracted out of original Records, Leiger Books, and other MSS. by SIR WILLIAM DUGDALE, KNT., with continuation to the present time, by SIR H. ELLIS, complete in 6 parts, folio, many plates	15 15 0	3 3 0
—— Another Copy, folio, plates, morocco, gilt edges	18 18 0	5 5 0
—— ANOTHER COPY, IMP. folio, LARGE PAPER, PROOF IMPRESSIONS of the Plates, blue morocco, super extra, gilt edges, by LEWIS	35 0 0	12 12 0

A few odd Parts to complete Sets.

JAMES BOHN, 12, KING WILLIAM STREET, STRAND.

BRADBURY AND EVANS,]   [PRINTERS, WHITEFRIARS.

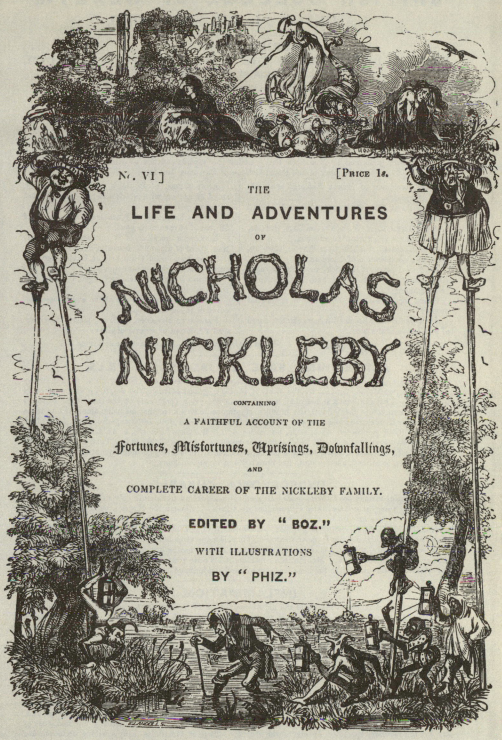

N°. VI] [Price 1s.

THE

LIFE AND ADVENTURES

OF

NICHOLAS NICKLEBY

CONTAINING

A FAITHFUL ACCOUNT OF THE

Fortunes, Misfortunes, Uprisings, Downfallings,

AND

COMPLETE CAREER OF THE NICKLEBY FAMILY.

EDITED BY "BOZ."

WITH ILLUSTRATIONS

BY "PHIZ."

LONDON: CHAPMAN AND HALL, 186, STRAND.

BRITISH COLLEGE OF HEALTH,

HAMILTON PLACE, NEW ROAD.

MORISON'S PILLS.
HYGEIAN DISPENSARY OF THE BRITISH COLLEGE OF HEALTH,
No. 38, PARIS STREET, EXETER.
SUPPORTED BY VOLUNTARY CONTRIBUTIONS.

PATRONS:—JAMES MORISON, THE HYGEIST.
GENERAL FARQUHAR, Early Bank, Perth.
PATRONESSES:—LADY SOPHIA GREY, Ashton Hayes, Chester.
Mrs. CHARLES GORDEN, Wiscombe Park, Devon.

Cases of Cure performed by MORISON'S PILLS, under the superintendence of RICHARD TOTHILL, Esq., Member of the Royal College of Surgeons, London.

ELIZA SYMONDS, of Mount Radford, aged 25, cured of hysteria.

MARY ANNE MAY, of Heavitree, aged 17, cured of hysteria.

ANNE LAYMAN, of Willock's-buildings, Exeter, aged 38, cured of a rheumatic affection.

JOHN UBESTER, of High-street, Exeter, aged 60, cured of a complication of disorders.

JANETIN TONKIN, of Exwick, near Exeter, aged 45, cured of an ulceration in both legs, of fifteen years' standing.

GRACE SCLATER, aged 28, cured of abdominal dropsy.

JOHN BENDING, of Broad Clift, near Exeter, cured of palpitation of the heart.

ANNE GIBBS, of Budleigh, Salterton, aged 52, cured of cancer, with which she had been afflicted for seven years.

THOMAS EDMUNDS, of West-street, Exeter, aged 56, cured of rheumatic gout.

ELIZABETH JOHNSON, of Woodbine-place, Heavitree, cured of a complication of disorders.

SARAH SYMONS, of Trinity-street, Exeter, aged 53, cured of erysipelatous inflammation.

THOMAS FORD, of Heavitree, aged 16, cured of rheumatic fever.

ELIZABETH FORD, mother of the above, aged 56, cured of abdominal dropsy.

ELIZABETH BENNETT, of Baring-place, Heavitree aged 27, cured of general debility.

(Signed)   RICHARD TOTHILL, Heavitree, near Exeter.

ASTONISHING SALE OF MORISON'S PILLS.

The following calculation is made from the evidence given by Mr. Joseph Wing, clerk to the Stamp Office, Somerset House, London, on the trial of Morison against Harmer, the proprietor of the *Weekly Dispatch*. That gentleman stated, that in a period of six years (part only of the time that Morison's Pills have been before the public), the number of stamps delivered for that medicine amounted to three millions nine hundred and one thousand; disposed of as follows:—1,800,000 stamps for boxes, at 1s. 1½d. each; 1,000,000 stamps for boxes, at 2s. 9d. each; 400,000 stamps for boxes, at 4s. 6d. each; 500,000 stamps for boxes, at 11s. each; 201,000 stamps for powders. Stamps, 3,901,000. Total number of pills, 590,000,000. Thus it appears, that in a period of six years, the above enormous quantity of Morison's Pills has been consumed, amounting to five hundred and ninety millions.

HYDROPHOBIA CURABLE.

This frightful malady has hitherto baffled all medical science and treatment. Everything has been tried but the right thing, as not according with medical doctrines. Although the Hygeian treatment has not yet to boast of any case of cure of Hydrophobia, nevertheless Mr. Morison, the Hygeist, has a strong conviction, that it would be successful if properly persevered with. Trial alone can decide; reasoning from analogy confirms this. By the Hygeian treatment, all poisonous virus is sucked or pumped out of the blood. This, very probably, may be a cure for Hydrophobia, the blood having become contaminated by a process similar to that of inoculation. Mr. Morison considers it his duty towards posterity, to give all publicity to his opinions on this subject, in the hope that some liberal and humane doctors may one day give it a fair trial.

INFLAMMATION.

To discover and expose to the world the nature and cause of Inflammation, and from thence to deduce a certain cure, proved so by experience, is to be considered as one of the greatest benefits that can be bestowed on mankind—if so it be, that health and exemption from chronic infirmities and premature death are still ranked as the greatest blessings, the Hygeian Theory assigns all inflammations to impurity of the blood. The practice has established the fact that vegetable purgation can alone be depended on as a real cure. The public would be astonished if made sensible of the fatal consequences of inflammation when treated according to present medical routine.

CAUTION TO PURCHASERS OF MORISON'S PILLS.

To prevent impositions the Honourable Commissioners of Stamps have directed the words " MORISON'S UNIVERSAL MEDICINES " to be engraved on the Government Stamp in white letters upon a red ground, without which none are genuine; and the public are further cautioned against purchasing the medicines of any but the regularly appointed Agents to the British College of Health, as many spurious imitations are now in circulation.
JAMES MORISON, THE HYGEIST.

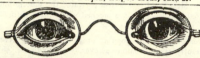
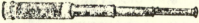

LABERN'S BOTANIC CREAM.

By appointment, patronised by her Most Gracious Majesty, celebrated for strengthening and promoting the growth of Hair, and completely freeing it from Scurf.—Sold by the Proprietor, H. Labern, Perfumer to her Majesty, 49, Judd Street, Brunswick Square, in pots, 1*s.* 6*d.*, 2*s.* 6*d.*, 3*s.* 6*d.*, and 5*s.*, and in Bottles 3*s.* 6*d.* and 5*s.* each, and by all Perfumers and Medicine Venders. Beware of counterfeits. Ask for "Labern's Botanic Cream."

** Trade Orders from the Country to come through the London Wholesale Houses.

PIERCE'S ECONOMICAL RADIATING STOVE-GRATE MANUFACTORY,

No. 5, JERMYN STREET, REGENT STREET.

The Nobility and Gentry are most respectfully solicited to examine a variety of new and elegant Stove Grates upon his so-much-approved Radiating Principle, from his own Designs, being the real Manufacturer of them. These Grates combine the useful and ornamental, blending Economy with Comfort—display a cheerful Fire and a clean Hearth—lessen materially the consumption of Fuel—diffuse a genial Warmth throughout the Apartment, and are adapted for general use. They retain the Heat many hours after the Fire is out—are executed in every style of Architecture—Grecian, Elizabethan, Louis Quatorze, and Gothic, agreeable to any Design.

W. P. has a grate expressly made for the Cure of Smoky Chimneys, and will guarantee its success. He invites attention to his Improved Method of Heating with Hot Water; also to the Domestic Pure Warm-Air Safety Stove, for Churches, Mansions, Houses, Galleries, Entrance-Halls, &c., with Pure Air, which may be seen in daily use at his Show Rooms and Manufactory, as well as an extentive assortment of Fenders, Fire-Irons, Ranges, Boilers, Patent Smoke-Jacks, Hot Plates, Broiling Plates, and all other articles of Kitchen requisites, with the latest Improvements. Baths of every Description, viz., Hot, Cold, Vapour, Douche, Shower, Leg, and Sponge; also Jekyll's Portable Baths.

W. Pierce, Locksmith, Bell-Hanger, &c., 5, Jermyn Street, Regent Street.

THE FALL OF THE LEAF.

" This phenomenon, so commonly observed and commented upon at this season of the year, but seldom suggests any other train of ideas than the ordinary one of its resemblance to the decline of life. It seems not to be generally understood, that the human being is subject to the same laws as those which govern the vegetable creation in the *Fall of the Leaf*. The present is found from experience and accurate observation to be the season when weak hair most rapidly falls of, and hair of strong luxuriant growth becomes relaxed—these evils, though long known to the medical world, were yet without a remedy till the discovery of the BALM OF COLUMBIA by OLDRIDGE—the introduction of which, as a powerful strengthener and preserver of the hair, has created an era in the annals of remedial agents, and from its unfailing effects in cases of baldness, has stamped it as one of the most important modern discoveries."

OLDRIDGE'S BALM causes whiskers and eyebrows to grow, prevents the Hair from turning grey, and the first application makes it curl beautifully, frees it from scurf, and stops the hair from falling off. Abundance of certificates from gentlemen of the first respectability are shown by the Proprietors, C. and A. OLDRIDGE, 1; Wellington Street, Strand, where the Balm is sold, price 3*s.* 6*d.*, 6*s.*, and 11*s.* per bottle. No other prices are genuine.

Some complaints have reached the Proprietors of a spurious Balm having been vended; they again caution the Public to be on their guard against base impostors, by especially asking for OLDRIDGE'S BALM OF COLUMBIA, 1, WELLINGTON STREET, STRAND, LONDON.

IMPORTANT TO GENTLEMEN GOING ABROAD.

R. KIPLING,

SHIRT MAKER AND GENERAL OUTFITTER, 7, LEICESTER SQUARE,

Respectfully invites the attention of the Nobility, Gentry, and Public, to his extensive Stock of Ready-made Linen. R. K. rests his claim for patronage upon superior quality and style, at the most moderate prices.

Where despatch is required, Gentlemen can be supplied with Ready-made Linen or India Cloth Shirts, of any size or quality, washed and ready for immediate use, at the following scale of prices:—

India Cloth	..	£1 16 0 per doz.	Stout Linen	..	8 6 each.
Do. with Linen Fronts, Collars, and Wristbands	3 0 0 ..		Do. Fine Fronts ..		9 6 ..
			Superfine do. ..		10 6 ..
Fine do.	..	3 18 0 ..	Fine do. Finest Fronts, Collars,		
Best do.	..	4 4 0 ..	and Wrists ..		12 6 ..
Aquatic do.	..	2 0 0 ..	Superfine ..		14 6 ..
Night Shirts	..	2 2 0 ..	Do. with French Cambric Fronts		16 6 ..

The above articles made to order on the shortest possible notice.

An extensive assortment of every description of Woollen, Cotton, and Silk Hosiery, and Under-Clothing. Bed and Table Linen, Flannels, Blankets, Calicoes, Linens, &c. &c.

7, LEICESTER SQUARE.—Two Doors East of Miss Linwood's Exhibition.

LITHOGRAPHY.

AT S. STRAKER'S Lithographic Establishment, 3, GEORGE YARD, LOMBARD STREET, LONDON,

Drawings, Maps, Plans, Elevations, Fac-Similes, and Writings, of every description,

Are executed in the best Style, with the utmost Expedition, and on the most moderate Terms.

STRAKER'S LITHOGRAPHIC PRESSES

To receive a Stone 8 by 14 Inches £5 5s. ; 14 by 18 £7 10s. ; 18 by 24 £9 10s. ; 20 by 26 £12 12s. ; larger Sizes in the same proportion.

Stones and every Material and Instrument used in the Art on the lowest Terms for Cash.—Stones on Hire, and forwarded to any Part of the Kingdom.—Country and Foreign Orders promptly attended to.

A. B. SAVORY and SONS, Goldsmiths,

No. 14, CORNHILL, opposite the Bank of England, LONDON.

PLATED CORNER DISHES, WITH SILVER EDGES AND SHIELDS FOR ENGRAVING.

THE GADROON PATTERN.   THE FLOWER PATTERN.

Four Dishes and Covers
  Strongly Plated,   small size ... £7 7 0
  Ditto   full size 10 10 0
  Extra strong Plating, full size 12 12 0

Four Dishes and Covers
  Extra strong Plating, full size... £13 10 0

Any of the above Sets form eight Dishes by removing the Handles from the Covers.

The Show Rooms of this Establishment occupy several floors and contain an extensive Stock of Plated Goods, Silver Plate, Jewellery, and Watches.

A Pamphlet, with Drawings and detailed Lists of Prices, may be had, on application free of cost.

ENGLISH GOLD WATCHES.—A. B. SAVORY & SONS, Watchmakers, No. 9, Cornhill, London, opposite the Bank of England, submit for selection a very large STOCK of GOLD WATCHES, the whole of which are made and finished under the careful inspection of experienced workmen on their own premises, and each warranted for correct performance.

SIZE FOR LADIES.

Fine Vertical Watches, jewelled, in engine-turned gold cases, and gold dials, warranted £10 10 0

Fine Vertical Watches, jewelled, with double-backed engine-turned gold cases, and gold dials, warranted £10 12 0

Patent Detached Lever Watches, jewelled in four holes, with double-backed gold cases, and gold dials, warranted £14 14 0

SIZE FOR GENTLEMEN.

Patent Detached Lever Watches, jewelled in four holes, seconds, and double-backed gold cases, warranted.................. £14 14 0

Patent Detached Lever Watches, capped, jewelled in six holes, seconds, double-backed gold cases and enamel dials, warranted. £17 17 0

Patent Detached Lever Watches, capped, jewelled in six holes, seconds, double-backed gold cases and gold dials, warranted .. £21 0 0

Either of the Gentlemen's Watches may be had in gold hunting cases for £3 3s. each extra.

N. B. Second-hand Watches purchased in exchange.

LONDON: BRADBURY AND EVANS, PRINTERS, WHITEFRIARS.

CHAPTER XVIII.

MISS KNAG, AFTER DOATING ON KATE NICKLEBY FOR THREE WHOLE
DAYS, MAKES UP HER MIND TO HATE HER FOR EVERMORE. THE
CAUSES WHICH LEAD MISS KNAG TO FORM THIS RESOLUTION.

THERE are many lives of much pain, hardship, and suffering, which,
having no stirring interest for any but those who lead them, are disregarded by persons who do not want thought or feeling, but who
pamper their compassion and need high stimulants to rouse it.

There are not a few among the disciples of charity who require in
their vocation scarcely less excitement than the votaries of pleasure in
theirs; and hence it is that diseased sympathy and compassion are
every day expended on out-of-the-way objects, when only too many
demands upon the legitimate exercise of the same virtues in a healthy
state, are constantly within the sight and hearing of the most unob-
servant person alive. In short, charity must have its romance, as the
novelist or playwright must have his. A thief in fustian is a vulgar
character, scarcely to be thought of by persons of refinement; but dress
him in green velvet, with a high-crowned hat, and change the scene of
his operations from a thickly-peopled city to a mountain road, and
you shall find in him the very soul of poetry and adventure. So it is
with the one great cardinal virtue, which, properly nourished and
exercised, leads to, if it does not necessarily include, all the others. It
must have its romance; and the less of real hard struggling work-a-
day life there is in that romance, the better.

The life to which poor Kate Nickleby was devoted, in consequence
of the unforeseen train of circumstances already developed in this narrative, was a hard one; but lest the very dullness, unhealthy confinement, and bodily fatigue, which made up its sum and substance, should
deprive it of any interest with the mass of the charitable and sympathetic, I would rather keep Miss Nickleby herself in view just now,
than chill them in the outset by a minute and lengthened description of
the establishment presided over by Madame Mantalini.

" Well, now, indeed Madame Mantalini," said Miss Knag, as Kate
was taking her weary way homewards on the first night of her
noviciate; " that Miss Nickleby is a very creditable young person—a
very creditable young person indeed—hem—upon my word, Madame
Mantalini, it does very extraordinary credit even to your discrimination
that you should have found such a very excellent, very well-behaved,
very—hem—very unassuming young woman to assist in the fitting
on. I have seen some young women when they had the opportunity
of displaying before their betters, behave in such a—oh, dear—well—
but you're always right, Madame Mantalini, always; and as I very
often tell the young ladies, how you do contrive to be always right,
when so many people are so often wrong, is to me a mystery indeed."

M

" Beyond putting a very excellent client out of humour, Miss Nickleby has not done anything very remarkable to-day—that I am aware of, at least," said Madame Mantalini in reply.

" Oh, dear !" said Miss Knag; "but you must allow a great deal for inexperience, you know."

" And youth ?" inquired Madame.

" Oh, I say nothing about that, Madame Mantalini," replied Miss Knag, reddening ; " because if youth were any excuse, you wouldn't have—"

" Quite so good a forewoman as I have, I suppose," suggested Madame.

" Well, I never did know anybody like you, Madame Mantalini," rejoined Miss Knag most complacently, " and that's the fact, for you know what one's going to say, before it has time to rise to one's lips. Oh, very good ! Ha, ha, ha !"

" For myself," observed Madame Mantalini, glancing with affected carelessness at her assistant, and laughing heartily in her sleeve, " I consider Miss Nickleby the most awkward girl I ever saw in my life."

" Poor dear thing," said Miss Knag, " it's not her fault. If it was, we might hope to cure it ; but as it's her misfortune, Madame Mantalini, why really you know, as the man said about the blind horse, we ought to respect it."

" Her uncle told me she had been considered pretty," remarked Madame Mantalini. " I think her one of the most ordinary girls I ever met with."

" Ordinary !" cried Miss Knag with a countenance beaming delight ; " and awkward ! Well, all I can say is, Madame Mantalini, that I quite love the poor girl; and that if she was twice as indifferent-looking, and twice as awkward as she is, I should be only so much the more her friend, and that's the truth of it."

In fact, Miss Knag had conceived an incipient affection for Kate Nickleby, after witnessing her failure that morning, and this short conversation with her superior increased the favourable prepossession to a most surprising extent ; which was the more remarkable, as when she first scanned that young lady's face and figure, she had entertained certain inward misgivings that they would never agree.

" But now," said Miss Knag, glancing at the reflection of herself in a mirror at no great distance, " I love her—I quite love her—I declare I do."

Of such a highly disinterested quality was this devoted friendship, and so superior was it to the little weaknesses of flattery or ill-nature, that the kind-hearted Miss Knag candidly informed Kate Nickleby next day, that she saw she would never do for the business, but that she need not give herself the slightest uneasiness on this account, for that she (Miss Knag) by increased exertions on her own part, would keep her as much as possible in the back ground, and that all she would have to do would be to remain perfectly quiet before company, and to shrink from attracting notice by every means in her power. This last suggestion was so much in accordance with the timid girl's own feelings and wishes, that she readily promised implicit reliance on the excellent spinster's advice: without questioning, or indeed bestowing a moment's reflection upon the motives that dictated it.

"I take quite a lively interest in you, my dear soul, upon my word," said Miss Knag; "a sister's interest, actually. It's the most singular circumstance I ever knew."

Undoubtedly it was singular, that if Miss Knag did feel a strong interest in Kate Nickleby, it should not rather have been the interest of a maiden aunt or grandmother, that being the conclusion to which the difference in their respective ages would have naturally tended. But Miss Knag wore clothes of a very youthful pattern, and perhaps her feelings took the same shape.

"Bless you!" said Miss Knag, bestowing a kiss upon Kate at the conclusion of the second day's work, "how very awkward you have been all day."

"I fear your kind and open communication, which has rendered me more painfully conscious of my own defects, has not improved me," sighed Kate.

"No, no, I dare say not," rejoined Miss Knag, in a most uncommon flow of good humour. "But how much better that you should know it at first, and so be able to go on straight and comfortable. Which way are you walking, my love?"

"Towards the city," replied Kate.

"The city!" cried Miss Knag, regarding herself with great favour in the glass as she tied her bonnet. "Goodness gracious me! now do you really live in the city?"

"Is it so very unusual for anybody to live there?" asked Kate, half smiling.

"I couldn't have believed it possible that any young woman could have lived there under any circumstances whatever, for three days together," replied Miss Knag.

"Reduced—I should say poor people," answered Kate, correcting herself hastily, for she was afraid of appearing proud, "must live where they can."

"Ah! very true, so they must; very proper indeed!" rejoined Miss Knag with that sort of half sigh, which, accompanied by two or three slight nods of the head, is pity's small change in general society; "and that's what I very often tell my brother, when our servants go away ill one after another, and he thinks the back kitchen's rather too damp for 'em to sleep in. These sort of people, I tell him, are glad to sleep anywhere! Heaven suits the back to the burden. What a nice thing it is to think that it should be so, isn't it?"

"Very," replied Kate, turning away.

"I'll walk with you part of the way, my dear," said Miss Knag, "for you must go very near our house; and as it's quite dark, and our last servant went to the hospital a week ago, with Saint Anthony's fire in her face, I shall be glad of your company."

Kate would willingly have excused herself from this flattering companionship, but Miss Knag having adjusted her bonnet to her entire

M 2

satisfaction, took her arm with an air which plainly showed how much she felt the compliment she was conferring, and they were in the street before she could say another word.

"I fear," said Kate, hesitating, "that mama—my mother, I mean—is waiting for me."

"You needn't make the least apology, my dear," said Miss Knag, smiling sweetly as she spoke; "I dare say she is a very respectable old person, and I shall be quite—hem—quite pleased to know her."

As poor Mrs. Nickleby was cooling—not her heels alone, but her limbs generally at the street corner, Kate had no alternative but to make her known to Miss Knag, who, doing the last new carriage customer at second-hand, acknowledged the introduction with condescending politeness. The three then walked away arm in arm, with Miss Knag in the middle, in a special state of amiability.

"I have taken such a fancy to your daughter, Mrs. Nickleby, you can't think," said Miss Knag, after she had proceeded a little distance in dignified silence.

"I am delighted to hear it," said Mrs. Nickleby; "though it is nothing new to me, that even strangers should like Kate."

"Hem!" cried Miss Knag.

"You will like her better when you know how good she is," said Mrs. Nickleby. "It is a great blessing to me in my misfortunes to have a child, who knows neither pride or vanity, and whose bringing-up might very well have excused a little of both at first. You don't know what it is to lose a husband, Miss Knag."

As Miss Knag had never yet known what it was to gain one, it followed very nearly as a matter of course that she didn't know what it was to lose one, so she said in some haste, "No, indeed I don't," and said it with an air intended to signify that she should like to catch herself marrying anybody—no no, she knew better than that.

"Kate has improved even in this little time, I have no doubt," said Mrs. Nickleby, glancing proudly at her daughter.

"Oh! of course," said Miss Knag.

"And will improve still more," added Mrs. Nickleby.

"That she will, I'll be bound," replied Miss Knag, squeezing Kate's arm in her own, to point the joke

"She always was clever," said poor Mrs. Nickleby, brightening up, "always, from a baby. I recollect when she was only two years and a half old, that a gentleman who used to visit very much at our house—Mr. Watkins, you know, Kate, my dear, that your poor papa went bail for, who afterwards ran away to the United States, and sent us a pair of snow shoes, with such an affectionate letter that it made your poor dear father cry for a week. You remember the letter, in which he said that he was very sorry he couldn't repay the fifty pounds just then, because his capital was all out at interest, and he was very busy making his fortune, but that he didn't forget you were his god-daughter, and he should take it very unkind if we didn't buy you a silver coral and put it down to his old account—dear me, yes, my dear, how stupid you are! and spoke so affectionately of the old port wine that he used to drink a bottle and a half of every time he came. You must remember, Kate ?"

" Yes, yes, mama ; what of him ?"

" Why, that Mr. Watkins, my dear," said Mrs. Nickleby slowly, as if she were making a tremendous effort to recollect something of paramount importance ; " that Mr. Watkins—he wasn't any relation, Miss Knag will understand, to the Watkins who kept the Old Boar in the village ; by the by, I don't remember whether it was the Old Boar or the George the Fourth, but it was one of the two, I know, and it's much the same—that Mr. Watkins said, when you were only two years and a half old, that you were one of the most astonishing children he ever saw. He did indeed, Miss Knag, and he wasn't at all fond of children, and couldn't have had the slightest motive for doing it. I know it was he who said so, because I recollect, as well as if it was only yesterday, his borrowing twenty pounds of her poor dear papa the very moment afterwards."

Having quoted this extraordinary and most disinterested testimony to her daughter's excellence, Mrs. Nickleby stopped to breathe ; and Miss Knag, finding that the discourse was turning upon family greatness, lost no time in striking in with a small reminiscence on her own account.

" Don't talk of lending money, Mrs. Nickleby," said Miss Knag, " or you'll drive me crazy, perfectly crazy. My mamma—hem—was the most lovely and beautiful creature, with the most striking and exquisite—hem—the most exquisite nose that ever was put upon a human face, I do believe, Mrs. Nickleby (here Miss Knag rubbed her own nose sympathetically) ; the most delightful and accomplished woman, perhaps, that ever was seen ; but she had that one failing of lending money, and carried it to such an extent that she lent—hem—oh ! thousands of pounds, all our little fortunes, and what's more, Mrs. Nickleby, I don't think, if we were to live till—till—hem—till the very end of time, that we should ever get them back again. I don't indeed."

After concluding this effort of invention without being interrupted, Miss Knag fell into many more recollections, no less interesting than true, the full tide of which Mrs. Nickleby in vain attempting to stem, at length sailed smoothly down, by adding an under-current of her own recollections ; and so both ladies went on talking together in perfect contentment : the only difference between them being, that whereas Miss Knag addressed herself to Kate, and talked very loud, Mrs. Nickleby kept on in one unbroken monotonous flow, perfectly satisfied to be talking, and caring very little whether anybody listened or not.

In this manner they walked on very amicably until they arrived at Miss Knag's brother's, who was an ornamental stationer and small circulating library keeper, in a by-street off Tottenham Court Road, and who let out by the day, week, month, or year, the newest old novels, whereof the titles were displayed in pen-and-ink characters on a sheet of pasteboard, swinging at his door-post. As Miss Knag happened at the moment to be in the middle of an account of her twenty-second offer from a gentleman of large property, she insisted upon their all going in to supper together ; and in they went.

"Don't go away, Mortimer," said Miss Knag as they entered the shop. "It's only one of our young ladies and her mother. Mrs. and Miss Nickleby."

"Oh, indeed!" said Mr. Mortimer Knag. "Ah!"

Having given utterance to these ejaculations with a very profound and thoughtful air, Mr. Knag slowly snuffed two kitchen candles on the counter and two more in the window, and then snuffed himself from a box in his waistcoat pocket.

There was something very impressive in the ghostly air with which all this was done, and as Mr. Knag was a tall lank gentleman of solemn features, wearing spectacles, and garnished with much less hair than a gentleman bordering on forty or thereabouts usually boasts, Mrs. Nickleby whispered her daughter that she thought he must be literary.

"Past ten," said Mr. Knag, consulting his watch. "Thomas, close the warehouse."

Thomas was a boy nearly half as tall as a shutter, and the warehouse was a shop about the size of three hackney coaches.

"Ah!" said Mr. Knag once more, heaving a deep sigh as he restored to its parent shelf the book he had been reading. "Well—yes—I believe supper is ready, sister."

With another sigh Mr. Knag took up the kitchen candles from the counter, and preceded the ladies with mournful steps to a back parlour, where a char-woman, employed in the absence of the sick servant, and remunerated with certain eighteenpences to be deducted from her wages due, was putting the supper out.

"Mrs. Blockson," said Miss Knag, reproachfully, "how very often I have begged you not to come into the room with your bonnet on."

"I can't help it, Miss Knag," said the char-woman, bridling up on the shortest notice. "There's been a deal o' cleaning to do in this house, and if you don't like it, I must trouble you to look out for somebody else, for it don't hardly pay me, and that's the truth, if I was to be hung this minute."

"I don't want any remarks, if *you* please," said Miss Knag, with a strong emphasis on the personal pronoun. "Is there any fire down stairs for some hot water presently?"

"No there is not, indeed, Miss Knag," replied the substitute; "and so I won't tell you no stories about it."

"Then why isn't there?" said Miss Knag.

"Because there an't no coals left out, and if I could make coals I would, but as I can't I won't, and so I make bold to tell you Mem," replied Mrs. Blockson.

"Will you hold your tongue—female?" said Mr. Mortimer Knag, plunging violently into this dialogue.

"By your leave, Mr. Knag," retorted the char-woman, turning sharp round. "I'm only too glad not to speak in this house, excepting when and where I'm spoke to, Sir; and with regard to being a female, Sir, I should wish to know what you considered yourself?"

"A miserable wretch," exclaimed Mr. Knag, striking his forehead. "A miserable wretch."

" I'm very glad to find that you don't call yourself out of your name, Sir," said Mrs. Blockson; " and as I had two twin children the day before yesterday was only seven weeks, and my little Charley fell down a airy and put his elber out last Monday, I shall take it as a favior if you'll send nine shillings for one week's work to my house, afore the clock strikes ten to-morrow."

With these parting words, the good woman quitted the room with great ease of manner, leaving the door wide open, while Mr. Knag, at the same moment, flung himself into the " warehouse," and groaned aloud.

" What is the matter with that gentleman, pray ?" inquired Mrs. Nickleby, greatly disturbed by the sound.

" Is he ill?" inquired Kate, really alarmed.

" Hush!" replied Miss Knag; " a most melancholy history. He was once most devotedly attached to—hem—to Madame Mantalini."

" Bless me!" exclaimed Mrs. Nickleby.

" Yes," continued Miss Knag, " and received great encouragement too, and confidently hoped to marry her. He has a most romantic heart, Mrs. Nickleby, as indeed—hem—as indeed all our family have, and the disappointment was a dreadful blow. He is a wonderfully accomplished man—most extraordinarily accomplished—reads—hem—reads every novel that comes out ; I mean every novel that—hem—that has any fashion in it, of course. The fact is, that he did find so much in the books he read applicable to his own misfortunes, and did find himself in every respect so much like the heroes—because of course he is conscious of his own superiority, as we all are, and very naturally—that he took to scorning everything, and became a genius ; and I am quite sure that he is at this very present moment writing another book."

" Another book!" repeated Kate, finding that a pause was left for somebody to say something.

" Yes," said Miss Knag, nodding in great triumph ; " another book, in three volumes post octavo. Of course it's a great advantage to him in all his little fashionable descriptions to have the benefit of my—hem — of my experience, because of course few authors who write about such things can have such opportunities of knowing them as I have. He's so wrapped up in high life, that the least allusion to business or worldly matters—like that woman just now for instance—quite distracts him ; but, as I often say, I think his disappointment a great thing for him, because if he hadn't been disappointed he couldn't have written about blighted hopes and all that ; and the fact is if it hadn't happened as it has, I don't believe his genius would ever have come out at all."

How much more communicative Miss Knag might have become under more favourable circumstances it is impossible to divine, but as the gloomy one was within ear-shot and the fire wanted making up, her disclosures stopped here. To judge from all appearances, and the difficulty of making the water warm, the last servant could not have been much accustomed to any other fire than St. Anthony's ; but a little brandy and water was made at last, and the guests, having been previously regaled with cold leg of mutton and bread and cheese, soon afterwards took leave ; Kate amusing herself all the way home with the recollection of her last glimpse of Mr. Mortimer Knag deeply abstracted in the shop, and Mrs. Nickleby by debating within herself whether the dress-making firm would ultimately become " Mantalini, Knag, and Nickleby," or " Mantalini, Nickleby, and Knag."

At this high point, Miss Knag's friendship remained for three whole days, much to the wonderment of Madame Mantalini's young ladies who had never beheld such constancy in that quarter before, but on the fourth it received a check no less violent than sudden, which thus occurred.

It happened that an old lord of great family, who was going to marry a young lady of no family in particular, came with the young lady, and the young lady's sister, to witness the ceremony of trying on two nuptial bonnets which had been ordered the day before ; and Madame Mantalini announcing the fact in a shrill treble through the speaking-pipe, which communicated with the work-room, Miss Knag darted hastily up stairs with a bonnet in each hand, and presented herself in the show-room in a charming state of palpitation, intended to demonstrate her enthusiasm in the cause. The bonnets were no sooner fairly on, than Miss Knag and Madame Mantalini fell into convulsions of admiration.

" A most elegant appearance," said Madame Mantalini.

" I never saw anything so exquisite in all my life," said Miss Knag.

Now the old lord, who was a *very* old lord, said nothing, but mumbled and chuckled in a state of great delight, no less with the nuptial bonnets and their wearers, than with his own address in getting such a fine woman for his wife ; and the young lady, who was a very lively young lady, seeing the old lord in this rapturous condition, chased the old lord behind a cheval-glass, and then and there kissed him, while Madame Mantalini and the other young lady looked discreetly another way.

But pending the salutation, Miss Knag, who was tinged with curiosity, stepped accidentally behind the glass, and encountered the lively young lady's eye just at the very moment when she kissed the old lord ; upon which the young lady in a pouting manner murmured something about " an old thing," and " great impertinence," and finished by darting a look of displeasure at Miss Knag and smiling contemptuously.

" Madam Mantalini," said the young lady.

" Ma'am," said Madame Mantalini.

" Pray have up that pretty young creature we saw yesterday."

" Oh yes, do," said the sister.

" Of all things in the world, Madame Mantalini," said the lord's intended, throwing herself languidly on a sofa, " I hate being waited upon by frights or elderly persons. Let me always see that young creature, I beg, whenever I come."

" By all means," said the old lord ; " the lovely young creature, by all means."

" Everybody is talking about her," said the young lady, in the same careless manner ; " and my lord, being a great admirer of beauty, must positively see her."

"She *is* universally admired," replied Madame Mantalini. "Miss Knag, send up Miss Nickleby. You needn't return."

"I beg your pardon, Madame Mantalini, what did you say last?" asked Miss Knag, trembling.

"You needn't return," repeated the superior sharply. Miss Knag vanished without another word, and in all reasonable time was replaced by Kate, who took off the new bonnets and put on the old ones: blushing very much to find that the old lord and the two young ladies were staring her out of countenance all the time.

"Why, how you colour, child!" said the lord's chosen bride.

"She is not quite so accustomed to her business as she will be in a week or two," interposed Madame Mantalini with a gracious smile.

"I am afraid you have been giving her some of your wicked looks, my lord," said the intended.

"No, no, no," replied the old lord, "no, no, I'm going to be married and lead a new life. Ha, ha, ha! a new life, a new life! ha, ha, ha!"

It was a satisfactory thing to hear that the old gentleman was going to lead a new life, for it was pretty evident that his old one would not last him much longer. The mere exertion of protracted chuckling reduced him to a fearful ebb of coughing and gasping, and it was some minutes before he could find breath to remark that the girl was too pretty for a milliner.

"I hope you don't think good looks a disqualification for the business, my lord," said Madame Mantalini, simpering.

"Not by any means," replied the old lord, "or you would have left it long ago."

"You naughty creature!" said the lively lady, poking the peer with her parasol; "I won't have you talk so. How dare you?"

This playful inquiry was accompanied with another poke and another, and then the old lord caught the parasol, and wouldn't give it up again, which induced the other lady to come to the rescue, and some very pretty sportiveness ensued.

"You will see that those little alterations are made, Madame Mantalini," said the lady. "Nay, my lord, you positively shall go first; I wouldn't leave you behind with that pretty girl, not for half a second. I know you too well. Jane, my dear, let him go first, and we shall be quite sure of him."

The old lord, evidently much flattered by this suspicion, bestowed a grotesque leer upon Kate as he passed, and receiving another tap with the parasol for his wickedness, tottered down stairs to the door, where his sprightly body was hoisted into the carriage by two stout footmen.

"Foh!" said Madame Mantalini, "how he ever gets into a carriage without thinking of a hearse, *I* can't think. There, take the things away, my dear, take them away."

Kate, who had remained during the whole scene with her eyes modestly fixed upon the ground, was only too happy to avail herself of the permission to retire, and hastened joyfully down stairs to Miss Knag's dominion.

The circumstances of the little kingdom had greatly changed, however, during the short period of her absence. In place of Miss Knag being stationed in her accustomed seat, preserving all the dignity and greatness of Madame Mantalini's representative, that worthy soul was reposing on a large box, bathed in tears, while three or four of the young ladies in close attendance upon her, together with the presence of hartshorn, vinegar, and other restoratives, would have borne ample testimony, even without the derangement of the head-dress and front row of curls, to her having fainted desperately.

"Bless me!" said Kate, stepping hastily forward, "What is the matter?"

This inquiry produced in Miss Knag violent symptoms of a relapse; and several young ladies, darting angry looks at Kate, applied more vinegar and hartshorn, and said it was "a shame."

"What is a shame?" demanded Kate. "What is the matter? What has happened? tell me."

"Matter!" cried Miss Knag, coming all at once bolt upright, to the great consternation of the assembled maidens; "Matter! Fie upon you, you nasty creature!"

"Gracious!" cried Kate, almost paralysed by the violence with which the adjective had been jerked out from between Miss Knag's closed teeth; "have *I* offended you?"

"*You* offended me!" retorted Miss Knag, "*You!* a chit, a child, an upstart nobody! Oh, indeed! Ha, ha!"

Now, it was evident as Miss Knag laughed, that something struck her as being exceedingly funny, and as the young ladies took their tone from Miss Knag—she being the chief—they all got up a laugh without a moment's delay, and nodded their heads a little, and smiled sarcastically to each other, as much as to say, how very good that was.

"Here she is," continued Miss Knag, getting off the box, and introducing Kate with much ceremony and many low curtseys to the delighted throng; "here she is—everybody is talking about her—the belle, ladies—the beauty, the—oh, you bold-faced thing!"

At this crisis Miss Knag was unable to repress a virtuous shudder, which immediately communicated itself to all the young ladies, after which Miss Knag laughed, and after that, cried.

"For fifteen years," exclaimed Miss Knag, sobbing in a most affecting manner, "for fifteen years I have been the credit and ornament of this room and the one up-stairs. Thank God," said Miss Knag, stamping first her right foot and then her left with remarkable energy, "I have never in all that time, till now, been exposed to the arts, the vile arts of a creature, who disgraces us all with her proceedings, and makes proper people blush for themselves. But I feel it, I do feel it, although I am disgusted."

Miss Knag here relapsed into softness, and the young ladies renewing their attentions, murmured that she ought to be superior to such things, and that for their part they despised them, and considered them beneath their notice; in witness whereof they called out more emphatically than before that it was a shame, and that they felt so angry, they did, they hardly knew what to do with themselves.

" Have I lived to this day to be called a fright!" cried Miss Knag, suddenly becoming convulsive, and making an effort to tear her front off.
" Oh no, no," replied the chorus, " pray don't say so ; don't, now."
" Have I deserved to be called an elderly person?" screamed Miss Knag, wrestling with the supernumeraries.
" Don't think of such things, dear," answered the chorus.
" I hate her," cried Miss Knag ; " I detest and hate her. Never let her speak to me again ; never let anybody who is a friend of mine speak to her ; a slut, a hussy, an impudent artful hussy !" Having denounced the object of her wrath in these terms, Miss Knag screamed once, hiccuped thrice, and gurgled in her throat several times : slumbered, shivered, woke, came to, composed her head-dress, and declared herself quite well again.

Poor Kate had regarded these proceedings at first in perfect bewilderment. She had then turned red and pale by turns, and once or twice essayed to speak ; but as the true motives of this altered behaviour developed themselves, she retired a few paces, and looked calmly on without deigning a reply. But although she walked proudly to her seat, and turned her back upon the group of little satellites who clustered round their ruling planet in the remotest corner of the room, she gave way in secret to some such bitter tears as would have gladdened Miss Knag inmost soul if she could have seen them fall.

CHAPTER XIX.

DESCRIPTIVE OF A DINNER AT MR. RALPH NICKLEBY'S, AND OF THE MANNER IN WHICH THE COMPANY ENTERTAINED THEMSELVES BEFORE DINNER, AT DINNER, AND AFTER DINNER.

THE bile and rancour of the worthy Miss Knag undergoing no diminution during the remainder of the week, but rather augmenting with every successive hour ; and the honest ire of all the young ladies rising, or seeming to rise, in exact proportion to the good spinster's indignation, and both waxing very hot every time Miss Nickleby was called up stairs, it will be readily imagined that that young lady's daily life was none of the most cheerful or enviable kind. She hailed the arrival of Saturday night, as a prisoner would a few delicious hours' respite from slow and wearing torture, and felt, that the poor pittance for her first week's labour would have been dearly and hardly earned had its amount been trebled.

When she joined her mother as usual at the street corner, she was not a little surprised to find her in conversation with Mr. Ralph Nickleby ; but her surprise was soon redoubled, no less by the matter of their conversation, than by the smoothed and retired manner of Mr. Nickleby himself.

" Ah! my dear!" said Ralph; " we were at that moment talking about you."

" Indeed !" replied Kate, shrinking, though she scarce knew why, from her uncle's cold glistening eye.

" That instant," said Ralph. " I was coming to call for you, making sure to catch you before you left ; but your mother and I have been talking over family affairs, and the time has slipped away so rapidly——"

" Well, now, hasn't it ?" interposed Mrs. Nickleby, quite insensible to the sarcastic tone of Ralph's last remark. " Upon my word, I couldn't have believed it possible, that such a——Kate, my dear, you're to dine with your uncle at half-past six o'clock to-morrow."

Triumphing in having been the first to communicate this extraordinary intelligence, Mrs. Nickleby nodded and smiled a great many times, to impress its full magnificence on Kate's wondering mind, and then flew off, at an acute angle, to a committee of ways and means.

" Let me see," said the good lady. " Your black silk frock will be quite dress enough, my dear, with that pretty little scarf, and a plain band in your hair, and a pair of black silk stock——Dear, dear," cried Mrs. Nickleby, flying off at another angle, " if I had but those unfortunate amethysts of mine—you recollect them, Kate, my love—how they used to sparkle, you know—but your papa, your poor dear papa —ah! there never was anything so cruelly sacrificed as those jewels were, never!" Overpowered by this agonising thought, Mrs. Nickleby shook her head in a melancholy manner, and applied her handkerchief to her eyes.

" I don't want them, mama, indeed," said Kate. " Forget that you ever had them."

" Lord, Kate, my dear," rejoined Mrs. Nickleby, pettishly, " how like a child you talk. Four-and-twenty silver tea spoons, brother-in-law, two gravies, four salts, all the amethysts—necklace, brooch, and ear-rings—all made away with at the same time, and I saying almost on my bended knees to that poor good soul, ' Why don't you do something, Nicholas? Why don't you make some arrangement?' I am sure that anybody who was about us at that time will do me the justice to own, that if I said that once, I said it fifty times a-day. Didn't I, Kate, my dear? Did I ever lose an opportunity of impressing it on your poor papa ?"

" No, no, mama, never," replied Kate. And to do Mrs. Nickleby justice, she never had lost—and to do married ladies as a body justice, they seldom do lose—any occasion of inculcating similar golden precepts, whose only blemish is, the slight degree of vagueness and uncertainty in which they are usually developed.

" Ah !" said Mrs. Nickleby, with great fervour, " if my advice had been taken at the beginning—Well, I have always done *my* duty, and that's some comfort."

When she had arrived at this reflection, Mrs. Nickleby sighed, rubbed her hands, cast up her eyes, and finally assumed a look of meek composure, thus importing that she was a persecuted saint, but that she wouldn't trouble her hearers by mentioning a circumstance which must be so obvious to everybody.

" Now," said Ralph, with a smile, which, in common with all other tokens of emotion, seemed to skulk under his face, rather than play boldly over it—" to return to the point from which we have strayed. I have a little party of—of—gentlemen with whom I am connected in business just now, at my house to-morrow ; and your mother has promised that you shall keep house for me. I am not much used to parties ; but this is one of business, and such fooleries are an important part of it sometimes. You don't mind obliging me ? "

" Mind ! " cried Mrs. Nickleby. " My dear Kate, why——"

" Pray," interrupted Ralph, motioning her to be silent. " I spoke to my niece."

" I shall be very glad, of course, uncle," replied Kate ; " but I am afraid you will find me very awkward and embarrassed."

" Oh no," said Ralph ; " come when you like, in a hackney coach —I'll pay for it. Good night—a—a—God bless you."

The blessing seemed to stick in Mr. Ralph Nickleby's throat, as if it were not used to the thoroughfare, and didn't know the way out. But it got out somehow, though awkwardly enough ; and having disposed of it, he shook hands with his two relatives, and abruptly left them.

" What a very strongly-marked countenance your uncle has," said Mrs. Nickleby, quite struck with his parting look. " I don't see the slightest resemblance to his poor brother."

" Mama ! " said Kate, reprovingly. " To think of such a thing ! "

" No," said Mrs. Nickleby, musing. " There certainly is none. But it's a very honest face."

The worthy matron made this remark with great emphasis and elocution, as if it comprised no small quantity of ingenuity and research ; and in truth it was not unworthy of being classed among the extraordinary discoveries of the age. Kate looked up hastily, and as hastily looked down again.

" What has come over you, my dear, in the name of goodness ? " asked Mrs. Nickleby, when they had walked on for some time in silence.

" I was only thinking, mama," answered Kate.

" Thinking ! " repeated Mrs. Nickleby. " Aye, and indeed plenty to think about, too. Your uncle has taken a strong fancy to you, that's quite clear ; and if some extraordinary good fortune doesn't come to you after this, I shall be a little surprised, that's all."

With this, she launched out into sundry anecdotes of young ladies, who had had thousand pound notes given them in reticules, by eccentric uncles ; and of young ladies who had accidentally met amiable gentlemen of enormous wealth at their uncles' houses, and married them, after short but ardent courtships ; and Kate, listening first in apathy, and afterwards in amusement, felt, as they walked home, something of her mother's sanguine complexion gradually awakening in her own bosom, and began to think that her prospects might be brightening, and that better days might be dawning upon them. Such is hope, Heaven's own gift to struggling mortals; pervading, like some subtle essence from the skies, all things, both good and bad ; as universal as death, and more infectious than disease.

The feeble winter's sun—and winter's suns in the city are very feeble indeed—might have brightened up as he shone through the dim windows of the large old house, on witnessing the unusual sight which one half-furnished room displayed. In a gloomy corner, where for years had stood a silent dusty pile of merchandise, sheltering its colony of mice, and frowning a dull and lifeless mass upon the panelled room, save when, responding to the roll of heavy waggons in the street without, it quaked with sturdy tremblings and caused the bright eyes of its tiny citizens to grow brighter still with fear, and struck them motionless, with attentive ear and palpitating heart, until the alarm had passed away—in this dark corner was arranged, with scrupulous care, all Kate's little finery for the day ; each article of dress partaking of that indescribable air of jauntiness and individuality which empty garments —whether by association, or that they become moulded as it were to the owner's form—will take, in eyes accustomed to, or picturing the wearer's smartness. In place of a bale of musty goods, there lay the black silk dress : the neatest possible figure in itself. The small shoes, with toes delicately turned out, stood upon the very pressure of some old iron weight ; and a pile of harsh discoloured leather had unconsciously given place to the very same little pair of black silk stockings, which had been the objects of Mrs. Nickleby's peculiar care. Rats and mice, and such small gear, had long ago been starved or emigrated to better quarters ; and in their stead appeared gloves, bands, scarfs, hair-pins, and many other little devices, almost as ingenious in their way as rats and mice themselves, for the tantalisation of mankind. About and among them all, moved Kate herself, not the least beautiful or unwonted relief to the stern old gloomy building.

In good time, or in bad time, as the reader likes to take it, for Mrs. Nickleby's impatience went a great deal faster than the clocks at that end of the town, and Kate was dressed to the very last hair-pin a full hour and a half before it was at all necessary to begin to think about it —in good time, or in bad time, the toilet was completed ; and it being at length the hour agreed upon for starting, the milkman fetched a coach from the nearest stand, and Kate, with many adieus to her mother, and many kind messages to Miss La Creevy, who was to come to tea, seated herself in it, and went away in state if ever any body went away in state in a hackney coach yet. And the coach, and the coachman, and the horses, rattled, and jangled, and whipped, and cursed, and swore, and tumbled on together, till they came to Golden Square.

The coachman gave a tremendous double knock at the door, which was opened long before he had done, as quickly as if there had been a man behind it with his hand tied to the latch. Kate, who had expected no more uncommon appearance than Newman Noggs in a clean shirt, was not a little astonished to see that the opener was a man in handsome livery, and that there were two or three others in the hall. There was no doubt about its being the right house , however, for there was the name upon the door, so she accepted the laced coat-sleeve

Miss Nickleby introduced to her Uncle's friends

which was tendered her, and entering the house, was ushered up stairs, into a back drawing-room, where she was left alone.

If she had been surprised at the apparition of the footman, she was perfectly absorbed in amazement at the richness and splendour of the furniture. The softest and most elegant carpets, the most exquisite pictures, the costliest mirrors; articles of richest ornament, quite dazzling from their beauty, and perplexing from the prodigality with which they were scattered around, encountered her on every side. The very staircase nearly down to the hall door, was crammed with beautiful and luxurious things, as though the house were brim-full of riches, which, with a very trifling addition, would fairly run over into the street.

Presently she heard a series of loud double knocks at the street-door, and after every knock some new voice in the next room; the tones of Mr. Ralph Nickleby were easily distinguishable at first, but by degrees they merged into the general buzz of conversation, and all she could ascertain was, that there were several gentlemen with no very musical voices, who talked very loud, laughed very heartily, and swore more than she would have thought quite necessary. But this was a question of taste.

At length the door opened, and Ralph himself, divested of his boots, and ceremoniously embellished with black silks and shoes, presented his crafty face.

" I couldn't see you before, my dear," he said, in a low tone, and pointing as he spoke, to the next room. " I was engaged in receiving them. Now—shall I take you in?"

" Pray uncle," said Kate, a little flurried, as people much more conversant with society often are when they are about to enter a room full of strangers, and have had time to think of it previously, " are there any ladies here?"

" No," said Ralph, shortly, " I don't know any."

" Must I go in immediately?" asked Kate, drawing back a little.

" As you please," said Ralph, shrugging his shoulders. " They are all come, and dinner will be announced directly afterwards—that's all."

Kate would have entreated a few minutes' respite, but reflecting that her uncle might consider the payment of the hackney-coach fare a sort of bargain for her punctuality, she suffered him to draw her arm through his and to lead her away.

Seven or eight gentlemen were standing round the fire when they went in, and as they were talking very loud were not aware of their entrance until Mr. Ralph Nickleby, touching one on the coat-sleeve, said in a harsh emphatic voice, as if to attract general attention—

" Lord Frederick Verisopht, my niece, Miss Nickleby."

The group dispersed as if in great surprise, and the gentleman addressed, turning round, exhibited a suit of clothes of the most superlative cut, a pair of whiskers of similar quality, a moustache, a head of hair, and a young face.

" Eh!" said the gentleman. " What—the—deyvle!"

With which broken ejaculations he fixed his glass in his eye, and stared at Miss Nickleby in great surprise.

" My niece, my lord," said Ralph.

" Well, then my ears did not deceive me, and it's not wa-a-x work," said his lordship. " How de do ? I'm very happy." And then his lordship turned to another superlative gentleman, something older, something stouter, something redder in the face, and something longer upon town, and said in a loud whisper that the girl was " deyvlish pitty."

" Introduce me, Nickleby," said this second gentleman, who was lounging with his back to the fire, and both elbows on the chimney-piece.

" Sir Mulberry Hawk," said Ralph.

" Otherwise the most knowing card in the pa-ack, Miss Nickleby," said Lord Frederick Verisopht.

" Don't leave me out, Nickleby," cried a sharp-faced gentleman, who was sitting on a low chair with a high back, reading the paper.

" Mr. Pyke," said Ralph.

" Nor me, Nickleby," cried a gentleman with a flushed face and a flash air, from the elbow of Sir Mulberry Hawk.

" Mr. Pluck," said Ralph. Then wheeling about again towards a gentleman with the neck of a stork and the legs of no animal in particular, Ralph introduced him as the Honorable Mr. Snobb; and a white-headed person at the table as Colonel Chowser. The colonel was in conversation with somebody, who appeared to be a make-weight, and was not introduced at all.

There were two circumstances which, in this early stage of the party, struck home to Kate's bosom, and brought the blood tingling to her face. One was the flippant contempt with which the guests evidently regarded her uncle, and the other the easy insolence of their manner towards herself. That the first symptom was very likely to lead to the aggravation of the second it needed no great penetration to foresee. And here Mr. Ralph Nickleby had reckoned without his host; for however fresh from the country a young lady (by nature) may be, and however unacquainted with conventional behaviour, the chances are that she will have quite as strong an innate sense of the decencies and proprieties of life as if she had run the gauntlet of a dozen London seasons—possibly a stronger one, for such senses have been known to blunt in this improving process.

When Ralph had completed the ceremonial of introduction, he led his blushing niece to a seat, and as he did so, glanced warily round as though to assure himself of the impression which her unlooked-for appearance had created.

" An unexpected playsure, Nickleby," said Lord Frederick Verisopht, taking his glass out of his right eye, where it had until now done duty on Kate, and fixing it in his left to bring it to bear on Ralph.

" Designed to surprise you, Lord Frederick," said Mr. Pluck.

" Not a bad idea," said his lordship, " and one that would almost warrant the addition of an extra two and a half per cent."

" Nickleby," said Sir Mulberry Hawk, in a thick coarse voice, " take the hint, and tack it on to the other five-and-twenty, or whatever it is, and give me half for the advice."

Sir Mulberry garnished this speech with a hoarse laugh, and terminated it with a pleasant oath regarding Mr. Nickleby's limbs, whereat Messrs. Pyke and Pluck " laughed consumedly."

These gentlemen had not yet quite recovered the jest when dinner was announced, and then they were thrown into fresh ecstacies by a similar cause ; for Sir Mulberry Hawk, in an excess of humour, shot dexterously past Lord Frederick Verisopht who was about to lead Kate down stairs, and drew her arm through his up to the elbow.

" No, damn it, Verisopht," said Sir Mulberry, " fair play's a jewel, and Miss Nickleby and I settled the matter with our eyes, ten minutes ago."

" Ha, ha, ha!" laughed the Honourable Mr. Snobb, " very good, very good."

Rendered additionally witty by this applause, Sir Mulberry Hawk leered upon his friends most facetiously, and led Kate down stairs with an air of familiarity, which roused in her gentle breast such disgust and burning indignation, as she felt it almost impossible to repress. Nor was the intensity of these feelings at all diminished, when she found herself placed at the top of the table, with Sir Mulberry Hawk and Lord Verisopht on either side.

" Oh, you've found your way into our neighbourhood, have you ? " said Sir Mulberry as his lordship sat down.

" Of course," replied Lord Frederick, fixing his eyes on Miss Nickleby, " how can you a-ask me ? "

" Well, you attend to your dinner," said Sir Mulberry, " and don't mind Miss Nickleby and me, for we shall prove very indifferent company, I dare say."

"I wish you'd interfere here, Nickleby," said Lord Verisopht.

" What is the matter, my lord ? " demanded Ralph from the bottom of the table, where he was supported by Messrs. Pyke and Pluck.

"This fellow, Hawk, is monopolising your niece," said Lord Frederick.

" He has a tolerable share of everything that you lay claim to, my lord," said Ralph with a sneer.

" 'Gad, so he has," replied the young man ; " deyvle take me if I know which is master in my house, he or I."

" I know," muttered Ralph.

" I think I shall cut him off with a shilling," said the young nobleman, jocosely.

" No, no, curse it," said Sir Mulberry. " When you come to the shilling—the last shilling—I'll cut you fast enough ; but till then, I'll never leave you—you may take your oath of it."

This sally (which was strictly founded on fact,) was received with a general roar, above which, was plainly distinguishable the laughter of Mr. Pyke and Mr. Pluck, who were evidently Sir Mulberry's toads in ordinary. Indeed, it was not difficult to see, that the majority of the company preyed upon the unfortunate young lord, who, weak and silly as he was, appeared by far the least vicious of the party. Sir Mulberry Hawk was remarkable for his tact in ruining, by himself

N

and his creatures, young gentlemen of fortune—a genteel and elegant profession, of which he had undoubtedly gained the head. With all the boldness of an original genius, he had struck out an entirely new course of treatment quite opposed to the usual method, his custom being, when he had gained the ascendancy over those he took in hand, rather to keep them down than to give them their own way; and to exercise his vivacity upon them openly and without reserve. Thus he made them butts in a double sense, and while he emptied them with great address, caused them to ring with sundry well-administered taps for the diversion of society.

The dinner was as remarkable for the splendour and complete-ness of its appointments as the mansion itself, and the company were remarkable for doing it ample justice, in which respect Messrs. Pyke and Pluck particularly signalised themselves; these two gentlemen eating of every dish, and drinking of every bottle, with a capacity and perseverance truly astonishing. They were remarkably fresh too, notwithstanding their great exertions: for, on the appearance of the dessert, they broke out again, as if nothing serious had taken place since breakfast.

" Well," said Lord Frederick, sipping his first glass of port, " if this is a discounting dinner, all I have to say is, deyvle take me, if it wouldn't be a good pla-an to get discount every day."

" You'll have plenty of it in your time," returned Sir Mulberry Hawk; " Nickleby will tell you that."

" What do you say, Nickleby ? " inquired the young man ; " am I to be a good customer ? "

" It depends entirely on circumstances, my lord," replied Ralph.

" On your lordship's circumstances," interposed Colonel Chouser of the Militia—and the race-courses.

The gallant Colonel glanced at Messrs. Pyke and Pluck as if he thought they ought to laugh at his joke, but those gentlemen, being only engaged to laugh for Sir Mulberry Hawk, were, to his signal dis-comfiture, as grave as a pair of undertakers. To add to his defeat, Sir Mulberry, considering any such efforts an invasion of his peculiar privilege, eyed the offender steadily through his glass as if astounded at his presumption, and audibly stated his impression that it was all " internal liberty," which being a hint to Lord Frederick, he put up his glass, and surveyed the object of censure as if he were some extra-ordinary wild animal then exhibiting for the first time. As a matter of course, Messrs. Pyke and Pluck stared at the individual whom Sir Mulberry Hawk stared at ; so the poor Colonel, to hide his con-fusion, was reduced to the necessity of holding his port before his right eye and affecting to scrutinise its colour with the most lively interest.

All this while Kate had sat as silently as she could, scarcely daring to raise her eyes, lest they should encounter the admiring gaze of Lord Frederick Verisopht, or, what was still more embarrassing, the bold looks of his friend Sir Mulberry. The latter gentleman was obliging enough to direct general attention towards her.

" Here is Miss Nickleby," observed Sir Mulberry, " wondering why the deuce somebody doesn't make love to her."

" No, indeed," said Kate, looking hastily up, " I——" and then she stopped, feeling it would have been better to have said nothing at all.

" I'll hold any man fifty pounds," said Sir Mulberry, " that Miss Nickleby can't look in my face, and tell me she wasn't thinking so."

" Done ! " cried the noble gull. " Within ten minutes."

" Done !" responded Sir Mulberry. The money was produced on both sides, and the Honourable Mr. Snobb was elected to the double office of stake-holder and time-keeper.

" Pray," said Kate, in great confusion, while these preliminaries were in course of completion. " Pray do not make me the subject of any bets. Uncle, I cannot really——."

" Why not, my dear ? " replied Ralph, in whose grating voice, however, there was an unusual huskiness, as though he spoke unwillingly, and would rather that the proposition had not been broached. " It is done in a moment ; there is nothing in it. If the gentlemen insist on it——"

" *I* don't insist on it," said Sir Mulberry, with a loud laugh. " That is, I by no means insist upon Miss Nickleby's making the denial, for if she does, I lose ; but I shall be glad to see her bright eyes, especially as she favours the mahogany so much."

" So she does, and it's too ba-a-d of you, Miss Nickleby," said the noble youth.

" Quite cruel," said Mr. Pyke.

" Horrid cruel," said Mr. Pluck.

" I don't care if I do lose," said Sir Mulberry, " for one tolerable look at Miss Nickleby's eyes is worth double the money."

" More," said Mr. Pyke.

" Far more," said Mr. Pluck.

" How goes the enemy, Snobb ?" asked Sir Mulberry Hawk.

" Four minutes gone."

" Bravo !"

" Won't you ma-ake one effort for me, Miss Nickleby ?" asked Lord Frederick, after a short interval.

" You needn't trouble yourself to inquire, my buck," said Sir Mulberry ; " Miss Nickleby and I understand each other ; she declares on my side, and shews her taste. You haven't a chance, old fellow. Time now, Snobb ?"

" Eight minutes gone."

" Get the money ready," said Sir Mulberry; " you'll soon hand over."

" Ha, ha, ha ! " laughed Mr. Pyke.

Mr. Pluck, who always came second, and topped his companion if he could, screamed outright.

The poor girl, who was so overwhelmed with confusion that she scarcely knew what she did, had determined to remain perfectly quiet ; but fearing that by so doing she might seem to countenance Sir Mulberry's boast, which had been uttered with great coarseness and vulgarity of manner, raised her eyes, and looked him in the face. There was something so odious, so insolent, so repulsive in the look which met her, that, without the power to stammer forth a syllable, she rose and hurried from the room. She restrained her tears by a great effort until she was alone up stairs, and then gave them vent.

"Capital!" said Sir Mulberry Hawk, putting the stakes in his pocket. "That's a girl of spirit, and we'll drink her health."

It is needless to say that Pyke and Co. responded with great warmth of manner to this proposal, or that the toast was drunk with many little insinuations from the firm, relative to the completeness of Sir Mulberry's conquest.   Ralph, who, while the attention of the other guests was attracted to the principals in the preceding scene, had eyed them like a wolf, appeared to breathe more freely now his niece was gone ; and the decanters passing quickly round, leant back in his chair, and turned his eyes from speaker to speaker, as they warmed with wine, with looks that seemed to search their hearts and lay bare for his distempered sport every idle thought within them.

Meantime Kate, left wholly to herself, had in some degree recovered her composure.   She had learnt from a female attendant, that her uncle wished to see her before she left, and had also gleaned the satisfactory intelligence, that the gentlemen would take coffee at table.   The prospect of seeing them no more contributed greatly to calm her agitation, and, taking up a book, she composed herself to read.

She started now and then when the sudden opening of the dining-room door let loose a wild shout of noisy revelry, and more than once rose in great alarm, as a fancied footstep on the staircase impressed her with the fear that some stray member of the party was returning alone.   Nothing occurring, however, to realise her apprehensions, she endeavoured to fix her attention more closely on her book, in which by degrees she became so much interested, that she had read on through several chapters without heed of time or place, when she was terrified by suddenly hearing her name pronounced by a man's voice close at her ear.

The book fell from her hand.   Lounging on an ottoman close beside her, was Sir Mulberry Hawk, evidently the worse—if a man be a ruffian at heart, he is never the better—for wine.

"What a delightful studiousness !" said this accomplished gentleman "Was it real, now, or only to display the eye-lashes ?"

Kate bit her lip, and looking anxiously towards the door, made no reply.

"I have looked at 'em for five minutes," said Sir Mulberry. "Upon my soul, they're perfect. Why did I speak, and destroy such a pretty little picture !"

"Do me the favour to be silent now, Sir," replied Kate.

"No, don't," said Sir Mulberry, folding his crush hat to lay his elbow on, and bringing himself still closer to the young lady ; "upon my life, you oughtn't to. Such a devoted slave of yours, Miss Nickleby —it's an infernal thing to treat him so harshly, upon my soul it is."

"I wish you to understand, Sir," said Kate, trembling in spite of herself, but speaking with great indignation, "that your behaviour offends and disgusts me. If you have one spark of gentlemanly feeling remaining, you will leave me instantly."

" Now why," said Sir Mulberry, " why will you keep up this appearance of excessive rigour, my sweet creature? Now, be more natural—my dear Miss Nickleby, be more natural—do."

Kate hastily rose; but as she rose, Sir Mulberry caught her dress, and forcibly detained her.

" Let me go, Sir," she cried, her heart swelling with anger. " Do you hear? Instantly—this moment."

" Sit down, sit down," said Sir Mulberry; " I want to talk to you."

" Unhand me, Sir, this instant," cried Kate.

" Not for the world," rejoined Sir Mulberry. Thus speaking, he leant over, as if to replace her in her chair; but the young lady making a violent effort to disengage herself, he lost his balance, and measured his length upon the ground. As Kate sprung forward to leave the room, Mr. Ralph Nickleby appeared in the door-way, and confronted her.

" What is this?" said Ralph.

" It is this, Sir," replied Kate, violently agitated : " that beneath the roof where I, a helpless girl, your dead brother's child, should most have found protection, I have been exposed to insult which should make you shrink to look upon me. Let me pass you."

Ralph *did* shrink, as the indignant girl fixed her kindling eye upon him; but he did not comply with her injunction, nevertheless; for he led her to a distant seat, and returning and approaching Sir Mulberry Hawk, who had by this time risen, motioned towards the door.

" Your way lies there, Sir," said Ralph, in a suppressed voice, that some devil might have owned with pride.

" What do you mean by that?" demanded his friend, fiercely.

The swoln veins stood out like sinews on Ralph's wrinkled forehead, and the nerves about his mouth worked as though some unendurable torture wrung them; but he smiled disdainfully, and again pointed to the door.

" Do you know me, you madman?" asked Sir Mulberry.

" Well," said Ralph. The fashionable vagabond for the moment quite quailed under the steady look of the older sinner, and walked towards the door, muttering as he went.

" You wanted the lord, did you?" he said, stopping short when he reached the door, as if a new light had broken in upon him, and confronting Ralph again. " Damme, I was in the way, was I?"

Ralph smiled again, but made no answer.

" Who brought him to you first?" pursued Sir Mulberry; " and how without me could you ever have wound him in your net as you have?"

" The net is a large one, and rather full," said Ralph. " Take care that it chokes nobody in the meshes."

" You would sell your flesh and blood for money; yourself, if you have not already made a bargain with the devil," retorted the other. " Do you mean to tell me that your pretty niece was not brought here as a decoy for the drunken boy down stairs?"

Although this hurried dialogue was carried on in a suppressed tone on both sides, Ralph looked involuntarily round to ascertain that Kate had not moved her position so as to be within hearing. His adversary saw the advantage he had gained, and followed it up.

" Do you mean to tell me," he asked again, " that it is not so ? Do you mean to say that if he had found his way up here instead of me, you wouldn't have been a little more blind, and a little more deaf, and a little less flourishing than you have been ? Come, Nickleby, answer me that."

" I tell you this," replied Ralph, " that if I brought her here, as a matter of business——"

" Aye, that's the word," interposed Sir Mulberry, with a laugh. " You're coming to yourself again now."

" — As a matter of business," pursued Ralph, speaking slowly and firmly, as a man who has made up his mind to say no more, " because I thought she might make some impression on the silly youth you have taken in hand and are lending good help to ruin, I knew—knowing him—that it would be long before he outraged her girl's feelings, and that unless he offended by mere puppyism and emptiness, he would, with a little management, respect the sex and conduct even of his usurer's niece. But if I thought to draw him on more gently by this device, I did not think of subjecting the girl to the licentiousness and brutality of so old a hand as you. And now we understand each other."

" Especially as there was nothing to be got by it—eh ?" sneered Sir Mulberry.

" Exactly so," said Ralph. He had turned away, and looked over his shoulder to make this last reply. The eyes of the two worthies met with an expression as if each rascal felt that there was no disguising himself from the other ; and Sir Mulberry Hawk shrugged his shoulders and walked slowly out.

His friend closed the door, and looked restlessly towards the spot where his niece still remained in the attitude in which he had left her. She had flung herself heavily upon the couch, and with her head drooping over the cushion and her face hidden in her hands, seemed to be still weeping in an agony of shame and grief.

Ralph would have walked into any poverty-stricken debtor's house, and pointed him out to a bailiff, though in attendance upon a young child's deathbed, without the smallest concern, because it would have been a matter quite in the ordinary course of business, and the man would have been an offender against his only code of morality. But here was a young girl, who had done no wrong but that of coming into the world alive ; who had patiently yielded to all his wishes ; who had tried so hard to please him—above all, who didn't owe him money—and he felt awkward and nervous.

Ralph took a chair at some distance, then another chair a little nearer, then moved a little nearer still, then nearer again, and finally sat himself on the same sofa, and laid his hand on Kate's arm.

" Hush, my dear !" he said, as she drew it back, and her sobs burst out afresh. " Hush, hush ! Don't mind it now ; don't think of it."

" Oh, for pity's sake, let me go home," cried Kate. " Let me leave this house, and go home."

" Yes, yes," said Ralph. " You shall. But you must dry your eyes first, and compose yourself. Let me raise your head. There —there."

" Oh, uncle ! " exclaimed Kate, clasping her hands. " What have I done—what have I done—that you should subject me to this ? If I had wronged you in thought, or word, or deed, it would have been most cruel to me, and the memory of one you must have loved in some old time ; but ——"

" Only listen to me for a moment," interrupted Ralph, seriously alarmed by the violence of her emotions. " I didn't know it would be so ; it was impossible for me to foresee it. I did all I could.—Come, let us walk about. You are faint with the closeness of the room, and the heat of these lamps. You will be better now, if you make the slightest effort."

" I will do anything," replied Kate, " if you will only send me home."

" Well, well, I will," said Ralph ; " but you must get back your own looks, for those you have will frighten them, and nobody must know of this but you and I. Now let us walk the other way. There. You look better even now."

With such encouragements as these, Ralph Nickleby walked to and fro, with his niece leaning on his arm ; quelled by her eye, and actually trembling beneath her touch.

In the same manner, when he judged it prudent to allow her to depart, he supported her down stairs, after adjusting her shawl and performing such little offices, most probably for the first time in his life. Across the hall, and down the steps Ralph led her too ; nor did he withdraw his hand, until she was seated in the coach.

As the door of the vehicle was roughly closed, a comb fell from Kate's hair, close at her uncle's feet ; and as he picked it up and returned it into her hand, the light from a neighbouring lamp shone upon her face. The lock of hair that had escaped and curled loosely over her brow, the traces of tears yet scarcely dry, the flushed cheek, the look of sorrow, all fired some dormant train of recollection in the old man's breast ; and the face of his dead brother seemed present before him, with the very look it wore on some occasion of boyish grief, of which every minutest circumstance flashed upon his mind, with the distinctness of a scene of yesterday.

Ralph Nickleby, who was proof against all appeals of blood and kindred—who was steeled against every tale of sorrow and distress— staggered while he looked, and reeled back into his house, as a man who had seen a spirit from some world beyond the grave.

CHAPTER XX.

WHEREIN NICHOLAS AT LENGTH ENCOUNTERS HIS UNCLE, TO WHOM
HE EXPRESSES HIS SENTIMENTS WITH MUCH CANDOUR.   HIS RESO-
LUTION.

LITTLE Miss La Creevy trotted briskly through divers streets at the
west end of the town early on Monday morning—the day after the
dinner—charged with the important commission of acquainting Madame
Mantalini that Miss Nickleby was too unwell to attend that day, but
hoped to be enabled to resume her duties on the morrow.   And as
Miss La Creevy walked along, revolving in her mind various genteel
forms and elegant turns of expression, with a view to the selection of
the very best in which to couch her communication, she cogitated a good
deal upon the probable causes of her young friend's indisposition.

" I don't know what to make of it," said Miss La Creevy.   " Her
eyes were decidedly red last night.   She said she had a head-ache;
head-aches don't occasion red eyes.   She must have been crying."

Arriving at this conclusion, which, indeed, she had established to her
perfect satisfaction on the previous evening, Miss La Creevy went on to
consider—as she had done nearly all night—what new cause of unhap-
piness her young friend could possibly have had.

" I can't think of any thing," said the little portrait painter.
" Nothing at all, unless it was the behaviour of that old bear.   Cross
to her, I suppose?   Unpleasant brute!"

Relieved by this expression of opinion, albeit it was vented upon
empty air, Miss La Creevy hurried on to Madame Mantalini's; and
being informed that the governing power was not yet out of bed,
requested an interview with the second in command, whereupon Miss
Knag appeared.

" So far as *I* am concerned," said Miss Knag, when the message had
been delivered, with many ornaments of speech ; " I could spare Miss
Nickleby for evermore."

" Oh, indeed, ma'am !" rejoined Miss La Creevy, highly offended.
" But you see you are not mistress of the business, and therefore it's of
no great consequence."

" Very good, ma'am," said Miss Knag.   " Have you any further
commands for me ? "

" No, I have not, ma'am," rejoined Miss La Creevy.

" Then good morning, ma'am," said Miss Knag.

" Good morning to you, ma'am ; and many obligations for your
extreme politeness and good-breeding," rejoined Miss La Creevy.

Thus terminating the interview, during which both ladies had
trembled very much, and been marvellously polite—certain indications
that they were within an inch of a very desperate quarrel—Miss La
Creevy bounced out of the room, and into the street.

" I wonder who that is," said the que◦   le soul.   " A nice person to know, I should think ! I wish I had t   ainting of her : *I'd* do her justice." So, feeling quite satisfied that ◦ ◦e had said a very cutting thing at Miss Knag's expense, Miss La C ◦eevy had a hearty laugh, and went home to breakfast, in great good humour.

Here was one of the advantages of having lived alone so long. The little bustling, active, cheerful creature, existed entirely within herself, talked to herself, made a confident of herself, was as sarcastic as she could be, on people who offended her, by herself ; pleased herself, and did no harm. If she indulged in scandal, nobody's reputation suffered ; and if she enjoyed a little bit of revenge, no living soul was one atom the worse. One of the many to whom, from st◦aitened circumstances, a consequent inability to form the associations they would wish, and a disinclination to mix with the society they could obtain, London is as complete a solitude as the plains of Syria, the humble artist had pursued her lonely, but contented way for many years ; and, until the peculiar misfortunes of the Nickleby family attracted her attention, had made no friends, though brimfull of the friendliest feelings to all mankind. There are many warm hearts in the same solitary guise as poor Miss La Creevy's.

However, that's neither here nor there, just now. She went home to breakfast, and had scarcely caught the full flavour of her first sip of tea, when the servant announced a gentleman, whereat Miss La Creevy, at once imagining a new sitter, transfixed by admiration at the street-door case, was in unspeakable consternation at the presence of the tea-things.

" Here, take 'em away ; run with 'em into the bed-room ; any-where," said Miss La Creevy. " Dear, dear ; to think that I should be late on this particular morning, of all others, after being ready for three weeks by half-past eight o'clock, and not a soul coming near the place!"

" Don't let me put you out of the way," said a voice Miss La Creevy knew. " I told the servant not to mention my name, because I wished to surprise you."

" Mr. Nicholas ! " cried Miss La Creevy, starting in great astonishment.

" You have not forgotten me, I see," replied Nicholas, extending his hand.

" Why I think I should even have known you if I had met you in the street," said Miss La Creevy, with a smile. " Hannah, another cup and saucer. Now I'll tell you what, young man ; I'll trouble you not to·repeat the impertinence you were guilty of on the morning you went away."

" You would not be very angry, would you ? " asked Nicholas.

" Wouldn't I !" said Miss La Creevy. " You had better try ; that's all."

Nicholas, with becoming gallantry, immediately took Miss La Creevy at her word, who uttered a faint scream and slapped his face ; but it was not a very hard slap, and that's the truth.

" I never saw such a rude creature !" exclaimed Miss La Creevy.

" You told me to try," said Nicholas.

" Well; but I was speaking ironically," rejoined Miss La Creevy.

" Oh! that's another thing," said Nicholas; " you should have told me that, too."

" I dare say you didn't know, indeed!" retorted Miss La Creevy. " But now I look at you again, you seem thinner than when I saw you last, and your face is haggard and pale. And how come you to have left Yorkshire?"

She stopped here; for there was so much heart in her altered tone and manner, that Nicholas was quite moved.

" I need look somewhat changed," he said, after a short silence; " for I have undergone some suffering, both of mind and body, since I left London. I have been very poor, too, and have even suffered from want."

" Good Heaven, Mr. Nicholas!" exclaimed Miss La Creevy, " what are you telling me!"

" Nothing which need distress you quite so much," answered Nicholas, with a more sprightly air; " neither did I come here to bewail my lot, but on matter more to the purpose. I wish to meet my uncle face to face. I should tell you that first."

" Then all I have to say about that is," interposed Miss La Creevy, " that I don't envy you your taste; and that sitting in the same room with his very boots, would put me out of humour for a fortnight."

" In the main," said Nicholas, " there may be no great difference of opinion between you and me, so far; but you will understand, that I desire to confront him; to justify myself, and to cast his duplicity and malice in his throat."

" That's quite another matter," rejoined Miss La Creevy. " God forgive me; but I shouldn't cry my eyes quite out of my head, if they choked him. Well."

" To this end I called upon him this morning," said Nicholas. " He only returned to town on Saturday, and I knew nothing of his arrival until late last night."

" And did you see him?" asked Miss La Creevy.

" No," replied Nicholas. " He had gone out."

" Hah!" said Miss La Creevy; " on some kind, charitable business, I dare say."

" I have reason to believe," pursued Nicholas, " from what has been told me by a friend of mine, who is acquainted with his movements, that he intends seeing my mother and sister to-day, and giving them his version of the occurrences that have befallen me. I will meet him there."

" That's right," said Miss La Creevy, rubbing her hands. " And yet, I don't know—" she added, " there is much to be thought of—others to be considered."

" I have considered others," rejoined Nicholas; " but as honesty and honour are both at issue, nothing shall deter me."

" You should know best," said Miss La Creevy.

" In this case I hope so," answered Nicholas. " And all I want you to do for me, is, to prepare them for my coming. They think me a long way off, and if I went wholly unexpected, I should frighten them. If you can spare time to tell them you have seen me, and that I shall be with them a quarter of an hour afterwards, you will do me a great service."

" I wish I could do you, or any of you, a greater," said Miss La Creevy ; " but the power to serve is as seldom joined with the will, as the will with the power."

Talking on very fast and very much, Miss La Creevy finished her breakfast with great expedition ; put away the tea-caddy and hid the key under the fender, resumed her bonnet, and, taking Nicholas's arm, sallied forth at once to the city. Nicholas left her near the door of his mother's house, and promised to return within a quarter of an hour at furthest.

It so chanced that Ralph Nickleby, at length seeing fit, for his own purposes, to communicate the atrocities of which Nicholas had been guilty, had (instead of first proceeding to another quarter of the town on business, as Newman Noggs supposed he would), gone straight to his sister-in-law. Hence when Miss La Creevy, admitted by a girl who was cleaning the house, made her way to the sitting-room, she found Mrs. Nickleby and Kate in tears, and Ralph just concluding his statement of his nephew's misdemeanours. Kate beckoned her not to retire, and Miss La Creevy took a seat in silence.

" You are here already, are you, my gentleman ?" thought the little woman. " Then he shall announce himself, and see what effect that has on you."

" This is pretty," said Ralph, folding up Miss Squeers's note ; " very pretty. I recommended him—against all my previous conviction, for I knew he would never do any good—to a man with whom, behaving himself properly, he might have remained in comfort for years. What is the result ? Conduct, for which he might hold up his hand at the Old Bailey."

" I never will believe it," said Kate, indignantly ; " never. It is some base conspiracy, which carries its own falsehood with it."

" My dear," said Ralph, " you wrong the worthy man. These are not inventions. The man is assaulted, your brother is not to be found ; this boy, of whom they speak, goes with him—remember, remember."

" It is impossible," said Kate. " Nicholas !—and a thief, too ! Mama, how can you sit and hear such statements ?"

Poor Mrs. Nickleby, who had at no time been remarkable for the possession of a very clear understanding, and who had been reduced by the late changes in her affairs to a most complicated state of perplexity, made no other reply to this earnest remonstrance than exclaiming from behind a mass of pocket-handkerchief, that she never could have believed it—thereby most ingeniously leaving her hearers to suppose that she did believe it.

" It would be my duty, if he came in my way, to deliver him up to justice," said Ralph, " my bounden duty ; I should have no other course, as a man of the world and a man of business, to pursue. And yet," said Ralph, speaking in a very marked manner, and looking furtively, but fixedly, at Kate, "and yet I would not, I would spare the feelings of his—of his sister. And his mother of course," added Ralph, as though by an afterthought, and with far less emphasis.

Kate very well understood that this was held out as an additional inducement to her, to preserve the strictest silence regarding the events of the preceding night. She looked involuntarily towards Ralph as he ceased to speak, but he had turned his eyes another way, and seemed for the moment quite unconscious of her presence.

"Everything," said Ralph, after a long silence, broken only by Mrs. Nickleby's sobs, "everything combines to prove the truth of this letter, if indeed there were any possibility of disputing it. Do innocent men steal away from the sight of honest folks, and skulk in hiding-places like outlaws? Do innocent men inveigle nameless vagabonds, and prowl with them about the country as idle robbers do? Assault, riot, theft, what do you call these?"

"A lie!" cried a furious voice, as the door was dashed open, and Nicholas burst into the centre of the room.

In the first moment of surprise, and possibly of alarm, Ralph rose from his seat, and fell back a few paces, quite taken off his guard by this unexpected apparition. In another moment, he stood fixed and immoveable with folded arms, regarding his nephew with a scowl of deadly hatred, while Kate and Miss La Creevy threw themselves between the two to prevent the personal violence which the fierce excitement of Nicholas appeared to threaten.

"Dear Nicholas," cried his sister, clinging to him. "Be calm, consider—"

"Consider, Kate!" cried Nicholas, clasping her hand so tight in the tumult of his anger, that she could scarcely bear the pain. "When I consider all, and think of what has passed, I need be made of iron to stand before him."

"Or bronze," said Ralph, quietly; "there is not hardihood enough in flesh and blood to face it out."

"Oh dear, dear!" cried Mrs. Nickleby, "that things should have come to such a pass as this!"

"Who speaks in a tone, as if I had done wrong, and brought disgrace on them?" said Nicholas, looking round.

"Your mother, Sir," replied Ralph, motioning towards her.

"Whose ears have been poisoned by you," said Nicholas; "by you —you, who under pretence of deserving the thanks she poured upon you, heaped every insult, wrong, and indignity, upon my head. You, who sent me to a den where sordid cruelty, worthy of yourself, runs wanton, and youthful misery stalks precocious; where the lightness of childhood shrinks into the heaviness of age, and its every promise blights, and withers as it grows. I call Heaven to witness," said Nicholas, looking eagerly round, "that I have seen all this, and that *that* man knows it."

"Refute these calumnies," said Kate, "and be more patient, so that you may give them no advantage. Tell us what you really did, and show that they are untrue."

" Of what do they—or of what does he accuse me?" said Nicholas.

" First, of attacking your master, and being within an ace of qualifying yourself to be tried for murder," interposed Ralph. " I speak
plainly, young man, bluster as you will."

" I interfered," said Nicholas, " to save a miserable wretched creature
from the vilest and most degrading cruelty. In so doing I inflicted
such punishment upon a wretch as he will not readily forget, though
far less than he deserved from me. If the same scene were renewed
before me now, I would take the same part ; but I would strike harder
and heavier, and brand him with such marks as he should carry to his
grave, go to it when he would."

" You hear?" said Ralph, turning to Mrs. Nickleby. " Penitence,
this !"

" Oh dear me !" cried Mrs. Nickleby, " I don't know what to think,
I really don't."

" Do not speak just now, mama, I entreat you," said Kate. " Dear
Nicholas, I only tell you, that you may know what wickedness can
prompt, but they accuse you of—a ring is missing, and they dare to
say that——"

" The woman," said Nicholas, haughtily, " the wife of the fellow
from whom these charges come, dropped—as I suppose—a worthless
ring among some clothes of mine, early in the morning on which I left
the house. At least, I know that she was in the bed-room where they
lay, struggling with an unhappy child, and that I found it when I
opened my bundle on the road. I returned it at once by coach, and
they have it now."

" I knew, I knew," said Kate, looking towards her uncle. " About
this boy, love, in whose company they say you left ?"

" That boy, a silly, helpless creature, from brutality and hard usage,
is with me now," rejoined Nicholas.

" You hear?" said Ralph, appealing to the mother again, " everything proved, even upon his own confession. Do you choose to restore
that boy, Sir ?"

" No, I do not," replied Nicholas.

" You do not ?" sneered Ralph.

" No," repeated Nicholas, " not to the man with whom I found
him. I would that I knew on whom he has the claim of birth : I
might wring something from his sense of shame, if he were dead to
every tie of nature."

" Indeed !" said Ralph. " Now, Sir, will you hear a word or two
from me ? "

" You can speak when and what you please," replied Nicholas,
embracing his sister. " I take little heed of what you say or threaten."

" Mighty well, Sir," retorted Ralph ; " but perhaps it may concern
others, who may think it worth their while to listen, and consider
what I tell them. I will address your mother, Sir, who knows the
world."

" Ah ! and I only too dearly wish I didn't," sobbed Mrs. Nickleby.

There really was no necessity for the good lady to be much distressed
upon this particular head, the extent of her worldly knowledge being,

to say the least, very questionable ; and so Ralph seemed to think, for
he smiled as she spoke.   He then glanced steadily at her and Nicholas
by turns, as he delivered himself in these words :—

    " Of what I have done, or what I meant to do, for you, ma'am, and
my niece, I say not one syllable.   I held out no promise, and leave
you to judge for yourself.   I hold out no threat now, but I say that this
boy, headstrong, wilful, and disorderly as he is, should not have one
penny of my money, or one crust of my bread, or one grasp of my hand,
to save him from the loftiest gallows in all Europe.   I will not meet
him, come where he comes, or hear his name.   I will not help him,
or those who help him.   With a full knowledge of what he brought
upon you by so doing, he has come back in his selfish sloth, to be an
aggravation of your wants, and a burden upon his sister's scanty wages.
I regret to leave you, and more to leave her, now, but I will not encourage this compound of meanness and cruelty, and, as I will not ask
you to renounce him, I see you no more."

    If Ralph had not known and felt his power in wounding those he
hated, his glances at Nicholas would have shown it him in all its
force, as he proceeded in the above address.   Innocent as the young
man was of all wrong, every artful insinuation stung, every well-con-
sidered sarcasm cut him to the quick, and when Ralph noted his pale
face and quivering lip, he hugged himself to mark how well he had
chosen the taunts best calculated to strike deep into a young and ardent
spirit.

    " I can't help it," cried Mrs. Nickleby, " I know you have been
very good to us, and meant to do a good deal for my dear daughter.
I am quite sure of that ; I know you did, and it was very kind of
you, having her at your house and all—and of course it would have
been a great thing for her, and for me too.   But I can't, you know,
brother-in-law, I can't renounce my own son, even if he has done all
you say he has—it's not possible, I couldn't do it ; so we must go to
rack and ruin, Kate, my dear.   I can bear it, I dare say."   Pouring
forth these, and a perfectly wonderful train of other disjointed expressions of regret, which no mortal power but Mrs. Nickleby's could ever
have strung together, that lady wrung her hands, and her tears fell faster.

    " Why do you say ' if Nicholas has done what they say he has,'
mama ? " asked Kate, with honest anger.   " You know he has not."

    " I don't know what to think, one way or other, my dear," said Mrs.
Nickleby ; " Nicholas is so violent, and your uncle has so much honest
composure, that I can only hear what he says, and not what Nicholas
does.   Never mind, don't let us talk any more about it.   We can go
to the Workhouse, or the Refuge for the Destitute, or the Magdalen
Hospital, I dare say ; and the sooner we go the better."   With this
extraordinary jumble of charitable institutions, Mrs. Nickleby again
gave way to her tears.

    " Stay," said Nicholas, as Ralph turned to go.   " You need not
leave this place, Sir, for it will be relieved of my presence in one
minute, and it will be long, very long, before I darken these doors again."

    " Nicholas," cried Kate, throwing herself on her brother's shoulder,
and clasping him in her arms, " do not say so.   My dear brother, you

Mr. Ralph Nickleby's "honest" composure.

will break my heart. Mama, speak to him. Do not mind her,
Nicholas; she does not mean it, you should know her better. Uncle,
somebody, for God's sake speak to him."

" I never meant, Kate," said Nicholas, tenderly, " I never meant to
stay among you; think better of me than to suppose it possible. I
may turn my back on this town a few hours sooner than I intended,
but what of that ? We shall not forget each other apart, and better
days will come when we shall part no more. Be a woman, Kate," he
whispered, proudly, " and do not make me one while *he* looks on."

" No, no, I will not," said Kate, eagerly, " but you will not leave
us. Oh! think of all the happy days we have had together, before
these terrible misfortunes came upon us ; of all the comfort and happiness of home, and the trials we have to bear now ; of our having no
protector under all the slights and wrongs that poverty so much favours,
and you cannot leave us to bear them alone, without one hand to
help us."

" You will be helped when I am away," replied Nicholas, hurriedly.
" I am no help to you, no protector ; I should bring you nothing but
sorrow, and want, and suffering. My own mother sees it, and her
fondness and fears for you point to the course that I should take. And
so all good angels bless you, Kate, till I can carry you to some home
of mine, where we may revive the happiness denied to us now, and
talk of these trials as of things gone by. Do not keep me here, but let
me go at once. There. Dear girl—dear girl."

The grasp which had detained him, relaxed, and Kate fainted in his
arms. Nicholas stooped over her for a few seconds, and placing her
gently in a chair, confided her to their honest friend.

" I need not entreat your sympathy," he said, wringing her hand,
" for I know your nature. You will never forget them."

He stepped up to Ralph, who remained in the same attitude which
he had preserved throughout the interview, and moved not a finger.

" Whatever step you take, Sir," he said, in a voice inaudible beyond
themselves, " I will keep a strict account of. I leave them to you, at
your desire. There will be a day of reckoning sooner or later, and it
will be a heavy one for you if they are wronged."

Ralph did not allow a muscle of his face to indicate that he heard
one word of this parting address. He hardly knew that it was concluded, and Mrs. Nickleby had scarcely made up her mind to detain
her son by force if necessary, when Nicholas was gone.

As he hurried through the streets to his obscure lodging, seeking to
keep pace, as it were, with the rapidity of the thoughts which crowded
upon him, many doubts and hesitations arose in his mind and almost
tempted him to return. But what would they gain by this ? Supposing he were to put Ralph Nickleby at defiance, and were even fortunate enough to obtain some small employment, his being with them
could only render their present condition worse, and might greatly im-
pair their future prospects, for his mother had spoken of some new
kindnesses towards Kate which she had not denied. " No," thought
Nicholas, " I have acted for the best."

But before he had gone five hundred yards, some other and different feeling would come upon him, and then he would lag again, and pulling his hat over his eyes, give way to the melancholy reflections which pressed thickly upon him.   To have committed no fault, and yet to be so entirely alone in the world ; to be separated from the only persons he loved, and to be proscribed like a criminal, when six months ago he had been surrounded by every comfort, and looked up to as the chief hope of his family—this was hard to bear.   He had not deserved it either. Well, there was comfort in that ; and poor Nicholas would brighten up again, to be again depressed, as his quickly-shifting thoughts presented every variety of light and shade before him.

Undergoing these alternations of hope and misgiving, which no one, placed in a situation of even ordinary trial, can fail to have experienced, Nicholas at length reached his poor room, where, no longer borne up by the excitement which had hitherto sustained him, but depressed by the revulsion of feeling it left behind, he threw himself on the bed, and turning his face to the wall, gave free vent to the emotions he had so long stifled.

He had not heard anybody enter, and was unconscious of the presence of Smike, until, happening to raise his head, he saw him standing at the upper end of the room, looking wistfully towards him.   He withdrew his eyes when he saw that he was observed, and affected to be busied with some scanty preparations for dinner.

" Well, Smike," said Nicholas, as cheerfully as he could speak, " let me hear what new acquaintances you have made this morning, or what new wonder you have found out in the compass of this street and the next one."

" No," said Smike, shaking his head mournfully ; " I must talk of something else to-day."

" Of what you like," replied Nicholas, good-humouredly.

" Of this ;" said Smike.   " I know you are unhappy, and have got into great trouble by bringing me away.   I ought to have known that, and stopped behind—I would, indeed, if I had thought it then.   You —you—are not rich : you have not enough for yourself, and I should not be here.   You grow," said the lad, laying his hand timidly on that of Nicholas, " you grow thinner every day ; your cheek is paler, and your eye more sunk.   Indeed I cannot bear to see you so, and think how I am burdening you.   I tried to go away to-day, but the thought of your kind face drew me back.   I could not leave you without a word."   The poor fellow could get no further, for his eyes filled with tears, and his voice was gone.

" The word which separates us," said Nicholas, grasping him heartily by the shoulder, " shall never be said by me, for you are my only comfort and stay.   I would not lose you now, for all the world could give.   The thought of you has upheld me through all I have endured to-day, and shall, through fifty times such trouble.   Give me your hand.   My heart is linked to yours.   We will journey from this place together, before the week is out.   What, if I am steeped in poverty ?   You lighten it, and we will be poor together."

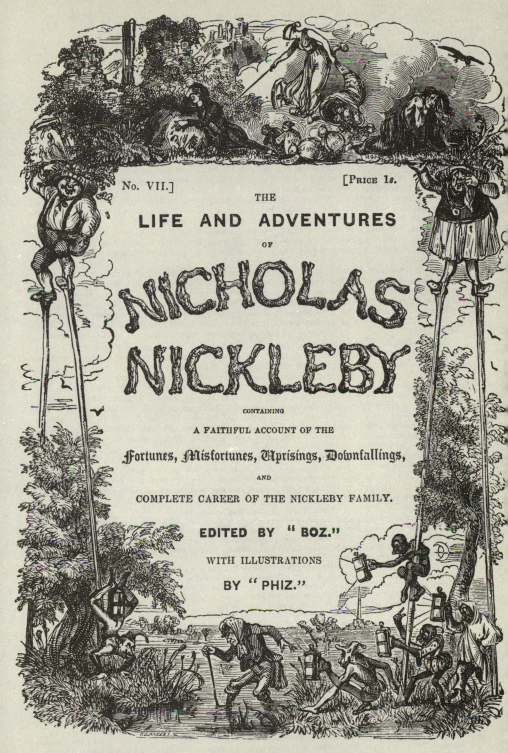

No. VII.]

[PRICE 1s.

THE

LIFE AND ADVENTURES

OF

NICHOLAS NICKLEBY

CONTAINING

A FAITHFUL ACCOUNT OF THE

Fortunes, Misfortunes, Uprisings, Downfallings,

AND

COMPLETE CAREER OF THE NICKLEBY FAMILY.

EDITED BY "BOZ."

WITH ILLUSTRATIONS

BY "PHIZ."

LONDON: CHAPMAN AND HALL, 186, STRAND.

SH COLLEGE OF HEALTH,
HAMILTON PLACE, NEW ROAD.

MORISON'S PILLS.

·····ES MORISON, Esq., President of the British College of Health.

St. Andrews, Norwich, Aug. 25, 1838.

SIR—Having lately witnessed a cure, almost as extraordinary as your own, from the use of Morison's Pills, I send you the particulars, which I think ought to be made public. The party I allude to is a respectable farmer; he had been suffering for years with violent palpitation of the heart, which, under medical treatment, got worse, and was at last pronounced to be an incurable case of ossification of the heart. To complete his despair of any relief, the doctor lent him a medical work, referring him to a part which pronounced his case beyond the reach of medicine. His own brother died of a similar complaint; and a gentleman in the same neighbourhood, under medical treatment, also died, who was opened, and from his case it was said that nothing that medical skill could devise would cure ossification of the heart.

Under the advice of the doctor and friends he gave up his farm, being assured that the least excitement from his servants or any other cause might prove fatal. Even the exertion of walking up stairs brought on the palpitation of the heart so violently, that he had to hold by the bed-post for some time before he could get his breath. In this state of utter despair he heard of Morison's Pills, and commenced with them in small doses; he felt their beneficial effect almost immediately at the seat of the disease. Notwithstanding, his wife said, "My dear, you hear the pills kill people; do give them up." But, as he was left to die by the doctors, he said "he could but die by the pills." He continued to take them in large and small doses, and, instead of death, is restored to good health · and, although in his 67th year, regrets that he has given up his farm.

I was in hopes that he would have published his case; he, however, objects to have his name made public, but will allow me to refer any one to him for the truth of the above, and much more than I have here stated. Through his recommendation two gentlemen have tried the pills for the same complaint, and have found great benefit, when every other means had failed. A gentleman in this county, who has been suffering under a complication of complaints for many years, under medical treatment, which at last ended in dropsy, after taking the pills a few months, is enjoying better health than he has done for the last 20 years. I remain, Sirs, yours respectfully, A. CHARLWOOD.

OBSERVATIONS.—The above forms a specimen of the cases which are treated by Morison's Pills; they may be termed "the incurables of the faculty." Were a census taken of the persons who have placed themselves under the Hygeian treatment, and the nature of their diseases, it most assuredly would appear that 99 out of every 100 had been given up as incurable by the faculty. Cases similar to the above are undeniable and convincing—they challenge inquiry. It is with such weapons that Hygeists take the field against the whole of the medical fraternity; not relying, as they do, on vain hypothesis, but on positive facts. They challenge the medical profession to contradict the theory on which they act, and they further challenge inquiry into the cases of cure effected under that theory. Had the Hygeists all the advantages of the medical profession, and was fairness the order of medical men, the contest might soon be decided; the day is not far distant, however, when the truth, notwithstanding all their efforts to the contrary, must be made manifest.

The following cases of cure by Morison's Pills have just been forwarded by Mr. Tothill, of Heavitree, Surgeon to the Exeter Hygeian Dispensary. With such undeniable facts constantly staring medical men in the face, it is not too harsh an expression when we say that the thousands who prematurely die every day under their treatment are short of being murdered, convinced as we are of the injurious and poisonous nature of their multifarious treatment.

MR. TOTHILL'S CASES FOR AUGUST 1838.

Mr. Wm. Kerswell's children, of the parish of Tedburn St Mary, seven miles from Exeter, one aged three years and a half, and the other fifteen months. These children took "Morison's Pills" previously, during, and after the small pox, and they did well. The small pox has prevailed greatly in that parish lately, and Mr. Kerswell's children had them in the natural way, and from their having been under the Hygeian treatment they have done better than any of the others in that neighbourhood.

James Sanders, aged 15, clerk to Mr. Avory, solicitor, Exeter, cured of an obstruction of the nostrils, which totally precluded his breathing through them, was thus afflicted for seven years : he is now in every respect in perfect health.

Sarah Trevillian, aged 55, of Exwick, two miles from Exeter, cured of scorbutic humour, with erysipelatous inflammation of many years' standing; she is now in perfect health.

Mr. Thos. Downing, of Heavitree, aged 27, cured of bilious fever.

Jane Goldsworthy, aged 52, of Heavitree, cured of chronic cough, with great general debility, of many years' standing.

Mary Hatterly, aged 45, of Heavitree, cured of chronic rheumatism, with general debility, of upwards of six years' standing.

John London, of the parish of Whimple, is a mail horse keeper, cured of consumption.

The Rev. Mr. Moxlay, of Heavitree, cured of an ulcerated leg, other treatment having failed.

Mr. Thos. Tuboy, Exeter, cured of quotidian ague of long standing, after the most skilful medical treatment having failed.

Mr. P. H. Wrighton, Exeter, cured of a severe bilious fever.

Mrs. Massis, Exeter, cured of chronic hepatitis, accompanied with general deranged state of the whole system, of many years' standing, after having been under the most skilful medical treatment.

(Signed) RICHARD TOTHILL, M.R.C.S.,
And Surgeon to the Exeter Hygeian Dispensary, August 1838.

The following is a list of the foreign general agents duly appointed by the British College of Health :— General Agent for the United States of America—Dr. George Taylor, 6½, Wall-street, New York; Mr. Thomas Gardner, Dacre's-lane, Calcutta, General Agent for India; Mr. Anderson, St. John's, New Brunswick; Mr. James Cochrane, Guernsey; Mr. Da Costa, Curaçoa; Mr. Charles Edwards, Sydney, New South Wales; Mr. V. Formosa, Malta; Mr. E. Lenington, Barbadoes; Messrs. J. Legge and Co., Quebec; Mr. Lobe, Cuba; Lieutenant J. M'Kinnon, Cape Breton, North America; Mr. T. H. Roberts, Church-street, Gibraltar; Messrs. Stiffel and Co., Odessa; Dr. Tollhausen, Jassy, Bucharest, Constantinople, and the whole of Turkey; Mr. H. W. Wells, British Guiana, George Town, Demerara.

No. VII.—OCTOBER 1, 1838.

THE
NICKLEBY ADVERTISER.

ADVANTAGEOUS BOOK SUPPLIES.
TO FAMILIES AND BOOK SOCIETIES
THROUGHOUT ENGLAND, SCOTLAND, AND IRELAND.

TERMS
OF THE
NEW SYSTEM AT BULL'S LIBRARY,
19, HOLLES STREET, FOUR DOORS FROM CAVENDISH SQUARE.
ESTABLISHED BY EDWARD BULL, LIBRARIAN.

THE SUBSCRIPTION FOR ONE FAMILY IS £6. 6s. THE YEAR—

Which entitles the Subscriber to 12 Volumes at a time in Town, and 24 in the Country, one half of which can be New Publications, and the remainder Books chosen from the Catalogues; or, if preferred, the Subscriber may order his supplies WHOLLY OF THE NEW AND VALUABLE PUBLICATIONS, for Four Guineas more the Year,—and they can be exchanged as often as desired. Every Subscriber is also entitled to have,—as a return, at the close of each Year,—Two Guineas' worth of any of the NEW WORKS TO KEEP, and is provided with Catalogues and Boxes free of expense.—THE SUBSCRIPTION TO BE PAID IN ADVANCE.

*** Two or more neighbouring Families, in the Country, are allowed to join in the above Subscription, by paying One Guinea for each extra Family. The regulations are the same as for Book Societies.

TERMS FOR BOOK SOCIETIES.

Societies Paying £10. 10s. the Year, are entitled to 30 vols. at a time, including, *if desired*, three Magazines and Reviews.

Societies Paying £12. 12s. the Year, are entitled to 36 vols. at a time, including four Magazines and Reviews.

Societies Paying £14. 14s. the Year, are entitled to 42 vols. at a time, including five Magazines and Reviews.

Societies Paying £16. 16s. the Year, are entitled to 48 vols. at a time, including six Magazines and Reviews.

*** Societies, however large, can be supplied at the same ratio as the above, which has been calculated so as to allow each Member to have *not less* than Three Volumes at all times in his possession.

More than half the Collection can be New Publications, and the remainder to be selected from other Modern or Standard Works, as described in the Library Catalogues and Select Lists. The supplies can be exchanged as often as desired.

REGULATIONS.

1. The Name and Address of one Party only are required at the Library.
2. THE SUBSCRIPTION TO BE PAID IN ADVANCE.
3. The expense of Carriage to and from the Library, Postage, &c. to be defrayed by Subscribers; but the Library Boxes and Catalogues are provided for them free of expense.

The preceding Terms E. BULL has endeavoured to give so fully and satisfactorily, that parties at remote distances from London, can at once commence subscribing, without the delay, trouble, and expense attending a correspondence. He also regularly publishes SELECT LISTS, so as to include all the valuable and popular New Publications, IN EVERY DEPARTMENT OF LITERATURE, of which nearly Eight Hundred are published annually. This List can be sent by post as a single letter, to assist Subscribers in making up their orders; but, to save time, E. BULL, on receiving intimation of the kind of Works desired, will take upon himself to form the first collection, and forward it at once, with the complete Catalogues of the Library.

MANUSCRIPTS FOR PUBLICATION.

The Nobility, Gentry, and Authors in general, are reminded that the present is the most opportune season for having their Manuscripts printed and published, which can be done with every advantage, under the active management of an experienced publisher. If required, the MSS. are prepared and conducted through the press by an able and practised writer. The Publisher can generally ensure among his connexions the sale of many copies of an edition for the party, who can receive the proceeds of his publication monthly. Apply (if by letter, post paid) to Mr. BULL, Publisher and Librarian, 19, Holles-street, London.

GOWLAND'S LOTION.

Perhaps there is no period of the Year when care is so requisite for the preservation of the Skin as the present. AUTUMN, with an essential change of temperature, induces also, in many habits, a return of Cutaneous irritation; and with others, the tendency to Impurities of this nature, alike unfavourable to Personal Appearance, and subversive of Agrémens, highly valued in Society. The entire SAFETY with which this elegant preparation is resorted to, as an effectual remedy in these cases, will therefore be found of great practical advantage, and especially so

IN THE DEPARTMENT OF THE TOILET,

Where the Lotion, recommended by the experience of nearly a CENTURY, continues to be the only article extant, upon which reliance may be placed, as a congenial preservative of a pure surface, and elastic state of the Skin, and sustainer of a pleasing delicacy and freshness of the Complexion.

GOWLAND'S LOTION has the Name of the Proprietor, **ROBERT SHAW, 33, QUEEN STREET, CHEAPSIDE, LONDON,** Engraved on the Government Stamp, by whom only (as Successor to the late Mrs. Vincent) this celebrated article is faithfully prepared from the original MS. Recipe of the late Doctor Gowland. Prices 2s. 9d., 5s. 6d., quarts 8s. 6d. The popular work, "The Theory of Beauty," accompanies each genuine package.

SHAW'S MINDORA OIL.

This admired exotic stays the falling of weak and attenuated Hair, and restores a vigorous growth, glossy and curling: Mindora Oil has also the remarkable peculiarity of being rendered in a state of NATIVE purity and fragrance, without CHEMICAL or other Admixture, and therefore differs in every requisite property from all COLOURED and factitious Compounds, as ensuring CLEANLINESS, preservation of the true COLOUR; and will be found, by both sexes, the most acceptable and effective article for every purpose connected with the Cultivation and Embellishment of the Hair.

Prepared for the Toilet, by the Proprietor, ROBERT SHAW, 33, QUEEN STREET, CHEAP-SIDE, LONDON, in Bottles at 3s., 5s. 6d., and in Stoppered Bottles at 10s. 6d., bearing his Signature on the label and wrapper. A Practical Treatise on the Hair accompanies each Package.

Sold as above, and by Sanger, Hannay, Oxford Street; Atkinsons, Rigge, Gattie & Co., Bond Street; Hendrie, Pell, Bateman, Low, Prout, Strand; Mattras, Fleet Street; Rigge, Butler, 4, Cheapside; Johnston, Cornhill; and by most respectable Perfumers and Medicine Venders.

AS SUPPLIED TO THE ROYAL TABLE.

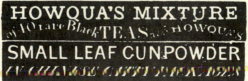

HOWQUA'S MIXTURE
of 40 rare Black TEAS, all HOWQUA'S
SMALL LEAF GUNPOWDER

TESTIMONIAL FROM DR. JAMES JOHNSON IN FAVOUR OF CAPTAIN PIDDING'S "HOWQUA'S MIXTURE TEA."

To Captain Pidding, Proprietor of the "Howqua's Mixture" Tea.

"Sir,—Ever since your 'Howqua's Mixture' Tea was first introduced to the public, myself and family have drunk it—indeed *only* it, and I have no hesitation in saying that I consider it superior to all others.—I am, Sir, yours, &c.

"8, Suffolk Place, Pall Mall.　　　(Signed)　　　Jas. Johnson, M.D."

The above copy of a letter, voluntarily addressed to Captain Pidding, the *sole proprietor* of the *only real* and *genuine* "Howqua's Mixture" and "Howqua's Small Leaf Gunpowder" Teas, by Dr. James Johnson, the celebrated physician, author of numerous works on Indigestion, &c., and Physician to his late Majesty, carries its own argument with it, for where a physician of such known eminence not only recommends to his numerous patients a particular tea, as superior to any other, but adds that "*he and his family consume it in preference to all others,*" it is impossible that any additional proofs of its superior excellence can strengthen such a recommendation.

The more rigid economist will also find that "Howqua's Mixture" tea, from its great strength, is cheaper at 6s. per lb. than any other tea, at 5s. or even 4s. per lb.

The teas consist of one kind of black, "Howqua's Mixture," of 40 rare teas all black, at 6s. per lb., being 8s. the catty package; one kind of green, "Howqua's Small Leaf Gunpowder," at 8s. 7½d. per lb., being 11s. 6d. the catty package. Both are sold in Chinese catty packages, containing 1 lb. and one-third net of tea, by C. Verry, Swiss Confectioner, 218, Regent Street, and T. Littlejohn and Son, Scotch Confectioners, 77, King William Street, City, whose names as the *sole London Agents* are upon every *genuine* catty. This should be particularly observed, as the unexampled celebrity of these two teas has induced many unprincipled grocers, tea-dealers, and others, to attempt a fraud upon the public by offering spurious imitations of the packages.

THE FOLLOWING

SPLENDID ANNUALS FOR 1839,

UNDER THE SUPERINTENDENCE OF

MR. CHARLES HEATH,

WILL APPEAR IN THE COURSE OF OCTOBER AND NOVEMBER.

I.

HEATH'S PICTURESQUE ANNUAL:

A HISTORY AND DESCRIPTION OF VERSAILLES.

BY LEITCH RITCHIE, ESQ.

With 20 Illustrations, comprising, among other highly-finished Works of Art, the following interesting subjects :—

VIEWS of the INTERIOR of the CHATEAU THEATRE during a Representation.	Whole-length PORTRAITS of Madame DE MAINTENON, Madlle. LA VALLIERE, Madame DE MONTESPAN, and MARIE ANTOINETTE, with accurate delineations of the Costume of their respective periods.
THE GALLERY of BATTLES.	
LA GALERIE des GLACES.	
THE INTERIOR of the CHAPEL.	

Super-royal 8vo, 1*l*. 1*s*. elegantly bound ; India Proofs, 2*l*. 2*s*.

II.

THE KEEPSAKE.

EDITED BY F. MANSELL REYNOLDS, ESQ.

Embellished with Engravings, including an exquisite Portrait of the Countess GUICCIOLI, after a Picture, painted expressly for " The KEEPSAKE," by CHALON.

Super-royal 8vo, 1*l*. 1*s*. ; India Proofs, 2*l*. 12*s*. 6*d*.

III.

THE BOOK OF BEAUTY.

EDITED BY THE COUNTESS OF BLESSINGTON.

The Engravings will consist entirely of richly-executed Portraits of English Nobility and Persons of Fashion ; viz.—

THE DUCHESS OF SUTHERLAND (Frontispiece).	MRS. MABERLY.
LADY FANNY COWPER.	MRS. MOUNTJOY MARTIN.
LADY W. STANHOPE.	MISS PURVESS.
LADY MAHON.	LADY FITZHARRIS.
	&c. &c.

Super-royal 8vo, 1*l*. 1*s*. elegantly bound ; India Proofs, 2*l*. 2*s*. 6*d*.

IV.

GEMS OF BEAUTY:

Displayed in a Series of Twelve highly-finished Engravings, from designs by eminent Artists ; with Poetical Illustrations by the COUNTESS OF BLESSINGTON.

Imperial 4to, 1*l*. 11*s*. 6*d*. richly bound in silk.

V.

PORTRAITS OF THE CHILDREN OF THE NOBILITY.

A Second Series of costly Engravings, from Drawings by CHALON, BOSTOCK, and other distinguished Artists.

EDITED BY MRS. FAIRLIE.

Royal 4to, 31*s*. 6*d*. handsomely bound ; Proofs on India Paper, 3*l*. 3*s*. morocco.

VI.

BEAUTY'S COSTUME.

SECOND SERIES.

Containing Twelve beautiful Engravings of Female Figures, in the Costume of various Times and Nations, after Designs by eminent Artists ; with descriptive Letter-press,

BY LEITCH RITCHIE, ESQ.

4to, 21*s*. elegantly bound ; or coloured in imitation of the Drawings, 2*l*. 2*s*.

LONDON : LONGMAN, ORME, AND CO.

CHAPTER XXI.

MADAME MANTALINI FINDS HERSELF IN A SITUATION OF SOME DIF-
FICULTY, AND MISS NICKLEBY FINDS HERSELF IN NO SITUATION
AT ALL.

THE agitation she had undergone rendered Kate Nickleby unable to
resume her duties at the dress-maker's for three days, at the expiration
of which interval she betook herself at the accustomed hour, and with
languid steps, to the temple of fashion where Madame Mantalini reigned
paramount and supreme.

The ill will of Miss Knag had lost nothing of its virulence in the
interval, for the young ladies still scrupulously shrank from all companionship with their denounced associate; and when that exemplary
female arrived a few minutes afterwards, she was at no pains to conceal
the displeasure with which she regarded Kate's return.

" Upon my word! " said Miss Knag, as the satellites flocked round
to relieve her of her bonnet and shawl; " I should have thought some
people would have had spirit enough to stop away altogether, when
they know what an incumbrance their presence is to right-minded
persons. But it's a queer world; oh! it's a queer world! "

Miss Knag having passed this comment on the world, in the tone in
which most people do pass comments on the world when they are out
of temper, that is to say, as if they by no means belonged to it, concluded by heaving a sigh, wherewith she seemed meekly to compassionate the wickedness of mankind.

The attendants were not slow to echo the sigh, and Miss Knag was
apparently on the eve of favouring them with some further moral
reflections, when the voice of Madame Mantalini, conveyed through the
speaking-tube, ordered Miss Nickleby up stairs to assist in the arrangement of the show-room; a distinction which caused Miss Knag to toss
her head so much, and bite her lips so hard, that her powers of conversation were for the time annihilated.

" Well, Miss Nickleby, child," said Madame Mantalini, when Kate
presented herself; " are you quite well again ? "

" A great deal better, thank you," replied Kate.

" I wish I could say the same," remarked Madame Mantalini, seating
herself with an air of weariness.

" Are you ill ? " asked Kate. " I am very sorry for that."

" Not exactly ill, but worried, child—worried," rejoined Madame.

" I am still more sorry to hear that," said Kate, gently. " Bodily
illness is more easy to bear than mental."

" Ah! and it's much easier to talk than to bear either," said Madame,
rubbing her nose with much irritability of manner. " There, get to
your work, child, and put the things in order, do."

While Kate was wondering within herself what these symptoms of

O

unusual vexation portended, Mr. Mantalini put the tips of his whiskers, and by degrees his head, through the half-opened door, and cried in a soft voice—

" Is my life and soul there ? "

" No," replied his wife.

" How can it say so, when it is blooming in the front room like a little rose in a demnition flower-pot ? " urged Mantalini. " May its poppet come in and talk ? "

" Certainly not," replied Madame ; " you know I never allow you here. Go along."

The poppet, however, encouraged perhaps by the relenting tone of this reply, ventured to rebel, and, stealing into the room, made towards Madame Mantalini on tiptoe, blowing her a kiss as he came along.

" Why will it vex itself, and twist its little face into bewitching nut-crackers ? " said Mantalini, putting his left arm round the waist of his life and soul, and drawing her towards him with his right.

" Oh ! I can't bear you," replied his wife.

" Not—eh, not bear me ! " exclaimed Mantalini. " Fibs, fibs. It couldn't be. There's not a woman alive that could tell me such a thing to my face—to my own face." Mr. Mantalini stroked his chin as he said this, and glanced complacently at an opposite mirror.

" Such destructive extravagance," reasoned his wife, in a low tone.

" All in its joy at having gained such a lovely creature, such a little Venus, such a demd enchanting, bewitching, engrossing, captivating little Venus," said Mantalini.

" See what a situation you have placed me in ! " urged Madame.

" No harm will come, no harm shall come to its own darling," rejoined Mr. Mantalini. " It is all over, there will be nothing the matter ; money shall be got in, and if it don't come in fast enough, old Nickleby shall stump up again, or have his jugular separated if he dares to vex and hurt the little——"

" Hush ! " interposed Madame. " Don't you see ? "

Mr. Mantalini, who, in his eagerness to make up matters with his wife, had overlooked, or feigned to overlook Miss Nickleby hitherto, took the hint, and laying his finger on his lip, sunk his voice still lower. There was then a great deal of whispering, during which Madame Mantalini appeared to make reference more than once to certain debts incurred by Mr. Mantalini previous to her coverture ; and also to an unexpected outlay of money in payment of the aforesaid debts ; and furthermore, to certain agreeable weaknesses on that gentleman's part, such as gaming, wasting, idling, and a tendency to horseflesh ; each of which matters of accusation Mr. Mantalini disposed of by one kiss or more, as its relative importance demanded, and the upshot of it all was, that Madame Mantalini was in raptures with him, and that they went up stairs to breakfast.

Kate busied herself in what she had to do, and was silently arranging the various articles of decoration in the best taste she could display, when she started to hear a strange man's voice in the room ; and started again to observe, on looking round, that a white hat, and a red neckerchief, and a broad round face, and a large head, and part of a green coat, were in the room too.

"Don't alarm yourself, Miss," said the proprietor of these appearances. "I say; this here's the mantie-making con-sarn, a'nt it?"

"Yes," rejoined Kate, greatly astonished. "What did you want?"

The stranger answered not; but first looking back, as though to beckon to some unseen person outside, came very deliberately into the room and was closely followed by a little man in brown, very much the worse for wear, who brought with him a mingled fumigation of stale tobacco and fresh onions. The clothes of this gentleman were much bespeckled with flue; and his shoes, stockings, and nether garments, from his heels to the waist buttons of his coat inclusive, were profusely embroidered with splashes of mud, caught a fortnight previous—before the setting-in of the fine weather.

Kate's very natural impression was, that these engaging individuals had called with the view of possessing themselves unlawfully of any portable articles that chanced to strike their fancy. She did not attempt to disguise her apprehensions, and made a move towards the door.

"Wait a minnit," said the man in the green coat, closing it softly, and standing with his back against it. "This is a unpleasant bisness. Vere's your govvernor?"

"My what—did you say?" asked Kate, trembling; for she thought 'governor' might be slang for watch or money.

"Mister Muntlehiney," said the man. "Wot's come of him? Is he at home?"

"He is above stairs, I believe," replied Kate, a little reassured by this inquiry. "Do you want him?"

"No," replied the visitor. "I don't ezactly want him, if it's made a favour on. You can jist give him that 'ere card, and tell him if he wants to speak to *me*, and save trouble, here I am, that's all."

With these words the stranger put a thick square card into Kate's hand, and turning to his friend remarked, with an easy air, "that the rooms was a good high pitch;" to which the friend assented, adding, by way of illustration, "that there was lots of room for a little boy to grow up a man in either on 'em, vithout much fear of his ever bringing his head into contract vith the ceiling."

After ringing the bell which would summon Madame Mantalini, Kate glanced at the card, and saw that it displayed the name of "Scaley," together with some other information to which she had not had time to refer, when her attention was attracted by Mr. Scaley himself, who, walking up to one of the cheval glasses, gave it a hard poke in the centre with his stick, as coolly as if it had been made of cast iron.

"Good plate this here, Tix," said Mr. Scaley to his friend.

"Ah!" rejoined Mr. Tix, placing the marks of his four fingers, and a duplicate impression of his thumb on a piece of sky-blue silk; "and this here article warn't made for nothing, mind you."

From the silk Mr. Tix transferred his admiration to some elegant

o 2

articles of wearing apparel, while Mr. Scaley adjusted his neckcloth at leisure before the glass, and afterwards, aided by its reflection, proceeded to the minute consideration of a pimple on his chin: in which absorbing occupation he was yet engaged when Madame Mantalini entering the room, uttered an exclamation of surprise which roused him.

" Oh! Is this the missis?" inquired Scaley.

" It is Madame Mantalini," said Kate.

" Then," said Mr. Scaley, producing a small document from his pocket and unfolding it very slowly, " this is a writ of execution, and if it's not conwenient to settle we'll go over the house at wunst, please, and take the inwentory."

Poor Madame Mantalini wrung her hands for grief, and rung the bell for her husband; which done, she fell into a chair and a fainting fit simultaneously. The professional gentlemen, however, were not at all discomposed by this event, for Mr. Scaley, leaning upon a stand on which a handsome dress was displayed (so that his shoulders appeared above it in nearly the same manner as the shoulders of the lady for whom it was designed would have done if she had had it on), pushed his hat on one side and scratched his head with perfect unconcern, while his friend Mr. Tix, taking that opportunity for a general survey of the apartment preparatory to entering upon business, stood with his inventory-book under his arm and his hat in his hand, mentally occupied in putting a price upon every object within his range of vision.

Such was the posture of affairs when Mr. Mantalini hurried in, and as that distinguished specimen had had a pretty extensive intercourse with Mr. Scaley's fraternity in his bachelor days, and was, besides, very far from being taken by surprise on the present agitating occasion, he merely shrugged his shoulders, thrust his hands down to the bottom of his pockets, elevated his eyebrows, whistled a bar or two, swore an oath or two, and, sitting astride upon a chair, put the best face upon the matter with great composure and decency.

" What's the demd total?" was the first question he asked.

" Fifteen hundred and twenty-seven pound, four and ninepence ha'penny," replied Mr. Scaley, without moving a limb.

" The halfpenny be demd," said Mr. Mantalini, impatiently.

" By all means if you vish it," retorted Mr. Scaley; " and the ninepence too."

" It don't matter to us if the fifteen hundred and twenty-seven pound went along with it, that I know on," observed Mr. Tix.

" Not a button," said Scaley.

" Well;" said the same gentleman, after a pause, " Wot's to be done —anythink? Is it only a small crack, or a out-and-out smash? A break-up of the constitootion is it—werry good. Then Mr. Tom Tix, esk-vire, you must inform your angel wife and lovely family as you won't sleep at home for three nights to come, along of being in possession here. Wot's the good of the lady a fretting herself?" continued Mr. Scaley, as Madame Mantalini sobbed. " A good half of wot's here isn't paid for I des-say, and wot a consolation oughtn't that to be to her feelings!"

The Professional Gentlemen at Madame Mantalinis.

With these remarks, combining great pleasantry with sound moral encouragement under difficulties, Mr. Scaley proceeded to take the inventory, in which delicate task he was materially assisted by the uncommon tact and experience of Mr. Tix, the broker.

" My cup of happiness's sweetener," said Mantalini, approaching his wife with a penitent air ; " will you listen to me for two minutes ?"

" Oh! don't speak to me," replied his wife, sobbing. " You have ruined me, and that's enough."

Mr. Mantalini, who had doubtless well considered his part, no sooner heard these words pronounced in a tone of grief and severity, than he recoiled several paces, assumed an expression of consuming mental agony, rushed headlong from the room, and was soon afterwards heard to slam the door of an up-stairs dressing-room with great violence.

" Miss Nickleby," cried Madame Mantalini, when this sound met her ear, " make haste for Heaven's sake, he will destroy himself! I spoke unkindly to him, and he cannot bear it from me. Alfred, my darling Alfred."

With such exclamations she hurried up stairs, followed by Kate ; who, although she did not quite participate in the fond wife's apprehensions, was a little flurried nevertheless. The dressing-room door being hastily flung open, Mr. Mantalini was disclosed to view with his shirt-collar symmetrically thrown back, putting a fine edge to a breakfast knife by means of his razor strop.

" Ah !" cried Mr. Mantalini, " interrupted !" and whisk went the breakfast knife into Mr. Mantalini's dressing-gown pocket, while Mr. Mantalini's eyes rolled wildly, and his hair floating in wild disorder, mingled with his whiskers.

" Alfred," cried his wife, flinging her arms about him, " I didn't mean to say it, I didn't mean to say it."

" Ruined !" cried Mr. Mantalini. " Have I brought ruin upon the best and purest creature that ever blessed a demnition vagabond! Demmit, let me go." At this crisis of his ravings Mr. Mantalini made a pluck at the breakfast knife, and being restrained by his wife's grasp, attempted to dash his head against the wall—taking very good care to be at least six feet from it, however.

" Compose yourself, my own angel," said Madame. " It was nobody's fault ; it was mine as much as yours, we shall do very well yet. Come, Alfred, come."

Mr. Mantalini did not think proper to come to all at once ; but after calling several times for poison, and requesting some lady or gentleman to blow his brains out, gentler feelings came upon him, and he wept pathetically. In this softened frame of mind he did not oppose the capture of the knife—which, to tell the truth, he was rather glad to be rid of, as an inconvenient and dangerous article for a skirt pocket—and finally he suffered himself to be led away by his affectionate partner.

After a delay of two or three hours, the young ladies were informed that their services would be dispensed with until further notice, and at the expiration of two days the name of Mantalini appeared in the list of bankrupts : Miss Nickleby receiving an intimation per post on

the same morning, that the business would be in future carried on under
the name of Miss Knag, and that her assistance would no longer be
required—a piece of intelligence with which Mrs. Nickleby was no
sooner made acquainted, than that good lady declared she had expected it all along, and cited divers unknown occasions on which she
had prophesied to that precise effect.

" And I say again," remarked Mrs. Nickleby (who, it is scarcely
necessary to observe, had never said so before), " I say again, that a
milliner's and dress-maker's is the very last description of business, Kate,
that you should have thought of attaching yourself to.   I don't make it
a reproach to you, my love; but still I will say, that if you had consulted your own mother——"

" Well, well, mama," said Kate, mildly ; " what would you recommend now ? "

" Recommend !" cried Mrs. Nickleby, " isn't it obvious, my dear,
that of all occupations in this world for a young lady situated as you
are, that of companion to some amiable lady is the very thing for
which your education, and manners, and personal appearance, and
everything else, exactly qualify you?   Did you never hear your poor
dear papa speak of the young lady who was the daughter of the old
lady who boarded in the same house that he boarded in once, when he
was a bachelor—what was her name again ?   I know it began with a
B, and ended with a g, but whether it was Waters or—no it couldn't
have been that either; but whatever her name was, don't you know
that that young lady went as companion to a married lady who died
soon afterwards, and that she married the husband, and had one of the
finest little boys that the medical man had ever seen—all within eighteen
months ?"

Kate knew perfectly well that this torrent of favourable recollection
was occasioned by some opening, real or imaginary, which her mother
had discovered in the companionship walk of life.   She therefore waited
very patiently until all reminiscences and anecdotes, bearing or not
bearing upon the subject, had been exhausted, and at last ventured to
inquire what discovery had been made.   The truth then came out.
Mrs. Nickleby had that morning had a yesterday newspaper of the
very first respectability from the public-house where the porter came
from, and in this yesterday's newspaper was an advertisement, couched
in the purest and most grammatical English, announcing that a married
lady was in want of a genteel young person as companion, and that
the married lady's name and address were to be known on application
at a certain library at the west end of the town, therein mentioned.

" And I say," exclaimed Mrs. Nickleby, laying the paper down in
triumph, " that if your uncle don't object, it's well worth the trial."

Kate was too sick at heart, after the rough jostling she had already
had with the world, and really cared too little at the moment what
fate was reserved for her, to make any objection.   Mr. Ralph Nickleby
offered none, but on the contrary highly approved of the suggestion ;
neither did he express any great surprise at Madame Mantalini's sudden
failure, indeed it would have been strange if he had, inasmuch as it

had been procured and brought about chiefly by himself. So the name and address were obtained without loss of time, and Miss Nickleby and her mama went off in quest of Mrs. Wititterly, of Cadogan Place, Sloane Street, that same forenoon.

Cadogan Place is the one slight bond that joins two great extremes ; it is the connecting link between the aristocratic pavements of Belgrave Square and the barbarism of Chelsea. It is in Sloane Street, but not of it. The people in Cadogan Place look down upon Sloane Street, and think Brompton low. They affect fashion too, and wonder where the New Road is. Not that they claim to be on precisely the same footing as the high folks of Belgrave Square and Grosvenor Place, but that they stand with reference to them rather in the light of those illegitimate children of the great who are content to boast of their connexions, although their connexions disavow them. Wearing as much as they can of the airs and semblances of loftiest rank, the people of Cadogan Place have the realities of middle station. It is the conductor which communicates to the inhabitants of regions beyond its limit, the shock of pride of birth and rank, which it has not within itself, but derives from a fountain-head beyond ; or, like the ligament which unites the Siamese twins, it contains something of the life and essence of two distinct bodies, and yet belongs to neither.

Upon this doubtful ground lived Mrs. Wititterly, and at Mrs. Wititterly's door Kate Nickleby knocked with trembling hand. The door was opened by a big footman with his head floured, or chalked, or painted in some way (it didn't look genuine powder), and the big footman, receiving the card of introduction, gave it to a little page ; so little indeed that his body would not hold, in ordinary array, the number of small buttons which are indispensable to a page's costume, and they were consequently obliged to be stuck on four abreast. This young gentleman took the card up-stairs on a salver, and pending his return, Kate and her mother were shown into a dining-room of rather dirty and shabby aspect, and so comfortably arranged as to be adapted to almost any purpose except eating and drinking.

Now, in the ordinary course of things and according to all authentic descriptions of high life, as set forth in books, Mrs. Wititterly ought to have been in her *boudoir*, but whether it was that Mr. Wititterly was at that moment shaving himself in the *boudoir* or what not, certain it is that Mrs. Wititterly gave audience in the drawing-room, where was everything proper and necessary, including curtains and furniture coverings of a roseate hue, to shed a delicate bloom on Mrs. Wititterly's complexion, and a little dog to snap at strangers' legs for Mrs. Wititterly's amusement, and the afore-mentioned page, to hand chocolate for Mrs. Wititterly's refreshment.

The lady had an air of sweet insipidity, and a face of engaging paleness ; there was a faded look about her, and about the furniture, and about the house altogether. She was reclining on a sofa in such a very unstudied attitude, that she might have been taken for an actress all ready for the first scene in a ballet, and only waiting for the drop curtain to go up.

" Place chairs."

The page placed them.

" Leave the room, Alphonse."

The page left it; but if ever there were an Alphonse who carried plain Bill in his face and figure, that page was the boy.

" I have ventured to call, ma'am," said Kate, after a few seconds of awkward silence, " from having seen your advertisement."

" Yes," replied Mrs. Wititterly, " one of my people put it in the paper.—Yes."

" I thought, perhaps," said Kate, modestly, " that if you had not already made a final choice, you would forgive my troubling you with an application."

" Yes," drawled Mrs. Wititterly again.

" If you have already made a selection——"

" Oh dear no," interrupted the lady, " I am not so easily suited. I really don't know what to say. You have never been a companion before, have you?"

Mrs. Nickleby, who had been eagerly watching her opportunity, came dexterously in before Kate could reply. " Not to any stranger, ma'am," said the good lady; " but she has been a companion to me for some years. I am her mother, ma'am."

" Oh!" said Mrs. Wititterly, " I apprehend you."

" I assure you, ma'am," said Mrs. Nickleby, " that I very little thought at one time that it would be necessary for my daughter to go out into the world at all, for her poor dear papa was an independent gentleman, and would have been at this moment if he had but listened in time to my constant entreaties and——"

" Dear mama," said Kate, in a low voice.

" My dear Kate, if you will allow me to speak," said Mrs. Nickleby, " I shall take the liberty of explaining to this lady——"

" I think it is almost unnecessary, mama."

And notwithstanding all the frowns and winks with which Mrs. Nickleby intimated that she was going to say something which would clench the business at once, Kate maintained her point by an expressive look, and for once Mrs. Nickleby was stopped upon the very brink of an oration.

" What are your accomplishments?" asked Mrs. Wititterly, with her eyes shut.

Kate blushed as she mentioned her principal acquirements, and Mrs. Nickleby checked them all off, one by one, on her fingers, having calculated the number before she came out. Luckily the two calculations agreed, so Mrs. Nickleby had no excuse for talking.

" You are a good temper?" asked Mrs. Wititterly, opening her eyes for an instant, and shutting them again.

" I hope so," rejoined Kate.

" And have a highly respectable reference for everything, have you?"

Kate replied that she had, and laid her uncle's card upon the table.

" Have the goodness to draw your chair a little nearer, and let me look at you," said Mrs. Wititterly; " I am so very near-sighted that I can't quite discern your features."

Kate complied, though not without some embarrassment, with this request, and Mrs. Wititterly took a languid survey of her countenance, which lasted some two or three minutes.

"I like your appearance," said that lady, ringing a little bell. "Alphonse, request your master to come here."

The page disappeared on this errand, and after a short interval, during which not a word was spoken on either side, opened the door for an important gentleman of about eight-and-thirty, of rather plebeian countenance and with a very light head of hair, who leant over Mrs. Wititterly for a little time, and conversed with her in whispers.

"Oh!" he said, turning round, "yes. This is a most important matter. Mrs. Wititterly is of a very excitable nature, very delicate, very fragile; a hothouse plant, an exotic."

"Oh! Henry, my dear," interposed Mrs. Wititterly.

"You are my love, you know you are; one breath—" said Mr. W., blowing an imaginary feather away. "Pho! you're gone."

The lady sighed.

"Your soul is too large for your body," said Mr. Wititterly. "Your intellect wears you out; all the medical men say so; you know that there is not a physician who is not proud of being called in to you. What is their unanimous declaration? 'My dear doctor,' said I to Sir Tumley Snuffim, in this very room, the very last time he came. 'My dear doctor, what is my wife's complaint? Tell me all. I can bear it. Is it nerves?' 'My dear fellow,' he said, 'be proud of that woman; make much of her; she is an ornament to the fashionable world, and to you. Her complaint is soul. It swells, expands, dilates—the blood fires, the pulse quickens, the excitement increases— Whew!'" Here Mr. Wititterly, who, in the ardour of his description, had flourished his right hand to within something less than an inch of Mrs. Nickleby's bonnet, drew it hastily back again, and blew his nose as fiercely as if it had been done by some violent machinery.

"You make me out worse than I am, Henry," said Mrs. Wititterly, with a faint smile.

"I do not, Julia, I do not," said Mr. W. "The society in which you move—necessarily move, from your station, connexion, and endowments—is one vortex and whirlpool of the most frightful excitement. Bless my heart and body, can I ever forget the night you danced with the baronet's nephew, at the election ball, at Exeter! It was tremendous."

"I always suffer for these triumphs afterwards," said Mrs. Wititterly.

"And for that very reason," rejoined her husband, "you must have a companion, in whom there is great gentleness, great sweetness, excessive sympathy, and perfect repose."

Here both Mr. and Mrs. Wititterly, who had talked rather at the Nicklebys than to each other, left off speaking, and looked at their two hearers, with an expression of countenance which seemed to say "What do you think of all that!"

"Mrs. Wititterly," said her husband, addressing himself to Mrs. Nickleby, "is sought after and courted by glittering crowds, and bril-

liant circles. She is excited by the opera, the drama, the fine arts, the
—the—the——"

"The nobility, my love," interposed Mrs. Wititterly.

"The nobility, of course," said Mr. Wititterly. "And the military.
She forms and expresses an immense variety of opinions, on an immense
variety of subjects. If some people in public life were acquainted with
Mrs. Wititterly's real opinion of them, they would not hold their heads
perhaps quite as high as they do."

"Hush, Henry," said the lady; "this is scarcely fair."

"I mention no names, Julia," replied Mr. Wititterly; "and nobody
is injured. I merely mention the circumstance to show that you are no
ordinary person; that there is a constant friction perpetually going on
between your mind and your body; and that you must be soothed and
tended. Now let me hear dispassionately and calmly, what are this
young lady's qualifications for the office."

In obedience to this request, the qualifications were all gone
through again, with the addition of many interruptions and cross-
questionings from Mr. Wititterly. It was finally arranged that
inquiries should be made, and a decisive answer addressed to Miss
Nickleby, under cover to her uncle, within two days. These conditions
agreed upon, the page showed them down as far as the staircase window,
and the big footman relieving guard at that point piloted them in
perfect safety to the street-door.

"They are very distinguished people, evidently," said Mrs. Nickleby,
as she took her daughter's arm. "What a superior person Mrs.
Wititterly is!"

"Do you think so, mama?" was all Kate's reply.

"Why who can help thinking so, Kate, my love?" rejoined her
mother. "She is pale, though, and looks much exhausted. I hope
she may not be wearing herself out, but I am very much afraid."

These considerations led the deep-sighted lady into a calculation of
the probable duration of Mrs. Wititterly's life, and the chances of the
disconsolate widower bestowing his hand on her daughter. Before reaching home, she had freed Mrs. Wititterly's soul from all bodily restraint,
married Kate with great splendour at Saint George's Hanover Square;
and only left undecided the minor question whether a splendid French-
polished mahogany bedstead should be erected for herself in the two-pair
back of the house in Cadogan Place, or in the three-pair front, between
which apartments she could not quite balance the advantages, and
therefore adjusted the question at last, by determining to leave it to the
decision of her son-in-law.

The inquiries were made. The answer—not to Kate's very great
joy—was favourable; and at the expiration of a week she betook herself, with all her moveables and valuables, to Mrs. Wititterly's mansion,
where for the present we will leave her.

CHAPTER XXII.

NICHOLAS, ACCOMPANIED BY SMIKE, SALLIES FORTH TO SEEK HIS
FORTUNE. HE ENCOUNTERS MR. VINCENT CRUMMLES ; AND WHO
HE WAS IS HEREIN MADE MANIFEST.

THE whole capital which Nicholas found himself entitled to, either
in possession, reversion, remainder, or expectancy, after paying his rent
and settling with the broker from whom he had hired his poor furniture,
did not exceed by more than a few halfpence the sum of twenty shillings.
And yet he hailed the morning on which he had resolved to quit London
with a light heart, and sprang from his bed with an elasticity of spirit
which is happily the lot of young persons, or the world would never be
stocked with old ones.

It was a cold, dry, foggy morning in early spring ; a few meagre
shadows flitted to and fro in the misty streets, and occasionally there
loomed through the dull vapour the heavy outline of some hackney-
coach wending homewards, which drawing slowly nearer, rolled jangling
by, scattering the thin crust of frost from its whitened roof, and soon
was lost again in the cloud. At intervals were heard the tread of slip-
shod feet, and the chilly cry of the poor sweep as he crept shivering to
his early toil; the heavy footfall of the official watcher of the night
pacing slowly up and down and cursing the tardy hours that still inter-
vened between him and sleep : the rumbling of ponderous carts and
waggons, the roll of the lighter vehicles which carried buyers and sellers
to the different markets: the sound of ineffectual knocking at the doors
of heavy sleepers—all these noises fell upon the ear from time to time,
but all seemed muffled by the fog, and to be rendered almost as indis-
tinct to the ear as was every object to the sight. The sluggish darkness thickened as the day came on ; and those who had the courage to
rise and peep at the gloomy street from their curtained windows, crept
back to bed again, and coiled themselves up to sleep.

Before even these indications of approaching morning were rife in
busy London, Nicholas had made his way alone to the city, and stood
beneath the windows of his mother's house. It was dull and bare to see,
but it had light and life for him ; for there was at least one heart
within its old walls to which insult or dishonour would bring the same
blood rushing that flowed in his own veins.

He crossed the road, and raised his eyes to the window of the room
where he knew his sister slept. It was closed and dark. " Poor
girl," thought Nicholas, " she little thinks who lingers here ! "

He looked again, and felt for the moment almost vexed that Kate
was not there to exchange one word at parting. " Good God ! " he
thought, suddenly correcting himself, " what a boy I am ! "

" It is better as it is," said Nicholas, after he had lounged on a few paces and returned to the same spot. " When I left them before, and could have said good bye a thousand times if I had chosen, I spared them the pain of leave-taking, and why not now ?" As he spoke, some fancied motion of the curtain almost persuaded him, for the instant, that Kate was at the window, and by one of those strange contradictions of feeling which are common to us all, he shrunk involuntarily into a door-way, that she might not see him. He smiled at his own weakness ; said " God bless them !" and walked away with a lighter step.

Smike was anxiously expecting him when he reached his old lodgings, and so was Newman, who had expended a day's income in a can of rum and milk to prepare them for the journey. They had tied up the luggage, Smike shouldered it, and away they went, with Newman Noggs in company, for he had insisted on walking as far as he could with them, over-night.

" Which way ?" asked Newman, wistfully.

" To Kingston first," replied Nicholas.

" And where afterwards ?" asked Newman. " Why won't you tell me ? "

" Because I scarcely know myself, good friend," rejoined Nicholas, laying his hand upon his shoulder ; " and if I did, I have neither plan nor prospect yet, and might shift my quarters a hundred times before you could possibly communicate with me."

" I am afraid you have some deep scheme in your head," said Newman, doubtfully.

" So deep," replied his young friend, " that even I can't fathom it. Whatever I resolve upon, depend upon it I will write you soon."

" You won't forget ? " said Newman.

" I am not very likely to," rejoined Nicholas. " I have not so many friends that I shall grow confused among the number, and forget my best one."

Occupied in such discourse as this they walked on for a couple of hours, as they might have done for a couple of days if Nicholas had not sat himself down on a stone by the way-side, and resolutely declared his intention of not moving another step until Newman Noggs turned back. Having pleaded ineffectually first for another half mile, and afterwards for another quarter, Newman was fain to comply, and to shape his course towards Golden Square, after interchanging many hearty and affectionate farewells, and many times turning back to wave his hat to the two wayfarers when they had become mere specks in the distance.

" Now listen to me, Smike," said Nicholas, as they trudged with stout hearts onwards. " We are bound for Portsmouth."

Smike nodded his head and smiled, but expressed no other emotion ; for whether they had been bound for Portsmouth or Port Royal would have been alike to him, so they had been bound together.

" I don't know much of these matters," resumed Nicholas ; " but Portsmouth is a sea-port town, and if no other employment is to be obtained, I should think we might get on board of some ship. I am young and active, and could be useful in many ways. So could you."

"I hope so," replied Smike. "When I was at that—you know where I mean?"

"Yes, I know," said Nicholas. "You needn't name the place."

"Well, when I was there," resumed Smike; his eyes sparkling at the prospect of displaying his abilities; "I could milk a cow, and groom a horse with anybody."

"Ha!" said Nicholas, gravely. "I am afraid they don't usually keep many animals of either kind on board ship, and even when they have horses, that they are not very particular about rubbing them down; still you can learn to do something else, you know. Where there's a will, there's a way."

"And I am very willing," said Smike, brightening up again.

"God knows you are," rejoined Nicholas; "and if you fail, it shall go hard but I'll do enough for us both."

"Do we go all the way to-day?" asked Smike, after a short silence.

"That would be too severe a trial, even for your willing legs," said Nicholas, with a good-humoured smile. "No. Godalming is some thirty and odd miles from London—as I found from a map I borrowed —and I purpose to rest there. We must push on again to-morrow, for we are not rich enough to loiter. Let me relieve you of that bundle, come."

"No, no," rejoined Smike, falling back a few steps. "Don't ask me to give it up to you."

"Why not?" asked Nicholas.

"Let me do something for you, at least," said Smike. "You will never let me serve you as I ought. You will never know how I think, day and night, of ways to please you."

"You are a foolish fellow to say it, for I know it well, and see it, or I should be a blind and senseless beast," rejoined Nicholas. "Let me ask you a question while I think of it, and there is no one by," he added, looking him steadily in the face. "Have you a good memory?"

"I don't know," said Smike, shaking his head sorrowfully. "I think I had once; but it's all gone now—all gone."

"Why do you think you had once?" asked Nicholas, turning quickly upon him as though the answer in some way helped out the purport of his question.

"Because I could remember when I was a child," said Smike, "but that is very, very long ago, or at least it seems so. I was always confused and giddy at that place you took me from; and could never remember, and sometimes couldn't even understand what they said to me. I—let me see—let me see."

"You are wandering now," said Nicholas, touching him on the arm.

"No," replied his companion, with a vacant look. "I was only thinking how——." He shivered involuntarily as he spoke.

"Think no more of that place, for it is all over," retorted Nicholas, fixing his eye full upon that of his companion, which was fast settling into an unmeaning stupified gaze, once habitual to him, and common even then. "What of the first day you went to Yorkshire?"

"Eh!" cried the lad.

" That was before you began to lose your recollection, you know," said Nicholas quietly. " Was the weather hot or cold?"

" Wet," replied the boy. " Very wet. I have always said when it rained hard that it was like the night I came: and they used to crowd round and laugh to see me cry when the rain fell heavily. It was like a child they said, and that made me think of it more. I turned cold all over sometimes, for I could see myself as I was then, coming in at the very same door."

" As you were then," repeated Nicholas, with assumed carelessness; " How was that?"

" Such a little creature," said Smike," that they might have had pity and mercy upon me, only to remember it."

" You didn't find your way there alone!" remarked Nicholas.

" No," rejoined Smike, " oh no."

" Who was with you?"

" A man—a dark withered man; I have heard them say so at the school, and I remembered that before. I was glad to leave him, I was afraid of him; but they made me more afraid of them, and used me harder too."

" Look at me," said Nicholas, wishing to attract his full attention. "There; don't turn away. Do you remember no woman, no kind gentle woman, who hung over you once, and kissed your lips, and called you her child?"

" No," said the poor creature, shaking his head, " no, never."

" Nor any house but that house in Yorkshire?"

" No," rejoined the youth, with a melancholy look : " a room—I remember I slept in a room, a large lonesome room at the top of a house, where there was a trap-door in the ceiling. I have covered my head with the clothes often, not to see it, for it frightened me, a young child with no one near at night, and I used to wonder what was on the other side. There was a clock too, an old clock, in one corner. I remember that. I have never forgotten that room, for when I have terrible dreams, it comes back just as it was. I see things and people in it that I had never seen then, but there is the room just as it used to be; *that* never changes."

" Will you let me take the bundle now?" asked Nicholas, abruptly changing the theme.

" No," said Smike, " no. Come, let us walk on."

He quickened his pace as he said this, apparently under the impression that they had been standing still during the whole of the previous dialogue. Nicholas marked him closely, and every word of this conversation remained indelibly fastened in his memory.

It was by this time within an hour of noon, and although a dense vapour still enveloped the city they had left as if the very breath of its busy people hung over their schemes of gain and profit and found greater attraction there than in the quiet region above, in the open country it was clear and fair. Occasionally in some low spots they came upon patches of mist which the sun had not yet driven from their strongholds; but these were soon passed, and as they laboured up the hills beyond, it was pleasant to look down and see how the sluggish mass rolled heavily off before the cheering influence of day. A broad fine honest sun lighted up the green pastures and dimpled water with the semblance of summer, while it left the travellers all the invigorating freshness of that early time of year. The ground seemed elastic under their feet; the sheep-bells were music to their ears; and exhilarated by exercise, and stimulated by hope, they pushed onwards with the strength of lions.

The day wore on, and all these bright colours subsided, and assumed a quieter tint, like young hopes softened down by time, or youthful features by degrees resolving into the calm and serenity of age. But they were scarcely less beautiful in their slow decline than they had been in their prime; for nature gives to every time and season some beauties of its own, and from morning to night, as from the cradle to the grave, is but a succession of changes so gentle and easy, that we can scarcely mark their progress.

To Godalming they came at last, and here they bargained for two humble beds, and slept soundly. In the morning they were astir, though not quite so early as the sun, and again afoot; if not with all the freshness of yesterday, still with enough of hope and spirit to bear them cheerily on.

It was a harder day's journey than that they had already performed, for there were long and weary hills to climb; and in journeys, as in life, it is a great deal easier to go down hill than up. However, they kept on with unabated perseverance, and the hill has not yet lifted its face to heaven that perseverance will not gain the summit of at last.

They walked upon the rim of the Devil's Punch Bowl, and Smike listened with greedy interest as Nicholas read the inscription upon the stone which, reared upon that wild spot, tells of a foul and treacherous murder committed there by night. The grass on which they stood had once been dyed with gore, and the blood of the murdered man had run down, drop by drop, into the hollow which gives the place its name. "The Devil's Bowl," thought Nicholas, as he looked into the void, "never held fitter liquor than that!"

Onward they kept with steady purpose, and entered at length upon a wide and spacious tract of downs, with every variety of little hill and plain to change their verdant surface. Here, there shot up almost perpendicularly into the sky a height so steep, as to be hardly accessible to any but the sheep and goats that fed upon its sides, and there stood a huge mound of green, sloping and tapering off so delicately, and merging so gently into the level ground, that you could scarce define its limits. Hills swelling above each other, and undulations shapely and uncouth, smooth and rugged, graceful and grotesque, thrown negligently side by side, bounded the view in each direction; while frequently, with unexpected noise, there uprose from the ground a flight of crows, who, cawing and wheeling round the nearest hills, as if uncertain of their course, suddenly poised themselves upon the wing and skimmed down the long vista of some opening valley with the speed of very light itself.

By degrees the prospect receded more and more on either hand, and as they had been shut out from rich and extensive scenery, so they emerged once again upon the open country. The knowledge that they were drawing near their place of destination, gave them fresh courage to proceed; but the way had been difficult, and they had loitered on the road, and Smike was tired. Thus twilight had already closed in, when they turned off the path to the door of a road-side inn, yet twelve miles short of Portsmouth.

"Twelve miles," said Nicholas, leaning with both hands on his stick, and looking doubtfully at Smike.

"Twelve long miles," repeated the landlord.

"Is it a good road?" inquired Nicholas.

"Very bad," said the landlord. As of course, being a landlord, he would say.

"I want to get on," observed Nicholas, hesitating. "I scarcely know what to do."

"Don't let me influence you," rejoined the landlord. "I wouldn't go on if it was me."

"Wouldn't you?" asked Nicholas, with the same uncertainty.

"Not if I knew when I was well off," said the landlord. And having said it he pulled up his apron, put his hands into his pockets, and taking a step or two outside the door, looked down the dark road with an assumption of great indifference.

A glance at the toil-worn face of Smike determined Nicholas, so without any further consideration he made up his mind to stay where he was.

The landlord led them into the kitchen, and as there was a good fire he remarked that it was very cold. If there had happened to be a bad one he would have observed that it was very warm.

"What can you give us for supper?" was Nicholas's natural question.

"Why—what would you like?" was the landlord's no less natural answer.

Nicholas suggested cold meat, but there was no cold meat—poached eggs, but there were no eggs—mutton chops, but there wasn't a mutton chop within three miles, though there had been more last week than they knew what to do with, and would be an extraordinary supply the day after to-morrow.

"Then," said Nicholas, "I must leave it entirely to you, as I would have done at first if you had allowed me."

"Why, then I'll tell you what," rejoined the landlord. "There's a gentleman in the parlour that's ordered a hot beef-steak pudding and potatoes at nine. There's more of it than he can manage, and I have very little doubt that if I ask leave, you can sup with him. I'll do that in a minute."

"No, no," said Nicholas, detaining him. "I would rather not. I— at least—pshaw! why cannot I speak out. Here; you see that I am travelling in a very humble manner, and have made my way hither on foot. It is more than probable, I think, that the gentleman may not

The Country Manager rehearses a Combat.

relish my company; and although I am the dusty figure you see, I am too proud to thrust myself into his."

"Lord love you," said the landlord, "it's only Mr. Crummles; he isn't particular."

"Is he not?" asked Nicholas, on whose mind, to tell the truth, the prospect of the savoury pudding was making some impression.

"Not he," replied the landlord. "He'll like your way of talking, I know. But we'll soon see all about that. Just wait a minute."

The landlord hurried into the parlour without staying for further permission, nor did Nicholas strive to prevent him: wisely considering that supper under the circumstances was too serious a matter to trifle with. It was not long before the host returned in a condition of much excitement.

"All right," he said in a low voice. "I knew he would. You'll see something rather worth seeing in there. Ecod, how they are a going of it!"

There was no time to inquire to what this exclamation, which was delivered in a very rapturous tone, referred, for he had already thrown open the door of the room; into which Nicholas, followed by Smike with the bundle on his shoulder (he carried it about with him as vigilantly as if it had been a purse of gold), straightway repaired.

Nicholas was prepared for something odd, but not for something quite so odd as the sight he encountered. At the upper end of the room were a couple of boys, one of them very tall and the other very short, both dressed as sailors—or at least as theatrical sailors, with belts, buckles, pigtails, and pistols complete—fighting what is called in play-bills a terrific combat with two of those short broad-swords with basket hilts which are commonly used at our minor theatres. The short boy had gained a great advantage over the tall boy, who was reduced to mortal strait, and both were overlooked by a large heavy man, perched against the corner of a table, who emphatically adjured them to strike a little more fire out of the swords, and they couldn't fail to bring the house down on the very first night.

"Mr. Vincent Crummles," said the landlord with an air of great deference. "This is the young gentleman."

Mr. Vincent Crummles received Nicholas with an inclination of the head, something between the courtesy of a Roman emperor and the nod of a pot companion; and bade the landlord shut the door and begone.

"There's a picture," said Mr. Crummles, motioning Nicholas not to advance and spoil it. "The little 'un has him; if the big 'un doesn't knock under in three seconds he's a dead man. Do that again, boys."

The two combatants went to work afresh, and chopped away until the swords emitted a shower of sparks, to the great satisfaction of Mr. Crummles, who appeared to consider this a very great point indeed. The engagement commenced with about two hundred chops administered by the short sailor and the tall sailor alternately, without producing any particular result until the short sailor was chopped down on one knee, but this was nothing to him, for he worked himself about on the one knee with the assistance of his left hand, and fought most desperately until the tall sailor chopped his sword out of his grasp. Now the inference was, that the short sailor, reduced to this extremity, would give in at once and cry quarter, but instead of that he all of a sudden drew a large pistol from his belt and presented it at the face of the tall sailor, who was so overcome at this (not expecting it) that he let the short sailor pick up his sword and begin again. Then the chopping recommenced, and a variety of fancy chops were administered on both sides, such as chops dealt with the left hand and under the leg and over the right shoulder and over the left, and when the short sailor made a vigorous cut at the tall sailor's legs, which would have shaved them clean off if it had taken effect, the tall sailor jumped over the short sailor's sword, wherefore to balance the matter and make it all fair, the tall sailor administered the same cut and the short sailor jumped over *his* sword. After this there was a good deal of dodging about and hitching up of the inexpressibles in the absence of braces, and then the short sailor (who was the moral character evidently, for he always had the best of it) made a violent demonstration and closed with the tall sailor, who, after a few unavailing struggles, went down and expired in great torture as the short sailor put his foot upon his breast and bored a hole in him through and through.

" That'll be a double *encore* if you take care, boys," said Mr. Crummles. " You had better get your wind now, and change your clothes."

Having addressed these words to the combatants, he saluted Nicholas, who then observed that the face of Mr. Crummles was quite proportionate in size to his body ; that he had a very full under-lip, a hoarse voice, as though he were in the habit of shouting very much, and very short black hair, shaved off nearly to the crown of his head—to admit (as he afterwards learnt) of his more easily wearing character wigs of any shape or pattern.

" What did you think of that, Sir ?" inquired Mr. Crummles.

" Very good, indeed—capital," answered Nicholas.

" You won't see such boys as those very often, I think," said Mr. Crummles.

Nicholas assented—observing, that if they were a little better match——

" Match !" cried Mr. Crummles.

" I mean if they were a little more of a size," said Nicholas, explaining himself.

" Size !" repeated Mr. Crummles ; " why, it's the very essence of the combat that there should be a foot or two between them. How are you to get up the sympathies of the audience in a legitimate manner, if there isn't a little man contending against a great one—unless there's at least five to one, and we haven't hands enough for that business in our company."

" I see," replied Nicholas. " I beg your pardon. That didn't occur to me, I confess."

" It's the main point," said Mr. Crummles. " I open at Portsmouth the day after to-morrow. If you're going there, look into the theatre, and see how that'll tell."

Nicholas promised to do so if he could, and drawing a chair near the fire, fell into conversation with the manager at once. He was very talkative and communicative, stimulated perhaps not only by his natural disposition, but by the spirits and water he sipped very plentifully, or the snuff which he took in large quantities from a piece of whitey-brown paper in his waistcoat pocket. He laid open his affairs without the smallest reserve, and descanted at some length upon the merits of his company, and the acquirements of his family, of both of which the two broad-sword boys formed an honourable portion. There was to be a gathering it seemed of the different ladies and gentlemen at Portsmouth on the morrow, whither the father and sons were proceeding (not for the regular season, but in the course of a wandering speculation), after fulfilling an engagement at Guildford with the greatest applause.

" You are going that way ? " asked the manager.

" Ye-yes," said Nicholas. " Yes, I am."

" Do you know the town at all ? " inquired the manager, who seemed to consider himself entitled to the same confidence as he had himself exhibited.

" No," replied Nicholas.

" Never there ? "

" Never."

Mr. Vincent Crummles gave a short dry cough, as much as to say, " If you won't be communicative, you won't ; " and took so many pinches of snuff from the piece of paper, one after another, that Nicholas quite wondered where it all went to.

While he was thus engaged, Mr. Crummles looked from time to time with great interest at Smike, with whom he had appeared considerably struck from the first. He had now fallen asleep, and was nodding in his chair.

" Excuse my saying so," said the manager, leaning over to Nicholas, and sinking his voice, " but—what a capital countenance your friend has got!"

" Poor fellow ! " said Nicholas, with a half smile, " I wish it were a little more plump and less haggard."

" Plump ! " exclaimed the manager, quite horrified, " you'd spoil it for ever."

" Do you think so ? "

" Think so, sir ! Why, as he is now," said the manager, striking his knee emphatically ; " without a pad upon his body, and hardly a touch of paint upon his face, he'd make such an actor for the starved business as was never seen in this country. Only let him be tolerably well up in the Apothecary in Romeo and Juliet with the slightest possible dab of red on the tip of his nose, and he'd be certain of three rounds the moment he put his head out of the practicable door in the front grooves O. P."

" You view him with a professional eye," said Nicholas, laughing.

" And well I may," rejoined the manager, " I never saw a young fellow so regularly cut out for that line since I've been in the profession, and I played the heavy children when I was eighteen months old."

The appearance of the beef-steak pudding, which came in simultaneously with the junior Vincent Crummleses, turned the conversation to other matters, and indeed for a time stopped it altogether. These two young gentlemen wielded their knives and forks with scarcely less address than their broad-swords, and as the whole party were quite as sharp set as either class of weapons, there was no time for talking until the supper had been disposed of.

The master Crummleses had no sooner swallowed the last procurable morsel of food than they evinced, by various half-suppressed yawns and stretchings of their limbs, an obvious inclination to retire for the night, which Smike had betrayed still more strongly: he having, in the course of the meal, fallen asleep several times while in the very act of eating. Nicholas therefore proposed that they should break up at once, but the manager would by no means hear of it, vowing that he had promised himself the pleasure of inviting his new acquaintance to share a bowl of punch, and that if he declined, he should deem it very unhandsome behaviour.

"Let them go," said Mr. Vincent Crummles, "and we'll have it snugly and cosily together by the fire."

Nicholas was not much disposed to sleep, being in truth too anxious, so after a little demur he accepted the offer, and having exchanged a shake of the hand with the young Crummleses, and the manager having on his part bestowed a most affectionate benediction on Smike, he sat himself down opposite to that gentleman by the fire-side to assist in emptying the bowl, which soon afterwards appeared, steaming in a manner which was quite exhilarating to behold, and sending forth a most grateful and inviting fragrance.

But, despite the punch and the manager, who told a variety of stories, and smoked tobacco from a pipe, and inhaled it in the shape of snuff, with a most astonishing power, Nicholas was absent and dispirited. His thoughts were in his old home, and when they reverted to his present condition, the uncertainty of the morrow cast a gloom upon him, which his utmost efforts were unable to dispel. His attention wandered; although he heard the manager's voice, he was deaf to what he said, and when Mr. Vincent Crummles concluded the history of some long adventure with a loud laugh, and an inquiry what Nicholas would have done under the same circumstances, he was obliged to make the best apology in his power, and to confess his entire ignorance of all he had been talking about.

"Why so I saw," observed Mr. Crummles. "You're uneasy in your mind. What's the matter?"

Nicholas could not refrain from smiling at the abruptness of the question, but thinking it scarcely worth while to parry it, owned that he was under some apprehensions lest he might not succeed in the object which had brought him to that part of the country.

"And what's that?" asked the manager.

"Getting something to do which will keep me and my poor fellow-traveller in the common necessaries of life," said Nicholas. "That's the truth; you guessed it long ago, I dare say, so I may as well have the credit of telling it you with a good grace."

" What's to be got to do at Portsmouth more than anywhere else ? " asked Mr. Vincent Crummles, melting the sealing-wax on the stem of his pipe in the candle, and rolling it out afresh with his little finger.

" There are many vessels leaving the port, I suppose," replied Nicholas. " I shall try for a berth in some ship or other. There is meat and drink there, at all events."

" Salt meat and new rum ; pease-pudding and chaff-biscuits," said the manager, taking a whiff at his pipe to keep it alight, and returning to his work of embellishment.

" One may do worse than that," said Nicholas. " I can rough it, I believe, as well as most men of my age and previous habits."

" You need be able to," said the manager, " if you go on board ship ; but you won't."

" Why not ? "

" Because there's not a skipper or mate that would think you worth your salt, when he could get a practised hand," replied the manager ; " and they as plentiful there as the oysters in the streets."

" What do you mean ? " asked Nicholas, alarmed by this prediction, and the confident tone in which it had been uttered. " Men are not born able seamen. They must be reared, I suppose ? "

Mr. Vincent Crummles nodded his head. " They must ; but not at your age, or from young gentlemen like you."

There was a pause. The countenance of Nicholas fell, and he gazed ruefully at the fire.

" Does no other profession occur to you, which a young man of your figure and address could take up easily, and see the world to advantage in ? " asked the manager.

" No," said Nicholas, shaking his head.

" Why, then, I'll tell you one," said Mr. Crummles, throwing his pipe into the fire, and raising his voice. " The stage."

" The stage ! " cried Nicholas, in a voice almost as loud.

" The theatrical profession," said Mr. Vincent Crummles. " I am in the theatrical profession myself, my wife is in the theatrical profession, my children are in the theatrical profession. I had a dog that lived and died in it from a puppy ; and my chaise-pony goes on in Timour the Tartar. I'll bring you out, and your friend too. Say the word. I want a novelty."

" I don't know anything about it," rejoined Nicholas, whose breath had been almost taken away by this sudden proposal. " I never acted a part in my life, except at school."

" There's genteel comedy in your walk and manner, juvenile tragedy in your eye, and touch-and-go farce in your laugh," said Mr. Vincent Crummles. " You'll do as well as if you had thought of nothing else but the lamps, from your birth downwards."

Nicholas thought of the small amount of small change there would remain in his pocket after paying the tavern bill : and he hesitated.

" You can be useful to us in a hundred ways," said Mr. Crummles. " Think what capital bills a man of your education could write for the shop-windows."

" Well, I think I could manage that department," said Nicholas.

" To be sure you could," replied Mr. Crummles. " ' For further particulars see small hand-bills '—we might have half a volume in every one of them. Pieces too ; why, you could write us a piece to bring out the whole strength of the company, whenever we wanted one."

" I am not quite so confident about that," replied Nicholas. " But I dare say I could scribble something now and then that would suit you."

" We'll have a new show-piece out directly," said the manager. " Let me see—peculiar resources of this establishment—new and splendid scenery—you must manage to introduce a real pump and two washing-tubs."

" Into the piece ! " said Nicholas.

" Yes," replied the manager.   " I bought 'em cheap, at a sale the other day ; and they'll come in admirably.   That's the London plan. They look up some dresses, and properties, and have a piece written to fit them.   Most of the theatres keep an author on purpose."

" Indeed ! " cried Nicholas.

" Oh yes," said the manager ; " a common thing.   It'll look very well in the bills in separate lines—Real pump !—Splendid tubs !— Great attraction !   You don't happen to be anything of an artist, do you ? "

" That is not one of my accomplishments," rejoined Nicholas.

" Ah !   Then it can't be helped," said the manager.   " If you had been, we might have had a large woodcut of the last scene for the posters, showing the whole depth of the stage, with the pump and tubs in the middle ; but however, if you're not, it can't be helped."

" What should I get for all this ? " inquired Nicholas, after a few moments' reflection.   " Could I live by it ? "

" Live by it ! " said the manager.   " Like a prince.   With your own salary, and your friend's, and your writings, you'd make—ah ! you'd make a pound a week ! "

" You don't say so."

" I do indeed, and if we had a run of good houses, nearly double the money."

Nicholas shrugged his shoulders, but sheer destitution was before him ; and if he could summon fortitude to undergo the extremes of want and hardship, for what had he rescued his helpless charge if it were only to bear as hard a fate as that from which he had wrested him ?   It was easy to think of seventy miles as nothing, when he was in the same town with the man who had treated him so ill and roused his bitterest thoughts ; but now it seemed far enough.   What if he went abroad, and his mother or Kate were to die the while ?

Without more deliberation he hastily declared that it was a bargain, and gave Mr. Vincent Crummles his hand upon it.

CHAPTER XXIII.

TREATS OF THE COMPANY OF MR. VINCENT CRUMMLES, AND OF HIS
AFFAIRS, DOMESTIC AND THEATRICAL.

As Mr. Crummles had a strange four-legged animal in the inn
stables, which he called a pony, and a vehicle of unknown design, on
which he bestowed the appellation of a four-wheeled phaeton, Nicholas
proceeded on his journey next morning with greater ease than he had
expected : the manager and himself occupying the front seat, and the
Master Crummleses and Smike being packed together behind, in company with a wicker basket defended from wet by a stout oilskin, in
which were the broad-swords, pistols, pigtails, nautical costumes, and
other professional necessaries of the aforesaid young gentlemen.

The pony took his time upon the road, and—possibly in consequence
of his theatrical education—evinced every now and then a strong inclination to lie down. However, Mr. Vincent Crummles kept him up
pretty well, by jerking the rein, and plying the whip ; and when these
means failed, and the animal came to a stand, the elder Master
Crummles got out and kicked him. By dint of these encouragements,
he was persuaded to move from time to time, and they jogged on (as
Mr. Crummles truly observed) very comfortably for all parties.

" He's a good pony at bottom," said Mr. Crummles, turning to
Nicholas.

He might have been at bottom, but he certainly was not at top,
seeing that his coat was of the roughest and most ill-favoured kind. So,
Nicholas merely observed, that he shouldn't wonder if he was.

" Many and many is the circuit this pony has gone," said Mr.
Crummles, flicking him skilfully on the eyelid for old acquaintance' sake.
" He is quite one of us. His mother was on the stage."

" Was she, indeed ? " rejoined Nicholas.

" She ate apple-pie at a circus for upwards of fourteen years," said
the manager ; " fired pistols, and went to bed in a nightcap ; and, in
short, took the low comedy entirely. His father was a dancer."

" Was he at all distinguished ? "

" Not very," said the manager. " He was rather a low sort of
pony. The fact is, that he had been originally jobbed out by the
day, and he never quite got over his old habits. He was clever in
melodrama too, but too broad—too broad. When the mother died, he
took the port-wine business."

" The port-wine business ! " cried Nicholas.

" Drinking port-wine with the clown," said the manager ; " but he
was greedy, and one night bit off the bowl of the glass, and choked
himself, so that his vulgarity was the death of him at last."

The descendant of this ill-starred animal requiring increased attention
from Mr. Crummles as he progressed in his day's work, that gentleman
had very little time for conversation, and Nicholas was thus left at

leisure to entertain himself with his own thoughts until they arrived at
the drawbridge at Portsmouth, when Mr. Crummles pulled up.

" We'll set down here," said the manager, " and the boys will take
him round to the stable, and call at my lodgings with the luggage.
You had better let yours be taken there for the present."

Thanking Mr. Vincent Crummles for his obliging offer, Nicholas
jumped out, and, giving Smike his arm, accompanied the manager up
High Street on their way to the theatre, feeling nervous and uncomfortable enough at the prospect of an immediate introduction to a scene
so new to him.

They passed a great many bills pasted against the walls and displayed in windows, wherein the names of Mr. Vincent Crummles, Mrs.
Vincent Crummles, Master Crummles, Master P. Crummles, and Miss
Crummles, were printed in very large letters, and everything else in
very small ones; and turning at length into an entry, in which was a
strong smell of orange-peel and lamp-oil, with an under-current of saw-
dust, groped their way through a dark passage, and, descending a step
or two, threaded a little maze of canvass screens and paint pots, and
emerged upon the stage of the Portsmouth Theatre.

" Here we are," said Mr. Crummles.

It was not very light, but Nicholas found himself close to the first
entrance on the prompter's side, among bare walls, dusty scenes, mil-
dewed clouds, heavily daubed draperies, and dirty floors. He looked
about him; ceiling, pit, boxes, gallery, orchestra, fittings, and decora-
tions of every kind,—all looked coarse, cold, gloomy, and wretched.

" Is this a theatre?" whispered Smike, in amazement; " I thought
it was a blaze of light and finery."

" Why, so it is," replied Nicholas, hardly less surprised; " but not
by day, Smike—not by day."

The manager's voice recalled him from a more careful inspection of
the building, to the opposite side of the proscenium, where, at a small
mahogany table with rickety legs and of an oblong shape, sat a stout,
portly female, apparently between forty and fifty, in a tarnished silk
cloak, with her bonnet dangling by the strings in her hand, and her
hair (of which she had a great quantity) braided in a large festoon over
each temple.

" Mr. Johnson," said the manager (for Nicholas had given the name
which Newman Noggs had bestowed upon him in his conversation with
Mrs. Kenwigs), " let me introduce Mrs. Vincent Crummles."

" I am glad to see you, Sir," said Mrs. Vincent Crummles, in a
sepulchral voice. " I am very glad to see you, and still more happy
to hail you as a promising member of our corps."

The lady shook Nicholas by the hand as she addressed him in these
terms; he saw it was a large one, but had not expected quite such an
iron grip as that with which she honoured him.

" And this," said the lady, crossing to Smike, as tragic actresses
cross when they obey a stage direction, " and this is the other. You
too, are welcome, Sir."

" He'll do, I think, my dear?" said the manager, taking a pinch of snuff.

" He is admirable," replied the lady. " An acquisition, indeed."

As Mrs. Vincent Crummles re-crossed back to the table, there bounded on to the stage from some mysterious inlet, a little girl in a dirty white frock with tucks up to the knees, short trousers, sandaled shoes, white spencer, pink gauze bonnet, green veil and curl-papers, who turned a pirouette, cut twice in the air, turned another pirouette, then looking off at the opposite wing shrieked, bounded forward to within six inches of the footlights, and fell into a beautiful attitude of terror, as a shabby gentleman in an old pair of buff slippers came in at one powerful slide, and chattering his teeth, fiercely brandished a walking-stick.

" They are going through the Indian Savage and the Maiden," said Mrs. Crummles.

" Oh ! " said the manager, " the little ballet interlude. Very good, go on. A little this way, if you please, Mr. Johnson. That'll do. Now."

The manager clapped his hands as a signal to proceed, and the Savage, becoming ferocious, made a slide towards the maiden, but the maiden avoided him in six twirls, and came down at the end of the last one upon the very points of her toes. This seemed to make some impression upon the savage, for, after a little more ferocity and chasing of the maiden into corners, he began to relent, and stroked his face several times with his right thumb and four fingers, thereby intimating that he was struck with admiration of the maiden's beauty. Acting upon the impulse of this passion, he (the savage) began to hit himself severe thumps in the chest, and to exhibit other indications of being desperately in love, which being rather a prosy proceeding, was very likely the cause of the maiden's falling asleep ; whether it was or not, asleep she did fall, sound as a church, on a sloping bank, and the savage perceiving it, leant his left ear on his left hand, and nodded sideways, to intimate to all whom it might concern that she *was* asleep, and no shamming. Being left to himself, the savage had a dance, all alone, and just as he left off the maiden woke up, rubbed her eyes, got off the bank, and had a dance all alone too—such a dance that the savage looked on in ecstasy all the while, and when it was done, plucked from a neighbouring tree some botanical curiosity, resembling a small pickled cabbage, and offered it to the maiden, who at first wouldn't have it, but on the savage shedding tears relented. Then the savage jumped for joy ; then the maiden jumped for rapture at the sweet smell of the pickled cabbage. Then the savage and the maiden danced violently together, and, finally, the savage dropped down on one knee, and the maiden stood on one leg upon his other knee ; thus concluding the ballet, and leaving the spectators in a state of pleasing uncertainty, whether she would ultimately marry the savage, or return to her friends.

" Very well indeed," said Mr. Crummles ; " bravo ! "

" Bravo ! " cried Nicholas, resolved to make the best of everything. "Beautiful ! "

"This, Sir," said Mr. Vincent Crummles, bringing the maiden forward, " this is the infant phenomenon—Miss Ninetta Crummles."

" Your daughter ? " inquired Nicholas.

" My daughter—my daughter," replied Mr. Vincent Crummles ; " the idol of every place we go into, Sir. We have had complimentary letters about this girl, Sir, from the nobility and gentry of almost every town in England."

" I am not surprised at that," said Nicholas ; " she must be quite a natural genius."

" Quite a ——— ! " Mr. Crummles stopped ; language was not powerful enough to describe the infant phenomenon. " I'll tell you what, Sir," he said ; " the talent of this child is not to be imagined. She must be seen, Sir—seen—to be ever so faintly appreciated. There ; go to your mother, my dear."

" May I ask how old she is ? " inquired Nicholas.

" You may, Sir," replied Mr. Crummles, looking steadily in his questioner's face as some men do when they have doubts about being implicitly believed in what they are going to say. " She is ten years of age, Sir."

" Not more ! "

" Not a day."

" Dear me ! " said Nicholas, " it's extraordinary."

It was ; for the infant phenomenon, though of short stature, had a comparatively aged countenance, and had moreover been precisely the same age—not perhaps to the full extent of the memory of the oldest inhabitant, but certainly for five good years. But she had been kept up late every night, and put upon an unlimited allowance of gin and water from infancy, to prevent her growing tall, and perhaps this system of training had produced in the infant phenomenon these additional phenomena.

While this short dialogue was going on, the gentleman who had enacted the savage came up, with his walking-shoes on his feet, and his slippers in his hand, to within a few paces, as if desirous to join in the conversation, and deeming this a good opportunity he put in his word.

" Talent there, Sir," said the savage, nodding towards Miss Crummles.

Nicholas assented.

" Ah ! said the actor, setting his teeth together, and drawing in his breath with a hissing sound, " she oughtn't to be in the provinces, she oughtn't."

" What do you mean ? " asked the manager.

" I mean to say," replied the other, warmly, " that she is too good for country boards, and that she ought to be in one of the large houses in London, or nowhere ; and I tell you more, without mincing the matter, that if it wasn't for envy and jealousy in some quarter that you know of, she would be. Perhaps you'll introduce me here, Mr. Crummles."

" Mr. Folair," said the manager, presenting him to Nicholas.

" Happy to know you, Sir." Mr. Folair touched the brim of his hat with his forefinger, and then shook hands. " A recruit, Sir, I understand ? "

" An unworthy one," replied Nicholas.

" Did you ever see such a set-out as that?" whispered the actor, drawing him away, as Crummles left them to speak to his wife.

" As what?"

Mr. Folair made a funny face from his pantomime collection, and pointed over his shoulder.

" You don't mean the infant phenomenon?"

" Infant humbug, Sir," replied Mr. Folair. " There isn't a female child of common sharpness in a charity school that couldn't do better than that. She may thank her stars she was born a manager's daughter."

" You seem to take it to heart," observed Nicholas, with a smile.

" Yes, by Jove, and well I may," said Mr. Folair, drawing his arm through his, and walking him up and down the stage. " Isn't it enough to make a man crusty to see that little sprawler put up in the best business every night, and actually keeping money out of the house, by being forced down the people's throats, while other people are passed over? Isn't it extraordinary to see a man's confounded family conceit blinding him even to his own interest? Why I *know* of fifteen and sixpence that came to Southampton one night last month to see me dance the Highland Fling, and what's the consequence? I've never been put up in it since—never once—while the 'infant phenomenon' has been grinning through artificial flowers at five people and a baby in the pit, and two boys in the gallery, every night."

" If I may judge from what I have seen of you," said Nicholas, "you must be a valuable member of the company."

" Oh!" replied Mr. Folair, beating his slippers together, to knock the dust out; " I *can* come it pretty well—nobody better perhaps in my own line—but having such business as one gets here, is like putting lead on one's feet instead of chalk, and dancing in fetters without the credit of it. Holloa, old fellow, how are you?"

The gentleman addressed in these latter words was a dark-complexioned man, inclining indeed to sallow, with long thick black hair, and very evident indications (although he was close shaved) of a stiff beard, and whiskers of the same deep shade. His age did not appear to exceed thirty, although many at first sight would have considered him much older, as his face was long and very pale, from the constant application of stage paint. He wore a checked shirt, an old green coat with new gilt buttons, a neckerchief of broad red and green stripes, and full blue trousers; he carried too a common ash walking-stick, apparently.more for show than use, as he flourished it about with the hooked end downwards, except when he raised it for a few seconds, and throwing himself into a fencing attitude, made a pass or two at the side-scenes, or at any other object, animate or inanimate, that chanced to afford him a pretty good mark at the moment.

" Well, Tommy," said this gentleman, making a thrust at his friend, who parried it dexterously with his slipper, " what's the news?"

" A new appearance, that's all," replied Mr. Folair, looking at Nicholas.

" Do the honours, Tommy, do the honours," said the other gentleman, tapping him reproachfully on the crown of the hat with his stick.

" This is Mr. Lenville, who does our first tragedy, Mr. Johnson,"
said the pantomimist.

" Except when old bricks and mortar takes it into his head to do it
himself, you should add, Tommy," remarked Mr. Lenville. " You
know who bricks and mortar is, I suppose, Sir ?"

" I do not, indeed," replied Nicholas.

" We call Crummles that, because his style of acting is rather in the
heavy and ponderous way," said Mr. Lenville.   " I mustn't be cracking
jokes though, for I've got a part of twelve lengths here which I must
be up in to-morrow night, and I haven't had time to look at it yet ;
I'm a confounded quick study, that's one comfort."

Consoling himself with this reflection, Mr. Lenville drew from his
coat-pocket a greasy and crumpled manuscript, and having made
another pass at his friend proceeded to walk to and fro, conning it to
himself, and indulging occasionally in such appropriate action as his
imagination and the text suggested.

A pretty general muster of the company had by this time taken
place ; for besides Mr. Lenville and his friend Tommy, there was
present a slim young gentleman with weak eyes, who played the low-
spirited lovers and sang tenor songs, and who had come arm-in-arm
with the comic countryman—a man with a turned-up nose, large
mouth, broad face, and staring eyes. Making himself very amiable to
the infant phenomenon, was an inebriated elderly gentleman in the last
depths of shabbiness, who played the calm and virtuous old men ; and
paying especial court to Mrs. Crummles was another elderly gentleman,
a shade more respectable, who played the irascible old men—those
funny fellows who have nephews in the army, and perpetually run about
with thick sticks to compel them to marry heiresses. Besides these,
there was a roving-looking person in a rough great-coat, who strode up
and down in front of the lamps, flourishing a dress cane, and rattling
away in an undertone with great vivacity for the amusement of an ideal
audience. He was not quite so young as he had been, and his figure
was rather running to seed ; but there was an air of exaggerated gentility about him, which bespoke the hero of swaggering comedy. There
was also a little group of three or four young men, with lantern jaws
and thick eyebrows, who were conversing in one corner ; but they
seemed to be of secondary importance, and laughed and talked together
without attracting any very marked attention.

The ladies were gathered in a little knot by themselves round the
rickety table before mentioned. There was Miss Snevellicci, who
could do anything from a medley dance to Lady Macbeth, and always
played some part in blue silk knee-smalls at her benefit, glancing from
the depths of her coal-scuttle straw bonnet at Nicholas, and affecting to be
absorbed in the recital of a diverting story to her friend Miss Ledrook,
who had brought her work, and was making up a ruff in the most
natural manner possible. There was Miss Belvawney, who seldom
aspired to speaking parts, and usually went on as a page in white
silk hose, to stand with one leg bent and contemplate the audience, or
to go in and out after Mr. Crummles in stately tragedy, twisting up the
ringlets of the beautiful Miss Bravassa, who had once had her like-

ness taken "in character" by an engraver's apprentice, whereof impressions were hung up for sale in the pastry-cook's window, and the green-grocer's, and at the circulating library, and the box-office, whenever the announce bills came out for her annual night. There was Mrs. Lenville in a very limp bonnet and veil, decidedly in that way in which she would wish to be if she truly loved Mr. Lenville; there was Miss Gazingi, with an imitation ermine boa tied in a loose knot round her neck, flogging Mr. Crummles, junior, with both ends in fun. Lastly, there was Mrs. Grudden in a brown cloth pelisse and a beaver bonnet, who assisted Mrs. Crummles in her domestic affairs, and took money at the doors, and dressed the ladies, and swept the house, and held the prompt book when everybody else was on for the last scene, and acted any kind of part on any emergency without ever learning it, and was put down in the bills under any name or names whatever that occurred to Mr. Crummles as looking well in print.

Mr. Folair having obligingly confided these particulars to Nicholas, left him to mingle with his fellows; the work of personal introduction was completed by Mr. Vincent Crummles, who publicly heralded the new actor as a prodigy of genius and learning.

"I beg your pardon," said Miss Snevellicci, sidling towards Nicholas, "but did you ever play at Canterbury?"

"I never did," replied Nicholas.

"I recollect meeting a gentleman at Canterbury," said Miss Snevellicci, "only for a few moments, for I was leaving the company as he joined it, so like you that I felt almost certain it was the same."

"I see you now for the first time," rejoined Nicholas with all due gallantry. "I am sure I never saw you before; I couldn't have forgotten it."

"Oh, I'm sure—it's very flattering of you to say so," retorted Miss Snevellicci with a graceful bend. "Now I look at you again, I see that the gentleman at Canterbury hadn't the same eyes as you—you'll think me very foolish for taking notice of such things, won't you?"

"Not at all," said Nicholas. "How can I feel otherwise than flattered by your notice in any way?"

"Oh! you men, you are such vain creatures!" cried Miss Snevellicci. Whereupon she became charmingly confused, and, pulling out her pocket handkerchief from a faded pink silk reticule with a gilt clasp, called to Miss Ledrook—

"Led, my dear," said Miss Snevellicci.

"Well, what is the matter?" said Miss Ledrook.

"It's not the same."

"Not the same what?"

"Canterbury—you know what I mean. Come here, I want to speak to you."

But Miss Ledrook wouldn't come to Miss Snevellicci, so Miss Snevellicci was obliged to go to Miss Ledrook, which she did in a skipping manner that was quite fascinating, and Miss Ledrook evidently joked Miss Snevellicci about being struck with Nicholas, for, after some playful whispering, Miss Snevellicci hit Miss Ledrook very hard on the backs of her hands, and retired up, in a state of pleasing confusion.

"Ladies and gentlemen," said Mr. Vincent Crummles, who had been writing on a piece of paper, "we'll call the Mortal Struggle to-morrow at ten; everybody for the procession. Intrigue, and Ways and Means, you're all up in, so we shall only want one rehearsal. Everybody at ten, if you please."

"Everybody at ten," repeated Mrs. Grudden, looking about her.

"On Monday morning we shall read a new piece," said Mr. Crummles; "the name's not known yet, but everybody will have a good part. Mr. Johnson will take care of that."

"Hallo!" said Nicholas, starting, "I——"

"On Monday morning," repeated Mr. Crummles, raising his voice, to drown the unfortunate Mr. Johnson's remonstrance; "that'll do, ladies and gentlemen."

The ladies and gentlemen required no second notice to quit, and in a few minutes the theatre was deserted, save by the Crummles' family, Nicholas, and Smike.

"Upon my word," said Nicholas, taking the manager aside, "I don't think I can be ready by Monday."

"Pooh, pooh," replied Mr. Crummles.

"But really I can't," returned Nicholas; "my invention is not accustomed to these demands, or possibly I might produce ——"

"Invention! what the devil's that got to do with it!" cried the manager, hastily.

"Everything, my dear Sir."

"Nothing, my dear Sir," retorted the manager, with evident impatience. "Do you understand French?"

"Perfectly well."

"Very good," said the manager, opening the table-drawer, and giving a roll of paper from it to Nicholas. "There, just turn that into English, and put your name on the title-page. Damn me," said Mr. Crummles, angrily, "if I haven't often said that I wouldn't have a man or woman in my company that wasn't master of the language, so that they might learn it from the original, and play it in English, and by that means save all this trouble and expense."

Nicholas smiled, and pocketed the play.

"What are you going to do about your lodgings?" said Mr. Crummles.

Nicholas could not help thinking that for the first week it would be an uncommon convenience to have a turn-up bedstead in the pit, but he merely remarked that he had not turned his thoughts that way.

"Come home with me then," said Mr. Crummles, "and my boys shall go with you after dinner, and show you the most likely place."

The offer was not to be refused: Nicholas and Mr. Crummles gave Mrs. Crummles an arm each, and walked up the street in stately array. Smike, the boys, and the phenomenon, went home by a shorter cut, and Mrs. Grudden remained behind to take some cold Irish stew and a pint of porter in the box-office.

Mrs. Crummles trod the pavement as if she were going to immediate execution with an animating consciousness of innocence and that heroic fortitude which virtue alone inspires. Mr. Crummles, on the other hand, assumed the look and gait of a hardened despot; but they both attracted some notice from many of the passers-by, and when they heard a whisper of " Mr. and Mrs. Crummles," or saw a little boy run back to stare them in the face, the severe expression of their countenances relaxed, for they felt it was popularity.

Mr. Crummles lived in Saint Thomas's Street, at the house of one Bulph, a pilot, who sported a boat-green door, with window-frames of the same colour, and had the little finger of a drowned man on his parlour mantel-shelf, with other maritime and natural curiosities. He displayed also a brass knocker, a brass plate, and a brass bell-handle, all very bright and shining; and had a mast, with a vane on the top of it, in his back yard.

" You are welcome," said Mrs. Crummles, turning round to Nicholas when they reached the bow-windowed front room on the first floor.

Nicholas bowed his acknowledgments, and was unfeignedly glad to see the cloth laid.

" We have but a shoulder of mutton with onion sauce," said Mrs. Crummles, in the same charnel-house voice; " but such as our dinner is, we beg you to partake of it."

" You are very good," replied Nicholas, " I shall do it ample justice."

" Vincent," said Mrs. Crummles, " what is the hour ? "

" Five minutes past dinner-time," said Mr. Crummles.

Mrs. Crummles rang the bell. " Let the mutton and onion sauce appear."

The slave who attended upon Mr. Bulph's lodgers disappeared, and after a short interval re-appeared with the festive banquet. Nicholas and the infant phenomenon opposed each other at the pembroke-table, and Smike and the master Crummleses dined on the sofa bedstead.

" Are they very theatrical people here ? " asked Nicholas.

" No," replied Mr. Crummles, shaking his head, " far from it—far from it."

" I pity them," observed Mrs. Crummles.

" So do I," said Nicholas ; " if they have no relish for theatrical entertainments, properly conducted."

" Then they have none, Sir," rejoined Mr. Crummles. " To the infant's benefit, last year, on which occasion she repeated three of her most popular characters, and also appeared in the Fairy Porcupine, as originally performed by her, there was a house of no more than four pound twelve."

" Is it possible ? " cried Nicholas.

" And two pound of that was trust, pa," said the phenomenon.

" And two pound of that was trust," repeated Mr. Crummles. " Mrs. Crummles herself has played to mere handfuls."

" But they are always a taking audience, Vincent," said the manager's wife.

" Most audiences are, when they have good acting—real good acting —the real thing," replied Mr. Crummles, forcibly.

" Do you give lessons, ma'am ? " inquired Nicholas.

" I do," said Mrs. Crummles.

" There is no teaching here, I suppose ? "

" There has been," said Mrs. Crummles. " I have received pupils here. I imparted tuition to the daughter of a dealer in ships' provivision ; but it afterwards appeared that she was insane when she first came to me. It was very extraordinary that she should come, under such circumstances."

Not feeling quite so sure of that, Nicholas thought it best to hold his peace.

" Let me see," said the manager cogitating after dinner. " Would you like some nice little part with the infant ? "

" You are very good," replied Nicholas hastily ; " but I think perhaps it would be better if I had somebody of my own size at first, in case I should turn out awkward. I should feel more at home perhaps."

" True," said the manager. " Perhaps you would, and you could play up to the infant in time you know."

" Certainly," replied Nicholas : devoutly hoping that it would be a very long time before he was honoured with this distinction.

" Then I'll tell you what we'll do," said Mr. Crummles. " You shall study Romeo when you've done that piece—don't forget to throw the pump and tubs in by-the-bye—Juliet Miss Snevellicci, old Grudden the nurse.—Yes, that'll do very well. Rover too ;—you might get up Rover while you were about it, and Cassio, and Jeremy Diddler. You can easily knock them off ; one part helps the other so much. Here they are, cues and all."

With these hasty general directions Mr. Crummles thrust a number of little books into the faltering hands of Nicholas, and bidding his eldest son go with him and show him where lodgings were to be had, shook him by the hand and wished him good night.

There is no lack of comfortable furnished apartments in Portsmouth, and no difficulty in finding some that are proportionate to very slender finances ; but the former were too good, and the latter too bad, and they went into so many houses, and came out unsuited, that Nicholas seriously began to think he should be obliged to ask permission to spend the night in the theatre, after all.

Eventually, however, they stumbled upon two small rooms up three pair of stairs, or rather two pair and a ladder, at a tobacconist's shop, on the Common Hard, a dirty street leading down to the dockyard. These Nicholas engaged, only too happy to have escaped any request for payment of a week's rent beforehand.

" There, lay down our personal property, Smike," he said, after showing young Crummles down stairs. " We have fallen upon strange times, and God only knows the end of them ; but I am tired with the events of these three days, and will postpone reflection till to-morrow —if I can."

ON THE FIRST OF NOVEMBER WILL BE PUBLISHED

No. I.,

(TO BE CONTINUED MONTHLY),

OF

HEADS OF THE PEOPLE:

PRICE ONE SHILLING.

AN INTRODUCTION.

"My Lord Duke"—(*Listen to the Head, most gracious Reader*)—"My Lord Duke, permit me to introduce to your Grace, Jack Heads-and-tails, the Mutton-pieman. Jack Heads-and-tails, his Grace the Duke of Manystars. Good folks, be acquainted."

"Sir Courcy Normanline, allow me to offer to your notice, Brightshovel Bill, the Flying Dustman. Brightshovel Bill, Sir Courcy Normanline, the oldest baronet of England. Know one another."

"Dear Duchess of Daffodils, may I be suffered to make known to you, poor little Alice Thousandstitch, the milliner's apprentice? Alice Thousandstitch, [*aside to her—* foolish thing, don't blush and tremble] know the condescending Duchess of Daffodils."

————

THE benevolent purpose of the gentleman whose *vera effigies*, or true likeness, adorns the page, is—if we err not—to make Englishmen intimate with Englishmen; to bring the ends of the Town and the Country together; to make May Fair known to the New Cut; New Cut to May Fair; to introduce the Daily Sempstress to the evening party of the Peeress; to shew and make the Duchess wonder at the three-shilling-per-week lodging of her little needle-woman.

In this goodly work, the worthy gentleman will be assisted by an Artist, as it would seem, "sent into this breathing world" for no meaner purpose than that of shewing to his countrymen the faces of each other; catching their visages in their most characteristic expression, and conveying at a glance the very "heart and mystery" of their function.

These Portraits—and their "name is Legion"—will not be Fancy Portraits. The purchaser will not be cheated with a Dustman in sugar-candy, or a Chimney-sweep in peppermint, after the modern fancy of face-making; neither will he have a Crockford in marmalade, or a Jack Ketch in barley-sugar; but true flesh and blood withal:—the stare—the squint—the leer—the eyes swimming with real innocent fun or with adulterated gin—the lips curled with pride or puckered with meanness—all is taken and will be given from *the life;* subjects of all ranks—all professions—all denominations—having unconsciously sat for the "HEADS OF THE PEOPLE."

The Work will in every respect be a National Work: and whether the Reader chance to be a Member of Parliament or a Mountebank—a Common Lawyer or a Common Thief—a Dealer in Stocks or a Dealer in other peoples' pocket-handkerchiefs—a trading Patriot or the Keeper of a *Fence* —a Cabinet Minister or a Quack Doctor—a Morality Monger or a Passer of Counterfeit Coin—a Police Magistrate or a Pantaloon—a Temperance Man of Toast-and-Water or a Man of Twenty *Goes*—a Peer who makes laws or a Peer who breaks windows—a Man with Stars and Garters or a Man with Hot Potatoes—be he one or more of these (and some of the functions might possibly be united) he will find the likeness of "*his Order*" among the "HEADS OF THE PEOPLE."

Each Number will contain four "HEADS," and a Description of the social habits and peculiarities of the subject will accompany every Portrait; this Description contributed by writers who have not studied human nature from Albums, but from beating hearts; who have not looked at life only through the plate-glass windows of a drawing-room, but have been pushed and elbowed by the living crowd:

LONDON:

ROBERT TYAS, 50, CHEAPSIDE:

J. MENZIES, EDINBURGH;

AND MACHEN AND CO. DUBLIN.

Vizetelly and Co. Printers,   135, Fleet Street. London.

IMMENSE SAVING IN THE PURCHASE OF TEA.

TO FAMILIES, THE CLERGY, HOTEL KEEPERS, LARGE SCHOOLS, &c.

On SATURDAY, THE 25TH OF AUGUST, we opened the spacious premises, **No. 8, Ludgate Hill,** for the sale of TEAS, COFFEES, SPICES, AND REFINED SUGARS.

The importance which the Tea Trade has of late years assumed, the enormous increase in the consumption, and the necessity there exists for purchasing so important an article of the best quality and at the cheapest rate, are ample reasons why a concern of first rate magnitude should be established.

Ludgate Hill, the centre of London, unquestionably one of the greatest thoroughfares in the metropolis, and through which hundreds of thousands are daily and hourly passing, is, from its situation, admirably calculated for the establishment of an extensive **Family and ready money business;** and though of late years high prices and indifferent qualities have lessened its reputation as a Tea Mart, yet we rest confident that the system which will be pursued by us, will, as our efforts are appreciated, restore it to its former influence.

The principles upon which we rest our claims for preference, are those which must be productive of confidence, and a permanent and increasing trade, viz: **Excellence in quality,** combined with **extreme moderation in price.** At our Establishment, Families in town or country, may rely upon obtaining every variety of Teas, at the lowest prices of the day.

The enormous quantity of Teas declared for the Quarterly Sale, in October, viz.: 243,019 packages, or 16,490,629 lbs., double the quantity ever disposed of at one Sale by the East India Company, has already had its effect upon the markets. Anticipating a still further reduction, we have lowered the prices of our Teas as follows:—

BLACK TEAS.

	s.	d.
	PER POUND.	
Genuine East India Compy.'s Congou (very good and strong Tea)	3	8

A short time since no Wholesale Dealer could purchase this Tea for less than Four Shillings per lb.

	s.	d.
Strong very full-bodied Congou	4	0
Fine blackish leaf Congou, (Pekoe kind)	4	4
The very finest Congou (Ripe Pekoe Souchong flavor)	4	8

This is the best Black Tea that can be obtained, and is sold by many houses at Six Shillings, and by **none, except ours,** at less than Five Shillings per pound.

	s.	d.
Good Bohea	2	10
Good Ordinary Congou	3	0
Good Common Congou	3	4

GREEN TEAS.

	s.	d.
Hyson Skin and Twankay	3	6
Curled and bright leaf Twankay, strong	3	8
Fine Bloom Tea, Hyson flavor	4	0
Genuine Hyson, good flavor	4	6
Fine Hyson, full flavor	5	0
Superfine Hyson, rich delicate flavor	6	0
Young Hyson, small leaf	3 10 to 4	4
Ouchain, or Young Hyson, small wiry bright leaf	4 8 to 5	0
Imperial Gunpowder	5 0 to 5	4
Gunpowder, small close leaf	5 4 to 6	0
Fine Gunpowder, small pearly leaf	6	6
Finest Gunpowder, small bright close twisted leaf	7	0

SIDNEY & COMPY.,

Importers of and Dealers in Tea.

8, LUDGATE HILL,

EIGHT DOORS FROM NEW BRIDGE STREET.

⁎₊⁎ Goods delivered within six miles of London, by our own Vans. Country Orders, per Post or Carrier, promptly executed.

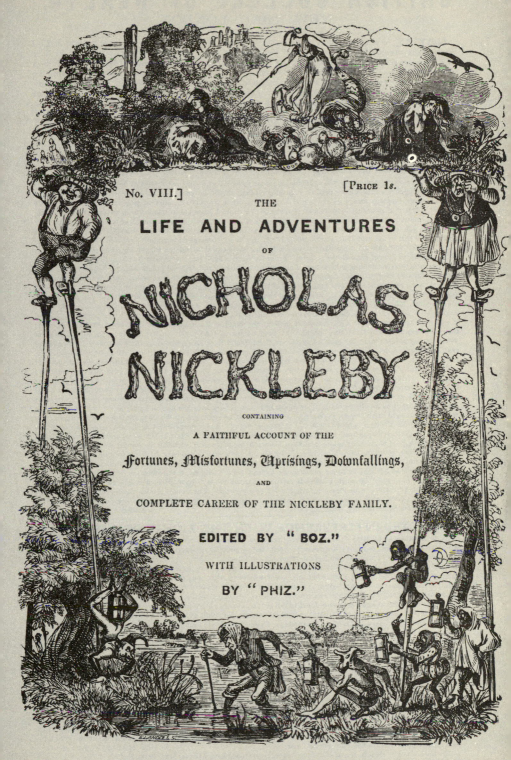

No. VIII.]   [Price 1s.

THE

LIFE AND ADVENTURES

OF

NICHOLAS NICKLEBY

CONTAINING

A FAITHFUL ACCOUNT OF THE

Fortunes, Misfortunes, Uprisings, Downfallings,

AND

COMPLETE CAREER OF THE NICKLEBY FAMILY.

EDITED BY " BOZ."

WITH ILLUSTRATIONS

BY " PHIZ."

LONDON: CHAPMAN AND HALL, 186, STRAND.

BRITISH COLLEGE OF HEALTH,
NEW ROAD, LONDON.

NOTICE.—Whereas a most unfair system of oppression is manifested by the lower grade of Medical Practitioners towards Mr. Morison and his Medicines, we, the undersigned, hereby declare, that we have for some years past used ourselves, and administered to others, the before-mentioned Medicines in all cases of disease, and are of opinion, first, that they are a cure for all curable diseases, and secondly, that the theory upon which such Medicines are administered is the only true one ; the whole of which we are ready and willing to verify whenever called upon. In conclusion, we cannot but regret that in such an important question to mankind generally, the Medical Profession should cautiously abstain from all fair and impartial investigation of the subject.

> ROBERT LYNCH, M.D.
> RICHARD TOTHILL, Surgeon to the Exeter Hygeian Dispensary, Heavitree, near Exeter.
> JOHNSON LINCOLN, Surgeon, R.N., Northallerton, Yorkshire.

September 21, 1838.

To James Morison, Esq., President of the British College of Health, London.

Sir,—It is now two years since you appointed me your general Agent for the counties of Somerset and Dorset. It might justly appear extraordinary that such an appointment should be conferred on a female. To many it might seem like presumptuous arrogance and a love of notoriety, while by others a desire of profit may be assigned as the reason. I feel it then a duty to myself, to you, and to the cause I advocate, to state why I, an unprotected woman, leaving my native retirement and home, thus boldly, as it might seem, come forward and place myself so conspicuously before the public. The details of my case and cure having been already published in the Morisoniana, &c., I will merely state that in the year 1832, after a whole life of suffering, I became (accidentally) acquainted with your medicines, but from being always accustomed to take only what my medical attendants suggested, I was prejudiced against everything which did not emanate from them. From the earliest age I had never been free from illness, in some form or other, erysipelas, amounting to blindness, and consequent internal and external inflammation ; frequent and violent spasm: ; diseased liver, with gall-stones. Then laid down for months with hip-joint malady, afterwards a cripple on crutches : then rheumatic fever and enlargements of the joints; then aphthæ, or thrush ; and after this, tic douloureux, typhus fever, &c., until what with my diseases and the severe treatment which was deemed necessary to attack them, viz., bleeding, blistering, cupping, leeching, salivating by calomel, &c. &c., I may truly add, gallons of medicines, I became an emaciated, useless, helpless creature, and life itself a burden. The medical men who attended me cannot, if this statement meets their eyes, contradict or deny the truth of these assertions. I received from the utmost of their skill, kindness, and attention ; but, like the poor woman in the Gospel, "I was not bettered, but rather grew worse, having suffered many things of many doctors," and should have, like her, spent all my substance in my anxious search after health, had I not providentially heard of your medicines. To be brief, I took them, without intermission, many months, and without allowing the opinions or persuasions of those opposed to them to prejudice my mind, I suffered long, but before a year elapsed all my former maladies were gone, as by a charm ! I became a new creature ! And now what remained for me to do ? How could I testify my gratitude to Him who had permitted your medicines to be thus blessed to one of the most unworthy of His creatures? All my sisters, six in number, had, after equal sufferings with myself, been laid in their tombs, in the bloom of life, and here was I, after a fortune spent in vain, thus marvellously, thus mercifully raised to enjoy robust health, and capable of the utmost bodily or mental exertion ! In whose service ought these powers, so freely, so newly given, to be employed ? Was I to content myself with selfishly sitting down, like a miser, to hoard my acquired treasure, or by a public devotedness to the alleviation of my fellow-creatures' sufferings, demonstrate the sincerity of my gratitude to Him "who has left us an example that we should trace his steps." I could not hesitate, and here I am a living monument, with the instrument which He has blessed in my possession, your invaluable medicines; and I should feel myself a recreant from my duty as a Christian, did I allow any selfish feeling, any false delicacy or shame, to prevent me from thus again publicly testifying my obligation.

I am aware that this may be called enthusiasm ; be it so. I can only say, that amidst the hundreds of cases of cure and of relief from suffering which I have witnessed by your medicines, I have derived more heartfelt delight than I ever did from all the praise, or pleasure, or friendship of the world. The time is coming when every man's work will be proved, and I wait with assured humble hope for that period, remaining, most faithfully, your obedient servant,

Crewkerne, Somersetshire, Sept. 24, 1838.   HARRIET BEANHAM.

PROJECTED INTERFERENCE WITH THE RIGHTS OF THE PEOPLE.

At the meetings of Medical Associations, measures have recently been adopted for what its members (overflowing with erudition and philanthropy) are pleased to term the suppression of Quackery, supported by articles which have recently appeared in a medical publication termed the "Lancet." Now, that all means have justly failed to put down MORISON'S PILLS, and that the errors of medical practice have been fully exposed, these champions of Esculapius are about petitioning Parliament to put down by force what they term "Quack Medicines," without considering that the greatest Quackery is to be found in their tottering profession, which they are so vainly endeavouring to support. But will not the public ask, what is it that in this enlightened age calls for legislative interference in such matters ? Is it that as knowledge is diffused to the people the medical profession retrogrades, and is compelled, for its support, to seek the assistance of Parliament, in order to make the public at large subservient to its cupidity ? Surely any act which would have for its effect the coercion of public opinion in such matters, would not only be an encroachment on the liberty of the subject, but a disgrace to the Statute-book.—British College of Health, New-road, London, October 1, 1838.

CAUTION.

Whereas spurious imitations of my Medicines are now in circulation, I, James Morison, the Hygeist, hereby give notice, That I am in *no wise* connected with the following Medicines purporting to be mine, and sold under the various names of "Dr. Morrison's Pills," "The Hygeian Pills," "The Improved Vegetable Universal Pills," "The Original Morison's Pills, as compounded by the late Mr. Moat," "The Original Hygeian Vegetable Pills," "The Original Morison's Pills," &c. &c. That my Medicines are prepared only at the British College of Health, Hamilton Place, King's Cross, and sold by the General Agents to the British College of Health and their Sub-Agents, and that no Chemist or Druggist is authorized by me to dispose of the same. None can be genuine without the words "MORISON'S UNIVERSAL MEDICINES" are engraved on the Government Stamp, in white letters upon a red ground.— In witness whereof I have hereunto set my hand.   JAMES MORISON, the Hygeist.

British College of Health, No. 2, Hamilton Place, New Road, King's Cross, May, 1838.

General Agent for the United States of America—Dr. George Taylor, 6½, Wall-street, New York. Mr. Thomas Gardner, Calcutta, General Agent for India.

PENNY AND SON'S POCKET-BOOKS—(*Continued*).

THE GENTLEMAN'S POCKET-BOOK ALMANACK

With an elegant Frontispiece, a View of the City of London Schools; contains, a comprehensive Summary of the Act abolishing Imprisonment for Debt, the Act for Legalising Contracts made by Companies with which Clergymen are connected, Recovery of Possession of Tenements under £20, and other Acts passed during 1838 ; Royal Family of Great Britain, Sovereigns of Europe, Her Majesty's Ministers, List of the House of Peers and Commons, and their Officers, with their Town residences, Law Intelligence—Terms, Quarter Sessions, Courts, Inns of Court, Poor-Law Commissioners, Official Assignees, Prisons, Heralds' College, Lords Lieutenants, Aldermen of London, Companies, Public Offices, Army and Navy Agents Societies, Bankers in London, Country Bankers in England, Scotland, Wales, and Ireland, and the Houses they draw upon in London, the Birmingham, Southampton, and Great Western Railway Stations and Fares; a Diary, of one hundred and twelve pages for Memorandums, Engagements, Cash Account, and Summary, for every day throughout the year, Almanack, with original information, and Astronomical Notices, for 1839, with other useful Commercial and General information.

Size, 5 in. by 3, bound in Mock Russia, or coloured Roan, with Tuck and Pockets, price 2s. 6d.

PENNY'S IMPROVED COMMERCIAL POCKET-BOOK.
WITH ALMANACK.

Carefully arranged, and adapted to the use of the Private Gentleman, Merchant, Trader, and Farmer, with a view of the new Houses of Parliament; containing a Summary of the Act abolishing Imprisonment for Debt, the Act for Legalising Contracts made by Companies with which clergymen are connected, the Act for recovering Possession of Tenements under £20 per annum, Repeal of certain Duties, and other Acts passed in the year 1838—State and Parliamentary Intelligence, Royal Family of Great Britain, Sovereigns of Europe, Her Majesty's Ministers, List of the Members of the Houses of Lords and Commons, with their Town residences, Officers of the two Houses, Officers of State, &c., Officers of Her Majesty's Household, Ladies of the Household, Her Majesty's Privy Council, the Lord Lieutenants, Heralds' College; Law Intelligence—Terms, Law Courts, Inns of Court, Official Assignees, Poor-Law Commissioners, Prisons; List of the Army, General Officers, Marine Corps, List of the Navy, Army and Navy Agents; Commercial and General information: Bankers in London, Country Bankers in England, Scotland, Wales, and Ireland, Aldermen, Companies, Offices, &c. of London, Mails made up in London, General and Twopenny Post, Birmingham, Southampton, and Great Western, Railway and Stations Fares, Public Offices, Societies, Window Duties, Porter's Fares, High-water Table, Astronomical Notices for 1839, Almanack for 1839, a Diary, of one hundred and twelve ruled pages for Memorandums and Cash Account for every day in the year, with a Cash Summary, and other useful information, Tables, &c.

Size 6 in. by 4, bound in Mock Russia, or coloured Roan, with Tuck and Pockets, price 3s. 6d.

CHEAP ANNUAL PRESENTS,
OR,
REWARDS FOR GOOD CONDUCT.

THE DIAMOND POCKET-BOOK ALMANACK,

With five elegant Plates. Contains—Fifty-four Engagement pages for the year, Cash Account for each month, Cash Summary, Almanack for 1839, Astronomical Notices. Answers to Enigmas and Charades of last year, Tales of the Young Robber, and Laconics. POETRY:—Rules for Exquisites, Forget Thee, a Song, On receiving a Portrait, Sunshine Sketch, To my Books, Do I remember it? and the Exile. Enigmas, Charades, New and Fashionable Dances, Bill and Receipt Stamps, Wages Table, Ready Reckoner, &c.

In Embossed Cover, Tuck and Pockets, price 1s.

DITTO, WITH NINE PLATES,
Embossed Roan Cover, Tuck, and Pockets, price 1s. 6d.

THE PEARL POCKET-BOOK ALMANACK,

With five elegant Plates. Contains—Fifty-four Engagement pages for the year, Cash Account for each month, Cash Summary, Almanack for 1839, Astronomical Notices. Answers to Enigmas and Charades of last year. Tales of the Shepherd Boy, Rose Allan, and on Hope. POETRY:—The Knight's Farewell, the French Governess, Sonnet,—Song, And canst thou say Farewell, Love, Song by Miss Mitford, and a Song. New and Fashionable Dances, Conundrums, Enigmas, Bill and Receipt Stamps, Wages Table, Ready Reckoner, &c.

In Embossed Cover, with Tuck, and Pockets, price 1s.

DITTO, WITH NINE PLATES,
Embossed Roan Cover, Tuck, and Pockets, price 1s. 6d.

PENNY'S Edition of the DIAMOND ALMANACK, price 1d. each. Ditto, interleaved, gilt edged, 2d. each. PENNY'S Edition of REES'S DIARY, with Almanack, price 6d. each.

The high character and ready sale which PENNY & SON's Annual Pocket-Book Annuals have for many years sustained, the moderate retail price of each Book, and the very liberal allowance to the Trade, will cause, as heretofore, a heavy demand on the publishing day, and will consequently require early applications to secure a supply.

THE FOLLOWING NEW WORKS ARE PUBLISHED BY

S. & J. FULLER, 34, RATHBONE PLACE.

IMITATIONS OF DRAWINGS IN COLOURS,

AFTER THOMAS SIDNEY COOPER.

Part I. Fitted up in a folio, gilt and lettered, price 2*l.* 12*s.* 6*d.*,

A SERIES OF TEN IMITATIONS OF DRAWINGS, MOUNTED, AFTER THOMAS SIDNEY COOPER.

Consisting of a variety of subjects illustrative of Rural Scenery, adapted for the use of the Artist, and for the amusement of the Amateur.

Part II. Consisting of

TEN IMITATIONS OF DRAWINGS,

As above, price 2*l.* 12*s.* 6*d.*

A NEW SERIES OF STUDIES OF CATTLE, DRAWN FROM NATURE, BY T. S. COOPER.

Now publishing, in Monthly Numbers, price 4*s.* each, or half-bound, price 2*l.* 2*s.*,

A NEW SERIES OF STUDIES OF CATTLE,

BY T. S. COOPER.

This beautiful work has the peculiar advantage of giving the most perfect imitation of Original Drawings by a process in Lithography, in which several tints are produced ; and will compose, not only the various Cattle seen in England, but also groups of rustic figures and rural character.

THE PETIT COURIER DES DAMES,

OR JOURNAL OF FRENCH FASHION.

S. & J. FULLER respectfully inform the Nobility and Gentry that the above elegant Journal, illustrated with Figures of Female Costume, and other departments of Fashionable Dress, beautifully coloured, arrives from Paris every week, and delivered to the Subscribers at 12*s.* the quarter, or 2*l.* 8*s.* the year, forming a most useful work of reference of elegant Female Costume.

STEEPLE CHASE, FOX HUNTING, & HORSE RACING.

S. and J. FULLER beg to inform their Friends and the Sporting World, that, having for many years past published some of the most favourite and popular Prints of STEEPLE CHASE, FOX HUNTING, HORSE RACING, and other subjects of the British Field Sports, with their much-admired and esteemed Portraits of the celebrated Winners of the Great St. Leger Stakes at Doncaster, and the Derby Stakes at Epsom, from the pencils of Messrs. HERRING, ALKEN, POLLARD, and other favourite Masters, many of these esteemed and favourite productions they have ready framed and varnished, in a novel kind of Frame, in imitation of the French, and which they can render, at very low prices, well adapted for the embellishment of the Shooting Box or Sportsman's Hall.

N.B. Orders for the East and West Indies, and the Colonies, executed at the shortest notice.

A SUPERIOR COLLECTION OF THE ANNUALS FOR 1839.

S. and J. FULLER have always on Sale an extensive Collection of LITHOGRAPHIC PRINTS from Paris, which are forwarded to them as soon as published, adapted for the new and ingenious Art of Transferring Prints to Wood. White Wood Articles of every description for the above, as Work Boxes, Card Boxes, Glove Boxes, Face Screens, Pole Screens, Chess Boards, Pier Tables, Work Tables, Baskets, Card Racks, &c. Flowers, Ornaments, &c. decorative and useful, for the Embellishment of Rooms.

N.B. Their new-invented TRANSFER VARNISH, sold in Bottles, with directions, price 1*s.* and 2*s.* each ; or fitted up in Boxes, with everything complete for the purpose, price 7*s.* 6*d.*

They continue to publish New Lithographic Prints, Medallions, Borders, &c. &c. weekly.

S. and J. FULLER have on Sale a superior Collection of fine Drawings, by Modern Masters ; and many Drawings on the Sports of the Field, by HENRY ALKEN and others.

SUPERIOR WORKS ON THE ART OF DRAWING,

NOW PUBLISHING BY S. & J. FULLER.

Studies of Cattle, drawn from Nature by Thomas Sidney Cooper ; consisting of Oxen, Bulls, Cows, Sheep, Asses, Goats, Deer, Rustic Figures, &c.

David Cox's Treatise on Landscape Painting and Effect in Water Colours, with Examples in Outline, Effect, and Colouring.

Cox's Progressive Lessons.

Cox's Young Artist's Companion for Drawing of Landscapes.

Cipriani's Rudiments for Drawing the Human Figure,

engraved by F. Bartolozzi, from the First Rudiments to the Finished Figure.

Studies of Trees, by S. Lines.

George Harley's Progressive Drawing Book of Landscapes, in 12 numbers, price One Shilling each.

Alken's New Sketch Book.

Alken's Rudiments for Drawing the Horse.

Alken's Illustrations for Landscape Scenery.

With numerous other Works on the Art of Drawing.

DRAWINGS LENT TO COPY.

APSLEY PELLATT'S

ABRIDGED LIST OF
Net Cash Prices for the best Flint Glass Ware.

DECANTERS.

25 Strong quart Nelson shape decanters, cut all over, bold flutes and cut brim & stopper, P.M. each 10s6d. to 12 0

26 Do. three-ringed royal shape, cut on and between rings, turned out stop, P.M. each 10 0
  Do. do. not cut on or between rings, nor turned out stopper, P.M. ea. 8s to 9 0

27 Fancy shapes, cut all over, eight flutes, spire stopper, &c. each, P.M. 16s. to 18 0
  Do. six flutes only, each, P.M. 24s. to 27 0

DISHES.

31 Dishes, oblong, pillar moulded, scolloped edges, cut star.

| 5-in. | 7-in. | 9-in. | 10-in. |
| 3s. 6d. | 6s. 6d. | 11s. | 13s. each. |

32 Oval cup sprig, shell pattern,

| 5-in. | 7-in. | 9-in. | 11-in. |
| 7s. 6d. | 9s. 6d. | 16s. | 19s. each. |

33 Square shape pillar, moulded star,

| 5-in. | 7-in | 9-in. | 10-in. |
| 4s. | 8s. | 12s. 6d. | 15s. each. |

FINGER CUPS.

37 Fluted finger-cups, strong, about 14 oz. each 2 6
  Do. plain flint, punted, per doz..... 18 0
  Do. coloured, per doz.......18s. to 21 0

38 Ten-fluted round, very strong, each . 5 0
  Eight-fluted do., each 8 0

39 Medicean shape, moulded pillar, pearl upper part, cut flat flutes, each .. 5 0

PICKLES.

46 Pickles, half fluted for 3 in. holes, RM ea. 4 6

47 Strong, moulded bottom, 3-in. hole, cut all over, flat flutes, R.M. each . 5 0
  Best cut star do. for 3½-in hole, PM ea. 7 6
  Very strong and best cut, P.M. each 14 6

WATER JUGS

59 Quarts, neatly fluted and cut rings, each.................14s. to 18 0

60 Ewer shape, best cut handles, &c.... 21 0

61 Silver do. scolloped edges, ex. lar. flutes 25 0

WATER BOTTLES

70 Moulded pillar body, cut neck, each . 3 0
71 Cut neck and star................. 3 0
72 Double fluted cut rings 3 6
73 Very strong pillar, moulded body, cut neck and rings 5 6
74 Grecian shape, fluted all over 7 0

TUMBLERS

	78	79	80	81	82	83	84	85	86	87	
Tale	5s.										
Flint,	7s.	10s.	12s.	12s.	10s.	12s.	14s.	18s.	18s.		Doz.
	to	to	to	to	to		to	to	to		
	8s.	12s	14s.	15s.	12s.		18s.	21s.	21s.	30s	do.

WINES

88	89	90	91	92	93	94	95	96	97	98	99
7s.	7s.	7s.	7s.	8s.	14s.	12s.	13s.	15s.	18s.	21s.	20s.
to	to	to	to								
8s.	9s.	9s.	9s.	10s.							

Glass Blowing, Cutting, and Engraving, may be inspected by Purchasers, at Mr. Pellatt's Extensive Flint Glass and Steam Cutting Works, in Holland Street, near Blackfriars' Bridge, any Tuesday, Wednesday, or Thursday.

Merchants and the Trade supplied on equitable Terms.

No Abatement from the above specified Ready Money Prices.

No Connexion with any other Establishment.

LABERN'S BOTANIC CREAM.

By appointment, patronised by her Most Gracious Majesty, celebrated for strengthening and promoting the growth of Hair, and completely freeing it from Scurf.—Sold by the Proprietor, H. Labern, Perfumer to her Majesty, 49, Judd Street, Brunswick Square, in pots, 1s. 6d., 2s. 6d., 3s. 6d., and 5s., and in Bottles 3s. 6d. and 5s. each, and by all Perfumers and Medicine Venders.   Beware of counterfeits.   Ask for "Labern's Botanic Cream."

⁎ Trade Orders from the Country to come through the London Wholesale Houses.

AUTUMNAL INFLUENCES.

That each season produces its appropriate and peculiar effects, both in the animal and vegetable economy, is pretty generally admitted ; though in its more minute operations, a sufficient accuracy of observation has rarely been attained. On the subject of the Hair, and the relaxing agency exercised on it at this particular season, enough has recently been set forth, to show the necessity of directing especial attention to this point.   A mild yet effectual stimulant is required to counteract this tendency ; and the popularity of OLDRIDGE'S BALM OF COLUMBIA points it out as the most salutary and efficient application.

OLDRIDGE'S BALM causes whiskers and eyebrows to grow, prevents the Hair from turning grey, and the first application makes it curl beautifully, frees it from scurf, and stops it from falling off.   Abundance of certificates from gentlemen of the first respectability are shown by the Proprietors, C. and A. OLDRIDGE, 1, Wellington Street, Strand, where the Balm is sold, price 3s. 6d., 6s., and 11s. per bottle.   No other prices are genuine.

Some complaints have reached the Proprietors of a spurious Balm having been vended ; they again caution the Public to be on their guard against the base impostors, by especially asking for OLDRIDGE'S BALM OF COLUM-BIA, 1, WELLINGTON STREET, STRAND, LONDON.

PERRY'S ESSENCE FOR THE TOOTH AND EAR-ACHE,
AND PAINS IN THE FACE AND JAWS.
Sold in Bottles, 11s., 2s. 9d., and 1s. 1½d.

PERRY'S ESSENCE has long been patronised by the most distinguished personages in the kingdom, eulogised in numerous highly respectable Medical Journals, and sanctioned by the first Physicians in Europe, who have declared it to be the "best Medicine ever discovered for the Tooth-Ache and Ear-Ache." Excruciating pain is instantaneously relieved by it, and the progress of decay in teeth arrested ; loose teeth are fastened, and kept firm, sound, and serviceable to the latest period.   It cures the scurvy in the gums, renders them healthy, effectually prevents Tooth-Ache, and also sweetens offensive breath.   The Essence retains its virtues in all climates ; but it must be very well corked, or it will be good for nothing.   By rubbing the hands &c. with pomatum, tallow, or spirits of wine, any stain made by the Essence will be removed.

From Professor Hertz's Popular Treatise on the Management of Teeth.—This eminent dentist, in his valuable work dedicated to QUEEN CHARLOTTE, recommends Perry's Essence as the only specific ever discovered for the Tooth-Ache ; and from the experience he has had with it, he states positively,—" That the composition is innocent, and it appears to check the progress of decay, instead of increasing it, which it is well known that remedies for the Tooth-Ache, from their caustic qualities, are apt to do."—See Fourth Edition of Hertz's Dissertation on Teeth, p. 19.

From the Monthly Gazette of Health, for October, 1818.—" The most effectual remedy for the Tooth-Ache with which we are acquainted is the Essence prepared by Mr. PERRY, of Farnham, in Surrey.   The remedy is perfectly mild, allays the pain almost immediately on being introduced into the carious Tooth, and by lining the internal surface with a resinous gum, it keeps off that disease, and checks the progress of decay."

Extract from the Medical Guide, for 1817.—" PERRY'S ESSENCE.—This composition, applied to the painful Tooth by means of lint, generally affords immediate relief, and is, no doubt, the most efficacious remedy for the Tooth-Ache that has been discovered, having been first prepared by Mr. PERRY, of Farnham."

From Dr. Reece's Dictionary of Medicine, 1813, sanctioned by his late Majesty, KING GEORGE THE FOURTH. —" I have made trial of a remedy for the Tooth-Ache, first recommended by Mr. PERRY, of Farnham, which in every instance (some of which were very violent) afforded instantaneous relief."

Extract from Dr. Jackson, 1806.—" Having had frequent opportunities of applying PERRY'S Essence to decayed Teeth, and from the instantaneous relief which it afforded to almost all to whom it has been administered, I do not hesitate to declare that it is, in my opinion, the best remedy for the Tooth-Ache, arising from decay, ever discovered."

Philosophical Journal for July, 1820.—" In an early Number we have given an analysis of PERRY's Essence : the favourable reports we have received from different parts of the country confirm the character we have given of it as a remedy for the Tooth-Ache.   It is free from any caustic quality, and is certainly incapable of doing any injury to the Teeth.   In cases of Caries, it appears to suspend the process of decomposition or decay."

From the Monthly Gazette of Health, for 1816.—The Editor, in his Preface, on the subject of " Proprietary Medicines," in remarking on the dangerous tendency of many of them, and of his exposure of their disgraceful practices, concludes by observing, that—" Some Patent Medicines he has discovered to possess merit superior to the London Pharmaco-pœia ; these he has not hesitated to recommend ; and of this number is PERRY's Essence for the Tooth-Ache."

See also the Commendations in No. I., p. 30, *of the same valuable publication,* under the head of " PERRY's Essence for the Tooth-Ache and Pains in the Face."—" This preparation does not contain any mineral production.   To allay pain in a hollow or carious Tooth, this composition, no doubt, affords an efficacious remedy ; in consequence of the de-composition which takes place, the internal surface of the caries is defended from the action of atmospheric air and acrid matter.   This Essence was discovered by Mr. PERRY, of Farnham, who in the printed wrapper of the bottle, asserts, that thousands of cases can be given to prove that his Essence is an infallible remedy for the Tooth-Ache and Ear-Ache, as not one instance has yet been produced in which it has failed, and through the solicitations and sanction of respectable medical men, it is offered to the public ; though not till it had passed a severe trial of seven years in private practice, when the Faculty declared it to be ' the best thing ever discovered, an excellent preserver of the Teeth and Gums, and that it must be a great blessing to the afflicted world.' "

Sold by Messrs. Barclay and Sons, 95, Farringdon-street, London (Sole Agents) ; also, Wholesale, by E. Edwards, 68, St. Paul's Churchyard ; Sutton and Co., Bow Churchyard ; and Retail, by Sanger, 150, Oxford street ; Heude-bourck, Middle-row, Holborn ; Burfield, 130, Strand ; Johnston, 68, Cornhill ; Willoughby, 61, Bishopsgate-street Without ; and by the principal Medicine Venders throughout the United Kingdom.

BEAUFOY'S
INSTANT CURE FOR THE TOOTH-ACHE.

This article has been extensively and successfully used for some time past in a populous Neighbourhood, and has proved to be an INSTANT CURE in most cases.

The Selling Price to the Public has been fixed purposely so low as to render the

"INSTANT CURE FOR THE TOOTH-ACHE"

accessible to all Classes.

MADE BY BEAUFOY & CO., SOUTH LAMBETH, LONDON,
And Sold by most Respectable Druggists and Patent Medicine Venders, in Town and Country.

The Bottles, with ample Directions for Use, Price 1s. 1½d. each, Stamp included.

[BRADBURY AND EVANS, PRINTERS, WHITEFRIARS.]

CHAPTER XXIV.

OF THE GREAT BESPEAK FOR MISS SNEVELLICCI, AND THE FIRST APPEARANCE OF NICHOLAS UPON ANY STAGE.

NICHOLAS was up betimes in the morning; but he had scarcely begun to dress, notwithstanding, when he heard footsteps ascending the stairs, and was presently saluted by the voices of Mr. Folair the pantomimist, and Mr. Lenville, the tragedian.

" House, house, house!" cried Mr. Folair.

" What, ho! within there!" said Mr. Lenville, in a deep voice.

Confound these fellows! thought Nicholas; they have come to breakfast, I suppose. " I'll open the door directly, if you'll wait an instant."

The gentlemen entreated him not to hurry himself; and to beguile the interval, had a fencing bout with their walking-sticks on the very small landing-place, to the unspeakable discomposure of all the other lodgers down stairs.

" Here, come in," said Nicholas, when he had completed his toilet. " In the name of all that's horrible, don't make that noise outside."

" An uncommon snug little box this," said Mr. Lenville, stepping into the front room, and taking his hat off before he could get in at all. " Pernicious snug."

" For a man at all particular in such matters it might be a trifle too snug," said Nicholas; " for, although it is undoubtedly a great convenience to be able to reach anything you want from the ceiling or the floor, or either side of the room, without having to move from your chair, still these advantages can only be had in an apartment of the most limited size."

" It isn't a bit too confined for a single man," returned Mr. Lenville. " That reminds me,—my wife, Mr. Johnson—I hope she'll have some good part in this piece of yours?"

" I glanced at the French copy last night," said Nicholas. " It looks very good, I think."

" What do you mean to do for me, old fellow?" asked Mr. Lenville, poking the struggling fire with his walking-stick, and afterwards wiping it on the skirt of his coat. " Anything in the gruff and grumble way?"

" You turn your wife and child out of doors," said Nicholas; " and in a fit of rage and jealousy stab your eldest son in the library."

" Do I though!" exclaimed Mr. Lenville. "That's very good business."

" After which," said Nicholas, " you are troubled with remorse till the last act, and then you make up your mind to destroy yourself. But just as you are raising the pistol to your head, a clock strikes— ten."

" I see," cried Mr. Lenville. " Very good."

Q

" You pause," said Nicholas ; " you recollect to have heard a clock strike ten in your infancy. The pistol falls from your hand—you are overcome—you burst into tears, and become a virtuous and exemplary character for ever afterwards."

" Capital!" said Mr. Lenville: " that's a sure card, a sure card. Get the curtain down with a touch of nature like that, and it 'll be a triumphant success."

" Is there anything good for me ?" inquired Mr. Folair, anxiously.

" Let me see," said Nicholas. " You play the faithful and attached servant ; you are turned out of doors with the wife and child."

" Always coupled with that infernal phenomenon," sighed Mr. Folair : " and we go into poor lodgings, where I won't take any wages, and talk sentiment, I suppose ? "

" Why—yes," replied Nicholas ; " that is the course of the piece."

" I must have a dance of some kind, you know," said Mr. Folair. " You'll have to introduce one for the phenomenon, so you'd better make it a *pas de deux*, and save time."

" There's nothing easier than that," said Mr. Lenville, observing the disturbed looks of the young dramatist.

" Upon my word I don't see how it's to be done," rejoined Nicholas.

" Why, isn't it obvious ?" reasoned Mr. Lenville. " Gadzooks, who can help seeing the way to do it?—you astonish me! You get the distressed lady, and the little child, and the attached servant, into the poor lodgings, don't you?—Well, look here. The distressed lady sinks into a chair, and buries her face in her pocket-handkerchief— ' What makes you weep, mama ?' says the child. ' Don't weep, mama, or you'll make me weep too !'—' And me !' says the faithful servant, rubbing his eyes with his arm. ' What can we do to raise your spirits, dear mama ?' says the little child. ' Aye, what *can* we do ?' says the faithful servant. ' Oh, Pierre !' says the distressed lady ; ' Would that I could shake off these painful thoughts.'—' Try, ma'am, try,' says the faithful servant ; ' rouse yourself, ma'am ; be amused.' —' I will,' says the lady, ' I will learn to suffer with fortitude. Do you remember that dance, my honest friend, which, in happier days, you practised with this sweet angel ? It never failed to calm my spirits then. Oh! let me see it once again before I die !'—There it is— cue for the band, *before I die*,—and off they go. That's the regular thing ; isn't it, Tommy ?"

" That's it," replied Mr. Folair. " The distressed lady, overpowered by old recollections, faints at the end of the dance, and you close in with a picture."

Profiting by these and other lessons, which were the result of the personal experience of the two actors, Nicholas willingly gave them the best breakfast he could, and when he at length got rid of them applied himself to his task, by no means displeased to find that it was so much easier than he had at first supposed. He worked very hard all day, and did not leave his room until the evening, when he went down to the theatre, whither Smike had repaired before him to go on with another gentleman as a general rebellion.

Here all the people were so much changed that he scarcely knew them. False hair, false colour, false calves, false muscles—they had become different beings. Mr. Lenville was a blooming warrior of most exquisite proportions; Mr. Crummles, his large face shaded by a profusion of black hair, a Highland outlaw of most majestic bearing; one of the old gentlemen a gaoler, and the other a venerable patriarch; the comic countryman, a fighting-man of great valour, relieved by a touch of humour; each of the master Crummleses a prince in his own right; and the low-spirited lover a desponding captive. There was a gorgeous banquet ready spread for the third act, consisting of two pasteboard vases, one plate of biscuits, a black bottle, and a vinegar cruet; and, in short, everything was on a scale of the utmost splendour and preparation.

Nicholas was standing with his back to the curtain, now contemplating the first scene, which was a Gothic archway, about two feet shorter than Mr. Crummles, through which that gentleman was to make his first entrance, and now listening to a couple of people who were cracking nuts in the gallery, wondering whether they made the whole audience, when the manager himself walked familiarly up and accosted him.

" Been in front to-night?" said Mr. Crummles.

"No," replied Nicholas, "not yet. I am going to see the play."

"We've had a pretty good Let," said Mr. Crummles. "Four front places in the centre, and the whole of the stage-box."

"Oh, indeed!" said Nicholas; "a family, I suppose?"

"Yes," replied Mr. Crummles, "yes. It's an affecting thing. There are six children, and they never come unless the phenomenon plays."

It would have been difficult for any party, family or otherwise, to have visited the theatre on a night when the phenomenon did *not* play, inasmuch as she always sustained one, and not uncommonly two or three, characters every night; but Nicholas, sympathising with the feelings of a father, refrained from hinting at this trifling circumstance, and Mr. Crummles continued to talk uninterrupted by him.

"Six," said that gentleman; "Pa and Ma eight, aunt nine, governess ten, grandfather and grandmother twelve. Then there's the footman, who stands outside, with a bag of oranges and a jug of toast-and-water, and sees the play for nothing through the little pane of glass in the box-door—it's cheap at a guinea; they gain by taking a box."

"I wonder you allow so many," observed Nicholas.

"There's no help for it," replied Mr. Crummles; "it's always expected in the country. If there are six children, six people come to hold them in their laps. A family-box carries double always. Ring in the orchestra, Grudden."

That useful lady did as she was requested, and shortly afterwards the tuning of three fiddles was heard. Which process having been protracted as long as it was supposed that the patience of the audience could possibly bear it, was put a stop to by another jerk of the bell,

which, being the signal to begin in earnest, set the orchestra playing a
variety of popular airs, with involuntary variations.

If Nicholas had been astonished at the alteration for the better
which the gentlemen displayed, the transformation of the ladies was
still more extraordinary. When, from a snug corner of the manager's
box, he beheld Miss Snevellicci in all the glories of white muslin with
a gold hem, and Mrs. Crummles in all the dignity of the outlaw's
wife, and Miss Bravassa in all the sweetness of Miss Snevellicci's confidential friend, and Miss Belvawney in the white silks of a page
doing duty everywhere and swearing to live and die in the service of
everybody, he could scarcely contain his admiration, which testified
itself in great applause, and the closest possible attention to the business of the scene. The plot was most interesting. It belonged to no
particular age, people, or country, and was perhaps the more delightful
on that account, as nobody's previous information could afford the
remotest glimmering of what would ever come of it. An outlaw had
been very successful in doing something somewhere, and came home in
triumph, to the sound of shouts and fiddles, to greet his wife—a lady of
masculine mind, who talked a good deal about her father's bones, which
it seemed were unburied, though whether from a peculiar taste on the
part of the old gentleman himself, or the reprehensible neglect of his
relations, did not appear. This outlaw's wife was somehow or other
mixed up with a patriarch, living in a castle a long way off, and this
patriarch was the father of several of the characters, but he didn't
exactly know which, and was uncertain whether he had brought up
the right ones in his castle, or the wrong ones, but rather inclined to
the latter opinion, and, being uneasy, relieved his mind with a banquet,
during which solemnity somebody in a cloak said " Beware!" which
somebody was known by nobody (except the audience) to be the
outlaw himself, who had come there for reasons unexplained, but
possibly with an eye to the spoons. There was an agreeable little
surprise in the way of certain love passages between the desponding
captive and Miss Snevellicci, and the comic fighting-man and Miss
Bravassa; besides which, Mr. Lenville had several very tragic scenes
in the dark, while on throat-cutting expeditions, which were all baffled
by the skill and bravery of the comic fighting-man (who overheard
whatever was said all through the piece) and the intrepidity of Miss
Snevellicci, who adopted tights, and therein repaired to the prison of
her captive lover, with a small basket of refreshments and a dark
lantern. At last it came out that the patriarch was the man who had
treated the bones of the outlaw's father-in-law with so much disrespect,
for which cause and reason the outlaw's wife repaired to his castle to
kill him, and so got into a dark room, where, after a great deal of
groping in the dark, everybody got hold of everybody else, and took
them for somebody besides, which occasioned a vast quantity of confusion, with some pistolling, loss of life, and torchlight; after which the
patriarch came forward, and observing, with a knowing look, that he
knew all about his children now, and would tell them when they got
inside, said that there could not be a more appropriate occasion for

marrying the young people than that, and therefore he joined their hands, with the full consent of the indefatigable page, who (being the only other person surviving) pointed with his cap into the clouds, and his right hand to the ground ; thereby invoking a blessing and giving the cue for the curtain to come down, which it did, amidst general applause.

" What did you think of that ?" asked Mr. Crummles, when Nicholas went round to the stage again. Mr. Crummles was very red and hot, for your outlaws are desperate fellows to shout.

" I think it was very capital, indeed," replied Nicholas ; " Miss Snevellicci in particular was uncommonly good."

" She's a genius," said Mr. Crummles ; " quite a genius, that girl. By-the-bye, I've been thinking of bringing out that piece of yours on her bespeak night."

" When ?" asked Nicholas.

" The night of her bespeak. Her benefit night, when her friends and patrons bespeak the play," said Mr. Crummles.

" Oh ! I understand," replied Nicholas.

" You see," said Mr. Crummles, " it's sure to go on such an occasion, and even if it should not work up quite as well as we expect, why it will be her risk, you know, and not ours."

" Yours, you mean," said Nicholas.

" I said mine, didn't I ?" returned Mr. Crummles. " Next Monday week. What do you say now ? You'll have done it, and are sure to be up in the lover's part long before that time."

" I don't know about ' long before,'" replied Nicholas ; " but by that time I think I can undertake to be ready."

" Very good," pursued Mr. Crummles, " then we 'll call that settled. Now, I want to ask you something else. There's a little—what shall I call it—a little canvassing takes place on these occasions."

" Among the patrons, I suppose ?" said Nicholas.

" Among the patrons ; and the fact is, that Snevellicci has had so many bespeaks in this place, that she wants an attraction. She had a bespeak when her mother-in-law died, and a bespeak when her uncle died ; and Mrs. Crummles and myself have had bespeaks on the anniversary of the phenomenon's birthday and our wedding-day, and occasions of that description, so that, in fact, there's some difficulty in getting a good one. Now won't you help this poor girl, Mr. Johnson?" said Crummles, sitting himself down on a drum, and taking a great pinch of snuff as he looked him steadily in the face.

" How do you mean ?" rejoined Nicholas.

" Don't you think you could spare half-an-hour to-morrow morning, to call with her at the houses of one or two of the principal people ?" murmured the manager in a persuasive tone.

" Oh dear me," said Nicholas, with an air of very strong objection, " I shouldn't like to do that."

" The infant will accompany her," said Mr. Crummles. " The moment it was suggested to me, I gave permission for the infant to go. There will not be the smallest impropriety—Miss Snevellicci, Sir, is the very soul of honour. It would be of material service—the gentleman from London—author of the new piece—actor in the new piece—first appearance on any boards—it would lead to a great bespeak, Mr. Johnson."

" I am very sorry to throw a damp upon the prospects of anybody, and more especially a lady," replied Nicholas; "but really I must decidedly object to making one of the canvassing party."

" What does Mr. Johnson say, Vincent?" inquired a voice close to his ear; and, looking round, he found Mrs. Crummles and Miss Snevellicci herself standing behind him.

" He has some objection, my dear," replied Mr. Crummles, looking at Nicholas.

" Objection!" exclaimed Mrs. Crummles. " Can it be possible?"

" Oh, I hope not!" cried Miss Snevellicci. " You surely are not so cruel—oh, dear me!—Well, I—to think of that now, after all one's looking forward to it."

" Mr. Johnson will not persist, my dear," said Mrs. Crummles. " Think better of him than to suppose it. Gallantry, humanity, all the best feelings of his nature, must be enlisted in this interesting cause."

" Which moves even a manager," said Mr. Crummles, smiling.

" And a manager's wife," added Mrs. Crummles, in her accustomed tragedy tones. " Come, come, you will relent, I know you will."

" It is not in my nature," said Nicholas, moved by these appeals, " to resist any entreaty, unless it is to do something positively wrong; and, beyond a feeling of pride, I know nothing which should prevent my doing this. I know nobody here either, and nobody knows me. So be it then. I yield."

Miss Snevellicci was at once overwhelmed with blushes and expressions of gratitude, of which latter commodity neither Mr. nor Mrs. Crummles was by any means sparing. It was arranged that Nicholas should call upon her at her lodgings at eleven next morning, and soon afterwards they parted : he to return home to his authorship; Miss Snevellicci to dress for the after-piece; and the disinterested manager and his wife to discuss the probable gains of the forthcoming bespeak, of which they were to have two-thirds of the profits by solemn treaty of agreement.

At the stipulated hour next morning, Nicholas repaired to the lodgings of Miss Snevellicci, which were in a place called Lombard-street, at the house of a tailor. A strong smell of ironing pervaded the little passage, and the tailor's daughter, who opened the door, appeared in that flutter of spirits which is so often attendant upon the periodical getting up of a family's linen.

" Miss Snevellicci lives here, I believe?" said Nicholas, when the door was opened.

The tailor's daughter replied in the affirmative.

" Will you have the goodness to let her know that Mr. Johnson is here?" said Nicholas.

" Oh, if you please, you're to come up stairs," replied the tailor's daughter, with a smile.

Nicholas followed the young lady, and was shown into a small apartment on the first floor, communicating with a back room; in which, as he judged from a certain half-subdued clinking sound as of cups and saucers, Miss Snevellicci was then taking her breakfast in bed.

" You're to wait, if you please," said the tailor's daughter, after a short period of absence, during which the clinking in the back room had ceased, and been succeeded by whispering—" She won't be long."

As she spoke she pulled up the window-blind, and having by this means (as she thought) diverted Mr. Johnson's attention from the room to the street, caught up some articles which were airing on the fender, and had very much the appearance of stockings, and darted off.

As there were not many objects of interest outside the window, Nicholas looked about the room with more curiosity than he might otherwise have bestowed upon it. On the sofa lay an old guitar, several thumbed pieces of music, and a scattered litter of curl-papers: together with a confused heap of play-bills, and a pair of soiled white satin shoes with large blue rosettes. Hanging over the back of a chair was a half-finished muslin apron with little pockets ornamented with red ribbons, such as waiting-women wear on the stage, and by consequence are never seen with anywhere else. In one corner stood the diminutive pair of top-boots in which Miss Snevellicci was accustomed to enact the little jockey, and, folded on a chair hard by, was a small parcel, which bore a very suspicious resemblance to the companion smalls.

But the most interesting object of all, was perhaps the open scrap-book, displayed in the midst of some theatrical duodecimos that were strewn upon the table, and pasted into which scrap-book were various critical notices of Miss Snevellicci's acting, extracted from different provincial journals, together with one poetic address in her honour, commencing—

> Sing, God of Love, and tell me in what dearth
> Thrice-gifted SNEVELLICCI came on earth,
> To thrill us with her smile, her tear, her eye,
> Sing, God of Love, and tell me quickly why.

Besides this effusion, there were innumerable complimentary allusions, also extracted from newspapers, such as—" We observe from an advertisement in another part of our paper of to-day, that tho charming and highly-talented Miss Snevellicci takes her benefit on Wednesday, for which occasion she has put forth a bill of fare that might kindle exhilaration in the breast of a misanthrope. In the confidence that our fellow-townsmen have not lost that high appreciation of public ability and private worth, for which they have long been so pre-eminently distinguished, we predict that this charming actress will be greeted with a bumper." " To Correspondents.—J. S. is misinformed when he supposes that the highly-gifted and beautiful Miss Snevellicci, nightly captivating all hearts at our pretty and commodious little theatre, is *not* the same lady to whom the young gentleman of immense fortune, residing within a hundred miles of the good city of York, lately made honourable proposals. We have reason to know that Miss Snevellicci *is* the lady who was implicated in that mysterious and romantic affair, and whose conduct on that occasion did no less honour to her head and heart, than do her histrionic triumphs to her brilliant genius." A most copious assortment of such paragraphs as these, with long bills of benefits all ending with " Come Early," in large capitals, formed the principal contents of Miss Snevellicci's scrap-book.

Nicholas had read a great many of these scraps, and was absorbed in a circumstantial and melancholy account of the train of events which had led to Miss Snevellicci's spraining her ancle by slipping on a piece of orange-peel flung by a monster in human form, (so the paper said,) upon the stage at Winchester,—when that young lady herself, attired in the coal-scuttle bonnet and walking-dress complete, tripped into the room, with a thousand apologies for having detained him so long after the appointed time.

" But really," said Miss Snevellicci, " my darling Led, who lives with me here, was taken so very ill in the night that I thought she would have expired in my arms."

" Such a fate is almost to be envied," returned Nicholas, " but I am very sorry to hear it nevertheless."

" What a creature you are to flatter !" said Miss Snevellicci, buttoning her glove in much confusion.

" If it be flattery to admire your charms and accomplishments," rejoined Nicholas, laying his hand upon the scrap-book, " you have better specimens of it here."

" Oh you cruel creature, to read such things as those. I'm almost ashamed to look you in the face afterwards, positively I am," said Miss Snevellicci, seizing the book and putting it away in a closet. " How careless of Led ! How could she be so naughty !"

" I thought you had kindly left it here, on purpose for me to read," said Nicholas. And really it did seem possible.

" I wouldn't have had you see it for the world !" rejoined Miss Snevellicci. " I never was so vexed—never. But she is such a careless thing, there's no trusting her."

The conversation was here interrupted by the entrance of the phenomenon, who had discreetly remained in the bedroom up to this moment, and now presented herself with much grace and lightness, bearing in her hand a very little green parasol with a broad fringe border, and no handle. After a few words of course, they sallied into the street.

The phenomenon was rather a troublesome companion, for first the right sandal came down, and then the left, and these mischances being repaired, one leg of the little white trowsers was discovered to be longer than the other ; besides these accidents, the green parasol was dropped down an iron grating, and only fished up again with great difficulty and by dint of much exertion. However it was impossible to scold her, as she was the manager's daughter, so Nicholas took it all in perfect good humour, and walked on with Miss Snevellicci, arm in arm on one side, and the offending infant on the other.

The first house to which they bent their steps, was situated in a terrace of respectable appearance. Miss Snevellicci's modest double-knock was answered by a foot-boy, who, in reply to her inquiry whether Mrs. Curdle was at home, opened his eyes very wide, grinned very much, and said he didn't know, but he'd inquire. With this, he showed them into a parlour where he kept them waiting, until the two women-servants had repaired thither, under false pretences, to see the play-actors, and having compared notes with them in the passage, and joined in a vast quantity of whispering and giggling, he at length went up stairs with Miss Snevellicci's name.

Now, Mrs. Curdle was supposed, by those who were best informed on such points, to possess quite the London taste in matters relating to literature and the drama; and as to Mr. Curdle, he had written a pamphlet of sixty-four pages, post octavo, on the character of the Nurse's deceased husband in Romeo and Juliet, with an inquiry whether he really had been a " merry man " in his lifetime, or whether it was merely his widow's affectionate partiality that induced her so to report him. He had likewise proved, that by altering the received mode of punctuation, any one of Shakspeare's plays could be made quite different, and the sense completely changed; it is needless to say, therefore, that he was a great critic, and a very profound and most original thinker.

" Well, Miss Snevellicci," said Mrs. Curdle, entering the parlour, " and how do *you* do ? "

Miss Snevellicci made a graceful obeisance, and hoped Mrs. Curdle was well, as also Mr. Curdle, who at the same time appeared. Mrs. Curdle was dressed in a morning wrapper, with a little cap stuck upon the top of her head ; Mr. Curdle wore a loose robe on his back, and his right fore-finger on his forehead after the portraits of Sterne, to whom somebody or other had once said he bore a striking resemblance.

" I ventured to call for the purpose of asking whether you would put your name to my bespeak, ma'am," said Miss Snevellicci, producing documents.

" Oh ! I really don't know what to say," replied Mrs. Curdle. " It's not as if the theatre was in its high and palmy days—you needn't stand, Miss Snevellicci—the drama is gone, perfectly gone."

" As an exquisite embodiment of the poet's visions, and a realisation of human intellectuality, gilding with refulgent light our dreamy moments, and laying open a new and magic world before the mental eye, the drama is gone, perfectly gone," said Mr. Curdle.

" What man is there now living who can present before us all those changing and prismatic colours with which the character of Hamlet is invested ? " exclaimed Mrs. Curdle.

" What man indeed—upon the stage ;" said Mr. Curdle, with a small reservation in favour of himself. " Hamlet ! Pooh ! ridiculous ! Hamlet is gone, perfectly gone."

Quite overcome by these dismal reflections, Mr. and Mrs. Curdle sighed, and sat for some short time without speaking. At length the lady, turning to Miss Snevellicci, inquired what play she proposed to have.

"Quite a new one," said Miss Snevellicci, "of which this gentleman is the author, and in which he plays; being his first appearance on any stage. Mr. Johnson is the gentleman's name."

"I hope you have preserved the unities, Sir?" said Mr. Curdle.

"The original piece is a French one," said Nicholas. "There is abundance of incident, sprightly dialogue, strongly-marked characters—"

"—All unavailing without a strict observance of the unities, Sir," returned Mr. Curdle. "The unities of the drama before everything."

"Might I ask you," said Nicholas, hesitating between the respect he ought to assume, and his love of the whimsical, "might I ask you what the unities are?"

Mr. Curdle coughed and considered. "The unities, Sir," he said, "are a completeness—a kind of a universal dove-tailedness with regard to place and time—a sort of a general oneness, if I may be allowed to use so strong an expression. I take those to be the dramatic unities, so far as I have been enabled to bestow attention upon them, and I have read much upon the subject, and thought much. I find, running through the performances of this child," said Mr. Curdle, turning to the phenomenon, "a unity of feeling, a breadth, a light and shade, a warmth of colouring, a tone, a harmony, a glow, an artistical development of original conceptions, which I look for in vain among older performers—I don't know whether I make myself understood?"

"Perfectly," replied Nicholas.

"Just so," said Mr. Curdle, pulling up his neckcloth. "That is my definition of the unities of the drama."

Mrs. Curdle had sat listening to this lucid explanation with great complacency, and it being finished, inquired what Mr. Curdle thought about putting down their names.

"I don't know, my dear; upon my word I don't know," said Mr. Curdle. "If we do, it must be distinctly understood that we do not pledge ourselves to the quality of the performances. Let it go forth to the world, that we do not give *them* the sanction of our names, but that we confer the distinction merely upon Miss Snevellicci. That being clearly stated, I take it to be, as it were, a duty, that we should extend our patronage to a degraded stage even for the sake of the associations with which it is entwined. Have you got two-and-sixpence for half-a-crown, Miss Snevellicci?" said Mr. Curdle, turning over four of those pieces of money.

Miss Snevellicci felt in all the corners of the pink reticule, but there was nothing in any of them. Nicholas murmured a jest about his being an author, and thought it best not to go through the form of feeling in his own pockets at all.

"Let me see," said Mr. Curdle; "twice four's eight—four shillings a-piece to the boxes, Miss Snevellicci, is exceedingly dear in the present state of the drama—three half-crowns is seven-and-six; we shall not differ about sixpence, I suppose. Sixpence will not part us, Miss Snevellicci?"

Poor Miss Snevellicci took the three half-crowns with many smiles and bends, and Mrs. Curdle, adding several supplementary directions relative to keeping the places for them, and dusting the seat, and sending two clean bills as soon as they came out, rang the bell as a signal for breaking up the conference.

"Odd people those," said Nicholas, when they got clear of the house.

"I assure you," said Miss Snevellicci, taking his arm, "that I think myself very lucky they did not owe all the money instead of being sixpence short. Now, if you were to succeed, they would give people to understand that they had always patronised you; and if you were to fail, they would have been quite certain of that from the very beginning."

The next house they visited they were in great glory, for there resided the six children who were so enraptured with the public actions of the phenomenon, and who, being called down from the nursery to be treated with a private view of that young lady, proceeded to poke their fingers into her eyes, and tread upon her toes, and show her many other little attentions peculiar to their time of life.

"I shall certainly persuade Mr. Borum to take a private box," said the lady of the house, after a most gracious reception. "I shall only take two of the children, and will make up the rest of the party, of gentlemen—your admirers, Miss Snevellicci. Augustus, you naughty boy, leave the little girl alone."

This was addressed to a young gentleman who was pinching the phenomenon behind, apparently with the view of ascertaining whether she was real.

"I am sure you must be very tired," said the mama, turning to Miss Snevellicci. "I cannot think of allowing you to go without first taking a glass of wine. Fie, Charlotte, I am ashamed of you. Miss Lane, my dear, pray see to the children."

Miss Lane was the governess, and this entreaty was rendered necessary by the abrupt behaviour of the youngest Miss Borum, who, having filched the phenomenon's little green parasol, was now carrying it bodily off, while the distracted infant looked helplessly on.

"I am sure, where you ever learnt to act as you do," said good-natured Mrs. Borum, turning again to Miss Snevellicci, "I cannot understand (Emma, don't stare so); laughing in one piece, and crying in the next, and so natural in all—oh, dear!"

"I am very happy to hear you express so favourable an opinion," said Miss Snevellicci. "It's quite delightful to think you like it."

"Like it!" cried Mrs. Borum. "Who can help liking it! I would go to the play twice a week if I could: I dote upon it—only you're too affecting sometimes. You do put me in such a state—into such fits of crying! Goodness gracious me, Miss Lane, how can you let them torment that poor child so?"

The phenomenon was really in a fair way of being torn limb from limb, for two strong little boys, one holding on by each of her hands, were dragging her in different directions as a trial of strength. However, Miss Lane (who had herself been too much occupied in contemplating the grown-up actors, to pay the necessary attention to these proceedings) rescued the unhappy infant at this juncture, who, being recruited with a glass of wine, was shortly afterwards taken away by her friends, after sustaining no more serious damage than a flattening of the pink gauze bonnet, and a rather extensive creasing of the white frock and trowsers.

It was a trying morning, for there were a great many calls to make, and everybody wanted a different thing; some wanted tragedies, and others comedies; some objected to dancing, some wanted scarcely anything else. Some thought the comic singer decidedly low, and others hoped he would have more to do than he usually had. Some people wouldn't promise to go, because other people wouldn't promise to go; and other people wouldn't go at all, because other people went. At length, and by little and little, omitting something in this place, and adding something in that, Miss Snevellicci pledged herself to a bill of fare which was comprehensive enough, if it had no other merit (it included among other trifles, four pieces, divers songs, a few combats, and several dances); and they returned home pretty well exhausted with the business of the day.

Nicholas worked away at the piece, which was speedily put into rehearsal, and then worked away at his own part, which he studied with great perseverance and acted—as the whole company said—to perfection. And at length the great day arrived. The crier was sent round in the morning to proclaim the entertainments with sound of bell in all the thoroughfares; extra bills of three feet long by nine inches wide, were dispersed in all directions, flung down all the areas, thrust under all the knockers, and developed in all the shops; they were placarded on all the walls too, though not with complete success, for an illiterate person having undertaken this office during the indisposition of the regular bill-sticker, a part were posted sideways and the remainder upside down.

At half-past five there was a rush of four people to the gallery-door; at a quarter before six there were at least a dozen; at six o'clock the kicks were terrific; and when the elder master Crummles opened the door, he was obliged to run behind it for his life. Fifteen shillings were taken by Mrs. Grudden in the first ten minutes.

Behind the scenes the same unwonted excitement prevailed. Miss Snevellicci was in such a perspiration that the paint would scarcely stay on her face. Mrs. Crummles was so nervous that she could hardly remember her part. Miss Bravassa's ringlets came out of curl with the heat and anxiety; even Mr. Crummles himself kept peeping through the hole in the curtain, and running back every now and then to announce that another man had come into the pit.

At last the orchestra left off, and the curtain rose upon the new piece. The first scene, in which there was nobody particular, passed off calmly enough, but when Miss Snevellicci went on in the second, accompanied by the phenomenon as child, what a roar of applause broke out! The people in the Borum box rose as one man, waving their hats and handkerchiefs, and uttering shouts of "bravo!" Mrs.

The great bespeak for Miss Snevellicci

Borum and the governess cast wreaths upon the stage, of which some fluttered into the lamps, and one crowned the temples of a fat gentleman in the pit, who, looking eagerly towards the scene, remained unconscious of the honour; the tailor and his family kicked at the panels of the upper boxes till they threatened to come out altogether; the very ginger-beer boy remained transfixed in the centre of the house; a young officer, supposed to entertain a passion for Miss Snevellicci, stuck his glass in his eye as though to hide a tear. Again and again Miss Snevellicci curtseyed lower and lower, and again and again the applause came down louder and louder. At length when the phenomenon picked up one of the smoking wreaths and put it on sideways over Miss Snevellicci's eye, it reached its climax, and the play proceeded.

But when Nicholas came on for his crack scene with Mrs. Crummles, what a clapping of hands there was! When Mrs. Crummles (who was his unworthy mother), sneered, and called him " presumptuous boy," and he defied her, what a tumult of applause came on! When he quarrelled with the other gentleman about the young lady, and producing a case of pistols, said, that if he *was* a gentleman, he would fight him in that drawing-room, till the furniture was sprinkled with the blood of one, if not of two—how boxes, pit, and gallery joined in one most vigorous cheer! When he called his mother names, because she wouldn't give up the young lady's property, and she relenting, caused him to relent likewise, and fall down on one knee and ask her blessing, how the ladies in the audience sobbed! When he was hid behind the curtain in the dark, and the wicked relation poked a sharp sword in every direction, save where his legs were plainly visible, what a thrill of anxious fear ran through the house! His air, his figure, his walk, his look, everything he said or did, was the subject of commendation. There was a round of applause every time he spoke. And when at last, in the pump-and-tub scene, Mrs. Grudden lighted the blue fire, and all the unemployed members of the company came in, and tumbled down in various directions—not because that had anything to do with the plot, but in order to finish off with a tableau—the audience (who had by this time increased considerably) gave vent to such a shout of enthusiasm, as had not been heard in those walls for many and many a day.

In short, the success both of new piece and new actor was complete, and when Miss Snevellicci was called for at the end of the play, Nicholas led her on, and divided the applause.

CHAPTER XXV.

CONCERNING A YOUNG LADY FROM LONDON, WHO JOINS THE COMPANY,
AND AN ELDERLY ADMIRER WHO FOLLOWS IN HER TRAIN; WITH
AN AFFECTING CEREMONY CONSEQUENT ON THEIR ARRIVAL.

THE new piece being a decided hit, was announced for every evening
of performance until further notice, and the evenings when the
theatre was closed, were reduced from three in the week to two.
Nor were these the only tokens of extraordinary success; for on the
succeeding Saturday Nicholas received, by favour of the indefatigable
Mrs. Grudden, no less a sum than thirty shillings; besides which substantial reward, he enjoyed considerable fame and honour, having a
presentation copy of Mr. Curdle's pamphlet forwarded to the theatre,
with that gentleman's own autograph (in itself an inestimable treasure)
on the fly-leaf, accompanied with a note, containing many expressions
of approval, and an unsolicited assurance that Mr. Curdle would be
very happy to read Shakspeare to him for three hours every morning
before breakfast during his stay in the town.

"I've got another novelty, Johnson," said Mr. Crummles one morning
in great glee.

"What's that?" rejoined Nicholas.   "The pony?"

"No, no, we never come to the pony till everything else has failed,"
said Mr. Crummles.   "I don't think we shall come to the pony at all
this season.   No, no, not the pony."

"A boy phenomenon, perhaps?" suggested Nicholas.

"There is only one phenomenon, Sir," replied Mr. Crummles impressively, "and that's a girl."

"Very true," said Nicholas.   "I beg your pardon.   Then I don't
know what it is, I am sure."

"What should you say to a young lady from London?" inquired
Mr. Crummles.   "Miss So-and-so, of the Theatre Royal, Drury Lane?"

"I should say she would look very well in the bills," said Nicholas.

"You're about right there," said Mr. Crummles; "and if you had
said she would look very well upon the stage too, you wouldn't have
been far out.   Look here; what do you think of that?"

With this inquiry Mr. Crummles severally unfolded a red poster, and
a blue poster, and a yellow poster, at the top of each of which public
notification was inscribed in enormous characters—"First appearance of
the unrivalled Miss Petowker, of the Theatre Royal, Drury Lane!"

"Dear me!" said Nicholas, "I know that lady."

"Then you are acquainted with as much talent as was ever compressed into one young person's body," retorted Mr. Crummles, rolling
up the bills again; "that is, talent of a certain sort—of a certain sort.
'The Blood Drinker,'" added Mr. Crummles with a prophetic sigh,
"'The Blood Drinker' will die with that girl; and she's the only sylph

I ever saw who could stand upon one leg, and play the tambourine on her other knee, *like* a sylph."

" When does she come down?" asked Nicholas.

" We expect her to-day," replied Mr. Crummles. " She is an old friend of Mrs. Crummles's. Mrs. Crummles saw what she could do—always knew it from the first. She taught her, indeed, nearly all she knows. Mrs. Crummles was the original Blood Drinker."

" Was she, indeed?"

" Yes. She was obliged to give it up though."

" Did it disagree with her?" asked Nicholas, smiling.

" Not so much with her, as with her audiences," replied Mr. Crummles. " Nobody could stand it. It was too tremendous. You don't quite know what Mrs. Crummles is, yet."

Nicholas ventured to insinuate that he thought he did.

" No, no, you don't," said Mr. Crummles; " you don't, indeed. *I* don't, and that's a fact; I don't think her country will till she is dead. Some new proof of talent bursts from that astonishing woman every year of her life. Look at her—mother of six children—three of 'em alive, and all upon the stage!"

" Extraordinary!" cried Nicholas.

" Ah! extraordinary indeed," rejoined Mr. Crummles, taking a complacent pinch of snuff, and shaking his head gravely. " I pledge you my professional word I didn't even know she could dance till her last benefit, and then she played Juliet and Helen Macgregor, and did the skipping-rope hornpipe between the pieces. The very first time I saw that admirable woman, Johnson," said Mr. Crummles, drawing a little nearer, and speaking in the tone of confidential friendship, " she stood upon her head on the butt-end of a spear, surrounded with blazing fireworks."

" You astonish me!" said Nicholas.

" *She* astonished *me!*" returned Mr. Crummles, with a very serious countenance. " Such grace, coupled with such dignity! I adored her from that moment."

The arrival of the gifted subject of these remarks put an abrupt termination to Mr. Crummles's eulogium, and almost immediately afterwards, Master Percy Crummles entered with a letter, which had arrived by the General Post, and was directed to his gracious mother; at sight of the superscription whereof, Mrs. Crummles exclaimed, " From Henrietta Petowker, I do declare!" and instantly became absorbed in the contents.

" Is it——?" inquired Mr. Crummles, hesitating.

" Oh yes, it's all right," replied Mrs. Crummles, anticipating the question. " What an excellent thing for her, to be sure!"

" It's the best thing altogether that I ever heard of, I think," said Mr. Crummles; and then Mr. Crummles, Mrs. Crummles, and Master Percy Crummles all fell to laughing violently. Nicholas left them to enjoy their mirth together, and walked to his lodgings, wondering very much what mystery connected with Miss Petowker could provoke such merriment, and pondering still more on the extreme surprise with which that lady would regard his sudden enlistment in a profession of which she was such a distinguished and brilliant ornament.

But in this latter respect he was mistaken ; for—whether Mr. Vincent Crummles had paved the way, or Miss Petowker had some special reason for treating him with even more than her usual amiability—their meeting at the theatre next day was more like that of two dear friends who had been inseparable from infancy, than a recognition passing between a lady and gentleman who had only met some half-dozen times, and then by mere chance. Nay, Miss Petowker even whispered that she had wholly dropped the Kenwigses in her conversations with the manager's family, and had represented herself as having encountered Mr. Johnson in the very first and most fashionable circles ; and on Nicholas receiving this intelligence with unfeigned surprise, she added with a sweet glance that she had a claim on his good-nature now, and might tax it before long.

Nicholas had the honour of playing in a slight piece with Miss Petowker that night, and could not but observe that the warmth of her reception was mainly attributable to a most persevering umbrella in the upper boxes ; he saw, too, that the enchanting actress cast many sweet looks towards the quarter whence these sounds proceeded, and that every time she did so the umbrella broke out afresh. Once he thought that a peculiarly shaped hat in the same corner was not wholly unknown to him, but being occupied with his share of the stage business he bestowed no great attention upon this circumstance, and it had quite vanished from his memory by the time he reached home.

He had just sat down to supper with Smike, when one of the people of the house came outside the door, and announced that a gentleman below stairs wished to speak to Mr. Johnson.

"Well, if he does, you must tell him to come up, that's all I know," replied Nicholas. "One of our hungry brethren, I suppose, Smike."

His fellow-lodger looked at the cold meat, in silent calculation of the quantity that would be left for dinner next day, and put back a slice he had cut for himself, in order that the visitor's encroachments might be less formidable in their effects.

"It is not anybody who has been here before," said Nicholas, "for he is tumbling up every stair. Come in, come in. In the name of wonder—Mr. Lillyvick !"

It was, indeed, the collector of water-rates who, regarding Nicholas with a fixed look and immoveable countenance, shook hands with most portentous solemnity and sat himself down in a seat by the chimney-corner.

"Why, when did you come here ?" asked Nicholas.

"This morning, Sir," replied Mr. Lillyvick.

"Oh ! I see ; then you were at the theatre to-night, and it was your umb——"

"This umbrella," said Mr. Lillyvick, producing a fat green cotton one with a battered ferrule : "what did you think of that performance ?"

"So far as I could judge, being on the stage," replied Nicholas, "I thought it very agreeable."

"Agreeable!" cried the collector. "I mean to say, Sir, that it was delicious."

Mr. Lillyvick bent forward to pronounce the last word with greater emphasis; and having done so, drew himself up, and frowned and nodded a great many times.

"I say, delicious," repeated Mr. Lillyvick. "Absorbing, fairy-like, toomultuous." And again Mr. Lillyvick drew himself up, and again he frowned and nodded.

"Ah!" said Nicholas, a little surprised at these symptoms of ecstatic approbation. "Yes—she is a clever girl."

"She is a divinity," returned Mr. Lillyvick, giving a collector's double knock on the ground with the umbrella before-mentioned. "I have known divine actresses before now, Sir; I used to collect—at least I used to *call for*—and very often call for—the water-rate at the house of a divine actress, who lived in my beat for upwards of four year, but never—no, never, Sir—of all divine creatures, actresses or no actresses, did I see a diviner one than is Henrietta Petowker."

Nicholas had much ado to prevent himself from laughing; not trusting himself to speak, he merely nodded in accordance with Mr. Lillyvick's nods, and remained silent.

"Let me speak a word with you in private," said Mr. Lillyvick.

Nicholas looked good-humouredly at Smike, who, taking the hint, disappeared.

"A bachelor is a miserable wretch, Sir," said Mr. Lillyvick.

"Is he?" asked Nicholas.

"He is," rejoined the collector. "I have lived in the world for nigh sixty year, and I ought to know what it is."

"You *ought* to know, certainly," thought Nicholas; "but whether you do or not, is another question."

"If a bachelor happens to have saved a little matter of money," said Mr. Lillyvick, "his sisters and brothers, and nephews and nieces, look *to* that money, and not to him; even if by being a public character he is the head of the family, or as it may be the main from which all the other little branches are turned on, they still wish him dead all the while, and get low-spirited every time they see him looking in good health, because they want to come into his little property. You see that?"

"O, yes," replied Nicholas: "it's very true, no doubt."

"The great reason for not being married," resumed Mr. Lillyvick, "is the expense; that's what's kept me off, or else—Lord!" said Mr. Lillyvick, snapping his fingers, "I might have had fifty women."

"Fine women?" asked Nicholas.

"Fine women, Sir!" replied the collector; "aye! not so fine as Henrietta Petowker, for she is an uncommon specimen, but such women as don't fall into every man's way, I can tell you that. Now suppose a man can get a fortune *in* his wife instead of with her—eh?"

"Why, then, he is a lucky fellow," replied Nicholas.

"That's what I say," retorted the collector, patting him benignantly on the side of the head with his umbrella; "just what I say: Hen-

R

rietta Petowker, the talented Henrietta Petowker, has a fortune in herself, and I am going to——."

"To make her Mrs. Lillyvick?" suggested Nicholas.

"No, Sir, not to make her Mrs. Lillyvick," replied the collector. "Actresses, Sir, always keep their maiden names, that's the regular thing—but I'm going to marry her; and the day after to-morrow, too."

"I congratulate you, Sir," said Nicholas.

"Thank you, Sir," replied the collector, buttoning his waistcoat. "I shall draw her salary, of course, and I hope after all that it's nearly as cheap to keep two as it is to keep one; that's a consolation."

"Surely you don't want any consolation at such a moment?" observed Nicholas.

"No," replied Mr. Lillyvick, shaking his head nervously: " no—of course not."

"But how come you both here, if you're going to be married, Mr. Lillyvick?" asked Nicholas.

"Why, that's what I came to explain to you," replied the collector of water-rate. "The fact is, we have thought it best to keep it secret from the family."

"Family!" said Nicholas. " What family?"

"The Kenwigses of course," rejoined Mr. Lillyvick. " If my niece and the children had known a word about it before I came away, they'd have gone into fits at my feet, and never have come out of 'em till I took an oath not to marry anybody—or they'd have got out a commission of lunacy, or some dreadful thing," said the collector, quite trembling as he spoke.

"To be sure," said Nicholas. " Yes; they would have been jealous, no doubt."

"To prevent which," said Mr. Lillyvick, " Henrietta Petowker (it was settled between us) should come down here to her friends, the Crummleses, under pretence of this engagement, and I should go down to Guildford the day before, and join her on the coach there, which I did, and we came down from Guildford yesterday together. Now, for fear you should be writing to Mr. Noggs, and might say anything about us, we have thought it best to let you into the secret. We shall be married from the Crummleses' lodgings, and shall be delighted to see you—either before church or at breakfast-time, which you like. It won't be expensive, you know," said the collector, highly anxious to prevent any misunderstanding on this point; " just muffins and coffee, with perhaps a shrimp or something of that sort for a relish, you know."

"Yes, yes, I understand," replied Nicholas. " Oh, I shall be most happy to come; it will give me the greatest pleasure. Where's the lady stopping—with Mrs. Crummles?"

"Why, no," said the collector; " they couldn't very well dispose of her at night, and so she is staying with an acquaintance of hers, and another young lady; they both belong to the theatre."

"Miss Snevellicci, I suppose?" said Nicholas.

"Yes, that's the name."

"And they'll be bridesmaids, I presume?" said Nicholas.

"Why," said the collector, with a rueful face, "they *will* have four bridesmaids; I'm afraid they'll make it rather theatrical."

"Oh no, not at all," replied Nicholas, with an awkward attempt to convert a laugh into a cough. "Who may the four be? Miss Snevellicci of course—Miss Ledrook—"

"The—the phenomenon," groaned the collector.

"Ha, ha!" cried Nicholas. "I beg your pardon, I don't know what I'm laughing at—yes, that'll be very pretty—the phenomenon—who else?"

"Some young woman or other," replied the collector, rising; "some other friend of Henrietta Petowker's. Well, you'll be careful not to say anything about it, will you?"

"You may safely depend upon me," replied Nicholas. "Won't you take anything to eat or drink?"

"No," said the collector; "I haven't any appetite. I should think it was a very pleasant life, the married one—eh?"

"I have not the least doubt of it," rejoined Nicholas.

"Yes," said the collector; "certainly. Oh yes. No doubt. Good night."

With these words, Mr. Lillyvick, whose manner had exhibited through the whole of this interview a most extraordinary compound of precipitation, hesitation, confidence and doubt; fondness, misgiving, meanness, and self-importance, turned his back upon the room, and left Nicholas to enjoy a laugh by himself if he felt so disposed.

Without stopping to enquire whether the intervening day appeared to Nicholas to consist of the usual number of hours of the ordinary length, it may be remarked that, to the parties more directly interested in the forthcoming ceremony, it passed with great rapidity, insomuch that when Miss Petowker awoke on the succeeding morning in the chamber of Miss Snevellicci, she declared that nothing should ever persuade her that that really was the day which was to behold a change in her condition.

"I never will believe it," said Miss Petowker; "I cannot really. It's of no use talking, I never can make up my mind to go through with such a trial!"

On hearing this, Miss Snevellicci and Miss Ledrook, who knew perfectly well that their fair friend's mind had been made up for three or four years, at any period of which time she would have cheerfully undergone the desperate trial now approaching if she could have found any eligible gentleman disposed for the venture, began to preach comfort and firmness, and to say how very proud she ought to feel that it was in her power to confer lasting bliss on a deserving object, and how necessary it was for the happiness of mankind in general that women should possess fortitude and resignation on such occasions; and that although for their parts they held true happiness to consist in a single life, which they would not willingly exchange—no, not for any worldly consideration—still (thank God), if ever the time *should* come, they hoped they knew their duty too well to repine, but would the rather submit with meekness and humility of spirit to a fate for which Providence had clearly designed them with a view to the contentment and reward of their fellow-creatures.

" I might feel it was a great blow," said Miss Snevellicci, " to break up old associations and what-do-you-callems of that kind, but I would submit my dear, I would indeed."

" So would I," said Miss Ledrook ; " I would rather court the yoke than shun it. I have broken hearts before now, and I'm very sorry for it : for it's a terrible thing to reflect upon."

" It is indeed," said Miss Snevellicci. " Now Led, my dear, we must positively get her ready, or we shall be too late, we shall indeed."

This pious reasoning, and perhaps the fear of being too late, supported the bride through the ceremony of robing, after which, strong tea and brandy were administered in alternate doses as a means of strengthening her feeble limbs and causing her to walk steadier.

" How do you feel now, my love ?" enquired Miss Snevellicci.

" Oh Lillyvick !" cried the bride—" If you knew what I am undergoing for you !"

" Of course he knows it, love, and will never forget it," said Miss Ledrook.

" Do you think he won't ?" cried Miss Petowker, really showing great capability for the stage. " Oh, do you think he won't ? Do you think Lillyvick will always remember it—always, always, always ?"

There is no knowing in what this burst of feeling might have ended, if Miss Snevellicci had not at that moment proclaimed the arrival of the fly, which so astounded the bride that she shook off divers alarming symptoms which were coming on very strong, and running to the glass adjusted her dress, and calmly declared that she was ready for the sacrifice.

She was accordingly supported into the coach, and there " kept up" (as Miss Snevellicci said) with perpetual sniffs of *sal volatile* and sips of brandy and other gentle stimulants, until they reached the manager's door, which was already opened by the two master Crummleses, who wore white cockades, and were decorated with the choicest and most resplendent waistcoats in the theatrical wardrobe. By the combined exertions of these young gentlemen and the bridesmaids, assisted by the coachman, Miss Petowker was at length supported in a condition of much exhaustion to the first floor, where she no sooner encountered the youthful bridegroom than she fainted with great decorum.

" Henrietta Petowker !" said the collector ; " cheer up, my lovely one."

Miss Petowker grasped the collector's hand, but emotion choked her utterance.

" Is the sight of me so dreadful, Henrietta Petowker ?" said the collector.

" Oh no, no, no," rejoined the bride ; " but all the friends—the darling friends—of my youthful days—to leave them all—it is such a shock !"

With such expressions of sorrow, Miss Petowker went on to

enumerate the dear friends of her youthful days one by one, and to call upon such of them as were present to come and embrace her. This done, she remembered that Mrs. Crummles had been more than a mother to her, and after that, that Mr. Crummles had been more than a father to her, and after that, that the Master Crummleses and Miss Ninetta Crummles had been more than brothers and sisters to her. These various remembrances being each accompanied with a series of hugs, occupied a long time, and they were obliged to drive to church very fast, for fear they should be too late.

The procession consisted of two flys; in the first of which were Miss Bravassa (the fourth bridesmaid), Mrs. Crummles, the collector, and Mr. Folair, who had been chosen as his second on the occasion. In the other were the bride, Mr. Crummles, Miss Snevellicci, Miss Ledrook, and the phenomenon. The costumes were beautiful. The bridesmaids were quite covered with artificial flowers, and the phenomenon, in particular, was rendered almost invisible by the portable arbour in which she was enshrined. Miss Ledrook, who was of a romantic turn, wore in her breast the miniature of some field-officer unknown, which she had purchased, a great bargain, not very long before ; the other ladies displayed several dazzling articles of imitative jewellery, almost equal to real ; and Mrs. Crummles came out in a stern and gloomy majesty, which attracted the admiration of all beholders.

But, perhaps the appearance of Mr. Crummles was more striking and appropriate than that of any member of the party. This gentleman, who personated the bride's father, had, in pursuance of a happy and original conception, " made up " for the part by arraying himself in a theatrical wig, of a style and pattern commonly known as a brown George, and moreover assuming a snuff-coloured suit, of the previous century, with grey silk stockings, and buckles to his shoes. The better to support his assumed character he had determined to be greatly overcome, and, consequently, when they entered the church, the sobs of the affectionate parent were so heart-rending that the pew-opener suggested the propriety of his retiring to the vestry, and comforting himself with a glass of water before the ceremony began.

The procession up the aisle was beautiful. The bride, with the four bridesmaids, forming a group previously arranged and rehearsed ; the collector, followed by his second, imitating his walk and gestures, to the indescribable amusement of some theatrical friends in the gallery ; Mr. Crummles, with an infirm and feeble gait ; Mrs. Crummles advancing with that stage walk, which consists of a stride and a stop alternately—it was the completest thing ever witnessed. The ceremony was very quickly disposed of, and all parties present having signed the register (for which purpose, when it came to his turn, Mr. Crummles carefully wiped and put on an immense pair of spectacles), they went back to breakfast in high spirits. And here they found Nicholas awaiting their arrival.

" Now then," said Crummles, who had been assisting Mrs. Grudden in the preparations, which were on a more extensive scale than was quite agreeable to the collector. " Breakfast, breakfast."

No second invitation was required. The company crowded and squeezed themselves at the table as well as they could, and fell to, immediately : Miss Petowker blushing very much when anybody was looking, and eating very much when anybody was *not* looking; and Mr. Lillyvick going to work as though with the cool resolve, that since the good things must be paid for by him, he would leave as little as possible for the Crummleses to eat up afterwards.

"It's very soon done, Sir, isn't it?" inquired Mr. Folair of the collector, leaning over the table to address him.

"What is soon done, Sir?" returned Mr. Lillyvick.

"The tying up—the fixing oneself with a wife," replied Mr. Folair. "It don't take long, does it?"

"No, Sir," replied Mr. Lillyvick, colouring. "It does not take long. And what then, Sir?"

"Oh! nothing," said the actor. "It don't take a man long to hang himself, either, eh? ha, ha!"

Mr. Lillyvick laid down his knife and fork, and looked round the table with indignant astonishment.

"To hang himself!" repeated Mr. Lillyvick.

A profound silence came upon all, for Mr. Lillyvick was dignified beyond expression.

"To hang himself!" cried Mr. Lillyvick again. "Is any parallel attempted to be drawn in this company between matrimony and hanging?"

"The noose, you know," said Mr. Folair, a little crest-fallen.

"The noose, Sir?" retorted Mr. Lillyvick. "Does any man dare to speak to me of a noose, and Henrietta Pe—"

"Lillyvick," suggested Mr. Crummles.

—"and Henrietta Lillyvick in the same breath?" said the collector. "In this house, in the presence of Mr. and Mrs. Crummles, who have brought up a talented and virtuous family, to be blessings and phenomenons, and what not, are we to hear talk of nooses?"

"Folair," said Mr. Crummles, deeming it a matter of decency to be affected by this allusion to himself and partner, "I'm astonished at you."

"What are you going on in this way at me for?" urged the unfortunate actor. "What have I done?"

"Done, Sir!" cried Mr. Lillyvick, "aimed a blow at the whole frame-work of society—"

"And the best and tenderest feelings," added Crummles, relapsing into the old man.

"And the highest and most estimable of social ties," said the collector. "Noose! As if one was caught, trapped into the married state, pinned by the leg, instead of going into it of one's own accord and glorying in the act!"

"I didn't mean to make it out, that you were caught and trapped, and pinned by the leg," replied the actor. "I'm sorry for it; I can't say any more."

"So you ought to be, Sir," returned Mr. Lillyvick; "and I am glad to hear that you have enough of feeling left to be so."

The quarrel appearing to terminate with this reply, Mrs. Lillyvick considered that the fittest occasion (the attention of the company being no longer distracted) to burst into tears, and require the assistance of all four bridesmaids, which was immediately rendered, though not without some confusion, for the room being small and the table-cloth long, a whole detachment of plates were swept off the board at the very first move. Regardless of this circumstance, however, Mrs. Lillyvick refused to be comforted until the belligerents had passed their words that the dispute should be carried no further, which, after a sufficient show of reluctance, they did, and from that time Mr. Folair sat in moody silence, contenting himself with pinching Nicholas's leg when anything was said, and so expressing his contempt both for the speaker and the sentiments to which he gave utterance.

There were a great number of speeches made, some by Nicholas, and some by Crummles, and some by the collector; two by the master Crummleses in returning thanks for themselves, and one by the phenomenon on behalf of the bridesmaids, at which Mrs. Crummles shed tears. There was some singing, too, from Miss Ledrook and Miss Bravassa, and very likely there might have been more, if the fly-driver, who stopped to drive the happy pair to the spot where they proposed to take steam-boat to Ryde, had not sent in a peremptory message intimating, that if they didn't come directly he should infallibly demand eighteen-pence over and above his agreement.

This desperate threat effectually broke up the party. After a most pathetic leave-taking, Mr. Lillyvick and his bride departed for Ryde, where they were to spend the next two days in profound retirement, and whither they were accompanied by the infant, who had been appointed travelling bridesmaid on Mr. Lillyvick's express stipulation, as the steam-boat people, deceived by her size, would (he had previously ascertained) transport her at half price.

As there was no performance that night, Mr. Crummles declared his intention of keeping it up till everything to drink was disposed of; but Nicholas having to play Romeo for the first time on the ensuing evening, contrived to slip away in the midst of a temporary confusion, occasioned by the unexpected development of strong symptoms of inebriety in the conduct of Mrs. Grudden.

To this act of desertion he was led, not only by his own inclinations, but by his anxiety on account of Smike, who, having to sustain the character of the Apothecary, had been as yet wholly unable to get any more of the part into his head than the general idea that he was very hungry, which—perhaps from old recollections—he had acquired with great aptitude.

"I don't know what's to be done, Smike," said Nicholas, laying down the book. "I am afraid you can't learn it, my poor fellow."

"I am afraid not," said Smike, shaking his head. "I think if you —but that would give you so much trouble."

"What?" inquired Nicholas. "Never mind me."

"I think," said Smike, "if you were to keep saying it to me in little bits, over and over again, I should be able to recollect it from hearing you."

"Do you think so!" exclaimed Nicholas. "Well said. Let us see who tires first. Not I, Smike, trust me. Now then. 'Who calls so loud?'"

"'Who calls so loud?'" said Smike.

"'Who calls so loud?'" repeated Nicholas.

"'Who calls so loud?'" cried Smike.

Thus they continued to ask each other who called so loud, over and over and over again; and when Smike had that by heart, Nicholas went to another sentence, and then to two at a time, and then to three, and so on, until at midnight poor Smike found to his unspeakable joy that he really began to remember something about the text.

Early in the morning they went to it again, and Smike, rendered more confident by the progress he had already made, got on faster and with better heart. As soon as he began to acquire the words pretty freely, Nicholas showed him how he must come in with both hands spread out upon his stomach, and how he must occasionally rub it, in compliance with the established form by which people on the stage always denote that they want something to eat. After the morning's rehearsal they went to work again, nor did they stop, except for a hasty dinner, until it was time to repair to the theatre at night.

Never had master a more anxious, humble, docile pupil. Never had pupil a more patient, unwearying, considerate, kind-hearted master.

As soon as they were dressed, and at every interval when he was not upon the stage, Nicholas renewed his instructions. They prospered well. The Romeo was received with hearty plaudits and unbounded favour, and Smike was pronounced unanimously, alike by audience and actors, the very prince and prodigy of Apothecaries.

CHAPTER XXVI.

IS FRAUGHT WITH SOME DANGER TO MISS NICKLEBY'S PEACE OF MIND.

THE place was a handsome suite of private apartments in Regent-street; the time was three o'clock in the afternoon to the dull and plodding, and the first hour of morning to the gay and spirited; the persons were Lord Frederick Verisopht, and his friend Sir Mulberry Hawk.

These distinguished gentlemen were reclining listlessly on a couple of sofas, with a table between them, on which were scattered in rich confusion the materials of an untasted breakfast. Newspapers lay strewn about the room, but these, like the meal, were neglected and unnoticed; not, however, because any flow of conversation prevented the attractions of the journals from being called into request, for not a word was exchanged between the two, nor was any sound uttered, save when one, in tossing about to find an easier resting-place for his aching head, uttered an

Nicholas instructs Smike in the Art of Acting.

exclamation of impatience, and seemed for the moment to communicate a new restlessness to his companion.

These appearances would in themselves have furnished a pretty strong clue to the extent of the debauch of the previous night, even if there had not been other indications of the amusements in which it had been passed. A couple of billiard balls, all mud and dirt, two battered hats, a champagne bottle with a soiled glove twisted round the neck, to allow of its being grasped more surely in its capacity of an offensive weapon; a broken cane; a card-case without the top; an empty purse; a watch-guard snapped asunder; a handful of silver, mingled with fragments of half-smoked cigars, and their stale and crumbled ashes;—these, and many other tokens of riot and disorder, hinted very intelligibly at the nature of last night's gentlemanly frolics.

Lord Frederick Verisopht was the first to speak. Dropping his slippered foot on the ground, and, yawning heavily, he struggled into a sitting posture, and turned his dull languid eyes towards his friend to whom he called in a drowsy voice.

"Hallo!" replied Sir Mulberry, turning round.

"Are we going to lie here all da-a-y?" said the Lord.

"I don't know that we're fit for anything else," replied Sir Mulberry; "yet awhile, at least. I haven't a grain of life in me this morning."

"Life!" cried Lord Verisopht. "I feel as if there would be nothing so snug and comfortable as to die at once."

"Then why don't you die?" said Sir Mulberry.

With which inquiry he turned his face away, and seemed to occupy himself in an attempt to fall asleep.

His hopeful friend and pupil drew a chair to the breakfast-table, and essayed to eat; but, finding that impossible, lounged to the window, then loitered up and down the room with his hand to his fevered head, and finally threw himself again on his sofa, and roused his friend once more.

"What the devil's the matter?" groaned Sir Mulberry, sitting upright on the couch.

Although Sir Mulberry said this with sufficient ill-humour, he did not seem to feel himself quite at liberty to remain silent; for, after stretching himself very often, and declaring with a shiver that it was "infernal cold," he made an experiment at the breakfast-table, and proving more successful in it than his less-seasoned friend, remained there.

"Suppose," said Sir Mulberry, pausing with a morsel on the point of his fork, "Suppose we go back to the subject of little Nickleby, eh?"

"Which little Nickleby; the money-lender or the ga-a-l?" asked Lord Verisopht.

"You take me, I see," replied Sir Mulberry. "The girl, of course."

"You promised me you'd find her out," said Lord Verisopht.

"So I did," rejoined his friend; "but I have thought further of the matter since then. You distrust me in the business—you shall find her out yourself."

"Na—ay," remonstrated Lord Verisopht.

"But I say yes," returned his friend. "You shall find her out

yourself. Don't think that I mean, when you can—I know as well as
you that if I did, you could never get sight of her without me. No.
I say you shall find her out—*shall*—and I'll put you in the way."

"Now, curse me, if you ain't a real, deyvlish, downright, thorough-
paced friend," said the young Lord, on whom this speech had produced
a most reviving effect.

"I'll tell you how," said Sir Mulberry. "She was at that dinner
as a bait for you."

"No!" cried the young Lord. "What the dey—"

"As a bait for you," repeated his friend; "old Nickleby told me
so himself."

"What a fine old cock it is!" exclaimed Lord Verisopht; "a noble
rascal!"

"Yes," said Sir Mulberry, "he knew she was a smart little creature—"

"Smart!" interposed the young lord. "Upon my soul, Hawk,
she's a perfect beauty—a—a picture, a statue, a—a—upon my soul
she is!"

"Well," replied Sir Mulberry, shrugging his shoulders and mani-
festing an indifference, whether he felt it or not; "that's a matter of
taste; if mine doesn't agree with yours, so much the better."

"Confound it!" reasoned the lord, "you were thick enough with
her that day, anyhow. I could hardly get in a word."

"Well enough for once, well enough for once," replied Sir Mulberry; "but not worth the trouble of being agreeable to again. If you
seriously want to follow up the niece, tell the uncle that you must know
where she lives, and how she lives, and with whom, or you are no
longer a customer of his. He'll tell you fast enough."

"Why didn't you say this before?" asked Lord Verisopht, "instead
of letting me go on burning, consuming, dragging out a miserable existence for an a-age?"

"I didn't know it, in the first place," answered Sir Mulberry carelessly; "and in the second, I didn't believe you were so very much in
earnest."

Now, the truth was that in the interval which had elapsed since the
dinner at Ralph Nickleby's, Sir Mulberry Hawk had been furtively
trying by every means in his power to discover whence Kate had so
suddenly appeared, and whither she had disappeared. Unassisted by
Ralph, however, with whom he had held no communication since their
angry parting on that occasion, all his efforts were wholly unavailing,
and he had therefore arrived at the determination of communicating to
the young lord the substance of the admission he had gleaned from that
worthy. To this he was impelled by various considerations; among
which the certainty of knowing whatever the weak young man knew
was decidedly not the least, as the desire of encountering the usurer's
niece again, and using his utmost arts to reduce her pride, and revenge
himself for her contempt, was uppermost in his thoughts. It was a
politic course of proceeding, and one which could not fail to redound to
his advantage in every point of view, since the very circumstance of
his having extorted from Ralph Nickleby his real design in introducing

his niece to such society, coupled with his extreme disinterestedness in communicating it so freely to his friend, could not but advance his interests in that quarter, and greatly facilitate the passage of coin (pretty frequent and speedy already) from the pockets of Lord Frederick Verisopht to those of Sir Mulberry Hawk.

Thus reasoned Sir Mulberry, and in pursuance of this reasoning he and his friend soon afterwards repaired to Ralph Nickleby's, there to execute a plan of operations concerted by Sir Mulberry himself, avowedly to promote his friend's object, and really to attain his own.

They found Ralph at home, and alone. As he led them into the drawing-room, the recollection of the scene which had taken place there seemed to occur to him, for he cast a curious look at Sir Mulberry, who bestowed upon it no other acknowledgment than a careless smile.

They had a short conference upon some money matters then in progress, which were scarcely disposed of when the lordly dupe (in pursuance of his friend's instructions) requested with some embarrassment to speak to Ralph alone.

" Alone, eh ? " cried Sir Mulberry, affecting surprise. " Oh, very good. I'll walk into the next room here. Don't keep me long, that's all."

So saying, Sir Mulberry took up his hat, and humming a fragment of a song disappeared through the door of communication between the two drawing-rooms, and closed it after him.

" Now, my lord," said Ralph, " what is it ? "

" Nickleby," said his client, throwing himself along the sofa on which he had been previously seated, so as to bring his lips nearer to the old man's ear, " what a pretty creature your niece is ! "

" Is she, my lord ? " replied Ralph. " Maybe—maybe—I don't trouble my head with such matters."

" You know she's a deyv'lish fine girl," said the client. " You must know that, Nickleby. Come, don't deny that."

" Yes, I believe she is considered so," replied Ralph. " Indeed, I know she is. If I did not, you are an authority on such points, and your taste, my lord—on all points, indeed—is undeniable."

Nobody but the young man to whom these words were addressed could have been deaf to the sneering tone in which they were spoken, or blind to the look of contempt by which they were accompanied. But Lord Frederick Verisopht was both, and took them to be complimentary.

" Well," he said, " p'raps you're a little right, and p'raps you're a little wrong—a little of both, Nickleby. I want to know where this beauty lives, that I may have another peep at her, Nickleby."

" Really—" Ralph began in his usual tones.

" Don't talk so loud," cried the other, achieving the great point of his lesson to a miracle. " I don't want Hawk to hear."

" You know he is your rival, do you ? " said Ralph, looking sharply at him.

" He always is, d-a-amn him," replied the client ; " and I want to steal a march upon him. Ha, ha, ha ! He'll cut up so rough,

Nickleby, at our talking together without him.   Where does she live, Nickleby, that's all ?   Only tell me where she lives, Nickleby."

"He bites," thought Ralph.   "He bites."

"Eh, Nickleby, eh ?" pursued the client.   "Where does she live ?"

"Really, my lord," said Ralph, rubbing his hands slowly over each other, "I must think before I tell you."

"No, not a bit of it, Nickleby; you mustn't think at all," replied Verisopht.   "Where is it ?"

"No good can come of your knowing," replied Ralph.   "She has been virtuously and well brought up; to be sure she is handsome, poor, unprotected—poor girl, poor girl."

Ralph ran over this brief summary of Kate's condition as if it were merely passing through his own mind, and he had no intention to speak aloud; but the shrewd sly look which he directed at his companion as he delivered it, gave this poor assumption the lie.

"I tell you I only want to see her," cried his client.   "A ma-an may look at a pretty woman without harm, mayn't he ?   Now, where *does* she live? You know you're making a fortune out of me, Nickleby, and upon my soul nobody shall ever take me to anybody else, if you only tell me this."

"As you promise that, my Lord," said Ralph, with feigned reluctance, "and as I am most anxious to oblige you, and as there's no harm in it—no harm—I'll tell you.   But you had better keep it to yourself, my Lord; strictly to yourself."   Ralph pointed to the adjoining room as he spoke, and nodded expressively.

The young Lord, feigning to be equally impressed with the necessity of this precaution, Ralph disclosed the present address and occupation of his niece, observing that from what he heard of the family they appeared very ambitious to have distinguished acquaintances, and that a Lord could, doubtless, introduce himself with great ease, if he felt disposed.

"Your object being only to see her again," said Ralph, "you could effect it at any time you chose by that means."

Lord Verisopht acknowledged the hint with a great many squeezes of Ralph's hard, horny hand, and whispering that they would now do well to close the conversation, called to Sir Mulberry Hawk that he might come back.

"I thought you had gone to sleep," said Sir Mulberry, re-appearing with an ill-tempered air.

"Sorry to detain you," replied the gull; "but Nickleby has been so ama-azingly funny that I couldn't tear myself away."

"No, no," said Ralph; "it was all his lordship.   You know what a witty, humorous, elegant, accomplished man Lord Frederick is. Mind the step, my Lord—Sir Mulberry, pray give way."

With such courtesies as these, and many low bows, and the same cold sneer upon his face all the while, Ralph busied himself in showing his visitors down stairs, and otherwise than by the slightest possible motion about the corners of his mouth, returned no show of answer to the look of admiration with which Sir Mulberry Hawk seemed to compliment him on being such an accomplished and most consummate scoundrel.

There had been a ring at the bell a few moments before, which was answered by Newman Noggs just as they reached the hall. In the ordinary course of business Newman would have either admitted the new-comer in silence, or have requested him or her to stand aside while the gentlemen passed out. But he no sooner saw who it was, than as if for some private reason of his own, he boldly departed from the established custom of Ralph's mansion in business hours, and looking towards the respectable trio who were approaching, cried in a loud and sonorous voice, " Mrs. Nickleby!"

" Mrs. Nickleby!" cried Sir Mulberry Hawk, as his friend looked back, and stared him in the face.

It was, indeed, that well-intentioned lady, who, having received an offer for the empty house in the city directed to the landlord, had brought it post-haste to Mr. Nickleby without delay.

" Nobody *you* know," said Ralph. " Step into the office, my—my—dear. I'll be with you directly."

" Nobody I know!" cried Sir Mulberry Hawk, advancing to the astonished lady. " Is this Mrs. Nickleby—the mother of Miss Nickleby—the delightful creature that I had the happiness of meeting in this house the very last time I dined here! But no;" said Sir Mulberry, stopping short. " No, it can't be. There is the same cast of features, the same indescribable air of—But no; no. This lady is too young for that."

" I think you can tell the gentleman, brother-in-law, if it concerns him to know," said Mrs. Nickleby, acknowledging the compliment with a graceful bend, " that Kate Nickleby is my daughter."

" Her daughter, my Lord!" cried Sir Mulberry, turning to his friend. " This lady's daughter, my Lord."

" My Lord!" thought Mrs. Nickleby. " Well, I never did—!"

" This, then, my Lord," said Sir Mulberry, " is the lady to whose obliging marriage we owe so much happiness. This lady is the mother of sweet Miss Nickleby. Do you observe the extraordinary likeness, my Lord ? Nickleby—introduce us."

Ralph did so, in a kind of desperation.

" Upon my soul, it's a most delightful thing," said Lord Frederick, pressing forward : " How de do ?"

Mrs. Nickleby was too much flurried by these uncommonly kind salutations, and her regrets at not having on her other bonnet, to make any immediate reply, so she merely continued to bend and smile, and betray great agitation.

" A—and how is Miss Nickleby ?" said Lord Frederick. " Well, I hope ?"

" She is quite well, I'm obliged to you, my lord," returned Mrs. Nickleby, recovering. " Quite well. She wasn't well for some days after that day she dined here, and I can't help thinking, that she caught cold in that hackney coach coming home : Hackney coaches, my lord, are such nasty things, that it's almost better to walk at any time, for although I believe a hackney coachman can be transported for life, if he has a broken window, still they are so reckless, that they nearly all

have broken windows. I once had a swelled face for six weeks, my
lord, from riding in a hackney coach—I think it was a hackney coach,"
said Mrs. Nickleby reflecting, " though I'm not quite certain, whether it
wasn't a chariot ; at all events I know it was a dark green, with a very
long number, beginning with a nought and ending with a nine—no,
beginning with a nine, and ending with a nought, that was it, and of
course the stamp office people would know at once whether it was a
coach or a chariot if any inquiries were made there—however that
was, there it was with a broken window, and there was I for six weeks
with a swelled face—I think that was the very same hackney coach,
that we found out afterwards, had the top open all the time, and
we should never even have known it, if they hadn't charged us a
shilling an hour extra for having it open, which it seems is the law, or
was then, and a most shameful law it appears to be—I don't understand the subject, but I should say the Corn Laws could be nothing to
that act of Parliament."

Having pretty well run herself out by this time, Mrs. Nickleby
stopped as suddenly as she had started off, and repeated that Kate was
quite well. " Indeed," said Mrs. Nickleby, " I don't think she ever
was better, since she had the hooping-cough, scarlet-fever and measles,
all at the same time, and that's the fact."

" Is that letter for me ? " growled Ralph, pointing to the little packet
Mrs. Nickleby held in her hand.

" For you, brother-in-law," replied Mrs. Nickleby, " and I walked
all the way up here on purpose to give it you."

" All the way up here ! " cried Sir Mulberry, seizing upon the chance
of discovering where Mrs. Nickleby had come from. " What a confounded distance ! How far do you call it now?"

" How far do I call it ! " said Mrs. Nickleby. " Let me see. It's
just a mile, from our door to the Old Bailey."

" No, no. Not so much as that," urged Sir Mulberry.

" Oh ! It is indeed," said Mrs. Nickleby. " I appeal to his lordship."

" I should decidedly say it was a mile," remarked Lord Frederick,
with a solemn aspect.

" It must be ; it can't be a yard less," said Mrs. Nickleby. " All
down Newgate Street, all down Cheapside, all up Lombard Street,
down Gracechurch Street, and along Thames Street, as far as Spig-
wiffin's Wharf. Oh ! It's a mile."

" Yes, on second thoughts I should say it was," replied Sir Mulberry.
" But you don't surely mean to walk all the way back ? "

" Oh no," rejoined Mrs. Nickleby. " I shall go back in an omnibus.
I didn't travel about in omnibuses, when my poor dear Nicholas was
alive, brother-in-law. But as it is, you know—"

" Yes, yes," replied Ralph impatiently, " and you had better get back
before dark."

" Thank you, brother-in-law, so I had," returned Mrs. Nickleby.
" I think I had better say good bye, at once."

" Not stop and—rest? " said Ralph, who seldom offered refreshments
unless something was to be got by it.

"Oh dear me no," returned Mrs. Nickleby, glancing at the dial.

"Lord Frederick," said Sir Mulberry, "we are going Mrs. Nickleby's way. We'll see her safe to the omnibus?"

"By all means. Ye-es."

"Oh! I really couldn't think of it!" said Mrs. Nickleby.

But Sir Mulberry Hawk and Lord Verisopht were peremptory in their politeness, and leaving Ralph, who seemed to think, not unwisely, that he looked less ridiculous as a mere spectator, than he would have done if he had taken any part in these proceedings, they quitted the house with Mrs. Nickleby between them; that good lady in a perfect ecstacy of satisfaction, no less with the attentions shown her by two titled gentlemen, than with the conviction, that Kate might now pick and choose, at least between two large fortunes, and most unexceptionable husbands.

As she was carried away for the moment by an irresistible train of thought, all connected with her daughter's future greatness, Sir Mulberry Hawk and his friend exchanged glances over the top of the bonnet which the poor lady so much regretted not having left at home, and proceeded to dilate with great rapture, but much respect, on the manifold perfections of Miss Nickleby.

"What a delight, what a comfort, what a happiness, this amiable creature must be to you," said Sir Mulberry, throwing into his voice an indication of the warmest feeling.

"She is indeed, Sir," replied Mrs. Nickleby; "she is the sweetest-tempered, kindest-hearted creature—and so clever!"

"She looks clayver," said Lord Verisopht, with the air of a judge of cleverness.

"I assure you she is, my lord," returned Mrs. Nickleby. "When she was at school in Devonshire, she was universally allowed to be beyond all exception the very cleverest girl there, and there were a great many very clever ones too, and that's the truth—twenty-five young ladies, fifty guineas a-year without the et-ceteras, both the Miss Dowdles, the most accomplished, elegant, fascinating creatures— Oh dear me!" said Mrs. Nickleby, "I never shall forget what pleasure she used to give me and her poor dear papa, when she was at that school, never—such a delightful letter every half-year, telling us that she was the first pupil in the whole establishment, and had made more progress than anybody else! I can scarcely bear to think of it even now. The girls wrote all the letters themselves," added Mrs. Nickleby, "and the writing-master touched them up afterwards with a magnifying glass and a silver pen; at least I think they wrote them, though Kate was never quite certain about that, because she didn't know the handwriting of hers again; but any way, I know it was a circular which they all copied, and of course it was a very gratifying thing—very gratifying."

With similar recollections Mrs. Nickleby beguiled the tediousness of the way, until they reached the omnibus, which the extreme politeness of her new friends would not allow them to leave until it actually started, when they took their hats, as Mrs. Nickleby solemnly assured her hearers on many subsequent occasions, "completely off," and kissed their straw-coloured kid gloves till they were no longer visible.

Mrs. Nickleby leant back in the furthest corner of the conveyance, and, closing her eyes, resigned herself to a host of most pleasing meditations. Kate had never said a word about having met either of these gentlemen; "that," she thought, "argues that she is strongly prepossessed in favour of one of them." Then the question arose, which one could it be. The lord was the youngest, and his title was certainly the grandest; still Kate was not the girl to be swayed by such considerations as these. "I will never put any constraint upon her inclinations," said Mrs. Nickleby to herself; "but upon my word I think there's no comparison between his lordship and Sir Mulberry—Sir Mulberry is such an attentive gentlemanly creature, so much manner, such a fine man, and has so much to say for himself. I hope it's Sir Mulberry—I think it must be Sir Mulberry!" And then her thoughts flew back to her old predictions, and the number of times she had said, that Kate with no fortune would marry better than other people's daughters with thousands; and, as she pictured with the brightness of a mother's fancy all the beauty and grace of the poor girl who had struggled so cheerfully with her new life of hardship and trial, her heart grew too full, and the tears trickled down her face.

Meanwhile, Ralph walked to and fro in his little back office, troubled in mind by what had just occurred. To say that Ralph loved or cared for—in the most ordinary acceptation of those terms—any one of God's creatures, would be the wildest fiction. Still, there had somehow stolen upon him from time to time a thought of his niece which was tinged with compassion and pity; breaking through the dull cloud of dislike or indifference which darkened men and women in his eyes, there was, in her case, the faintest gleam of light —a most feeble and sickly ray at the best of times—but there it was, and it showed the poor girl in a better and purer aspect than any in which he had looked on human nature yet.

"I wish," thought Ralph, "I had never done this. And yet it will keep this boy to me, while there is money to be made. Selling a girl—throwing her in the way of temptation, and insult, and coarse speech. Nearly two thousand pounds profit from him already though. Pshaw! match-making mothers do the same thing every day."

He sat down, and told the chances, for and against, on his fingers.

"If I had not put them in the right track to-day," thought Ralph, "this foolish woman would have done so. Well. If her daughter is as true to herself as she should be from what I have seen, what harm ensues? A little teazing, a little humbling, a few tears. Yes," said Ralph, aloud, as he locked his iron safe. "She must take her chance. She must take her chance."

113, FLEET STREET.

STANDARD LIBRARY EDITIONS

OF

𝔓𝔬𝔭𝔲𝔩𝔞𝔯 𝔚𝔬𝔯𝔨𝔰.

BEAUTIFULLY PRINTED,

IN MEDIUM OCTAVO,

ON FINE PAPER.

UNIFORM WITH " BYRON'S

WORKS," " CURIOSITIES OF

LITERATURE," &c. &c.

UNDER the above general title, a series of works is now in course of publication, on a plan combining such high LITERARY MERIT, ELEGANCE OF FORM AND EXECUTION, and CHEAPNESS, as will render them accessible to all classes of the community.

The novelty of this plan does not consist in an issue of merely cheap books. Hitherto, CHEAP books, though low in price, have been correspondingly low in execution. The design is *still* to make them low in price, but in every respect excellent; and to enable every one of limited means, but cultivated mind, to possess a library of well-printed, handsome books, at a very moderate price.

Ten Works have been already published, viz. :—

	s.	*d.*
THE LADY OF THE LAKE. BY SIR W. SCOTT	1	0
THE LAY OF THE LAST MINSTREL. BY SIR W. SCOTT	1	0
MARMION. BY SIR W. SCOTT	1	2
THE VICAR OF WAKEFIELD. BY OLIVER GOLDSMITH	1	0
THE BOROUGH. A POEM. BY THE REV. GEORGE CRABBE	1	4
NARRATIVE OF THE MUTINY OF THE BOUNTY. BY LIEUT. BLIGH	1	4
POETICAL WORKS OF H. KIRKE WHITE. WITH A BIOGRAPHICAL NOTICE	1	0
POEMS AND SONGS OF ROBERT BURNS. WITH A BIOGRAPHICAL NOTICE	2	6
MRS. HUTCHINSON'S MEMOIRS OF HER HUSBAND, COLONEL HUTCHINSON; *Governor of Nottingham Castle during the Civil War*	2	6
PAUL AND VIRGINIA; AND ELIZABETH.		

From the foregoing list, it will be obvious that no particular arrangement has been attempted. On the contrary, in making the selection, care has been taken that the works produced should be of a miscellaneous character, so that all tastes might in turn be gratified. Hereafter, when the number is sufficiently increased, they may be formed into volumes, to suit the wishes of the purchaser; and in the mean time, as each work is protected by a wrapper, it may be preserved in a fit condition for binding. Many other works are in preparation; and they will be brought forward as speedily as is consistent with the care they require.

OPINIONS OF THE PRESS.

" The first real People's Editions we have seen, that combine high literary merit with a cheapness that places them within the reach, we should say, of all who can wish for them ; whilst their mechanical execution is such as to render them fit for any book shelf where Mr. MURRAY's, Mr. CADELL's, or Mr. MOXON's single volume editions are admitted, have emanated from the shop of Mr. Smith, of Fleet Street."—*Spectator*.

" We lately copied an article from the *Spectator*, in commendation of the system of publishing the Standard Works of England at a cheap rate ; and from the specimens of the edition before us, we cordially join in the opinion of that paper. It is surely an object of considerable importance in times like these, when there is so great a struggle for the spread of education and general knowledge, that the treasures of English literature should be made as generally available as possible. This Standard Edition is well calculated to insure the general perusal of the best English works, from the cheapness with which they are now supplied. To show the advantages of this edition, it is only necessary to state that " Scott's Lay " and " The Lady of the Lake," are to be had *for 1s. each, and "Marmion"* for 1s. 2d. Crabbe's " Borough " is published at 1s. 4d., and " The Vicar of Wakefield" at 1s. We hear a great deal about cheap Continental editions ; but when a work, equal in extent to " The Vicar of Wakefield," is to be had in a handsome form, on good paper, and handsomely printed, for One Shilling, we think it will be admitted that we manage these things quite as well in England."—*Courier*.

" The elegance with which these works are brought out is a strong recommendation, and certainly, in point of economy, they are not exceeded by any publication of the day. The works selected are of the highest order, and already stamped with fame. The typography is exceedingly beautiful, and the press appears to have been corrected with more than ordinary care. ' Lieutenant Bligh's Narrative of the Mutiny of the Bounty,' is followed by an interesting account of the subsequent history of the Mutineers, and the colony of Pitcairn's Island, which completes a tale of startling reality."—*Atlas*.

" ' The Borough,' by the Rev. G. Crabbe, LL.B. ; ' The Vicar of Wakefield ;' ' Marmion ;' ' The Lay of the Last Minstrel :' At a trifling cost we here have each of these works, admirably printed in double columns, royal 8vo. ' Nature's sternest painter, yet her best,' is a poet whose works should be brought within the means of the working classes. ' The Vicar of Wakefield,' everybody's favourite, the book for all ages, reads as freshly as ever ; and the re-publication, in such a form, of the stirring poems of Scott, is matter to rejoice over."—*Sunday Times*.

" We have often called the attention of our readers to this very cheap and elegant edition of the Standard Works of our language. The publisher still continues this work, and we trust with success, for it is a pleasing and very useful acquisition to the many who are capable of enjoying elegant literature, but not so capable of paying for dear books. We have now before us four numbers of this work, containing ' Marmion,' ' The Lay of the Last Minstrel,' the delightful novel of ' The Vicar of Wakefield,' and Crabbe's celebrated poem, ' The Borough.' "—*Weekly Dispatch*.

" Uniform with Murray's single volume of Byron, we have here ' The Lady of the Lake,' ' The Lay of the Last Minstrel,' and ' Marmion,' with all the notes, most beautifully and correctly printed, at a price beyond all comparison cheap. We augur that this Standard Library Edition will be one of the most successful and popular publications in this country."—*Naval and Military Gazette*.

Souvenir Classics,

FORMING

ELEGANT AND APPROPRIATE PRESENTS.

The following editions of the most popular and Classical Authors are particularly adapted for PRESENTS, being printed in small octavo, in the very best style, embellished with Frontispieces engraved on Steel, and elegantly bound. Several others are in preparation, and will shortly be published.

I.

Price 3s. 6d. cloth, and 7s. 6d. morocco elegant,

MARMION.

BY

SIR WALTER SCOTT.

II.

Price 3s. 6d. cloth, gilt, and 7s. 6d. morocco elegant,

THE

LADY OF THE LAKE.

BY

SIR WALTER SCOTT.

III.

Price 2s. 6d. cloth, gilt, & 6s. 6d. morocco elegant,

ELIZABETH;

OR,

THE EXILES OF SIBERIA.

IV.

Price 3s. 6d. cloth, gilt, and 7s. 6d. mor. elegant,

GOLDSMITH'S POEMS AND ESSAYS.

V.

Price 3s. 6d. cloth, gilt, & 7s. 6d. morocco elegant,

ROMANTIC TALES.

BY M. G. LEWIS.

CONTAINING

MY UNCLE'S GARRET WINDOW; THE ANACONDA; AND AMORASSAN.

VI.

Price 3s. cloth, gilt, and 7s. morocco elegant,

THE

VICAR OF WAKEFIELD.

BY DR. GOLDSMITH.

VII.

Price 3s. 6d. cloth, gilt, & 7s. 6d. morocco elegant,

THOMSON'S SEASONS

AND

CASTLE OF INDOLENCE.

VIII.

Price 2s. 6d. cloth gilt; 3s. silk; 5s. morocco, royal 32mo, with a Portrait,

THREE CENTURIES OF MEDITATIONS & VOWS, Divine and Moral.

BY JOSEPH HALL, D.D., BISHOP OF NORWICH.

IX.

Price 2s. 6d. cloth gilt; 3s. silk; 5s. morocco, royal 32mo, with a Portrait,

SELECT THOUGHTS;

OR

Choice Helps for a Pious Spirit.

BY JOSEPH HALL, D.D., BISHOP OF NORWICH.

In the Press.

LAY OF THE LAST MINSTREL.
PAUL AND VIRGINIA.

BURNS'S SONGS AND POEMS.
COWPER'S POEMS.

THE WORKS OF WILLIAM PALEY, D.D.,

ARCHBISHOP OF CARLISLE.

COMPLETE.

WITH A PORTRAIT, AND NUMEROUS ILLUSTRATIVE NOTES.

In One Volume, super-royal 8vo, price 17s. cloth.

BISHOP BURNET'S HISTORY OF HIS OWN TIMES.

COMPLETE.

With a Portrait, and copious Historical and Biographical Notes.

In One Volume, super-royal 8vo, price 17s. cloth.

ON THE BREEDING, REARING, DISEASES, AND GENERAL MANAGEMENT OF POULTRY.

BY WALTER B. DICKSON.

In foolscap 8vo, with 14 Woodcuts, price 6s. cloth.

SIR JOHN FROISSART'S CHRONICLES OF ENGLAND, FRANCE, SPAIN, &c.

This Edition will be printed from the Translation of the late Thomas Johnes, Esq., and collated throughout with that of Lord Berners; numerous additional Notes will also be given, and the whole will be embellished with upwards of One Hundred Engravings on Wood, illustrating the Costume and Manners of the period, chiefly taken from the illuminated MS. copies of the Author, in the British Museum, and elsewhere.

Publishing monthly in Parts, price 2s. each.

THE FLORAL CABINET,

AND

Magazine of Exotic Botany.

Publishing monthly in Numbers, price 2s. 6d. each. Each Number containing Four beautiful Plates, accurately coloured from Nature; with Descriptions of the Plants, their Cultivation, &c.; and other original Articles.

The First Volume, containing Nos. 1 to 12, may be had, half-bound Morocco, price 36s.

LODGE'S PORTRAITS

OF ILLUSTRIOUS PERSONAGES OF GREAT BRITAIN.

Just published,

Number 21, price 2s. 6d.; or India Paper, 4s. Part 21, price 5s.; or India Paper, 8s. Volume 5, price 22s.; or India Paper, 34s.

TO BE COMPLETED IN EIGHTY NUMBERS, OR FORTY PARTS, OR TEN VOLS.

LETTERS FROM A FATHER TO HIS SON,

On various Topics relative to Literature and the Conduct of Life.

BY JOHN AIKIN, M.D.

A NEW EDITION.

In Foolscap 8vo, price 5s. cloth; or 10s. morocco elegant.

[BRADBURY AND EVANS, PRINTERS, WHITEFRIARS.]

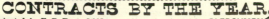

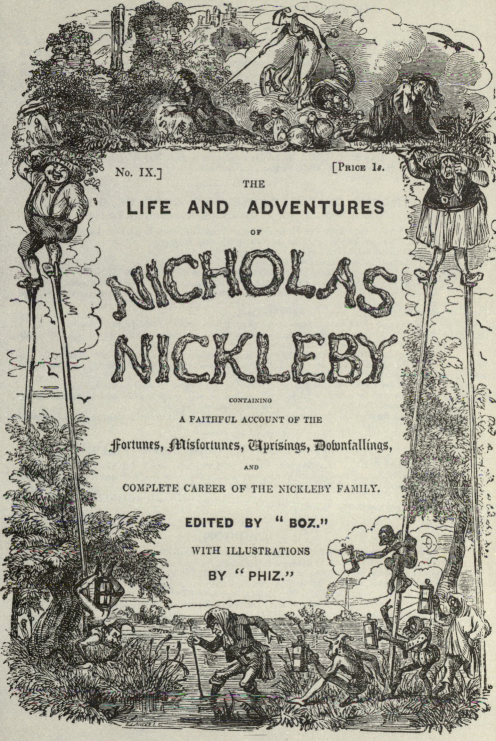

No. IX.]   [Price 1s.

THE
LIFE AND ADVENTURES
OF
NICHOLAS NICKLEBY

CONTAINING

A FAITHFUL ACCOUNT OF THE

Fortunes, Misfortunes, Uprisings, Downfallings,

AND

COMPLETE CAREER OF THE NICKLEBY FAMILY.

EDITED BY "BOZ."

WITH ILLUSTRATIONS

BY "PHIZ."

LONDON: CHAPMAN AND HALL, 186, STRAND.

BRITISH COLLEGE OF HEALTH,
HAMILTON PLACE, NEW ROAD.

NOTICE.—Whereas a most unjustifiable application is about being made to Parliament by the Medical Profession, for a Medical Inquisition in this Country, which will have for its object to prevent the establishing of any system of Medicine, HOWEVER BENEFICIAL TO THE PUBLIC at large, because such *system may militate against the pecuniary interests of the Medical Body ;* We, the undersigned, being three Medical Practitioners duly licensed, hereby declare, that we have for some years past used ourselves, and administered to others, Morison's Medicines in all cases of disease, and are of opinion, 1st, that they are a cure for all curable diseases ; and, 2dly, that the *theory upon which such medicines are administered is the only true one ;* the whole of which we are ready and willing to verify whenever called upon. In conclusion, we cannot but regret that in such an important question to mankind generally, the Medical Profession should cautiously abstain from all fair and impartial investigation on the subject.

ROBERT LYNCH, M.D.
RICHARD TOTHILL, Surgeon to the Exeter Hygeian Dispensary, Heavitree, near Exeter.
JOHNSON LINCOLN, Surgeon, R.N., Northallerton, Yorkshire.
September 21, 1838.

SYNOPSIS OF THE CAUSE AND CURE OF DISEASE,
ACCORDING TO THE HYGEIAN, OR MORISONIAN SYSTEM.

A knowledge of the best means for preserving and restoring health is the most important of human pursuits. This knowledge is *only* to be acquired by following *Nature.*
1.—All animal bodies consist of *fluids* and *solids.*
2.—It is from and by the fluids that the solids are *formed.*
3.—The fluids contained in the human body are *four times* the weight of the solids.
4.—The chief of the fluids is the blood, from which all the others are derived and derivable.
5.—The blood is the *life*—the *primum mobile*—the *first agent*—from which all others derive their origin.
6.—Health depends upon the *purity* of the blood.
7.—The purity of the blood depends upon its having *free outlets* for its acquired impurities.
8.—Disease is induced by the choking up of these outlets in the bowels, by an accumulation of mucus on the inner surface of the intestines, &c.
9.—This accumulation is occasioned by anything that weakens the circulation or hurts digestion.
10.—The impurities thus detained in the blood occasion *every* species of disease, according to the particular locality in which they become lodged.
11.—All diseases proceed from *one* source, therefore they may all be cured by *one* medicine.
12.—This medicine must be a *purgative*, innoxious in itself, yet sufficiently powerful to carry off the above-mentioned mucus, and by improving digestion, improve the blood.
13.—This discovery has been made by Mr. James Morison, Hygeist, in the composition of the *Universal Medicines.*

INSANITY CURED BY MORISON'S PILLS.

" I, Richard Tothill, of Heavitree, near Exeter, Surgeon, hereby certify, that Samuel Crabb, aged 55, residing at Pin Hoe, three miles from Exeter, was cured, under my notice, of Insanity, solely by the use of the Vegetable Universal Medicines of the British College of Health, after having been in the Exeter Asylum. RICHARD TOTHILL, M.R.C.S.I.
" Heavitree, near Exeter, October 1, 1000."

CAUTION.

Whereas spurious imitations of my Medicines are now in circulation, I, JAMES MORISON, the Hygeist, hereby give notice, That I am in no*wise* connected with the following Medicines purporting to be mine, and sold under the various names of " Dr. Morrison's Pills," " The Hygeian Pills," " The Improved Vegetable Universal Pills," " The Original Morison's Pills, as compounded by the late Mr. Moat," " The Original Hygeian Vegetable Pills," " The Original Morison's Pills," &c. &c.

That my Medicines are prepared only at the British College of Health, Hamilton Place, King's Cross, and sold by the General Agents to the British College of Health and their Sub-Agents, and that no Chemist or Druggist is authorized by me to dispose of the same.

None can be genuine without the words " MORISON'S UNIVERSAL MEDICINES " are engraved on the Government Stamp, in white letters upon a red ground. In witness whereof I have hereunto set my hand.

BRITISH COLLEGE OF HEALTH,
No. 2, Hamilton Place, New Road, King's Cross, *May*, 1838.

JAMES MORISON,
The Hygeist.

Sold in Boxes, at 1*s.* 1½*d.*, 2*s.* 9*d.*, 4*s.* 6*d.*, and Family Packets, containing three 4*s.* 6*d.* Boxes, 11*s.* each.

Dr. George Taylor, 6½, Wall-street, New York, General Agent for the United States of America.
Mr. Thomas Gardner, Calcutta, General Agent for India.

On the 1st of November was published, and will be continued Monthly, in super-royal 8vo, price 2s. 6d.

THE PICTORIAL EDITION OF SHAKSPERE.

PART I.—TWO GENTLEMEN OF VERONA.

The Notes and Notices will embrace every subject that appears necessary to be investigated for the complete information of the reader. The almost endless variety of objects presented in the text, will call for the best assistance that the Editor can procure from gentlemen conversant with particular departments.

In the Design and Engraving of the Woodcuts, the most eminent Artists will be employed. The same desire will preside over the artistical as the literary department—namely, to produce an edition of Shakspere that, whilst it may be more interesting to the general reader, as well as more attractive as a work of art, than any which has yet been published, shall aim at the most complete accuracy; and thus offer a not unworthy tribute to the great Poet, which may be acceptable not only to England, but to every country where his works are welcomed as the universal property of the civilized world.

In this edition the Comedies and Tragedies will be published, as nearly as can be ascertained, in the order in which they were written, but in separate classes; and the Histories according to the order of events. Whilst this arrangement is preserved with reference to the completion of the work in volumes, a necessary variety will be offered in the periodical publication of Plays taken from each of the three classes, as for example:—

Part 1.—Two Gentlemen of Verona	COMEDY.
2.—King John	HISTORY.
3.—Romeo and Juliet	TRAGEDY.

The Plays will occupy Thirty-seven Parts. The entire work, including Shakspere's Sonnets and other Poems, and a Life of Shakspere, with local Illustrations, as well as other introductory matter, will extend to Forty-two Parts. The ultimate arrangement will be as follows:—

Comedies	14 Parts.	2 Vols.
Histories	10	1
Tragedies	13 }	2
Index	1 }	
Poems, Life, &c.	6	1
	44 Parts.	6 Vols.

LONDON: CHARLES KNIGHT AND CO., 22, LUDGATE STREET.

This day is published, dedicated by express permission, and under the immediate Patronage of Her Majesty the QUEEN DOWAGER,

FINDEN'S FEMALE PORTRAITS OF THE COURT OF QUEEN VICTORIA.

Part IV., containing
ADA, COUNTESS OF LOVELACE (Daughter of Lord Byron).
THE LADY ASHLEY.
THE LADY CAPEL.
India Proofs Folio, 21s.   Plain Proofs Folio, 15s.   Prints, 12s.

London:—Published by the Proprietors, at Nos. 18 and 19, Southampton-place, Euston-square; sold also by Ackermann and Co., 96, Strand; James Fraser, 215, Regent-street; Ryley and Co., 8, Regent-street, and by every respectable Bookseller in the Kingdom.

UNDER THE SUPERINTENDENCE OF MR. CHARLES HEATH.

This day is published, in sup.-roy. 8vo, 21s. elegantly bound; India Proofs, 2l. 12s. 6d.,

THE BOOK OF BEAUTY.

EDITED BY THE COUNTESS OF BLESSINGTON.

The Engravings consist entirely of richly-executed Portraits, after Paintings by Chalon, E. Landseer, Bostock, Lucas, and Ross, of English Nobility and Persons of Fashion, viz.;—

Duchess of Sutherland,	Lady Wilhelmina Stanhope,	The Viscountess Fitzharris,
Viscountess Mahon,	Lady Fanny Cowper,	Mrs. Verschoyle,
Viscountess Vallétort,	Mrs Maberly,	Miss Ellen Home Purves,
Viscountess Powerscourt,	Mrs. Mountjoy Martyn,	Miss Cockayne.

LONDON: LONGMAN, ORME, & CO.

This day, One Shilling, No. II. of

HEADS OF THE PEOPLE;

A SKETCH-BOOK OF LIFE.

CONTAINING

THE "LION" (OF A CIRCLE).	THE MAID OF ALL-WORK.
THE MEDICAL STUDENT.	THE FASHIONABLE PHYSICIAN.

"Nothing can be more life-like and original than these Portraits, which mark out the class they are intended to represent as distinctly as if the real specimens of the genus were before the eye. The characters are also described with considerable fidelity and humour; and if the work proceed to give "The Heads" of other classes with as much truth as those of the present number, the volume, when completed, must be popular both as "Heads and Tales."—*Courier.*

*** This National Work is published Monthly, each Number containing Four Plates; with Letter-press Descriptions by the most distinguished writers of the day.

ROBERT TYAS, 50, CHEAPSIDE; J. MENZIES, EDINBURGH; AND MACHEN & CO., DUBLIN.

NEW WORKS

PUBLISHED BY CHAPMAN AND HALL.

THE PICKWICK PAPERS COMPLETE.

In one volume 8vo, bound in cloth, price 1*l.* 1*s.* ; half-bound morocco, 1*l.* 4*s.* 6*d.* ; whole-bound morocco, 1*l.* 6*s.* 6*d.*

THE

POSTHUMOUS PAPERS OF THE PICKWICK CLUB.

BY "BOZ."

WITH FORTY-THREE ILLUSTRATIONS BY "PHIZ."

UNIFORM WITH THE PICKWICK PAPERS.

No. XIV., to be completed in Twenty Numbers, 8vo, price One Shilling each,

SKETCHES BY "BOZ."

ILLUSTRATIVE OF EVERY-DAY LIFE AND EVERY-DAY PEOPLE.

A New Edition.

COMPRISING BOTH THE SERIES,

AND EMBELLISHED WITH FORTY ILLUSTRATIONS,

BY GEORGE CRUIKSHANK.

ECARTE.

Neatly bound, with gilt edges, price 2*s.* 6*d.*

A TREATISE ON THE GAME OF ECARTE;

COMPRISING

THE RULES OF THE GAME, AND TABLES SHOWING THE ODDS AT ANY POINT OF IT.

ALSO,

EXAMPLES OF DIFFICULT HANDS,

WITH DIRECTIONS FOR PLAYING THEM; TO WHICH ARE ADDED, RULES FOR CALCULATING BETS ON ANY EVENTS.

In one volume, small 8vo, price 5*s.*, neatly bound,

A VISIT TO THE BRITISH MUSEUM.

CONTAINING

A FAMILIAR DESCRIPTION OF EVERY OBJECT OF INTEREST IN THE VARIOUS DEPARTMENTS OF THAT ESTABLISHMENT.

WITH NUMEROUS ILLUSTRATIONS.

" A very useful and interesting little work, containing a description of every object of interest in the various departments of the establishment."—*Herald.*

In one volume, square 16mo, neatly bound, price 3s. 6d.,

MORALS FROM THE CHURCHYARD,

In a Series of Cheerful Fables for the Youth of both Sexes.

WITH EIGHT BEAUTIFULLY ENGRAVED ILLUSTRATIONS ON WOOD, FROM DESIGNS BY

H. K. BROWNE.

" This neat little volume is a very pretty companion to Mrs. Austin's ' Story without an End,' written in the same agreeable style of mixed liveliness and tenderness, and illustrated with several charming engravings on wood, from designs of a very superior character. The object of the Fable is to exhibit a moral estimate of human pursuits, adapted to the minds of children, and to show that, finally, nothing can stand the test of that universal leveller, the grave, excepting virtue and religion. The manner is healthy and cheerful, as a child's book should be, and a vein of actual interest gives life and shape to the allegory."—*Examiner.*

TRAVELLING AND HUNTING MAPS.

MOUNTED IN CASES ADAPTED TO THE WAISTCOAT POCKET, 1s. 6d. EACH,

MAPS OF THE ENGLISH COUNTIES,

ENGRAVED BY SYDNEY HALL.

WITH THE MAIL AND COACH ROADS CORRECTLY COLOURED.

In one volume, square 16mo, price 5s., neatly bound,

THE JUVENILE BUDGET;

Or, Stories for Little Readers.

BY MRS. S. C. HALL.

WITH SIX ILLUSTRATIONS BY H. K. BROWNE.

" These stories are chiefly collected from the ' Juvenile Forget-me-Not,' and long since received our word of commendation ; but thus collected they form a very pretty and pleasant volume, and will be a most welcome present to our young friends."—*Athenæum.*

One volume, royal 16mo, neatly bound, price 5s. 6d.,

CHESS FOR BEGINNERS;

In a Series of Progressive Lessons,

SHOWING THE MOST APPROVED METHODS OF BEGINNING AND ENDING THE GAME, TOGETHER WITH VARIOUS SITUATIONS AND CHECK MATES.

BY WILLIAM LEWIS,

Author of several Works on the Game.

WITH TWENTY-FOUR DIAGRAMS PRINTED IN COLOURS. SECOND EDITION, CORRECTED.

FRENCH POETRY.

In one volume 12mo, neatly bound in cloth, gilt edges, price 4s.,

FLEURS DE POESIE MODERNE;

CONTAINING

THE BEAUTIES OF A. DE LAMARTINE, VICTOR HUGO, DE BERANGER, C. DE LAVIGNE.

" A selection made in the spirit of the day. Instead of a collection from other and old collections, the compiler has chosen the best of modern French writers, and presented us with the very best of their thoughts."—*Spectator.*

SEVENTH EDITION.

In one volume, small 8vo, price 3s. boards,

SKETCHES OF YOUNG LADIES;

WITH SIX ILLUSTRATIONS BY " PHIZ."

The Busy Young Lady.	The Young Lady who is engaged.	The Whimsical Young Lady.
The Romantic Young Lady.	The Petting Young Lady.	The Sincere Young Lady.
The Matter-of-Fact Young Lady.	The Natural Historian Young Lady.	The Affirmative Young Lady.
The Young Lady who Sings.	The Indirect Young Lady.	The Natural Young Lady.
The Plain Young Lady.	The Stupid Young Lady.	The Clever Young Lady.
The Evangelical Young Lady.	The Hyperbolical Young Lady.	The Mysterious Young Lady.
The Manly Young Lady.	The Interesting Young Lady.	The Lazy Young Lady.
The Literary Young Lady.	The Abstemious Young Lady.	The Young Lady from School.

FIFTH EDITION.

In one volume, small 8vo, price 3s. boards,

SKETCHES OF YOUNG GENTLEMEN;

CONTENTS.

Dedication to the Young Ladies.	The ' Throwing-off' Young Gentleman	The Military Young Gentleman.
The Out-and-out Young Gentleman.	The Poetical Young Gentleman.	The Political Young Gentleman.
The Domestic Young Gentleman.	The Funny Young Gentleman.	The Censorious Young Gentleman.
The Bashful Young Gentleman.	The Theatrical Young Gentleman.	The Young Ladies' Young Gentleman,
The very Friendly Young Gentleman.		

WITH SIX ILLUSTRATIONS BY " PHIZ."

In two volumes, small 8vo, with Frontispieces, price 9s.,

EDWARD, THE CRUSADER'S SON.
A Tale.

ILLUSTRATING THE HISTORY, MANNERS, AND CUSTOMS OF ENGLAND IN THE ELEVENTH CENTURY.

BY MRS. BARWELL.

" The intelligent and accomplished lady who has written these volumes was urged to the undertaking by an idea that a tale founded on, and illustrating the manners, customs, architecture, and costume of the eleventh century, would be valuable, not only to the young, but to that class of instructors who disapprove of the too stimulating pages of historical romance, and yet desire something more than dull details for their pupils. The task was difficult, but it has been fully conquered."—*New Monthly Magazine.*

One volume, foolscap, handsomely bound in embossed cloth, gilt edges, price 12s.; or in morocco, 16s.,

THE ARTIST;

Or, Young Ladies' Instructor in Ornamental Painting, Drawing, &c.

CONSISTING OF LESSONS IN

GRECIAN PAINTING	ORIENTAL TINTING	TRANSFERRING
JAPAN PAINTING	MEZZOTINTING	INLAYING

AND MANUFACTURING ARTICLES FOR FANCY FAIRS, ETC.

BY B. F. GANDEE, Teacher.

EMBELLISHED WITH A BEAUTIFUL FRONTISPIECE AND TITLE-PAGE, PRINTED IN OIL COLOURS BY BAXTER, AND SEVENTEEN OTHER ILLUSTRATIVE ENGRAVINGS.

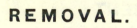

BEDS, FEATHERS, BEDTICKS, AND MATTRESSES.

Seasoned Feather Beds, 18*s.* to 5*l.*; Prime Dressed Feathers, 9*d.* to 2*s.* 6*d.* per lb.; Ticks, 3*s.* to 24*s.*; Field Tent Bedsteads, 20*s.*; Alva Marina Mattresses to fit, 10*s.*; Soft Wool Flocks, 2*d.*, 3*d.*, and 4*d.* per lb. Every description of Bedsteads, Mattresses, Palliasses, and Bedding, full 30 per cent. cheaper. Merchants, Captains, Upholsterers, Brokers, and Proprietors of Schools, supplied at D. TIMOTHY'S old-established Manufactory, No. 31, Barbican, corner of Redcross-street, City.

LABERN'S BOTANIC CREAM.

By appointment, patronised by her Most Gracious Majesty, celebrated for strengthening and promoting the growth of Hair, and completely freeing it from Scurf.—Sold by the Proprietor, H. Labern, Perfumer to her Majesty, 49, Judd Street, Brunswick Square, in pots, 1*s.* 6*d.*, 2*s.* 6*d.*, 3*s.* 6*d.*, and 5*s.*, and in Bottles 3*s.* 6*d.* and 5*s.* each, and by all Perfumers and Medicine Venders. Beware of counterfeits. Ask for "Labern's Botanic Cream."

*** Trade Orders from the Country to come through the London Wholesale Houses.

PIERCE'S ECONOMICAL RADIATING STOVE-GRATE MANUFACTORY, N⁰ 5, JERMYN STREET, REGENT STREET.

The Nobility and Gentry are most respectfully solicited to examine a variety of new and elegant Stove Grates upon his so-much-approved Radiating Principle, from his own Designs, being the real Manufacturer of them. These Grates combine the useful and ornamental, blending Economy with Comfort—display a cheerful Fire and a clean Hearth—lessen materially the consumption of Fuel—diffuse a genial Warmth throughout the Apartment, and are adapted for general use. They retain the Heat many hours after the Fire is out—are executed in every style of Architecture—Grecian, Elizabethan, Louis Quatorze, and Gothic, agreeable to any Design.

W. P. has a grate expressly made for the Cure of Smoky Chimneys, and will guarantee its success. He invites attention to his Improved Method of Heating with Hot Water; also to the Domestic Pure Warm-Air Safety Stove, for Churches, Mansions, Houses, Galleries, Entrance-Halls, &c., with Pure Air, which may be seen in daily use at his Show Rooms and Manufactory; as well as an extensive assortment of Fenders, Fire-Irons, Ranges, Boilers, Patent Smoke-Jacks, Hot Plates, Broiling Plates, and all other articles of Kitchen requisites, with the latest Improvements. Baths of every Description, viz., Hot, Cold, Vapour, Douche, Shower, Leg, and Sponge; also Jekyll's Portable Baths.

MANUFACTURER OF Dᴿ ARNOTT'S STOVE,

(Which may be seen in use in various patterns,) adapted for Churches, Halls, and Offices.

GREAT NOVELTY IN HAIR BRUSHES.
MECHI'S PATENT REGULATING BRUSHES,

By which they may, in one moment, be made excessively hard or soft, as required.

MECHI, NO. 4, LEADENHALL STREET, LONDON,

Has purchased of the Patentee the right of manufacturing this extraordinary invention, which, whilst it affords such great advantages, is not much more costly than the common hair brush.

The same principle is also applied to Cloth Brushes.

MECHI IS SOLE INVENTOR OF
THE CASTELLATED TOOTH-BRUSHES,

Of which spurious imitations are offered all over the country. He will be responsible for those only which bear his name and address.

Mechi has an immense stock of Hair, Cloth, Tooth, Nail, and Shaving Brushes, Flesh Brushes, Table Brushes and Comb Brushes, comprising the most elegant work of that kind ever presented to the Public. Hair Brushes in Ivory and Tortoiseshell, 3*l.* to 5*l.* per pair.

MOSLEY'S METALLIC PENS.

R. MOSLEY & CO. beg to call the attention of Mercantile Men, and the Public in general, to their superior Metallic Pens. They possess the highest degree of elasticity and flexibility, and are found perfectly free from all those inconveniences which have prevented so many persons making use of Metallic Pens.

Every description of writer may be suited, as these pens are manufactured of various qualities, degrees of hardness, &c. They may be had at all respectable Stationers throughout the kingdom.

Observe that every Pen is stamped, R. MOSLEY & CO., LONDON.

PHYSICAL CHANGES IN MAN.

It is an acknowledged fact in medical science, that man undergoes a continuous, though imperceptible corporeal change, and that an entire physical renewal takes place several times in the course of an ordinary life-time; the changes arising from the variable influences of the seasons appear not so generally familiar, but it is no less important to know, that with the periodical decline of the year a slight but gradual relaxation takes place throughout the surface of the skin, and is shown more particularly at the roots of the Hair, which, but for a judicious stimulative treatment, is apt to thin and fall off. For the strengthening and renovating of this important auxiliary to beauty, the most valuable modern discovery has been proved to be OLDRIDGE'S BALM OF COLUMBIA, the effects of which in thickening, preserving, and renovating the Human Hair, are now indisputably established.

OLDRIDGE'S BALM causes whiskers and eyebrows to grow, prevents the Hair from turning grey, and the first application makes it curl beautifully, frees it from scurf, and stops it from falling off. Abundance of certificates from gentlemen of the first respectability are shown by the Proprietors, C. and A. OLDRIDGE, 1, Wellington Street, Strand, where the Balm is sold, price 3*s.* 6*d.*, 6*s.*, and 11*s.* per bottle. No other prices are genuine.

Some complaints have reached the Proprietors of a spurious Balm having been vended; they again caution the Public to be on their guard against the base impostors, by especially asking for OLDRIDGE'S BALM OF COLUMBIA, 1, WELLINGTON STREET, STRAND, LONDON.

APSLEY PELLATT'S
ABRIDGED LIST OF
Net Cash Prices for the best Flint Glass Ware.

DECANTERS.

25 Strong quart Nelson shape decanters,
cut all over, bold flutes and cut
brim & stopper, P.M. each 10s6d. to 12 0
26 Do. three-ringed royal shape, cut on
and between rings, turned out stop,
P.M. each 10 0
  Do. do. not cut on or between rings,
nor turned out stopper, P.M. ea. 8s to 9 0
27 Fancy shapes, cut all over, eight flutes,
spire stopper, &c. each, P.M. 16s. to 18 0
  Do. six flutes only, each, P.M. 24s. to 27 0

DISHES.

31 Dishes, oblong, pillar moulded, scolloped
edges, cut star.

5-in.	7-in.	9-in.	10-in.
3s. 6d.	6s. 6d.	11s.	13s. each.

32 Oval cup sprig, shell pattern,

5-in.	7-in.	9-in.	11-in.
7s. 6d.	9s. 6d.	16s.	19s. each.

33 Square shape pillar, moulded star,

5-in.	7-in	9-in.	10-in.
4s.	8s.	12s. 6d.	15s. each.

FINGER CUPS.

37 Fluted finger-cups, strong, about 14
oz. each 2 6
  Do. plain flint, punted, per doz..... 18 0
  Do. coloured, per doz.......18s. to 21 0
38 Ten-fluted round, very strong, each . 5 0
  Eight-fluted do., each 8 0
39 Medicean shape, moulded pillar, pearl
upper part, cut flat flutes, each .. 5 0

PICKLES

46 Pickles, half fluted for 3 in. holes, RM ea. 4 6
47 Strong, moulded bottom, 3-in. hole,
cut all over, flat flutes, R.M. each . 5 0
  Best cut star do. for 3½-in. hole, PM ea. 7 6
  Very strong and best cut, P.M. each 14 6

WATER JUGS

59 Quarts, neatly fluted and cut rings,
each....................14s. to 18 0
60 Ewer shape, best cut handles, &c... 21 0
61 Silver do. scolloped edges, ex. lar. flutes 25 0

WATER BOTTLES

70 Moulded pillar body, cut neck, each . 3 0
71 Cut neck and star............... 3 0
72 Double fluted cut rings 3 6
73 Very strong pillar, moulded body, cut
neck and rings 5 6
74 Grecian shape, fluted all over 7 0

TUMBLERS

	78	79	80	81	82	83	84	85	86	87	
Tale	5s.										
Flint,	7s.	10s.	12s.	12s.	10s.	12s.	14s.	18s.	18s.		Doz.
	to	to	to	to	to	to	to	to	to		
	8s.	12s	14s.	15s.	12s.		18s.	21s.	21s.	30s	do.

WINES

88	89	90	91	92	93	94	95	96	97	98	99
7s.	7s.	7s.	7s.	8s.	14s.	12s.	13s.	15s.	18s.	21s.	20s.
to	to	to	to								
8s.	9s.	9s.	9s.	10s.							

Glass Blowing, Cutting, and Engraving, may
be inspected by *Purchasers,* at Mr. Pellatt's Ex-
tensive *Flint Glass and Steam Cutting Works, in
Holland Street, near Blackfriars' Bridge, any
Tuesday, Wednesday,* or *Thursday.*
Merchants and the **Trade** supplied on **equitable
Terms.**
No Abatement from the above specified Ready Money Prices.
No Connexion with any other Establishment.

M. & W. Collis, Printers, 104, Bishopsgate Street Within.

HARRISON'S FAMILY MEDICINES.

ANODYNE LINIMENT,

FOR THE CURE OF

RHEUMATISM, GOUT, LUMBAGO, SCIATICA, TIC DOLOREUX, CROUP, QUINSY, SORE THROAT, STIFF NECK, INFLAMMATION OF THE CHEST, &c. &c.

ADDRESS.—Without pretending to more than he is able to perform ; or having the Charlatanism to promulgate a false theory in medicine ; or, *above all,* the desire to impose upon the credulity of the public, the Proprietor of the Anodyne Liniment fearlessly asserts, that this preparation is the most valuable and effective remedy extant, for the relief and cure of the above diseases, and of local pain, in whatever part of the body situate. It is a sedative, and cures by relieving the irritation of the sentient nerves of the diseased part. A single trial will carry conviction of its wonderful remedial virtues to the minds of the most sceptical, and increase the reputation it has already established.

COUGH PILLS,

(WITHOUT OPIUM, OR ANY OTHER INJURIOUS DRUG).

ADDRESS.—At this season of the year, when Cough is the unwelcome intruder at almost every domestic hearth, public attention cannot be too often or too forcibly drawn to those remedies which assist Nature to rid herself of the baneful effects of that most insidious and dangerous of all diseases,—Cough !— The proprietor of these Pills assures the invalid, that they will be found a most efficient remedy for Cough, Asthma, and all Pulmonary Affections, of however long standing,—performing a cure, by increasing expectoration, and insensible perspiration,—and that they do not cause either Headache, or Constipation of Bowels, the usual effects of remedies for this class of diseases.

APERIENT PILLS,

(WITHOUT CALOMEL, OR ANY DRASTIC DRUG).

ADDRESS.—The utility of aperient medicines is too well known and acknowledged, by every person of common sense in the present day, to require comment. It is not the *use,* but the *abuse* of this remedy that is objectionable. There are numberless forms of aperient and antibilious pills, of one kind and another, daily advertised, to all of which *some* objections may, with truth, be made. The proprietor of these Aperient Pills, however, asserts, with the confidence founded on many years' successful experience of the remedy, that they will be found to possess a decided superiority over all preparations of the kind hitherto brought before the public,—performing, *in moderate doses,* all that is required of them, *without griping, or any inconvenience* to the patient, merely unloading the bowels, and keeping up, for a day or two, such gentle action as would be effected by Nature in a healthy state,—differing in this respect from all other Aperient Medicines, which generally leave a state of constipation, requiring a constant repetition of the remedy. They are, indeed, so mild in their operation, that they may be taken by the infant ; and are confidently recommended to pregnant women. The proprietor, conscious that they would be sanctioned, is willing to submit his prescriptions to the ordeal of any medical body, except of those visionaries, the Homœopathists, of whose pretended remedies it may be said,

" The effect was great, because the dose was small ;
'Twould been greater, had there been none at all ! "

NOTE.—Full directions and remarks are enclosed with each packet of these medicines, to which the attention of the invalid is particularly requested.

The above medicines are faithfully prepared by the proprietor from the prescriptions of MR. HARRISON, Surgeon, late of Blandford, Dorset ; and sold wholesale by Barclay and Sons, Farringdon Street ; Edwards, St. Paul's ; Constable and Finden, Borough ; and retail by Sanger, Oxford Street ; Butler, Cheapside ; March, Old Patent Medicine Warehouse, Middle Row, Holborn ; Priest, Parliament Street ; and by all Patent Medicine Venders throughout the kingdom.

BRITANNIA LIFE ASSURANCE COMPANY,

No. 1, PRINCES STREET, BANK, LONDON.

CAPITAL, ONE MILLION.

Directors.

WILLIAM BARDGETT, ESQ.
SAMUEL BEVINGTON, ESQ.
WILLIAM FECHNEY BLACK, ESQ.
JOHN BRIGHTMAN, ESQ.
GEORGE COHEN, ESQ.
MILLIS COVENTRY, ESQ.
JOHN DREWETT, ESQ.

ROBERT EGLINTON, ESQ.
ERASMUS ROBERT FOSTER, ESQ.,
ALEX. ROBERT IRVINE, ESQ.
PETER MORRISON, ESQ.
WILLIAM SHAND, JUN., ESQ.
HENRY LEWIS SMALE, ESQ.
THOMAS TEED, ESQ.

Auditors.

EDWARD BEVAN, ESQ. | ANDREW JOPP, ESQ.

Medical Officers.

WILLIAM STROUD, M.D., Great Coram Street, Russell Square.
EBENEZER SMITH, ESQ., Surgeon, Billiter Square.

Standing Counsel.

The HON. JOHN ASHLEY, New Square, Lincoln's-Inn.

Solicitor.

WILLIAM BEVAN, ESQ., Old Jewry.

Bankers.

MESSRS. DREWETT & FOWLER, Princes Street, Bank.

This Institution is so constituted as to afford the benefits of Life Assurance in their fullest extent to Policy holders, and to present greater facilities and accommodation than can be obtained in any similar establishment. Among others, the following improvements on the system usually adopted, are recommended to the attention of the Public.

A most economical set of Tables—computed expressly for the use of this Institution, from authentic and complete data; *and presenting the lowest rates of Assurance that can be offered, without compromising the safety of the Institution.*

A Table of increasing rates of Premium, on a new and remarkable plan, peculiarly advantageous in cases where Assurances are effected, by way of securing loans or debts, a less immediate payment being required on a policy for the whole term of life, than in any other office; and the holder having the option of paying a periodically-increasing rate; or of having the sum assured diminished, according to an equitable scale of reduction.

A Table of decreasing rates of Premium, also on a novel and remarkable plan: the Policy-holder having the option of discontinuing the payment of all further premiums after *twenty, fifteen, ten,* and even *five* years; and the Policy still remaining in force,—in the first case, for the full amount originally assured; and in either of the three other cases, for a portion of the same, according to a fixed and equitable scale, endorsed upon the Policy.

Policies effected by persons on their own lives, not rendered void in case of death by duelling, or the hands of justice. In the event of suicide, if the Policy be assigned to a *bonâ fide* creditor, the sum assured paid without deduction; if not so assigned, the full amount of premiums returned to the family of the assured.

Policies revived without the exaction of a fine within twelve months, on the production of satisfactory evidence as to health, and payment of interest on the premiums due.

Age of the assured in every case admitted in the Policy.

All claims payable within one month after proof of death.

A liberal commission allowed to solicitors and agents.

Extract from increasing Rates of Premium for an Assurance of £100, for whole Term of Life.

Age.	Annual Premium payable during				
	First Five Years.	Second Five Years.	Third Five Years.	Fourth Five Years.	Remainder of Life.
	£ s. d.	£ s. d.	£ s. d.	£ s. d.	£ s. d.
20	1 1 4	1 5 10	1 10 11	1 16 9	2 3 8
30	1 6 4	1 12 2	1 19 1	2 7 4	2 17 6
40	1 16 1	2 4 4	2 14 6	3 7 3	4 3 4
50	2 16 7	3 9 4	4 5 5	5 6 3	6 13 7

PETER MORRISON, *Resident Director.*

[BRADBURY AND EVANS, PRINTERS, WHITEFRIARS.]

CHAPTER XXVII.

MRS. NICKLEBY BECOMES ACQUAINTED WITH MESSRS. PYKE AND
PLUCK, WHOSE AFFECTION AND INTEREST ARE BEYOND ALL BOUNDS.

MRS. NICKLEBY had not felt so proud and important for many a
day, as when, on reaching home, she gave herself wholly up to the
pleasant visions which had accompanied her on her way thither.
Lady Mulberry Hawk—that was the prevalent idea. Lady Mulberry
Hawk!—On Tuesday last, at St. George's, Hanover Square, by the
Right Reverend the Bishop of Llandaff, Sir Mulberry Hawk, of Mulberry Castle, North Wales, to Catherine, only daughter of the late
Nicholas Nickleby, Esquire, of Devonshire. "Upon my word!" cried
Mrs. Nicholas Nickleby, " it sounds very well."

Having despatched the ceremony, with its attendant festivities, to
the perfect satisfaction of her own mind, the sanguine mother pictured
to her imagination a long train of honours and distinctions which could
not fail to accompany Kate in her new and brilliant sphere. She
would be presented at court, of course. On the anniversary of her
birth-day, which was upon the nineteenth of July ("at ten minutes
past three o'clock in the morning," thought Mrs. Nickleby in a parenthesis, " for I recollect asking what o'clock it was,") Sir Mulberry
would give a great feast to all his tenants, and would return them
three and a half per cent. on the amount of their last half-year's rent,
as would be fully described and recorded in the fashionable intelligence, to the immeasurable delight and admiration of all the readers
thereof. Kate's picture, too, would be in at least half-a-dozen of the
annuals, and on the opposite page would appear, in delicate type,
" Lines on contemplating the Portrait of Lady Mulberry Hawk. By
Sir Dingleby Dabber." Perhaps some one annual, of more comprehensive design than its fellows, might even contain a portrait of the
mother of Lady Mulberry Hawk, with lines by the father of Sir
Dingleby Dabber. More unlikely things had come to pass. Less
interesting portraits had appeared. As this thought occurred to the
good lady, her countenance unconsciously assumed that compound
expression of simpering and sleepiness which, being common to all such
portraits, is perhaps one reason why they are always so charming and
agreeable.

With such triumphs of aërial architecture did Mrs. Nickleby occupy
the whole evening after her accidental introduction to Ralph's titled
friends ; and dreams, no less prophetic and equally promising, haunted
her sleep that night. She was preparing for her frugal dinner next
day, still occupied with the same ideas—a little softened down per·
haps by sleep and daylight—when the girl who attended her, partly
for company, and partly to assist in the household affairs, rushed into
the room in unwonted agitation, and announced that two gentlemen
were waiting in the passage for permission to walk up stairs.

s

" Bless my heart ! " cried Mrs. Nickleby, hastily arranging her cap and front, " if it should be—dear me, standing in the passage all this time—why don't you go and ask them to walk up, you stupid thing ?"

While the girl was gone on this errand, Mrs. Nickleby hastily swept into a cupboard all vestiges of eating and drinking; which she had scarcely done, and seated herself with looks as collected as she could assume, when two gentlemen, both perfect strangers, presented themselves.

" How do you *do ?*" said one gentleman, laying great stress on the last word of the inquiry.

" *How* do you do ?" said the other gentleman, altering the emphasis, as if to give variety to the salutation.

Mrs. Nickleby curtseyed and smiled, and curtseyed again, and remarked, rubbing her hands as she did so, that she hadn't the—really —the honour to—

" To know us," said the first gentleman.   " The loss has been ours, Mrs. Nickleby.   Has the loss been ours, Pyke ?"

" It has, Pluck," answered the other gentleman.

" We have regretted it very often, I believe, Pyke ? " said the first gentleman.

" Very often, Pluck," answered the second.

" But now," said the first gentleman, " now we have the happiness we have pined and languished for.   Have we pined and languished for this happiness, Pyke, or have we not ?"

" You know we have, Pluck," said Pyke, reproachfully.

" You hear him, ma'am ?" said Mr. Pluck, looking round ; " you hear the unimpeachable testimony of my friend Pyke—that reminds me,—formalities, formalities, must not be neglected in civilized society. Pyke—Mrs. Nickleby."

Mr. Pyke laid his hand upon his heart, and bowed low.

" Whether I shall introduce myself with the same formality," said Mr. Pluck—" whether I shall say myself that my name is Pluck, or whether I shall ask my friend Pyke (who being now regularly introduced, is competent to the office) to state for me, Mrs. Nickleby, that my name is Pluck ; whether I shall claim your acquaintance on the plain ground of the strong interest I take in your welfare, or whether I shall make myself known to you as the friend of Sir Mulberry Hawk—these, Mrs. Nickleby, are considerations which I leave to you to determine."

" Any friend of Sir Mulberry Hawk's requires no better introduction to me," observed Mrs. Nickleby, graciously.

" It is delightful to hear you say so," said Mr. Pluck, drawing a chair close to Mrs. Nickleby, and sitting himself down.   " It is refreshing to know that you hold my excellent friend, Sir Mulberry, in such high esteem.   A word in your ear, Mrs. Nickleby.   When Sir Mulberry knows it, he will be a happy man—I say, Mrs. Nickleby, a happy man.   Pyke, be seated."

" *My* good opinion," said Mrs. Nickleby, and the poor lady exulted in the idea that she was marvellously sly,—" my good opinion can be of very little consequence to a gentlemen like Sir Mulberry."

" Of little consequence!" exclaimed Mr. Pluck. " Pyke, of what consequence to our friend, Sir Mulberry, is the good opinion of Mrs. Nickleby ? "

" Of what consequence ?" echoed Pyke.

" Aye," repeated Pluck ; " is it of the greatest consequence ?"

" Of the very greatest consequence," replied Pyke.

" Mrs. Nickleby cannot be ignorant," said Mr. Pluck, " of the immense impression which that sweet girl has— "

" Pluck !" said his friend, " beware !"

" Pyke is right," muttered Mr. Pluck, after a short pause ; " I was not to mention it. Pyke is very right. Thank you, Pyke."

" Well now, really," thought Mrs. Nickleby within herself. " Such delicacy as that, I never saw !"

Mr. Pluck, after feigning to be in a condition of great embarrassment for some minutes, resumed the conversation by entreating Mrs. Nickleby to take no heed of what he had inadvertently said—to consider him imprudent, rash, injudicious. The only stipulation he would make in his own favour was, that she should give him credit for the best intentions.

" But when," said Mr. Pluck, " when I see so much sweetness and beauty on the one hand, and so much ardour and devotion on the other, I—pardon me, Pyke, I didn't intend to resume that theme. Change the subject, Pyke."

" We promised Sir Mulberry and Lord Frederick," said Pyke, " that we'd call this morning and inquire whether you took any cold last night."

" Not the least in the world last night, Sir ;" replied Mrs. Nickleby, " with many thanks to his Lordship and Sir Mulberry for doing me the honour to inquire ; not the least—which is the more singular, as I really am very subject to colds, indeed—very subject. I had a cold once," said Mrs. Nickleby, " I think it was in the year eighteen hundred and seventeen ; let me see, four and five are nine, and—yes, eighteen hundred and seventeen, that I thought I never should get rid of ; actually and seriously, that I thought I never should get rid of. I was only cured at last by a remedy that I don't know whether you ever happened to hear of, Mr. Pluck. You have a gallon of water as hot as you can possibly bear it, with a pound of salt and sixpen'orth of the finest bran, and sit with your head in it for twenty minutes every night just before going to bed ; at least, I don't mean your head —your feet. It's a most extraordinary cure—a most extraordinary cure. I used it for the first time, I recollect, the day after Christmas Day, and by the middle of April following the cold was gone. It seems quite a miracle when you come to think of it, for I had it ever since the beginning of September."

" What an afflicting calamity !" said Mr. Pyke.

" Perfectly horrid !" exclaimed Mr. Pluck.

s 2

"But it's worth the pain of hearing, only to know that Mrs. Nickleby recovered it, isn't it, Pluck?" cried Mr. Pyke.

"That is the circumstance which gives it such a thrilling interest, replied Mr. Pluck.

"But come," said Pyke, as if suddenly recollecting himself; "we must not forget our mission in the pleasure of this interview. We come on a mission, Mrs. Nickleby."

"On a mission," exclaimed that good lady, to whose mind a definitive proposal of marriage for Kate at once presented itself in lively colours.

"From Sir Mulberry," replied Pyke. "You must be very dull here."

"Rather dull, I confess," said Mrs. Nickleby.

"We bring the compliments of Sir Mulberry Hawk, and a thousand entreaties that you'll take a seat in a private box at the play to-night," said Mr. Pluck.

"Oh dear!" said Mrs. Nickleby," "I never go out at all, never."

"And that is the very reason, my dear Mrs. Nickleby, why you should go out to-night," retorted Mr. Pluck. "Pyke, entreat Mrs. Nickleby."

"Oh, pray do," said Pyke.

"You positively must," urged Pluck.

"You are very kind," said Mrs. Nickleby hesitating; "but—"

"There's not a but in the case, my dear Mrs. Nickleby," remonstrated Mr. Pluck; "not such a word in the vocabulary. Your brother-in-law joins us, Lord Frederick joins us, Sir Mulberry joins us, Pyke joins us—a refusal is out of the question. Sir Mulberry sends a carriage for you—twenty minutes before seven to the moment—you'll not be so cruel as to disappoint the whole party, Mrs. Nickleby?"

"You are so very pressing, that I scarcely know what to say," replied the worthy lady.

"Say nothing; not a word, not a word, my dearest madam," urged Mr. Pluck. "Mrs. Nickleby," said that excellent gentleman, lowering his voice, "there is the most trifling, the most excusable breach of confidence in what I am about to say; and yet if my friend Pyke there overheard it—such is that man's delicate sense of honour, Mrs. Nickleby —he'd have me out before dinner-time."

Mrs. Nickleby cast an apprehensive glance at the warlike Pyke, who had walked to the window; and Mr. Pluck, squeezing her hand, went on—

"Your daughter has made a conquest—a conquest on which I may congratulate you. Sir Mulberry, my dear ma'am, Sir Mulberry is her devoted slave. Hem!"

"Hah!" cried Mr. Pyke at this juncture, snatching something from the chimney-piece with a theatrical air. "What is this! what do I behold!"

"What *do* you behold, my dear fellow?" asked Mr. Pluck.

"It is the face, the countenance, the expression," cried Mr. Pyke, falling into his chair with a miniature in his hand; "feebly portrayed, imperfectly caught, but still *the* face, *the* countenance, *the* expression."

Affectionate behaviour of Messrs Pyke & Pluck.

"I recognise it at this distance!" exclaimed Mr. Pluck in a fit of enthusiasm. "Is it not, my dear madam, the faint similitude of—"

"It is my daughter's portrait," said Mrs. Nickleby, with great pride. And so it was. And little Miss La Creevy had brought it home for inspection only two nights before.

Mr. Pyke no sooner ascertained that he was quite right in his conjecture, than he launched into the most extravagant encomiums of the divine original; and in the warmth of his enthusiasm kissed the picture a thousand times, while Mr. Pluck pressed Mrs. Nickleby's hand to his heart, and congratulated her on the possession of such a daughter, with so much earnestness and affection, that the tears stood, or seemed to stand, in his eyes. Poor Mrs. Nickleby, who had listened in a state of enviable complacency at first, became at length quite overpowered by these tokens of regard for, and attachment to, the family; and even the servant girl, who had peeped in at the door, remained rooted to the spot in astonishment at the ecstasies of the two friendly visiters.

By degrees these raptures subsided, and Mrs. Nickleby went on to entertain her guests with a lament over her fallen fortunes, and a picturesque account of her old house in the country: comprising a full description of the different apartments, not forgetting the little store-room, and a lively recollection of how many steps you went down to get into the garden, and which way you turned when you came out at the parlour-door, and what capital fixtures there were in the kitchen. This last reflection naturally conducted her into the wash-house where she stumbled upon the brewing utensils, among which she might have wandered for an hour, if the mere mention of those implements had not, by an association of ideas, instantly reminded Mr. Pyke that he was "amazing thirsty."

"And I'll tell you what," said Mr. Pyke; "if you'll send round to the public-house for a pot of mild half-and-half, positively and actually I'll drink it."

And positively and actually Mr. Pyke did drink it, and Mr. Pluck helped him, while Mrs. Nickleby looked on in divided admiration of the condescension of the two, and the aptitude with which they accommodated themselves to the pewter-pot; in explanation of which seeming marvel it may be here observed, that gentlemen who, like Messrs. Pyke and Pluck, live upon their wits (or not so much, perhaps, upon the presence of their own wits as upon the absence of wits in other people) are occasionally reduced to very narrow shifts and straits, and are at such periods accustomed to regale themselves in a very simple and primitive manner.

"At twenty minutes before seven, then," said Mr. Pyke, rising, "the coach will be here. One more look—one little look—at that sweet face. Ah! here it is. Unmoved, unchanged!" This by the way was a very remarkable circumstance, miniatures being liable to so many changes of expression—"Oh, Pluck! Pluck!"

Mr. Pluck made no other reply than kissing Mrs. Nickleby's hand with a great show of feeling and attachment; Mr. Pyke having done the same, both gentlemen hastily withdrew

Mrs. Nickleby was commonly in the habit of giving herself credit for a pretty tolerable share of penetration and acuteness, but she had never felt so satisfied with her own sharp-sightedness as she did that day. She had found it all out the night before. She had never seen Sir Mulberry and Kate together—never even heard Sir Mulberry's name—and yet hadn't she said to herself from the very first, that she saw how the case stood ? and what a triumph it was, for there was now no doubt about it. If these flattering attentions to herself were not sufficient proof, Sir Mulberry's confidential friend had suffered the secret to escape him in so many words. " I am quite in love with that dear Mr. Pluck, I declare I am," said Mrs. Nickleby.

There was one great source of uneasiness in the midst of this good fortune, and that was the having nobody by, to whom she could confide it. Once or twice she almost resolved to walk straight to Miss La Creevy's and tell it all to her. " But I don't know," thought Mrs. Nickleby ; " she is a very worthy person, but I am afraid too much beneath Sir Mulberry's station for us to make a companion of. Poor thing !" Acting upon this grave consideration she rejected the idea of taking the little portrait-painter into her confidence, and contented herself with holding out sundry vague and mysterious hopes of preferment to the servant girl, who received these obscure hints of dawning greatness with much veneration and respect.

Punctual to its time came the promised vehicle, which was no hackney coach, but a private chariot, having behind it a footman, whose legs, although somewhat large for his body, might, as mere abstract legs, have set themselves up for models at the Royal Academy. It was quite exhilarating to hear the clash and bustle with which he banged the door and jumped up behind after Mrs. Nickleby was in ; and as that good lady was perfectly unconscious that he applied the gold-headed end of his long stick to his nose, and so telegraphed most disrespectfully to the coachman over her very head, she sat in a state of much stiffness and dignity, not a little proud of her position.

At the theatre entrance there was more banging and more bustle, and there were also Messrs. Pyke and Pluck waiting to escort her to her box ; and so polite were they, that Mr. Pyke threatened with many oaths to " smifligate " a very old man with a lantern who accidentally stumbled in her way—to the great terror of Mrs. Nickleby, who, conjecturing more from Mr. Pyke's excitement than any previous acquaintance with the etymology of the word that smifligation and bloodshed must be in the main one and the same thing, was alarmed beyond expression, lest something should occur. Fortunately, however, Mr. Pyke confined himself to mere verbal smifligation, and they reached their box with no more serious interruption by the way, than a desire on the part of the same pugnacious gentleman to " smash " the assistant box-keeper for happening to mistake the number.

Mrs. Nickleby had scarcely been put away behind the curtain of the box in an arm chair, when Sir Mulberry and Lord Verisopht arrived, arrayed from the crowns of their heads to the tips of their gloves, and from the tips of their gloves to the toes of their boots, in the most elegant and costly manner. Sir Mulberry was a little hoarser than on the previous day, and Lord Verisopht looked rather sleepy and queer; from which tokens, as well as from the circumstance of their both being to a trifling extent unsteady upon their legs, Mrs. Nickleby justly concluded that they had taken dinner.

"We have been—we have been—toasting your lovely daughter, Mrs. Nickleby," whispered Sir Mulberry, sitting down behind her.

"Oh, ho!" thought that knowing lady; "wine in; truth out.— You are very kind, Sir Mulberry."

"No, no, upon my soul!" replied Sir Mulberry Hawk. "It's you that's kind, upon my soul it is. It was so kind of you to come to-night."

"So very kind of you to invite me, you mean, Sir Mulberry," replied Mrs. Nickleby, tossing her head, and looking prodigiously sly.

"I am so anxious to know you, so anxious to cultivate your good opinion, so desirous that there should be a delicious kind of harmonious family understanding between us," said Sir Mulberry, "that you mustn't think I'm disinterested in what I do. I'm infernal selfish; I am—upon my soul I am."

"I am sure you can't be selfish, Sir Mulberry!" replied Mrs. Nickleby. "You have much too open and generous a countenance for that."

"What an extraordinary observer you are!" said Sir Mulberry Hawk.

"Oh no, indeed, I don't see very far into things, Sir Mulberry," replied Mrs. Nickleby, in a tone of voice which left the baronet to infer that she saw very far indeed.

"I am quite afraid of you," said the baronet. "Upon my soul," repeated Sir Mulberry, looking round to his companions; "I am afraid of Mrs. Nickleby. She is so immensely sharp."

Messrs. Pyke and Pluck shook their heads mysteriously, and observed together that they had found that out long ago; upon which Mrs. Nickleby tittered, and Sir Mulberry laughed, and Pyke and Pluck roared.

"But where's my brother-in-law, Sir Mulberry?" inquired Mrs. Nickleby. "I shouldn't be here without him. I hope he's coming."

"Pyke," said Sir Mulberry, taking out his tooth-pick and lolling back in his chair, as if he were too lazy to invent a reply to this question. "Where's Ralph Nickleby?"

"Pluck," said Pyke, imitating the baronet's action, and turning the lie over to his friend, "where's Ralph Nickleby?"

Mr. Pluck was about to return some evasive reply, when the bustle caused by a party entering the next box seemed to attract the attention of all four gentlemen, who exchanged glances of much meaning. The new party beginning to converse together, Sir Mulberry suddenly assumed the character of a most attentive listener, and implored his friends not to breathe—not to breathe.

"Why not?" said Mrs. Nickleby. "What is the matter?"

"Hush!" replied Sir Mulberry, laying his hand on her arm. "Lord Frederick, do you recognize the tones of that voice?"

" Deyvle take me if I didn't think it was the voice of Miss Nickleby."

" Lor, my Lord !" cried Miss Nickleby's mamma, thrusting her head round the curtain. " Why, actually—Kate, my dear, Kate."

" *You* here, mamma ! Is it possible !"

" Possible, my dear ? Yes."

" Why who—who on earth is that you have with you, mamma ?" said Kate, shrinking back as she caught sight of a man smiling and kissing his hand.

" Who do you suppose, my dear ?" replied Mrs. Nickleby, bending towards Mrs. Wititterly, and speaking a little louder for that lady's edification. " There's Mr. Pyke, Mr. Pluck, Sir Mulberry Hawk, and Lord Frederick Verisopht."

" Gracious Heaven !" thought Kate hurriedly. " How comes she in such society !"

Now, Kate thought thus *so* hurriedly, and the surprise was so great, and moreover brought back so forcibly the recollection of what had passed at Ralph's delectable dinner, that she turned extremely pale and appeared greatly agitated, which symptoms being observed by Mrs. Nickleby, were at once set down by that acute lady as being caused and occasioned by violent love.   But, although she was in no small degree delighted by this discovery which reflected so much credit on her own quickness of perception, it did not lessen her motherly anxiety in Kate's behalf ; and accordingly, with a vast quantity of trepidation, she quitted her own box to hasten into that of Mrs. Wititterly.   Mrs. Wititterly, keenly alive to the glory of having a lord and a baronet among her visiting acquaintance, lost no time in signing to Mr. Wititterly to open the door, and thus it was that in less than thirty seconds Mrs. Nickleby's party had made an irruption into Mrs. Wititterly's box, which it filled to the very door, there being in fact only room for Messrs. Pyke and Pluck to get in their heads and waistcoats.

" My dear Kate," said Mrs. Nickleby, kissing her daughter affectionately.   " How ill you looked a moment ago ! You quite frightened me, I declare !"

" It was mere fancy, mamma,—the—the—reflection of the lights perhaps," replied Kate, glancing nervously round, and finding it impossible to whisper any caution or explanation.

" Don't you see Sir Mulberry Hawk, my dear ?"

Kate bowed slightly, and biting her lip turned her head towards the stage.

But Sir Mulberry Hawk was not to be so easily repulsed, for he advanced with extended hand ; and Mrs. Nickleby officiously informing Kate of this circumstance, she was obliged to extend her own. Sir Mulberry detained it while he murmured a profusion of compliments, which Kate, remembering what had passed between them, rightly considered as so many aggravations of the insult he had already put upon her.   Then followed the recognition of Lord Verisopht, and then the greeting of Mr. Pyke, and then that of Mr. Pluck, and finally, to complete the young lady's mortification, she was compelled at Mrs. Wititterly request to perform the ceremony of introducing the odious persons, whom she regarded with the utmost indignation and abhorrence.

" Mrs. Wititterly is delighted," said Mr. Wititterly, rubbing his hands ; " delighted, my Lord, I am sure, with this opportunity of contracting an acquaintance which, I trust, my Lord, we shall improve. Julia, my dear, you must not allow yourself to be too much excited, you must not. Indeed you must not. Mrs. Wititterly is of a most excitable nature, Sir Mulberry. The snuff of a candle, the wick of a lamp, the bloom on a peach, the down on a butterfly. You might blow her away, my Lord ; you might blow her away."

Sir Mulberry seemed to think that it would be a great convenience if the lady could be blown away. He said, however, that the delight was mutual, and Lord Verisopht added that it was mutual, whereupon Messrs. Pyke and Pluck were heard to murmur from the distance that it was very mutual indeed.

" I take an interest, my Lord," said Mrs. Wititterly, with a faint smile, " such an interest in the drama."

" Ye—es. It's very interasting," replied Lord Verisopht.

" I'm always ill after Shakspeare," said Mrs. Wititterly. " I scarcely exist the next day ; I find the re-action so very great after a tragedy, my Lord, and Shakspeare is such a delicious creature."

" Ye—es !" replied Lord Verisopht. " He was a clayver man."

" Do you know, my Lord," said Mrs. Wititterly, after a long silence, " I find I take so much more interest in his plays, after having been to that dear little dull house he was born in ! Were you ever there, my Lord ?"

" No, nayver," replied Verisopht.

" Then really you ought to go, my Lord," returned Mrs. Wititterly, in very languid and drawling accents. " I don't know how it is, but after you've seen the place and written your name in the little book, somehow or other you seem to be inspired ; it kindles up quite a fire within one."

" Ye—es !" replied Lord Verisopht. " I shall certainly go there."

" Julia, my life," interposed Mr. Wititterly, " you are deceiving his lordship—unintentionally, my Lord, she is deceiving you. It is your poetical temperament, my dear—your ethereal soul—your fervid imagination, which throws you into a glow of genius and excitement. There is nothing in the place, my dear—nothing, nothing."

" I think there must be something in the place," said Mrs. Nickleby, who had been listening in silence ; " for, soon after I was married, I went to Stratford with poor dear Mr. Nickleby, in a post-chaise from Birmingham—was it a post-chaise though !" said Mrs. Nickleby, considering ; " yes, it must have been a post-chaise, because I recollect remarking at the time that the driver had a green shade over his left eye ;—in a post-chaise from Birmingham, and after we had seen Shakspeare's tomb and birth-place, we went back to the inn there, where we slept that night, and I recollect that all night long I dreamt of nothing but a black gentleman, at full length, in plaster-of-Paris, with a lay down collar tied with two tassels, leaning against a post and thinking; and when I woke in the morning and described him to Mr. Nickleby, he said it was Shakspeare just as he had been when he was alive, which was very curious indeed.   Stratford—Stratford," continued Mrs. Nickleby, considering.   " Yes, I am positive about that, because I recollect I was in the family way with my son Nicholas at the time, and I had been very much frightened by an Italian image boy that very morning. In fact, it was quite a mercy, ma'am," added Mrs. Nickleby, in a whisper to Mrs. Wititterly, " that my son didn't turn out to be a Shakspeare, and what a dreadful thing that would have been !"

When Mrs. Nickleby had brought this interesting anecdote to a close, Pyke and Pluck, ever zealous in their patron's cause, proposed the adjournment of a detachment of the party into the next box ; and with so much skill were the preliminaries adjusted, that Kate, despite all she could say or do to the contrary, had no alternative but to suffer herself to be led away by Sir Mulberry Hawk.   Her mother and Mr. Pluck accompanied them, but the worthy lady, pluming herself upon her discretion, took particular care not so much as to look at her daughter during the whole evening, and to seem wholly absorbed in the jokes and conversation of Mr. Pluck, who, having been appointed sentry over Mrs. Nickleby for that especial purpose, neglected, on his side, no possible opportunity of engrossing her attention.

Lord Frederick Verisopht remained in the next box to be talked to by Mrs. Wititterly, and Mr. Pyke was in attendance to throw in a word or two when necessary.   As to Mr. Wititterly, he was sufficiently busy in the body of the house, informing such of his friends and acquaintance as happened to be there, that those two gentlemen up stairs, whom they had seen in conversation with Mrs. W., were the distinguished Lord Frederick Verisopht and his most intimate friend, the gay Sir Mulberry Hawk—a communication which inflamed several respectable housekeepers with the utmost jealousy and rage, and reduced sixteen unmarried daughters to the very brink of despair.

The evening came to an end at last, but Kate had yet to be handed down stairs by the detested Sir Mulberry ; and so skilfully were the manœuvres of Messrs. Pyke and Pluck conducted, that she and the baronet were the last of the party, and were even—without an appearance of effort or design—left at some little distance behind.

" Don't hurry, don't hurry," said Sir Mulberry, as Kate hastened on, and attempted to release her arm.

She made no reply, but still pressed forward.

" Nay, then—" coolly observed Sir Mulberry, stopping her outright.

" You had best not seek to detain me, sir !" said Kate, angrily.

" And why not ?" retorted Sir Mulberry.   " My dear creature, now why do you keep up this show of displeasure ?"

" Show !" repeated Kate, indignantly.   " How dare you presume to speak to me, Sir—to address me—to come into my presence ?"

" You look prettier in a passion, Miss Nickleby," said Sir Mulberry Hawk, stooping down, the better to see her face.

" I hold you in the bitterest detestation and contempt, sir," said Kate. " If you find any attraction in looks of disgust and aversion, you—let me rejoin my friends, sir, instantly. Whatever considerations may have withheld me thus far, I will disregard them all, and take a course that even *you* might feel, if you do not immediately suffer me to proceed."

Sir Mulberry smiled, and still looking in her face and retaining her arm, walked towards the door.

" If no regard for my sex or helpless situation will induce you to desist from this coarse and unmanly persecution," said Kate, scarcely knowing, in the tumult of her passions, what she said,—" I have a brother who will resent it dearly, one day."

" Upon my soul ! " exclaimed Sir Mulberry, as though quietly communing with himself; passing his arm round her waist as he spoke, " she looks more beautiful, and I like her better in this mood, than when her eyes are cast down, and she is in perfect repose ! "

How Kate reached the lobby where her friends were waiting she never knew, but she hurried across it without at all regarding them, and disengaged herself suddenly from her companion, sprang into the coach, and throwing herself into its darkest corner burst into tears.

Messrs. Pyke and Pluck, knowing their cue, at once threw the party into great commotion by shouting for the carriages, and getting up a violent quarrel with sundry inoffensive bystanders ; in the midst of which tumult they put the affrighted Mrs. Nickleby in her chariot, and having got her safely off, turned their thoughts to Mrs. Wititterly, whose attention also they had now effectually distracted from the young lady, by throwing her into a state of the utmost bewilderment and consternation. At length, the conveyance in which she had come rolled off too with its load, and the four worthies, being left alone under the portico, enjoyed a hearty laugh together.

" There," said Sir Mulberry, turning to his noble friend. " Didn't I tell you last night that if we could find where they were going by bribing a servant through my fellow, and then established ourselves close by with the mother, these people's honour would be our own ? Why here it is, done in four-and-twenty hours."

" Ye-es," replied the dupe. " But I have been tied to the old woman all ni-ight."

" Hear him," said Sir Mulberry, turning to his two friends. " Hear this discontented grumbler. Isn't it enough to make a man swear never to help him in his plots and schemes again ? Isn't it an infernal shame ? "

Pyke asked Pluck whether it was not an infernal shame, and Pluck asked Pyke ; but neither answered.

" Isn't it the truth ? " demanded Verisopht. " Wasn't it so ? "

" Wasn't it so ! " repeated Sir Mulberry. " How would you have had it ? How could we have got a general invitation at first sight— come when you like, go when you like, stop as long as you like, do what you like—if you, the lord, had not made yourself agreeable to the foolish mistress of the house? Do *I* care for this girl, except as your friend? Haven't I been sounding your praises in her ears, and bearing her pretty sulks and peevishness all night for you? What sort of stuff do you think I'm made of? Would I do this for every man— Don't I deserve even gratitude in return?"

" You're a deyvlish good fellow," said the poor young lord, taking his friend's arm. " Upon my life, you're a deyvlish good fellow, Hawk."

" And I have done right, have I?" demanded Sir Mulberry.

" Quite ri-ght."

" And like a poor, silly, good-natured, friendly dog as I am, eh?"

" Ye-es, ye-es—like a friend," replied the other.

" Well then," replied Sir Mulberry, " I'm satisfied. And now let's go and have our revenge on the German baron and the Frenchman, who cleaned you out so handsomely last night."

With these words the friendly creature took his companion's arm and led him away, turning half round as he did so, and bestowing a wink and a contemptuous smile on Messrs. Pyke and Pluck, who, cramming their handkerchiefs into their mouths to denote their silent enjoyment of the whole proceedings, followed their patron and his victim at a little distance.

CHAPTER XXVIII.

MISS NICKLEBY, RENDERED DESPERATE BY THE PERSECUTION OF SIR MULBERRY HAWK, AND THE COMPLICATED DIFFICULTIES AND DISTRESSES WHICH SURROUND HER, APPEALS, AS A LAST RESOURCE, TO HER UNCLE FOR PROTECTION.

THE ensuing morning brought reflection with it, as morning usually does; but widely different was the train of thought it awakened in the different persons who had been so unexpectedly brought together on the preceding evening, by the active agency of Messrs. Pyke and Pluck.

The reflections of Sir Mulberry Hawk—if such a term can be applied to the thoughts of the systematic and calculating man of dissipation, whose joys, regrets, pains, and pleasures, are all of self, and who would seem to retain nothing of the intellectual faculty but the power to debase himself, and to degrade the very nature whose outward semblance he wears—the reflections of Sir Mulberry Hawk turned upon Kate Nickleby, and were, in brief, that she was undoubtedly handsome; that her coyness *must* be easily conquerable by a man of his address and experience, and that the pursuit was one which could not fail to redound to his credit, and greatly to enhance his reputation with the world. And lest this last consideration—no mean or secondary one with Sir Mulberry—should sound strangely in the ears of some, let it be remembered that most men live in a world of their own, and that in that limited circle alone are they ambitious for distinction and applause. Sir Mulberry's world was peopled with profligates, and he acted accordingly.

Thus, cases of injustice, and oppression, and tyranny, and the most extravagant bigotry, are in constant occurrence among us every day. It is the custom to trumpet forth much wonder and astonishment at the chief actors therein setting at defiance so completely the opinion of the world; but there is no greater fallacy; it is precisely because they do consult the opinion of their own little world that such things take place at all, and strike the great world dumb with amazement.

The reflections of Mrs. Nickleby were of the proudest and most complacent kind; and under the influence of her very agreeable delusion she straightway sat down and indited a long letter to Kate, in which she expressed her entire approval of the admirable choice she had made, and extolled Sir Mulberry to the skies; asserting, for the more complete satisfaction of her daughter's feelings, that he was precisely the individual whom she (Mrs. Nickleby) would have chosen for her son-in-law, if she had had the picking and choosing from all mankind. The good lady then, with the preliminary observation that she might be fairly supposed not to have lived in the world so long without knowing its ways, communicated a great many subtle precepts applicable to the state of courtship, and confirmed in their wisdom by her own personal experience. Above all things she commended a strict maidenly reserve, as being not only a very laudable thing in itself, but as tending materially to strengthen and increase a lover's ardour. " And I never," added Mrs. Nickleby, " was more delighted in my life than to observe last night, my dear, that your good sense had already told you this." With which sentiment, and various hints of the pleasure she derived from the knowledge that her daughter inherited so large an instalment of her own excellent sense and discretion (to nearly the full measure of which she might hope, with care, to succeed in time), Mrs. Nickleby concluded a very long and rather illegible letter.

Poor Kate was well nigh distracted on the receipt of four closely-written and closely-crossed sides of congratulation on the very subject which had prevented her closing her eyes all night, and kept her weeping and watching in her chamber; still worse and more trying was the necessity of rendering herself agreeable to Mrs. Wititterly, who, being in low spirits after the fatigue of the preceding night, of course expected her companion (else wherefore had she board and salary ?) to be in the best spirits possible. As to Mr. Wititterly, he went about all day in a tremor of delight at having shaken hands with a lord, and having actually asked him to come and see him in his own house. The lord himself, not being troubled to any inconvenient extent with the power of thinking, regaled himself with the conversation of Messrs. Pyke and Pluck, who sharpened their wit by a plentiful indulgence in various costly stimulants at his expense.

It was four in the afternoon—that is, the vulgar afternoon of the sun and the clock—and Mrs. Wititterly reclined, according to custom, on the drawing-room sofa, while Kate read aloud a new novel in three volumes, entitled " The Lady Flabella," which Alphonse the doubtful had procured from the library that very morning. And it was a production admirably suited to a lady labouring under Mrs. Wititterly's complaint, seeing that there was not a line in it, from beginning to end, which could, by the most remote contingency, awaken the smallest excitement in any person breathing.

Kate read on.

" ' Cherizette,' said the lady Flabella, inserting her mouse-like feet in the blue satin slippers, which had unwittingly occasioned the half-playful half-angry altercation between herself and the youthful Colonel Befillaire, in the Duke of Mincefenille's *salon de danse* on the previous night. ' *Chérizette, ma chère, donnez-moi de l'eau-de-Cologne, s'il vous plaît, mon enfant.*

" ' *Mercie*—thank you,' said the Lady Flabella, as the lively but devoted Cherizette plentifully besprinkled with the fragrant compound the Lady Flabella's *mouchoir* of finest cambric, edged with richest lace, and emblazoned at the four corners with the Flabella crest, and gorgeous heraldic bearings of that noble family ; ' *Mercie*—that will do.'

" ' At this instant, while the Lady Flabella yet inhaled that delicious fragrance by holding the *mouchoir* to her exquisite, but thoughtfully-chiselled nose, the door of the *boudoir* (artfully concealed by rich hangings of silken damask, the hue of Italy's firmament) was thrown open, and with noiseless tread two valets-de-chambre, clad in sumptuous liveries of peach-blossom and gold, advanced into the room followed by a page in *bas de soie*—silk stockings—who, while they remained at some distance making the most graceful obeisances, advanced to the feet of his lovely mistress, and dropping on one knee presented, on a golden salver gorgeously chased, a scented *billet*.

" ' The Lady Flabella, with an agitation she could not repress, hastily tore off the *envelope* and broke the scented seal. It *was* from Befillaire—the young, the slim, the low-voiced—*her own* Befillaire.' "

" Oh, charming ! " interrupted Kate's patroness, who was sometimes taken literary ; " Poetic, really. Read that description again, Miss Nickleby."

Kate complied.

" Sweet, indeed ! " said Mrs. Wititterly, with a sigh. " So voluptuous, is it not—so soft ? "

" Yes, I think it is," replied Kate, gently ; " very soft."

" Close the book, Miss Nickleby," said Mrs. Wititterly. " I can hear nothing more to-day ; I should be sorry to disturb the impression of that sweet description. Close the book."

Kate complied, not unwillingly ; and, as she did so, Mrs. Wititterly raising her glass with a languid hand, remarked, that she looked pale.

" It was the fright of that—that noise and confusion last night," said Kate.

" How very odd ! " exclaimed Mrs. Wititterly, with a look of surprise. And certainly, when one comes to think of it, it *was* very odd that anything should have disturbed a companion. A steam-engine, or other ingenious piece of mechanism out of order, would have been nothing to it.

" How did you come to know Lord Frederick, and those other delightful creatures, child ? " asked Mrs. Wititterly, still eyeing Kate through her glass.

" I met them at my uncle's," said Kate, vexed to feel that she was colouring deeply, but unable to keep down the blood which rushed to her face whenever she thought of that man.

" Have you known them long ? "

" No," rejoined Kate.   " Not long."

" I was very glad of the opportunity which that respectable person, your mother, gave us of being known to them," said Mrs. Wititterly, in a lofty manner.   " Some friends of ours were on the very point of introducing us, which makes it quite remarkable."

This was said lest Miss Nickleby should grow conceited on the honour and dignity of having known four great people (for Pyke and Pluck were included among the delightful creatures), whom Mrs. Wititterly did not know.   But as the circumstance had made no impression one way or other upon Kate's mind, the force of the observation was quite lost upon her.

" They asked permission to call," said Mrs. Wititterly.   " I gave it them of course."

" Do you expect them to-day ?" Kate ventured to inquire.

Mrs. Wititterly's answer was lost in the noise of a tremendous rapping at the street-door, and, before it had ceased to vibrate, there drove up a handsome cabriolet, out of which leaped Sir Mulberry Hawk and his friend Lord Verisopht.

" They are here now," said Kate, rising and hurrying away.

" Miss Nickleby !" cried Mrs. Wititterly, perfectly aghast at a companion's attempting to quit the room, without her permission first had and obtained.   " Pray don't think of going."

" You are very good !" replied Kate.   " But—"

" For goodness' sake, don't agitate me by making me speak so much," said Mrs. Wititterly, with great sharpness.   " Dear me, Miss Nickleby, I beg—"

It was in vain for Kate to protest that she was unwell, for the footsteps of the knockers, whoever they were, were already on the stairs.   She resumed her seat, and had scarcely done so, when the doubtful page darted into the room and announced, Mr. Pyke, and Mr. Pluck, and Lord Verisopht, and Sir Mulberry Hawk, all at one burst.

" The most extraordinary thing in the world," said Mr. Pluck saluting both ladies with the utmost cordiality ; " the most extraordinary thing.   As Lord Frederick and Sir Mulberry drove up to the door, Pyke and I had that instant knocked."

" That instant knocked," said Pyke.

" No matter how you came, so that you are here," said Mrs. Wititterly, who, by dint of lying on the same sofa for three years and a half, had got up quite a little pantomime of graceful attitudes, and now threw herself into the most striking of the whole series, to astonish the visiters. "I am delighted, I am sure."

"And how is Miss Nickleby?" said Sir Mulberry Hawk, accosting Kate, in a low voice—not so low, however, but that it reached the ears of Mrs. Wititterly.

"Why, she complains of suffering from the fright of last night," said the lady. "I am sure I don't wonder at it, for my nerves are quite torn to pieces."

"And yet you look," observed Sir Mulberry, turning round; "and yet you look—"

"Beyond everything," said Mr. Pyke, coming to his patron's assist-ance. Of course Mr. Pluck said the same.

"I am afraid Sir Mulberry is a flatterer, my Lord," said Mrs. Wititterly, turning to that young gentleman, who had been sucking the head of his cane in silence, and staring at Kate.

"Oh, deyvlish!" replied Verisopht. Having given utterance to which remarkable sentiment, he occupied himself as before.

"Neither does Miss Nickleby look the worse," said Sir Mulberry, bending his bold gaze upon her. "She was always handsome, but, upon my soul, ma'am, you seem to have imparted some of your own good looks to her besides."

To judge from the glow which suffused the poor girl's countenance after this speech, Mrs. Wititterly might, with some show of reason, have been supposed to have imparted to it some of that artificial bloom which decorated her own. Mrs. Wititterly admitted, though not with the best grace in the world, that Kate *did* look pretty. She began to think too, that Sir Mulberry was not quite so agreeable a creature as she had at first supposed him; for, although a skilful flatterer is a most delightful companion if you can keep him all to yourself, his taste becomes very doubtful when he takes to complimenting other people.

"Pyke," said the watchful Mr. Pluck, observing the effect which the praise of Miss Nickleby had produced.

"Well, Pluck," said Pyke.

"Is there anybody," demanded Mr. Pluck, mysteriously, "anybody you know, that Mrs. Wititterly's profile reminds you of?"

"Reminds me of!" answered Pyke. "Of course there is."

"Who do you mean?" said Pluck, in the same mysterious manner. "The D. of B.?"

"The C. of B.," replied Pyke, with the faintest trace of a grin lingering in his countenance. "The beautiful sister is the countess; not the duchess."

"True," said Pluck, "the C. of B. The resemblance is won-derful?"

"Perfectly startling," said Mr. Pyke.

Here was a state of things! Mrs. Wititterly was declared, upon the testimony of two veracious and competent witnesses, to be the very picture of a countess! This was one of the consequences of getting into good society. Why, she might have moved among grovelling people for twenty-years, and never heard of it. How could she, indeed? what did *they* know about countesses!

The two gentlemen having by the greediness with which this little bait was swallowed, tested the extent of Mrs. Wititterly's appetite for adulation, proceeded to administer that commodity in very large doses, thus affording to Sir Mulberry Hawk an opportunity of pestering Miss Nickleby with questions and remarks to which she was absolutely obliged to make some reply. Meanwhile, Lord Verisopht enjoyed unmolested the full flavour of the gold knob at the top of his cane, as he would have done to the end of the interview if Mr. Wititterly had not come home, and caused the conversation to turn to his favorite topic.

" My Lord," said Mr. Wititterly, " I am delighted—honoured— proud. Be seated again, my Lord, pray. I am proud, indeed—most proud."

It was to the secret annoyance of his wife that Mr. Wititterly said all this, for, although she was bursting with pride and arrogance, she would have had the illustrious guests believe that their visit was quite a common occurrence, and that they had lords and baronets to see them every day in the week. But Mr. Wititterly's feelings were beyond the power of suppression.

" It is an honour, indeed!" said Mr. Wititterly. " Julia, my soul, you will suffer for this to-morrow."

" Suffer!" cried Lord Verisopht.

" The reaction, my Lord, the reaction," said Mr. Wititterly. " This violent strain upon the nervous system over, my Lord, what ensues? A sinking, a depression, a lowness, a lassitude, a debility. My Lord, if Sir Tumley Snuffim was to see that delicate creature at this moment, he would not give a—a—*this* for her life." In illustration of which remark, Mr. Wititterly took a pinch of snuff from his box and jerked it lightly into the air as an emblem of instability.

" Not *that*," said Mr. Wititterly, looking about him with a serious countenance. " Sir Tumley Snuffim would not give that for Mrs. Wititterly's existence."

Mr. Wititterly told this with a kind of sober exultation, as if it were no trifling distinction for a man to have a wife in such a desperate state, and Mrs. Wititterly sighed and looked on, as if she felt the honour, but had determined to bear it as meekly as might be.

" Mrs. Wititterly," said her husband, " is Sir Tumley Snuffim's favourite patient. I believe I may venture to say, that Mrs. Wititterly is the first person who took the new medicine which is supposed to have destroyed a family at Kensington Gravel Pits. I believe she was. If I am wrong, Julia, my dear, you will correct me."

" I believe I was," said Mrs. Wititterly, in a faint voice.

As there appeared to be some doubt in the mind of his patron how he could best join in this conversation, the indefatigable Mr. Pyke threw himself into the breach, and, by way of saying something to the point, inquired—with reference to the aforesaid medicine—whether it was nice.

T

" No, Sir, it was not.   It had not even that recommendation,"
said Mr. W.

" Mrs. Wititterly is quite a martyr," observed Pyke, with a complimentary bow.

" I *think* I am," said Mrs. Wititterly, smiling.

" I think you are, my dear Julia," replied her husband, in a tone
which seemed to say that he was not vain, but still must insist upon
their privileges.   " If anybody, my Lord," added Mr. Wititterly,
wheeling round to the nobleman, " will produce to me a greater martyr
than Mrs. Wititterly, all I can say is, that I shall be glad to see that
martyr, whether male or female—that's all, my Lord."

Pyke and Pluck promptly remarked that certainly nothing could be
fairer than that ; and the call having been by this time protracted to a
very great length, they obeyed Sir Mulberry's look, and rose to go.   This
brought Sir Mulberry himself and Lord Verisopht on their legs also.
Many protestations of friendship, and expressions anticipative of the
pleasure which must inevitably flow from so happy an acquaintance,
were exchanged, and the visiters departed, with renewed assurances
that at all times and seasons the mansion of the Wititterlys would be
honoured by receiving them beneath its roof.

That they came at all times and seasons—that they dined there one
day, supped the next, dined again on the next, and were constantly to
and fro on all—that they made parties to visit public places, and met
by accident at lounges—that upon all these occasions Miss Nickleby
was exposed to the constant and unremitting persecution of Sir Mulberry Hawk, who now began to feel his character, even in the estimation of his two dependants, involved in the successful reduction of her
pride—that she had no intervals of peace or rest, except at those hours
when she could sit in her solitary room and weep over the trials of
the day—all these were consequences naturally flowing from the well-
laid plans of Sir Mulberry, and their able execution by the auxiliaries,
Pyke and Pluck.

And thus for a fortnight matters went on.   That any but the
weakest and silliest of people could have seen in one interview that
Lord Verisopht, though he was a lord, and Sir Mulberry Hawk,
though he was a baronet, were not persons accustomed to be the best
possible companions, and were certainly not calculated by habits, manners, tastes, or conversation, to shine with any very great lustre in the
society of ladies, need scarcely be remarked.   But with Mrs. Wititterly
the two titles were all-sufficient ; coarseness became humour, vulgarity
softened itself down into the most charming eccentricity ; insolence
took the guise of an easy absence of reserve, attainable only by those
who had had the good fortune to mix with high folks.

If the mistress put such a construction upon the behaviour of her
new friends, what could the companion urge against them ?   If they
accustomed themselves to very little restraint before the lady of the
house, with how much more freedom could they address her paid
dependent !   Nor was even this the worst.   As the odious Sir Mulberry
Hawk attached himself to Kate with less and less of disguise, Mrs.

Wititterly began to grow jealous of the superior attractions of Miss Nickleby. If this feeling had led to her banishment from the drawing-room when such company was there, Kate would have been only too happy and willing that it should have existed, but unfortunately for her she possessed that native grace and true gentility of manner, and those thousand nameless accomplishments which give to female society its greatest charm; if these be valuable anywhere, they were especially so where the lady of the house was a mere animated doll. The consequence was, that Kate had the double mortification of being an indispensable part of the circle when Sir Mulberry and his friends were there, and of being exposed, on that very account, to all Mrs. Wititterly's ill-humours and caprices when they were gone. She became utterly and completely miserable.

Mrs. Wititterly had never thrown off the mask with regard to Sir Mulberry, but when she was more than usually out of temper, attributed the circumstance, as ladies sometimes do, to nervous indisposition. However, as the dreadful idea that Lord Verisopht also was somewhat taken with Kate, and that she, Mrs. Wititterly, was quite a secondary person, dawned upon that lady's mind and gradually developed itself, she became possessed with a large quantity of highly proper and most virtuous indignation, and felt it her duty, as a married lady and a moral member of society, to mention the circumstance to "the young person" without delay.

Accordingly, Mrs. Wititterly broke ground next morning, during a pause in the novel-reading.

"Miss Nickleby," said Mrs. Wititterly, "I wish to speak to you very gravely. I am sorry to have to do it, upon my word I am very sorry, but you leave me no alternative, Miss Nickleby." Here Mrs. Wititterly tossed her head—not passionately, only virtuously—and remarked, with some appearance of excitement, that she feared that palpitation of the heart was coming on again.

"Your behaviour, Miss Nickleby," resumed the lady, "is very far from pleasing me—very far. I am very anxious indeed that you should do well, but you may depend upon it, Miss Nickleby, you will not, if you go on as you do."

"Ma'am!" exclaimed Kate, proudly.

"Don't agitate me by speaking in that way, Miss Nickleby, don't," said Mrs. Wititterly, with some violence, "or you'll compel me to ring the bell."

Kate looked at her, but said nothing.

"You needn't suppose," resumed Mrs. Wititterly, "that your looking at me in that way, Miss Nickleby, will prevent my saying what I am going to say, which I feel to be a religious duty. You needn't direct your glances towards me," said Mrs. Wititterly, with a sudden burst of spite; "I am not Sir Mulberry, no nor Lord Frederick Verisopht, Miss Nickleby; nor am I Mr. Pyke, nor Mr. Pluck either."

Kate looked at her again, but less steadily than before; and resting her elbow on the table, covered her eyes with her hand.

"If such things had been done when I was a young girl," said Mrs.

Wititterly (this, by the way, must have been some little time before),
" I don't suppose anybody would have believed it."

" I don't think they would," murmured Kate. " I do not think
anybody would believe, without actually knowing it, what I seem
doomed to undergo!"

" Don't talk to me of being doomed to undergo, Miss Nickleby, if
you please," said Mrs. Wititterly, with a shrillness of tone quite
surprising in so great an invalid. " I will not be answered, Miss
Nickleby. I am not accustomed to be answered, nor will I permit it
for an instant. Do you hear?" she added, waiting with some apparent inconsistency *for* an answer.

" I do hear you, Ma'am," replied Kate, " with surprise—with
greater surprise than I can express."

" I have always considered you a particularly well-behaved young
person for your station in life," said Mrs. Wititterly; " and as you are
a person of healthy appearance, and neat in your dress and so forth, I
have taken an interest in you, as I do still, considering that I owe a
sort of duty to that respectable old female, your mother. For these
reasons, Miss Nickleby, I must tell you once for all, and begging you
to mind what I say, that I must insist upon your immediately altering
your very forward behaviour to the gentlemen who visit at this house.
It really is not becoming," said Mrs. Wititterly, closing her chaste
eyes as she spoke; " it is improper—quite improper."

" Oh!" cried Kate, looking upwards and clasping her hands, " is
not this, is not this, too cruel, too hard to bear! Is it not enough that
I should have suffered as I have, night and day; that I should almost
have sunk in my own estimation from very shame of having been
brought into contact with such people; but must I also be exposed to
this unjust and most unfounded charge!"

" You will have the goodness to recollect, Miss Nickleby," said
Mrs. Wititterly, " that when you use such terms as ' unjust,' and
' unfounded,' you charge me, in effect, with stating that which is
untrue."

" I do," said Kate, with honest indignation. " Whether you make
this accusation of yourself, or at the prompting of others, is alike to
me. I say it *is* vilely, grossly, wilfully untrue. Is it possible!" cried
Kate, " that any one of my own sex can have sat by, and not have
seen the misery these men have caused me! Is it possible that you,
ma'am, can have been present, and failed to mark the insulting freedom that their every look bespoke? Is it possible that you can have
avoided seeing, that these libertines, in their utter disrespect for you,
and utter disregard of all gentlemanly behaviour and almost of decency,
have had but one object in introducing themselves here, and that the
furtherance of their designs upon a friendless, helpless girl, who, without this humiliating confession, might have hoped to receive from one
so much her senior something like womanly aid and sympathy? I do
not—I cannot believe it!"

If poor Kate had possessed the slightest knowledge of the world,
she certainly would not have ventured, even in the excitement into

which she had been lashed, upon such an injudicious speech as this. Its effect was precisely what a more experienced observer would have foreseen. Mrs. Wititterly received the attack upon her veracity with exemplary calmness, and listened with the most heroic fortitude to Kate's account of her own sufferings. But allusion being made to her being held in disregard by the gentlemen, she evinced violent emotion, and this blow was no sooner followed up by the remark concerning her seniority, than she fell back upon the sofa, uttering dismal screams.

"What is the matter!" cried Mr. Wititterly, bouncing into the room. "Heavens, what do I see! Julia! Julia! look up, my life, look up!"

But Julia looked down most perseveringly, and screamed still louder! so Mr. Wititterly rang the bell, and danced in a frenzied manner round the sofa on which Mrs. Wittitterly lay; uttering perpetual cries for Sir Tumley Snuffim, and never once leaving off to ask for any explanation of the scene before him.

"Run for Sir Tumley," cried Mr. Wititterly, menacing the page with both fists. "I knew it, Miss Nickleby," he said, looking round with an air of melancholy triumph, "that society has been too much for her. This is all soul, you know, every bit of it." With this assur-ance Mr. Wititterly took up the prostrate form of Mrs. Wititterly, and carried her bodily off to bed.

Kate waited until Sir Tumley Snuffim had paid his visit and looked in with a report, that, through the special interposition of a merciful Providence (thus spake Sir Tumley), Mrs. Wititterly had gone to sleep. She then hastily attired herself for walking, and leaving word that she should return within a couple of hours, hurried away towards her uncle's house.

It had been a good day with Ralph Nickleby,—quite a lucky day; and as he walked to and fro in his little back room with his hands clasped behind him, adding up in his own mind all the sums that had been, or would be, netted from the business done since morning, his mouth was drawn into a hard, stern smile; while the firmness of the lines and curves that made it up, as well as the cunning glance of his cold, bright eye, seemed to tell, that if any resolution or cunning would increase the profits, they would not fail to be excited for the purpose.

"Very good!" said Ralph, in allusion, no doubt, to some proceeding of the day. "He defies the usurer, does he? Well, we shall see. 'Honesty is the best policy,' is it? We'll try that, too.'

He stopped, and then walked on again.

"He is content," said Ralph, relaxing into a smile, "to set his known character and conduct against the power of money—dross, as he calls it. Why, what a dull blockhead this fellow must be! Dross too—dross!—Who's that?"

"Me," said Newman Noggs, looking in. "Your niece."

"What of her?" asked Ralph sharply.

"She's here."

"Here!"

Newman jerked his head towards his little room, to signify that she was waiting there.

"What does she want?" asked Ralph.

"I don't know," rejoined Newman. "Shall I ask?" he added quickly.

"No," replied Ralph. "Show her in—stay." He hastily put away a padlocked cash-box that was on the table, and substituted in its stead an empty purse. "There," said Ralph. "*Now* she may come in."

Newman, with a grim smile at this manœuvre, beckoned the young lady to advance, and having placed a chair for her retired; looking stealthily over his shoulder at Ralph as he limped slowly out.

"Well," said Ralph, roughly enough; but still with something more of kindness in his manner than he would have exhibited towards anybody else. "Well, my—dear. What now?"

Kate raised her eyes, which were filled with tears; and with an effort to master her emotion strove to speak, but in vain. So drooping her head again, she remained silent. Her face was hidden from his view, but Ralph could see that she was weeping.

"I can guess the cause of this!" thought Ralph, after looking at her for some time in silence. "I can—I can guess the cause. Well! Well!"—thought Ralph—for the moment quite disconcerted, as he watched the anguish of his beautiful niece. "Where is the harm? only a few tears; and it's an excellent lesson for her—an excellent lesson."

"What is the matter?" asked Ralph, drawing a chair opposite, and sitting down.

He was rather taken aback by the sudden firmness with which Kate looked up and answered him.

"The matter which brings me to you, sir," she said, "is one which should call the blood up into your cheeks, and make you burn to hear, as it does me to tell. I have been wronged; my feelings have been outraged, insulted, wounded past all healing, and by your friends."

"Friends!" cried Ralph, sternly. "*I* have no friends, girl."

"By the men I saw here, then," returned Kate, quickly. "If they were no friends of yours, and you knew what they were,—oh, the more shame on you, uncle, for bringing me among them. To have subjected me to what I was exposed to here, through any misplaced confidence or imperfect knowledge of your guests, would have required some strong excuse; but if you did it—as I now believe you did—knowing them well, it was most dastardly and cruel."

Ralph drew back in utter amazement at this plain speaking, and regarded Kate with his sternest look. But she met his gaze proudly and firmly, and although her face was very pale, it looked more noble and handsome, lighted up as it was, than it had ever appeared before.

"There is some of that boy's blood in you, I see," said Ralph, speaking in his harshest tones, as something in the flashing eye reminded him of Nicholas at their last meeting.

"I hope there is!" replied Kate. "I should be proud to know it. I am young, uncle, and all the difficulties and miseries of my situation have kept it down, but I have been roused to-day beyond all endurance, and, come what may, *I will not*, as I am your brother's child, bear these insults longer."

"What insults, girl?" demanded Ralph, sharply.

"Remember what took place here, and ask yourself," replied Kate, colouring deeply. "Uncle, you must—I am sure you will—release me from such vile and degrading companionship as I am exposed to now. I do not mean," said Kate, hurrying to the old man, and laying her arm upon his shoulder; "I do not mean to be angry and violent— I beg your pardon if I have seemed so, dear uncle,—but you do not know what I have suffered, you do not indeed. You cannot tell what the heart of a young girl is—I have no right to expect you should; but when I tell you that I am wretched, and that my heart is breaking, I am sure you will help me. I am sure, I am sure you will!"

Ralph looked at her for an instant; then turned away his head, and beat his foot nervously upon the ground.

"I have gone on day after day," said Kate, bending over him, and timidly placing her little hand in his, "in the hope that this persecution would cease; I have gone on day after day, compelled to assume the appearance of cheerfulness, when I was most unhappy. I have had no counsellor, no adviser, no one to protect me. Mamma supposes that these are honourable men, rich and distinguished, and how *can* I— how can I undeceive her—when she is so happy in these little delu·· sions, which are the only happiness she has? The lady with whom you placed me, is not the person to whom I could confide matters of so much delicacy, and I have come at last to you, the only friend I have at hand—almost the only friend I have at all—to entreat and implore you to assist me."

"How can *I* assist you, child?" said Ralph, rising from his chair, and pacing up and down the room in his old attitude.

"You have influence with one of these men, I *know*," rejoined Kate, emphatically. "Would not a word from you induce them to desist from this unmanly course?"

"No," said Ralph, suddenly turning; "at least—that—I can't say it, if it would."

"Can't say it!"

"No," said Ralph, coming to a dead stop, and clasping his hands more tightly behind him. "I can't say it."

Kate fell back a step or two, and looked at him, as if in doubt whether she had heard aright.

"We are connected in business," said Ralph, poising himself alternately on his toes and heels, and looking coolly in his niece's face, "in business, and I can't afford to offend them. What is it after all? We have all our trials, and this is one of yours. Some girls would be proud to have such gallants at their feet."

"Proud!" cried Kate.

"I don't say," rejoined Ralph, raising his fore-finger, "but that you do right to despise them ; no, you show your good sense in that, as indeed I knew from the first you would. Well. In all other respects you are comfortably bestowed. It's not much to bear. If this young lord does dog your footsteps, and whisper his drivelling inanities in your ears, what of it ? It's a dishonourable passion. So be it ; it won't last long. Some other novelty will spring up one day, and you will be released. In the mean time —"

" In the mean time," interrupted Kate, with becoming pride and indignation, " I am to be the scorn of my own sex, and the toy of the other ; justly condemned by all women of right feeling, and despised by all honest and honourable men ; sunken in my own esteem, and degraded in every eye that looks upon me. No, not if I work my fingers to the bone, not if I am driven to the roughest and hardest labour. Do not mistake me. I will not disgrace your recommendation. I will remain in the house in which it placed me, until I am entitled to leave it by the terms of my engagement ;—though, mind, I see these men no more. When I quit it, I will hide myself from them and you, and, striving to support my mother by hard service, I will live at least, in peace, and trust in God to help me."

With these words, she waved her hand, and quitted the room, leaving Ralph Nickleby motionless as a statue.

The surprise with which Kate, as she closed the room-door, beheld, close beside it, Newman Noggs standing bolt upright in a little niche in the wall like some scarecrow or Guy Faux laid up in winter quarters, almost occasioned her to call aloud. But, Newman laying his finger upon his lips, she had the presence of mind to refrain.

" Don't," said Newman, gliding out of his recess, and accompanying her across the hall. " Don't cry, don't cry." Two very large tears, by-the-bye, were running down Newman's face as he spoke.

" I see how it is," said poor Noggs, drawing from his pocket what seemed to be a very old duster, and wiping Kate's eyes with it, as gently as if she were an infant. " You're giving way now. Yes, yes, very good ; that's right, I like that. It was right not to give way before him. Yes, yes ! Ha, ha, ha ! Oh, yes. Poor thing !"

With these disjointed exclamations, Newman wiped his own eyes with the afore mentioned duster, and, limping to the street-door, opened it to let her out.

" Don't cry any more," whispered Newman. " I shall see you soon. Ha ! ha ! ha ! And so shall somebody else too. Yes, yes. Ho ! ho !"

" God bless you," answered Kate, hurrying out, " God bless you."

" Same to you," rejoined Newman, opening the door again a little way, to say so. " Ha, ha, ha ! Ho ! ho ! ho !"

And Newman Noggs opened the door once again to nod cheerfully, and laugh—and shut it, to shake his head mournfully, and cry.

Ralph remained in the same attitude till he heard the noise of the closing door, when he shrugged his shoulders, and after a few turns about the room—hasty at first, but gradually becoming slower, as he relapsed into himself—sat down before his desk.

It is one of those problems of human nature, which may be noted down, but not solved ;—although Ralph felt no remorse at that moment for his conduct towards the innocent, true-hearted girl ; although his libertine clients had done precisely what he had expected, precisely what he most wished, and precisely what would tend most to his advantage, still he hated them for doing it, from the very bottom of his soul.

"Ugh !" said Ralph, scowling round, and shaking his clenched hand as the faces of the two profligates rose up before his mind ; "you shall pay for this. Oh ! you shall pay for this !"

As the usurer turned for consolation to his books and papers, a performance was going on outside his office-door, which would have occasioned him no small surprise, if he could by any means have become acquainted with it.

Newman Noggs was the sole actor. He stood at a little distance from the door, with his face towards it ; and with the sleeves of his coat turned back at the wrists, was occupied in bestowing the most vigorous, scientific, and straightforward blows upon the empty air.

At first sight, this would have appeared merely a wise precaution in a man of sedentary habits, with the view of opening the chest and strengthening the muscles of the arms. But the intense eagerness and joy depicted in the face of Newman Noggs, which was suffused with perspiration; the surprising energy with which he directed a constant succession of blows towards a particular panel about five feet eight from the ground, and still worked away in the most untiring and per-severing manner, would have sufficiently explained to the attentive observer, that his imagination was threshing, to within an inch of his life, his body's most active employer, Mr. Ralph Nickleby.

CHAPTER XXIX.

OF THE PROCEEDINGS OF NICHOLAS, AND CERTAIN INTERNAL DIVI-SIONS IN THE COMPANY OF MR. VINCENT CRUMMLES.

THE unexpected success and favour with which his experiment at Portsmouth had been received, induced Mr. Crummles to prolong his stay in that town for a fortnight beyond the period he had originally assigned for the duration of his visit, during which time Nicholas per-sonated a vast variety of characters with undiminished success, and attracted so many people to the theatre who had never been seen there before, that a benefit was considered by the manager a very promising speculation. Nicholas assenting to the terms proposed, the benefit was had, and by it he realized no less a sum than twenty pounds.

Possessed of this unexpected wealth, his first act was to inclose to honest John Browdie the amount of his friendly loan, which he accom-panied with many expressions of gratitude and esteem, and many cordial wishes for his matrimonial happiness. To Newman Noggs he forwarded one half of the sum he had realized, entreating him to take an opportunity of handing it to Kate in secret, and conveying to her the warmest assurances of his love and affection. He made no mention of the way in which he had employed himself; merely informing Newman that a letter addressed to him under his assumed name at the Post Office, Portsmouth, would readily find him, and entreating that worthy friend to write full particulars of the situation of his mother and sister, and an account of all the grand things that Ralph Nickleby had done for them since his departure from London.

" You are out of spirits," said Smike, on the night after the letter had been despatched.

" Not I !" rejoined Nicholas, with assumed gaiety, for the confession would have made the boy miserable all night ; " I was thinking about my sister, Smike."

" Sister !"

" Aye."

" Is she like you ?" inquired Smike.

" Why, so they say," replied Nicholas, laughing, " only a great deal handsomer."

" She must be *very* beautiful," said Smike, after thinking a little while with his hands folded together, and his eyes bent upon his friend.

" Anybody who didn't know you as well as I do, my dear fellow, would say you were an accomplished courtier," said Nicholas.

" I don't even know what that is," replied Smike, shaking his head. " Shall I ever see your sister ?"

" To be sure," cried Nicholas ; " we shall all be together one of these days—when we are rich, Smike."

" How is it that you, who are so kind and good to me, have nobody to be kind to you ?" asked Smike.   " I cannot make that out."

" Why, it is a long story," replied Nicholas, " and one you would have some difficulty in comprehending, I fear. I have an enemy—you understand what that is ?"

" Oh, yes, I understand that," said Smike.

" Well, it is owing to him," returned Nicholas. " He is rich, and not so easily punished as *your* old enemy, Mr. Squeers. He is my uncle, but he is a villain, and has done me wrong."

" Has he though ?" asked Smike, bending eagerly forward. " What is his name ? Tell me his name."

" Ralph—Ralph Nickleby."

" Ralph Nickleby," repeated Smike.   " Ralph.   I'll get that name by heart."

He had muttered it over to himself some twenty times, when a loud knock at the door disturbed him from his occupation. Before he could open it, Mr. Folair, the pantomimist, thrust in his head.

Mr. Folair's head was usually decorated with a very round hat, unusually high in the crown, and curled up quite tight in the brims. On the present occasion he wore it very much on one side, with the back part forward in consequence of its being the least rusty; round his neck he wore a flaming red worsted comforter, whereof the straggling ends peeped out beneath his threadbare Newmarket coat, which was very tight and buttoned all the way up. He carried in his hand one very dirty glove, and a cheap dress cane with a glass handle ; in short, his whole appearance was unusually dashing, and demonstrated a far more scrupulous attention to his toilet, than he was in the habit of bestowing upon it.

"Good evening, sir," said Mr. Folair, taking off the tall hat, and running his fingers through his hair. "I bring a communication. Hem!"

"From whom, and what about?" inquired Nicholas. "You are unusually mysterious to-night."

"Cold, perhaps," returned Mr. Folair; "cold, perhaps. That is the fault of my position—not of myself, Mr. Johnson. My position as a mutual friend requires it, sir." Mr. Folair paused with a most impressive look, and diving into the hat before noticed, drew from thence a small piece of whity-brown paper curiously folded, whence he brought forth a note which it had served to keep clean, and handing it over to Nicholas, said—

"Have the goodness to read that, sir."

Nicholas, in a state of much amazement, took the note and broke the seal, glancing at Mr. Folair as he did so, who, knitting his brow and pursing up his mouth with great dignity, was sitting with his eyes steadily fixed upon the ceiling.

It was directed to blank Johnson Esq., by favour of Augustus Folair Esq. ; and the astonishment of Nicholas was in no degree lessened, when he found it to be couched in the following laconic terms :

"Mr. Lenville presents his kind regards to Mr. Johnson, and will feel obliged if he will inform him at what hour to-morrow morning it will be most convenient to him to meet Mr. L. at the Theatre, for the purpose of having his nose pulled in the presence of the company.

"Mr. Lenville requests Mr. Johnson not to neglect making an appointment, as he has invited two or three professional friends to witness the ceremony, and cannot disappoint them upon any account whatever.

"*Portsmouth, Tuesday night.*"

Indignant as he was at this impertinence, there was something so exquisitely absurd in such a cartel of defiance, that Nicholas was obliged to bite his lip and read the note over two or three times before he could muster sufficient gravity and sternness to address the hostile messenger, who had not taken his eyes from the ceiling, nor altered the expression of his face in the slightest degree.

"Do you know the contents of this note, sir?" he asked, at length.

"Yes," rejoined Mr. Folair, looking round for an instant, and immediately carrying his eyes back again to the ceiling.

"And how dare you bring it here, sir?" asked Nicholas, tearing it into very little pieces, and jerking it in a shower towards the messenger. "Had you no fear of being kicked down stairs, sir?"

Mr. Folair turned his head—now ornamented with several fragments of the note—towards Nicholas, and with the same imperturbable dignity briefly replied " No."

" Then," said Nicholas, taking up the tall hat and tossing it towards the door, " you had better follow that article of your dress, sir, or you may find yourself very disagreeably deceived, and that within a dozen seconds."

" I say, Johnson," remonstrated Mr. Folair, suddenly losing all his dignity, " none of that, you know. No tricks with a gentleman's wardrobe."

" Leave the room," returned Nicholas. " How could you presume to come here on such an errand, you scoundrel ? "

" Pooh ! pooh !" said Mr. Folair, unwinding his comforter, and gradually getting himself out of it. " There—that's enough."

" Enough !" cried Nicholas, advancing towards him. " Take yourself off, sir."

" Pooh ! pooh ! I tell you," returned Mr. Folair, waving his hand in deprecation of any further wrath ; " I wasn't in earnest. I only brought it in joke."

" You had better be careful how you indulge in such jokes again," said Nicholas, " or you may find an allusion to pulling noses rather a dangerous reminder for the subject of your facetiousness. Was it written in joke too, pray ? "

" No no, that's the best of it," returned the actor ; " right down earnest—honour bright."

Nicholas could not repress a smile at the odd figure before him, which, at all times more calculated to provoke mirth than anger, was especially so at that moment, when with one knee upon the ground Mr. Folair twirled his old hat round upon his hand, and affected the extremest agony lest any of the nap should have been knocked off—an ornament which, it is almost supe_fluous to say, it had not boasted for many months.

" Come, sir," said Nicholas, laughing in spite of himself. " Have the goodness to explain."

" Why, I'll tell you how it is," said Mr. Folair, sitting himself down in a chair with great coolness. " Since you came here, Lenville has done nothing but second business and, instead of having a reception every night as he used to have, they have let him come on as if he was nobody."

" What do you mean by a reception ?" asked Nicholas.

" Jupiter !" exclaimed Mr. Folair, " what an unsophisticated shepherd you are, Johnson ! Why, applause from the house when you first come on. So he has gone on night after night, never getting a hand and you getting a couple of rounds at least, and sometimes three, till at length he got quite desperate, and had half a mind last night to play Tybalt with a real sword, and pink you—not dangerously, but just enough to lay you up for a month or two."

" Very considerate," remarked Nicholas.

" Yes, I think it was under the circumstances ; his professional reputation being at stake," said Mr. Folair, quite seriously. " But his heart failed him, and he cast about for some other way of annoying you, and making himself popular at the same time—for that's the point. Notoriety, notoriety, is the thing. Bless you, if he had pinked you," said Mr. Folair, stopping to make a calculation in his mind, " it would have been worth—ah, it would have been worth eight or ten shillings a week to him. All the town would have come to see the actor who nearly killed a man by mistake; I shouldn't wonder if it had got him an engagement in London. However, he was obliged to try some other mode of getting popular, and this one occurred to him. It's a clever idea, really. If you had shown the white feather, and let him pull your nose, he'd have got it into the paper; if you had sworn the peace against him, it would have been in the paper too, and he'd have been just as much talked about as you—don't you see ? "

" Oh certainly," rejoined Nicholas ; " but suppose I were to turn the tables, and pull *his* nose, what then ? Would that make his fortune ?"

" Why, I don't think it would," replied Mr. Folair, scratching his head, " because there wouldn't be any romance about it, and he wouldn't be favourably known. To tell you the truth though, he didn't calculate much upon that, for you're always so mild-spoken, and are so popular among the women, that we didn't suspect you of showing fight. If you did, however, he has a way of getting out of it easily, depend upon that."

" Has he ?" rejoined Nicholas. " We will try, to-morrow morning. In the meantime, you can give whatever account of our interview you like best. Good night."

As Mr. Folair was pretty well known among his fellow-actors for a man who delighted in mischief, and was by no means scrupulous, Nicholas had not much doubt but that he had secretly prompted the tragedian in the course he had taken, and, moreover, that he would have carried his mission with a very high hand if he had not been disconcerted by the very unexpected demonstrations with which it had been received. It was not worth his while to be serious with him, however, so he dismissed the pantomimist, with a gentle hint that if he offended again it would be under the penalty of a broken head ; and Mr. Folair, taking the caution in exceedingly good part, walked away to confer with his principal, and give such an account of his proceedings as he might think best calculated to carry on the joke.

He had no doubt reported that Nicholas was in a state of extreme bodily fear ; for when that young gentleman walked with much deliberation down to the theatre next morning at the usual hour, he found all the company assembled in evident expectation, and Mr. Lenville, with his severest stage face, sitting majestically on a table, whistling defiance.

Now the ladies were on the side of Nicholas, and the gentlemen (being jealous) were on the side of the disappointed tragedian ; so that the latter formed a little group about the redoubtable Mr. Lenville, and the former looked on at a little distance in some trepidation and anxiety. On Nicholas stopping to salute them, Mr. Lenville laughed a scornful laugh, and made some general remark touching the natural history of puppies.

"Oh!" said Nicholas, looking quietly round, "are you there?"

"Slave!" returned Mr. Lenville, flourishing his right arm, and approaching Nicholas with a theatrical stride. But somehow he appeared just at that moment a little startled, as if Nicholas did not look quite so frightened as he had expected, and came all at once to an awkward halt, at which the assembled ladies burst into a shrill laugh.

"Object of my scorn and hatred!" said Mr. Lenville, "I hold ye in contempt."

Nicholas laughed in very unexpected enjoyment of this performance; and the ladies, by way of encouragement, laughed louder than before; whereat Mr. Lenville assumed his bitterest smile, and expressed his opinion that they were " minions."

"But they shall not protect ye!" said the tragedian, taking an upward look at Nicholas, beginning at his boots and ending at the crown of his head, and then a downward one, beginning at the crown of his head, and ending at his boots—which two looks, as everybody knows, express defiance on the stage. "They shall not protect ye— boy!"

Thus speaking, Mr. Lenville folded his arms, and treated Nicholas to that expression of face with which, in melo-dramatic performances, he was in the habit of regarding the tyrannical kings when they said, 'Away with him to the deepest dungeon beneath the castle moat;' and which, accompanied with a little jingling of fetters, had been known to produce great effects in its time.

Whether it was the absence of the fetters or not, it made no very deep impression on Mr. Lenville's adversary, however, but rather seemed to increase the good humour expressed in his countenance; in which stage of the contest, one or two gentlemen, who had come out expressly to witness the pulling of Nicholas's nose, grew impatient, murmuring that if it were to be done at all it had better be done at once, and that if Mr. Lenville didn't mean to do it he had better say so, and not keep them waiting there. Thus urged, the tragedian adjusted the cuff of his right coat sleeve for the performance of the operation, and walked in a very stately manner up to Nicholas, who suffered him to approach to within the requisite distance, and then, without the smallest discomposure, knocked him down.

Before the discomfited tragedian could raise his head from the boards, Mrs. Lenville (who, as has been before hinted, was in an interesting state) rushed from the rear rank of ladies, and uttering a piercing scream threw herself upon the body.

"Do you see this, monster? Do you see this?" cried Mr. Lenville, sitting up, and pointing to his prostrate lady, who was holding him very tight round the waist.

"Come," said Nicholas, nodding his head, "apologize for the insolent note you wrote to me last night, and waste no more time in talking."

"Never !" cried Mr. Lenville.

"Yes—yes—yes— " screamed his wife. "For my sake—for mine, Lenville—forego all idle forms, unless you would see me a blighted corse at your feet."

"This is affecting!" said Mr. Lenville, looking round him, and drawing the back of his hand across his eyes. "The ties of nature are strong. The weak husband and the father—the father that is yet to be—relents. I apologize."

"Humbly and submissively ?" said Nicholas.

"Humbly and submissively," returned the tragedian, scowling upwards. "But only to save her,—for a time will come——"

"Very good," said Nicholas ; "I hope Mrs. Lenville may have a good one ; and when it does come, and you are a father, you shall retract it if you have the courage. There. Be careful, sir, to what lengths your jealousy carries you another time ; and be careful, also, before you venture too far, to ascertain your rival's temper." With this parting advice Nicholas picked up Mr. Lenville's ash stick which had flown out of his hand, and breaking it in half, threw him the pieces and withdrew, bowing slightly to the spectators as he walked out.

The profoundest deference was paid to Nicholas that night, and the people who had been most anxious to have his nose pulled in the morning, embraced occasions of taking him aside, and telling him with great feeling, how very friendly they took it that he should have treated that Lenville so properly, who was a most unbearable fellow, and on whom they had all, by a remarkable coincidence, at one time or other contemplated the infliction of condign punishment, which they had only been restrained from administering by considerations of mercy ; indeed, to judge from the invariable termination of all these stories, there never was such a charitable and kind-hearted set of people as the male members of Mr. Crummles's company.

Nicholas bore his triumph, as he had his success in the little world of the theatre, with the utmost moderation and good humour. The crest-fallen Mr. Lenville made an expiring effort to obtain revenge by sending a boy into the gallery to hiss, but he fell a sacrifice to popular indignation, and was promptly turned out without having his money back.

"Well, Smike," said Nicholas when the first piece was over, and he had almost finished dressing to go home, "is there any letter yet ?"

"Yes," replied Smike, "I got this one from the post-office."

"From Newman Noggs," said Nicholas, casting his eye upon the cramped direction ; "it's no easy matter to make his writing out. Let me see—let me see."

By dint of poring over the letter for half an hour, he contrived to make himself master of the contents, which were certainly not of a nature to set his mind at ease. Newman took upon himself to send back the ten pounds, observing that he had ascertained that neither Mrs. Nickleby nor Kate was in actual want of money at the moment, and that a time might shortly come when Nicholas might want it more. He entreated him not to be alarmed at what he was about to say;—there was no bad news—they were in good health—but he thought circumstances might occur, or were occurring, which would render it absolutely necessary that Kate should have her brother's protection, and if so, Newman said, he would write to him to that effect, either by the next post or the next but one.

Nicholas read this passage very often, and the more he thought of it the more he began to fear some treachery upon the part of Ralph Once or twice he felt tempted to repair to London at all hazards without an hour's delay, but a little reflection assured him that if such a step were necessary, Newman would have spoken out and told him so at once.

" At all events I should prepare them here for the possibility of my going away suddenly," said Nicholas ; " I should lose no time in doing that." As the thought occurred to him, he took up his hat and hurried to the green-room.

" Well, Mr. Johnson," said Mrs. Crummles, who was seated there in full regal costume, with the phenomenon as the maiden in her maternal arms, " next week for Ryde, then for Winchester, then for ——"

" I have some reason to fear," interrupted Nicholas, " that before you leave here my career with you will have closed."

" Closed !" cried Mrs. Crummles, raising her hands in astonishment.

" Closed !" cried Miss Snevellicci, trembling so much in her tights that she actually laid her hand upon the shoulder of the manageress for support.

" Why, he don't mean to say he's going !" exclaimed Mrs. Grudden, making her way towards Mrs. Crummles. " Hoity toity ! nonsense."

The phenomenon, being of an affectionate nature and moreover excitable, raised a loud cry, and Miss Belvawney and Miss Bravassa actually shed tears. Even the male performers stopped in their conversation, and echoed the word " Going !" although some among them (and they had been the loudest in their congratulations that day) winked at each other as though they would not be sorry to lose such a favoured rival ; an opinion, indeed, which the honest Mr. Folair, who was ready dressed for the savage, openly stated in so many words to a demon with whom he was sharing a pot of porter.

Nicholas briefly said that he feared it would be so, although he could not yet speak with any degree of certainty ; and getting away as soon as he could, went home to con Newman's letter once more, and speculate upon it afresh.

How trifling all that had been occupying his time and thoughts for many weeks seemed to him during that sleepless night, and how constantly and incessantly present to his imagination was the one idea that Kate in the midst of some great trouble and distress might even then be looking—and vainly too—for him !

WORKS OF ART,

PUBLISHED BY

ACKERMANN & CO. LONDON.

Ackermann's Annuals for 1839.

THE BOOK OF ROYALTY,

Or, Characteristics of British Palaces. Edited by Mrs. S. C. Hall. Containing Thirteen Facsimiles, illustrating incidents during various Reigns of the British Court, after Coloured Drawings by W. Perring and J. Brown. Elegantly bound in Scarlet Morocco, richly Emblazoned, and forming the most splendid and the only coloured Annual hitherto produced. Imperial 4to., price 2l. 12s. 6d.

" The volume is pictorially gay looking, and its literature is pleasant."—*Literary Gazette.*

" The binding is so gorgeous, as not merely to call for praise, but claims precedence in our three-fold commendation of this volume. The illustrations are so carefully finished, as closely to approach what they are intended to represent, viz. coloured drawings." — *Athenæum.*

" The BOOK OF ROYALTY must, of course, take precedence. The prints are on a new plan, and not, we think, an unhappy one. A dozen or more of these brightly coloured designs adorn the volume, and pretty little stories and ballads by Mrs. Hall illustrate the illustrations."—*Times.*

" The binding is elegant and chaste. The embellishments have the recommendation of novelty, a sure passport to success. On the whole, among the Annuals, none will better merit the favour with which it is certain to be received."—*Courier.*

" The most novel and beautiful of all the Annuals. The book opens a new field. Mrs. Hall has put her high powers and correct discrimination to work out an ingenious and delicate design, and has completed an Annual that honestly and fairly fulfils its title of BOOK OF ROYALTY. Its illustrations are full of skilful grouping and general artistical expression, founded upon historical data."— *Morning Post.*

" The BOOK OF ROYALTY is the most splendid of all the Annuals."—*Conservative Journal.*

" This superb and gorgeous folio is finished and executed in a style so as closely to represent coloured drawings."—*Naval and Military Gazette.*

FORGET ME NOT, FOR 1839.

A Christmas, New Year's, and Birthday Present. Edited by Frederick Shoberl. Containing Engravings by C. and H. Rolls, Davenport, Simmons, Outrim, Stocks, Periam, Allen, and Hinchcliff; from Paintings and Drawings by Cooper, R.A., Parris, Barrett, Jones, Middleton, Joy, Nash, Jennings, Mrs. M'Ian, Miss Adams, and Bell; and Literary Compositions by T. K. Hervey, D. Jerrold, Calder Campbell, P. H. Fleetwood, Esq. M.P., Dr. Mackenzie, H. F. Chorley, Swain, Michell, Richard and Mary Howitt, Miss Landon, Miss Lawrance, Mrs. Lee, Mrs. Sigourney, Miss Gould, Mrs. Walker, Miss M. A. Browne, Miss L. H. Sheridan, &c. &c. &c. Elegantly bound in Maroon Morocco, price 12s.

HINTS ON LIGHT AND SHADOW, 'COMPOSITION, &c., as applicable to Landscape Painting. By Samuel Prout, Esq. F.S.A., Painter in Water Colours in Ordinary to Her Majesty. 20 plates, containing 83 examples, executed in the improved method of two tints. Imperial 4to. cloth, lettered, price 2l. 2s.

" To all who have taste and power to appreciate what is excellent in art, this work will recommend itself: it will be found useful to professed Artists."—*Literary Gazette.*

" As maxims of experience, they deserve to be written in letters of gold."—*Spectator.*

" This publication is no less elegant than valuable: it would be difficult, indeed, to point out a more useful guide for the student."—*Naval and Military Gazette.*

" The slightest sketch here given as illustrative of effect, is full of the power of the author's genius."—*John Bull.*

" For taste in selection, clearness and precision of execution, and fidelity of representation, these exquisite little sketches can hardly be surpassed."—*United Service Journal.*

" We think this one of the cleverest works extant; to the student it will be invaluable: each respective plate is a beautiful specimen of talent and genius."—*Bell's Messenger.*

" Mr. Prout could not have presented the basis of his practice, and the result of his experience, in a more instructive, more attractive, or a more advantageous form."—*Atlas.*

WILKINSON'S SKETCHES AND SCENERY IN THE BASQUE PROVINCES OF SPAIN, with a Selection of National Music; illustrated by Notes and Reminiscences. Imperial 4to. bound, price 2*l.* 2*s.* plain; coloured, in imitation of the originals, 3*l.* 3*s.*

"The Author is induced to hope, that the Drawings contained in this Work will prove a welcome addition to the libraries of those officers who have served in Spain, whether belonging to the army of the Duke of Wellington, to the present force stationed on the coast of Cantabria under the command of Lord John Hay, or the late expedition intrusted to the guidance of Sir George De Lacy Evans."

WORKS DRAWN AND ENGRAVED BY AUGUSTUS PUGIN.

1. Designs for Gothic Furniture, 25 plates.
2. Designs for Iron and Brass Work, 27 plates.
3. Designs for Gold and Silversmiths, 27 plates.
4. Details of Ancient Timber Houses, 22 plates.

Royal 4to. 1*l.* 1*s.* each volume, bound in cloth.

New Prints.

The Measurement given refers to the Subjects, exclusive of blank Margin or Inscription.

THE MARTYRS IN PRISON. Dedicated by special permission to Her Majesty. Painted from original portraits by J. R. Herbert, and engraved in Mezzotinto by S. W. Reynolds. Size, 27¼ inches by 20. Prints, 2*l.* 2*s.*; Proofs, 3*l.* 13*s.* 6*d.*; India Paper, 5*l.* 5*s.*

We have here portraits of four Protestant Martyrs, Latimer, Cranmer, Ridley, and Bradford, to whose zeal and courage we are indebted for the Reformed Religion of our Established Church, when confined in one room of the Tower for preaching Christ's Gospel. A brief Memoir, with fac-simile Autographs, of these eminent Martyrs, accompanies this interesting Engraving.

JACOB'S DREAM. (From the celebrated Picture at Devonshire House.) Painted by Salvator Rosa; in Mezzotinto, by S. W. Reynolds. Size, 27¼ inches by 19¼. Prints, 2*l.* 2*s.*; Proofs, 3*l.* 13*s.* 6*d.*; Before Letters, 5*l.* 5*s.*

"This example of the style and manner of this great Painter is justly considered one of his choicest productions: it is beautifully engraved."—*Literary Gazette.*

ANCIENT JERUSALEM, during the approach of the Miraculous Darkness which attended the Crucifixion. Painted by W. Linton; in Mezzotinto, by W. Lupton. Size, 28 inches by 18. Prints, 2*l.* 2*s.*; Proofs, 4*l.* 4*s.*; Before Letters, 6*l.* 6*s.*

THE MANUSCRIPT. (Vide Tristram Shandy.) Engraved in Line by H. W. Watt, after a Picture by Leslie, R.A. Size, 13½ by 10. Price 1*l.* 1*s.*; Proofs, 2*l.* 2*s.*; India Proofs, 3*l.* 3*s.*; Before Letters, 4*l.* 4*s.*

THE ETON MONTEM, as celebrated last June, when attended by Her Majesty, enlivened with the interesting Costumes exhibited on the occasion. Size of the plate, 15¼ by 22½; highly coloured, 1*l.* 1*s.*

A SUPERB PORTRAIT OF HER MOST GRACIOUS MAJESTY THE QUEEN, engraved in the first style of Mezzotint by W. O. Geller, from the original and celebrated Picture by G. Swandale, Esq. Price to Subscribers: Prints, 1*l.* 1*s.*; Proofs, 2*l.* 2*s.*; fine Proofs before Letters, 3*l.* 3*s.* Size of the Engraving, 26½ inches by 20, including margin.

"This portrait may be considered a surprising resemblance of the illustrious original."—*Literary Gazette.*

"Mr. Swandale's portrait of Her Majesty is a dignified work, excellently conceived and executed."—*Athenæum.*

"This is a splendid production: the likeness is the best we have seen."—*Literary Journal.*

"This is the first portrait—at least, the first worthy of being called a portrait—of Her Majesty."—*Morning Advertiser.*

"This very graceful picture presents us with the best likeness we have seen of Her Majesty."—*Morning Chronicle.*

"This is decidedly the best portrait of Her Majesty which has hitherto appeared: it is a faithful likeness."—*Sunday Times.*

ALSO, THE FOLLOWING PORTRAITS OF HER MAJESTY, &c.

Painted by H. Collen; Engraved in Stipple, by T. Woolnoth. 5¾ inches by 4¼. Prints, 5s.; Proofs, 7s. 6d.; Before Letters, 10s. 6d.

Painted by A. Chalon, R.A.; in Mezzotinto, by S. Cousins, A.R.A. Size, 21 inches by 30; Prints, 3l. 3s.; Proofs, 5l. 5s.; Before Letters, 8l. 8s.

Painted by E. T. Parris; in Mezzotinto, by E. Wagstaff. Size, 9¾ inches by 12¾ high. Price 1l. 1s.; Proofs, 2l. 2s.; India, 3l. 3s.

Painted by Stewart; in Mezzotinto, by E. H. Every. Size, 11 inches by 13¼ high. Price 7s. 6d.

Painted by R. J. Lane, R. A.; Engraved in the Chalk Manner, by F. C. Lewis. In a circle 7¼ inches in diameter. Prints, 5s.; Proofs, 7s. 6d.; Before Letters, 10s. 6d.

Painted by G. Hayter; in Mezzotinto, by H. Cousins. 26 inches by 16. Prints, 2l. 2s.; Proofs, 4l. 4s.; Before Letters, 6l. 6s.

In Stipple, from "Finden's Female Aristocracy." 10 inches by 8. Prints, 7s. 6d.; Proofs, 10s. 6d.

By T. Sully, for the United States; in Mezzotinto, by C. E. Wagstaff. Prints, 1l. 1s.; Proofs, 2l. 2s.; Before Letters, 4l. 4s.

By A. Aglio; in Mezzotinto, by James Scott. 22 inches by 17. Price 1l. 1s.; Proofs, 2l. 2s.

HER MAJESTY, AND H. R. H. THE DUCHESS OF KENT. A Pair. By Chalon; on Stone, by R. J. Lane. Size, 17½ inches by 12. Price 1l. 1s.; 2l. 2s.; Proofs, 3l. 3s., in Colours.

HER MAJESTY THE QUEEN, AND H. R. H. THE DUCHESS OF KENT (Whole Lengths). A Pair. By G. Hayter; in Mezzotinto, by J. Bromley. 24½ inches by 16¼. Prints, 1l. 11s. 6d.; Proofs, 3l. 3s. each.

HER MAJESTY QUEEN ADELAIDE. By A. Grahl; in Mezzotinto, by S. W. Reynolds. 9 inches by 7½. Prints, 10s. 6d.; Proofs, 15s.

THE ORIENTAL PORTFOLIO; or, Scenery, Manners, and Customs, of the East. In Parts, containing Five Plates, imperial folio, published quarterly. Price 1l. 1s.

NIMROD'S SPORTING. Illustrated with Twenty-six Line Engravings, after E. Landseer, R.A.; A. Cooper, R.A.; C. Hancock, &c. Imperial 4to. cloth, bound elegant, price 2l. 2s.; ditto, Proofs on India Paper, 3l. 3s.

ALBUM COSMOPOLITE. Containing Autographs and Drawings by Sovereigns, Statesmen, Poets, &c. of every Country. From the Album of M. Alexander Vattemere. Price 7s. per Part; Proofs, 12s. each.

THE SPORTING REVIEW. A New Monthly Magazine. Price 2s. 6d. per Number.

MEMOIRS OF THE LIFE OF THE LATE JOHN MYTTON, ESQ., of Halston, Shropshire; with Notices of his Hunting, Shooting, Driving, Racing, Eccentric and Extravagant Exploits. By Nimrod. Second Edition, with numerous Coloured Illustrations, by H. Alken and T. J. Rawlins. 8vo., cloth, elegant. Price 1l. 5s.

GAMONIA; or, the Art of Preserving Game, and an Improved Method of making Plantations and Covers. By Lawrence Rawstorne, Esq. With Fifteen Coloured Engravings. Price 1l. 1s., bound in Green Morocco.

THEORY OF PAINTING. To which is added, an Index of Mixed Tints, and an Introduction to Painting in Water Colours, with Precepts. By T. H. Fielding, Teacher at the Hon. East India Company's Seminary, Addiscombe. 8vo. Price 1l. 6s.

THE CIVIL ENGINEER AND MECHANIST. A Practical Treatise designed for the use of Engineers, Iron Masters, Manufacturers, and Operative Mechanics, &c. By C. J. Blunt, and R. M. Stephenson, Civil Engineers, Architects, &c. In Parts, with descriptive Letterpress to each Part. Price, each, 1l. 1s. I. to V. have appeared.

PROUT'S FACSIMILES OF FIFTY SKETCHES IN FLANDERS AND GERMANY. Price, on India Paper, 6l. 6s.

PROUT'S INTERIORS AND EXTERIORS. Forty-eight Plates, half-bound, imperial 4to. Price 3*l*. 3*s*.

J. S. PROUT'S ANTIQUITIES OF BRISTOL. Thirty Plates, half-bound, imperial 4to. Price 2*l*. 10*s*.

THE ALHAMBRA. Shewing the Plans, Elevations, Sections, and Details, of this beautiful Specimen of Moorish Architecture. Printed in Colours. Folio Columbier, price 1*l*. 5*s*.; folio Grand Aigle, heightened in Gold, 2*l*. 2*s*. each Part.

SIX COLOURED VIEWS ON THE LONDON AND BIRMINGHAM RAILWAY. By T. T. Bury. Price, the set, 12*s*.

TWELVE DITTO OF THE LIVERPOOL AND MANCHESTER RAILWAY. By T. T. Bury. In Two Parts, price, each, 12*s*.

VIEW OF THE COURT OF LIONS IN THE ALHAMBRA. By Owen Jones, Architect. Printed in Colours, from Nine Lithographic Stones, and relieved in Gold. Size, 1 foot 5½ inches by 2 feet 2 high. Price 2*l*. 12*s*. 6*d*.

THE VILLAGE CHURCH. By Mrs. Seyffarth; in Mezzotinto, by J. Egan. 21¼ inches by 14¾. Prints, 1*l*. 1*s*.; Proofs, 1*l*. 11*s*. 6*d*.; Before Letters, 2*l*. 2*s*.

HAFED. (Portrait of a celebrated Deer Hound.) By E. Landseer, R.A.; in Mezzotinto, by C. G. Lewis. 23½ inches by 17½. Prints, 15*s*.; Proofs, 1*l*. 5*s*.; Before Letters, 2*l*. 2*s*.

THE BRITISH QUEEN AND GREAT WESTERN STEAM SHIPS. A Pair; highly Coloured. Price 10*s*. 6*d*. each.

THE SLEEPING BLOODHOUND, and SUSPENSE. A Pair. By E. Landseer, R.A.; in Mezzotinto. 20 inches by 15¼. Prints, 12*s*.; Proofs, 1*l*. 1*s*.; Before Letters, 1*l*. 11*s*. 6*d*. each.

LOOKING IN AND LOOKING OUT. By H. P. PARKER; in Mezzotinto, by W. O. Geller. 22¼ inches by 18. Prints, 15*s*.; Proofs, 1*l*. 5*s*. Coloured, 1*l*. 11*s*. 6*d*. each.

SMUGGLER'S QUARRELLING. By H. P. Parker; in Mezzotinto, by T. Lupton. 21 inches by 16. Prints, 1*l*. 1*s*.; Proofs, 2*l*. 2*s*.; Before Letters, 2*l*. 12*s*. 6*d*.

THE SPANISH CONTRABANDISTA. By J. F. Lewis; in Mezzotinto, by C. Turner, A.R.A. 26 inches by 21. Prints, 2*l*. 2*s*.; Proofs, 4*l*. 4*s*.; Before Letters, 5*l*. 5*s*.

WELLINGTON AT WATERLOO. By A. Cooper, R.A.; in Mezzotinto, by T. Bromley. 22 inches by 17. Prints, 1*l*. 1*s*.; Proofs, 2*l*. 2*s*.

NAPOLEON AT WATERLOO. Painted by Steuben; in Mezzotinto, by W. H. Simmons. Companion to the above. Same Size and Price.

INDULGING. By W. Kidd; in Line, by W. H. Watt. 11¼ inches by 8¾. Prints, 10*s*. 6*d*.; Proofs, 1*l*. 1*s*.; Before Letters, 2*l*. 2*s*.

SMUGGLERS ATTACKED. By H. P. Parker; on Stone, by T. Fairland. 21 inches by 17. Prints, on India Paper, 7*s*. 6*d*.; Coloured, 15*s*.

WOLVES ATTACKING DEER. A Scene in the Tyrol. By F. Gauermann; in Line, by B. P. Gibson. 10 inches by 8¼. Prints, 7*s*. 6*d*.; Proofs, 15*s*.

THE LAST SUPPER. By Leonardo da Vinci; Engraved by A. Collas. In the Numismatique style. 15¼ inches by 6¾. Prints, 7*s*. 6*d*.

BELSHAZZAR'S FEAST. In Mezzotinto, by J. Martin. 28½ inches by 18½. Prints, 2*l*. 12*s*. 6*d*.; Proofs, 5*l*. 5*s*.; Before Letters, 10*l*. 10*s*.

THE FALL OF BABYLON. By the Same. Same Size and Price.

THE DEATH OF THE FIRST-BORN. By the Same. 29 inches by 17¼. Same Price.

THE DESTROYING ANGEL. By the Same. Same Size and Price.

THE FALL OF NINEVEH. By the Same. 32 inches by 21. Prints, 5*l*. 5*s*.; Proofs, 10*l*. 10*s*.; Before Letters, 21*l*.

JOSHUA COMMANDING THE SUN TO STAND STILL. By the Same. 27 inches by 17. Prints, 3*l*. 13*s*. 6*d*.; Proofs, 7*l*. 7*s*.; Before Letters, 14*l*. 14*s*.

THE DELUGE. By the Same. 28 inches by 18¾. Prints, 3*l.* 3*s.*; Proofs, 6*l.* 6*s.*; Before Letters, 12*l.* 12*s.*

THE CRUCIFIXION. By the Same. 28¼ inches by 18¼. Prints, 2*l.* 12*s.* 6*d.*; Proofs, 5*l.* 5*s.*; Before Letters, 10*l.* 10*s.*

HISTORICAL ILLUSTRATIONS TO THE BIBLE, for the use of Schools and Home Education—the Old Testament. Twenty Plates. Price 20*s.*

PROGRESS OF INTEMPERANCE. (A series of Six Plates.) Painted by E. V. Rippingille. In Mezzotinto, by S. W. Reynolds. Size, 18 inches by 13. Price, the Set; Prints, 3*l.* 3*s.*; Proofs, 5*l.* 5*s.*; Before Letters, 7*l.* 7*s.*

THE KEEPER GOING ROUND HIS TRAPS. By C. Hancock. In Mezzotinto, by H. Beckwith. 16½ inches by 11½. Prints, 10*s.* 6*d.*; Proofs, 15*s.*; First Proofs, 1*l.* 1*s.*

THE FORESTER IN SEARCH OF GAME. Companion to the above. By the Same. Same Size and Price.

A SHIPWRECK. By J. M. W. Turner, R.A. In Mezzotinto, by C. Turner, A.R.A. 30 inches by 20¾. Prints, 1*l.* 1*s.*; in Colours, 2*l.* 2*s.*

WRECKERS OFF FORT ROUGE. (Calais in the Distance.) By C. Stanfield. In Mezzotinto, by J. P. Quilly. 26½ inches by 19¼. Prints, 1*l.* 1*s.*; Proofs, 2*l.* 2*s.*

THE PORT OF LIVERPOOL. By. S. Walters; in Aquatint, by R. G. Reeve. 24½ inches by 17¼. Prints, 12*s.*; in Colours, 1*l.* 4*s.*

SOLICITING A VOTE. By Buss. In Mezzotinto, by T. Lupton. 18¼ inches by 12½. Prints, 12*s.*; Proofs, 1*l.* 1*s.*; Before Letters, 1*l.* 7*s.* 6*d.*

THE TIGHT SHOE. By H. Richter. In Mezzotinto, by T. P. Quilly. Companion to the above. Same Size and Price.

WAITING FOR "THE TIMES" (after an adjourned Debate). By R. B. Haydon. In Mezzotinto, by T. Lupton. 14 inches by 10½. Prints, 7*s.* 6*d.*; Proofs, 12*s.*

READING THE SCRIPTURES. By R. B. Haydon. In Mezzotinto, by J. E. Coombs. 12 inches by 10. Prints, 7*s.* 6*d.*; Proofs, 12*s.*

THE LOVE LETTER. By J. Graham. In Mezzotinto, by W. Ward. 14⅞ inches by 11¼. Prints, 12*s.* Proofs, 1*l.* 1*s.*; in Colours, 1*l.* 4*s.*

THE SEAL OF AFFECTION. By J. Stewart. Engraved by O. Geller. Companion to the above. Same Size and Price.

HINDA. By G. Beechey. In Mezzotinto, by G. H. Phillips. 21½ inches by 17½. Prints, 15*s.*; Proofs, 1*l.* 5*s.*; in Colours, 1*l.* 11*s.* 6*d.*

THE HAPPY DREAM (after the Ball). By J. Stewart. In Mezzotinto, by W. Nicholas. 16¼ inches by 13¼. Prints, 10*s.* 6*d.*; Proofs, 1*l.* 1*s.*; in Colours, 1*l.* 5*s.*

HIGH AND LOW LIFE. By E. Landseer, R.A. On Stone, by R. J. Lane, A.R.A. A Pair. 15 inches by 12. Prints, on India Paper, 9*s.*; Proofs, 15*s.*; in Colours, 18*s.* each.

JACK IN OFFICE. By E. Landseer, R.A In Line, by Gibbon. 16½ inches by 12¾. Prints, 15*s.*; Proofs, 1*l.* 10*s.*

THE DANGEROUS PLAYFELLOW. By W. Etty, R.A. On Stone, by E. Morton. 11 inches by 11. Prints, on India Paper, 5*s.*; Proofs, 7*s.* 6*d.*; Coloured, 10*s.* 6*d.*

THE GAMEKEEPER'S STABLE AND DOWN CHARGE. By A. Cooper, R.A. In Mezzotinto, by F. Bromley. A Pair. 12 inches by 9¾. Prints, 7*s.* 6*d.*; Coloured, 15*s.* each.

THE WANTON COURSER (from Homer's Iliad). By S. Gilpin, R.A. In Mezzotinto, by S. W. Reynolds. 30 inches by 20. Prints, 1*l.* 11*s.* 6*d.*; Proofs, 2*l.* 12*s.* 6*d.*; Before Letters, 3*l.* 3*s.*

GUILT AND INNOCENCE. By J. R. Herbert. In Mezzotinto, by J. Egan. 18¼ inches by 14¼. Prints, 15*s.*; Proofs, 1*l.* 1*s.*; Before Letters, 1*l.* 11*s.* 6*d.*

VIEWS OF QUEBEC, AND THE FALLS OF NIAGARA (a Series of Twelve Coloured Views). By Lieut.-Col. Cockburn. 26 inches by 17¼. Price 10*l.* 10*s.* the Set; or separate Plates, 1*l.* 1*s.* each.

ECCE HOMO; from the Original in the National Gallery. By Correggio. On Stone, by W. Franquinet. 22 inches by 19. Prints, on India Paper, 10*s.* 6*d.*; Proofs, 15*s.*; finely Coloured, 1*l.* 1*s.*

A HIGHLAND SHEPHERD'S DOG rescuing a Sheep from a Snow-drift. By E. Landseer, R.A. On Stone, by R. J. Lane, A.R.A. 16½ inches by 12¾. Prints, on India Paper, 10*s.* 6*d.*; in Colours, 1*l.* 1*s.*

THE SHEPHERD'S GRAVE. Painted by E. Landseer, R.A. In Line, by B. P. Gibbon. Size, 12 inches by 10¼. Prints, 12*s.*; Proofs, 1*l.* 1*s.*; Before Letters, 1*l.* 11*s.* 6*d.*

THE SHEPHERD'S CHIEF MOURNER. Painted by E. Landseer, R. A. In Line, by B. P. Gibbon. Companion to the above. Same Size and Price.

BURNET'S CARTOONS. Engraved on Steel by himself. Size, 18½ inches by 23½. Price 4*s.* each.

GULLIVER IN BROBDIGNAG. (Exhibited on the Farmer's Table.) Painted by R. Redgrave. Engraved by J. Mollison. Size, 9 inches 3-8ths by 7 inches 3-8ths. Prints, 7*s.* 6*d.*; Proofs, 12*s.*; First Proofs, 15*s.*

THE RAT-CATCHER. Painted by C. Hancock. In Line, by W. Raddon. Size, 10¼ inches by 7¼. Prints, 7*s.* 6*d.*; Proofs, 12*s.*; Before Letters, 15*s.*

Portraits.

THE DUKE OF WELLINGTON (whole length). By W. Simpson. In Mezzotinto, by G. H. Phillips. 25½ inches by 16⅝. Prints, 1*l.* 11*s.* 6*d.*; Proofs, 3*l.* 3*s.*; Before Letters, 5*l.* 5*s.*

THE DUKE OF WELLINGTON. By Sir T. Lawrence. In Mezzotinto, by S. Cousins. 11¼ inches by 9¼. Prints, 1*l.* 1*s.*; Proofs, 2*l.* 12*s.*

SIR ROBERT PEEL, Bart. By J. Wood. In Mezzotinto, by W. Ward. 11¼ inches by 9¼. Prints, 1*l.* 1*s.*; Proofs, 2*l.* 2*s.*

ANNE, COUNTESS OF MORNINGTON. Painted by the Hon. Lady Burghersh. In Mezzotinto, by W. Hodgetts. Size, 17 by 24 high. Prints, 1*l.* 1*s.*; Proofs, 2, 3, and 4 guineas.

EARL OF EGREMONT. By G. Clint. In Mezzotinto, by T. Lupton. 23¼ inches by 15½. Prints, 1*l.* 1*s.*; Proofs, 2*l.* 2*s.*

RICE WYNNE, ESQ. Painted by J. Pardon. Engraved in Mezzotinto, by W. O. Geller. Size, 24 inches by 18½. Price, 1*l.* 5*s.*

PAUL OURY, ESQ., a Fox-hunter, rough and ready. Painted by R. R. Scanlan. Engraved by Thomas Landseer. Size, 20 inches by 15½. Price 1*l.* 1*s.*

Sporting Prints.

PORTRAITS OF THE WINNERS OF THE DERBY, OAKS, AND GREAT ST. LEGER STAKES. By J. Ferneley, C. Hancock, F. C. Turner, &c. 16½ inches by 12¼. Coloured, 15*s.* each. Rowton, Priam, Velocipede, Glencoe, Cadland, Spaniel, Riddlesworth, Bay Middleton, Chorister, St. Giles, Sultan, Dangerous, Cyprian, Hornsea, Mundig, Queen of Trumps, Elis Mango, Phosphorus, Miss Letty, Amato, Don John.

THE ROYAL HUNT. Meeting of Her Majesty's Staghounds on Ascot Heath. By F. Grant. In Mezzotinto, by F. Bromley. 32 inches by 21. Prints, 3*l.* 3*s.*; Proofs, 5*l.* 5*s.*; Before Letters, 6*l.* 6*s.*

THE HUNTER'S ANNUAL. Four Plates on India Paper. Price 2*l.* 2*s.* By R. B. Davis. On Stone, by J. W. Giles. (To be continued annually.)

R. B. DAVIS'S KENNEL SCENES. On Stone, by J. W. Giles. 16*s.*; in Colours, 1*l.* 4*s.*

STABLE SCENES, AND FIELD SCENES. By the Same. Each, Four Plates. Same Size and Price.

DONCASTER RACES, 1836, FOR THE GREAT ST. LEGER STAKES. Four Coloured Plates. By J. Pollard. 24½ inches by 14¾. Price 3*l*. 13*s*. 6*d*. the Set.

STAG HUNT. Four Plates, illustrating the Song, Hey ho! Tantivy. By F. C. Turner. Coloured, 3*l*. 3*s*. the Set.

THE AYLESBURY STEEPLE CHASE, 1836. Four Highly Coloured Plates, the Light Weight Stakes. 19¾ inches by 13¾. Price 2*l*. 2*s*. the Set.

THE LEAMINGTON STEEPLE CHASE. Four Coloured Plates, after F. C. Turner. 23½ inches by 14½. Price 3*l*. 3*s*. the Set.

ALKEN'S SHOOTINGS. Four Coloured Plates; the Moor, the Field, the Wood, and the Water. 18 inches by 13. Price 2*l*. 2*s*. the Set.

LOYAL FOX HUNTERS. Highly Coloured. 7*s*. 6*d*.

R. B. DAVIS'S SHOOTINGS; Grouse, Partridge, Pheasant, Snipe, Woodcock, and Water Fowl. Six Coloured Plates. 17½ inches by 13¾. Price 3*l*. 3*s*. the Set.

EPSOM RACES; a Series of Six Finely Coloured Plates. By J. Pollard. 18½ inches by 11¾. Price 3*l*. 3*s*. the Set.

MOVING ACCIDENTS BY FLOOD AND FIELD. Four Highly Coloured Plates. By F. C. Turner. 14½ inches by 10¼. Price 1*l*. 16*s*. the Set.

THE QUORN HUNT. Eight Beautifully Coloured Plates. 20¼ inches by 12½. Price 4*l*. 14*s*. 6*d*. the Set.

F. C. TURNER'S FOX CHASE. Four Coloured Plates. 19 inches by 14¼. Price 2*l*. 2*s*. the Set.

COUNT SANDOR'S HUNTING EXPLOITS. Ten Highly Coloured Plates. By J. Ferneley. 13¾ inches by 10½. Price 3*l*. 3*s*. the Set.

HODGE'S FOX HUNTING. Eight Highly Coloured Plates. By H. Alken. 20½ inches by 12½. Price 4*l*. 14*s*. 6*d*. the Set.

THE LAST GRAND STEEPLE CHASE OVER LEICESTERSHIRE. Eight Coloured Plates. 18 inches by 14. Price 3*l*. 3*s*. the Set.

ST. ALBAN'S GRAND STEEPLE CHASE. By J. Pollard. Six Coloured Prints. 17 inches by 12. Price 2*l*. 12*s*. 6*d*. the Set.

ASCOT HEATH RACES, 1836. 24 inches by 14¼. Highly Coloured. Price 1*l*. 1*s*.

THE GRAND STAND AT DONCASTER RACES; with Portraits of the Winning Horses for the last Twenty Years. 24¼ inches by 21. Highly Coloured. Price 1*l*. 1*s*.

SPORTING IN THE SCOTTISH ISLES. By W. Heath. Four Coloured Plates. 12½ inches by 8¾. Price 1*l*. the Set.

TURPIN'S RIDE TO YORK. By E. Hall. Six Coloured Plates. 15 inches by 11. Price 2*l*. 2*s*. the Set.

DONCASTER, ASCOT, GOODWOOD, AND EPSOM RACES. 24¼ inches by 14. Highly Coloured. Price 1*l*. 1*s*.

GOODWOOD RACE COURSE AND GRAND STAND; Priam winning the Cup in 1831. 26½ by 16¼. Coloured. Price 1*l*. 1*s*.

DEER STALKING. By J. Ferneley. Engraved by Duncan. Two Coloured Plates. 24 inches by 18¼. Price 1*l*. 5*s*. each.

GROUSE SHOOTING. By N. Fielding. A Pair. 11¾ inches by 9. Price, Coloured, 6*s*. each.

RED DEER SHOOTING. By N. Fielding. A Pair. 12 inches by 9. Price, Coloured, 6*s*. each.

THE RIGHT AND THE WRONG SORT.   By H. Alken.   A Pair. 17½ inches by 11¼.   Price, each, 12s. 6d., Coloured.

HODGE'S HARE HUNTING ; a Pair.   20 inches by 13.   Price 12s. 6d., each, Coloured.

R. B. DAVIS'S COURSING ; a Pair.   17½ inches by 14.   Price, Coloured, 10s. 6d. each.

ALKEN'S SPORTING ANECDOTES.   13 inches by 8½.   3s. 6d. each. The Hunting Sweep; Sporting Miller; Three Blind Uns and a Bolter; Jorrocks's Hunt Breakfast; Lord Marrowbones and his Man; Swell and the Surrey, Two Plates; the Sporting Tailor; the Hunted Tailor; the Sporting Parson's Hunting Lecture; Fox Hunting *versus* Politics; the Sporting Bishop; Mungo for a Hundred; the Hunting Sweep and the Duke; the Spree at Melton Mowbray, Two Plates.   To be continued.

ACKERMANN *and* Co. *will supply the following* ANNUALS *for* 1839.

	£.	s.	d.
THE BOOK OF ROYALTY, splendidly bound in Scarlet Morocco, Thirteen Highly Coloured Drawings	2	12	6
FORGET ME NOT, elegantly bound in Crimson Morocco	0	12	0
THE AMARANTH, bound in Silk	1	11	6
THE DIADEM, bound in Turkey Morocco	1	11	6
THE KEEPSAKE, bound in Crimson Silk	1	1	0
———————— India Proofs, large paper	2	12	6
GEMS OF BEAUTY, Imperial 4to	1	11	6
HEATH'S BOOK OF BEAUTY, bound in Blue Morocco	1	1	0
———————————— India Proofs, large paper	2	12	6
HEATH'S PICTURESQUE ANNUAL, bound in Morocco	1	1	0
———————————— India Proofs, large paper	2	12	6
PORTRAITS OF THE CHILDREN OF THE NOBILITY	1	11	6
BEAUTY'S COSTUME, 4to	1	1	0
THE BELLE OF THE SEASON, Imperial 8vo	1	11	6
A BOOK OF THE PASSIONS	1	11	6
LANDSCAPE ANNUAL (PORTUGAL), bound in Morocco	1	1	0
———————————————— India Proofs, large paper	2	12	6
DRAWING-ROOM SCRAP-BOOK, elegantly bound	1	1	0
ORIENTAL ANNUAL	1	1	0
———————— large paper	2	12	6
CAUNTER AND DANIEL'S ORIENTAL ANNUAL, Morocco	1	1	0
FINDEN'S TABLEAUX, Imperial 4to., splendidly bound in Morocco	2	2	0
———————— India Proofs	3	3	0
FRIENDSHIP'S OFFERING	0	12	0
BRITISH LANDSCAPE SCENERY, by Copley Fielding, Cox, &c.	0	12	0
FISHER'S JUVENILE SCRAP-BOOK	0	8	0
HOOD'S COMIC ANNUAL, half-bound Morocco	0	12	0
BIJOU ALMANACK	0	1	6
CRUIKSHANK'S COMIC ALMANACK	0	2	6
ORACLE OF RURAL LIFE AND SPORTING ALMANACK	0	2	6
N. B.—FLOWERS OF LOVELINESS, in a unique and novel binding, Imperial 4to., the volumes for 1836, 1837, 1838	1	11	6
———————————— India Proofs, large paper	2	12	6
ROGERS'S POEMS, and ITALY, illustrated with the original Proofs. Morocco, gilt edges, 2 vols. royal 4to., each	2	2	0

London : Printed by James Moyes, Castle Street, Leicester Square.

TO FAMILIES, SCHOOLS, &c.

PRICES OF
Genuine Drugs & Medicines,
SOLD BY
J. GRIFFITHS,
CHEMIST,
CLERKENWELL GREEN, LONDON.

	per oz.	per lb.		per oz.	per lb
Æther, strongest	6 — 6	6	Essence, Almonds	— 1	4
Antimony Wine	2 — 2	0	———— Bergamot	— 1	4
Almonds, Jordan Sweet	2 — 2	6	———— Lemons	— 0	8
Do., Bitter	— 1	6	———— Musk	— 2	0
Alum, lump or powder	—	2	———— Pennyroyal	— 1	6
Alkanet Root	1 — 1	0	———— Peppermint	— 1	0
Adhesive Plaister, per yard	. . 1	0	———— Ginger	— 0	6
Blue Pill	6 — 5	0	———— Rose	— 1	6
Borax	1 — 1	0	———— Cinnamon	— 1	4
Blue Vitriol	1 —	8	For flavouring confectionary, and scents.		
Burgundy Pitch	1 —	10	Purified Epsom Salts, lb. 6d. 3 lbs. 1 0		
Camomiles	0 — 1	4	French Chalk . . oz. 0 2 — 1 6		
Cascarilla Bark	1 — 1	0	———— Polish	2	6
Carbonate of Soda	1 — 1	0	Gentian Root . . . . 0 1½— 1 6		
Castor Oil, white and tasteless	3 — 2	0	Ginger, Barbadoes	0	9
Calumba Root	1 — 1	0	———— Jamaica	1	2
Camphor	4 — 4	0	Galls, Aleppo	3	10
Carmine, drachm 1s. 6d.	10s.		Glauber's Salts. 6d. per lb. or 3 lbs. for 1s.		
Canada Balsam	3 — 3	0	Graduated Medicine Glasses . each 1 6		
Castile Soap	2 — 2	0	Gum, Arabic . per lb. 9d., 1s., & 1 6		
Carraway Seeds	1 —	9	———— White and Picked . 2 6		
Coriander Seeds	1 —	8	Gum, Dragon . . — 0 3 — 3 0		
Cloves, fine new	4 — 4	0	——— Gamboge . . — 0 4 — 5 0		
Cochineal	8 —10	0	——— Myrrh, in powder — 0 4 — 4 0		
Copperas	. .	2	——— Scammony do. per dr. 0 6		
Conserve of Hips	2 — 2	0	——— Mastic . . per oz. 0 3 — 3 0		
Roses	2 — 2	0	——— Sandrac . . — 0 1 — 1 0		
Chloride of Lime, in Powder	. .	8	——— Shellac . . . per lb. 10d., & 1 2		
Solution . . pint 6d.	gal. 3s.		Hartshorn Shavings . . . 1½— 1 6		
Comp. Extract of Colocynth 1	0 —12	0	Hay Saffron . . . . dram 4 oz. 2 0		
Sarsaparilla 1	0 —11	0	Hiera Picræ . . . oz. 4 lb. 4 0		
Cream of Tartar		10	Honey, New English . . . 1 4		
Digestive Pills, prepared from			Iceland Moss . . . . . 1 — 1 0		
Rhubarb, Ginger, and Ca-			Ipecacuanha Wine . . . . 3 — 3 0		
momile Flowers 4d. doz., 4 doz. 1	0		Isinglass . . . . . . 10 —12 0		
Distilled Peppermint, Cinna-			Issue Peas . . . per 100 1 0		
mon, Dill, Carraway, Pimen-			——— Plasters . . per box 9		
to, Elderflower, Pennyroyal,			Jalap Powder . . . 4 — 4 0		
Rose Waters, and Camphor			Laudanum . . . . . 4 — 4 0		
Julep, at 6d., per pint.			Lenitive Electuary . . 1½— 1 6		
Elixir Paregoric, for Coughs	3 — 3	0	Lint (Patent) . . lb. 1 4, 2 0 & 3 0		
Vitriol	2 — 2	0	Linseed 4		

	per oz.	per lb.
Linseed Meal . . .4d. lb.	3 lbs. 1	0
Liquorice Root	1	0
Linseed Oil		6
Leeches, per dozen . . .	2 0 & 3	0
Logwood . . . . . lb.		2
Mustard, best Durham . .	1	4
Magnesia	3 — 2	0
——— Calcined . . .	6 — 5	0
Manna, Small	4 — 4	0
——— Finest	6 — 7	0
Naptha, purified, per pint . .	1	3
——— Polish	1	3
Nitre, Powder		8
Nitric Acid	1	0
Nitrous Acid (strongest) . .	0	10
Nutmegs	8 —10	0
Oil of Sweet Almonds . .	2 — 2	0
Olive or Salad Oil . .	1 — 1	2
Opodeldoc . . . , .	3 — 2	6
Orris Root and Powder . .	2 — 2	0
Orange Peel, dried . .	3 — 3	0
——— candied . .	1½— 1	8
Otto Roses dram 3s. oz.	—20	0
Oxalic Acid	2 — 2	0
Ointments, various		
Pearl Barley	0 — 0	4
—— Sago	0 — 0	4
Pearlash (American) . .	0 — 0	5
Peruvian Bark . . .	6 — 6	0
Pil Cochia	6 — 6	0
Prepared charcoal . . .	2 — 2	0
——— Barley (Robinson's) ea. 6 dz. 5		0
——— Chalk	0 — 0	6
——— Hartshorn . . .	0 — 1	0
——— Jamaica Ginger .	2 — 2	0
Plate Powder (white) . .	0 — 2	0
——— (rouge) . .	0 — 4	0
Pyrolyneous Acid, . .	1½— 1	6
Rezin, Black and Yellow lb. 2d.	7lb. 1	0
Red Sanders Wood . . .	1 — 1	0
Rose Pink	0 — 0	8
Rhubarb Root, Indian . .	8 — 7	0
——— Powder . . .,	1s. — 8	0
——— best Turkey . .	1 —12	0
——— Powder . . .	1s. 6d.—18	0
Rochelle or Tasteless Salts . .	1 — 1	0

	per oz.	per lb.
Rose Leaves	4 — 5	0
Roche Alum	1 — 0	6
Rouge, best (Jewellers) . .	4 — 4	0
Salts Sorrel	3 — 2	8
Salt Petre. . . . 5d. —	7 lb. for 2	6
Sal Ammoniac . . 7d. —	7 lb. for 3	6
Salt of Tartar	0	8
Sassafras Chips	0	8
Sarsaparilla Root	4 — 4	0
Senna Leaves, Indian . .	2 — 2	0
——— Alexandria .	3 — 3	6
Spermaceti, lump . . .	2 — 2	6
——— powder . .	3 — 3	0
Spirits of Camphor . . .	3 — 3	0
——— Hartshorn . . .	1½— 1	0
——— Salts	0	2
——— Sal Volatile . .	3 — 3	0
——— Sweet Nitre . .	3 — 2	6
——— Turpentine . . .	0	9
Sugar of Lead	1½— 1	0
Sulphur, flour . lb. 6d. —	3 lb. 1	0
——— milk . . .	1 — 1	0
Sulphate of Iron (pure) . .	0	9
Tamarinds	1	0
Tapioca	0	10
Tartaric Acid	2 — 2	0
Tincture of Bark, compound .	3 — 3	6
——— Lavender, ditto . .	3 — 3	6
——— Myrrh	4 — 4	0
——— Rhubarb, compound	3 — 3	0
——— Senna (Daffy's Elixir)	3	0
——— Gum Guaicum, for rheu-		
matism	4 — 4	0
Turmeric	0	10
Verdigris	2	0
——— Distilled	5	0
Vermillion	4 — 5	0
Volatile Salts	1 — 0	8
Bees' Wax	2 — 2	0
White Wax	2½— 2	6
——— Vitriol	1 — 0	8

Wine of Colchicum for inflammatory rheumatism, the pain of which is increased by warmth; it should be properly combined to secure its purgative effects, and counteract its injurious tendency.

MISCELLANEOUS ARTICLES.

Ginger Beer Powders per doz. 6d, 3 doz. 1 3
Lemonade ditto . . — 6d. — 1 3
Seidlitz ditto . . — 9d. — 2 0
Soda Water ditto . . — 4d. 4 doz. 1 0
Each dozen makes six draughts.
Eau de Cologne, per bottle . 2 0
Fragrant Lavender Water, half-pint bot. 2s. 0d.
——— pint 3s. 6d.
Marking Ink per case, 9d., 1s., & 1s. 6d.
Lucifer Matches 1d. per box, & 7d. per doz.
Pink Saucers 4d. each, 4 for 1s.
Pomatums 4d., 4 for 1s.

Preston Salts, 6d. bottle.
Tooth Brushes, 3d. & 6d. each.
——— Powder 6d. each, 5s. dozen boxes.
Court Plaster, & Gold Beaters Skin, 3d. & 6d.
White and Brown Windsor soap, 2d sq. 7 for 1s.
Maccaroni & Vermicelli, 1s. 6d. lb.
Violet Hair Powder 1s. 2d. lb.
Plain ditto, 1s.
Shields and Teats, 6d. each.
Salts of Lemons, 6d. oz. or box.
Fumigating Pastiles, 10d. oz., 10s. lb.

LOZENGES, &c.

Acidulated Drops . .	oz:	0	1¼lb.	1	6	Jujubes	oz.	0	3 lb.	3	0
Aniseed Candy . .	—	0	1 —	1	2	——— Liquorice . .	—	0	3 —	3	0
Barley Sugar . . .	—	0	1½—	1	6	Magnesia Lozenges .	—	0	3 —	3	0
Black Currant Lozenges	—	0	3 —	3	0	Nitre ditto . .	—	0	3 —	3	0
Bath Pipe	—	0	3 —	3	0	Peppermint Pipes .	—	0	2 —	2	0
Candied Horehound .	—	0	1 —	1	2	——— Lozenges, strong		0	3 —	3	0
Coltsfoot Rock . .	—	0	2 —	2	0	Quinine Lozenges .	—	0	8 —	0	0
Ginger Pipe . . .	—	0	2 —	2	0	Refined Juice . . .	—	0	2 —	2	0
—— Lozenges, very strong		0	3 —	3	0	Worm Lozenges for Children					
Ipecacuanha Lozenges	—	0	3 —	3	0	of all Ages . .	oz.	0	8 —		
Italian Juice, best . .	—	1½	0 —	1	6						

COUGH PLASTERS,

The best preventative against, and remedy for Coughs, Colds, Asthma, Consumption, Shortness of Breath, Rheumatisms, Lumbago, and Pains and Weakness of the Back and Limbs. They cause no irritation, and have no unpleasant smell. 2d., 3d., and 4d. each.

KERR'S COUGH PILLS,

Recommended as a safe and efficacious remedy in all Disorders of the Breast and Lungs; are peculiarly adapted for promoting a free and easy expectoration; they speedily remove the most obstinate and violent Coughs, and in moist or phlegmatic Asthmas, approaching to Consumption, their effect is truly beneficial. They heal, cleanse, and strengthen the Lungs, soothe the inflamed Membranes, dissolve thick tenacious Juices, give due tone to the Solids, and consequently that necessary invigoration so essential to persons of a weak or Consumptive habit. In Boxes, containing 30 Pills, 1s. 1½d. Three Boxes, for 3s.

The Price of the Stamps allowed on Patent Medicines.

Cupping on the new principle, at a moderate price.

FAMILY APERIENT
VEGETABLE PILLS,

For assisting Digestion and preventing Flatulence, Acidity, Heartburn, Giddiness, Sick Head-ache, Disorders of the Stomach, and Bilious Affections generally.

Of all complaints to which the human frame is liable, none perhaps is more distressing and at the same time more common, than a weak and impaired state of the stomach and digestive organs; it not only prevents a participation in the ordinary enjoyments of life, from that denial which it imposes on those who are subject to it, but brings with it, as a necessary consequence, a train of accompanying evils—as Flatulence, Acidity, Pain in the Stomach, Habitual Costiveness, Sickness, Head-Ache, and that distressing complaint usually termed Heartburn. Thus the constitution is weakened and deprived of all nourishment and support, while acrid and vitiated juices overspread the system, forbid the return of health and become the source of almost every species of complaint. In Boxes, containing 30 Pills, 1s. 1½d.. each. Three Boxes for 3s.

Directions.—Take two every other night, at bed-time, as a gentle Aperient; and for Indigestion one an hour before dinner.

CARRAGEEN, OR IRISH MOSS.

This Vegetable Substance has long been highly esteemed by the Peasants on the western coasts of Ireland, as a dietetic remedy for various diseases; more especially for Coughs, Colds, Consumptions, and affections of the Chest, Lungs, and Kidneys. It is particularly recommended for such as are delicate and weakly; for Infants brought up by hand, and for Children afflicted with Rickets or Scrofulous Diseases. Dissolved by being boiled in water it forms a thick mucilage, more pure and agreeable than that produced from any other vegetable; and the Jelly made from it is found to agree better with the stomach than any of those prepared from animal substances.

Directions for making Jelly.—Steep a quarter of an ounce of the Moss in cold water for five minutes, then take it out, shake out the water, and boil it in a quart of new milk until it is of the consistency of warm Jelly; strain and sweeten it to the taste with white sugar or honey.

For Consumptive Persons.—A small tea cupful should be taken in the morning, and repeated every four hours. 10d. per Pound.

CONCENTRATED

ESSENCE OF SARSAPARILLA,

For Purifying the Blood. Warranted to keep in all Climates; and to contain the due proportions of Sarsaparilla, Sassafras, Lignum Vitæ, Liquorice and Mezereon Roots. A dessert spoonful, or half an ounce, in a tumbler of cold water, makes the Compound Decoction of Sarsaparilla, of the London Pharmacopœia. In Bottles, containing 4 oz., 3s. 6d. each, or 1s. per oz.

COMPOUND

DECOCTION OF SARSAPARILLA,

Made PRECISELY according to the London Pharmacopœia, and warranted to contain the due proportions of Sarsaparilla, Sassafras, Lignum-Vitæ, Liquorice, and Mezereon Roots, well known as a remedy for eruptions on the skin, and other complaints arising from impurity of the blood. Sold in Wine Bottles, 2s. 6d. each.

THE BLACK DRAUGHT AND BLUE PILL.

Although no one cause can be assigned for ALL diseases, it is still the opinion of Medical Men that the greater number arise from an obstructed, or disordered state of the Digestive Organs. Mr. ABERNETHY supposes that local diseases are produced by the same cause, and recommends the above Medicine as the best for obtaining a healthy action of the Liver and Bowels, at the commencement of all complaints attended with costiveness.

It has long been known as a safe and efficacious remedy for Heartburn, Acidity, Giddiness, Sick Head-ache, and Bilious Affections generally. Price 6d.

A PHYSICIAN in attendance every Morning, from 10 to 12 o'Clock, to give ADVICE GRATIS, and a SURGEON may be consulted at any time of the day, free of all expense, except for the requisite Medicines, which are charged at the usual Chemists' prices.—Prescriptions are dispensed with the utmost care—the Medicines used are of the *purest character—the prices charged will be found very moderate.*

NOTE.—*Orders from the Country (post paid), enclosing a Remittance, will be executed on the shortest notice, and the Carriage paid when the value exceeds five pounds.*

OSBORNE, Printer, 126, Chancery Lane.

TO MEDICINE VENDERS GENERALLY,

AND

TO MERCHANTS, CAPTAINS, AND OTHERS INTERESTED IN FOREIGN COMMERCE.

SHARP'S ROYAL BRITISH CERATES AND LINIMENT.

THE high character which was early acquired by these preparations with the leading members of the Medical profession, and amongst all classes of the population, in Great Britain, and which is gradually tending to nearly every country in the four quarters of the Globe, leaves them unrivalled in value and importance. They are, consequently, offered to the Mercantile classes and the Public, with the full conviction that they will be found the most useful and valuable external remedies ever submitted to general notice.

The series consists of a Liniment, with the Plain, and four combinations of Cerates :—Namely, No. 1, Plain; No. 2, Camphorated; No. 3, Emollient; No. 4, Balsamic; and No. 5, Sulphurated; severally applicable to the cure of the following diseases and injuries, in the manner clearly laid down in the full printed directions which accompany each packet.

To the PUBLIC AT LARGE they are offered as yielding prompt and effectual relief for Gout—in some states, Rheumatic Affections, Lumbago, Glandular Swellings, many instances of Scrofulous Sores and Swellings, Tumours, Relaxed Sore Throats, Hooping Cough, Croup, Swelled Face or Gums, Nervous Headaches, some cases of Deafness, external Inflammation—in all its shapes, Boils, Ulcerated and other Wounds, Sprains, Cramp, Bruises, Burns, Scalds, Erysipelas, Venomous Stings, Itch, Ringworm, Scaldhead, Grocers' Itch, Chilblains, Chapped Hands or Lips, Bunions, Corns, Tender Feet, Paralysis of a local character, and Tic-douloureux.

For the use of the NEGRO POPULATION, in our own Colonial possessions and other tropical countries, they will be found most serviceable, as remedies for the diseases known as Yaws, Chigua, and Crawcraws; and as affording immediate relief from the pain caused by the bites of Musquitoes, and many venomous insects and reptiles.

As PLANTATION STORES, therefore, for the cure of all the diseases and injuries above enumerated, either in the white or coloured population, they must be invaluable.

In all NEW SETTLEMENTS, for the use of PRIVATE FAMILIES, with detached residences, and for LARGE ESTABLISHMENTS of any kind, they will especially be found of the greatest importance ; from their rendering such parties, in a great degree, independent of regular medical advice ; which is often, in those situations, difficult to be obtained.

As SHIPS' STORES, and in all MINING DISTRICTS, their value is highly appreciated; as the several preparations are found of the greatest utility in the rapid cure of Rheumatic complaints, Sprains, Bruises, and the several other diseases and injuries to which both sailors and miners are constantly, and in a peculiar degree, exposed.

Free from everything in the most remote degree allied to quackery—equally powerful in their effects and innocent in their composition—and calculated to keep for any length of time, and in all climates—these preparations are confidently offered by the Proprietors to every class of persons, in the various assortments specially prepared to meet the whole, or any limited portion, of the cases here enumerated.

Prepared only by SHARP, WEST, and Co., sole Proprietors, 153, Fleet Street, London ; and sold in Packets of four sizes, at 1s. 1½d., 2s. 9d., 4s. 6d., and 11s. each ; and expressly for Ship and Plantation Stores, in large brown Jars and Bottles, at 7s. each, including, in all cases, the Government Stamp, having the name and residence of the Proprietors engraved upon it, without which none can be genuine. Merchants, Captains, and others may be provided, gratuitously, with all the requisite documents in the several European languages, with the prices stated in the currency of the respective countries.

Sold also by the Patent Medicine Venders in and round the Metropolis ; by one or more Chemists, Druggists, or other licensed Venders, in every Town in the Three Kingdoms ; and by established Agents in the several British Dependencies in all parts of the world, as well as in most Foreign States ; from all the requisite documents, and numerous Testimonials of the highest character, may be obtained.

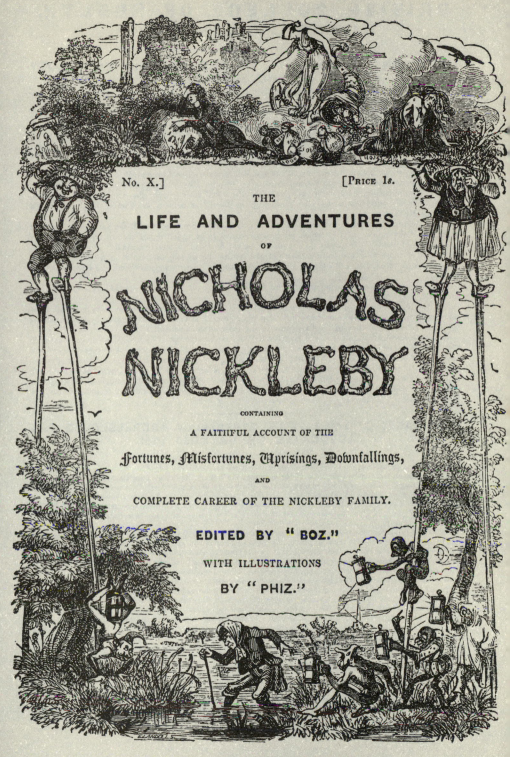

No. X.] [Price 1s.

THE
LIFE AND ADVENTURES
OF
NICHOLAS NICKLEBY

CONTAINING

A FAITHFUL ACCOUNT OF THE

Fortunes, Misfortunes, Uprisings, Downfallings,

AND

COMPLETE CAREER OF THE NICKLEBY FAMILY.

EDITED BY "BOZ."

WITH ILLUSTRATIONS

BY "PHIZ."

LONDON: CHAPMAN AND HALL, 186, STRAND.

BRITISH COLLEGE OF HEALTH,
HAMILTON PLACE, NEW ROAD.

OBJECTIONS OF HYGEISTS TO THE ORGANIC PATHOLOGY OF THE FACULTY.

1st.—Because no disease whatsoever primarily occurs in the solids, but on the contrary, through an impurity in the fluids—the blood!

2nd.—Because no organ as an organ is possessed of an acting or living principle, without the agency of the blood, *more than any other part of the body;* thus showing that when such an organ is affected, it is the blood which has been the cause thereof, and that it is only by purifying the principle of its existence (the blood) *that can restore it (the organ)* to its proper functions.

3rd.—Because what are termed nervous complaints under an organic pathology, have their origin, as all other complaints or diseases, in the blood, and should not therefore be treated specifically. The symptoms manifested in such cases are merely effects, and *not* causes, as asserted by the medical profession—it is the blood which stimulates the nervous system, in a healthy or unhealthy state, like all other parts of the body; purify it (the circulating fluid) sufficiently, and the effects will cease; hence the firm belief of Hygeists, that hydrophobia, and all other maladies termed by the faculty as nervous, are curable by the Vegetable Universal Medicines.

4th.—Because the stomach and bowels are what may be most properly termed, the natural emunctories or outlets of the human body, by which all impurities are to be expelled, but that an organic pathology (and therefore the objection) treats those most important functions as merely secondary (to the disgrace, be it said, of those who have had the health of the community so long confided to their care), its object being to *attack* specifically, and *independently* of the *blood,* the organs supposed from the symptoms to be affected.

5th.—Because it is made manifest, that the faculty, *acting on an organic pathology,* are not more successful in the cure of disease (nor by far so much so) as they were 2000 years ago, when the multifarious specifics they now make use of were unknown; and that at the present moment, it is an art most completely "founded on conjecture and improved by murder," as is lamentably proved by the numerous poisonous medicines administered at hap-hazard to the too-credulous patient.

READER—Above are the objections of Hygeists to the organic pathology of doctors; the difference between it and the Hygeian theory will be sufficient to account for the unparalleled success which has attended the medicines of the British College of Health, notwithstanding the opposition. All persons desirous of investigating this important question, should read the Morisoniana, price 6d., and the other Hygeian publications, to be had at the Medical Dissenter Office, 368, Strand, and of all the Hygeian agents throughout the kingdom.

It is most confidently suggested, that medical men cannot give good and sufficient reasons against the Hygeian system. If they can, let them be submitted to the world.

TWO CASES OF SMALL-POX, ESPECIALLY ADDRESSED TO THE ADVOCATES OF VACCINATION.

TO MR. MORISON.

On Saturday, January 6th, one of my daughters became ill and very feverish; I gave her a dose of twelve No. 1 pills bruised to powder, but such was the state of her body they did not operate further than cleansing the stomach and relieving the chest. I then administered a strong dose, which gave her complete relief. On the Tuesday following she began with the small-pox; as soon as I discovered this, I acted upon her with No. 1 pills powdered, in doses from ten to twelve, up to the fourth day, and in six days she was literally covered with them, the pustules being very large and remarkably full. On the Tuesday following they were at the crisis; she began immediately to recover, and is now stout and hearty.

On Tuesday, January 23rd, my youngest daughter took them. I followed the same course precisely as in the other case; they reached the crisis in the same period, and she is now hearty and well. What is remarkable in the Hygeian treatment of the above cases is, that, although they were literally covered with large pustules, and of course exceedingly painful, they were able to eat and drink throughout the disorder, and were quite free from any fever. In order to test the medicine and our system thoroughly, I ordered them to have whatever they wished for, either to eat or drink; consequently they ate bread, meat, potatoes, bread and cheese, pastry and confectionary, and drank water, milk, tea, coffee, ale and porter; but so thoroughly was the system fortified by the medicine that not the slightest inconvenience resulted, and although they had such a quantity upon their faces, I fully believe they will not have three marks on either of them. I wish just to mention here, that this has been the result in all the small-pox cases which I have undertaken since my labours commenced in this country. I deem it proper to publish these cases while the facts are well known and the red marks appear, so that any person opposed to the system may see for themselves, by proofs which cannot be counterfeited, and that others may see the erroneous method pursued by the faculty, in leaving the body unpurged until after the crisis of the disorder; the awful consequences of their mode of treatment being too well known to need stating by me.—Remaining, yours respectfully,   J. J. LEES.

Bridge-street, Manchester, Feb. 12th, 1838.

CAUTION.

To prevent impositions, the Honourable Commissioners of Stamps have directed the words "Morison's Universal Medicines" to be engraved on the Government Stamp, in white letters upon a red ground, without which none are genuine; and the public is further cautioned against purchasing Morison's Pills except of the regularly appointed agents to the British College of Health, as spurious imitations are in circulation. The public are cautioned against a base imitation, called "Dr. Morrison's Pills." Observe the mean subterfuge of the double "r."

PREPARING FOR PUBLICATION.

In One Volume, small Octavo,

SONGS & BALLADS.

BY SAMUEL LOVER.

These Popular Lyrics, including the celebrated " Superstitions of Ireland," will be now, for the first time, collected and revised by the Author.

In One Volume, small Octavo.

WITH ILLUSTRATIONS BY PHIZ,

A PAPER —— OF TOBACCO;

TREATING OF THE

RISE, PROGRESS, PLEASURES, AND ADVANTAGES OF SMOKING;

WITH

REMARKS ON THE USE AND ABUSE OF THE FASCINATING WEED.

ANECDOTES OF DISTINGUISHED SMOKERS.

MEMS. ON PIPES & TOBACCO BOXES.

And an Essay, Tritical, Critical, Practical, and Theoretical, on SNUFF.

BY JOSEPH FUME.

" You see the drift, Sir ; you take it ;
You *smoke.*"—TATLER.

In oblong Quarto, the First Part of

PHIZ'S FANCIES;

CONTAINING

THREE SHEETS OF DESIGNS AND SKETCHES,

DRAWN AND ETCHED BY HIMSELF.

LONDON: CHAPMAN AND HALL, 186, STRAND.

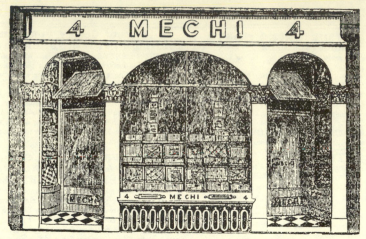

LEADENHALL STREET, LONDON.

MECHI'S NEW YEAR'S PRESENTS.

MANUFACTORY No. 4, LEADENHALL STREET, LONDON.

LADIES' COMPANIONS, or Work Cases   15s. to 2l.

LADIES' CARD CASES, in Pearl, Ivory, and Tortoiseshell . . . .   10s. to 5l. each.

LADIES' WORK BOXES .   25s. to 10 Guineas.

LADIES' DRESSING CASES 2l. 10s. to 50 Guineas.

LADIES' SCOTCH WORK BOXES at all prices.

LADIES' ROSEWOOD AND MAHOGANY DESKS   12s. 6d. to 10 Guineas.

LADIES' MOROCCO AND RUSSIA LEATHER WRITING CASES . . . .   5s. to 5l.

LADIES' ENVELOPE CASES, various prices.

LADIES' TABLE INKSTANDS, made of British Coal (quite a novelty) . . . .   7s. 6d. to 30s.

LADIES' SCOTCH TOOTH-PICK CASES.

LADIES' IVORY AND TORTOISESHELL HAIR BRUSHES . . .   at 2l. to 5l. per Pair.

LADIES' SCENT AND TOILET BOTTLES in great variety.

LADIES' SCOTCH TEA CADDIES .   21s. to 40s.

LADIES' PLAYING CARD BOXES .   30s. to 5l.

LADIES' JAPAN DRESSING CASES .   7s. to 15s.

LADIES' TORTOISESHELL DRESSING & SIDE COMBS.

LADIES' HAND GLASSES.

LADIES' PATENT INSTANTANEOUS PEN-MAKERS . . . .   10s. 6d. and 12s. 6d.

LADIES' ELEGANT PENKNIVES AND SCISSORS   5s. to 30s.

TRY MECHI'S Magic STROP.

MISCELLANEOUS.

BAGATELLE TABLES .	£3 10 0 to £5	0 0
BACKGAMMON TABLES . .	1 0 0 to 5	10 0
CHESS BOARDS . .	0 4 0 to 3	0 0
POPE JOAN BOARDS . .	0 13 0 to 1	0 0
IVORY CHESSMEN .	1 1 0 to 10	10 0
BONE AND WOOD DITTO .	Various Prices.	
WHIST MARKERS, COUNTERS, &c.		

GENT.'S DRESSING CASES, in Wood   2l. to 50l.

GENT.'S LEATHER DRESSING CASES 25s. to 24l.

GENT.'S WRITING DESKS, in Wood   30s. to 16l.

GENT.'S LEATHER WRITING DESKS 24s. 6d. to 5l.

GENT.'S WRITING & DRESSING CASE COMBINED . . . . .   5l. to 16l.

GENT.'S POCKET BOOKS WITH INSTRUMENTS   20s. to 40s.

GENT.'S ELEGANT CASES OF RAZORS 12s. to 3l.

GENT.'S SEVEN DAY RAZORS, in Fancy Woods   25s. to 5l.

GENT.'S RAZOR STROPS .   2s. to 30s.

GENT.'S SPORTING KNIVES .   12s. to 5l.

GENT.'S FANCY PENKNIVES   5s. to 15s.

GENT.'S PEARL AND SHELL POCKET COMBS   3s. 6d. to 15s.

GENT.'S SCOTCH CIGAR BOXES 3s. 6d. to 40s.

GENT.'S COAL AND EBONY INKSTANDS   7s. 6d. to 50s.

GENT.'S IVORY AND FANCY WOOD HAIR BRUSHES . . . .   20s. to 3l. 10s.

GENT.'S SETS OF BRUSHES, in Russia Cases   25s. to 4l. 10s.

GENT.'S SILVER AND IVORY SHAVING BRUSHES In elegant Patterns.

GENT.'S SILVER AND SHELL TABLETS.

MECHI,  MECHI,

4, LEADENHALL St. LONDON.

Submits, to public inspection, his Manufactures as being of the finest quality this kingdom can produce, and at moderate prices.

A large Stock of Table Cutlery, Plated Tea and Coffee Services, Dish Covers, Hash Covers, &c.

TO THE HEADS OF PUBLIC AND PRIVATE SCHOOLS, AND PARENTS GENERALLY.

PATRONIZED BY

THE ROYAL FAMILY & THE NOBILITY.

SHARP'S ROYAL BRITISH CERATES AND LINIMENT.

Numerous highly respectable principals of public schools and private academies, both ladies' and gentlemen's, who have had the fullest opportunities of observing, in their establishments, the beneficial effects of these preparations, in the rapid cure of the complaints and injuries to which children are, in a peculiar degree, liable, have strongly urged the proprietors to bring them in an especial manner to the notice of the heads of similar establishments throughout the country, as entitled to their universal support. It is in accordance with this suggestion, that the proprietors have determined thus publicly to draw the attention of all who have the charge of youth, of either sex—whether for the purposes of education, or as parents, in their respective domestic circles—to the fact, that their Cerates and Liniment constitute, in their several modifications, prompt and efficient remedies for Chilblains, Chapped Hands or Lips, Ringworm, Scald-Head, Hooping-Cough, Croup, Sore Throats, Glandular Swellings, Sprains, Bruises, Burns, Scalds, Boils, and the various other external diseases or injuries to which Children are especially subject.

The preparations consist of a Liniment, with the plain, and four combinations of Cerates; namely, No. 1, Plain; No. 2, Camphorated; No. 3, Emollient; No. 4, Balsamic; and No. 5, Sulphurated; which are most delicate in their external character; free from everything unpleasant in their use; and severally applicable to the cure of the above diseases or injuries, in the manner clearly laid down in the full printed directions which accompany each packet.

The Proprietors give their solemn assurance, that every fact stated, with respect to the powers of these substances, is not only quite within the strictest limits of the truth, but has been fully established, in every class of cases, in the practice of medical men of great respectability, in the metropolis and elsewhere; and that the several preparations, although most effectual in their remedial character, are quite free from every deleterious ingredient, and in the highest degree innocent in their entire composition. They may, consequently, be used with perfect safety, for even the most delicate children. The Proprietors, therefore, feel persuaded, that when these preparations have been once introduced in the various establishments for the education of youth of both sexes, as well as in private families, they will ever after be regarded as essential domestic stores for all seasons, and more especially for winter.

Although a separate enumeration is given above, of the disorders which belong chiefly to children and young persons, the Proprietors beg to state, that their preparations are equally valuable in the following additional cases; namely, Gout in some states, Rheumatic Affections, Lumbago, many instances of Scrofulous Sores and Swellings, Tumours, Swelled Face or Gums, Nervous Headaches, some cases of Deafness, External Inflammation, in all its shapes, Ulcerated and other Wounds, Cramp, Erysipelas, Venomous Stings, Itch, Grocer's Itch, Bunions, Corns, Tender Feet, Paralysis of a local character, and Tic-Douloureux. As no class of society is exempt from the liability to some or other of these attacks, so to every rank must access to such a powerful series of simple, but effectual remedies, be highly desirable.

The ROYAL BRITISH CERATES are made up, in all their modifications, in boxes of four sizes, at 13½d., 2s. 9d., 4s. 6d., and 11s. each; and the LINIMENT in bottles of three sizes, with ground-glass stoppers, at 2s. 9d., 4s. 6d., and 11s. each. Stamps in all cases included. Also, in boxes, containing every variety of kind and size, prepared expressly for the use of families and schools, or other large establishments.

Sold by SHARP, WEST, & CO., 153, Fleet Street, London, sole Proprietors, whose names and address are upon the Stamp; and by the established licensed Medicine Venders throughout the Three Kingdoms; from whom may be obtained, gratuitously, all the requisite documents; including strong Testimonials from numerous persons of the highest respectability.

APSLEY PELLATT'S

ABRIDGED LIST OF
Net Cash Prices for the best Flint Glass Ware.

DECANTERS.

25 Strong quart Nelson shape decanters, cut all over, bold flutes and cut brim & stopper, P.M. each 10s6d. to 12 0

26 Do. three-ringed royal shape, cut on and between rings, turned out stop, P.M. each 10 0
   Do. do. not cut on or between rings, 'nor turned out stopper, P.M. ea. 8s to 9 0

27 Fancy shapes, cut all over, eight flutes, spire stopper, &c. each, P.M. 16s. to 18 0
   Do. six flutes only, each, P.M. 24s. to 27 0

DISHES.

31 Dishes, oblong, pillar moulded, scolloped edges, cut star.

5-in.	7-in.	9-in.	10-in.
3s. 6d.	6s. 6d.	11s.	13s. each.

32 Oval cup sprig, shell pattern,

5-in.	7-in.	9-in.	11-in.
7s. 6d.	9s. 6d.	16s.	19s. each.

33 Square shape pillar, moulded star,

5-in.	7-in	9-in.	10-in.
4s.	8s.	12s. 6d.	15s. each.

FINGER CUPS.

37 Fluted finger-cups, strong, about 14 oz. each 2 6
   Do. plain flint, punted, per doz..... 18 0
   Do. coloured, per doz.......18s. to 21 0

38 Ten-fluted round, very strong, each . 5 0
   Eight-fluted do., each 8 0

39 Medicean shape, moulded pillar, pearl upper part, cut flat flutes, each .. 5 0

PICKLES

46 Pickles, half fluted for 3 in. holes, RM ea. 4 6

47 Strong, moulded bottom, 3-in. hole, cut all over, flat flutes, R.M. each . 5 0
   Best cut star do. for 3½-in. hole, PM ea. 7 6
   Very strong and best cut, P.M. each 14 6

WATER JUGS

59 Quarts, neatly fluted and cut rings, each.....................14s. to 18 0

60 Ewer shape, best cut handles, &c... 21 0

61 Silver do. scolloped edges, ex. lar. flutes 25 0

WATER BOTTLES

70 Moulded pillar body, cut neck, each . 3 0

71 Cut neck and star................. 3 0

72 Double fluted cut rings 3 6

73 Very strong pillar, moulded body, cut neck and rings 5 6

74 Grecian shape, fluted all over 7 0

TUMBLERS

	78	79	80	81	82	83	84	85	86	87	
Tale bs.											
Flint,	7s.	10s.	12s.	12s.	10s.	12s.	14s.	18s.	18s.		Doz.
	to	to	to	to	to	to	to	to	to		
	8s.	12s	14s.	15s.	12s.		19s.	21s.	21s.	30s	do.

WINES

88	89	90	91	92	93	94	95	96	97	98	99
7s.	7s.	7s.	7s.	8s.	14s.	12s.	13s.	15s.	18s.	21s.	20s.
to	to	to	to								
8s.	9s.	9s.	9s.	10s.							

Glass Blowing, Cutting, and Engraving, may be inspected by Purchasers, at Mr. Pellatt's Extensive Flint Glass and Steam Cutting Works, in Holland Street, near Blackfriars' Bridge, any Tuesday, Wednesday, or Thursday.

Merchants and the Trade supplied on equitable Terms.

No Abatement from the above specified Ready Money Prices.

No Connexion with any other Establishment.

BEAUFOY'S
INSTANT CURE FOR THE TOOTH-ACHE.

This article has been extensively and successfully used for some time past in a populous Neighbourhood, and has proved to be an INSTANT CURE in most cases.

The Selling Price to the Public has been fixed purposely so low as

to render the

"INSTANT CURE FOR THE TOOTH-ACHE"

accessible to all Classes.

MADE BY BEAUFOY & CO., SOUTH LAMBETH, LONDON,

And Sold by most Respectable Druggists and Patent Medicine Venders
in Town and Country.

The Bottles, with ample Directions for Use, Price 1s. 1½d. each, Stamp included.

[BRADBURY AND EVANS, PRINTERS, WHITEFRIARS.]

CHAPTER XXX.

FESTIVITIES ARE HELD IN HONOUR OF NICHOLAS, WHO SUDDENLY WITHDRAWS HIMSELF FROM THE SOCIETY OF MR. VINCENT CRUMMLES AND HIS THEATRICAL COMPANIONS.

MR. VINCENT CRUMMLES was no sooner acquainted with the public announcement which Nicholas had made relative to the probability of his shortly ceasing to be a member of the company, than he evinced many tokens of grief and consternation ; and, in the extremity of his despair, even held out certain vague promises of a speedy improvement not only in the amount of his regular salary, but also in the contingent emoluments appertaining to his authorship. Finding Nicholas bent upon quitting the society—for he had now determined that, even if no further tidings came from Newman, he would, at all hazards, ease his mind by repairing to London and ascertaining the exact position of his sister—Mr. Crummles was fain to content himself by calculating the chances of his coming back again, and taking prompt and energetic measures to make the most of him before he went away.

" Let me see," said Mr. Crummles, taking off his outlaw's wig, the better to arrive at a cool-headed view of the whole case. " Let me see. This is Wednesday night. We'll have posters out the first thing in the morning, announcing positively your last appearance for to-morrow."

" But perhaps it may not be my last appearance, you know," said Nicholas. " Unless I am summoned away, I should be sorry to inconvenience you by leaving before the end of the week."

" So much the better," returned Mr. Crummles. " We can have positively your last appearance, on Thursday—re-engagement for one night more, on Friday—and, yielding to the wishes of numerous influential patrons, who were disappointed in obtaining seats, on Saturday. That ought to bring three very decent houses."

" Then I am to make three last appearances, am I ? " inquired Nicholas, smiling.

" Yes," rejoined the manager, scratching his head with an air of some vexation ; " three is not enough, and it's very bungling and irregular not to have more, but if we can't help it we can't, so there's no use in talking. A novelty would be very desirable. You couldn't sing a comic song on the pony's back, could you ? "

" No," replied Nicholas, " I couldn't indeed."

" It has drawn money before now," said Mr. Crummles, with a look of disappointment. " What do you think of a brilliant display of fireworks ? "

" That it would be rather expensive," replied Nicholas, drily.

" Eighteenpence would do it," said Mr. Crummles. " You on the top of a pair of steps with the phenomenon in an attitude ; ' Farewell' on a transparency behind ; and nine people at the wings with a squib

U

in each hand—all the dozen and a half going off at once—it would be very grand—awful from the front, quite awful."

As Nicholas appeared by no means impressed with the solemnity of the proposed effect, but, on the contrary, received the proposition in a most irreverent manner and laughed at it very heartily, Mr. Crummles abandoned the project in its birth, and gloomily observed that they must make up the best bill they could with combats and hornpipes, and so stick to the legitimate drama.

For the purpose of carrying this object into instant execution, the manager at once repaired to a small dressing-room adjacent, where Mrs. Crummles was then occupied in exchanging the habiliments of a melo-dramatic empress for the ordinary attire of matrons in the nineteenth century. And with the assistance of this lady, and the accomplished Mrs. Grudden (who had quite a genius for making out bills, being a great hand at throwing in the notes of admiration, and knowing from long experience exactly where the largest capitals ought to go), he seriously applied himself to the composition of the poster.

"Heigho!" sighed Nicholas, as he threw himself back in the prompter's chair, after telegraphing the needful directions to Smike, who had been playing a meagre tailor in the interlude, with one skirt to his coat, and a little pocket handkerchief with a large hole in it, and a woollen nightcap, and a red nose, and other distinctive marks peculiar to tailors on the stage. "Heigho! I wish all this were over."

"Over, Mr. Johnson!" repeated a female voice behind him, in a kind of plaintive surprise.

"It was an ungallant speech, certainly," said Nicholas, looking up to see who the speaker was, and recognising Miss Snevellicci. "I would not have made it if I had known you had been within hearing."

"What a dear that Mr. Digby is!" said Miss Snevellicci, as the tailor went off on the opposite side, at the end of the piece, with great applause. (Smike's theatrical name was Digby.)

"I'll tell him presently, for his gratification, that you said so," returned Nicholas.

"Oh you naughty thing!" rejoined Miss Snevellicci. "I don't know, though, that I should much mind *his* knowing my opinion of him; with some other people, indeed, it might be—" Here Miss Snevellicci stopped, as though waiting to be questioned, but no questioning came, for Nicholas was thinking about more serious matters.

"How kind it is of you," resumed Miss Snevellicci, after a short silence, "to sit waiting here for him night after night, night after night, no matter how tired you are; and taking so much pains with him, and doing it all with as much delight and readiness as if you were coining gold by it!"

"He well deserves all the kindness I can show him, and a great deal more," said Nicholas. "He is the most grateful, single-hearted, affectionate creature, that ever breathed."

"So odd, too," remarked Miss Snevellicci, "isn't he?"

"God help him, and those who have made him so, he is indeed," rejoined Nicholas, shaking his head

"He is such a devilish close chap," said Mr. Folair, who had come up a little before, and now joined in the conversation. " Nobody can ever get anything out of him."

"What *should* they get out of him ?" asked Nicholas, turning round with some abruptness.

" Zooks ! what a fire-eater you are, Johnson !" returned Mr. Folair, pulling up the heel of his dancing shoe. " I'm only talking of the natural curiosity of the people here, to know what he has been about all his life."

" Poor fellow ! it is pretty plain, I should think, that he has not the intellect to have been about anything of much importance to them or anybody else," said Nicholas.

" Ay," rejoined the actor, contemplating the effect of his face in a lamp reflector, " but that involves the whole question, you know."

"What question ?" asked Nicholas.

" Why, the who he is and what he is, and how you two, who are so different, came to be such close companions," replied Mr. Folair, delighted with the opportunity of saying something disagreeable. " That's in everybody's mouth."

" The ' everybody ' of the theatre, I suppose ?" said Nicholas, contemptuously.

" In it and out of it too," replied the actor. " Why, you know, Lenville says— "

" I thought I had silenced him effectually," interrupted Nicholas, reddening.

" Perhaps you have," rejoined the immovable Mr. Folair ; " if you have, he said this before he was silenced : Lenville says that you're a regular stick of an actor, and that it's only the mystery about you that has caused you to go down with the people here, and that Crummles keeps it up for his own sake ; though Lenville says he don't believe there's anything at all in it, except your having got into a scrape and run away from somewhere, for doing something or other."

" Oh !" said Nicholas, forcing a smile.

" That's a part of what he says," added Mr. Folair. " I mention it as the friend of both parties, and in strict confidence. *I* don't agree with him, you know. He says he takes Digby to be more knave than fool ; and old Fluggers, who does the heavy business you know, *he* says that when he delivered messages at Covent Garden the season before last, there used to be a pickpocket hovering about the coach-stand who had exactly the face of Digby ; though, as he very properly says, Digby may not be the same, but only his brother, or some near relation."

" Oh !" cried Nicholas again.

" Yes," said Mr. Folair, with undisturbed calmness, " that's what they say. I thought I'd tell you, because really you ought to know. Oh ! here's this blessed phenomenon at last. Ugh, you little imposition, I should like to — quite ready, my darling,—humbug—Ring up Mrs. G., and let the favourite wake 'em."

Uttering in a loud voice such of the latter allusions as were com-

plimentary to the unconscious phenomenon, and giving the rest in a
confidential "aside" to Nicholas, Mr. Folair followed the ascent of the
curtain with his eyes, regarded with a sneer the reception of Miss
Crummles as the Maiden, and, falling back a step or two to advance
with the better effect, uttered a preliminary howl, and "went on"
chattering his teeth and brandishing his tin tomahawk as the Indian
Savage.

"So these are some of the stories they invent about us, and bandy
from mouth to mouth!" thought Nicholas. "If a man would commit
an inexpiable offence against any society, large or small, let him be
successful. They will forgive him any crime but that."

"You surely don't mind what that malicious creature says, Mr.
Johnson?" observed Miss Snevellicci in her most winning tones.

"Not I," replied Nicholas. "If I were going to remain here, I
might think it worth my while to embroil myself. As it is, let them
talk till they are hoarse. But here," added Nicholas, as Smike
approached, "here comes the subject of a portion of their good-nature,
so let he and I say good night together."

"No, I will not let either of you say anything of the kind," returned
Miss Snevellicci. "You must come home and see mama, who only
came to Portsmouth to-day, and is dying to behold you. Led, my
dear, persuade Mr. Johnson."

"Oh, I'm sure," returned Miss Ledrook, with considerable vivacity,
"if *you* can't persuade him—" Miss Ledrook said no more, but
intimated, by a dexterous playfulness, that if Miss Snevellicci couldn't
persuade him, nobody could.

"Mr. and Mrs. Lillyvick have taken lodgings in our house, and
share our sitting-room for the present," said Miss Snevellicci. "Won't
that induce you?"

"Surely," returned Nicholas, "I can require no possible inducement
beyond your invitation."

"Oh no! I dare say," rejoined Miss Snevellicci. And Miss
Ledrook said, "Upon my word!" Upon which Miss Snevellicci said
that Miss Ledrook was a giddy thing; and Miss Ledrook said that
Miss Snevellicci needn't colour up quite so much; and Miss Snevellicci
beat Miss Ledrook, and Miss Ledrook beat Miss Snevellicci.

"Come," said Miss Ledrook, "it's high time we were there, or we
shall have poor Mrs. Snevellicci thinking that you have run away with
her daughter, Mr. Johnson; and then we should have a pretty to do."

"My dear Led," remonstrated Miss Snevellicci, "how you do talk!"

Miss Ledrook made no answer, but taking Smike's arm in hers, left
her friend and Nicholas to follow at their pleasure; which it pleased
them, or rather pleased Nicholas who had no great fancy for a *tête-à-
tête* under the circumstances, to do at once.

There were not wanting matters of conversation when they reached
the street, for it turned out that Miss Snevellicci had a small basket to
carry home, and Miss Ledrook a small band-box, both containing such
minor articles of theatrical costume as the lady performers usually
carried to and fro every evening. Nicholas would insist upon carrying

the basket, and Miss Snevellicci would insist upon carrying it herself, which gave rise to a struggle, in which Nicholas captured the basket and the band-box likewise. Then Nicholas said, that he wondered what could possibly be inside the basket, and attempted to peep in, whereat Miss Snevellicci screamed, and declared that if she thought he had seen, she was sure she should faint away. This declaration was followed by a similar attempt on the band-box, and similar demonstrations on the part of Miss Ledrook, and then both ladies vowed that they wouldn't move a step further until Nicholas had promised that he wouldn't offer to peep again. At last Nicholas pledged himself to betray no further curiosity, and they walked on: both ladies giggling very much, and declaring that they never had seen such a wicked creature in all their born days—never.

Lightening the way with such pleasantry as this, they arrived at the tailor's house in no time; and here they made quite a little party, there being present, besides Mr. Lillyvick and Mrs. Lillyvick, not only Miss Snevellicci's mama, but her papa also. And an uncommonly fine man Miss Snevellicci's papa was, with a hook nose, and a white forehead, and curly black hair, and high cheek bones, and altogether quite a handsome face, only a little pimply as though with drinking. He had a very broad chest had Miss Snevellicci's papa, and he wore a threadbare blue dress coat buttoned with gilt buttons tight across it; and he no sooner saw Nicholas come into the room, than he whipped the two forefingers of his right hand in between the two centre buttons, and sticking his other arm gracefully a-kimbo seemed to say, "Now, here I am, my buck, and what have you got to say to me?"

Such was, and in such an attitude sat, Miss Snevellicci's papa, who had been in the profession ever since he had first played the ten-year-old imps in the Christmas pantomimes; who could sing a little, dance a little, fence a little, act a little, and do everything a little, but not much; who had been sometimes in the ballet, and sometimes in the chorus, at every theatre in London; who was always selected in virtue of his figure to play the military visitors and the speechless noblemen; who always wore a smart dress, and came on arm-in-arm with a smart lady in short petticoats,—and always did it too with such an air that people in the pit had been several times known to cry out "Bravo!" under the impression that he was somebody. Such was Miss Snevellicci's papa, upon whom some envious persons cast the imputation that he occasionally beat Miss Snevellicci's mama, who was still a dancer, with a neat little figure and some remains of good looks; and who now sat, as she danced,—being rather too old for the full glare of the foot-lights,—in the back ground.

To these good people Nicholas was presented with much formality. The introduction being completed, Miss Snevellicci's papa (who was scented with rum and water) said that he was delighted to make the acquaintance of a gentleman so highly talented; and furthermore remarked, that there hadn't been such a hit made—no, not since the first appearance of his friend Mr. Glavormelly, at the Coburg.

"You have seen him, sir?" said Miss Snevellicci's papa.

" No, really I never did," replied Nicholas.

" You never saw my friend Glavormelly, Sir ! " said Miss Snevellicci's papa. " Then you have never seen acting yet. If he had lived——"

" Oh, he is dead, is he ?" interrupted Nicholas.

" He is," said Mr. Snevellicci, " but he isn't in Westminster Abbey, more's the shame. He was a——. Well, no matter. He is gone to that bourne from whence no traveller returns. I hope he is appreciated *there*."

So saying, Miss Snevellicci's papa rubbed the tip of his nose with a very yellow silk handkerchief, and gave the company to understand that these recollections overcame him.

" Well, Mr. Lillyvick," said Nicholas, " and how are you ?"

" Quite well, Sir," replied the collector. " There is nothing like the married state, Sir, depend upon it."

" Indeed !" said Nicholas, laughing.

" Ah ! nothing like it Sir," replied Mr. Lillyvick solemnly. " How do you think," whispered the collector, drawing him aside, " How do you think she looks to-night ?"

" As handsome as ever," replied Nicholas, glancing at the late Miss Petowker.

" Why, there's a air about her, Sir," whispered the collector, " that I never saw in anybody. Look at her now she moves to put the kettle on. There ! Isn't it fascination, Sir ?"

" You're a lucky man," said Nicholas.

" Ha, ha, ha !" rejoined the collector. " No. Do you think I am though, eh ? Perhaps I may be, perhaps I may be. I say, I couldn't have done much better if I had been a young man, could I ? You couldn't have done much better yourself, could you—eh—could you ?" With such inquiries, and many more such, Mr. Lillyvick jerked his elbow into Nicholas's side, and chuckled till his face became quite purple in the attempt to keep down his satisfaction.

By this time the cloth had been laid under the joint superintendence of all the ladies, upon two tables put together, one being high and narrow, and the other low and broad. There were oysters at the top, sausages at the bottom, a pair of snuffers in the centre, and baked potatoes wherever it was most convenient to put them. Two additional chairs were brought in from the bedroom ; Miss Snevellicci sat at the head of the table, and Mr. Lillyvick at the foot ; and Nicholas had not only the honour of sitting next Miss Snevellicci, but of having Miss Snevellicci's mama on his right hand, and Miss Snevellicci's papa over the way. In short, he was the hero of the feast ; and when the table was cleared and something warm introduced, Miss Snevellicci's papa got up and proposed his health in a speech containing such affecting allusions to his coming departure, that Miss Snevellicci wept, and was compelled to retire into the bedroom.

" Hush ! Don't take any notice of it, said Miss Ledrook, peeping in from the bedroom. " Say, when she comes back, that she exerts herself too much."

Miss Ledrook eked out this speech with so many mysterious nods and frowns before she shut the door again, that a profound silence came upon all the company, during which Miss Snevellicci's papa looked very big indeed—several sizes larger than life—at everybody in turn, but particularly at Nicholas, and kept on perpetually emptying his tumbler and filling it again, until the ladies returned in a cluster, with Miss Snevellicci among them.

" You needn't alarm yourself a bit, Mr. Snevellicci," said Mrs. Lilly-vick. " She is only a little weak and nervous ; she has been so ever since the morning."

" Oh," said Mr. Snevellici, " that's all, is it ?"

" Oh yes, that's all. Don't make a fuss about it," cried all the ladies together.

Now this was not exactly the kind of reply suited to Mr. Snevellicci's importance as a man and a father, so he picked out the unfortunate Mrs. Snevellicci, and asked her what the devil she meant by talking to him in that way.

" Dear me, my dear——" said Mrs. Snevellicci.

" Don't call me your dear, ma'am," said Mr. Snevellicci, " if you please."

" Pray, pa, don't," interposed Miss Snevellicci.

" Don't what, my child ?"

" Talk in that way."

" Why not ?" said Mr. Snevellicci. " I hope you don't suppose there's anybody here who is to prevent my talking as I like ?"

" Nobody wants to, pa," rejoined his daughter.

" Nobody would if they did want to," said Mr. Snevellicci. " I am not ashamed of myself. Snevellicci is my name ; I'm to be found in Broad Court, Bow Street, when I'm in town. If I'm not at home, let any man ask for me at the stage door. Damme, they know me at the stage door I suppose. Most men have seen my portrait at the cigar shop round the corner. I've been mentioned in the newspapers before now, haven't I ? Talk ! I'll tell you what ; if I found out that any man had been tampering with the affections of my daughter, I wouldn't talk. I'd astonish him without talking ;—that's my way."

So saying, Mr. Snevellicci struck the palm of his left hand three smart blows with his clenched fist : pulled a phantom nose with his right thumb and fore finger, and swallowed another glassful at a draught. " That's my way," repeated Mr. Snevellicci.

Most public characters have their failings ; and the truth is that Mr. Snevellicci was a little addicted to drinking ; or, if the whole truth must be told, that he was scarcely ever sober. He knew in his cups three distinct stages of intoxication,—the dignified—the quarrelsome—the amorous. When professionally engaged he never got beyond the dignified ; in private circles he went through all three, passing from one to another with a rapidity of transition often rather perplexing to those who had not the honour of his acquaintance.

Thus Mr. Snevellicci had no sooner swallowed another glassful than he smiled upon all present in happy forgetfulness of having exhibited symptoms of pugnacity, and proposed "The ladies—bless their hearts!" in a most vivacious manner.

"I love 'em," said Mr. Snevellicci, looking round the table, "I love 'em, every one."

"Not every one," reasoned Mr. Lillyvick, mildly.

"Yes, every one," repeated Mr. Snevellicci.

"That would include the married ladies, you know," said Mr. Lillyvick.

"I love them too, Sir," said Mr. Snevellicci.

The collector looked into the surrounding faces with an aspect of grave astonishment, seeming to say, "This is a nice man!" and appeared a little surprised that Mrs. Lillyvick's manner yielded no evidences of horror and indignation.

"One good turn deserves another," said Mr. Snevellicci. "I love them and they love me." And as if this avowal were not made in sufficient disregard and defiance of all moral obligations, what did Mr. Snevellicci do? He winked — winked, openly and undisguisedly; winked with his right eye—upon Henrietta Lillyvick!

The collector fell back in his chair in the intensity of his astonishment. If anybody had winked at her as Henrietta Petowker, it would have been indecorous in the last degree; but as Mrs. Lillyvick! While he thought of it in a cold perspiration, and wondered whether it was possible that he could be dreaming, Mr. Snevellicci repeated the wink, and drinking to Mrs. Lillyvick in dumb show, actually blew her a kiss! Mr. Lillyvick left his chair, walked straight up to the other end of the table, and fell upon him—literally fell upon him—instantaneously. Mr. Lillyvick was no light weight, and consequently when he fell upon Mr. Snevellicci, Mr. Snevellicci fell under the table. Mr. Lillyvick followed him, and the ladies screamed.

"What is the matter with the men,—are they mad!" cried Nicholas, diving under the table, dragging up the collector by main force, and thrusting him, all doubled up, into a chair, as if he had been a stuffed figure. "What do you mean to do? what do you want to do? what is the matter with you?"

While Nicholas raised up the collector, Smike had performed the same office for Mr. Snevellicci, who now regarded his late adversary in tipsy amazement.

"Look here, Sir," replied Mr. Lillyvick, pointing to his astonished wife, "here is purity and elegance combined, whose feelings have been outraged—violated, Sir!"

"Lor, what nonsense he talks!" exclaimed Mrs. Lillyvick in answer to the inquiring look of Nicholas. "Nobody has said anything to me."

"Said, Henrietta!" cried the collector. "Didn't I see him——"

Mr. Lillyvick couldn't bring himself to utter the word, but he counterfeited the motion of the eye.

"Well!" cried Mrs. Lillyvick. "Do you suppose nobody is ever to look at me? A pretty thing to be married indeed, if that was law!"

"You didn't mind it?" cried the collector.

" Mind it !" repeated Mrs. Lillyvick contemptuously. "You ought to go down on your knees and beg everybody's pardon, that you ought."

" Pardon, my dear ?" said the dismayed collector.

" Yes, and mine first," replied Mrs. Lillyvick. " Do you suppose *I* ain't the best judge of what's proper and what's improper ?"

" To be sure," cried all the ladies. " Do you suppose *we* shouldn't be the first to speak, if there was anything that ought to be taken notice of ?"

" Do you suppose *they* don't know, Sir ?" said Miss Snevellicci's papa, pulling up his collar, and muttering something about a punching of heads, and being only withheld by considerations of age. With which Miss Snevellicci's papa looked steadily and sternly at Mr. Lillyvick for some seconds, and then rising deliberately from his chair, kissed the ladies all round, beginning with Mrs. Lillyvick.

The unhappy collector looked piteously at his wife, as if to see whether there was any one trait of Miss Petowker left in Mrs. Lillyvick, and finding too surely that there was not, begged pardon of all the company with great humility, and sat down such a crest-fallen, dispirited, disenchanted man, that despite all his selfishness and dotage, he was quite an object of compassion.

Miss Snevellicci's papa being greatly exalted by this triumph, and incontestible proof of his popularity with the fair sex, quickly grew convivial, not to say uproarious; volunteering more than one song of no inconsiderable length, and regaling the social circle between-whiles with recollections of divers splendid women who had been supposed to entertain a passion for himself, several of whom he toasted by name, taking occasion to remark at the same time that if he had been a little more alive to his own interest, he might have been rolling at that moment in his chariot-and-four. These reminiscences appeared to awaken no very torturing pangs in the breast of Mrs. Snevellicci, who was sufficiently occupied in descanting to Nicholas upon the manifold accomplishments and merits of her daughter. Nor was the young lady herself at all behind-hand in displaying her choicest allurements; but these, heightened as they were by the artifices of Miss Ledrook, had no effect whatever in increasing the attentions of Nicholas, who, with the precedent of Miss Squeers still fresh in his memory steadily resisted every fascination, and placed so strict a guard upon his behaviour that when he had taken his leave the ladies were unanimous in pronouncing him quite a monster of insensibility.

Next day the posters appeared in due course, and the public were informed, in all the colours of the rainbow, and in letters afflicted with every possible variation of spinal deformity, how that Mr. Johnson would have the honour of making his last appearance that evening, and how that an early application for places was requested, in consequence of the extraordinary overflow attendant on his performances,—it being a remarkable fact in theatrical history, but one long since established beyond dispute, that it is a hopeless endeavour to attract people to a theatre unless they can be first brought to believe that they will never get into it.

Nicholas was somewhat at a loss, on entering the theatre at night, to account for the unusual perturbation and excitement visible in the countenances of all the company, but he was not long in doubt as to the cause, for before he could make any inquiry respecting it Mr. Crummles approached, and in an agitated tone of voice, informed him that there was a London manager in the boxes.

" It's the phenomenon, depend upon it, Sir," said Crummles, dragging Nicholas to the little hole in the curtain that he might look through at the London manager. " I have not the smallest doubt it's the fame of the phenomenon—that's the man; him in the great-coat and no shirt-collar. She shall have ten pound a-week, Johnson; she shall not appear on the London boards for a farthing less. They shan't engage her either, unless they engage Mrs. Crummles too—twenty pound a-week for the pair; or I'll tell you what, I'll throw in myself and the two boys, and they shall have the family for thirty. I can't say fairer than that. They must take us all, if none of us will go without the others. That's the way some of the London people do, and it always answers. Thirty pound a-week—it's too cheap, Johnson. It's dirt cheap."

Nicholas replied, that it certainly was; and Mr. Vincent Crummles taking several huge pinches of snuff to compose his feelings, hurried away to tell Mrs. Crummles that he had quite settled the only terms that could be accepted, and had resolved not to abate one single farthing.

When everybody was dressed and the curtain went up, the excitement occasioned by the presence of the London manager increased a thousandfold. Everybody happened to know that the London manager had come down specially to witness his or her own performance, and all were in a flutter of anxiety and expectation. Some of those who were not on in the first scene, hurried to the wings, and there stretched their necks to have a peep at him; others stole up into the two little private boxes over the stage-doors, and from that position reconnoitred the London manager. Once the London manager was seen to smile— he smiled at the comic countryman's pretending to catch a blue-bottle, while Mrs. Crummles was making her greatest effect. " Very good, my fine fellow," said Mr. Crummles, shaking his fist at the comic countryman when he came off, " you leave this company next Saturday night."

In the same way, everybody who was on the stage beheld no audience but one individual; everybody played to the London manager. When Mr. Lenville in a sudden burst of passion called the emperor a miscreant, and then biting his glove, said, " But I must dissemble," instead of looking gloomily at the boards and so waiting for his cue, as is proper in such cases, he kept his eye fixed upon the London manager. When Miss Bravassa sang her song at her lover, who according to custom stood ready to shake hands with her between the verses, they looked, not at each other but at the London manager. Mr. Crummles died point blank at him; and when the two guards came in to take the body off after a very hard death, it was seen to open its eyes and glance at the London manager. At length the London manager was discovered to be asleep, and shortly after that he woke up and went away, whereupon all the company fell foul of the unhappy comic countryman, declaring that his buffoonery was the sole cause ; and Mr. Crummles said, that he had put up with it a long time, but that he really couldn't stand it any longer, and therefore would feel obliged by his looking out for another engagement.

All this was the occasion of much amusement to Nicholas, whose only feeling upon the subject was one of sincere satisfaction that the great man went away before he appeared. He went through his part in the two last pieces as briskly as he could, and having been received with unbounded favour and unprecedented applause—so said the bills for next day, which had been printed an hour or two before —he took Smike's arm and walked home to bed.

With the post next morning came a letter from Newman Noggs, very inky, very short, very dirty, very small, and very mysterious, urging Nicholas to return to London instantly ; not to lose an instant ; to be there that night if possible.

" I will," said Nicholas. " Heaven knows I have remained here for the best, and sorely against my own will ; but even now I may have dallied too long. What can have happened ? Smike, my good fellow, here—take my purse. Put our things together, and pay what little debts we owe—quick, and we shall be in time for the morning coach. I will only tell them that we are going, and will return to you immediately."

So saying, he took his hat, and hurrying away to the lodgings of Mr. Crummles, applied his hand to the knocker with such hearty good-will, that he awakened that gentleman, who was still in bed, and caused Mr. Bulph the pilot to take his morning's pipe very nearly out of his mouth in the extremity of his surprise.

The door being opened, Nicholas ran up-stairs without any ceremony, and bursting into the darkened sitting-room on the one pair front, found that the two Master Crummleses had sprung out of the sofa-bedstead and were putting on their clothes with great rapidity, under the impression that it was the middle of the night, and the next house was on fire.

Before he could undeceive them, Mr. Crummles came down in a flannel-gown and nightcap ; and to him Nicholas briefly explained that circumstances had occurred which rendered it necessary for him to repair to London immediately.

" So good bye," said Nicholas ; " good bye, good bye."

He was half-way down stairs before Mr. Crummles had sufficiently recovered his surprise to gasp out something about the posters.

" I can't help it," replied Nicholas. " Set whatever I may have earned this week against them, or if that will not repay you, say at once what will. Quick, quick."

" We'll cry quits about that," returned Crummles. " But can't we have one last night more ?"

" Not an hour—not a minute," replied Nicholas, impatiently.

"Won't you stop to say something to Mrs. Crummles?" asked the manager, following him down to the door.

"I couldn't stop if it were to prolong my life a score of years," rejoined Nicholas. "Here, take my hand, and with it my hearty thanks.—Oh! that I should have been fooling here!"

Accompanying these words with an impatient stamp upon the ground, he tore himself from the manager's detaining grasp, and darting rapidly down the street was out of sight in an instant.

"Dear me, dear me," said Mr. Crummles, looking wistfully towards the point at which he had just disappeared; "if he only acted like that, what a deal of money he'd draw! He should have kept upon this circuit; he'd have been very useful to me. But he don't know what's good for him. He is an impetuous youth. Young men are rash, very rash."

Mr. Crummles being in a moralizing mood, might possibly have moralized for some minutes longer if he had not mechanically put his hand towards his waistcoat pocket, where he was accustomed to keep his snuff. The absence of any pocket at all in the usual direction, suddenly recalled to his recollection the fact that he had no waistcoat on; and this leading him to a contemplation of the extreme scantiness of his attire, he shut the door abruptly, and retired up-stairs with great precipitation.

Smike had made good speed while Nicholas was absent, and with his help everything was soon ready for their departure. They scarcely stopped to take a morsel of breakfast, and in less than half an hour arrived at the coach-office: quite out of breath with the haste they had made to reach it in time. There were yet a few minutes to spare, so, having secured the places, Nicholas hurried into a slopseller's hard by, and bought Smike a great-coat. It would have been rather large for a substantial yeoman, but the shopman averring (and with considerable truth) that it was a most uncommon fit, Nicholas would have purchased it in his impatience if it had been twice the size.

As they hurried up to the coach, which was now in the open street and all ready for starting, Nicholas was not a little astonished to find himself suddenly clutched in a close and violent embrace, which nearly took him off his legs; nor was his amazement at all lessened by hearing the voice of Mr. Crummles exclaim "It is he—my friend, my friend!"

"Bless my heart," cried Nicholas, struggling in the manager's arms, "what are you about?"

The manager made no reply, but strained him to his breast again, exclaiming as he did so, "Farewell, my noble, my lion-hearted boy!"

In fact, Mr. Crummles, who could never lose any opportunity for professional display, had turned out for the express purpose of taking a public farewell of Nicholas; and to render it the more imposing, he was now, to that young gentleman's most profound annoyance, inflicting upon him a rapid succession of stage embraces, which, as everybody knows, are performed by the embracer's laying his or her chin on the shoulder of the object of affection, and looking over it. This Mr. Crummles did in the highest style of melo-drama, pouring forth at the

Theatrical emotion of Mr Vincent Crummles.

same time all the most dismal forms of farewell he could think of, out of the stock pieces. Nor was this all, for the elder Master Crummles was going through a similar ceremony with Smike ; while Master Percy Crummles, with a very little second-hand camlet cloak, worn theatrically over his left shoulder, stood by, in the attitude of an attendant officer, waiting to convey the two victims to the scaffold.

The lookers-on laughed very heartily, and as it was as well to put a good face upon the matter, Nicholas laughed too when he had succeeded in disengaging himself; and rescuing the astonished Smike, climbed up to the coach roof after him, and kissed his hand in honour of the absent Mrs. Crummles as they rolled away.

CHAPTER XXXI.

OF RALPH NICKLEBY AND NEWMAN NOGGS, AND SOME WISE PRECAU-
TIONS, THE SUCCESS OR FAILURE OF WHICH WILL APPEAR IN
THE SEQUEL.

In blissful unconsciousness that his nephew was hastening at the utmost speed of four good horses towards his sphere of action, and that every passing minute diminished the distance between them, Ralph Nickleby sat that morning occupied in his customary avocations, and yet unable to prevent his thoughts wandering from time to time back to the interview which had taken place between himself and his niece on the previous day. At such intervals, after a few moments of abstraction, Ralph would mutter some peevish interjection, and apply himself with renewed steadiness of purpose to the ledger before him, but again and again the same train of thought came back despite all his efforts to prevent it, confusing him in his calculations, and utterly distracting his attention from the figures over which he bent. At length Ralph laid down his pen, and threw himself back in his chair as though he had made up his mind to allow the obtrusive current of reflection to take its own course, and, by giving it full scope, to rid himself of it effectually.

" I am not a man to be moved by a pretty face," muttered Ralph sternly. " There is a grinning skull beneath it, and men like me who look and work below the surface see that, and not its delicate covering. And yet I almost like the girl, or should if she had been less proudly and squeamishly brought up. If the boy were drowned or hanged, and the mother dead, this house should be her home. I wish they were, with all my soul."

Notwithstanding the deadly hatred which Ralph felt towards Nicholas, and the bitter contempt with which he sneered at poor Mrs. Nickleby—notwithstanding the baseness with which he had behaved, and was then behaving, and would behave again if his interest prompted him, towards Kate herself—still there was, strange though it may seem, something humanizing and even gentle in his thoughts at that moment. He thought of what his home might be if Kate were there ; he placed her in the empty chair, looked upon her, heard her speak ; he felt again upon his arm the gentle pressure of the trembling hand ; he strewed his costly rooms with the hundred silent tokens of feminine presence and occupation ; he came back again to the cold fireside and the silent dreary splendour ; and in that one glimpse of a better nature, born as it was in selfish thoughts, the rich man felt himself friendless, childless, and alone. Gold, for the instant, lost its lustre in his eyes, for there were countless treasures of the heart which it could never purchase.

A very slight circumstance was sufficient to banish such reflections from the mind of such a man. As Ralph looked vacantly out across the yard towards the window of the other office, he became suddenly aware of the earnest observation of Newman Noggs, who, with his red nose almost touching the glass, feigned to be mending a pen with a rusty fragment of a knife, but was in reality staring at his employer with a countenance of the closest and most eager scrutiny.

Ralph exchanged his dreamy posture for his accustomed business attitude : the face of Newman disappeared, and the train of thought took to flight, all simultaneously and in an instant.

After a few minutes, Ralph rang his bell. Newman answered the summons, and Ralph raised his eyes stealthily to his face, as if he almost feared to read there, a knowledge of his recent thoughts .

There was not the smallest speculation, however, in the countenance of Newman Noggs. If it be possible to imagine a man, with two eyes in his head, and both wide open, looking in no direction whatever, and seeing nothing, Newman appeared to be that man while Ralph Nickleby regarded him.

" How now ?" growled Ralph.

" Oh !" said Newman, throwing some intelligence into his eyes all at once, and dropping them on his master, " I thought you rang. With which laconic remark Newman turned round and hobbled away.

" Stop !" said Ralph.

Newman stopped ; not at all disconcerted.

" I did ring."

" I knew you did."

" Then why do you offer to go if you know that ?"

" I thought you rang to say you didn't ring," replied Newman. " You often do."

" How dare you pry, and peer, and stare at me, sirrah ?" demanded Ralph.

" Stare !" cried Newman, " at you ! Ha, ha !" which was all the explanation Newman deigned to offer.

" Be careful, sir," said Ralph, looking steadily at him. " Let me have no drunken fooling here. Do you see this parcel ?"

" It's big enough," rejoined Newman.

" Carry it into the City ; to Cross, in Broad Street, and leave it there—quick. Do you hear ?"

Newman gave a dogged kind of nod to express an affirmative reply, and, leaving the room for a few seconds, returned with his hat. Having made various ineffective attempts to fit the parcel (which was some two feet square) into the crown thereof, Newman took it under his arm, and after putting on his fingerless gloves with great precision and nicety, keeping his eyes fixed upon Mr. Ralph Nickleby all the time, he adjusted his hat upon his head with as much care, real or pretended, as if it were a bran-new one of the most expensive quality, and at last departed on his errand.

He executed his commission with great promptitude and despatch, only calling at one public-house for half a minute, and even that might be said to be in his way, for he went in at one door and came out at the other; but as he returned and had got so far homewards as the Strand, Newman began to loiter with the uncertain air of a man who has not quite made up his mind whether to halt or go straight forwards. After a very short consideration, the former inclination prevailed, and making towards the point he had had in his mind, Newman knocked a modest double-knock, or rather a nervous single one, at Miss La Creevy's door.

It was opened by a strange servant, on whom the odd figure of the visitor did not appear to make the most favourable impression possible, inasmuch as she no sooner saw him than she very nearly closed it, and placing herself in the narrow gap, inquired what he wanted. But Newman merely uttering the monosyllable " Noggs," as if it were some cabalistic word, at sound of which bolts would fly back and doors open, pushed briskly past and gained the door of Miss La Creevy's sitting-room, before the astonished servant could offer any opposition.

" Walk in if you please," said Miss La Creevy in reply to the sound of Newman's knuckles; and in he walked accordingly.

" Bless us!" cried Miss La Creevy, starting as Newman bolted in ; " what did you want, Sir ?"

" You have forgotten me," said Newman, with an inclination of the head. " I wonder at that. That nobody should remember me who knew me in other days, is natural enough; but there are few people who, seeing me once, forget me *now*." He glanced, as he spoke, at his shabby clothes and paralytic limb, and slightly shook his head.

" I did forget you, I declare," said Miss La Creevy, rising to receive Newman, who met her half-way, " and I am ashamed of myself for doing so ; for you are a kind, good creature, Mr. Noggs. Sit down and tell me all about Miss Nickleby. Poor dear thing! I haven't seen her for this many a week."

" How's that ?" asked Newman.

" Why, the truth is, Mr. Noggs," said Miss La Creevy, " that I have been out on a visit—the first visit I have made for fifteen years."

" That is a long time," said Newman, sadly.

" So it is a very long time to look back upon in years, though, somehow or other, thank Heaven, the solitary days roll away peacefully and happily enough," replied the miniature painter. " I have a brother, Mr. Noggs—the only relation I have—and all that time I never saw him once. Not that we ever quarrelled, but he was apprenticed down in the country, and he got married there, and new ties and affections springing up about him, he forgot a poor little woman like me, as it was very reasonable he should, you know. Don't suppose that I complain about that, because I always said to myself, ' It is very natural ; poor dear John is making his way in the world, and has a wife to tell his cares and troubles to, and children now to play about him, so God bless him and them, and send we may all meet together one day where we shall part no more.' But what do you think, Mr. Noggs," said the miniature painter, brightening up and clapping her hands, " of that very same brother coming up to London at last, and never resting till he found me out ; what do you think of his coming here and sitting down in that very chair, and crying like a child because he was so glad to see me—what do you think of his insisting on taking me down all the way into the country to his own house (quite a sumptuous place, Mr. Noggs, with a large garden and I don't know how many fields, and a man in livery waiting at table, and cows and horses and pigs and I don't know what besides), and making me stay a whole month, and pressing me to stop there all my life—yes, all my life—and so did his wife, and so did the children— and there were four of them, and one, the eldest girl of all, they—they had named her after me eight good years before, they had indeed. I never was so happy ; in all my life I never was !" The worthy soul hid her face in her handkerchief, and sobbed aloud ; for it was the first opportunity she had had of unburdening her heart, and it would have its way.

" But bless my life," said Miss La Creevy, wiping her eyes after a short pause, and cramming her handkerchief into her pocket with great bustle and despatch ; " what a foolish creature I must seem to you, Mr. Noggs ! I shouldn't have said anything about it, only I wanted to explain to you how it was I hadn't seen Miss Nickleby."

" Have you seen the old lady ?" asked Newman.

" You mean Mrs. Nickleby ?" said Miss La Creevy. " Then I tell you what, Mr Noggs, if you want to keep in the good books in that quarter, you had better not call her the old lady any more, for I suspect she wouldn't be best pleased to hear you. Yes, I went there the night before last, but she was quite on the high ropes about something, and was so grand and mysterious, that I couldn't make anything of her ; so, to tell you the truth, I took it into my head to be grand too, and came away in state. I thought she would have come round again before this, but she hasn't been here."

" About Miss Nickleby— " said Newman.

" Why she was here twice while I was away," returned Miss La Creevy. " I was afraid she mightn't like to have me calling on her among those great folks in what's-its-name Place, so I thought I'd wait a day or two, and if I didn't see her, write."

" Ah !" exclaimed Newman, cracking his fingers.

" However, I want to hear all the news about them from you," said

Miss La Creevy. "How is the old rough and tough monster of Golden Square? Well, of course; such people always are. I don't mean how is he in health, but how is he going on; how is he behaving himself?"

"Damn him!" cried Newman, dashing his cherished hat on the floor; "like a false hound."

"Gracious, Mr. Noggs, you quite terrify me!" exclaimed Miss La Creevy, turning pale.

"I should have spoilt his features yesterday afternoon if I could have afforded it," said Newman, moving restlessly about, and shaking his fist at a portrait of Mr. Canning over the mantel-piece. "I was very near it. I was obliged to put my hands in my pockets, and keep 'em there very tight. I shall do it some day in that little back-parlour, I know I shall. I should have done it before now, if I hadn't been afraid of making bad worse. I shall double-lock myself in with him and have it out before I die, I'm quite certain of it."

"I shall scream if you don't compose yourself, Mr. Noggs," said Miss La Creevy; "I'm sure I shan't be able to help it."

"Never mind," rejoined Newman, darting violently to and fro. "He's coming up to-night: I wrote to tell him. He little thinks I know; he little thinks I care. Cunning scoundrel! he don't think that. Not he, not he. Never mind, I'll thwart him—*I*, Newman Noggs. Ho, ho, the rascal!"

Lashing himself up to an extravagant pitch of fury, Newman Noggs jerked himself about the room with the most eccentric motion ever beheld in a human being: now sparring at the little miniatures on the wall, and now giving himself violent thumps on the head, as if to heighten the delusion, until he sank down in his former seat quite breathless and exhausted.

"There," said Newman, picking up his hat; "that's done me good. Now I'm better, and I'll tell you all about it."

It took some little time to reassure Miss La Creevy, who had been almost frightened out of her senses by this remarkable demonstration; but that done, Newman faithfully related all that had passed in the interview between Kate and her uncle, prefacing his narrative with a statement of his previous suspicions on the subject, and his reasons for forming them; and concluding with a communication of the step he had taken in secretly writing to Nicholas.

Though little Miss La Creevy's indignation was not so singularly displayed as Newman's, it was scarcely inferior in violence and intensity. Indeed if Ralph Nickleby had happened to make his appearance in the room at that moment, there is some doubt whether he would not have found Miss La Creevy a more dangerous opponent than even Newman Noggs himself.

"God forgive me for saying so," said Miss La Creevy, as a wind-up to all her expressions of anger, "but I really feel as if I could stick this into him with pleasure."

It was not a very awful weapon that Miss La Creevy held, it being in fact nothing more nor less than a black-lead pencil; but discovering

x

her mistake, the little portrait painter exchanged it for a mother-of-pearl fruit knife, wherewith, in proof of her desperate thoughts, she made a lunge as she spoke, which would have scarcely disturbed the crumb of a half-quartern loaf.

"She won't stop where she is, after to-night," said Newman. "That's a comfort."

"Stop!" cried Miss La Creevy, "she should have left there, weeks ago."

—"If we had known of this," rejoined Newman. "But we didn't. Nobody could properly interfere but her mother or brother. The mother's weak—poor thing—weak. The dear young man will be here to-night."

"Heart alive!" cried Miss La Creevy. "He will do something desperate, Mr. Noggs, if you tell him all at once."

Newman left off rubbing his hands, and assumed a thoughtful look.

"Depend upon it," said Miss La Creevy, earnestly, "if you are not very careful in breaking out the truth to him, he will do some violence upon his uncle or one of these men that will bring some terrible calamity upon his own head, and grief and sorrow to us all."

"I never thought of that," rejoined Newman, his countenance falling more and more. "I came to ask you to receive his sister in case he brought her here, but——"

"But this is a matter of much greater importance," interrupted Miss La Creevy; "that you might have been sure of before you came, but the end of this, nobody can foresee, unless you are very guarded and careful."

"What can I do?" cried Newman, scratching his head with an air of great vexation and perplexity. "If he was to talk of pistolling 'em all, I should be obliged to say, 'Certainly—serve 'em right.'"

Miss La Creevy could not suppress a small shriek on hearing this, and instantly set about extorting a solemn pledge from Newman that he would use his utmost endeavours to pacify the wrath of Nicholas; which, after some demur, was conceded. They then consulted together on the safest and surest mode of communicating to him the circumstances which had rendered his presence necessary.

"He must have time to cool before he can possibly do any thing," said Miss La Creevy. "That is of the greatest consequence. He must not be told until late at night."

"But he'll be in town between six and seven this evening," replied Newman. "*I* can't keep it from him when he asks me."

"Then you must go out, Mr. Noggs," said Miss La Creevy. "You can easily have been kept away by business, and must not return till nearly midnight."

"Then he'll come straight here," retorted Newman.

"So I suppose," observed Miss La Creevy; "but he won't find me at home, for I'll go straight to the City the instant you leave me, make up matters with Mrs. Nickleby, and take her away to the theatre, so that he may not even know where his sister lives."

Upon further discussion, this appeared the safest and most feasible mode of proceeding that could possibly be adopted. Therefore it was finally determined that matters should be so arranged, and Newman, after listening to many supplementary cautions and entreaties, took his leave of Miss La Creevy and trudged back to Golden Square; ruminating as he went upon a vast number of possibilities and impossibilities which crowded upon his brain, and arose out of the conversation that had just terminated.

CHAPTER XXXII.

RELATING CHIEFLY TO SOME REMARKABLE CONVERSATION, AND SOME REMARKABLE PROCEEDINGS TO WHICH IT GIVES RISE.

"London at last!" cried Nicholas, throwing back his great-coat and rousing Smike from a long nap. "It seemed to me as though we should never reach it."

"And yet you came along at a tidy pace too," observed the coachman, looking over his shoulder at Nicholas with no very pleasant expression of countenance.

"Ay, I know that," was the reply; "but I have been very anxious to be at my journey's end, and that makes the way seem long."

"Well," remarked the coachman, "if the way seemed long with such cattle as you've sat behind, you *must* have been most uncommon anxious;" and so saying, he let out his whip-lash and touched up a little boy on the calves of his legs by way of emphasis.

They rattled on through the noisy, bustling, crowded streets of London, now displaying long double rows of brightly-burning lamps, dotted here and there with the chemists' glaring lights, and illuminated besides with the brilliant flood that streamed from the windows of the shops, where sparkling jewellery, silks and velvets of the richest colours, the most inviting delicacies, and most sumptuous articles of luxurious ornament, succeeded each other in rich and glittering profusion. Streams of people apparently without end poured on and on, jostling each other in the crowd and hurrying forward, scarcely seeming to notice the riches that surrounded them on every side; while vehicles of all shapes and makes, mingled up together in one moving mass like running water, lent their ceaseless roar to swell the noise and tumult.

As they dashed by the quickly-changing and ever-varying objects, it was curious to observe in what a strange procession they passed before the eye. Emporiums of splendid dresses, the materials brought from every quarter of the world; tempting stores of every thing to stimulate and pamper the sated appetite and give new relish to the oft-repeated feast; vessels of burnished gold and silver, wrought into every exquisite form of vase, and dish, and goblet; guns, swords pistols, and patent engines of destruction; screws and irons for the crooked, clothes for the newly-born, drugs for the sick, coffins for the dead, and churchyards for the buried—all these jumbled each with the other and flocking side by side, seemed to flit by in motley dance like the fantastic groups of the old Dutch painter, and with the same stern moral for the unheeding restless crowd.

Nor were there wanting objects in the crowd itself to give new point and purpose to the shifting scene. The rags of the squalid ballad-singer fluttered in the rich light that showed the goldsmith's treasures, pale and pinched-up faces hovered about the windows where was tempting food, hungry eyes wandered over the profusion guarded by one thin sheet of brittle glass—an iron wall to them; half-naked shivering figures stopped to gaze at Chinese shawls and golden stuffs of India. There was a christening party at the largest coffin-maker's, and a funeral hatchment had stopped some great improvements in the bravest mansion. Life and death went hand in hand; wealth and poverty stood side by side; repletion and starvation laid them down together.

But it was London; and the old country lady inside, who had put her head out of the coach-window a mile or two this side Kingston, and cried out to the driver that she was sure he must have passed it and forgotten to set her down, was satisfied at last.

Nicholas engaged beds for himself and Smike at the inn where the coach stopped, and repaired, without the delay of another moment, to the lodgings of Newman Noggs; for his anxiety and impatience had increased with every succeeding minute, and were almost beyond controul.

There was a fire in Newman's garret, and a candle had been left burning; the floor was cleanly swept, the room was as comfortably arranged as such a room could be, and meat and drink were placed in order upon the table. Every thing bespoke the affectionate care and attention of Newman Noggs, but Newman himself was not there.

"Do you know what time he will be home?" inquired Nicholas, tapping at the door of Newman's front neighbour.

"Ah, Mr. Johnson!" said Crowl, presenting himself. "Welcome, Sir.—How well you're looking! I never could have believed——"

"Pardon me," interposed Nicholas. "My question—I am extremely anxious to know."

"Why, he has a troublesome affair of business," replied Crowl, "and will not be home before twelve o'clock. He was very unwilling to go, I can tell you, but there was no help for it. However, he left word that you were to make yourself comfortable till he came back, and that I was to entertain you, which I shall be very glad to do."

In proof of his extreme readiness to exert himself for the general entertainment, Mr. Crowl drew a chair to the table as he spoke, and helping himself plentifully to the cold meat, invited Nicholas and Smike to follow his example.

Disappointed and uneasy, Nicholas could touch no food, so, after he had seen Smike comfortably established at the table, he walked out (despite a great many dissuasions uttered by Mr. Crowl with his mouth full), and left Smike to detain Newman in case he returned first.

As Miss La Creevy had anticipated, Nicholas betook himself straight to her house. Finding her from home, he debated within himself for some time whether he should go to his mother's residence and so compromise her with Ralph Nickleby. Fully persuaded, how-ever, that Newman would not have solicited him to return unless there was some strong reason which required his presence at home, he re-solved to go there, and hastened eastwards with all speed.

Mrs. Nickleby would not be at home, the girl said, until past twelve, or later. She believed Miss Nickleby was well, but she didn't live at home now, nor did she come home except very seldom. She couldn't say where she was stopping, but it was not at Madame Man-talini's—she was sure of that.

With his heart beating violently, and apprehending he knew not what disaster, Nicholas returned to where he had left Smike. New-man had not been home. He wouldn't be, till twelve o'clock ; there was no chance of it. Was there no possibility of sending to fetch him if it were only for an instant, or forwarding to him one line of writing to which he might return a verbal reply ? That was quite impracticable. He was not at Golden Square, and probably had been sent to execute some commission at a distance.

Nicholas tried to remain quietly where he was, but he felt so nervous and excited that he could not sit still. He seemed to be losing time unless he was moving. It was an absurd fancy, he knew, but he was wholly unable to resist it. So, he took up his hat and rambled out again.

He strolled westward this time, pacing the long streets with hurried footsteps, and agitated by a thousand misgivings and apprehensions which he could not overcome. He passed into Hyde Park, now silent and deserted, and increased his rate of walking as if in the hope of leaving his thoughts behind. They crowded upon him more thickly, however, now there were no passing objects to attract his attention ; and the one idea was always uppermost, that some stroke of ill-fortune must have occurred so calamitous in its nature that all were fearful of disclosing it to him. The old question arose again and again —What could it be ? Nicholas walked till he was weary, but was not one bit the wiser ; and indeed he came out of the Park at last a great deal more confused and perplexed than when he went in.

He had taken scarcely any thing to eat or drink since early in the morning, and felt quite worn out and exhausted. As he returned languidly towards the point from which he had started, along one of the thoroughfares which lie between Park Lane and Bond Street, he passed a handsome hotel, before which he stopped mechanically.

" An expensive place, I dare say," thought Nicholas ; " but a pint of wine and a biscuit are no great debauch wherever they are had. And yet I don't know."

He walked on a few steps, but looking wistfully down the long vista of gas-lamps before him, and thinking how long it would take to reach the end of it—and being besides in that kind of mood in which a man is most disposed to yield to his first impulse—and being, besides, strongly attracted to the hotel, in part by curiosity, and in part by some odd mixture of feelings which he would have been troubled to define—Nicholas turned back again, and walked into the coffee-room.

It was very handsomely furnished. The walls were ornamented with the choicest specimens of French paper, enriched with a gilded cornice of elegant design. The floor was covered with a rich carpet ; and two superb mirrors, one above the chimney-piece and one at the opposite end of the room reaching from floor to ceiling, multiplied the other beauties and added new ones of their own to enhance the general effect. There was a rather noisy party of four gentlemen in a box by the fire-place, and only two other persons present—both elderly gentlemen, and both alone.

Observing all this in the first comprehensive glance with which a stranger surveys a place that is new to him, Nicholas sat himself down in the box next to the noisy party, with his back towards them, and postponing his order for a pint of claret until such time as the waiter and one of the elderly gentlemen should have settled a disputed question relative to the price of an item in the bill of fare, took up a news-paper and began to read.

He had not read twenty lines, and was in truth half-dozing, when he was startled by the mention of his sister's name. " Little Kate Nickleby" were the words that caught his ear. He raised his head in amazement, and as he did so, saw by the reflection in the opposite glass, that two of the party behind him had risen and were standing before the fire. " It must have come from one of them," thought Nicholas. He waited to hear more with a countenance of some indig-nation, for the tone of speech had been anything but respectful, and the appearance of the individual whom he presumed to have been the speaker was coarse and swaggering.

This person—so Nicholas observed in the same glance at the mirror which had enabled him to see his face—was standing with his back to the fire conversing with a younger man, who stood with his back to the company, wore his hat, and was adjusting his shirt collar by the aid of the glass. They spoke in whispers, now and then bursting into a loud laugh, but Nicholas could catch no repetition of the words, nor anything sounding at all like the words, which had attracted his attention.

At length the two resumed their seats, and more wine being ordered, the party grew louder in their mirth. Still there was no reference made to anybody with whom he was acquainted, and Nicholas became persuaded that his excited fancy had either imagined the sounds alto-gether, or converted some other words into the name which had been so much in his thoughts.

" It is remarkable too," thought Nicholas: " if it had been ' Kate' or ' Kate Nickleby,' I should not have been so much surprised ; but ' little Kate Nickleby !' "

.... was attracted by the mention of his Sister's name in the Coffee Room.

The wine coming at the moment prevented his finishing the sentence. He swallowed a glassful and took up the paper again. At that instant——

" Little Kate Nickleby !" cried a voice behind him.

" I was right," muttered Nicholas as the paper fell from his hand. " And it was the man I supposed."

" As there was a proper objection to drinking her in heeltaps," said the voice, " we'll give her the first glass in the new magnum. Little Kate Nickleby !"

" Little Kate Nickleby," cried the other three. And the glasses were set down empty.

Keenly alive to the tone and manner of this slight and careless mention of his sister's name in a public place, Nicholas fired at once ; but he kept himself quiet by a great effort, and did not even turn his head.

" The jade !" said the same voice which had spoken before. " She's a true Nickleby—a worthy imitator of her old uncle Ralph—she hangs back to be more sought after—so does he ; nothing to be got out of Ralph unless you follow him up, and then the money comes doubly welcome, and the bargain doubly hard, for you're impatient and he isn't. Oh ! infernal cunning."

" Infernal cunning," echoed two voices.

Nicholas was in a perfect agony as the two elderly gentlemen opposite, rose one after the other and went away, lest they should be the means of his losing one word of what was said. But the conversation was suspended as they withdrew, and resumed with even greater freedom when they had left the room.

" I am afraid," said the younger gentleman, " that the old woman has grown jea-a-lous, and locked her up. Upon my soul it looks like it."

" If they quarrel and little Nickleby goes home to her mother, so much the better," said the first. " I can do any thing with the old lady. She'll believe anything I tell her."

" Egad that's true," returned the other voice. " Ha, ha, ha ! Poor devyle !"

The laugh was taken up by the two voices which always came in together, and became general at Mrs. Nickleby's expense. Nicholas turned burning hot with rage, but he commanded himself for the moment, and waited to hear more.

What he heard need not be repeated here. Suffice it that as the wine went round he heard enough to acquaint him with the characters and designs of those whose conversation he overheard ; to possess him with the full extent of Ralph's villany, and the real reason of his own presence being required in London. He heard all this and more. He heard his sister's sufferings derided, and her virtuous conduct jeered at and brutally misconstrued ; he heard her name banded from mouth to mouth, and herself made the subject of coarse and insolent wagers, free speech, and licentious jesting.

The man who had spoken first, led the conversation and indeed almost engrossed it, being only stimulated from time to time by some slight observation from one or other of his companions. To him then Nicholas addressed himself when he was sufficiently composed to stand before the party, and force the words from his parched and scorching throat.

"Let me have a word with you, Sir," said Nicholas.

"With me, Sir?" retorted Sir Mulberry Hawk, eyeing him in disdainful surprise.

"I said with you," replied Nicholas, speaking with great difficulty, for his passion choked him.

"A mysterious stranger, upon my soul!" exclaimed Sir Mulberry, raising his wine-glass to his lips, and looking round upon his friends.

"Will you step apart with me for a few minutes, or do you refuse?" said Nicholas, sternly.

Sir Mulberry merely paused in the act of drinking, and bade him either name his business or leave the table.

Nicholas drew a card from his pocket, and threw it before him.

"There, Sir," said Nicholas; "my business you will guess."

A momentary expression of astonishment, not unmixed with some confusion, appeared in the face of Sir Mulberry as he read the name; but he subdued it in an instant, and tossing the card to Lord Verisopht, who sat opposite, drew a toothpick from a glass before him, and very leisurely applied it to his mouth.

"Your name and address?" said Nicholas, turning paler as his passion kindled.

"I shall give you neither," replied Sir Mulberry.

"If there is a gentleman in this party," said Nicholas, looking round and scarcely able to make his white lips form the words, "he will acquaint me with the name and residence of this man."

There was a dead silence.

"I am the brother of the young lady who has been the subject of conversation here," said Nicholas. "I denounce this person as a liar, and impeach him as a coward. If he has a friend here, he will save him the disgrace of the paltry attempt to conceal his name—an utterly useless one—for I will find it out, nor leave him until I have"

Sir Mulberry looked at him contemptuously, and, addressing his companions, said—

"Let the fellow talk, I have nothing serious to say to boys of his station; and his pretty sister shall save him a broken head, if he talks till midnight."

"You are a base and spiritless scoundrel!" said Nicholas, "and shall be proclaimed so to the world. I *will* know you; I will follow you home if you walk the streets till morning."

Sir Mulberry's hand involuntarily closed upon the decanter, and he seemed for an instant about to launch it at the head of his challenger. But he only filled his glass, and laughed in derision.

Nicholas sat himself down, directly opposite to the party, and, summoning the waiter, paid his bill.

"Do you know that person's name?" he inquired of the man in an audible voice; pointing out Sir Mulberry as he put the question.

Sir Mulberry laughed again, and the two voices which had always spoken together, echoed the laugh; but rather feebly.

"That gentleman, Sir?" replied the waiter, who, no doubt, knew his cue, and answered with just as little respect, and just as much impertinence as he could safely show: "no, Sir, I do not, Sir."

"Here, you Sir," cried Sir Mulberry, as the man was retiring; "do you know *that* person's name?"

"Name, Sir? No, Sir."

"Then you'll find it there," said Sir Mulberry, throwing Nicholas's card towards him; "and when you have made yourself master of it, put that piece of pasteboard in the fire—do you hear me?"

The man grinned, and, looking doubtfully at Nicholas, compromised the matter by sticking the card in the chimney-glass. Having done this, he retired.

Nicholas folded his arms, and, biting his lip, sat perfectly quiet; sufficiently expressing by his manner, however, a firm determination to carry his threat of following Sir Mulberry home, into steady execution.

It was evident from the tone in which the younger member of the party appeared to remonstrate with his friend, that he objected to this course of proceeding, and urged him to comply with the request which Nicholas had made. Sir Mulberry, however, who was not quite sober, and who was in a sullen and dogged state of obstinacy, soon silenced the representations of his weak young friend, and further seemed—as if to save himself from a repetition of them—to insist on being left alone. However this might have been, the young gentleman and the two who had always spoken together, actually rose to go after a short interval, and presently retired, leaving their friend alone with Nicholas.

It will be very readily supposed that to one in the condition of Nicholas, the minutes appeared to move with leaden wings indeed, and that their progress did not seem the more rapid from the monotonous ticking of a French clock, or the shrill sound of its little bell which told the quarters. But there he sat; and in his old seat on the opposite side of the room reclined Sir Mulberry Hawk, with his legs upon the cushion, and his handkerchief thrown negligently over his knees: finishing his magnum of claret with the utmost coolness and indifference.

Thus they remained in perfect silence for upwards of an hour—Nicholas would have thought for three hours at least, but that the little bell had only gone four times. Twice or thrice he looked angrily and impatiently round; but there was Sir Mulberry in the same attitude, putting his glass to his lips from time to time, and looking vacantly at the wall, as if he were wholly ignorant of the presence of any living person.

At length he yawned, stretched himself, and rose; walked coolly to the glass, and having surveyed himself therein, turned round and honoured Nicholas with a long and contemptuous stare. Nicholas stared again with right good-will; Sir Mulberry shrugged his shoulders, smiled slightly, rang the bell, and ordered the waiter to help him on with his great-coat.

The man did so, and held the door open.

" Don't wait," said Sir Mulberry ; and they were alone again.

Sir Mulberry took several turns up and down the room, whistling carelessly all the time :` stopped to finish the last glass of claret which he had poured out a few minutes before, walked again, put on his hat, adjusted it by the glass, drew on his gloves, and, at last, walked slowly out.   Nicholas, who had been fuming and chafing until he was nearly wild, darted from his seat, and followed him—so closely, that before the door had swung upon its hinges after Sir Mulberry's passing out, they stood side by side in the street together.

There was a private cabriolet in waiting ; the groom opened the apron, and jumped out to the horse's head.

" Will you make yourself known to me ?" asked Nicholas, in a suppressed voice.

" No," replied the other fiercely, and confirming the refusal with an oath. " No."

" If you trust to your horse's speed, you will find yourself mistaken," said Nicholas. " I will accompany you. By Heaven I will, if I hang on to the footboard."

" You shall be horsewhipped if you do," returned Sir Mulberry.

" You are a villain," said Nicholas.

" You are an errand-boy for aught I know," said Sir Mulberry Hawk.

" I am the son of a country gentleman," returned Nicholas, " your equal in birth and education, and your superior I trust in everything besides. I tell you again, Miss Nickleby is my sister. Will you or will you not answer for your unmanly and brutal conduct ?"

" To a proper champion—yes. To you—no," returned Sir Mulberry, taking the reins in his hand. " Stand out of the way, dog. William, let go her head."

" You had better not," cried Nicholas, springing on the step as Sir Mulberry jumped in, and catching at the reins. " He has no command over the horse, mind. You shall not go—you shall not, I swear —till you have told me who you are."

The groom hesitated, for the mare who was a high-spirited animal and thorough-bred, plunged so violently that he could scarcely hold her.

" Leave go, I tell you ! " thundered his master.

The man obeyed. The animal reared and plunged as though it would dash the carriage into a thousand pieces, but Nicholas, blind to all sense of danger, and conscious of nothing but his fury, still maintained his place and his hold upon the reins.

" Will you unclasp your hand ?"

" Will you tell me who you are ?"

" No !"

" No !"

In less time than the quickest tongue could tell it, these words were exchanged, and Sir Mulberry shortening his whip, applied it furiously to the head and shoulders of Nicholas. It was broken in the struggle ;

Nicholas gained the heavy handle, and with it laid open one side of his antagonist's face from the eye to the lip. He saw the gash ; knew that the mare had darted off at a wild mad gallop ; a hundred lights danced in his eyes, and he felt himself flung violently upon the ground.

He was giddy and sick, but staggered to his feet directly, roused by the loud shouts of the men who were tearing up the street, and screaming to those ahead to clear the way. He was conscious of a torrent of people rushing quickly by—looking up, could discern the cabriolet whirled along the foot pavement with frightful rapidity—then heard a loud cry, the smashing of some heavy body, and the breaking of glass—and then the crowd closed in in the distance, and he could see or hear no more.

The general attention had been entirely directed from himself to the person in the carriage, and he was quite alone. Rightly judging that under such circumstances it would be madness to follow, he turned down a bye-street in search of the nearest coach-stand, finding after a minute or two that he was reeling like a drunken man, and aware for the first time of a stream of blood that was trickling down his face and breast.

CHAPTER XXXIII

IN WHICH MR. RALPH NICKLEBY IS RELIEVED, BY A VERY EXPEDITIOUS PROCESS, FROM ALL COMMERCE WITH HIS RELATIONS.

SMIKE and Newman Noggs, who in his impatience had returned home long before the time agreed upon, sat before the fire, listening anxiously to every footstep on the stairs, and the slightest sound that stirred within the house, for the approach of Nicholas. Time had worn on, and it was growing late. He had promised to be back in an hour ; and his prolonged absence began to excite considerable alarm in the minds of both, as was abundantly testified by the blank looks they cast upon each other at every new disappointment.

At length a coach was heard to stop, and Newman ran out to light Nicholas up the stairs. Beholding him in the trim described at the conclusion of the last chapter, he stood aghast in wonder and consternation.

" Don't be alarmed," said Nicholas, hurrying him back into the room. " There is no harm done, beyond what a bason of water can repair."

" No harm !" cried Newman, passing his hands hastily over the back and arms of Nicholas, as if to assure himself that he had broken no bones. " What have you been doing ?"

" I know all," interrupted Nicholas ; " I have heard a part, and guessed the rest. But before I remove one jot of these stains, I must hear the whole from you. You see I am collected. My resolution is taken. Now, my good friend, speak out ; for the time for any palliation or concealment is past, and nothing will avail Ralph Nickleby now."

" Your dress is torn in several places ; you walk lame, and I am sure are suffering pain," said Newman. " Let me see to your hurts first."

" I have no hurts to see to, beyond a little soreness and stiffness that will soon pass off," said Nicholas, seating himself with some difficulty. " But if I had fractured every limb, and still preserved my senses, you should not bandage one till you had told me what I have the right to know.   Come," said Nicholas, giving his hand to Noggs.   " You had a sister of your own, you told me once, who died before you fell into misfortune.   Now think of her, and tell me, Newman."

" Yes, I will, I will," said Noggs.   " I'll tell you the whole truth."

Newman did so.   Nicholas nodded his head from time to time, as it corroborated the particulars he had already gleaned ; but he fixed his eyes upon the fire, and did not look round once.

His recital ended, Newman insisted upon his young friend's stripping off his coat, and allowing whatever injuries he had received to be properly tended.   Nicholas, after some opposition, at length consented, and while some pretty severe bruises on his arms and shoulders were being rubbed with oil and vinegar, and various other efficacious remedies which Newman borrowed from the different lodgers, related in what manner they had been received.   The recital made a strong impression on the warm imagination of Newman ; for when Nicholas came to the violent part of the quarrel, he rubbed so hard, as to occasion him the most exquisite pain, which he would not have exhibited, however, for the world, it being perfectly clear that, for the moment, Newman was operating on Sir Mulberry Hawk, and had quite lost sight of his real patient.

This martyrdom over, Nicholas arranged with Newman that while he was otherwise occupied next morning, arrangements should be made for his mother's immediately quitting her present residence, and also for despatching Miss La Creevy to break the intelligence to her.   He then wrapped himself in Smike's great-coat, and repaired to the inn where they were to pass the night, and where (after writing a few lines to Ralph, the delivery of which was to be entrusted to Newman next day,) he endeavoured to obtain the repose of which he stood so much in need.

Drunken men, they say, may roll down precipices, and be quite unconscious of any serious personal inconvenience when their reason returns.   The remark may possibly apply to injuries received in other kinds of violent excitement ; certain it is, that although Nicholas experienced some pain on first awakening next morning, he sprung out of bed as the clock struck seven, with very little difficulty, and was soon as much on the alert as if nothing had occurred.

Merely looking into Smike's room, and telling him that Newman Noggs would call for him very shortly, Nicholas descended into the street, and calling a hackney-coach, bade the man drive to Mrs. Wititterly's, according to the direction which Newman had given him on the previous night.

It wanted a quarter to eight when they reached Cadogan Place. Nicholas began to fear that no one might be stirring at that early hour, when he was relieved by the sight of a female servant, employed in cleaning the door-steps. By this functionary he was referred to the doubtful page, who appeared with dishevelled hair and a very warm and glossy face, as of a page who had just got out of bed.

By this young gentleman he was informed that Miss Nickleby was then taking her morning's walk in the gardens before the house. On the question being propounded whether he could go and find her, the page desponded and thought not; but being stimulated with a shilling, the page grew sanguine and thought he could.

" Say to Miss Nickleby that her brother is here, and in great haste to see her," said Nicholas.

The plated buttons disappeared with an alacrity most unusual to them, and Nicholas paced the room in a state of feverish agitation which made the delay even of a minute insupportable. He soon heard a light footstep which he well knew, and before he could advance to meet her, Kate had fallen on his neck and burst into tears.

"My darling girl," said Nicholas as he embraced her. " How pale you are !"

" I have been so unhappy here, dear brother," sobbed poor Kate ; " so very, very, miserable. Do not leave me here, dear Nicholas, or I shall die of a broken heart."

" I will leave you nowhere," answered Nicholas—" never again. Kate," he cried, moved in spite of himself as he folded her to his heart. " Tell me that I acted for the best. Tell me that we parted because I feared to bring misfortune on your head ; that it was a trial to me no less than to yourself, and that if I did wrong it was in ignorance of the world and unknowingly."

" Why should I tell you what we know so well ?" returned Kate soothingly. " Nicholas—dear Nicholas—how can you give way thus ?"

" It is such bitter reproach to me to know what you have undergone," returned her brother ; " to see you so much altered, and yet so kind and patient—God !" cried Nicholas, clenching his fist and suddenly changing his tone and manner, " it sets my whole blood on fire again. You must leave here with me directly ; you should not have slept here last night, but that I knew all this too late. To whom can I speak, before we drive away ? "

This question was most opportunely put, for at that instant Mr. Wititterly walked in, and to him Kate introduced her brother, who at once announced his purpose, and the impossibility of deferring it.

" The quarter's notice," said Mr. Wititterly, with the gravity of a man on the right side, " is not yet half expired. Therefore— "

" Therefore," interposed Nicholas, " the quarter's salary must be lost, Sir. You will excuse this extreme haste, but circumstances require that I should immediately remove my sister, and I have not a moment's time to lose. Whatever she brought here I will send for, if you will allow me, in the course of the day."

Mr. Wititterly bowed, but offered no opposition to Kate's immediate departure ; with which, indeed, he was rather gratified than otherwise, Sir Tumley Snuffim having given it as his opinion, that she rather disagreed with Mrs. Wititterly's constitution.

" With regard to the trifle of salary that is due," said Mr. Wititterly, " I will—" here he was interrupted by a violent fit of coughing—" I will—owe it to Miss Nickleby."

Mr. Wititterly, it should be observed, was accustomed to owe small accounts, and to leave them owing. All men have some little pleasant way of their own; and this was Mr. Wititterly's.

" If you please," said Nicholas. And once more offering a hurried apology for so sudden a departure, he hurried Kate into the vehicle, and bade the man drive with all speed into the City.

To the City they went accordingly, with all the speed the hackney-coach could make; and as the horses happened to live at Whitechapel and to be in the habit of taking their breakfast there, when they breakfasted at all, they performed the journey with greater expedition than could reasonably have been expected.

Nicholas sent Kate up-stairs a few minutes before him, that his unlooked-for appearance might not alarm his mother, and when the way had been paved, presented himself with much duty and affection. Newman had not been idle, for there was a little cart at the door, and the effects were hurrying out already.

Now, Mrs. Nickleby was not the sort of person to be told anything in a hurry, or rather to comprehend anything of peculiar delicacy or importance on a short notice. Wherefore, although the good lady had been subjected to a full hour's preparation by little Miss La Creevy, and was now addressed in most lucid terms both by Nicholas and his sister, she was in a state of singular bewilderment and confusion, and could by no means be made to comprehend the necessity of such hurried proceedings.

" Why don't you ask your uncle, my dear Nicholas, what he can possibly mean by it?" said Mrs. Nickleby.

" My dear mother," returned Nicholas, " the time for talking has gone by. There is but one step to take, and that is to cast him off with the scorn and indignation he deserves. Your own honour and good name demand that, after the discovery of his vile proceedings, you should not be beholden to him one hour, even for the shelter of these bare walls."

" To be sure," said Mrs. Nickleby, crying bitterly, " he is a brute, a monster; and the walls are very bare, and want painting too, and I have had this ceiling white-washed at the expense of eighteen pence, which is a very distressing thing, considering that it is so much gone into your uncle's pocket. I never could have believed it—never."

" Nor I, nor anybody else," said Nicholas.

" Lord bless my life!" exclaimed Mrs. Nickleby. " To think that that Sir Mulberry Hawk should be such an abandoned wretch as Miss La Creevy says he is, Nicholas, my dear; when I was congratulating myself every day on his being an admirer of our dear Kate's, and thinking what a thing it would be for the family if he was to become connected with us, and use his interest to get you some profitable government place. There are very good places to be got about the court, I know; for the brother of a friend of ours (Miss Cropley, at

Exeter, my dear Kate, you recollect), he had one, and I know that it was the chief part of his duty to wear silk stockings, and a bag wig like a black watch-pocket; and to think that it should come to this after all—oh, dear, dear, it's enough to kill one, that it is!" With which expressions of sorrow, Mrs. Nickleby gave fresh vent to her grief, and wept piteously.

As Nicholas and his sister were by this time compelled to superintend the removal of the few articles of furniture, Miss La Creevy devoted herself to the consolation of the matron, and observed with great kindness of manner that she must really make an effort, and cheer up.

" Oh I dare say, Miss La Creevy," returned Mrs. Nickleby, with a petulance not unnatural in her unhappy circumstances, " it's very easy to say cheer up, but if you had had as many occasions to cheer up as I have had —— and there," said Mrs. Nickleby, stopping short, " Think of Mr. Pyke and Mr. Pluck, two of the most perfect gentlemen that ever lived, what am I to say to them—what can I say to them ? Why, if I was to say to them, ' I'm told your friend Sir Mulberry is a base wretch,' they'd laugh at me."

" They will laugh no more at us, I take it," said Nicholas, advancing. " Come mother, there is a coach at the door, and until Monday, at all events, we will return to our old quarters."

—" Where every thing· is ready, and a hearty welcome into the bargain," added Miss La Creevy. " Now, let me go with you down stairs."

But Mrs. Nickleby was not to be so easily moved, for first she insisted on going up stairs to see that nothing had been left, and then on going down stairs to see that every thing had been taken away ; and when she was getting into the coach she had a vision of a forgotten coffee-pot on the back-kitchen hob, and after she was shut in, a dismal recollection of a green umbrella behind some unknown door. At last Nicholas, in a condition of absolute despair, ordered the coachman to drive away, and in the unexpected jerk of a sudden starting, Mrs. Nickleby lost a shilling among the straw, which fortunately confined her attention to the coach until it was too late to remember any thing else.

Having seen every thing safely out, discharged the servant, and locked the door, Nicholas jumped into a cabriolet and drove to a bye place near Golden Square where he had appointed to meet Noggs ; and so quickly had every thing been done, that it was barely half past nine when he reached the place of meeting.

" Here is the letter for Ralph," said Nicholas, " and here the key. When you come to me this evening, not a word of last night. Ill news travels fast, and they will know it soon enough. Have you heard if he was much hurt ?"

Newman shook his head.

" I will ascertain that myself without loss of time," said Nicholas.

" You had better take some rest," returned Newman. " You are fevered and ill."

Nicholas waved his hand carelessly, and concealing the indisposition he really felt, now that the excitement which had sustained him was over, took a hurried farewell of Newman Noggs, and left him.

Newman was not three minutes' walk from Golden Square, but in the course of that three minutes he took the letter out of his hat and put it in again twenty times at least. First the front, then the back, then the sides, then the superscription, then the seal, were objects of Newman's admiration. Then he held it at arm's length as if to take in the whole at one delicious survey, and then he rubbed his hands in a perfect ecstacy with his commission.

He reached the office, hung his hat on its accustomed peg, laid the letter and key upon the desk, and waited impatiently until Ralph Nickleby should appear. After a few minutes, the well-known creaking of his boots was heard on the stairs, and then the bell rung.

" Has the post come in ? "

" No."

" Any other letters ? "

" One." Newman eyed him closely, and laid it on the desk.

" What's this ? " asked Ralph, taking up the key.

" Left with the letter ;—a boy brought them—quarter of an hour ago, or less."

Ralph glanced at the direction, opened the letter, and read as follows :—

" You are known to me now. There are no reproaches I could heap upon your head which would carry with them one thousandth part of the grovelling shame that this assurance will awaken even in your breast.

" Your brother's widow and her orphan child spurn the shelter of your roof, and shun you with disgust and loathing. Your kindred renounce you, for they know no shame but the ties of blood which bind them in name with you.

" You are an old man, and I leave you to the grave. May every recollection of your life cling to your false heart, and cast their darkness on your death-bed."

Ralph Nickleby read this letter twice, and frowning heavily, fell into a fit of musing ; the paper fluttered from his hand and dropped upon the floor, but he clasped his fingers, as if he held it still.

Suddenly, he started from his seat, and thrusting it all crumpled into his pocket, turned furiously to Newman Noggs, as though to ask him why he lingered. But Newman stood unmoved, with his back towards him, following up, with the worn and blackened stump of an old pen, some figures in an Interest-table which was pasted against the wall, and apparently quite abstracted from every other object.

ESTABLISHED 1820.

RIPPON AND BURTON'S

FURNISHING IRONMONGERY WAREHOUSES,

12, WELLS STREET, OXFORD STREET, LONDON.

CATALOGUE of ARTICLES, which, if purchased for Town, must be paid for on delivery; if for the Country, or for Exportation, the money must be remitted, postage free, with the order. On any other terms RIPPON & BURTON respectfully decline doing business at the Prices herein named.

The Frequent ROBBERIES of PLATE

Have induced RIPPON & BURTON to manufacture a SUBSTITUTE for SILVER, possessing all its advantages in point of appearance and durability, at less than one-tenth the cost. Their BRITISH PLATE is of such a superior quality, that it requires the strictest scrutiny to distinguish it from silver, than which it is more durable, every article being made of solid wrought material; it improves with use, and is warranted to stand the test of the strongest of acids—aquafortis.

BRITISH PLATE.

			£ s. d.
Fiddle-handle Table Spoons & Forks, per doz. 12s & 16s			0
Ditto	ditto	very strong	£1 0 0
Ditto	Dessert Spoons and Forks 10s. &		0 14 0
Ditto	ditto,	very strong	0 16 0
Ditto	Tea Spoons	5s. and	0 6 0
Ditto	Ditto, very strong		0 10 0
Ditto	Gravy Spoons	each	0 4 0
Ditto	ditto very strong		0 5 0
Ditto	Salt and Mustard Spoons		0 0 6
Ditto	Ditto and Ditto, with gilt bowls		0 1 0
Ditto	Sauce Ladles		0 1 6
Ditto	ditto very strong		0 2 0
Ditto	Soup Ladles		0 8 0
Ditto	ditto very strong		0 9 0
Ditto	Fish Knives		0 7 0
Ditto	Butter Knives		0 2 0
Ditto	Sugar Bows	per pair	0 1 0
Ditto	Ditto, very strong		0 1 6
Ivory handle Fish Knives		each	0 9 6
Ditto	Butter Knives		0 3 0
Pearl handle	Ditto		0 4 6

Round Waiters, with rich shell mountings and feet, centre elegantly chased, 8 in. diameter 1 5 0
Ditto, ditto, 10 in. ditto ... 1 10 0
Ditto, ditto, 12 in. ditto ... 2 2 0
Ditto, ditto, 16 in. ditto ... 3 3 0
Cruet Frames, with 4 rich cut glasses, shell mountings, and feet each 1 8 0
Ditto, ditto, 5 glasses 2 0 0
Ditto, ditto, 7 Glasses 2 15 0
Liquor Frames, with 3 richly cut glasses 3 15 0
Decanter Stands, with shell mountings, per pair 1 1 0
Bread Baskets, richly chased, and with rich shell mountings 2 10 0
Toast Racks 0 10 6
Asparagus Tongs, per pair 0 12 0

			£ s. d.
King's Pattern Table Spoons & Forks, per doz.			£1 15s 0
Ditto	Dessert ditto	do...	1 8 0
Ditto	Tea Spoons	do...	0 15 0
Ditto	Gravy ditto	each	0 8 0
Ditto	Fish Knives	do...	0 13 0
Ditto	Salt and Mustard Spoons..do...		0 1 3
Ditto	Soup Ladles	do...	0 14 0
Ditto	Sauce Ladles	do...	0 3 6
Ditto	Sugar Tongs	do...	0 3 0

Table Candlesticks, 8 inches high ......per pair 0 16 0
Ditto, with gadroon mountings, 8 inches high 1 0 0
Ditto, ditto, 10 ditto 1 5 0
Ditto, with shell mountings, 8 ditto 1 5 0
Ditto, ditto, 10 ditto 1 10 0
Ditto, Antique Silver Pattern, 10 ditto 1 15 0
Chamber Candlesticks, with Snuffers and Extinguisher ......each from 0 9 6
Snuffers, per pair ......from 5s. 6d. to 0 8 6
Snuffer Trays, with gadroon mountings ... each 0 10 6
Do. with shell do. & richly chased centres, 9s. 6d to 12 0
Skewers......per inch 0 0 4
Handsome modern pattern Teapots, to hold 1 qt. 1 10 0
Newest Silver Pattern ditto 2 2 0
Coffee Pots, Sugar Basins, and Cream Ewers to match.
Steak Dishes and Covers, with rich shell mountings and loose handles, per pair 3 3 0
Teakettle, with ivory handle, and with stand and spirit lamp 6 10 0
Salt Cellars, richly mounted, with insides gilt, per pair 0 14 0

CAUTION.—In consequence of the objections so justly urged against the use of the article called German Silver, the Manufacturers of that Metal are now calling it British Plate, although the materials of which it is made remain unchanged. The British Plate manufactured by RIPPON & BURTON UNDERGOES a CHEMICAL PROCESS, by which it is rendered pure, and superior to any other so called.

** From the continual accession of fresh Patterns and Articles, this List is necessarily incomplete. The above may however be taken as a criterion of prices, and are always on sale.

Superior TABLE CUTLERY.

Every Knife and Fork warranted Steel, and exchanged if not found good.	Table Knives, per doz.	Table Forks, per doz.	Dessert Knives, per doz.	Dessert Forks, per doz.	Carvers, per pair.	The set of 50 pieces.
3½-inch Octagon Ivory Handles, with Rimmed Shoulders...	14s. 0d.	7s. 0d.	12s. 0d.	6s. 0d.	4s. 6d.	£2 0s. 0d.
The same size to balance	16 0	8 0	14 0	7 0	5 6	2 10 0
3¾-inch Octagon Ivory Handles, with Rimmed Shoulders...	18 0	9 0	15 0	7 0	6 0	2 15 0
The same size to balance	21 0	10 6	16 0	8 0	7 6	3 0 0
4-inch Octagon Ivory Balance Handles	28 0	14 0	18 0	9 0	8 6	3 17 6
4-inch ditto, with Waterloo Balance Shoulders	28 0	14 0	18 0	9 0	8 6	3 17 6
White Bone octagon shape Handles	8 8	4 4	6 8	3 4	3 0	1 6 0
Ditto ditto, with Rimmed Shoulders	11 4	5 8	9 4	3 4	3 6	1 14 6
Black Horn octagon shape Handles	7 4	3 8	6 0	3 0	2 6	1 2 6
Ditto ditto, with Rimmed Shoulders	11 4	5 8	9 4	4 8	3 6	1 14 6
Very strong Rough Bone Handles	7 4	3 8	6 0	3 0	2 6	1 2 6
Black Wood Handles	5 4	2 8	4 0	2 0	2 0	0 16 0
Oval shape White Bone Handles	6 0	3 0	4 0	2 0	2 0	0 17 0

The Forks priced in the above Scale are all forged Steel. Cast Steel Forks 2s. per doz. less.

Richly Carved Rosewood Cases, containing of Transparent Ivory Handles, with Silver Ferules, 18 Table Knives 18 Dessert Knives, 2 pair large Carvers, and 1 pair of Poultry or Game Carvers, £10.

January 1st, 1839.

Shower Baths, Japanned Bamboo, with Brass Force-pump attached, to throw the water into the shower cistern, the very best made, with copper conducting tubes, and curtains complete, £5. 10s.

Hip Baths, Japanned Bamboo, £1.

Spunging Baths, Round, 30 inches diameter, 7 inches deep, 18s.

Open Baths, 3 ft. 6 in. long, 30s. ; 4 ft. long, 35s. ; 4 ft. 6in. long, 50s.; 5 ft. long, 60s.; 5 ft. 6 in. long, 70s.

Feet Baths, Japanned Bamboo, small size, 6s. 6d. ; large, 7s 6d.; tub shape, with hoops, 11s.

Table Lamps, Bronze or Gilt, with ground glass globe shades.

Hall Lamps or Lanterns, with glass shade over top, complete with burner, Bronzed or Gilt.

Bottle Jacks, Japanned, 7s. 6d.; Brass, 9s. 6d. each.

Brass Stair Rods, per doz. 21 inches long, 3s. 6d.; 24 in. 4s. 3d. ; 27 in. 5s.; 30 in. 5s. 6d.

Brass Curtain Poles, warranted solid, 1½ inch diameter, 1s. 6d. per foot ; 2 in. 2s. 2d. per foot.

Brass Poles, complete with end ornaments, rings, hooks & brackets, 3ft. long, 15s.; 3ft. 6 in. 17s.; 4ft. 20s.

Brass Curtain Bands, 1½ in. wide, 2s. 6d.per pair, 1½ in. 3s.; 2 in. 4s. Richer patterns, 1½ in. 4s. ; 2 in. 5s.

Finger Plates for Doors, newest and richest patterns, long, 1s. 2d. ; short, 10d. each.

Copper Coal Scoops, small, 10s. 6d. ; middle, 13s. large, 14s. 6d.. Helmet Shape, 14s. 6d., 18s., 20s.; Square Shape, with Hand Scoop, 28s.

Copper Tea Kettles, Oval Shape, very strong, with barrel handle, 2 quarts, 5s. 6d.; 3 quarts, 6s. ; 4 quarts, 7s. The strongest quality made, 2 quarts 8s. ; 3 quarts, 10s.; 4 quarts, 11s.

Copper Stewpans; Soup or Stock Pots, and Fish Kettles, with Brazing Pan; Saucepans & Preserving Pans; Cutlet Pans, Frying Pans, and Omelette Pans, at prices proportionate with the above.

Copper Warming Pans, with handles, for fire, 6s. 6d. to 9s. 6d. ; Ditto, for water, 9s. 6d.

Fire Irons.

Large strong Wrought Iron, for Kitchens, 5s. 6d. to 12s. 0
Wrought Iron, suitable for Servants' Bed Rooms 2 0
Small Polished Steel, for better Bed Rooms . 5 0
Large ditto, for Libraries . : . 7 0
Ditto ditto, for Dining Rooms . . 8 6
Ditto ditto, with Cut Heads, for ditto . . 11 6
Ditto very highly polished Steel, plain good pattern 20 0
Ditto ditto, richly cut . . . 25s. to 40 0

Corkscrews, Patent, 3s. 6d. each ; Common ditto, 6d., 9d., 1s., 1s. 6d., and 2s.

Smoke Jack, with Chains and Spit, £6. Superior Self-acting do. with Dangle and Horizontal Spit, £10.

N. B. Experienced Workmen employed to clean, repair, and oil Smoke Jacks, which are so constantly put out of order by the treatment they meet with from chimney sweepers.

Captains' Cabin Lamps, with 1 quart kettles, 6s.

Britannia Metal Goods.

To hold	-	1½ Pts.	1 Qt.	2½ Pts.
Teapots, with Black Handles and Black Knobs	.	1s. 6d.	2s. 0d.	2s. 9d.
Ditto, very strong	.	3 0	3 6	4 0
Ditto, with Pearl Knobs	.	4 6	5 6	6 6
Ditto with Pearl Knobs and Metal Handles	.	6 6	8 0	9 6

Coffee Biggins, 1s. 6d. each size extra.
Table Candlesticks, 8 in. 3s. per pair; 9 in. 4s. 6d.; 10 in. 7s. 6d.
Chamber Candlesticks with Extinguishers, 2s. each.
Ditto with Gadroon Edges, complete with Snuffers and Extinguisher, 4s. each.
Mustards, with Blue Earthen Lining, 1s. each.
Salt Cellars with ditto, 1s. 4d. per pair.
Pepper Boxes, 1s. each.

Britannia Metal Hot Water Dishes, with wells for gravy, and gadroon edges, 16 inches long, 30s. ; 18in., 35s. ; 20 in., 42s. ; 22 in., 50s. ; 24 in., 55s. Hot Water Plates, 6s. 6d. each.

Cruet Frames, Black Japanned, with 3 Glasses, 3s. 8d.; 4 Glasses, 4s. 9d. ; 5 Glasses, 6s.; 6 Glasses, 7s.

Reading Candlesticks, with Shade and Light to slide, one light, 5s. 6d.; two lights, 7s. 6d.

Coffee Filterers, for making Coffee without boiling.

To hold	.	1 Pint.	1½ Pts.	1 Qt.	3 Pts.
Best Block Tin	.	4s. 0d.	4s. 6d.	5s. 6d.	7s. 0d.
Bronzed	. . .	5 6	6 6	7 6	9 6

Etnas, for boiling a Pint of Water in three minutes, 3s. each.

Coffee and **Pepper Mills,** small, 3s.; middle, 4s.; large, 4s. 6d.
Ditto, to fix, small, 4s. 6d.; middle, 5s. 6d.; large, 6s. 6d.

Iron Digesters, for making Soup, to hold 2 galls. 9s. ; 3 galls. 10s. 6d.; 4 galls. 16s.

Tea Urns, Globe shape. to hold four quarts, 27s. each. Modern Shapes, to hold 6 quarts, 45s. to 60s. each.

Improved Wove Wire Gauze Window Blinds, in mahogany frames, made to any size, and painted to any shade of colour, 2s. 3d. per square foot.
Ornamenting with shaded lines, 1s. 6d. each blind.
Ditto, with lines and corner ornaments, 2s. 6d. each blind.
Blinds, ornamented with landscape, in mahogany frames, 4s. per square foot.
Old Blind Frames filled with new wire, and painted any colour, at 1s. 4d. per square foot.

Servants' Wire Lanterns, Open Tops, with Doors, 1s. 6d. each. Closed Tops, with Doors, 2s.

Rush Safes, Open Tops, 2s. 3d. each. Closed Tops, with Doors, 2s. 9d. each.

Fire Guards, painted Green, with Dome Tops, 14 inch, 1s. 6d.; 16 in. 1s. 9d. ; 18 in. 2s. 3d. Brass Wire, 6s., 6s. 6d., and 7s. 6d.

Egg Whisks, Tinned Wire, 9d. each.

Wire Work.—All kinds of useful and ornamental Wire Work made to order.

Family Weighing Machines, or Balances, complete, with weights from ¼ oz. to 14 lbs., 26s.

Ditto Patent Spring Weighing Machines, which do not require weights, 6s. 6d. to 20s.

DISH COVERS.

Inches long .	9	10	11	12	14	16	18	Set of 6.	Set of 7.
The commonest are in sets of the six first sizes, which cannot be separated .									
Block Tin .	1s. 6d	1s. 9d	2s. 0d	2s. 6d	3s. 3d	3s. 6d	5s. 6d	£0 6s. 0d	
Ditto, Anti-Patent shape . .	1 9	2 0	2 6	3 0	4 0	4 6	8 0	0 11 6	£0 17s. 0d
Ditto, O. G. shape . .	2 0	2 6	3 0	3 6	4 6	6 0	8 6	0 16 0	1 4 0
Ditto, Patent Imperial Silver shape. The Tops raised in one piece, the very best made, except Plated or Silver .	3 6	4 0	4 9	6 0	7 6	9 6	11 6	1 1 0	1 9 6
Wove Wire Fly-proof, tin rims, japanned	...	2 6	...	3 3	4 0	5 0	5 6	1 15 0	2 5 0

FENDERS.

The immense variety which the Show Rooms contain, and the constant change of patterns of Fenders, render it impossible to give the prices of but a small portion of them. The following Scale, however, may be taken as a guide, and the prices generally will be found about 25 per cent. below any other house whatever.

	3 Feet.	3 Feet 3.	3 Feet 6.	3 Feet 9.	4 Feet.
	3s. 0d.	3s. 6d.	4s. 0d.		
Green, with Brass Top, suitable for Bed Rooms	9 6	10 6	12 0	13s. 6d.	15s. 0d.
All Brass	12 0	13 0	14 0	15 0	16 0
Black Iron for Dining Rooms or Libraries	15 0	16 0	17 0	18 0	19 0
Bronzed for ditto	18 0	20 0	21 0	23 0	25 0
Ditto, with bright Steel Tops	21 0	23 0	25 0	27 0	29 6
Ditto, very handsome, with Steel Tops and Steel Bottom Moulding					
Very rich Pattern, with Scroll Centre, Steel Rod and Steel Ends, for Drawing Rooms [all sizes]	...	...	...	from	50 0
Green painted Wire Nursery Guard Fenders, Brass Tops, 18 in. high	15 0	16 3	17 6	18 9	20 0
Ditto, 24 inches high	18 0	19 6	21 0	22 6	24 0
Iron Kitchen Fenders, with Sliding Bars	6 0	6 6	7 0	7 6	

STOVES.

Inches wide	18	20	22	24	26	28	30	32	34	36
Elliptic or Rumford Stoves, for Bed Rooms	6s. 0d.	6s. 8d.	7s. 4d.	8s. 0d.	8s. 8d.	9s. 4d.	10s. 0d	10s. 8d	11s. 4d	12s. 0d
Common half register Stoves	9 0	10 0	11 0	12 0	13 0	14 0	15 0	16 0	17 0	18 0
Best do. bold Fronts and Bannister Bars	-	-	-	-	-	-	-	28 0	30 0	32 0
Register Stoves of superior patterns	-	-	18 0	19 6	21 0	22 6	24 0	25 6	27 0	

Register Stoves, fine Cast, 3 feet wide, 2*l.* 5*s.*, 2*l.* 10*s.*, and 3*l.*—Ground Bright Front Register Stoves with Bronzed and Steel Ornaments, and with bright and black bars, 3 feet wide, 4*l.* 10*s.*, 5*l.* and 5*l.* 10*s.*
Ironing Stoves for Laundries, complete, with Frame and Ash Pan, 1*l.* 6*s.*

KITCHEN RANGES.

To fit an opening of	3 Ft. 2.	3 Ft. 4.	3 Ft. 6.	4 Ft.	4 Ft. 4.	5 Ft.
With Oven and Boiler	50s.	54s.	58s.			
Self-acting ditto, with Oven and Boiler, Sliding Cheek, and Wrought Iron Bars (recommended)	90	95	100	110s.	126s.	140s.

Iron Saucepans and Tea Kettles.

	1 pint.	1½ pint.	1 Quart.	3 pint.	2 Quart.	3 Quart.	4 Quart.	6 Quart.	8 Quart.
Iron Saucepan and Cover	0s. 11d.	1s. 1d.	1s. 3d.	1s. 6d.	1s. 9d.	2s. 2d.	2s. 8d.	3s. 6d.	4s. 0d.
Iron Stewpan and Cover	...	...	1 4	1 10	2 3	3 3	4 0	5 6	6 6
Round Iron Tea Kettles	...	...	...	...	2 9	4 3	5 0	7 0	9 0
Oval ditto	...	...	...	...	3 3	4 9	5 6	7 6	9 6

Iron Boiling Pots.

	2¼ Gall.	3 Gall.	3½ Gall.	4 Gall.	5 Gall.	6 Gall.
Oval Iron Boiling Pot and Cover	5s. 6d.	6s. 6d.	7s. 0d.	8s. 6d.	10s. 0d.	11s. 6d.
Tea Kitchens, or Water Fountains, with Brass Pipe & Cock		13 0	14 0	14 6	16 0	18 6

Iron Coal Scoops and Boxes.

	14 in. long.	16 in. long.	18 in. long.
Coal Boxes, Japanned with Covers, ornamented with Gold Lines	12s. 0d.	14s. 0d.	16s. 0d.
Coal Scoops, Iron, for Kitchen Use	1 9	2 6	3 6
Ditto, lined with Zinc, the most serviceable article of the kind ever made	5 0	6 6	7 6
Upright Hods	1 9	2 6	3 6

Japanned Goods.

Inches long	18	20	22	24	26	28	30
TEA TRAYS, good common quality	1s. 3d.	1s. 6d.	1s. 9d.	2s. 3d.	2s. 9d.	3s. 3d.	3s. 9d.
Ditto, best common quality	2 6	3 0	3 6	4 6	5 6	6 0	7 0
Ditto, paper shape, black	5 6	7 0	8 0	9 6	11 0	12 6	14 0
Ditto, Gothic paper shape, black	9 6	11 0	12 6	14 0	15 6	17 0	19 0
Ditto, ditto, Marone, ornamented all over	11 0	12 6	14 0	16 0	17 6	19 0	21 0

Bread and Knife Trays, each 9d., 1s., 1s. 6d., 2s. & 2s. 6d.
Middle quality ditto, at 2s. and 2s. 6d.
Best quality ditto, Gothic shape, 3s. 6d., 4s. 6d. and 5s. 6d. each.
Tea Trays, paper, Gothic shape, in sets of one each of 18, 24, and 30 inches, £5.
Ditto, richest patterns, the set, £6. and £7.
Toast Racks, plain black; 1s. 6d. Ornamented, 2s.
Ditto, marone or green, ornamented all over, 2s. 9d.
Cheese Trays, 2s., 2s. 6d., 3s., and 3s. 6d.
Snuffer Trays, 6d., 9d., 1s., 1s. 3d., and 1s. 6d.
Paper ditto, 2s., 2s. 6d., 3s., 3s. 6d., and 4s.
Paper Decanter Stands, plain black, 3s. 6d. per pair.
Ditto, red, 4s. per pair.
Ditto, ornamented black or marone, 4s. 6d. per pair.

Plate Warmers, upright shape, with gilt lines, 21s.
Ditto, long shape, £1. 5s.
Toilet Cans and Toilet Pails, 7s. 6d. each.
Chamber Slop Pails, japanned green outside and red inside, small, 3s.; middle, 4s.; large, 5s. 6d.
Chamber Candlesticks, complete, with Snuffers and Extinguisher, 6d. Ditto, better, 9d. to 3s.
Cash Boxes, with Tumbler Locks, small size, 5s. 6d.
Ditto, ditto, middle size, 6s. 6d.; large size, 7s. 6d.
Ditto, ditto, with Patent Locks, 10s. 6d.
Deed Boxes, Japanned Brown, with Locks, 12 inches long, 11s.; 14 in. 15s.; 16 in. 18s.; 18 in. 21s.
Candle Boxes, 1s. 4d. each.
Candle or Rush Safes, 2s. 6d. each.
Cinder Pails or Sifters, Japanned Brown, 11s. each.

TIN GOODS.

	1 Pt.	1 Qt.	3 Pt.	2 Qf.	3 Qt.	4 Qt.	6 Qt.	8 Qt.	9 Qt.	10 Qt.
To hold										
SAUCEPANS, strong common. with Covers	0s. 4d	0s. 5d	0s. 6d	0s. 8d	0s. 10	1s. 2d	1s. 3d	1s. 4d	1s. 8d	2s. 0d
Strongest Tin, with Iron Handles	0 9	1 0	1 4	1 10	2 2	2 9	3 6	4 0	4 6	5 0
Block Tin	1 4	2 0	2 6	3 0	3 9	4 6	6 0			
Saucepans and Steamers	—	—	—	—	2 9	3 6	4 0	4 6		

Coffee and Chocolate Pots, Block Tin, to hold 1 quart,
  1s. 4d.; 3 pints, 1s. 10d.; 2 quarts, 2s. 3d
Colanders, small, 1s.; large, 1s. 6d.
Ditto, Block Tin, small, 3s. 6d.; large, 4s. 6d.
Dripping Pans, with wells, small, 3s.; mid., 5s.: large, 7s.
Fish Kettles, small, 4s. 6d.; middle, 5s. 6d.; large, 6s. 6d.

Turbot Pans, or Kettles, Turbot shape, 21s.
Meat Screens for Bottle Jacks, 15s. each.
Ditto, Wood, Elliptic Shape, lined with Tin, upon
  Rollers, with Shelf and Door, 3 feet wide, £1. 10s.
  Larger sizes in proportion.
Stomach Warmers, each 2s. 6d.

	3 Pts.	2 Qts.	3 Qts.	4 Qts.
To hold				
TEA KETTLES, Oval shape, strong Common Tin	1s. 0d.	1s. 2d.	1s. 4d.	1s. 6d.
Ditto, strongest Tin	2 0	2 6	3 0	3 6
Block Tin, with Iron Handles and Iron Spouts	4 0	4 3	5 3	6 3
Oblong shape, with round Barrel Handles and Iron Spout	4 9	5 6	6 0	6 6

RIPPON & BURTON'S Prices of STRONG SETS of IRON and TIN
KITCHEN FURNITURE.

Small Set.

1 Bread Grater	0s. 6
1 Pair Brass Candlesticks	2 6
1 Bottle Jack	7 6
1 Tin Candlestick	1 3
1 Candle Box	0 10
1 Meat Chopper	1 6
1 Cinder Sifter	1 0
1 Coffee Pot	1 0
1 Colander	1 0
1 Dripping Pan & Stand	5 0
1 Dust Pan	0 6
1 Slice	0 6
1 Fish Kettle	4 0
1 Flour Box	0 8
2 Flat Irons	1 8
1 Fryingpan	1 2
1 Gridiron	1 0
1 Mustard Pot	1 0
1 Salt Cellar	0 8
1 Pepper Box	0 6
1 Block Tin Butter Sauce-pan	1 6
2 Iron Saucepans	6 0
2 Iron Stewpans	3 6
1 Boiling Pot, Iron	7 0
1 Set of Skewers	0 6
6 Knives and Forks	4 6
3 Spoons	0 9
1 Tea Pot and 1 Tea Tray	6 0
1 Toasting Fork	0 6
1 Tea Kettle	4 6
£3 10 0	

Middle Set.

1 Bread Grater	1s. 0
1 Pair Brass Candlesticks	3 0
1 Bottle Jack	7 6
1 Pair of Bellows	1 4
2 Tin Candlesticks	2 6
1 Candle Box	1 4
1 Cheese Toaster	1 4
1 Chopper	1 9
1 Cinder Sifter	1 3
1 Coffee Pot	1 3
1 Colander	1 3
1 Dripping Pan & Stand	5 6
1 Dust Pan	0 8
1 Fish Slice	1 0
1 Fish Kettle	5 6
Pepper and Flour Boxes	1 2
3 Flat Irons	3 0
1 Fryingpan	1 9
1 Gridiron	1 3
2 Jelly Moulds	5 6
1 Mustard Pot	1 0
1 Salt Cellar	0 8
1 Plate Basket	5 6
2 Block Tin Saucepans	3 6
3 Iron Saucepans	7 6
1 Saucepan and Steamer	3 6
1 Large Boiling Pot	9 6
3 Stewpans	7 0
1 Set of Skewers	0 6
6 Knives and Forks	5 6
6 Iron Spoons	1 6
1 Tea Pot & 1 Tea Tray	6 0
1 Toasting Fork	0 6
1 Tea Kettle	6 6
£5 7 6	

Large Set.

1 Bread Grater	1s. 0
1 Pair Brass Candlesticks	3 6
1 Bottle Jack	9 6
1 Pair of Bellows	2 0
2 Deep Tin Candlesticks	2 6
1 Candle Box	1 4
1 Cheese Toaster	1 10
1 Chopper, for Meat	2 0
1 Cinder Sifter	1 6
1 Coffee Pot	2 3
1 Coal Shovel	2 6
1 Colander	1 6
1 Dripping Pan and Stand	7 0
1 Dust Pan	0 8
1 Egg Slice	0 6
1 Fish Slice	1 2
2 Fish Kettles	10 6
1 Flour Box	1 0
3 Flat Irons	4 0
2 Fryingpans	4 6
1 Gridiron, with fluted Bars	3 6
1 Wood Meat Screen	30 0
3 Jelly Moulds	6 0
1 Mustard Pot	1 0
1 Salt Cellar	0 8
1 Pepper Box	0 6
1 Wicker Plate Basket, lined with Tin	7 6
3 Block Tin Saucepans	5 6
4 Iron Saucepans	12 3
1 Saucepan and Steamer	1 6
1 Large Boiling Pot, Iron	10 6
4 Stewpans, Iron	9 0
2 Sets of Skewers	1 0
6 Knives and Forks	5 6
6 Iron Spoons	1 6
1 Tea Pot	3 0
1 Tea Tray	4 0
1 Toasting Fork	1 0
1 Egg Whisk	0 9
1 Tea Kettle	7 6
£7 16 0	

In submitting to the Public the foregoing Catalogue, RIPPON & BURTON beg to state, that they will continue to offer Articles of the VERY BEST MANUFACTURE only, as they have hitherto done, at prices which, when compared with others of the same quality, will be found much lower than any that have ever yet been quoted. The knowledge which RIPPON & BURTON have obtained by their long connexion with the largest Manufacturers, and the principle upon which they conduct their business, afford great advantages to the purchaser; all Articles being bought in very large quantities for Cash, and marked for sale at Cash prices, which are not subject to discount or abatement of any kind; thus giving the ready money purchaser all the advantages that can be obtained over the plan usually adopted by others, of marking their goods at prices which will enable them to give credit, and pay for that credit which they take; allowing those, who pay cash, 5 per cent. discount from prices 25 per cent. higher than they should fairly be charged. The many years RIPPON & BURTON'S business has been established, and the very extensive patronage they have met with, will be some proof that the public have not been deceived by them; but, as a further security against the impositions practised by many, RIPPON & BURTON will continue to exchange, or return the money for every article that is not approved of, if returned in good condition and free of expense within one month of the time it was purchased.

J. Bradley, Printer, 78, Great Titchfield-street, London.

STEEL PENS.

JOSEPH GILLOTT,
STEEL PEN MANUFACTURER,
AND PATENTEE OF THE

ELONGATED EQUI-POINTED METALLIC PEN,

59, *Newhall Street and Graham Street,*

BIRMINGHAM.

WHOLESALE AND FOR EXPORTATION.

JOSEPH GILLOTT has been for nearly twenty years engaged in the manufacture of STEEL PENS, and during that time has devoted his unceasing attention to the improving and perfecting this useful and necessary article—the result of his persevering efforts, and numerous experiments upon the properties of the metal used, has been the construction of a pen upon a principle entirely new, combining all the advantages of the elasticity and fineness of the quill, with the durability of the metallic pen, and thus obviating the objections which have hitherto existed against the use of steel pens.

The Patentee is proud to acknowledge, that a discerning public has paid the most gratifying tribute to his humble, though useful labours, by a demand for his pens far exceeding his highest expectations.

The number of steel pens manufactured at Joseph Gillott's Works, from October, 1837, to October, 1838,

was **35,808,452**

or **2,984,037** $\frac{8}{12}$ dozens.

or **248,659** gross, **9** dozen and **8** pens.

This statement will shew the estimation in which these pens are held, and it is presumed will be an inducement to those who desire to have a really good article, at least to make a trial of Joseph Gillott's steel pen.

Manufactured by Joseph Gillott, at his Works, 59, Newhall Street, and Graham Street, Birmingham, and may be had of all stationers and other respectable dealers in steel pens throughout the kingdom.

Pearson, Printer, 36, Bishopsgate Street Within.

BRITANNIA LIFE ASSURANCE COMPANY,

No. 1, PRINCES STREET, BANK, LONDON.

CAPITAL, ONE MILLION.

Directors.

WILLIAM BARDGETT, ESQ.
SAMUEL BEVINGTON, ESQ.
WILLIAM FECHNEY BLACK, ESQ.
JOHN BRIGHTMAN, ESQ.
GEORGE COHEN, ESQ.
MILLIS COVENTRY, ESQ.
JOHN DREWETT, ESQ.

ROBERT EGLINTON, ESQ.
ERASMUS ROBERT FOSTER, ESQ.
ALEX. ROBERT IRVINE, ESQ.
PETER MORRISON, ESQ.
WILLIAM SHAND, JUN., ESQ.
HENRY LEWIS SMALE, ESQ.
THOMAS TEED, ESQ.

Medical Officers.
WILLIAM STROUD, M.D., Great Coram Street, Russell Square.
EBENEZER SMITH, ESQ., Surgeon, Billiter Square.

Standing Counsel.
The HON. JOHN ASHLEY, New Square, Lincoln's-Inn.

Solicitor.
WILLIAM BEVAN, ESQ., Old Jewry.

Bankers.
MESSRS. DREWETT & FOWLER, Princes Street, Bank.

This Institution is so constituted as to afford the benefits of Life Assurance in their fullest extent to Policy holders, and to present greater facilities and accommodation than can be obtained in any similar establishment. Among others, the following improvements on the system usually adopted, are recommended to the attention of the Public.

A most economical set of Tables—computed expressly for the use of this Institution, from authentic and complete data ; *and presenting the lowest rates of Assurance that can be offered, without compromising the safety of the Institution.*

A Table of increasing rates of Premium, on a new and remarkable plan, peculiarly advantageous in cases where Assurances are effected, by way of securing loans or debts, a less immediate payment being required on a policy for the whole term of life, than in any other office ; and the holder having the option of paying a periodically-increasing rate ; or of having the sum assured diminished, according to an equitable scale of reduction.

A Table of decreasing rates of Premium, also on a novel and remarkable plan ; the Policy-holder having the option of discontinuing the payment of all further premiums after *twenty, fifteen, ten,* and even *five* years ; and the Policy still remaining in force,—in the first case, for the full amount originally assured ; and in either of the three other cases, for a portion of the same, according to a fixed and equitable scale, endorsed upon the Policy.

Policies effected by persons on their own lives, not rendered void in case of death by duelling, or the hands of justice. In the event of suicide, if the Policy be assigned to a *bonâ fide* creditor, the sum assured paid without deduction ; if not so assigned, the full amount of premiums returned to the family of the assured.

Policies revived without the exaction of a fine within twelve months, on the production of satisfactory evidence as to health, and payment of interest on the premiums due.

Age of the assured in every case admitted in the Policy.

All claims payable within one month after proof of death.

A liberal commission allowed to solicitors and agents.

Extract from increasing Rates of Premium for an Assurance of £100, for whole Term of Life.

Age.	First Five Years.	Second Five Years.	Third Five Years.	Fourth Five Years.	Remainder of Life.
	£ s. d.	£ s. d.	£ s. d.	£ s. d.	£ s. d.
20	1 1 4	1 5 10	1 10 11	1 16 9	2 3 8
30	1 6 4	1 12 2	1 19 1	2 7 4	2 17 6
40	1 16 1	2 4 4	2 14 6	3 7 3	4 3 4
50	2 16 7	3 9 4	4 5 5	5 6 3	6 13 7

PETER MORRISON, *Resident Director.*